BERLIN SONG

Other novels by Alan Gold

The Gift of Evil
(Book I in Amra's Journey)

The Marmara Contract
(Book II in Amra's Journey)

The Final Candidate

The Lost Testament

The Jericho Files

Minyan

Alan Gold's website and email addresses are:

HTTP://www.cg.com.au

alangold@zeta.org.au

BERLIN SONG

ALAN GOLD

HarperCollins*Publishers*

HarperCollins*Publishers*

First published in Australia in 1999
by HarperCollins*Publishers* Pty Limited
ACN 009 913 517
A member of HarperCollins*Publishers* (Australia) Pty Limited Group
http://www.harpercollins.com.au

HarperCollins*Publishers*

25 Ryde Road, Pymble, Sydney, NSW 2073, Australia
31 View Road, Glenfield, Auckland 10, New Zealand
77–85 Fulham Palace Road, London W6 8JB, United Kingdom
Hazelton Lanes, 55 Avenue Road, Suite 2900, Toronto, Ontario M5R 3L2
and 1995 Markham Road, Scarborough, Ontario M1B 5M8, Canada
10 East 53rd Street, New York NY 10022, USA

National Library Cataloguing-in-Publication data:

Gold, Alan, 1945–.
   Berlin Song.
   ISBN 0 7322 6585 1.
   I. Title.
A823.3

Cover images: Castle, Peter Scholey—Wildlight.
                     Woman's face, International Photographic Library.
Printed in Australia by Griffin Press Pty Ltd on 50 gsm Ensobulky

5 4 3 2 1
02 01 00 99

This book is dedicated to the memory of Yossi and Bella Weiss, as well as their parents, brothers and sisters, nieces and nephews, and to all those whose lives were foreshortened by the Nazis.

ACKNOWLEDGEMENTS

Berlin Song is the third book in Amra's Journey, an odyssey over three and a half thousand years, a tale recording the way in which events shape the actions and decisions of three very different women. The theme common to all of the books is an amulet created in the times of the Hittites, 1545 years before Christ. The charm was made by Amra's father to protect her against the difficulties of her journey to Troy to find the secret of making iron. I chose this historical period, and this particular talisman, because the Hittites gave us some of our most enduring legends, our earliest myths.

In the first book of the series, *The Gift of Evil*, I portrayed the unwritten horrors of Stalinism; the second book, *The Marmara Contract*, depicts the cyclical nature of history — that if we fail to learn the lessons of history, then we are doomed to repeat our mistakes (the recent genocides of Rwanda and Yugoslavia are tragic proofs of this axiom); and this novel, *Berlin Song*, demonstrates the resourcefulness and indomitability of the human spirit, despite the attempts of Nazism, the greatest crime in all human history, to crush humanity.

The trilogy began with a journey to Slovakia which I took with my wife Eva to try to trace her roots. It was there that I realised for the first time the enormity of the horrors suffered by refugees when dispossessed from their homes, their lives, their loved ones. My wife was fortunate; her parents escaped Stalin's grasp and thrived in the welcoming embrace of Australia. Tens of millions of refugees throughout the world today are far less fortunate.

Many people throughout the world have helped me research and write this book, kind friends from Slovakia, England, America and Germany as well as in Australia. People from all walks of life have been unstinting in their assistance. I have been privileged to enjoy long and detailed conversations with leading academics in the field of Holocaust Studies, and with Ministers of Religion, philosophers, and historians as well as men and women who were victims of the greatest crime in the long history of humanity.

Of the many who assisted me, the efforts of a few come into sharper focus: Professor Ronald Newton of Simon Fraser University in Burnaby, Canada, the world's leading expert on the Nazi menace in Argentina; Professor Colin Tatz of the Department of Politics at Macquarie University, Sydney, and Mrs Sandra Tatz who were the models of generosity whenever I needed to know anything about the Holocaust; Dr Vera Ranki who helped me with the politics of inclusion and exclusion; Dr Ruth Wajnryb who assisted me in understanding the difficulties of the language of Holocaust transmission; Adrian Collette, general manager of the Australian Opera who facilitated my learning about the details of a production of *Tosca*; and Henry Aram for his assistance in providing reference material concerning the underground Jews of Berlin during the War.

As always, my publisher HarperCollins deserves a particular vote of thanks for the confidence, generosity and most especially the support in bringing the novels of the Amra trilogy into existence. My friends at HarperCollins shared my vision and have been wonderful in their encouragement. Particular thanks to Barrie Hitchon, Angelo Loukakis, Jim Demetriou, Darian Causby, Karen-Maree Griffiths and especially to my wonderful editor, Belinda Lee. It was Andrew Wilkins' eagle eye and keen intelligence during the long and difficult structural edit which enabled me to see more in this book than I first realised.

Whilst writing a novel is a long and solitary act, it could never have been done without the support of people whom I love and who have been willing to sacrifice much on my behalf. My wife, Eva, my children Raffe, Jonathan and Georgina, my dear friend and assistant, Jenny Roberts, and the world's most sympathetic and understanding bank manager, Leigh Clarke.

PROLOGUE

RUTHENIA, EASTERN EUROPE, 1903

In the grey of the early morning, Serel and her children crept with the stealth of animals out of their burrows, and up to the crest of the river bank. She peered over the edge, looking at her blackened home to ensure the madmen weren't still there. She knew the risks. If the men hadn't left, if they were lying in a drunken sleep, then she and her children would be killed.

Throughout the long cold night she'd listened intently, her family depending on her, trying to discern whether a cry or a moan or a screech was made by an animal or by one of the drunken demons. All night long she'd strained and concentrated, too terrified to breathe in case it gave a warning to the men who had destroyed her home that there were more Jews to kill.

But as morning rose above the pitiless ground, a silence enveloped the river and its bank. It encouraged her to stir her children, to walk together as a family, timorously forwards, cowering low to the ground, inching towards the swirling shroud of smoke draping over their home.

Familiar shapes slowly took on new and intimidating forms. So different from how they had been the previous night. A torn chair, its innards burst like a suppurating wound; a sofa slashed, the stuffing bleeding out of it; curtains and rugs littering the ground, precious possessions now fouled with the contempt of men who hated her, men whom she didn't even know. And her heart dropped when she saw the contents of her wardrobe, all her dresses and underwear, scattered and slashed and trodden into the dirt as a sign of the men's contempt. Now what was she going to wear? And why her underthings? Why them? And why their furniture? She and Nussan had worked so hard to afford what the men last night had treated with such derision.

As she walked closer to the house, its shape loomed like a spectre, evolving from out of the wisps of smoke and mist. And the nearer she came, the clearer, the more awful, were the things she saw. When she had peered over the river's bank, her distant home looked like a shrouded apparition. Now, as she trudged closer, Serel and her children became part of the dream. She stared at her home in mute incomprehension, shaking her head to try to make it a reality. She closed and opened her eyes, but nothing changed. It once was, but now it was no more. Everything was burnt, black, empty. There was no roof, no walls. Standing in her back garden, alive with vegetables, Serel looked right through her dead house, and could see the familiar road in the front and the pathway which led from her front door to the street. 'How could that be?' she wondered. Only the door posts were left. Not the walls whose plaster had collapsed as the heat made the house disintegrate. Only the door frame. Its posts and lintel were still smoking like cheap black cigars.

The damp fresh air of the river bank was overwhelmed by the acrid stench of the charred wood and plaster. Serel moved slowly forward, her children hugging her skirt in terror. She walked through the archway of the door. Why, she wondered? Why was she walking through the door when there were no walls? Because that's the way it should have been, some inner voice told her. But it was absurd! The house had no walls. She shook her head in consternation.

The burnt and charred walls which once kept her warm and safe from Ruthenia's frosts, which once protected her, only last night had enclosed her loving family. Late last evening, while Nussan was in the inn getting drunk and bemoaning his fate at being married to a woman who could reject a sudden fortune, Serel had held baby Eva close to her breast and felt the child suckling. Now this same baby was cold and dirty and was beginning to stir, her nose wrinkling in the smoke-filled atmosphere; her other children, Rosl and Yitzchok, were clinging desperately to her skirts, their closeness making it difficult for her to walk through whatever it was that had once been her home.

Serel looked down at her sleeping baby, insulating her from the cold. It was strangely comforting to feel Eva suckling early-morning milk from her breast.

Last night this devastated shell had been the home where she and her family had lived. Only last night, Serel had sung a lullaby to each of her children, waiting for her husband Nussan to return from the inn. She knew he would be drunk and angry, that his fury at her would be reignited by the drink, and that he would have spent the evening boasting about the treasure he'd dug up, and ridiculing Serel's madness in wanting to give it over to the Constable. From the moment he had brought the amulet and its heavy gold chain home to her, exulting in their sudden good fortune, Serel knew that it was trouble. The amulet was tainted by death. Nussan had found it in a grave. It was inside the chest cavity of some skeleton. He'd put it around her neck and she had snatched it off in horror. Four times that night, she'd spat over her shoulder and said blessings to the Almighty. She'd even poured salt over her hands. But in the end, the amulet's curse had been stronger than her prayers to the Almighty. And look at the trouble it had brought. Another pogrom, another visit from the Christian madmen from Hell.

The grave where Nussan had found the amulet was very old. Some people said it was thousands of years old. Did Serel care? These were the times before God, before the God of Abraham, Isaac and Jacob. No wonder it was cursed. Even now, she felt her hands tingling from where she had touched the amulet and her neck still prickled from where its gold chain had hung.

Night after night since she'd told him to give it away, he'd become angrier and angrier and had gone to the inn to drink his anger into unconsciousness. But last night had been the worst. He hadn't even come home after the inn had closed. Serel kept watch after the children were asleep. Then she saw the lights burning in the sky, the flames of torches, the shadows of evil men, spectres who had been sent by the forces beyond the grave to take back their amulet.

Last night! Last night was so long ago. Not a night, but a lifetime. Before they went to bed, Serel had brushed the children's hair, kissed them on their foreheads, said a silent prayer in Yiddish and Hebrew over each of them, begging Almighty God to protect them against the spectres which whirled and whined in the blackness beyond. She'd said her usual prayer, the one her mother had taught her after the last pogrom three years ago. It had protected them till now. And again, they'd returned. After the last time, when twenty people had been killed, she never believed that another pogrom could happen again in her lifetime. How could God allow it?

And not once in her wildest nightmares did she imagine that her imprecations to the Almighty might fail … never once did she think that the evil Christian men would attack their village as they'd done in years past. Why all the prayers to God if He didn't listen?

But gather, they did. And all because of Nussan and that God-damned amulet he'd dug up from the hill at the top of his field. From a gravesite of some poor person who'd died hundreds, maybe even thousands of years earlier.

Long after the children were asleep, the Banshees began their screaming, flames leapt into the bitter night, and Jewish men and women wailed in fear of the spectres on horseback whose swords gleamed in the holocaust.

Serel had heard the horsemen when they were almost on top of the village. They came from the other direction, thank God, because that gave her time to gather her precious children and escape. She heard them before she realised what they were. And then she smelled them. She smelled the fire of their flaming torches. She smelled the excitement of their horses. She smelled the drunken fury of the men.

When the noise had begun, Serel dashed out into the front garden to look up the road towards the centre of the village and see what was happening; and what she saw frightened her more than anything she'd seen before. Horsemen towering above the roads and shops, swinging flaming brands and swords and screaming in fury because the Jews of the village were hiding in their homes. It terrified her, because she was on her own. Nussan was still in the inn. She moaned prayers out loud so that Almighty God might hear them, and make the attackers miss her little house.

The men on horseback spurred their mounts until the vibration of the animals' hooves had roused all the villagers from their sleep. And when they saw the flames of the torches, they realised that soon their houses could become conflagrations. So men and women in nightgowns suddenly appeared and scurried from homes into fields to hide like mice from the swords and flames.

Serel could sense the fear of the villagers within their houses. She saw lights being lit in rooms and then disappearing down into cellars. And the horsemen, swirling like a malignant cloud of locusts in the middle of the village began to chase the fleeing villagers for sport. Two elderly people scampered in terror across the road to try to escape the madmen. But there was no escape. Instead the horsemen impaled the elderly *yidden* with their spears. Serel recognised one as she fell sprawling into the dirt. It was Malka, the butcher's wife. She and Malka were in a sewing circle together. God Almighty! Malka was now lying dead by the side of the road.

Serel couldn't move, she was so terrified. Yet in the dark night the horsemen, their faces illuminated by their flaming brands, still hadn't finished. Men, women and children were screaming. People clutched their bleeding, broken limbs. Some lay dead in the streets. Everywhere, prayers were being shouted to a deaf God. But still the madmen weren't finished. They wheeled their horses around as though it were a children's playground, and threw their torches up into the straw roofs which exploded into the flames of a cremation.

But that was last night. This morning, the day was cold and grey and the air stank of smoke. Serel clutched her children closer to her as they walked through their charred home. She was cold, damp, exhausted. She needed to act decisively if she was going to save herself and the children. She had to find Nussan, give back the amulet and see what she could rescue from the ruination around her. She had to find her family and friends and neighbours and apologise to them for the harm which Nussan had brought to the village.

But her mind wouldn't allow her the luxury of thinking about the future for long. Instead, she closed her eyes and last night's madness again reappeared in her mind like a malignancy. Swords flashing in the flames; the glistening skins of horses, mouths foaming with fear and excitement.

And then, the horsemen had joined up at the south end of the village as though looking for her. Like a pack of wolves eagerly anticipating an attack, they coalesced in a terrifying formation, swords held aloft in pride and power. And then they slowly, arrogantly, trotted down the road out of the village and towards her.

In front of them, illuminated by the glow of the fires, stumbling like a drunkard, was her husband Nussan. He had been running down the road towards her, shouting out, 'Serel!' He'd thrown himself into the front garden, but she'd swept up her children as soon as she saw the horsemen gathering and riding towards her house. She had to protect them. But before she left the house, she'd turned and stopped for a moment; she'd hidden behind a chair, looking out of the front window into the garden. She could see her husband was too drunk to help her, and she called out to him to get into the house. But he couldn't hear her in the noise. She ran to the front screaming, 'Nussan. Come quick. Nussan.' But he didn't understand what was happening. He just sat on the ground in the front of their garden, holding his head, mumbling words which were inaudible. Prayers to a God he'd sworn forever to forsake? Words of regret that he'd brought all this misery on his family and friends?

Serel had been so terrified, she'd raced down towards the river, pulling her two older tearful children as she desperately clutched a screaming Eva. Where was her husband when she most needed him? Drunk and useless. Sitting in the front garden, in the lettuce patch, moaning his sorrow to the world.

That was last night, but now that everything was in ruins, she bitterly regretted her anger towards him. For even though she'd been denying it all night, Serel knew in her heart of hearts that Nussan was dead. Her emotions were confused. Where was her husband when the madmen destroyed everything she possessed? Wasn't it his job to protect his family?

Serel and her family walked slowly to what was once the front of the house. Chickens were there, grubbing on the ground for grains, impervious to the madness of the Christians. In the distance, she heard a dog barking. She heard the lowing of cattle, anxious to be milked. But the milkman might be dead. Or might be wandering through the burnt-out shell of his house. And Serel heard the wailing of women, appealing to the Almighty for assistance for the horrors which they had undergone the previous night. Appeals? Why appeals? Why not curses? Or imprecations? Where was God when all this happened? And where was His servant, Nussan?

Serel listened, and heard men crying, and shouting prayers into the cloudy sky. They were praying outdoors. There was no *shul* for them to pray in; it had been torched by the hate of the madmen.

And in the front of her burnt-down home, propped up against the wall of the barn as though he was resting among the vegetables after a day of ploughing his field, indistinctly through the smoky haze of the grey morning, Serel saw the body of Nussan, her husband.

She walked closer to him in trepidation, in full understanding of his death, and of the future her life would now follow. She hated him and she loved him. But when she saw what the men had done to her Nussan, any residual anger towards him immediately evaporated. She stared in incomprehension at the man with whom she had shared her life, who until now had been a part of her. She winced at his stillness. He was as grey as the early-morning light, as though blending into the earth and the air. And then she saw his death. Unlike Nussan, who shot lame horses and helped birth goats and sheep and cows, Serel avoided much of the brutality of Nature. So the barbarity of her husband's death, his lack of life, at first shocked her; then it numbed her. She was too horrified to cry as she looked at the vicious serrated hole where his chest had once been. She hid her children's eyes when they began to react in hysteria to the thing on the ground that had once been their father. Only the previous day, this body had played with them, thrown them to the ceiling, laughed at their cavorting.

Serel's hate had gone, but not her contempt. She looked at her Nussan in pity. He had sat there for the entire night, dead, while Serel hugged and protected her terrified children beside the river, being eaten alive by gnats and mosquitos and frightened by slithering things that rustled in the long reeds.

She'd warned him, begged him. The moment he'd brought the amulet home and put it around her neck, she'd told him her fears of what it might bring. He started to shout, telling her that at last they were rich, and could afford to leave this God-forsaken part of the world and travel to America, the *goldeneh medina*. He'd woken up the children with his shouting. Baby Eva started to cry. Nussan became increasingly annoyed that Serel's reaction wasn't what he'd hoped. Then she told him that the amulet meant nothing but trouble. Hadn't she said to him that people like them, poor Jews, didn't own expensive golden necklaces with huge gold pendants. He said he'd found it in some grave on the new land he'd just cleared.

Did she care? No. All she wanted was for Nussan to hand the thing into the Constable, and perhaps earn a few *kopeks* reward. That at least would put candles on the *Shabbos* table.

Serel sent the older children Rosl and Yitzchok to fetch the Rabbi, so that he could help her in her moment of despair. By now, Baby Eva was fully awake and had stopped suckling. She was smiling, God bless her, and reaching up with her pudgy little hands to play with Serel's dark eyebrows. They always seemed to fascinate her.

It was the innocence of the baby's reaction that made Serel begin to cry; an innocent cry which broke through the solitary cordon she had built, to insulate herself from the grief which threatened to overwhelm her. Serel smiled at her baby while tears coursed down her cheeks. Her body began to shake and Baby Eva thought it was a game. Another smile. Serel wanted to weep, to lay on the ground and wail to the Almighty for what had suddenly happened to her life. But she couldn't. Not yet. She had three children to protect. She had herself to look after.

Serel looked away from the body of the man who was once her husband. She couldn't think of him as her Nussan. He wasn't her Nussan. The man she married loved life. He loved to drink, to dance, to eat, to make love. Always making love. Always finding an excuse to go to their room, warn off the children with lies about mummy and daddy wanting to sleep, close the door and stifle his movements and moans until they would emerge from their room, feeling guilty that their children were looking bored and abandoned. That was her Nussan. A man who belly-laughed at adversity; a man who always left for work in the early hours, confident that this day good things would happen. A man who returned from ploughing the fields, or fighting the plagues which God threw at Ruthenia as if it was a garbage heap and who would stand outside their door, aching from exhaustion, and fighting back the agony of frustration; a man who could end the day desolate, yet who entered their house each night as though he was seeing his family for the first time … a massive smile on his face, kisses for everybody, throwing the children around the room, stroking little Eva's head, and kissing her as though he was blowing gently on a feather.

She heard Nussan's horse moving around in the barn, kicking at the wooden posts which held him tethered. He must be terrified of the smell of burning and death. But he was only a horse and she had people to worry about. She would attend to him later.

Serel looked again at the ghoul in front of her, the grey-skinned thing on the ground. But there was no Nussan there any longer. The pain was too great. She turned, and walked towards the gate. Looking down the street, she saw the full horror of what the Christians had done the previous night. Houses along the street were gutted; the communal hall was still on fire – nobody was trying to put out the dying embers. And the *shul*. It was nothing more than a blackened frame. Only the thick wooden doors were still standing. They were enclosing nothing. They looked ridiculous. Just standing on their own. Serel laughed bitterly. Baby Eva giggled. How ridiculous.

Men and women were searching the *shul*. What for? For God? Trying to find scraps of the holy *Torah* so that they could continue to pray and read the services. The Rabbi was standing in the middle of the street, stroking the heads of other peoples' children, talking to bereft men and women, trying to convince them that God had known, and probably ordained what had happened in order to test the faith of the community. Serel knew what he would be saying. 'Now, more than ever, we must pray to God Almighty, and ask his help and forgiveness. Blessed art thou, oh Lord, our God, King of the Universe, who, in Your infinite wisdom, hath made thy people…'

Suddenly she was disgusted. With the Christians, with the village, with her husband, Nussan, with the Rabbi, with herself. She wanted to get away. She called the children back. They had only gone a few paces, stunned into inaction by the horror of what was their village. They returned instantly, glad to turn away from the adults' wailing and beating of breasts.

Serel breathed in deeply to control herself. She had to be a mother. She would go to pieces later. Cry and scream and wail at the moon in her misery, but now she had to present the image of a woman of calm and resolve so the children didn't panic.

'Rosl, I want you to find me a big pot which we can use for water for the journey. Yitzchok go find whatever clothes are still clean and any pillows and blankets in case we have to sleep in the fields tonight. Rosl,' she said to her daughter who had already turned and started to search through the piles of debris in the garden, 'While you're looking, see if you can find food. Anything. Just to get us on our way. We'll drink water from streams.'

Rosl looked at her mother. 'But can't we fill up at the village pump?'

Serel smiled and walked over to her daughter, stroking her head. 'If people let us fill our bottles, then of course we will.'

Yitzchok stopped what he was doing and walked over to stand close to his mother. It was the first time she had spoken properly since they had crept away from the river. Yitzchok couldn't take his eyes off his dead father. He was in shock. But he was now the man. He knew the customs. He must protect his mother, even though he was only still a boy, not yet *bar mitzvah*.

'Mother, how are we going to eat? What if there's no food left?'

She bent down and kissed his hair. '*Bubeleh*, we'll find beautiful juicy potatoes in the fields. Every night, we'll have a meal, a banquet for a king. Thank God it's summer but because of the rains, the crops haven't yet been fully brought in. There'll still be plenty of carrots and lettuce and beans and, who knows, we might find apple and pear trees. There's God's gifts out there.'

Serel felt Rosl drawing close to her skirts again. She had no time for this. She had to get away. She had to leave in case the madmen came back. But she could feel the girl sobbing as she held on to her leg.

Serel stroked her hair. 'Rosl, you're a big girl. You must understand that we're in trouble. Now isn't the time to cry nor to do anything but leave this place.'

'But it's my home. My friends are here,' wept the little girl.

'You can make friends elsewhere, in other towns, in other cities. People here don't like us. They want to hurt us. They've already hurt your poor father, *alav ha shalom*. We must leave if we don't want the same to happen to us.'

'I don't want to go. I'm frightened.'

Yitzchok felt himself grow tall and important. He put his arm around Rosl. 'Rosl, I'm here as well as Mummy. Don't be afraid.'

'Yitzchok, what about my toys? What about my doll?'

'You can bring those with you,' said Serel. 'Whatever you can carry.'

Serel bent down and looked closely at Yitzchok's face. My God, she thought, was he already becoming a man? Nussan will be so proud. She corrected herself. Nussan would have been proud. She fought back tears. She cupped her hands over his cheeks. 'Listen to me, *bubeleh*. You have to be very big and strong for Mummy. And at night you have to creep into a farmer's barn and play some games. You have to see how many eggs you can take without the chickens squawking.'

The boy looked at her in shock. 'But that's stealing.'

'No,' she said. 'No, it's a game. Life is a game from now on. And you, Rosl, you have to go to the back doors and kitchens and ask for bread and see if you can persuade people to give you other food as well. Maybe the homes of *yidden*. Maybe not. Who knows?'

The children looked at each other in consternation. Their mother was asking them to steal and beg. What would daddy say?

Serel stood and looked at the choices before her. One possibility was to stay here, and be a pauper in the village, begging *tzedokoh* from the community, a *kopek* here, a loaf of bread and some milk there like Reb Abram the beggar and other widows who threw themselves on the charity of others; or to uproot her family, face the dangers of the journey across the face of Europe, and go to America. Or Palestine? No, not Palestine. She'd heard tales of how rugged the life was there, of how hard people had to work to drain the swamps, of the malaria, of the fights between Jews and Moslems. No! She'd already suffered enough. She'd go to America. The land of opportunity. There she'd work as a seamstress or as a cook or something.

Because, in her heart, she knew precisely what she would do. She had been born into poverty; she had been treated as dirt by the Christians in the main town, who despised her just because she was a Jew; her marriage was to a poor farmer who broke his back throughout the whole year just so they could eat; and now she was a young widow with a lifetime of misery ahead of her. Yesterday her poverty had been a burden to bear. Now yesterday looked like a paradise.

Why was she thinking of pogroms when she should be on the road already? There had been an average of one pogrom every three or four years. Drunks from the big city who swept through the land killing innocent Jews just because they were Jews. Burning down synagogues, destroying Holy books, murdering Rabbis, making them urinate on ancient scrolls, burning fields so Jews would starve. They seemed to sweep through the Jewish areas at the behest of the church or some prince or rich landowner. Whenever the Christians wanted something they would drive the Jews away and just take it. But what had happened in the past would be like a paradise compared to what faced her tomorrow.

It took only a few moments for the family to gather up what remained of their possessions. She bundled them into a large sheet, and slung it over her shoulder. It was hard, carrying Eva and the bundle … and she hadn't even left her front garden, let alone walk God knows how many thousands of miles to America. But others had done it, and so would she.

She hurried the children onto the road, telling them not to keep looking at their poor father. Yitzchok and Rosl weren't yet old enough to understand that he needed to be buried, and prayers said over his soul. The Rabbi could do that. It was his job. Meantime, she had to protect her children, and get out before the madmen came back, which they almost certainly would. They would meet in the inn tonight and laugh at their exploits of the previous evening. They would tell each other how they had speared this Jew with a sword, or run that Jew down with their horses' hooves. They would laugh as they remembered the flames from the straw roofs, leaping up into the sky. And they would drink more and more, until they decided to do the same thing again tonight, to relive the same thrill of killing and burning. Well, not to Serel they wouldn't. She and her children wouldn't be there to give these animals more pleasure. They would be long gone.

They walked into the road and looked towards the West. The road looked horribly long, stretching into the distance. She and Nussan knew the road well. It led to his fields. In her twenty-six years, she had only ever been a few miles past the outskirts of her village, and now she was planning to leave it. She had been for picnics on the river bank. She had helped Nussan in the fields. She had seen the distant mountains but she had never been close to them. She had only ever stayed where she belonged.

She smiled bravely and looked at her two eldest children. 'Come, Yitzchok. Come, Rosl. We're going on an adventure.'

Rosl looked at her in horror. She pointed to the body of her father, propped up against the barn.

'But Daddy? What about Daddy? We can't leave him behind.'

'Daddy is staying here, my love. Daddy isn't coming with us. It's just the four of us now. We'll have such fun on the road. It'll be such an adventure.'

Yitzchok shook his head. 'But I have *cheder* tomorrow. The Rabbi will be angry if I'm not there to learn my Hebrew.'

'No *cheder*. There are other more important things now than learning your *alef bez*. Now we have to go on a long journey. It's full of fun. Much better than school. Come, children.'

Despite their mother's injunction, they both looked at the body of their father. Serel realised she should have covered him with a blanket for his dignity. But the dead had no dignity. Neither did the living, not if you were a Jew.

Now she was going. Every step of the way would be like treading on quicksand. How would she cope? What would she do for money? The Christians had stolen all the money. They had killed her husband. How would she buy new clothes for the children? How would she sole their shoes? Where would she find money for powder to delouse them? Castor oil when they were sick? God Almighty, how was she going to manage?

They started to follow their mother but then she stopped, thinking to herself. She shook her head and sighed. It had brought ruin and destruction on them. It had killed her husband. It was cursed but it was her lifeline. It was the only way she would be able to survive.

'Stay here children. I'm just going back to the barn to get something.'

She dropped the bundle at the children's feet and told Yitzchok to hold baby Eva for a while. She ran to the barn, deliberately avoiding looking at Nussan. There was a blanket. She picked it up and took it outside to cover him but then realised that when the Jews came to her house to see if they were alright, they might miss him and then he wouldn't be buried. So, she threw the horse blanket on the floor.

The barn was hot even in the early-morning sun. It stank of horse shit and the flies buzzed angrily as she disturbed them. Nussan had told her the previous night where he had hidden the amulet. She got a spade and shovelled a pile of horse shit aside. Nothing showed so she threw the shovel aside and picked up a rake. She carefully separated the matted straw and the stinking boluses of droppings in the hope of finding it and then when she pulled the rake out, a long dirty object clung to it. The amulet and its necklace. She carried them over on the rake and tipped them into a pail of water. Wrinkling her nose in disgust she plunged her hands into the pail and washed the amulet.

It was large and chunky, the size of a big coin. The necklace was finely wrought like filigree. It was beautiful, and it was horrible. It was like the seductress Jezebel, full of charm and danger but deadly to those who came too close.

In the distance, Yitzchok shouted, 'Momma, Eva is crying.'

She bundled the amulet and necklace into a ball in the palm of her hand, opened her bodice and manoeuvred it so that it was below her breast. If thieves felt her breasts, there was a good chance that they wouldn't feel the amulet. Nussan's horse whinnied as she moved towards him. He was a good old horse. He only had a couple more years left in him before he went to be boiled down in the nearby town but he was still strong. She would take him. He would carry the children while she walked beside. That would ease everybody's burden.

'Come,' she said to him, patting his nose. But then she realised that a woman alone with three children could hide herself in a hedgerow. A woman with a horse would attract everybody's attention. She sighed. What would Nussan do? Did it matter? 'I have to leave you, old boy. Somebody will come along and look after you. Be well in your freedom.'

She walked outside and said a silent prayer over her husband's dead body, shaking her head in sorrow. Now she wanted to mourn for him, to grieve for the man who was the father of her three children, the man who wanted more and more and more children as though he was repopulating the world of every Jew killed in all the pogroms the Christians had thrown at them for two thousand years. Never mind about their poverty or where the extra food was coming from, Nussan wanted more children. Well, God rest his soul, may he rest in peace, he would never know the joys. Neither would she. Who would marry a widow with three children?

She walked towards the gate, kissed Yitzchok and Rosl and took baby Eva back. She picked up the bundle and threw it over her shoulder again.

'Come children. We're going to America.'

'America!' said Yitzchok.

'Let me tell you about America. Your Uncle Yossl is there. We had a letter from him last year. He lives in a huge house with servants. He doesn't do any work. It's a wonderful land. And he eats beef and chicken every day. And chocolate. You've never tasted chocolate. Just wait. It's unbelievable. That's where we're going to live, kinder. That's where we're going to live.'

Rosl turned around to take a last look at her father. She wanted to ask what was going to happen, why he wasn't coming with them, why he was just lying there with that red thing all over his chest, why he looked grey. There was so much she didn't understand but her mother was happy. She would follow her mother.

And they began to walk to America.

CHAPTER ONE

NEW YORK, PRESENT DAY

It was Sunday, the best day of the week. There were four Sundays in every month – some wonderful months had five – but only two of these Sundays were the best days. On the other two Sundays, they were forced to fulfil family obligations, one to his parents, one to hers.

As Sarah Kaplan Rose and her husband, David Rose drove towards the house, feelings of claustrophobia began to grow into trepidation. Visits to Sarah's family home were always like this. The warm greeting cooled by the time she was through the door and transmuted into guilt imposed by her parents at the entry to the lounge room. Within half an hour, Sarah was usually searching for excuses to leave early. David, of course, was different. He had so much gentleness and understanding that he would nod his head tolerantly as Sarah's parents (actually her mother; her father merely went along for the ride) unburdened themselves of their litany of complaints against the world in general, and, by subtle innuendo, their daughter's misdemeanours in particular. Her crime was invariably the same … 'shame you didn't phone, there were things we needed to talk about …' 'pity you didn't send your Aunt Bernice a "get well soon" card …' The list was endless.

And today's visit was going to be no less tense than any previous occasion. On Saturday morning, Sarah had received a call from her father, Sol. He needed her legal assistance. As they turned into her parents' street, the thought of it made her smile. It was a year since she'd given up being a lawyer and married, yet her father still saw her as an attorney.

She reached over and touched David's shoulder as he negotiated the twisting streets in the suburb where her parents lived. A year. A whole year of beautiful blissful marriage. In her mind, she had assumed that the year of living together as husband and wife would be little different from their years sharing an apartment in New York City. She loved being married. She loved its security and especially the fact that she no longer felt prey to unwanted advances by young men she met for the first time. She could now approach men socially without being concerned that she might be giving the wrong messages. The wedding bands she and David had chosen together were like a force-field around her. She and David were securely locked within that force-field, loving every moment of their married lives together as well as their professional lives apart. And despite the accusation by militant feminist colleagues of selling out the sisterhood by becoming traditional, she'd latterly incorporated David's surname into her own. One small step for a woman, one giant step for humankind …

Sarah was formulating the words to deflect her father's plea for legal help. She knew what he'd done; he'd used her name as a weapon. She could almost hear his voice: 'Listen, mister. You get this *farcochteneh* thing fixed, or I'll get my daughter on you, and she's a top lawyer in a big city firm. She spits out guys like you after breakfast.'

Right at the beginning, when she returned from Turkey and took up her new post, she'd told her father that she wouldn't be able to help him with whatever legal entanglement he always seemed to get himself into. As Chief Executive Officer of a new, and very public lobby group, Sarah was precluded by the terms of her contract as well as her public profile from acting in any private legal capacity.

But for her father, she was still, and would always be, the young girl sent to study law at New York Jewish Women's College and then in Graduate School at Harvard. For Sol Kaplan, she would always be 'Sarah, the lawyer, my daughter,' even if she became Secretary-General of the United Nations!

David slowed the car to turn left into the road leading towards her parent's home. She glanced over as he concentrated on the road. As so often, she looked at his calm and gentle face, and glanced lovingly at the way his long sensitive fingers gripped the wheel. They were a cellist's fingers. They were a lover's fingers. Love and music. So closely allied. And the thing which Sarah enjoyed most of all was watching David's look of ecstasy when he gripped the throat and the bow of his beloved cello and stroked it to produce the most glorious music she had ever heard.

Sometimes, when they were alone, she asked him to play the first few bars of the Haydn or Boccherini or Dvořák cello concertos. Just the first few bars, to hear the dark sexual, resonant voice of the cello transport her from an enervating and nerve-racking day at the office onto a plane of serenity and quiet contemplation. How lucky she was! Most women coming home from a day at work reached for a glass of wine and sat for ten minutes to calm down, to re-fire their momentum. But when she came home, she got her virtuoso cellist husband to play her enough blissful bars to make her body yearn for his. She was happy. He was happy. And the cello rarely got beyond the introduction of a piece's opening themes.

The car slowed as they entered the suburban street in which Sarah's family had lived from when she was born.

In two weeks' time, they would drive into New Jersey to visit David's parents. They recognised how lucky they were that both sets of parents were still alive, but ever since they started to go out together, and especially since they were married, an interesting relationship crossover had taken place. David adored and in turn was adored by Sarah's parents; and Sarah was adored and was in turn adored by David's. However, David's relationship with his own parents and Sarah's with hers was polite, formal and occasionally fraught with feelings which made both ashamed as they lay in bed later that night.

Sarah's mother had the irritating habit of nodding sagely whenever Sarah told her of things that had been happening in Manhattan, either in their private or professional lives. She would comment, 'That's wonderful dear,' or 'Gee, that's great,' but the subtext, the unwritten message was so visibly published in the air between them that no further conversation was necessary … or possible without Sarah causing even more of a disruption to their relationship.

Her mother's comments would be patent disapproval of Sarah's way of doing things or living or experiencing or behaving. Things had improved since she and David had married, but only marginally. Only over dinner or coffee or when they went out for a walk would her mother delicately refer to her disapproval and say, as if the subject had been dragged up from some long-faded memory, 'Do you remember what you were saying about …? Well, are you really sure you should …'

Sarah now realised that any residual feelings of personal inadequacy and insufficiency had diminished since the time she left home. Only by being free of the suffocating atmosphere of her parents' home had she gained a perspective about herself. Her friends at Harvard had made her realise that she was adequate; more than adequate. She'd always been popular both at school and in her society, but when the front door closed on the outside world and she faced the reality of her mother, she immediately became a child again, treated with love, but which quickly transmuted to condescension and aloofness; the triumphs and successes of days were often subsumed within the one or two misdemeanours she'd committed against the integrity of the family – bed not made the way it should have been … dresser not as tidy … soiled underwear not in the right coloured piles … the list of possible infringements against the way her mother had constructed their home seemingly endless. And all the while, her father Sol tried to act as moderator, as honest broker, mediating a line between her mother's love and irritation, between her need for love and her exasperation.

But all that changed for Sarah when she began to live with David, an up-and-coming cellist. They'd met at Harvard; they lived together in the strictest of secrecy; and now they were married. And with her security in her relationship with David came a new and more mature relationship with her mother … from Sarah's side at least. Now she was a married woman, she no longer put up with the slurs and asides and nuances which peppered her mother's mealtime conversation. It irritated David the way in which Sarah picked up on her mother's complaints and threw them back at her, acting like an attorney with a hostile witness; but no matter how she promised on the way there to behave herself when she was in her mother's home, some remark always seemed to goad Sarah to adopt the stand of the lawyer and question why and under what circumstances the allegation had been levelled.

When she was living at home, she often wondered why it was that somebody so admired by friends, social groups and a wide community could be viewed so differently by a daughter? When Sarah had brought schoolfriends home, they'd raved about her mom. They'd tell her that her mom was cool, totally with it, and they'd compare her with their own callous, strict and indifferent mothers. Was Sarah the only one who could see the truth? The only one capable of seeing the real person behind the image. A mother always finding fault with everything she did; who constantly organised and created and performed tasks for and on behalf of Sarah in order to prove what a wonderful mother she was; who drove herself to exhaustion and then ensured that everybody in the vicinity knew that she was acting in the role of martyr. Bertha Kaplan was an amalgam of the Saint, the slave and the spinster, working till she dropped to ensure that everybody knew that everything was precise and a result of her endeavours.

But when it came to warmth, when it came to the open and unshackled expressions of love, there was a void. All the untrammelled love Sarah had enjoyed as a child had come from her father, who also suffered the tyranny of the household. Her mother was the one who assaulted the school when she heard her daughter had been falsely accused of theft; her mother was the one who organised her birthday parties down to the colour of the frosting on the cupcakes; her mother was the one who stayed up late when she came home from a date.

And it wasn't until Sarah left home to go to Harvard that she understood why. It wasn't affection or responsibility. It was control.

Well, it was all too late now. Sarah had taken control of her own life – even though she and David had already lived together for a year before she'd been caught out and been forced to admit it to her mother.

Most mothers recognise they can have little direct influence upon the lives of a thirty-year-old daughter. Certainly, this had been a growing problem between Sarah and her mother since Sarah had turned eighteen … and the problem had continued to grow in intensity year by year. The era of command ameliorated by reward, a regimen which her mother had entertained during most of Sarah's youth, was long past. Sarah no longer obeyed instructions and was no longer swayed by reward, so her mother had been forced to learn a whole new language of relationship; a new way of maintaining control without the directness of command. It was a delicate balance, a new field of endeavour which she found interfered with the relationship she wanted to enjoy with her daughter.

It was David who saw the relationship in its true light, David who explained to Sarah what she had instinctively known all her life but refused to admit to herself. Bertha sought a loving, maternal relationship with Sarah and couldn't come to an accommodation with Sarah's independence, her feminism, her antipathy to the normal and traditional ways in which Jewish wives behaved. Sarah wouldn't be, now or ever, a typical, normal young Jewish woman. It was only by the grace of God that she had fallen in love with a Jewish man. She rarely went to synagogue. She attended few Jewish clubs or societies. Many Friday nights as she was growing into adulthood, she had refused to be present at the family's Sabbath dinner, instead going to lectures on international politics or to dinner with friends.

But it was David who rationalised Bertha's discomfort with her daughter. He had seen it in the first few weeks of their relationship when Sarah suggested that they share an apartment together.

'I think your mother would have problems with that,' he'd said.

Sarah had burst out laughing. 'Every mother would have problems with it, but that's not going to stop me doing it.'

'But your mother is in a special situation,' David had told her. 'She's never had a father. She never knew a father's love. Her father died after he'd been brutalised in a concentration camp. She has a fear which you will never begin to understand, and that fear comes out as a need to protect and control.'

David's explanation of something which Sarah had always known instinctively, yet which she'd never espoused so clearly, stayed with her every time she saw her mother; but it didn't stop Sarah's years of frustration erupting with some biting remark.

It hadn't stopped her moving in with David either. And true to form, Bertha Kaplan came to an accommodation in her own mind, but still said to her friends that Sarah was living in a nice Manhattan apartment. And David was living in a nice apartment too.

Having spoken to dozens of women in her situation, Bertha Kaplan's consolation at the gulf which was part of her adult relationship with Sarah was that few mothers had succeeded in maintaining the nexus with their children, once they left home. Most managed to alienate their children with words and deeds. The only reason that Sarah wasn't alienated from her parents was David's calming voice and his gentle way of nudging Sarah's mother back across the line which she occasionally over-stepped, and of rationalising the afternoon's conversation, of defusing Sarah as they drove back to Manhattan.

They entered the driveway of Bertha and Sol Kaplan's whiteboard home with its delicate lawns and geometrically trimmed paths. When Sarah was growing up, she hadn't been allowed to use toys like bikes or carts on the grass in case she damaged the manicured surface with tyre tracks. To this day, Sarah felt a sense of prohibition as she walked out of her car and across the grass to approach the doorway.

'Sarah,' her mother said in delight as she opened the door. Despite the heat of the day, they were greeted by a blast of warm kitchen air, suffused with the smell of roasting chicken, pumpkin, roast potatoes and apple strudel.

'David,' she shouted in a slightly – but noticeably – louder and more enthusiastic voice, throwing both arms around their necks and hugging them in a three-way embrace.

'How come you're so late? I've been in the kitchen worrying', she said as she led them into the lounge room where Sarah's father was ensconced in his easychair reading the Sunday edition of the paper. Her mother continued, 'You should have been here half an hour ago. Not that it matters, don't worry. Except about the food. It's nothing. I'll try to rescue it while you talk to your father.'

Bertha walked out of the lounge room towards the kitchen, unaware of the way in which she had caused an atmosphere of tension. Sol put the paper down and sighed. It was what he'd been doing, unconsciously, for their entire marriage; these days, sighing was like breathing. He stood, wordlessly kissing his daughter and David on the cheeks. He wore the look of a man who has lost the rhythm of living and the energy of life, like an elderly dog, no longer good for anything other than being kept around the house.

Sarah was glad to see him, but felt her usual sense of unease as she stood in his front parlour, a room from which, because of its porcelains, rugs and furniture, her mother had restricted her until she was in the last years of high school. The room remained a chintz nightmare and the lingering smell of her father's cigars, expunged from the house ten years earlier by the shrill health warnings of her mother, still hung faintly in the air.

'So, what's new with you kids? Sarah, how's the job? You still enjoying getting peoples' property back? And you,' he said, transferring his attention to David. 'I read the reviews of your concert with the Chicago Symphony. I'm proud of you. What did they say, "The Rostropovich of the new millenium". Wonderful, David. Y'know, I heard Rostropovich when he played Carnegie. Just like you played there. Even then, he was old. He waddled onto the stage. Could hardly stand. He *schlumps* into a chair. I thought he was a gonner, but for the next hour, he plays the cello like he's a spring chicken. I'll never forget it. Passion? You want passion? You listen to Rostropovich's records. Now there's passion! And now you! They're calling you the next Rostropovich. Wonderful. *Mazeltov.*

'Eh, I'm rambling. So, tell me children, what's new with you?'

Without waiting for an answer, he continued, 'You wanna know what's new with me? Remember I bought that new ride-on motor mower. *Cut the grass sitting on your ass* ... Some advert. Twelve hundred bucks that *schmuck* of a thing cost me. It broke down after the first three days. *Punkt.* Stops in the middle of the lawn like it's gone out on strike. I'm sitting there and people are walking down the street saying things to me like, "Hey buddy, you broken down. Wanna lift?" I feel humiliated. I take it back to the guy. I'm reasonable. I tell him I've been humiliated and that it's a brand-new machine. You know what that *mumser* says ... ?'

'Dad,' Sarah interrupted. 'You haven't got a problem. It's under warranty.'

'Problem! What do you know about problems! You think I don't know it's under warranty. What does a warranty mean these days! *Gurnisht*! My day, a warranty meant something. I tell that to the smartass behind the counter. He says he'll fix it. I say what am I going to use to cut the grass while you're fixing it? I tell him I got grass outside you could lose a sheep in. He says, use what you used before. I tell him I've thrown the old mower away. *Farcochteneh* piece of Japanese crap. I say I bought a new motor mower so I wouldn't have to yig my *kishkers* out on the lawn. He says to me "so if your grass is that long, call in a lawn mower service", like I'm some Rockefeller. I say to him you want me to call a service, I'll send the bill to you. He tells me take it or leave it.'

Sol looked at his daughter, 'Sarah, I want you to handle it. I want you to write me a letter. No, I want you to phone him. He won't listen to me. I was jumping up and down shouting. He says you want to sue? Sue. I told him, "Sure, I'll sue. I've got a daughter, a Harvard lawyer. You think I'm some *schmuck* from the stetls you can play games with." I tell him he'll have the biggest lawsuit this side of the Supreme Court. I haven't closed my eyes one night since I started with this son of a bitch. You've got to help. You're a lawyer. Do something.'

'Dad, we've just driven two hours. You think we can have a drink before we seek leave to petition the Supreme Court? A drink would be nice.'

Sarah looked at David who was fighting back a smile.

Sol scowled. 'You want a drink? I should serve you? You're my daughter. You know where the drinks are. Go get a drink.'

David turned and walked over to the drink cabinet in the corner of the room, where he opened the fridge, got himself a Dr Peppers and Sarah a club soda.

'So what are you going to do about my motor mower? You saw the condition of the lawn. I'm ashamed to stick my head out the door. My neighbours are laughing at me.'

'Dad, your grass is perfect. We could use it for a tablecloth. You don't need a lawyer for this. You need somebody like David who can negotiate, talk sense to the guy. You get too emotional, too involved. Me too. I'll just get angry.'

Irate, he said, 'Involved. Of course I'm involved. What? You think this is happening to somebody else? I'm your father. I paid for you to go to Harvard. You think you got there on thin air? This is a legal matter. Right up your alley. It's up to you to do something.'

David sipped from his Dr Peppers and intervened, 'Give me his name and telephone number, Sol. Tomorrow morning I'll give him a ring and see what I can negotiate.'

Sol smiled and nodded. He turned to Sarah and said, 'I love this boy. Y'know, if you stop making it as a musician, you'll never want for business. You can become a lawyer. And you,' he said to Sarah, 'you should learn from David. He's not too big to help out family.' Sol picked up the motor mower salesman's business card from the mantlepiece, and said to him, 'David, you've got a tongue on you sweeter than honey. Tell him all I want is a replacement mower until mine's fixed. I wanted to tell him that, but I got so angry I just left. That's not too much to ask. They do that in car showrooms for good public relations.'

'I'll ask, Sol. I'll ask.'

He turned to his daughter. 'Thank God you married him. Keep him, for Christ's sake, Sarah. No more running off to Czechoslovakia or Turkey. Look what I could lose out on if he gets fed up and dumps you.'

He moved over to David and kissed him again on the forehead.

Sarah smiled, 'Dad, this is some kind of record. I've been in the house less than two minutes and already a guilt trip. Enough, okay.'

Sol shrugged. 'What guilt trips? Guilt don't exist in this house.'

Before David could intervene and prevent Sarah from launching into a full-scale philippic, her mother came out of the kitchen. 'I think we're lucky. Hold your breath, because I think I've managed to rescue the chicken. It's on the table. Come children. Eat. You must be starving.'

CHAPTER TWO

BUENOS AIRES, ARGENTINA, PRESENT DAY

The Jews of Argentina shifted uncomfortably in their seats. Two thousand of them in the rebuilt Jewish Communal Hall, one of Buenos Aires' larger auditoriums. Armed security guards, as well as a contingent of Jewish militia trained by Mossad, stood at every entry and exit way in the hall as the Rabbi spoke.

Not only were there armed guards outside the hall but, within a two kilometre radius of the hall, security personnel stood on street corners to give early warnings of a possible raid by neo-Nazis.

The reason that the Jews, leaders of the 300 000 strong Argentine Jewish community, felt discomforted was because Rabbi Noah Friedman, head of the Los Angeles-based Simon Wiesenthal Centre, was telling them things that everybody knew but nobody wanted to have said out loud. Standing on the podium, he was like a Jeremiah, shaking his finger in accusation at the Argentine government, its police force and even at the Jewish community leaders for having allowed the memory of the 120 Jews who had been killed in two bomb attacks to have been muted by the passage of time.

'I know what you're thinking,' he shouted. 'You're thinking it's easy for me, living in Los Angeles, to come down here and to accuse you of indifference. I don't know the circumstances of living in Argentina, where the police force and the government are anti-Semitic and where your next-door neighbour could very well have been a Nazi storm-trooper. Sure, I don't know the difficulties first hand. But what I do know is that indifference kills. Not today. Maybe not tomorrow, but through indifference, through allowing the memory of the Jews killed in the hideous bombings of the Israeli Embassy and the Jewish Community Centre to fade, these crimes *will* be repeated. Every time we Jews close our eyes to the crimes of history, every time we say to ourselves, "Listen, things aren't so bad now. Let's keep quiet and continue living the way we're living," every time some Jew says that, he's signing a death sentence for another Jew in a generation to come.'

He took a sip of water and cleared his throat. He looked at the audience. They were all decent people. There wasn't one of them with whom he wouldn't proudly associate. These were his own people; Jews just like himself. Some were probably as religious as him, some were maybe cultural Jews. Who knows? But one thing was absolutely certain. No Los Angeles Jew would even begin to understand what it was like to live in Buenos Aires, in Argentina; a nation whose government had allowed the greatest criminals in history, the Nazi elite, to flood across its borders after the war and find safe haven for their money and assets. Most had died, of course, in the fifty years since the war, but in the last ten-to-fifteen years, young neo-Nazis had been rampaging around Jewish communities in Argentina and causing utter mayhem. And the police, as anti-Semitic and as full of ignorance and hatred as the neo-Nazis, were totally indifferent to their Fascist activities.

Rabbi Friedman continued. 'I've written a letter to your President demanding that action be taken against those responsible for the obscenities committed in 1992 at the Israeli Embassy and 1994 at the Jewish Community Centre. Years have dragged by since these outrages in which more than one hundred of our people died. Years of pathetic investigations and culpable criminality. Of course the government knows who the criminals are! Of course the government knows that it was people here, working with Hezbollah guerillas, working with Iran and assisted by your local police force. There's not much *we* can do against the Hezbollah, though Mossad have got them as one of their international priorities. But there's a hell of a lot that your government can do against the police and the Army who were hand in glove with the evil swine who murdered our people.'

One member of the audience was Dr Luis Forenjo, an elderly man from Avellaneda just outside Buenos Aires. He wasn't squirming at all. He was listening intently to the translation of the Rabbi's words. He had a letter on his desk from a young woman, which he would now answer. What the Rabbi said was right. It was up to him. Instead of going home to bed, he would return to his office that very night and answer the young woman's letter. And while he was doing that, he would deal with another matter as well.

NEW YORK, PRESENT DAY

Joshua Krantz used all of the net profits from his shares in his latest movie, twenty-two and a half million dollars, to perpetuate the memory of his family. He was fulfilling a promise made to his father only days before Hermann Krantz had died of a stroke a couple of years earlier; but it was really an unspoken promise made on behalf of his grandparents, whom he had only known as a boy.

It was a vast amount of money, a fortune by anybody's account, but it was only seed money. Krantz, one of

Hollywood's most successful movie directors, had spent six months using his legendary leverage and powers of persuasion to encourage Los Angeles banks, finance houses, movie studios, and wealthy actors to match his generosity. Just as Ted Turner had given a billion dollars to the United Nations and persuaded other members of the mega-rich community to dip into their pockets, so Josh had spent the past half a year hitting the phones.

In the year after he had returned from Slovakia, he had managed to raise over $70 million, rent office premises in uptown New York, persuade his lawyer Sarah Kaplan to become his new Chief Executive Officer, and inform the entire American ethnic community that the *Moishe, Vilma and Hermann Krantz Institute for Justice for the Victims of Evil*, was open for business.

Despite a desperate plea from Sarah that the name was too long and unwieldy for any letterhead, Josh Krantz insisted that his grandparent's and father's names must be perpetuated. Eventually the lobby and activist group became known, simply, as The Krantz Institute. Its purpose was to fight on behalf of powerless refugees who had been dispossessed of their homes or lands, to begin the process of reclaiming property, money, jewellery, business, or any other asset stolen when some invading force of conquerors swept through a country. The victims could be anybody – Jews, Africans, central Europeans, Asians – religion, race, political belief and colour had no bearing on whether The Institute took up the challenge to fight for the rights of a dispossessed victim against the nation from which he or she had been expelled. The only criterion was that the applicant had to have left the country of origin under duress. And neither was time a determining factor in whether The Institute would take up the cudgels on behalf of somebody seeking help; if the property had been stolen from a great-great-grandparent, then inquiries would still be made, though staff took great pains to explain to victims that the further back in time a wrong existed, the lower the chance of it being righted.

Josh had originally insisted that The Institute fight only for Jewish victims and descendants of the Eastern European anti-Semitism, the Holocaust, Stalinism and neo-Nazism, but Sarah had insisted just as vehemently that justice meant justice for everyone, and that justice was blind to a person's colour, religion, sex or nationality. Josh was eventually persuaded. After a year of high-profile operation in which the activities of The Institute were lauded by the media, he was satisfied. Indeed, whenever he flew to New York and entered The Institute, he was always gratified to see a waiting room full of faces from Asia, Africa, South America, as well as Europe.

His visit this morning was unexpected. Sarah thought he was in Denver, Colorado filming some new movie. He had only just completed his quarterly inspection of the books, the personnel, and the results of The Institute's work. As with everything Sarah did, there was almost nothing with which he could find fault. He did manage to criticise overspending on aspects of human resources relating to staff training, but Sarah insisted that it was money well and necessarily spent.

So his sudden unscheduled appearance surprised the front-office staff, as well as Sarah's assistants. It was a Monday morning, and she was held up in traffic on her way into the office. Josh sat in her office, waiting. Outside, a concerned PA got hold of her on her mobile phone.

'Sarah, it's Mandy. Josh Krantz's here. He's sitting in your office.' Her voice sounded concerned and conspiratorial.

'So?'

'What do you want me to do?' she asked.

'Mandy, you've got plenty of things to get on with. Get on with them.'

Twenty minutes later, Sarah breezed into her office, acknowledged Josh, walked over and kissed him on the cheek. 'So, to what do I owe this unexpected honour?'

He shrugged. 'I'm in the middle of a shit-fight over a claim for plagiarism from some author I've never heard of. Apparently he sent his manuscript into my office ten years ago. Somebody rejected it. Last year I make *The Sayer Connection*, and the asshole claims he sees aspects of his plot plus a couple of lines of dialogue which are the same as in his book. In the middle of making a fucking movie, I'm suddenly slapped with an injunction on a film I made last year. Now I have to stop all work at a zillion dollars a day because I'm ordered to appear in court in New York. For God's sake! My lawyers can't get the judge to see reason. He wants to make a name for himself by hauling my ass into court and interrogating me personally. Publicity, the works. I reckon he's about to run for office.'

Sarah shook her head. Since she left the law, she had grown to see justice from the point of view of the victim. And so often, ordinary people were victims of lawyers. 'Can't you …'

He shook his head. 'We've tried everything. I'll be in contempt if I don't appear, just for the record. Then I can smile, my lawyers will assure His Honour that I never even read the book, we'll settle for a hundred grand, and I'll be back on a plane tonight. Which means we can have lunch.'

'No can do. I'm having lunch with Senator Graceling. He's head of the Appropriations Committee. It's an important meeting because I want to follow through that letter I sent him two months back about the government putting money into The Institute instead of everything coming from donations. Federal funding will ease the burden.'

'Can I come?' he asked hesitantly. He sounded timorous, socially inept; hardly the warlord of Hollywood. She smiled. So potent in Hollywood, so insecure in the real world. She had been so near to having a full-on relationship with him when she was representing him in his quest to reclaim his father's and grandparent's home in Slovakia. Only common sense and restraint on both sides had prevented it. When Josh offered her the job of CEO of his new foundation, she had at first rejected it out of hand. She was frightened that her fondness of him, and their close encounter of the sexual kind in Eastern Europe could affect her judgements both professionally and in her marriage. By any criteria, Joshua Krantz was a very attractive man. Stunningly wealthy, divorced, and still wearing the crown as Hollywood's most creative mind for a decade and a half, most of the women in The Institute were in love with him. Some of the men too.

It had been a tough decision, but she had chosen David over Josh. Substance over image. Josh had been terrific. He was understanding, generous, and gave them an extraordinary wedding present, though declining their invitation, citing his need to be on location in South America. But there was always something in the background. Some deeply contrived subtext between them. She could feel it, whenever they were alone together; some buried desire, some reminiscence of a past potential, the use of a word or look which wasn't quite appropriate to the occasion. Sarah knew that the last thing Josh wanted was to come between her and David; he loved them both. He'd even persuaded David to score music for his last movie, for an obscene amount of money. But she would never allow herself to be in a situation with him that might be compromising. She'd done that once in Slovakia. She'd so nearly given in. It had nearly ruined her relationship with David.

'I said, can I come with you?'

She smiled, and apologised. 'Sorry, I'm miles away. Of course you can come. You're the boss. And frankly, Senator Graceling would love to have lunch with you. He's such a poseur, he'd be the first to recognise that being seen with you is worth a couple of thousand votes.'

Mandy knocked on the door, and walked in with a tray of coffee for them both. Deliberately waiting until she'd left, Sarah asked, 'Is your court appearance the only reason for this visit?'

He sipped his coffee and smiled. She was so much like a wife … she knew way in advance when he was obfuscating. He looked at her, deliberating on how to broach the subject, the silence testimony to the difficulty of what he needed to say. 'No, seeing the judge is the reason I'm in New York, not the reason I came to The Institute.

'Sarah, over the past year, you and me, we've had times when we disagreed with each other about the direction in which The Institute was heading. We've compromised, but essentially, we both agree that our primary function is to help people who were thrown out of their homes; that we're here to help them get their property back. Money, jewellery, businesses … doesn't matter.'

Sarah nodded. She was somewhat concerned by the sudden change in his mood. She wondered if perhaps she was in some sort of trouble … maybe overstepping her authority as Chief Executive … maybe spending too much.

He mulled over the next thoughts before he said, 'Most of our work here deals in issues of the past. Getting back property stolen by Hitler's Nazis, by the Nazi Poles and Hungarians and Ustasha; getting back what Stalin and his henchmen stole; helping people in Africa and South America reclaim what was stolen from them.'

'That's our job, Josh. That's our Mission Statement.'

'And that's what we all agreed on a year ago when the Board met in its first session, and hammered out why we're all here.'

Again, Sarah agreed. Now she was more mystified than ever.

'Two months ago, I was making a film in Argentina. They're very keen to turn Buenos Aires into a southern Hollywood, a production centre for movies. They stand a chance, as well. The country's got a lot going for it. Snow and ice in the south, jungle in the interior, a city which looks like Paris … it's all there. Tell me, Sarah, how much do you know about South America today?' he asked.

She shrugged. 'About as much as any other North American, I guess.'

'And modern-day Germany? And Austria?' he asked.

'A lot more about Europe than I know about South America. I travel to Europe a couple of times a year dealing with the governments. Why Josh? Where's all this leading?'

'Sarah, you'd be the first to know about the growth of neo-Nazism in Europe. Young people, skinheads, brainless fascists giving Nazi salutes and screaming out '*Heil Hitler*' and burning migrant hostels. But it's travelling like a virus around the world, Sarah. It's beginning to happen in South America and Australia and Asia and Russia. Not the *Heil Hitler* stuff, but young unemployed, uneducated men joining extreme right-wing Nazi-style organisations, beating the shit out of foreigners and homosexuals and Jews. South America, North America, Britain, France, Eastern Europe, Central Europe. It's like Germany in the early thirties all over again. They're Hitler's grandchildren. That bastard's been resurrected.'

Sarah Kaplan looked at her boss, her friend. This was information which was carried in every news magazine. Now she was really wondering where he was going with all this. 'Okay. Now tell me the punchline. Should I start packing for a warm climate, or for a cold climate?'

He smiled at her. Disarmingly. 'I want us, this Institute, to start a new division. A whole new arena of activity. Not just getting back the property for victims, but preventing property from being stolen and people being made refugees in the first place. To warn the world about what's really happening. To open the sewer covers, and expose the filth that's gathering in the dark corners underground and in cellars and places where the sun doesn't shine.'

He had that Messianic look in his eyes; she'd seen it several times before. A look that told her he had a goal, a mission, and would allow nothing to get in the way of his objective. And she certainly knew him well enough to know that he'd thought the concept through carefully before coming to see her; he had a plan in mind, something which was probably outrageous and brilliant and which nobody had thought of before. But even she was stunned when he continued, 'Think back, Sarah, to the time of the Jews being expelled from Judea by the Romans. They spread all over what was then known of the world. How do you think they kept in touch, warned each other of the dangers which faced Judaism, told every community, no matter where, just what was going on? They created an unbelievable way of communicating with each other.'

She looked at him in amazement. 'The *Responsa*,' she said.

'Right! The *Responsa*. Communities were always able to keep in touch with each other, letting each other know what was going on because the Rabbis answered the questions of distant communities about Jewish laws and custom. Sometimes it was something simple like explaining what one Rabbi had decided about the modern interpretation of some ancient law. But sometimes, the *Responsa* was all about warning communities of the growth of problems, telling them that they were in the path of some future cataclysm. How do you think they coped with life in totally different worlds from the biblical lands, and still kept their religion intact, still kept themselves intact?'

Sarah looked at him, a sinking feeling settling in her guts. When he was in one of these moods, he was like a biblical prophet ... unbendable, self-righteous, incapable of listening to contradictory arguments.

'That's what I want to do, Sarah. I want to set up a new *Responsa*. I want community leaders all over the world to tell a central organisation what problems are growing in their area. Tell the world what's going on. Tell our organisation, so that, with our powers of communication, we can tell the world and tread on evil before it takes hold. Imagine how many lives could have been saved if Hitler's plans had been stopped in their tracks in the 1920s.'

'Josh, that's what the United Nations, and the Anti-Defamation League, and Amnesty International and dozens of other organisations are doing right now. How can we, with relatively modest funds, and a limited staff, possibly do what you're suggesting?'

Joshua Krantz looked at her with bemusement, stunned that her normally wonderful mind hadn't followed the trail his own mind had been working on for the past months. 'There's a Jewish community in almost every town in almost every country in the world. We write to everybody, and get them to send us the information about what's happening in their area. Anything to do with fascism and anti-Semitism and Nazism and skin-heads and revisionism. Then we collate it all, and get the Israeli Ambassador in the United Nations to alert the world to what's going on in the world's most public forum.'

She looked at him in amazement.

'So,' he said, standing. 'I've got things to do. What time's lunch?'

CHAPTER THREE

RUTHENIA, 1903

Serel left her village, making a promise to God that as soon as she landed in New York she would mourn the death of her husband. She had no idea how long it would take her to get to the new promised land but however long the journey, she would never forget her obligations to God or her husband. She knew that she should already begin the ritual of sitting *sheva* for her husband. These were the seven days of intense mourning, days when she and her children must sit on low stools as the entire *stetl* came by her house, men offering their prayers and consolation, the women offering their consolation and poppyseed cake. She and the children mustn't wash their hair, nor look in a mirror, nor lift a finger to prepare themselves a meal; all they had to do was to think of Nussan, husband and father, and the joy he had brought to their lives. Then the entire village would know what a good wife she was, what wonderful, tragic children they had raised, and the Rabbi would say prayers for the eternal peace of her dead husband.

After the first seven days, God and age-old customs demanded that she should continue to grieve for the *shloshim* period, thirty days in all, during which the mourning wasn't quite as intense as in the first seven; days when she could occasionally get up from the low stool, wash more than just her hands and face and perform other acts which were prohibited to grieving widows during the first week of their bereavement. She knew that without a son who was past the age of his *bar mitzvah*, there would be nobody in her family to say the *kaddish* prayers for her husband, and the Rabbi would take on the responsibility. He would do it without being asked. She knew that he would gladly act on her behalf. He was a good man, a kind man. Not a learned man, but then a small *stetl* such as the one where she lived couldn't afford a learned Rabbi, not like the ones in the great *yeshivas* where hundreds of students gathered to sit at the feet of a *maggid*, a man whose learning encompassed everything, who had all the answers; and who, when he died, sat at the right hand of God.

How long had she been on the road now? She'd lost count of time. She'd hardly rested since they first left the village. She thought back with shame to what had happened two, or was it four, hours earlier. She had stood for a moment at the signpost, her children still clustered around her legs like newborn ducks just emerged from their nest. She read the name of the village, mouthed it, almost tasted it. Was it for a last lingering memory? Just the name left a acidic bitter taste in her mouth. Please God, she would never have to say it again. She had stood there, looking back at the grey smoky pall which hung over the village. In the distance, she could see men and women walking around, still in a daze. Further up the hill, where the Christian town sat smugly atop the crest, men and women were beginning to stand in the middle of the street and look down upon the Jews in their *stetl* in the lower town. How arrogant they were, standing, pointing. Were they laughing, or just deciding what Jewish property they could steal?

Serel remembered clearly the wave of nausea which had swept over her and she remembered feeling that, while the journey ahead was so long and frightening, anything was better than the misery of her people and the hatred of her Christian neighbours. Even leaving her family to protect her children was necessary in her mind. And she had burst into tears and terrified her three children.

Now she reached up underneath her breasts and felt the amulet and its gold chain hang heavily in her bodice; she could feel the additional weight on her shoulders. The foul thing was cursed, that she knew. Her every inclination, the screaming nightmares in her mind, told her to rip it from her neck and throw it into a distant field, to get rid of it, to expunge it from her body, away from the presence of her children, and out of her memory. But the rational part of her, the part which had enabled her to survive marriage to Nussan and all his wild schemes, told her that without it, she was dead, a woman with no money, with no way of buying food or transport or passage to America … what could a woman do?

And so she would take the devil whose grasp was around her neck and carry it with her until she could sell it and then, perhaps then, she would pass on the misery that it had brought.

She turned her attention to the road. The first step beyond the village had been the most difficult. It had been a step into the unknown. Not that she hadn't trodden that same road leading to her husband's field a thousand times, but never before as a widow, knowing she would not be returning later that night to the security of her little home.

That seemed hours ago. Yet even now, after she'd been walking for so long, it was still only early morning and she was exhausted. Serel thought back to the events of the night and to just a few hours earlier when in the grey half-light of the morning she had crept from the river bank with her children. What a night it had been, she sighed to herself. She had enjoyed no sleep for the whole night; she had lain with her children on the river bank while her house, her clothes, and her bed had been debased by the madmen. The feather doona, the bolster, the lovely pillows which her head used to sink into as she drifted exhausted off to sleep, all had been strewn shamelessly over the filthy ground outside her house. Her bed had been burned in the conflagration. She had loved that bed. It was a gift from her father, given to them with smiles and nudges and embarrassing remarks, when she and Nussan were first married. On the first night of their wedding, she had been frightened of the bed. Would the sheets be stained with enough of her blood of purity? Would her mother be able to hang the sheet out of her bedroom window the following morning to show all their neighbours that her daughter was a virgin on her wedding night?

She felt herself beginning to cry but fought to hold it back so as not to alarm her already frightened children. Her wedding. Would she ever again know the joy of a wedding ceremony, of the comfort of a husband? Nussan, her mother and her father, were proud of her the following morning after her marriage. There was sufficient of her own blood, even though her mother was at their bedroom door early the following morning with a vial full of sheep's blood. When she made love for the first time to Nussan, it hurt her; but a week or so later she began to enjoy it. During their first year together, her body began to respond to Nussan's warmth, his gentleness and his strength. And when she'd been married for years, Serel looked forward to the time when the children were asleep in their room and she and Nussan could sink down into the deep pillows, into the enfolding mattress which moulded to fit their bodies, and they would hold each other.

In the warming early-morning air, mist still gripping

the ground from the cold night, Serel shook her head sadly in memory of a life that would be no more. Unless God smiled on her, what man, except somebody poor and old and feeble, would want to take on the responsibility of a widow with three children. A madman maybe? Oh well! She had more important things to think about now than her own enjoyment. She must protect her children. She didn't even have time to bury her husband.

They continued their walk into the unknown road ahead and Serel began to sing a song that she knew the children liked. It was a lullaby. Her mother had sung it to her when she was a little girl and had comforted her in the cold depths of winter when bare branches scratched the outside of the windows, as the wind blew from the distant mountains in howling gales.

> Come children. Come. The summer is here.
> The winter's defeated, it's now time to cheer.
> Life is so happy. Things are so good.
> Come children. Come. There's plenty of food.
> Come children. Come. The Lord blesses you.
> Don't make Him sad, so smile at Him too.

Yitzchok and Rosl smiled and instinctively reached out to hold their mother. Yitzchok began to join in. Rosl followed. Baby Eva stirred. The road ahead still stretched far into the distance in spite of how far they'd already walked. So strange. So unfamiliar. As the morning mists slowly evaporated, the countryside became sharply defined.

It was a long, long way from Roznava to Poprad. In the early days of their marriage, she'd so badly wanted to go there; to see the beautiful shops, and the women in their fine dresses and carriages with horses, and houses built on three levels with running water and electric lights. But they couldn't afford such a journey. And anyway, Nussan had said that it would take at least four days for a strong man to walk … how could they do it with young children; but in their fantasies, lying in bed at night, dreaming their dreams, they'd talked about going there one year for a break from the farm. What a joke, she thought. The impossible past now became the improbable future.

Four days for a strong man; but she was only a woman carrying a baby with two children at her heels. She had all their possessions of her world slung over her back. She had just a handful of *kopeks* in her bag in case, God forbid, she had to buy food. She was terrified, but everything in her heart told her that this was the right decision, that she had to get away, that behind her was where her husband had been killed, the place where she was surrounded by enemies which the villagers were powerless to fight; and she knew with absolute certainty that the madmen who had rampaged and killed last night were sobering up now, and in the evening when they'd drunk more, they would come back again until they had found the amulet.

She felt the warmth of the heavy charm inside her bodice, pulling down on her breasts. She had no spare hand with which to feel it or take it out and have a look at its strange carvings. It had brought evil into her village, her home. Perhaps the markings were the markings of the devil. Perhaps she was carrying the evil eye. Her mother and her aunts and the women of the *stetl* warned each other about the evil eye, *kin ein ahora*. Beware of the evil eye. Dear God, what could she do? Without the amulet and without the necklace, she had nothing. It might be evil, but how would they survive without the money it would bring? Her plan was to sell them in Poprad and have enough money to pay for the rest of the journey. Maybe she could even afford tickets on a coach which could take her to Kraków, then Wroclaw, and maybe even to Berlin. Who knows? Maybe she could even ride like a proper lady all the way to Hamburg. If she could sell the cursed amulet. If she could survive. Serel realised that she had stopped walking. The children were looking at her in surprise. What could she do? Every time she thought, every time her fear struck her, she stopped to think. She must learn to think and walk at the same time.

It was already well into the afternoon and the land had long ago lost its familiarity. Serel continued to look behind her as they walked down the long narrow road, most of the fields hidden by tall hedgerows. Twice, Rosl had slipped in one of the muddy ruts and yelped in pain, grabbing at her ankle. Fortunately she hadn't damaged herself. Although she hobbled, it was more for sympathy than for reality. What would Serel do if Rosl became lame? How could she carry two children? Yitzchok continued to help Serel by taking Eva and carrying her, but he wasn't a big boy and his help was given for increasingly short distances as his energy began to drain from him.

They had been walking for at least six hours. Maybe seven. Or so she guessed from the position of the sun. All of them had begun their journey carrying bottles of water tied into the straps around their bodies. Periodically they became increasingly light, only to become heavy again when they filled them in nearby streams. Fortunately, water wasn't a problem. There were plenty of little springs and rivers crisscrossing the area. They used them as a way of washing their feet, and they splashed themselves with cold water and filled up their bottles; it was an excuse to cool down, and to rest.

But what they didn't find was food. She had been so frightened of staying in the *stetl* that she'd rushed away, unprepared. Now Serel was beginning to fear starvation. She had imagined that food would be as plentiful along the road as it was when she and Nussan went out for a picnic. There were always berries and fruit from pear or apple trees. But then she realised her own stupidity. When they went on a picnic, they always had a basket and in the basket were bread and cheese and pickles and sometimes if they were lucky, some chicken or duck or even sometimes some lamb if the butcher had just slaughtered a sheep. In her mind, she remembered the joy of finding the branches of trees bursting with apples and other fruits. Reality now made her understand that they were just delights to eat when her stomach was already full. And this wasn't the growing time for apples.

Now, her stomach was empty and her children were complaining. There hadn't been any food left in the house. The evil men last night may have eaten it or more likely it was destroyed when they burned her home. She should have asked neighbours for help. They would have been more than willing to help a widow; but Serel had been too terrified for herself and her children to delay. She hadn't said goodbye to anybody. She'd just thrown together a few clothes and other belongings, and a cooking pot, and tried to escape the return of the madmen.

What was she going to do for her children? Eva, she could feed. There was still some milk in her breasts. Not much. The child was eating minced-up meats and vegetables. But what about Yitzchok? What about Rosl? What about herself? How were they going to eat? Every farmhouse they had passed on the road was a Christian home. Farmers in the fields looked at her and her family in suspicion, in hostility. Everywhere, there were pigs in sties, grovelling in the filth and snorting at their approach.

The last thing she would do would be to eat *chazereih*; and the last thing those Christian *mumsers* would do is feed a hungry Jewish widow and her children.

There would be no Jews until Poprad. Of that she was sure. Her village was only twenty kilometres from Kosice, a big town with many Jews. There she could have found a dozen people to help her, take her and her children in. But she wasn't heading in that direction. Kosice was the gateway to the East, to the North, to Poland and Russia and more hatred and pogroms. No. She was on her way to America, the *goldeneh medina*, the new home in which she'd find peace and security for herself and her children. And now she was on the road to Poprad, and to things which she didn't know about. Were there villages on the road? And if so were there *stetls* on the outskirts of the villages where Jews huddled together in fear of the Christian madmen?

Yitzchok pulled at Serel's skirt. 'Mummy, I'm hungry. When can we stop and eat?'

'Soon *bubeleh*. In good time. In God's time, but we want to go to America. If we stop and eat all the while, we'll never get there.'

'But Mummy,' said Rosl. 'We must eat. I want some bread and *schmaltz*. With a glass of lime water. Where can we get it?'

She looked at her children and smiled bravely. The realisation had been slowly growing in her mind that soon she might have to turn back. She had been impetuous and stupid like her husband. There was no way that she could possibly walk with her children to America. Not without careful planning and lots of money. Eight hours on the road had brought that reality into sharp focus. Nussan her husband may God rest his soul, was impetuous, a fool, that's why he had brought destruction on the village.

'Children,' she said as they stopped to regain their breath. 'Children, what about we go to America another day?' Her voice was dry and rasping.

Yitzchok looked up at her and shook his head in wonder. 'Really?' he asked.

'Of course. We don't have to go to America today. We can go tomorrow or the day after. Why don't we go back and see our friends in the village. Would you like to do that?'

Rosl said nothing. Neither did Yitzchok. They knew that their mother didn't mean it. This wasn't a game. They had walked too far. This was unknown territory for them. Their mother was tired. Sometimes she spoke like this when she'd been working hard in the house or the fields.

As though by instinct she knew they didn't believe her. She stroked their heads, one after the other, clutching baby Eva closely to her bosom and walked on. How could she possibly go back? What would she say to her neighbours? They would already have come to her house looking for her. They would have found Nussan and taken him to bury, to say prayers. They would be frantic worrying about her, thinking that she and the children had been swept up by the madmen and abducted, maybe raped or killed. How would she explain her absence? Fool, she said to herself. Fool, just like your husband. A fool.

They rounded a corner in the rutted road, walking between the tracks made by carts and carefully avoided the horse and cow droppings which festooned their path. Would she turn back now or would she keep walking just a few kilometres, just in case. In case what? In case God in His infinite mercy provided for them. She laughed. The children smiled, happy that she was happy. God provide for them! Where was God when they needed

Him? Serel had always been a believer. Not like Nussan. He used to taunt her with his blasphemies and his ungodly ways. Well, he had certainly suffered God's punishment but if there was a God, why was Serel suffering? Why was He punishing the wife and the children for the crimes of the husband? But then, why did God punish widows and orphans? The Rabbi used to say, 'Who knows the mind of God?' But Serel didn't care about the mind. All she cared about was justice. She found herself stroking Eva's hair and kissing her, holding her so tightly that the little girl began to shift her body in discomfort.

They walked until in the distance, they saw a field with a low hedgerow. The field was being prepared for the summer harvest. Serel's heart stopped. She'd seen people in fields before, but the people always seemed to be at a distance from where they were. These people were working near to the road. There was no way that she could avoid their seeing her. God protect her. She averted her head from their gaze, and spat three times onto the ground to protect her and the children from evil. Then she instinctively put her hand to her breast and felt for the solid outline of the amulet, and said another quick prayer; then she let the accursed thing go. Why was she putting her faith in something which had only brought misery?

The people in the field hadn't noticed her. But they soon would. Then she'd be in terrible trouble. There were wagons in the middle of the field, horses tethered under trees and six or seven people working with hoes, making long lines in the earth. Some were weeding, others were throwing straw into the ground to give it nourishment and to prevent more weeds and frost ravaging next season's crops. Serel's fear intensified. There were women working with the men, but that probably wouldn't save her. Sometimes women could be vicious and nasty. They might look at her with suspicion. Christian women often hated Jewish women, calling them sluts and whores and accusing them of bewitching their husbands.

Serel continued walking towards the field in increasing trepidation. As she drew level, one of the men, tall and bearded, stood up, adjusted his cap and undid the buttons on his tunic. He exposed his chest to the hot sun. It was matted with curly black hair and even from the distance, Serel could see that he was sweating. The man wiped his brow with his shirt sleeve and walked away from the others to where his horse was tethered at a tree near to the road. She approached the tree at the same time as him. He looked at her and at the three children. His face was hard and suspicious. Serel looked away, casting her eyes to the road, terrified. She quickened her pace to walk beyond his look.

He called out, 'Alone, little mother?'

She walked on, ignoring him.

'Your children look hot. Have you a drink for them?'

She continued to ignore him.

'Don't be afraid, little mother. I'm not going to hurt you. Your children look hot and tired. How long have you been on the road?'

Yitzchok stopped and turned to the man. 'Since early morning,' he replied.

Serel pulled Yitzchok back towards her and smacked him with her free hand. 'Don't talk to the man,' she whispered urgently in Yiddish.

They continued to walk but the man ran beyond the tree and out of the entrance of the field to stand in front of their path on the road. Serel stopped and looked at him in horror, her heart pounding. The man was flushed with sweat. He was taller and stronger than she. Taller even than Nussan. He was a big, healthy man. A

Christian. Serel stood in the ruts of the road and, like a protective swan, gathered her children around her. She glanced over into the field to see the other men and women who had stopped their work and were looking at the interchange.

The man bowed theatrically. 'You're frightened. I didn't mean to startle you. I saw a woman alone on a road with two children and a baby. Being a Christian man, I am bound to think to myself, how can I help this woman? I have food and I have wine. I'm sure my family and friends will be happy to share God's grace, and our good fortune with you, if you will sit with us in the shade of the tree.'

Serel was still utterly terrified. She looked at the man and he must have seen the fear register in her face. He shook his head in surprise. 'Why are you so frightened, little mother? My wife is in the field, as is her sister, as is my brother. God forbid I should feel any desire or ill will towards you. I say again that we're a Christian family. We want to share God's bounty with you. By your look of exhaustion, you've been walking for hours. You must rest, if only for the sake of the children. Come, mother,' he said more softly. 'Come, sit with us. Or let the children sit with us and you stand in the road if you're still uncertain. But either way, let the children rest. Christ said, "suffer the little children to come unto me".'

Serel's eyes opened wide in shock. The last time she'd heard Christ's words, they'd been screamed from the lips of a priest who was leading a crowd of villagers down the main street of their *stetl*, threatening every Jew with death unless they converted. If this man reported her to the priest, they would surely die.

'Do you speak our language?' he asked in Ruthenian. He asked the same question in Slovak, then in Russian. Serel only spoke Slovakian and Yiddish. Some

Hungarian, but not enough for a conversation. Still, she remained silent.

Giving up, the man again bowed theatrically, and told her, 'I'll return to the field and I apologise for upsetting you. Carry on with your journey. May God show you mercy, and give you sustenance.'

He turned and slowly walked back from where he had come. Yitzchok pulled at his mother's arm. 'Mummy, he wants to give us food. I'm hungry.'

'Please Mummy,' said Rosl.

Serel's heart ached. Going with this man was danger. Not going with him would see her children hungry and exhausted. What would Nussan do? The man stopped, having heard what the children said. He called out to his wife, 'Magdalena! Bring cheese and bread and apple juice for the children. These travellers will not sit with us, but wish to eat on the road. We'll eat under the trees.'

'Wait,' said Serel in Slovakian. 'Please wait.'

The man stopped and looked at her.

She didn't know how to address him. She had only spoken to a handful of Christians in her life, mostly officials in the village, who treated her with contempt, as though she was a beast in the field. Falteringly, she said to the man, 'We've just begun our journey. I'm sorry if I … I mean, we're alone and …'

He silenced her with a gesture. Softly, he said, 'Follow me into the field, dear friends. Rest with us. Then, if you wish, when the sun goes down, we'll be going in the direction that you're now walking. If you walk, you'll only get more tired, so ride with us on our cart. Stay in our village. There's an inn there, and it's clean.'

She nodded. She would leave immediately after she'd shared their food. She couldn't afford to pay for an inn but she didn't dare tell this man. She followed him into the field. The others walked out of the ruts they had been making ready to harvest the crop. They introduced themselves. Serel deliberately didn't tell them her name, nor the names of her children. They had Yiddish names. They would be identified as Jews. It was too risky.

The women made a fuss of Yitzchok and Rosl. The men were courteous and attentive to Serel's hunger and tiredness. Indeed, they were charming. Serel unloaded herself of her burdens and sat properly for the first time since early in the morning and greedily ate the bread they gave her. It was Christian bread. She said a silent blessing, hoping that God wouldn't notice it wasn't kosher. When the man broke off a lump of cheese, spearing it with his knife and handing it to her, she felt tears welling up in her eyes. She fought them back unsuccessfully. The adults looked at her in astonishment. Serel sat cross-legged under a willow tree in the middle of a field, surrounded by Christian men and women she had never before met, and she sobbed her heart out.

She masked her face with a rag soaked in cold water, squeezing it from time to time so that the water washed away the streaks made by her tears. After a while, she was able to put down the rag, and face the strangers, who watched her in concern. But what upset her most was that Yitzchok and Rosl were staring at her in horror, frightened by her sudden loss of self-control. And then Serel looked from her older children to little Eva. Her baby was in the lap of one of the Christian women, who was helping the child sip milk from a cup. Her Eva! Her baby! In the lap of a Christian!

Pleading, Serel said, 'Can I have my baby back? We must go. I'm sorry we've caused you so much trouble.' She started to rise, but the Christian man who had accosted them in the road put his strong hand on her shoulder. It was a forceful gesture, though in his eyes, she could see that there was no malice.

'You aren't going anywhere, little mother. You're in great distress. You'll stay with us until you're able to travel. You've eaten nothing but a piece of bread. Apart from your baby, your children won't eat properly until you do. Now, if my knowledge of Judaism is correct, you can eat this cheese and bread without danger of transgressing your dietary laws. There's no pork or other meats to prevent your enjoying it.'

Serel stared at him in horror. The man smiled.

In explanation, he said, 'You might be frightened by my knowledge, but please don't be. I am a man of education. I have been a student at the Charles University in Kosice where I studied philosophy. It is my choice to return to my roots and the soil and to be a farmer. That's how I know about your religion. You see, I now know that your son is named Yitzchok, as he was called by his sister, whose name I don't know. Yitzchok is a Hebrew name. Your reluctance to join us tells me that as Jews, you are probably outcasts from a community for reasons at which I can only guess. Perhaps you were victims of Christian people. Perhaps you were expelled from your village by your own people. Perhaps none of these; maybe you're visiting relatives from another village. But my guess is that you're escaping the madness of Christians who hate you. We've heard of these attacks against the Jews. We, my wife and family and friends, do not follow the teaching of the Elders of the Catholic Church. We have a preacher, a Godly man, who tells us that God loves all men and women, regardless of whether they follow Christ, or Mohammed, or Moses. Our love is for all, not just for Christians. In our community, we permit no condemnation of the beliefs of others. Rather, we hope to learn from others, and to create a universe of peace and harmony in which all men will be brothers, no matter their race, the colour of their skin, or their beliefs.'

He looked at her, hoping she understood. She was a woman in deep distress, alone in the world, harbouring feelings of loneliness, utterly dispirited.

Serel thought she understood what the man was saying; she also knew it was a trap to make her confess her Judaism. Hadn't Jews been accused throughout the centuries of drinking the blood of Christian boys and girls? Hadn't they been accused by this new book, the *Protocols of the Elders of Zion*, a horrible lie which was frightening everybody, that the Jews were trying to take over the world? What did these people think? Jews in her *stetl* hadn't enough money to buy themselves coal for heating in the winter, and yet the *Goyim* thought that they were trying to take over the world! *Mishuggas*. Now this *goy* was holding out the hand of friendship and speaking of things which she barely understood. Why? So he could rob her of money she didn't have? Or report her to the priest or the Constable and earn himself a reward? Again she couldn't understand why? Had she committed a crime? She was just walking from her village to the next village. Why shouldn't she? Christians could. And Jews had been able to for the past five years, since the edict from the Government saying that Jews didn't need travel permits any more to leave their villages.

Serel stood, bowed in politeness, and said sternly to her children, 'Come, *kinder*, we must leave. Thank these people for their food, and we're on our way.'

Reluctantly, the children stood, complaint in their every movement. The Christians were mystified.

'Do you still think we intend to harm you? Why? What have we done which makes you so afraid of us?' the tall man asked, genuinely astonished at Serel's actions.

His lack of understanding angered her. And she had made a fool of herself by crying in front of them. Hadn't her mother said to her, 'Serel, never show your true feelings to anybody except me and Almighty God. Not even to your husband.' Serel looked at the man, and was unable to contain the fury which was building up inside her. But now it had been released when her wall of insensibility had been demolished by the tears. Now she felt vulnerable again. And her vulnerability made her see her husband's murderers as this man and his brothers.

'Harm me,' she said looking at him, and then at the other Christians sitting in the shade of the tree. 'Of course you want to harm me. Last night your people destroyed my village. Last night, my husband was murdered by drunken men on horses, Christians just like you. You sit here, all holy and loving. But when you've had too much to drink or when the priests or the constables tell you, you get on your horses and ride down on unarmed men and women and children and murder them and break their bones and set fire to their houses. Harm me? Yes, you want to harm me, just because I don't believe in Jesus. Come Yitzchok. Come Rosl.' She looked at the Christian woman in anger. 'Give me back my baby. Aren't you frightened she'll make you dirty?' Serel reached down, and picked up baby Eva, who began to cry as she was suddenly wrenched away from the comforting arms of a woman who was feeding her.

Serel turned around, her heart thumping against the amulet inside her bodice. Her mouth would get her into trouble again. She should have stayed silent. Fool that she was. She was no better than her husband. She rushed her children towards the gate of the field.

Suddenly, the Christian man shouted, 'Stop!'

Panic! Serel knew that if she stopped, she would be in dire peril. Arrest, police, judges, prison. What about her children? But if she didn't stop, it would rouse the Christian to even greater anger. He would know for sure that she should be reported to the police. Reason was her only weapon. She stopped, her back to him.

But to her surprise, in a gentle and calming voice, he said, 'My name is Adolphus. My wife is Magdalena. Like you, we are all God's children. I beg of you, sister, do not judge us as you judge those who hurt you. You have no reason to think harshly of us. We have offered you food and rest. I'm sorry about the death of your husband. I grieve for your loss. I understand how you must feel towards Christians, but not all Christians are evil. Just as not all Jews are good. There are Jews in Kosice who deliberately robbed my father in a trade when he was selling some family jewellery during the last famine. Yet, we don't blame all Jews. We blame an evil man, just as you, my dear sister, cannot blame me and my family for the evil that these men yesterday did to you and your family. Though we are not responsible, I beg you, share in our fortune and be part of us if only for an hour.'

Serel stood on the spot, not knowing what to do. She could feel Yitzchok straining against her hand, wanting to return. He was starving. Rosl was limp with tiredness. Although they had only been walking for eight hours, they had eaten nothing and had only drunk water from streams. If she continued like this, both children would soon become ill, as would she herself.

Yet … His words were sweet and reasonable. Could she take the risk of stopping? Could she take the risk of going on? Slowly, she turned and looked at him, his face was neither smiling nor scowling. Neither was the rest of the group showing any emotion. They were waiting for her to decide. Sunlight dappled the ground through the leaves of the trees and fell upon the tall Christian who called himself Adolphus. Such a German name. Such a silly name. She smiled at the ridiculousness of her situation. Smiling was all she could do. She might be dead if she did and dead if she didn't. And all through her own lack of preparedness and stupidity. Adolphus smiled at the change in her face.

'Good,' he said. 'Wonderful. Come. Sit and eat and then tell me about your religion. We know so little. We read the Bible and we read of Abraham, Isaac and Jacob and of the great Moses but these Patriarchs, these great warrior priests, are so different from the Jews we see in villages around here, huddled together wearing peculiar clothes and ringlets in front of their ears and prayer shawls and little boxes on their heads.'

Serel's smile broadened. She was increasingly confident that he wasn't ridiculing her, that his question was genuine. Instinctively he continued. 'and why can't you eat pork and ham and bacon? Why are these prohibited? The Old Testament Book of Exodus says that they're forbidden but Jesus said that those laws no longer apply. Now, I know you don't believe in Jesus, but surely after two thousand years…'

Adolphus' wife Magdalena, who was sitting on the ground at the feet of her husband, slapped him on the back of his leg. 'Quiet, fool. She's exhausted. So are the children. Let them sit down and eat before you talk theology.'

Magdalena stood and walked over to Serel, taking Yitzchok by the hand. 'Please sister. May I take your young son and give him food? Please.'

Serel let go of his hand and Yitzchok eagerly followed the other woman to sit beside a basket of food. Another woman in the group stood and without asking, smiled at Serel and grasped Rosl gently by the hand. Serel was left holding baby Eva and watched in pleasure as her two children sat beside the baskets of food and eagerly ate cheese and onion and pickled cabbage and bread. She was standing looking at Adolphus. He walked slowly over to her and held out his arms. Serel, exhausted, confused and still unable to overcome her reluctance, handed her baby over to him. It wasn't a sign of acceptance, more of defeat. She was so tired that she had no more fight left in her. Adolphus carried the baby over to another woman in the group and lay the child in her arms. The woman broke off bits of cheese from her own groundcloth and placed them on baby Eva's tongue. The child tested the texture and taste and began to eat greedily. Serel's breasts were empty, having fed the baby as they walked along the road.

Adolphus walked back and accompanied Serel to the spot in which she had previously sat beneath the tree. He took a small groundcloth and spread it before her, then broke a large chunk of bread and with a knife, shaved a nob of butter and a wedge of cheese which he placed on top of the bread. Serel nodded in thanks and began to eat. A woman tipped a pitcher and milk poured into a glass which she handed to Serel. It was still warm from the cow in a next-door field, and tasted better than any food or drink she had ever eaten. The creamy smooth textures, the delicious fresh roughness of the bread, its crustiness and nutty flavours enlivened her spirits. The more she ate, the more hungry she became.

The Christians watched her in amusement. She drank some milk, wiped her mouth and said, 'If my behaviour has offended you, I apologise. I hope that you can understand. My husband died yesterday at the hands of the Christians. I haven't yet fully understood what's happening to me. I didn't even have time to bury him, because the madmen were coming back. I escaped carrying almost nothing except clothes for the children to wear and blankets to cover them at night. There was no food left. The madmen had eaten it or burned it all when they set fire to my house.'

There was obvious sorrow and consternation in the group, before Magdalena said, 'There are many evil men in this world. That's why we believe in Christ. We believe that His death enabled sinners to find comfort and in comfort comes understanding.'

Serel didn't want a theological argument. She didn't know enough and she was too tired. She yawned, and lay back on the ground. She tried to keep her eyes open looking up at the burning sky through the tree. The leaves made beautiful patterns in the clouds, which scudded high above the land.

She was awoken by a hand gently shaking her shoulder. She was in the middle of a dream but the moment she opened her eyes the dream evaporated. She looked up and the sky had changed. When she closed her eyes, it had been a burning blue. Now it was much softer, more muted. She looked around her and saw Magdalena looking down smiling.

'You've been asleep all afternoon,' said Magdalena. 'Yitzchok was telling me that you've had no sleep in two days. He said you hid by a river bank and were awake the whole night while the men burned your home. He's a brave little boy. He knows what happened to his father. He also knows that you have to get away. Rosl is different. She is confused and worried. I have comforted her but only you can reassure her.'

Serel's body was stiff. She tried to sit up but ached from the long walk and the deep sleep. Magdalena put her arm behind her back and helped her to sit.

'Your name is Serel?' Serel nodded. 'Yitzchok is a very bright boy. He reminds me of my son, Krystof. He died of diphtheria when he was six, may the Lord Jesus and all His Angels, and God Almighty the Father rest his soul. Yitzchok has told me much about your family. He was keen to talk.'

Serel nodded. She had no secrets now. Her only secret, her Jewishness, was known by everybody.

'Serel, we'll be finishing work, and leaving here within the hour. We're going back to our village. You can't continue on your own. At night, the road will be too dangerous to travel, and there's no reason why you and the children should sleep in a ditch. I know you have no money. Stay with us in our house. We have cheese and milk and bread. Tonight I'll make a vegetable soup and we'll roast turnips and potatoes and carrots. You don't have to eat meat in my home, for I know that it offends your religion. My house is comfortable and you and the children can sleep on the kitchen floor. Then in the morning, we can decide how best you can be helped.' It was a fait accompli. Magdalena stood and began to walk off, but Serel reached out and grabbed her by the skirt.

'Why?' Serel asked her simply as she turned. Magdalena frowned. 'Why are you doing this for me, for my children? We're Jews. You're Christians. I know what your husband said but I don't understand why you're being so kind.'

Magdalena nodded and thought for a moment. 'If you found a sick child in your village with no mother or father, would you help that child? Would you take him in and make him better? Even if you knew that the child was a Christian!'

Serel shrugged. 'Of course.'

'Our Lord told us to take care of the weak and the poor. He never made any distinction between Jews and Christians. We see you and your children as those in need of help. No more. No less. Learn to trust us. When you are well and when you have food, then we'll send you on your way to wherever it is that you want to go. Until then, rely upon us just as one day we may come to rely upon you.'

CHAPTER FOUR

The week that Serel spent in the home of Adolphus and Magdalena and their six children was one of the most extraordinary of her young life. It was only the third home she'd ever lived in; the first was her parents'; then her marriage home, which had originally belonged to Nussan's parents, and which they shared with the couple until their deaths. And now, by circumstances which she could hardly accept as reality, she was living in the home of a Christian family.

Living with a group of people whose conversation she found strange and whose customs were unnatural, a group with whom she hadn't grown up nor known since she was a child, was at first unnerving. But she quickly adapted, blocking her ears night and morning when they said their prayers. And Serel quickly re-adjusted to the comforts of many people under the same roof. She had four brothers and sisters, and constantly fought with them when she lived with her parents. But that was different. Here, in a large and peaceful Christian household, where everybody respected one another, there was less tension, fewer arguments.

For reasons which she reluctantly explained at Adolphus' request, and only admitted when he consistently repeated his questions, Serel insisted on spending night after night in the home sitting on a low cushion. They invited her to sit with them at the table or in the front room of the house where the family gathered at night to talk and pray. Wherever she went,

Serel carried her cushion and sat closer to the floor than any of the others. It was three days before she was willing to tell Adolphus that even though there were no Jews in his tiny village of Vlachovo, she felt compelled to follow the traditional Jewish mourning rituals of sitting on a low seat in memory of her husband. Adolphus understood and quietly informed the rest of his family why their guest was acting in this unusual fashion. The women of the Christian household began to join her on the floor by sitting on their own cushions out of respect for her grief for Nussan, until she gently thanked them but assured them that only wives and children were expected to do so.

In the meantime, Adolphus' and Magdalena's children did whatever they could to relieve Serel of the strain of attending to her own. The Christian children's ages ranged between three and fourteen and although there were understandable though buried tensions and jealousies, they behaved with tolerance to the interlopers in their house. The older children happily took Yitzchok and Rosl for visits to local relatives and friends, explaining that they were visiting from a nearby village. Under instructions from their father, nobody mentioned their guests' religion.

Serel recovered remarkably quickly from the trauma of the past few days. Some inner strength enabled her to put her husband's murder and the family's dramatically altered fortunes into a new perspective. The fact that the Christian family had been so unbelievably, indeed extraordinarily kind, generous and liberal-minded impressed her tremendously. If only other Christians behaved like these, the Jews of Slovakia and the Ukraine and other parts of Eastern Europe might actually be able to live in some sort of peace and harmony with their neighbours.

One night, the fourth of their stay, Serel broached the subject which she failed to understand, asking Adolphus why it was that Christians hated Jews so vehemently.

He weighed his answer carefully before saying, 'Imagine this. You're shipwrecked upon an island. It's the most beautiful island in the whole world. Tall snow-capped mountains, gushing rivers, gentle valleys, an island of peace and harmony and tranquillity. But when you arrive, you suddenly realise that all the inhabitants of the island are blind. They can't see a thing. And so you make it your mission to share your joy, and describe to them what you can see.

'But suddenly, you realise that the residents of the island are not blind at all. Instead, they live all their lives with their eyes tightly shut, refusing to look out and see the world. From your original feelings of pity for their blindness, you suddenly become angry. You shout at them, "Open your eyes, you fools. Why don't you comprehend the beauty of these sights. Why don't you see the majesty, the wonders on this island?" That I'm afraid, my dear Serel, is how most Christians see the Jews. Not blind, but refusing to open their eyes to the wonders and truth of Jesus. If your people, the Sons of Abraham, Isaac and Jacob, were truly blind, we Christians would understand and have great pity. We would feel sorrow that you couldn't see what we could see. But instead many Christians feel fury towards you, because you are able to see and yet you refuse to open your eyes and follow the truth of the New Testament. And it was that very blindness, in the beginning of our Lord's journey through the Holy Land, which caused the Jews to hunt Him down, and persecute Him. That's why Christians hate Jews. That's what makes some of us very angry.'

Serel nodded. For the first time, she understood. 'But not you, Adolphus. You and Magdalena and the other people in your family, and your friends. You're different. You don't treat us like that. You treat us kindly. Why are you different?'

Again, he thought carefully before replying. 'Christ's words are capable of infinite interpretation. It was St Paul who was angry with the Jews for being stiff-necked. After him, many of the Popes continued the fury. Now we have these horrible lies about Jewish people using the blood of Christian children to make their Passover bread. Nonsense. Superstition. But unfortunately it's added fuel to the fire. My family, my friends, have a priest who ministers to several of the local villages. He is a man of modesty, decency and a man completely different from other priests we've had, who treat themselves like the lord in the castle near here. They think that just because they're God's messenger on earth, they too should be worshipped. At least that's the way they behave. We, my family and friends, think that Christ's message of love will bring peace to the entire world. If only His message is followed.'

Serel continued to sit on her low cushion and thought deeply about his words. They were so appealing and she wanted to accept that this was a Christianity which would not abuse her; but Serel had seen a very different kind of Christianity; a Christianity which came not from the heart, but from wherever hatred dwelt. She and her family had been brutalised by the ugly side of Christianity, a side which had little or nothing to do with the Christ of whom Adolphus spoke. Those who committed the pogroms and the attacks of hatred were Christians who were driven to revulsion by fear or ignorance or goaded on by the priests in their rich churches or the dukes and princes and kings in their fine palaces. Christians whom she wanted nothing to do with but who continued to assault her people as they had been assaulted by the Christian Church from its very beginning.

She could have stayed with them forever, but three days later, Serel and her children set off along the road to Poprad. She knew that Adolphus and Magdalena would be happy for her to stay longer. They continually assured her that she was no burden to them. Indeed, she had been enormously useful to the household, because, despite the contravention to the rituals of mourning, Serel insisted on cleaning and tidying the house when the family went into the fields to work. Not only that, but the workers came home to a beautifully prepared meal. The only thing which Serel refused to do was to touch the family's unkosher meat. That, however, wasn't a problem, because during the time that she was in their house, she cooked traditional Jewish dishes which they found delicious. She made them *lokshen kugel* with cheese, cheese *kreplach*, plum and apricot *barenikes*, and a dish which Adolphus insisted she teach Magdalena, *kasha*, roasted buckwheat made with vegetable oil.

Just before she left the house, Magdalena insisted upon giving her a bag full of food, the sort which would last for many days. Salted fish, hard-boiled eggs, cheeses wrapped in wax paper, nuts and dried fruit, and bread, as well as a knife to help her slice the food to feed her family. Not only that, but after his family had left for the fields early in the morning, their eldest son Leon drove back from the fields with the transport wagon and gave Serel, Yitzchok, Rosl and the baby a ride all the way to Stratena where he kissed them all, blessed them and promised to say prayers for a week to ensure their safe delivery to Poprad.

What Leon didn't know and what she wouldn't tell

anybody was that Poprad wasn't the end of their journey, but little more than a beginning. From there, she would somehow have to find her way to Kraków. From Kraków, she must journey to the centre of Poland and from there across into Germany to catch the boat from Hamburg to America. It was so daunting a prospect that, as she watched Leon retreating into the distance, the horses' hooves clopping on the dry rutted road, she was in half a mind to shout and ask him to wait, to run back to the safety of the Christian house where she had been staying, to enjoy their hospitality, to be a part of their family. Although everything about them was alien, it was comforting. But it wasn't secure. For one day, some inquisitive neighbour would ask too many questions about the strangers and discover that they were Jewish; then a land-holder would be told or the priest from another town would come and visit; and then Serel and her new friends would find men with flaming torches and swords brandished in the air, riding on huge horses outside their home shouting curses and spitting hate.

That was why she'd left their home. Safety was in moving from place to place so she wasn't recognised, so she was invisible. Serel was now alone with her three children in a wild and inhospitable area, frightening because she had never trodden this path before. She looked around and only two things stretched before her. The road to Poprad and the road back from where she had come. She knew she couldn't retreat. Not now. But she also knew that continuing the journey would be far harder than before. Then she was running for her life. Now, she was leaving a comforting security.

She took the children and kissed them all, saying a prayer in Hebrew for their safe delivery at the beginning of their journey.

May it be thy will, Oh Lord, our God and God of our
    fathers
To conduct us in peace; to direct our steps in peace
To uphold us in peace and to leave us in life, joy and
    peace.
Deliver us from every enemy, ambush and hurt by the
    way.

She couldn't remember the rest. Her father had said it
when he had travelled to Kiev and he had returned safely.
Please God, it would help her and her children. She
began to sing a song. It was the same song she had sung
when she set out from her tiny village of Roznava. Then
there had been no music in her voice, only fear. Then she
was escaping her husband's murderers and the destruction
of everything she loved. Now she was striking out in a
new direction. Ready and able to face the dangers. She
had food in her belly, food on her back and friends to
support her if she needed to turn around.

It was two days to Poprad where she was sure there
would be a Jewish community. All she needed to do was to
survive the next two days. She would sleep in the warmth
of the summer nights in a comfortable field. She would
feed her children and replenish her supplies by the charity
of the Jews in the town she was heading towards. She
would sell the chain of the amulet, and hopefully have
enough money to buy the tickets she'd need to sail from
Hamburg to New York. Then when she was in America,
she would finally sell the damned amulet and let some other
poor *schmuck* have the problems. The money would be in
dollars and it would enable her to set up a business. Then
she would be alright. Now she suddenly felt confident
again, even though the road ahead was frightening. The
melody grew louder and the children smiled.

NEW YORK, PRESENT DAY

For the past three months, much of Sarah Kaplan's time had been devoted to organising for the proper disposal of the sacks-full of mail that were now flowing from Jewish communities around the world, into her office. The task diverted her from her main work as CEO of a major refugee and humanitarian charity, and it also forced her to work many increased hours, but when the operation began to show results, she grudgingly accepted that the idea was right. In admiration of his amazing foresight and perception, Sarah sent an email to Josh that made her boss particularly proud. It said simply, 'Damn you Krantz. Do you have to be right all the time!'

Joshua Krantz's inspiration, the *Responsa*, had sparked everybody's imagination. Three months ago, Sarah, as Chief Executive Officer of the *Moishe, Vilma and Hermann Krantz Institute for Justice for the Victims of Evil* had written to every Jewish community throughout the world registered somewhere with an international organisation. Letters from her had been received by presidents of synagogues, rabbis, chairmen and women of B'nai B'rith, Jewish schools, elderly peoples' homes and many more in every town in every country in the world where there was a Jewish population of more than fifty souls.

Sarah's letter had been translated by The Institute's linguists into over thirty distinct languages, and sent out. Within weeks, a flood of completed form letters, some typed or handwritten, as well as correspondence of congratulations, and some of condemnation, began to arrive back into New York.

In the initial letter which she sent to the community leaders, Sarah introduced herself and The Institute, explaining why they had embarked on the organisation of a new *Responsa* along the lines in which the ancient disparate Jewish communities kept in touch with each other on matters of customs, habits, news and theology. She didn't dwell too much on the growth of fascism, neo-Nazism, and other manifestations of racism; instead her letter talked in generalities about collecting a central intelligence of government, church, community, political, factional and social anti-Semitic statements and actions. This collection of intelligence would then be collated and faxed or emailed as a monthly bulletin to all Jewish communities throughout the world … a sort of early warning system.

The responses which came back to The Institute were little short of amazing, and they came in their thousands. Some were effusive and promised to be vigilant in reporting any rise in intolerance, anti-Semitism or general racial prejudice in their area and to fill in the forms which they had been sent; in this way, thousands of communities would be reporting on a monthly basis. Other communities and their leadership were lukewarm to the idea, but assured Sarah that at their next annual meeting they would ask approval of the community and would respond shortly thereafter at the appropriate time. A few Jewish leaders were outright hostile, telling Sarah that the idea was preposterous, that there already existed adequate official bodies to investigate this type of intolerance and an additional body could only cause confusion and anxiety and give the fascists additional notoriety, playing into their hands about a new Jewish conspiracy like the *Protocols of the Elders of Zion*.

A new suite of rooms on another floor was devoted to the *Responsa*. Additional staff were hired to handle the cataract of mail that poured into the office every day. Huge maps of every continent and most large geographical areas had been pinned up on the walls and floors carried flags which nominated four distinct categories of response. A computer programme had been written to enable the directors of The Institute to monitor trends to see if they could link a rise in one country's Fascism to Fascism in other parts of Europe, or former European colonies. The logic was applied for every country in the world, and specified the activities of the French, German, British, Russian, American, Australian, South African, Arabic, South American and other racist and anti-Semitic groups operating in significant areas where Jews had settled and had an influence.

At the same time as this was being done, an analysis was prepared by The Institute's linguists to determine whether the literature pumped out by the hate groups had a common theme. What phrases kept recurring in hate literature produced by neo-Nazis in widely separated parts of the world? What aspects of the hatred towards Jews in particular communities seemed to have roots in other parts. Ultimately, Josh and Sarah wanted to be able to determine whether the mindless rhetoric, the eternal lies told about the Jews, were sourced from one or two centres of evil … perhaps belonging to well-known anti-Semites in Canada or America or Germany or Austria. If they could prove that most of the world's anti-Semitic groups were goosestepping to the same centrally composed tune, then they would be in a position to bring pressure to bear to get the authorities to attack the source.

In a way, Sarah understood the criticism she was receiving from a few community groups and herself felt uncomfortable undertaking this task. For centuries, Christians had complained about a central Jewish/Zionist conspiracy to take over the world. Now the Jews were searching for a Christian conspiracy. One day the world would be free of conspiracy theories ... as soon as the world was free of conspirators!

Much of Sarah's time since setting up the *Responsa* had also been devoted to talking to B'nai B'rith, university departments studying global terrorism and racism, the FBI, the CIA, Departments of Defence, embassies, Holocaust study centres and other groups in order to patch into their databases so that the *Responsa* would be running at full pelt within months.

It had been a frenetic three months since she and Josh had met one morning in her office and he had discussed the idea with her. At first she was sceptical, bemused, even resistant. There was plenty of work in The Institute to keep her and her staff busy looking after the needs of families who were dispossessed from their land-holdings or assets, be they Jewish, Christian or Moslem, white, black or yellow.

But, in his perennial fashion, Josh had gently insisted upon her following his ideas through and the more she did, the more they grew into a reality. Now, when she thought back over the work they had managed to accomplish over the past three months, she was astounded that she hadn't thought about doing something like it herself, criticism or no.

Suddenly almost every Jewish community except for a handful of recalcitrant ones who were happy to bury their collective heads in the sand, was talking to each other through the New York Headquarters. Communications were established through the Internet in which each community could contact others; there were five different levels of passwords issued for the huge Internet site which linked each community, a mammoth task in itself, bearing in mind how many communities were connected to the web.

The communities were using the *Responsa* and reporting in potentially dangerous trends and influences. The computers were working flat out to coordinate all the information. Sarah spent the first two hours of each of her working days upstairs in the *Responsa's* offices planning strategy and approaches, and then came downstairs to The Institute offices to see to her normal working day.

But this morning was different, as was one of the dozens of letters referred to her for special attention. As well as the usual letters addressed to the director of the *Responsa*, a letter had arrived addressed personally to Sarah Kaplan and marked *strictly private and confidential*. Many respondents ignored the international reply-paid envelope which was sent out with all their mail and instead sent back their own. In some cases, the letter was addressed to Sarah personally as the signatory. These were usually ignored by the *Responsa's* staff, and dealt with in the normal way. But even the most junior member of the *Responsa's* postal clerks recognised that this particular letter, one from South America, was different and very personal. The office manager handed it to Sarah the moment she arrived.

Sarah glanced at it, tore it open, read the first couple of paragraphs in a cursory way, and then, frowning, read the rest much more closely. She shook her head and smiled at the office manager, making a throw-away remark about the letter being something to do with her family. She put it into her briefcase, telling the office manager she would attend to it downstairs later in the day. The matter was forgotten upstairs.

During the two hours in the *Responsa's* office, Sarah's mind kept on wandering back to the letter. The first thing she did when she went downstairs and closed the door of her own office was to open and re-read the letter.

Three times. The more she read it, the less sense it made. She put it away, intending to talk to her mother the next time they met, which would be the following weekend.

She had tried to get on with her work. She made phone calls. She dictated letters. Sarah answered email from around the world. She phoned Josh on location in the Orkney Islands of Scotland and chatted for ten minutes. Her diary told her she had three meetings that day. Enough time to re-read the letter a fourth time.

She took it out of her briefcase and checked that the door to her office was closed. Why? There was nothing that she had done wrong. Why did she feel this need for secrecy? She re-read the letter. It was from an address in Argentina, a place called Avellaneda. Before she left the *Responsa's* offices, she'd looked it up on a map. It was just south of the capital, Buenos Aires. The letter was stiffly formal and showed the patent unfamiliarity of the writer with the English language, but there was also a touch of gentleness in the man's style.

Dear Miss Sarah Kaplan,

As one of the leaders of our small but pious Jewish community in Avellaneda, I have been pleased to read your recent letter. I am sending you another response to that first letter, with which you will be pleased, bearing in mind my country's terrible history of Nazis. But in the meantime forgive me for corresponding to you with another, more personal issue.

Miss Kaplan, I hope you are the Miss Sarah Kaplan I've been trying to find for a number of years now. If you are not, this letter will be meaningless to you and I ask you to allow me to apologise and to write back and tell me that you are not the Miss Sarah Kaplan I'm seeking. Let me firstly introduce myself. I am Dr Luis Forenjo. Although now retired, for many years, I was a doctor of medicine. One of my patients, as well as a very old and close friend was a man whose name was Ricardo Padrone. Of course, I and everybody knew that he wasn't Argentinian or Spanish. In fact, before coming to Argentina, he was a communist whose youth was destroyed in a German Labour Camp during the terrible Second World War and who in 1945 came to Argentina to seek a new life.

So, why am I telling you all of this my dear Miss Kaplan? Before his death, Ricardo Padrone appointed me his executor. On going through his papers I discovered many things about him which came as a surprise. My dear friend Ricardo died four years ago. He was a very elderly man, aged 92, and for years had been nearly bedridden. Occasionally walking outside his home to sit on the verandah. He was blind with glaucoma and his whole body was racked with arthritis. He was a pathetic sight compared to the robust man I knew when I first met him nearly four decades earlier. He was then in his mid-fifties and was a horse man, an adventurer, a marvellous chess player, a wit, a man of great culture and with a wonderful knowledge of the world and its politics. We spent many enjoyable holidays together in Patagonia and riding in the wilds of the Pampas.

But I ramble. I will come to the point before you despair of this letter having any point. As his executor, I opened his security box In the Banco de la Plata in Buenos Aires. As you would expect, it was full of old papers, many share certificates, title deeds to property in Germany (most of them are no longer valid). And letters. Many letters. There were no details of his early life, indeed, no letters were written before 1946, but there was one letter which captured my interest. It was dated in 1950.

You see, when I first met Ricardo he had been married for some years to a lovely woman called Rosaria. They had no children but were a loving couple. I never for one minute thought that Rosaria wasn't his first wife. It never occurred to me. I assumed that he had been thrown into the Camps in Germany as a young man, and had had no chance to marry before migrating to South America. He never made any mention of another wife, certainly never told Rosaria of such a woman, and rarely spoke of his days in Germany, telling me they were very painful to recall.

Yet, in his safety deposit box I found many references to his Germany days. Some photographs, many documents, but the most extraordinary was a letter to a woman called Eva. It was a very strange letter, dated August 13, 1950. It was a letter which he had obviously written in anger, though there was much compassion in the letter for a child whom he seemed to love; a child called Bettina. He blamed this woman Eva for leaving him in his hour of need, and cursed her in an ungallant fashion … yet he still offered to pay money for the welfare and upkeep of the child Bettina as well as to continue paying for a woman called Annelise who lived in Germany.

The letter was returned to him with a message scrawled on the letter by this woman Eva. She denied she was any longer his wife. She said she never wanted to see him again. She said that now he had tracked her down in New York, she would move and change her name so that he would never be able to find him. He wrote her a second letter dated a month later. The letter (and I only have a carbon copy in his deposit box) said that he would never give up hope that she would forgive him and was always available if she needed help with the upbringing of their child. There is no record of a reply.

So why am I writing to you Miss Kaplan? Simply this. As executor of his estate, and in consideration for the fact that his poor wife Rosaria died from a motor car accident only two months after his death, then Bettina his only child (if this letter is true), is his rightful heir. Not that there is a vast fortune for her to inherit. A farm still in the family name, shares in several Argentine companies, some of which are worth quite a lot of money, and some money in his account.

This is why I need to find Bettina. For the past four years I have searched for her. I followed the trail of people who migrated from Argentina to New York around June, July and August of 1950. I have found a woman called Eva Arpel, who seems to fit the picture of what I am looking for, as far as dates and such like is concerned.

It appears that this Eva Arpel settled in New York, Queens I believe, and was registered as a migrant from Argentina. She was accompanied by a baby called Bertha. Only very recently have I received replies from the Jewish Agencies in NY and been able to ascertain that Bertha Arpel grew up in and I believe married a man called Sol Kaplan. They have a daughter whose name is Sarah Kaplan.

I was about to write to Bertha Kaplan a letter similar to this one I am writing to you, when as if by some divine intervention, your letter arrived at the offices of the Rabbi in Avellaneda. As I have told you, I am one of the leaders of our community. On receipt of this letter, I telephoned your office, and asked a few innocent questions about you. I'm sure you won't mind. Your staff was very correct and proper. I said that I was an uncle from Argentina, and asked whether your mother and father were Bertha and Sol. They told me that my assumption was correct. Forgive your staff, Miss Kaplan. I can be very persuasive, and the information they gave me about you was hardly a secret.

So, you may also have gathered that I now believe there's a chance you may be the same Sarah Kaplan who is the daughter of the Bettina (Bertha) whom I seek. This means that if you write and tell me you are, then I can contact your mother. If not, you will not hear from me again, other than replying to your request for information about fascists in this area, of which, I'm afraid, there are many, both young and old. Ah, will we Jews never be free of them?

If you are not related to the Bertha Kaplan I seek, would you be kind enough to reply and perhaps inform me whether you know of other Bertha Kaplan's in New York. It's a big Jewish community and I know there could be many. I'm taking a chance that you are the Sarah Kaplan whose mother is the right Bertha, and in turn, whose mother is the right Eva, whose first husband may have been the man whose estate I execute.

Thank you for your time in reading this letter.

Sincerely,
Luis Forenjo
(Retired Doctor of Medicine)

Sarah put the letter down and took a sip of water. South America? It was all nonsense. Sure, her mother was Bertha, her father's name was Sol. And yes, her grandmother, God rest her soul, was Eva; she'd died in 1975 when Sarah was only eight. She vaguely remembered her *Bubba* Eva on her mother's side, but had much clearer memories of her father's parents. They had lived until the mid, and late eighties, when Sarah was already a young woman. She'd been devastated by their deaths; not so when *Bubba* Eva died, Sarah regretfully recalled.

She remembered her mother's tears at *Bubba* Eva's funeral, and then going back to the cold and tiny apartment to sit *sheva*. And most of all, Sarah remembered the seven days of mourning, when her mother cried during every *minyan*, when Sol had said prayers, when relatives had gathered around and told her that she must have strength, that *Bubba* Eva had now gone to God and would no longer suffer. Sarah didn't even know her grandmother was suffering. She remembered the huge and frightening beard of the Rabbi and the smell of tobacco and wine on his breath; she remembered the claustrophobia she felt every time the family entered the small lounge room with its intricate laces and old-fashioned furniture and crowds of people gathered in the room to mumble prayers and then to wolf down poppyseed cake and *laikach* and honey cake and wash it down with a *schlugg* of schnapps (to keep out the cold) or *slivovitz*, or whisky. But that was all she remembered. Nothing about *Bubba* Eva.

Only later did she plainly remember her mother's rambling about *Bubba* Eva's suffering. The memory of those days flooded back. *Bubba* Eva's suffering became a mantra of her youth, an absolute truth, an article of faith like that creed the Christians said … what was it? The Nicene Creed. Bertha could never mention her mother without talking about the way *Bubba* Eva had suffered all her life; how she had been a widow in her earliest days of marriage; how she had struggled through the concentration camp; how her husband had survived five years in a labour camp and then died of exhaustion a few years after the war was over; how Eva and her baby had travelled on a cattle ship to New York and, not speaking the language and knowing nobody, had managed to establish herself with a good life and good friends. It was a miraculous story of hard work, dedication and lifelong suffering, a twentieth-century morality tale, a Jewish *Pilgrim's Progress*.

This was her *Bubba* Eva. This was the woman that Sarah remembered vaguely from her childhood thoughts. What she didn't remember was her young tears when *Bubba* Eva died, only the confusion that other people were crying. And the guilt that she wasn't.

She hadn't thought of Eva in years. Only when Sarah visited her parent's house once a month for Sunday dinner did she see the memory of *Bubba* Eva; and then it was only through the medium of grainy, black-and-white photographs on a mantlepiece. There were all sorts of pictures recording *Bubba* Eva's life from her earliest times in New York, snaps taken by friends at picnics or down at Coney Island, or in a holiday shack in the Adirondacks to more formal photographs when *Bubba* Eva was in her sixties and Bertha was getting married to Sol. Then there were photographs taken when Sarah was born in 1967. The last photograph was of an elegant tired, sad-faced old lady taken at a school play, in which Sarah played the part of Esther in the biblical story. Bertha and Sol were beaming at the diminutive, fresh-faced Sarah as she stood proudly between them, resplendent in her costume. But there was no smile on Eva's face, only a look of infinite sadness. Now that Sarah thought about it, the other pictures were all of an elegant elderly woman, stiffly formal, looking into the camera lens as though it had no right to be pointing at her.

It was as if *Bubba* Eva's life was little more than a historical transcript, a record of only the most vague visual memory; like a family movie buried in a rarely opened drawer, taken out and played occasionally for the benefit of record, but having no connection, no reality or presence in Sarah's mind.

Her memory of Eva was of an old woman, thin as a wisp, with straggly grey hair; smelling of heavy perfume and hairspray. Her hair was always worn in a contorted architectural bun, placed strategically above her head, a constructed wonder which Sarah, as a little girl, always wanted to pull apart. Sarah smiled. The memories were beginning to return, grudgingly and fleetingly. The more she tried to remember, the more concrete was the picture of the woman she had known in the first few years of her life.

Sarah had no memory of her grandfather, Bertha's father, *Bubba* Eva's husband, but his story was a part of the family legend. His name was Saul; he'd been interned in a concentration camp for much of the war. The family originally came from a village called Michalovce in the eastern part of Slovakia. In 1903, Sarah's great-grandfather Nathan, whom Bertha called Nussan, had been the victim of a pogrom, murdered by drunken Christians. His wife, Sarah's great-grandmother Serel – after whom she was named – had walked across Europe with three small children, one of them was still a tiny baby. They were her great uncles and aunts, Isaac, Rose and her grandmother, Eva. She'd never met Isaac and Rose; they were victims of the Nazis. Eva and her mother Serel lived in Berlin. Both Eva's mother Serel, and Eva's husband Saul had been victims of the Nazis. Nobody had any idea how Serel had died, though they knew that Saul somehow managed to outlive Adolf Hitler.

Sarah was racking her brains to remember the scant and long-forgotten details of her family history. No! That wasn't true. As a young girl, her interest in the family history was trampled by the emotion of her mother.

Every time Sarah asked questions, the rawness of the emotions would cause the young girl embarrassment. And so she patiently listened to the stories her family told around the dinner table. And when her mother became emotional, Sarah managed to excuse herself, not wishing to see her mother upset and cursing somebody called Hitler, and people called the Nazi swine. Now, as an adult, she bitterly regretted not having remained.

What had happened to her grandparents? Sarah closed her eyes, and desperately tried to re-focus on long-forgotten snippets of information. She remembered being told that at the start of the war the family was in Berlin, having moved there from Slovakia after the pogrom. According to her mother, Sarah was told that her grandfather, *Zaida* Saul had been arrested and brutalised by the SS. Apparently, he belonged to some form of Bund, or Jewish Socialist movement in Berlin. He was one of the first that the Nazis saw to. In 1941, Saul was sent to Sachsenhausen Concentration Camp. Because he was strong, he was one of the hideously treated *Schuhläufer-Kommando*, a pathetic squad of young men whose job it was to wear newly made Wehrmacht boots in order to test their durability; the *Schuhläufer-Kommando* squad was forced to march for mile after mile, day after day, in concentric circles. Anybody who fell or fainted or stopped was shot on the spot. Sarah could only imagine the misery of walking in circles for ten hours a day, every day for years in painfully new shoes. Among concentration camp inmates, it was the most hideous of all the tasks the prisoners had to perform.

At the end of the war, when Sachsenhausen was liberated by the Russians, Saul managed to escape to the West and in 1946, he and Eva were miraculously re-united in the ruins of Berlin; Sarah's mother, Bertha, was the result of their joyous reunion; but tragically they were only together a matter of a few pleasant years. Saul had become so ill, and was so undernourished, so racked by the poisons and experiments which camp doctors carried out on him, that in 1950, he died in Eva's arms, smiling one last time. Immediately after that, *Bubba* Eva took her young child, Bertha and came to make a new life in America. The only item of value she brought with her was the amulet, which her own father had unearthed in a Bronze Age grave which was on the plot of land he was farming.

And that was it! End of story. South America? It was all nonsense. Neither she, nor her family had any connection with South America. They had never been there, nor did they know anyone who lived there. Obviously this doctor was wrong. She was not the Sarah Kaplan he was seeking. She would write back to the gentle Jewish doctor, and kindly explain where he had gone wrong. But she would most certainly help him. With her databases and her computer wizardry, she would be able to find the correct family, and set things to right.

But no matter how much she tried to work for the rest of the day, the letter from South America kept insinuating itself on her mind. Maybe her mother might know something.

CHAPTER FIVE

MUNICH, BAVARIA, 1905

Two year old Reinholdt Stricher awoke with a start and began to wail the moment his father slammed the door of the family's tiny apartment. His mother Lotte, her nose continually wrinkling at the reek of boiling cabbages which their neighbours were always cooking, tried to comfort her baby, stroking the back of his head, something that usually worked. When that failed, she put her hand into his pants, and gently stroked his penis. The baby sighed and immediately began to settle. The last thing Lotte wanted was for baby Reinholdt's yelling to disturb his father. Normally when Otto returned from one of his meetings, he was euphoric. She was treated to a detailed, and always glowing description of how the comrades had drunken, eaten, toasted and made grandiose gestures; he would relive every glorious detail, and, with the tears of beer in his eyes, retell how, towards the end of the evening, everybody in the Society swore eternal loyalty to the flag, the Fatherland and to each other.

Sometime he would find it hard to talk as emotion infused his mind; he would tell Lotte of the way in which his comrades in the *Ringvereine* would slap each other's *Lederhosen*, flick the braces, even make fun of the Society's Most High and Holy and Courageous Knight-Commander-In-Chief. The Society provided such comradeship, such a warmth of communality. It was what

Otto lived for, throughout every day of the week; that, and his beloved family. It was what kept him going, working fifty-five hours in five and a half days a week in a stinking factory, and then coming home to a dark and dingy block of apartments with no sunlight between the buildings, no air to breathe in summer, and the windows frosty and steamy in winter. What a life!

Were it not for his beautiful family, and the company of his Society, he'd pack it all in, and go somewhere else. Munich, glorious as it was, was becoming less friendly, more intransigent, hostility everywhere. All except in the Society. Tuesday was the night he devoted to joining his hundreds of comrades in the Bavarian Society of the Officers of the Teutonic Empire. Three weeks ago, it had been called the Bavarian Society for the Glorification of German Manhood; but several wives had ridiculed the old name, commenting that they hadn't seen manhood from their husbands in years. And so a motion declaring the Teutonic Brotherhood alive and well had been carried unanimously by the comrades. Now they were all Teutons. Who the Teutons were in history had been explained to the members of the Society, but Otto was drunk at the time, and hadn't subsequently thought to ask what a Teuton was. And their main enemies were the members of the *Glaube, Leibe, Hoffnung Ringvereine* society. Morons! He explained to Lotte that the closest these buffoons got to Faith, Love and Hope was when they all got together at the end of the night to see who could piss the highest up a wall. Fools!

But his return tonight was different. There was no jollity, no feeling of harmony with the world. Tonight Otto hadn't returned from his Society as a Teuton. Neither had he returned as a comrade; nor had he come back to his home as a drunk but happy father and husband. From the moment Lotte heard his efforts trying to put the key into the lock she knew that tonight was different. He had thrust open the front door of their apartment and slammed it shut so hard that it reverberated through all the walls. Even the neighbours' conversation next door had come to an abrupt end. The noise had woken up baby Reinholdt and startled him. When he began to cry, Lotte ran into his room so that the noise of his crying wouldn't further exacerbate her husband's temper.

The little boy was comforted and she kissed him, whispering a lullaby into his ears, covering him with his favourite blue blanket. She waited breathless until he returned to a state of sleep, and then gently closed the door of their communal bedroom.

When she emerged into the hot and airless central room of their apartment, Lotte saw her husband standing in front of the toilet, his legs astride, a long and never-ending stream of urine seeming to pacify his anger. Why was he angry? What had happened? He would tell her when he was ready. She waited until he had finished. Without washing his hands, he came into the living-kitchen area of their cramped, three-room home.

'What's wrong darling?' she asked.

He shook his head. 'You wouldn't understand.'

She nodded. He was probably right. She never did understand the politics he came home with. The words were meaningless to her, yet they were thrown around like epithets; Socialists, Bundists, Marxists, Jews, Nationalists, militarists, Imperialists. To her they were just words. To her husband, they were reasons for ecstasy or anger, depending on which word he used at the time. She would never understand what he was talking about. She had no education, having spent only three years at school and could barely read or write but she was a good wife and a good mother and she loved her husband dearly. And she especially knew what little sexual tricks made him big and hard and strong so that in the morning, he always woke up with a smile on his face.

'Can I make you a coffee?'

He shook his head and belched. 'Get me a beer darling,' he said. He was beginning to calm down. There would be no more shouting. Nor should there be. She gave him sex every night, even sometimes when she was bleeding with her monthlies. He had no reason to complain about her. She wasn't like the other wives who hated and avoided sex, pretending to be asleep, or sick, or saying that their periods were going on and on. Otto was the envy of everyone at his factory because it wasn't something he kept to himself.

So if it wasn't her, then it must have been something which happened tonight. Otto sat in an armchair and picked up the paper but he didn't read it. Instead, he threw it down and, as she opened the ice cabinet to get him his beer, he shouted to her in the kitchen, 'They're going to take over, you know.'

'Who are, darling?' she said, her voice muted to indicate to her husband that he should not shout.

'These Russians. The Jewish Bolsheviks. We had word today. One of the Brotherhood invited Von Tritzka to address us. He told us all about them, this man Lenin, filthy rabblerouser, socialist gone mad, follower of that Jew, Marx. I tell you, you put the bits together and it's terrifying. They held their conference last month. Big meeting. The Bolshevik Communist Party. You know what they want to do? Take over the world. Worldwide revolution. International socialism. God help us all.'

Lotte finished pouring his beer from the jug and returned it into the ice cabinet. It was just how he liked it; cold with a frothy head, served in a pewter stein. He had been given it to commemorate thirty years faithful service in the woollen mills. Five years ago, he had been made foreman and that had eased the financial pressures considerably; certainly enough for them to get married.

She stood over him and stroked his head, just like she had stroked little Reinholdt's penis. He reached up and put his arm around her waist, then down to fondle the cheeks of her buttocks. Then he put his hand between her legs, something that they both enjoyed. He rubbed his hand in and out of her crotch. She smiled at him and sat on his lap, knowing what her movement would do to his manhood. She squirmed all over his crotch, just the way he liked it. Then she kissed him on the forehead and then on each of his eyes, and licked his eyelids, and then his nose and then she licked up the froth of the beer from his mouth. It was something she knew that he loved very much and which she was happy to do for her husband.

All would have been well, had she kept quiet. But what she did next, though innocent, was entirely the wrong thing to do at the worst possible moment.

'These Jews,' she asked. 'Isn't the owner of your wool factory a Jew?'

She felt her husband's body tense. 'He's different. He's okay. He's good to us. Not like these Marxist Jews. My boss doesn't want to take over the world. All he wants to do is to make money. But it's the other Jews that I hate. The Communists. These new Bolsheviks. God help us.' He sipped his beer, then asked, 'Did you read the book?'

She felt her body slump in despair. 'I tried, Otto, darling. Truly I did. When I finished the washing, when your dinner was cooking, I sat down and I tried to read it. It's very hard. I didn't understand much.'

'It's a short book,' he said in frustration. 'I thought you'd be able to read it.' He saw she was distressed, and placated her. 'I understand. It is difficult. Even some of the members of the Society have difficulty reading it. The leader had to explain what some of it meant.'

'What's a protocol? I understand some bits, but what's a protocol? And what's a Zion?'

He shook his head sadly. How on earth could he get this lovely young woman, the pride and joy of his life, his comfort, his mistress, his wife, to understand the danger that she and little Reinholdt and everybody else in Bavaria faced? The world was being manipulated by an international Jewish conspiracy, the banks, the munitions factories, heavy industry, international finance. It was all under the control of the Jews. And they were like spiders, sitting in a dark corner weaving a web to entrap hard-working Germans like himself. And why? So they could build this Palestine State. This Jew journalist, Herzl, he had even announced it in public. That was the aim. To build a Jewish State and from Jerusalem to control the whole of the world.

Well, Otto Stricher and all his colleagues in the Bavarian Society of the Officers of the Teutonic Empire, and soon every other good German, would put a stop to it. The leader had told them precisely what he was going to do. He would follow General Wittelsbach to the ends of the earth. He had trust in the General. The General had even met Hindenburg personally. The General had connections. And once the General began to march to free the world of this web of intrigue, nothing would stop him.

Now he was thinking about it again, Otto's fury returned. Not even Lotte's comforts could calm him down. He was suddenly back there in the Beer Hall, feeling the same ire he and his colleagues had felt as the General, and then Von Tritzka were explaining about the Jewish conspiracy and how imminent was the danger to all of them.

Otto swallowed another mouthful of beer. Lotte bent down and again licked the foam from his upper lip. She smiled and began to kiss him. He stiffened and put the beer stein down. The Jews could wait for another day.

NEW YORK, PRESENT DAY

Sarah began to write her letter to Dr Forenjo the following morning. She wrote four paragraphs and then deleted them from her computer. In the afternoon, she managed to put three paragraphs together before deleting them as well. She was uncomfortable about writing back and denying help to a man who seemed so kind and open and who was obviously trying to do the best for an old friend, as well as discharging a moral and legal duty. Instead she would delay writing for a day or two and search databases in order to assist him in finding out precisely who he was seeking.

Even though post-war Europe had been in tatters and Nazi records were destroyed *holus bolus*, in the 1940s and '50s the records of the American Immigration Service were accurate and today there were no difficulties or obstacles in accessing them. A friend in the Public Records section of the Department of Immigration told her he should have an answer back within hours.

No answer came back that day, and the following day Sarah continued to wait in frustration. She phoned him in the middle of the afternoon. He apologised, explaining that cutbacks in his staff had delayed the response, which had come back to him that morning. He delayed sending it, because he wanted to re-check personally the details he'd received from his department. The same answer resurfaced.

It appeared from the records of the Department of Customs and Immigration, and the old Department of Immigrant Administration that for the months of June, July and August 1950, no woman named Eva Arpel, travelling with a daughter Bertha or Bettina, had passed through any immigration point in continental America from Europe. The famous Ellis Island, through which seventeen million immigrants had passed to enter America, had closed in 1943 and since then, processing of migrants was undertaken in New York City proper, so the Island's records were of no value.

He had widened the search to include immigrants coming to America from the rest of the world and had come up with only one name which matched Sarah's inquiry for those particular months. An Eva Arpel, travelling with her daughter Bertha had arrived from Buenos Aires into New York on July 28, 1950. She had given no forwarding address, nor had she any relatives in the country with whom she would be living. Because she was a Jewish woman immigrant without a supporting male, and because she had no relations in America to assist her, the Department of Immigration had placed her in the Betty Freyer Hostel for Displaced Jewish Immigrants for processing by the relevant authorities. That was the last that US Immigrant Administration knew of her.

Sarah listened in incomprehension. 'Where did she go after she left the hostel?' she asked.

Her friend replied, 'Sorry, Sarah, but we don't have access to those records. You'll have to go to the State Department or the Jewish Agency or B'nai B'rith or the Betty Freyer Hostel records to find out, assuming that the records are still in existence.'

Sarah thanked him and put the phone down. She shook her head in confusion. Was it possible that her grandmother, *Bubba* Eva, had left Europe and gone to South America before coming to New York? Why would she do that? It was nonsense. The only way out of Europe for a migrant in those days was a ship from

Hamburg or Rotterdam. First stop London. Second stop New York. But South America? It was impossible. What the hell was going on?

David held her hand and listened attentively as she explained what she had discovered that afternoon.

'Sarah, you know how confused things were straight after the war. There's been a stuff up. We both know it. The Immigration records aren't necessarily accurate, or your grandmother was confused, or the retelling of the family history was wrong. Something happened, God knows what, but don't you think that your own mother would remember she'd been born in South America?'

Sarah nodded her head in agreement. It was the only logical explanation. Joining his theme, she asked rhetorically, 'Can you remember what you were doing before you were five? My mother came here when she was a toddler. All the experiences would have been new. She would have known German fluently. If she had been born in South America, for God's sake, she would have remembered some words, wouldn't she? She remembers German. I've never known her to speak a word of Spanish. Doesn't that prove she was born in Germany and came here when she was five?'

David wondered whether she was trying to convince him, or herself.

Sarah waited patiently for the following Sunday when they drove to Long Island. She entered the house and smiled again at the familiar heavy smell of cooking. *Nouvelle Cuisine* had no place in her mother's home. Somewhere in Bertha's mind was the equation that food equals love, and the more food, the more love was on display.

Her parents began their usual litany of examination the

moment Sarah and her husband crossed the threshold, and her mother immediately excused herself to walk into the kitchen to finish preparation of the meal.

'Mom, let the meal go for a minute, will you. There's something I want to talk to you about,' said Sarah. Her mother looked surprised. Sarah walked over to her, and put her arm around her shoulder, something she hadn't done in a long time. Bertha responded warmly and snuggled up to her daughter.

'Mom, remember when we used to talk about the old days. Around the dinner table. Dad and you used to tell us about how things were when you were kids in America.'

'And you would listen?' Her mother turned to David, 'You think I could get her to listen. The minute I used the word "family" she'd spring out of her chair like a jackrabbit and bound upstairs. Any excuse. Homework, have to phone a girlfriend … I used to say to Sol that when she grew up she'd have to wear a name tag to family get-togethers so that people would know her.'

Her mother stood at the door wearing an old apron and smiled. 'Darling, we can talk while we eat. I should let the meal go to hell because you want to talk about our family? All of a sudden you're interested? You want to eat burned lamb. Who eats burned lamb?'

'Mom, please. Just turn it down. I only want to talk to you for a few minutes.'

'What, turn it down? You can't just turn lamb down. I've got the vegetables cooking so they'll be ready together. We'll talk over lunch.'

'No Mom. I want to talk to you quietly, without the sound of knives and forks.'

Sol intervened, 'Sarah, in the city you're a *gantzer macher*, here you'll eat lamb same time as the rest of us. This can wait, surely?'

Sarah remained silent. There was no use responding. Bertha and Sol looked at their daughter. Then Sol looked at his wife quizzically, wondering why Sarah was making such a fuss. He sighed, and Bertha realised that she was beginning to look petty in front of David, so she decided to concede on this issue. She shrugged her shoulders and walked out to turn off the stove.

'So, what is this?' asked her father. 'You back to prosecuting attorney? What's your mother done, you're putting her in the witness box?' He tried to make it sound like a joke, but for some reason of inner tension, Sarah took him seriously.

'Mom's done nothing. Something's come up at work which I have to discuss with her.'

'You want to talk in private? If I wasn't so hungry, I'd take my son-in-law for a walk around the block.'

David smiled. Sol was so proud, that he spoke of him in titles; my son-in-law the cellist; my son-in-law, the musician … he couldn't remember Sol ever calling him David.

'No,' said Sarah. 'No, there's nothing private.'

Bertha returned and sat down on the couch next to Sol. All of a sudden, comprehension dawned, and Bertha Kaplan beamed a smile. She grasped Sol's hand tighter. 'I know what it is,' she burst out laughing and shouted for joy.

Sol looked at her in surprise. 'What?' he demanded.

'She's pregnant. I'm going to have a grandchild. I told you she's been looking flushed. Didn't I say that to you, a fortnight ago?'

'Mom,' said Sarah interrupting quickly. 'I'm not pregnant.'

Her mother's face fell.

'Mom, I need to talk to you about *Bubba* Eva.'

'*Bubba* Eva, God rest her soul?' her mother said, surprised that her infallible intuition had let her down.

'Tell me, where did *Bubba* Eva come from?' asked Sarah.

'Michalovce. She was born in Michalovce. Slovakia. In the *humsht*. You've been there. You went with Josh Krantz when you went over to Czechoslovakia to get his house back.'

'And when she was a baby, what happened?'

'You know what happened,' her mother said.

'Tell me.'

'My grandmother, your great-grandmother Serel, God rest her soul, saw her husband Nathan killed by madmen. It was the beginning of the century … 1900 or something. So she up's the children and carries Eva and Isaac and Rose all the way to Berlin. Serel wanted to come to America, I think, but she got caught up with things before the war and couldn't get out of Germany. She was a widow. It must have been so hard for her.'

'After Berlin, what happened?'

'After Berlin, I don't know. I think *mamma* Eva grew up and became a woman and married your grandfather Saul, God rest his soul. My father. I never even knew him. He was put into Sachsenhausen Concentration Camp by those murdering Nazi swine. God knows how he survived those bastards, may Almighty God make them rot in Hell. Anyway, by some miracle, your *Bubba* and *Zeida* were reunited after the war. I was born in 1946. He died in 1950 of a broken heart. After that, there was no reason for *Bubba* Eva to stay in that *farstinkeneh* hole of a country, so your grandmother and I left Germany and came here to America. Like her mother before her had saved her children when she was a young widow, so my mother carried me as a little girl across Europe and into America. And that's it. End of story.'

Sarah nodded. 'How old was *Bubba* Eva when she left Michalovce?'

'She was just born. She was a baby. Serel your great-grandmother had to carry her.'

'And that was in 1903?'

'Yes, as far as I know.'

'It couldn't have been later?'

'Maybe. Maybe 1904, 1905. From what I was told, Serel, my grandmother, remarried when she got to Berlin. But my mother was very hazy about the details. She always used to say, "better you don't know the *mishugas* what went on before the war." So that's the story! That's what I was told.'

'Then think about this,' said Sarah. 'If grandmother Eva was born in 1903, and she died in 1975, she would have been 72.'

'Nah,' said her mother dismissively. 'She was 65 when she died. That's one thing I'm sure of. At the time when she died, Sol and I said how sad it was that she was so young.'

Sarah said gently, 'Then she must have been born in 1910. After they got to Berlin. She must have been the child of the second husband.'

'Nah, you've made a mistake. Your grandmother told me her life story. I know these things.' But there was a frown on Bertha's face.

'Next question,' Sarah said.

David interrupted. From the moment her mother had returned from the kitchen, Sarah's demeanour had changed from a daughter to that of an inquisitor. 'Honey', he said, 'do you think now would be a good time to have lunch and then perhaps continue this after lunch.'

'No, David. I'd rather we continued. If that's alright with you, Mom.'

Sol asked, 'Sarah, what's going on?'

'Dad, I had some news this week about the family. And it doesn't make sense. There's nothing wrong, I promise you. I just have to get things clear for my own sake.'

'Your mother's told you what happened.'

'Dad, just a couple things, and then I'm finished. I promise.' She turned to her mother and walked over to sit beside her, holding her other hand. 'Mom, when you and *Bubba* Eva came to America, you were about five, right?'

'Yes. I was born at the beginning of 1946. We got here some time in 1950. If not five, I was four and eleven months or something. I don't know exactly when I got here.'

'And you came from where?'

'From Germany. Why, where should I have come from?'

'Do you remember anything about South America?'

'Excuse me?'

'Do you remember going to South America from Germany?'

'South America?' She burst out laughing. 'Your father and I wouldn't even go there for a holiday. Why should your *Bubba* Eva take me to South America before we came to New York?'

'I think you ought to read this.'

Sarah took a letter from the top inside breast pocket of her jacket and gave it to her mother. Bertha looked at it as though it was a court summons and opened it in trepidation. She read the letterhead at the top and then turned to the bottom of the third page where she read the signature.

She looked at Sarah and asked, 'Who is this, Dr Luis Forenjo?'

'Read the letter, Mom,' said Sarah gently.

Sol peeked over and read along with his wife. They waited for each other at the end of the first page. Then at the end of the second page. The letter finished in the middle of the third. Bertha looked up and shook her head.

'You've got the wrong people. It's a mistake. I feel sorry for the guy but it ain't us. We didn't come from South America.'

'Mom, I've just checked all the records. There's no record of entry around that time for Eva Arpel with a daughter Bertha or Bettina coming in from Europe but there's a record of them coming in from Buenos Aires, in Argentina.'

'It ain't us,' Bertha said quietly. 'That's all I can tell you. Listen, *bubeleh*. Don't waste your time on this rubbish. Meanwhile, me?' she stood, ending the conversation, 'I'm going to put back on the lamb. If not, it'll get greasy. David,' she said turning to her son-in-law, 'I've made potatoes the way you like them.'

Sol handed back the letter which Sarah folded and put into her inside breast pocket. It sat right above the amulet which Sarah always wore, the family heirloom given to her by Bertha when Sarah reached twenty-one; just as Eva had given it to Bertha, and Serel had given it to Eva, and for which Nussan the farmer had died nearly a century earlier in a bloody pogrom in a tiny *stetl* in the East of Slovakia.

God Almighty, Sarah thought. This was what she and her mother had believed … what they'd known absolutely … all their lives.

How could it possibly be otherwise?

CHAPTER SIX

THE HIGH TARTRA MOUNTAINS, SLOVAKIA, 1903

Nobody told her that Poprad was so high. For all of her life Serel had lived in a valley beside a river. It was a beautiful river, fast flowing and freezing in the spring with the mountain melt-water, and then with languid, cooling waters in the height of the summer. She knew that the water for her river came from somewhere. She knew of course that it came from high far-away mountains, but she had no idea how high the mountains were. Serel now realised that the mountains had been a barrier preventing her from leaving.

During her marriage to Nussan, Serel had speculated about the adventure of leaving but how could she? Tied to a farm and a horse and two cows. Now she was leaving. Now, she was climbing the mountain to get to the other side. She had been climbing for three days. People told her that Poprad was further up the hill. But how far?

Now she was dealing with more confidence with the people she met on the way. The Christians who had been so kind to her had instilled her with vigour and self-respect. She was still cautious. She was still a Jew but she smiled at people as they passed her on their carts. She even nodded to a rich-looking man on horseback as he rode towards her. Disdainfully, he avoided her look, but couldn't help noticing young Yitzchok bowing in mock solemnity as the rich man rode past them. A smile appeared on the man's mustachioed face, just a flicker, but enough for Serel to know that she could now talk to all level of people from the very low to much more important, to Christians, to Atheists and Socialists. She could now speak as a woman and no longer as a Jew.

A farmer whom she passed in the morning taking a load of vegetables to some town passed her again on his return in the middle of the day. He stopped and doffed his cap. He asked her if she wanted a lift with the children. She was immensely grateful and told him so. He took her up the hill to Poprad. He didn't speak much. He was taciturn. He hummed a tune which Serel didn't recognise. He dropped her at the outskirts of the town. The last thing the farmer wanted to do was to take her to a priest or a church, damn their bones. And neither did he want to be seen with her. His wife was a shrew, and would listen to any gossip. Serel alighted and again thanked the man, blessing him for his kindness. He whipped the horse along.

Serel stood at the entry to the town, too frightened to move. This was the first big place she'd ever been to. Nussan had been to Kosice, the big city twenty miles from their home but she had stayed at home to feed the horse and milk the cows, and look after the children. Poprad was overwhelming. There were people and horses and dogs and carts everywhere, all moving constantly in between rows of houses which seemed to be going in all directions. It was nothing like her village. Row after row of houses stretching as far as the eye could see. In Kosice, she knew that there were tall buildings, overshadowed by the spires of churches, and lording over everything was St Elizabeth's Cathedral.

Poprad must be as large and as magnificent as the images she carried in her mind of Kosice, pictures painted at night in bed when Nussan returned. Serel looked up in the sky and saw four spires, each with crosses at the top. One was different. It was shaped like an onion. She knew what the difference was.

'Come children,' she said, and they began walking, cautiously, into the centre of Poprad, past shops selling all sorts of diverse and unusual items. Yitzchok could hardly believe his eyes. Every few moments he stopped and stood outside a shop window, looking in at the wonders it contained, things of which he'd only ever dreamed. Bolts of cloth and sewing machines in one. Daggers, knives and cutlery in another. And next door, jewellery of the most extraordinary beauty, scintillating with light as the late-afternoon sun gleamed on the silver and gold. Rosl was more circumspect, more frightened. She had never seen anything like this. She clung to her mother's skirts while baby Eva slept.

'Come Yitzchok,' said Serel. 'We must find our people. Now we will be safe.'

The question was how was she to find the Jewish quarter? She knew there was one. People who visited her *stetl* had talked of the wealthy and important Jews of Poprad. But where did they live? Were they the same as the Jews she'd grown up with, living all in one place, with only two or three roads to the entire village; or were they like the Jews she had heard about in New York who lived in every part of the city, and who were free to move without having to show papers if the police suddenly demanded it?

The signs on the shops gave no clue. The names were clearly Slovak or Hungarian. Some were even German. She crossed the street and with the increase in the numbers of horses and wagons, she realised she was getting closer and closer to the centre. It was a maze of streets. She stopped to look in admiration at the organisation of life around her.

Things were so different here. It was the middle of the afternoon, and there were hundreds of people on the street. Didn't they work? Weren't the women at home preparing the evening meal for their husbands? And why were so many men in the streets, dressed in their best clothes? Why weren't they working?

This place was very strange. Serel's entire existence, her whole life, was governed by nature, and the sun. Living in her *stetl*, she woke up to the sun and she went to bed shortly after the sun had gone down. Candles and oil lamps had defied nature but nature fought back by making her tired the minute candles were lit.

But here! She looked along the streets. There were street lamps everywhere. The roads had pavements where ladies and gentlemen would walk. And all the streets seemed to lead towards the central square, an area of huge proportions. But where were the trees? Where were the fields? She felt uncomfortable; she'd never in her life been so far from the earth.

Because the buildings on the other side of the square were further away, Serel's view of the skyline gave her an understanding of where Poprad was in relation to the nearby mountains in which the city nestled. To reach Poprad, she had climbed and climbed, all the while seeing snow-capped mountains in the distance. But now that she was in the centre she could see how close the mountains were. It was as if Poprad was a sleeping child in the cradle which the mountains formed.

Her attention was suddenly changed as a covered wagon carrying passengers passed close enough to prove a danger. She pulled Rosl closer to her, away from the edge of the pavement. She looked through the windows of the carriage and when it had passed, she realised that she was looking directly into a shop on the other side of the street. It was a jewellery shop and above the door was the name *M. J. Moses*.

Could it be?

She crossed the street, forgetting to check whether any horses or carts were coming. She just wasn't used to traffic. She entered the shop with her children in tow. A bell tinkled as she closed the door, which attracted Rosl's attention and made the child smile. A small man, balding, dressed in a shirt with a strange winged collar, a waistcoat and shirt sleeves, with a fob watch hanging from one of the pockets in his waistcoat like the amulet she had secreted in her bodice, smiled at her and said, 'Good afternoon, may I help you?'

Serel suddenly realised that she had no idea what to ask. She flushed in embarrassment. What if he wasn't Jewish? Perhaps a Christian was called Moses. The old fears suddenly resurfaced, a spectre rising to haunt her. The shopkeeper frowned. 'Can I help you?' he asked again.

Then he looked at her more carefully. Her clothes and those of her children were extremely crude, made of the roughest linens and wools. The children looked filthy, indeed from the look of them they had been sleeping rough in gutters. The last thing he wanted in his exclusive emporium were beggars. He walked urgently around the counter, shooing them away as though they were refuse.

'I'm afraid you'll have to leave now,' he said. 'Please get out of my shop.'

Serel was mystified. From the look of him, he was a Jew. Couldn't he recognise her as a sister in Abraham?

'I need help,' she said. 'Most of my food is gone.'

'Get out,' he suddenly commanded, his voice becoming aggressive. 'Get out or I'll call the police.'

'Are you a Jew?' she asked.

His face froze in fear. 'Get out immediately if you know what's good for you.' He put his hand on her shoulder and started to push her.

Yitzchok reacted angrily. 'Stop it,' he shouted. 'Stop hurting my mother.'

The man stopped. The last thing he wanted was an embarrassing fuss.

Serel said, 'Please, don't push me. I just want to know if you can help me. I need to find the Jews of this town. I've come from Roznava. There was a pogrom. My husband was killed. I need help.'

The shopkeeper's anger immediately subsided. He withdrew his hand and looked at her closely. 'You're a Jew?' he asked cautiously.

The woman nodded.

'When was the pogrom?'

She shrugged her shoulders. 'I don't know when it was. I've lost count of the days. I've been staying with a family who were kind to me and since then I've been walking to Poprad, except for the last bit where a farmer gave me a lift. We've been sleeping in fields and the nights have been getting colder. We've used up all the food that they gave us.'

'You're a Jew?' the man repeated.

Serel nodded.

His voice urgent, he glanced around the empty shop and whispered, 'Tell me the blessing over the lighting of the *shabbos* candles.'

Serel frowned.

'Tell me the blessing over the candles,' he repeated, this time more insistently.

She covered Yitzchok's head and said the *ba'rucha*. It was a prayer she said in Hebrew every *shabbos* of her life when the family sat down for their evening meal. The shopkeeper nodded, his face became less tense. He walked back to his counter, took a slip of paper and wrote some words.

Then he stopped and looked at her. 'Do you read and write?'

She nodded. 'Here,' he said. 'You'll find our Rabbi at this address.' He gave her clear indications of how to get there. 'Walk towards the centre of Poprad. Take the second street left, the third street on the right and you'll see the *shul*. The Rabbi's house is next door. Tell him I sent you. My name and address are on the back of the card. He'll see to your needs.'

Serel tried to kiss his hand in gratitude, but he withdrew it, not wanting to be offended by her roughness. He smelled of some sort of perfume, maybe eau de Cologne. She'd smelt it before. The butcher's wife had been given it as a present by her husband when he returned once from Kiev. The jeweller's hands were soft. Nothing like the hands of Nussan or his friends. She took the children under her wing and walked towards the door.

'A moment,' he said. Serel stopped and looked at him in expectation. 'I'm sure the Rabbi will help you. I hope he does. But if he doesn't, there's no point in your returning. In fact, I don't want you to come back here. I have customers from the very best parts of Poprad society. If they see you or your children in my shop, what will they think?'

Serel nodded sadly and started to walk out of his emporium. But then she suddenly stopped, thinking for a moment. She turned and looked at Mr Moses, feeling a sense of anger. Why should he treat her like this? Yes, he was rich. You could see that by his waistcoat, and his shiny shoes, the pomade in his hair, the softness of the skin on his cheek and his hands. All these things spoke of a man who didn't have to work in the fields. But that didn't give him the right to treat her like she was dirt under his leather shoes. In her home, she was the *balaboosta*. She had clean linen, white tablecloths, lace head scarfs and the children never went without. She walked back towards him in indignation.

'I have something to sell. You're a jeweller. Will you buy it?'

He frowned. 'I'm sorry. We don't trade in second-hand merchandise.'

'It's not second hand. It was' … She hesitated for a moment, ' … made by my husband. He's a craftsman.'

'His name?' Mr Moses asked.

'His name is … was Nussan. He sold his jewellery in Kiev.' The lies became bigger as she told them.

'Kiev?'

'Yes,' said Serel. 'In Kiev, to a trader there.'

Moses remained quiet, confused. Her look, her clothes, the ragged children, spoke of a farming *stetl* family, not a wealthy man connected with the elite of the jewellery trade in the provincial capital. He didn't believe her. She could have told him Vienna for all she knew about Kiev. Or Paris. Or New York. What game was she playing?

Serel turned her back away from him and reached into her blouse; she took out the heavy gold amulet and necklace. Mr Moses looked at it in surprise. He could tell immediately that it was valuable, if indeed it was gold and not lead painted as gold. He'd fallen for that trick before.

'Your husband made this?'

Serel nodded. She put it in his hands. He felt the chain, then he felt the amulet in his other hand. It was solid gold, of that he had no doubt, but the working was crude, rough, almost primitive. The chain was attractive, but it wasn't the fine filigree which was all the fashion now in Paris and St Petersburg and Prague. But the chain had an innocence about it. The links were beautifully done. Some were twisted, some were straight. It was definitely the work of a craftsman, not an artisan. It might even appeal to some of the ladies in Poprad because it had a dimension which was rare in jewellery. He tried to find a word to equate to his feelings, but all he could think was that the chain was innocent.

Then he looked at the amulet. This was strange indeed. He squeezed his eye into his magnifying eyepiece and looked more closely. It was amazing. There was a crude drawing of an animal on one side. Perhaps a bull. On the other, there was a drawing of an owl and on both sides were interesting striations, amazingly carved. Could they be waves of the sea, or perhaps the markings of a bumble bee or a wasp? Wavy lines, the like of which he had never seen before. Again, he was struck by its primitiveness, as though it had been made by a child … but there was also a sophistication about it which he found intriguing. It was an object he would like to possess.

But how to deal with this woman? She was impoverished. That was obvious. The pogrom had stripped her of whatever wealth or assets a woman like this once possessed. Well, that wasn't his problem. He took the eyeglass out of his eye and placed the amulet and necklace onto a scale.

'No,' said Serel suddenly. 'Not both. Just the necklace. How much will you give me for the necklace?'

He undid the clasp and slipped the necklace out of the loop, freeing the amulet. He put on several gram weights. It was heavier than he thought. It weighed more than even his experienced eye could judge. He did a quick mental calculation and mentioned a price. It was half the real value but business was business.

Serel's eyes widened in shock. 'As much as that?'

'Yes,' he said, regretting he hadn't offered her a quarter of the real value. How was he to tell that she had no idea of the price of gold.

'I'll take it,' she said.

'It's not that simple,' said Mr Moses. 'How do I know it's yours? You could have stolen it.'

'It's mine. My husband … made it two weeks ago, before the pogrom.'

'Two weeks ago?' Moses said. He looked at the chain again. There were markings on it, the black indentations of great age. And the closer he examined, the older it looked. Indeed, it now was obvious that this chain was old, many years old. 'This wasn't made recently,' he said. 'It has no shine to it. It has no feel of newness. What lies are you telling me, woman?'

Tears began to well up in her eyes. She was so tired. She just wanted to be safe and secure and have enough money in her pocket that she didn't have to worry.

'Well?' demanded Moses.

'My husband dug it up,' she said quietly. 'He found it buried in a grave. It was the reason for the pogrom. He got drunk and told people about it.'

Moses nodded. That explained things.

'This is buried treasure. It belongs to the State. I can't touch it.'

Her shoulders shrugged. She held out her hand.

'No,' he said. 'I'm not giving this back to you. It's my duty to give it to the constabulary.'

Serel's face drained of blood. It was the only thing of value that she possessed. Without it, she was truly, utterly desperate.

'Please,' she said. 'I have nothing.'

He looked at her, his mind scheming. 'I'll give you half of its value. I can melt the chain down and make your criminality disappear. I can make it into something else. Gold always remains gold no matter when it was dug out of the ground or buried into it. As to the other thing, the amulet, I'm sorry. You must take that. That has markings on it which I don't like. Even if I melt it down, it would worry me. The evil eye.'

'So how much will you give me for the chain?' she asked, desperation growing in her voice.

He went to his cash drawer and took out a wad of money. He counted out notes one-quarter of the true value of the gold. 'That's all I'm giving you. Take that and keep your mouth shut. Refuse it and I'll take both of them straight around to the Constable. And understand this, woman. If you breathe a word of our transaction, I'll deny everything. Once its melted down you'll have no proof, and then you'll be arrested and your children will go to a poorhouse.'

She pocketed the money quickly. It was enough to ensure food and comfort and warmth for her and her children until they got to America. She turned and walked quickly out of the shop. This was her nest egg. This was the money she would use to buy passage. She would tell nobody she had it. Nobody. Not the Rabbi. Not the people who would help her. She would still be poor until she got to America and then she would spend her fortune buying a new life for herself and her children.

Mr Moses watched her leave. He picked up the chain and smiled. But then, suddenly, he realised that he had made a mistake. The calibration he had used to weigh the gold was far lighter than he should have done. He'd weighed the chain as if it was silver. He smiled to himself. It was a genuine mistake. A stupid mistake. He re-calibrated his scale and put on extra weights. The chain was far more valuable than he believed. Amazing! He had made more money in this one day than he had in the last two months. What a piece of luck! If only he hadn't been so silly about the amulet, he could have made six months' profit. Why did he give it back? Oh well, it was too late now. The woman was already disappearing down the road.

The joy of the money in her pocket evaporated quickly. As she walked down the road, she realised that she had been tricked. Anger started to grow in her mind. Her husband had died for the damned necklace and the amulet. Yet, she had only got half of its value. Why? She didn't trust Moses at all. He would not have taken it to the Constable. He would have kept it himself and profited. She breathed deeply. She hated being a woman on her own. Nussan, for all his gullibility would never have allowed Moses to get away with it. Still, it was too late now. She couldn't go back. She couldn't create a scene. Knowing him, he'd call the police and then the amulet would be found and she'd be hanged for theft and who would look after her children then? And anyway, she didn't want to go back.

She had no money in her pocket! Nothing! She was still poor. Her hand was in her pocket, but it felt nothing. The money that she had clutched in her hand as she left his shop was no longer there. She had already stuck it into her bodice and she wouldn't take it out again until she was well away from Poprad. She wouldn't even take transport from Poprad to the next town. She wouldn't dare be accused of having money. When she got to Hamburg she would buy tickets for America. She would convince herself that she was as poor now as she had been before she entered Moses' shop.

She walked in a daze. She didn't really understand where she was, or what she was doing. As they left the Rabbi's house, the children had tried to talk to her, but she merely smiled, and nodded, and continued to walk.

How could these people have been so cruel. What had they called her? 'A peasant!' She was a Jew, yet she'd been treated as if she suffered from leprosy. Even the Rabbi had been aloof and condescending, not even showing her into his rich and luxurious home, but directing her to a woman who dealt with the ... what had he called her? ... *'unfortunates'* of this city. She'd gone to the woman, who had demanded even more proof of her Jewishness. Then, when she was satisfied, she had directed Serel to the house of a wealthy Jewish family on the outskirts of Poprad who often gave to charity, where the woman was confident that Serel and her children could sleep for a few nights.

She approached the house from the rear, as instructed. Even from the back garden, Serel could tell that it was a large house. Inside, she found that the family was attended by four servants. The man who owned the house was a businessman, dealing in gas and oil. Or so she understood from the servants. She was instructed to enter and leave the house only by the back door. Her accommodation would always be downstairs, where she and her children would be fed. And that was the way it was. They slept the night on cots set up in the scullery. It was cold, but they were given plenty of blankets. In the morning, Yitzchok was told to go to the coalhouse, and fill up a dozen scuttles, to be stored outside the back door. These would replace the empty scuttles which were to be used to light fires in all the rooms as soon as the sun started to fall. Poprad was so high up that even in summer, the nights could get very cold.

Rosl was set to work polishing the cutlery which had been used for a dinner party the family had given the previous night. She had never seen so much silverware. Soup tureens; massive silver dishes; oddly shaped plates with large silver domes; huge ladles with intricate handles; exquisite salt and pepper pots; salvers which contained the bone and skin remnants of some massive fish; sauce bowls; silver platters with fearsome spikes in the middle on which large joints of meat had stood, their fat now congealed in the runnels on the outside of the dish; and so many knives and forks and spoons in so many different sizes and shapes that she wondered what they could possibly be used for. In her house, there was one spoon or one knife and fork for each meal, even when *Mamma* made a soup and some meat and something to eat afterwards, like *lockshen kuggle*.

Serel was told to help in the kitchen. The cook, a fat and florid-faced elderly Jewess, was like an old hag. She bossed and ordered everybody around, as if she were a *Rebbitzen*. The whole family worked and slept and then in the morning when they woke up early, they worked only to await the night when they would fall asleep again. She had no right to expect more. She and the children were fed and they were warm at night, but her hopes were that her life wouldn't continue to be this hard. She was working as she worked in her own house, only everything was on a much bigger scale and there was no Nussan at home to kiss her and cuddle her and help her when he had rested.

On one of the mornings, when the cook was preparing a lunch for the guests of the mistress of the house, Serel had noticed what the woman was making. She had placed all the ingredients in a large brown mixing bowl into which she was placing handfuls of food. Raisins, finely chopped nuts, a bit more flour, a little bit of milk, stirring and stirring in order to get the consistency right. But one of the ingredients she was missing out was schnapps. Serel made this particular dessert at least two or three times a month. It was a recipe her mother had taught her. The schnapps gave it a heady lightness, a moistness. Especially pear schnapps. That was the best.

She walked over to the cook and told her what she did with such a dish in her own home. The cook looked at her in utter contempt, a look that quickly transmuted to anger. She shouted, 'I take no advice from peasants like you. What do you know about fine kosher food? People like you! Get back to washing the dishes or I'll have you thrown out of my kitchen.'

All the servants stopped their work and looked at the vicious exchange. Everybody loved raised voices in the kitchen. It overcame the monotony. They wanted to see how Serel would respond. But instead of saying anything she turned and walked back to her scullery sink, where she continued to scrape the pots, her back to everybody else. She couldn't see them laughing at her but they couldn't see the tears welling up in her eyes at the humiliation, at the feeling of impotence. In her own home, she was the *balaboosta*, the mistress of the house; but she no longer had a home. Not any more. She was a poor Jew, relying upon charity. Is this what she had come to? The tears coarsed down her cheeks. She stopped her body from shaking in sobs, masking it by coughing. She determined to leave the following morning.

When she woke, she packed only the goods she had brought with her. One of the maids who arrived in the kitchen early to fetch her mistress a cup of coffee, saw her packing. When Serel first arrived, the maid had felt contempt for her but she recognised her now as a loving and caring mother who had fallen on hard times. It could happen to anybody.

'You're leaving us?' she asked.

Serel nodded.

'You must take food and clothing.'

Serel shook her head. 'I want nothing. I just want to leave here.'

'Is it because of what the cook said to you last night?'

Serel nodded and then shook her head. 'No. It's not just the cook. It's everything. I'm a peasant, according to everybody. I don't belong in a fine house. Yet before the

Christians destroyed my home, I was a *balaboosta*. A somebody. Now, I'm a nobody. I'm going to America if this is the way I'm treated. I don't want to stay.'

'Where will you go from here? How will you get there?' asked the maid.

'To Kraków. Then to Wroclaw, and then, please God, to Hamburg to catch the boat.'

The maid registered her shock. 'How will you get to Kraków? You can't walk over the mountains. Some people do, but they're young men, hikers, mountain climbers; not mothers with three small children. You'll have to go around the Tartras; then north. But it's a terrible journey. Can't you take a coach?'

Serel shook her head. 'I have no money,' she said softly.

'Then how?' queried the maid. What Serel was planning was beyond her comprehension.

'How I got here,' answered Serel. 'Walking.'

'With three children? You're mad.'

'What else can I do? Others have done it.'

'Not with three children.'

Serel shrugged. 'I would rather die on the road than live here.'

The maid sighed. 'Don't leave just yet. Please wait. There's something I want to do.'

The maid turned and walked quickly out of the kitchen carrying the coffee cup on a silver tray. Serel continued to pack her goods. She woke up the children and told them to get ready to leave. The maid came back in a hurry, a smile on her face. 'Come with me,' she said urgently. Mystified, Serel followed the woman out of the kitchen and up the stairs which she had only ever seen from a distance, but never once ascended. She knew they led up to where the rich family lived. She had no right being up there.

She gasped as she walked up the steps. She was entering

a palace, huge rooms with dark wood – mahogany – everywhere. The walls were lined with wood. The floors were wooden and carpeted with thick piled multicoloured rugs and carpets. Heavy red drape curtains hung across every window. There was the perfumed smell of a man in the house; it could be expensive tobacco, not that Serel had ever smelt tobacco whose aroma was like delicate herbs. The cheap tobacco that Nussan had smoked was not completely dissimilar, though it reeked throughout her house, and whenever he returned from the inn in Roznava, his clothes stank of it.

There were sideboards and credenzas groaning with gold and silver statues or delicate porcelain maidens, their arms uplifted or outstretched; and there was a huge clock in the entry hall, reaching nearly to the ceiling, which ticked imperiously in the corner, the only noise which could be heard in the draped quietness of the massive room.

'Come,' said the maid, and hurried Serel across the floor and up yet another flight of stairs. Two flights? What kind of a house was this? How tall could it possibly be?

As they ascended the stairs, the colours changed. Downstairs they were dark, mahogany, red, and with deep velvet shades and curtains. Upstairs was a much lighter pastel blue like a delicate eggshell of a duck, or a hint of sky in the walls. The top of the stairs divided into a corridor which ran around the entire floor. There was no sound from their footsteps, the floor was thickly carpeted. This was luxury the like of which Serel simply didn't understand. Nowhere had she seen this wealth, this fineness. And the house belonged to Jews … amazing!

The maid knocked gently on a cream-painted door so as not to disturb the rest of the still-sleeping household. A muffled command came from within the room. The maid opened the door and walked in. She stood within the frame of the door, curtsying.

'The woman is here, Madam,' she said.

The maid ushered Serel into the room. Serel didn't have time to appreciate its beauty, except to see a profusion of yellow and white, like a field of daisies. The most delicate of nets hung over the large bed, a dressing table with a gilt-edged mirror took up most of one corner of the huge room; a window whose view looked out towards the nearby mountain was covered with the finest netted tracery she had ever seen, blowing gently in the cold early-morning breeze. The heat from the fire in the room warmed a middle-aged, extremely elegant woman as she sat in an armchair sipping a cup of coffee and reading a letter. She was a woman of obvious refinement, and as Serel stared at her beauty, she realised that the face was nothing short of exquisite. The dark hair, though flecked with grey strands, was piled up in luxuriant waves above her head. She wore a delicious nightdress which was covered by a chemise whose gold and silver trim shimmered in the light from the window. The woman put the letter down and stared at Serel.

'This is the woman I was telling you about, Madam,' said the maid. 'She came here sent by the Rabbi and she's about to leave.'

The mistress of the house nodded. Serel wondered where her husband was. Obviously they slept in separate bedrooms.

'And how have you enjoyed your stay with us?' asked the woman. Her voice was as refined as her face and body and clothes. It had a musical lilt, a tone of confidence and self-regard.

'Very well thank you, Madam,' Serel lied.

'And where will you go after you leave us?'

'I'm heading towards Kraków.'

The woman smiled. 'My favourite city. My husband and I go there two or three times a year. He goes on business. I go because I have many friends.'

Serel nodded. The maid intervened. 'Madam, this woman is leaving without food or clothing for her children. I'm worried that she will be cold if she sleeps in fields in the night.'

A look of concern swept across the mistress's face. 'Nonsense,' she said. 'You can't possibly leave in that state. How many children do you have?'

The maid told her what Serel's circumstances were. The mistress of the house turned to the maid. 'See to it that this woman has plenty of food as well as clothing for her children. Give her blankets and ensure that she eats well before she sets off on the road. And especially the children. They must have hot milk and chocolate. See that cook follows my orders.'

The maid curtsied again. Serel attempted to curtsy but didn't know how. The maid took Serel by the arm but before she left, she turned and said, 'Thank you so much. I and my children bless you.'

The woman nodded and returned to her correspondence.

She was beginning to regret her decision to walk out of Poprad. She'd done it to prove to anybody who looked at her that she had no money. She intended to catch a coach at the next town, to use some of the money from the sale of the necklace to make life easier for her and her children. But it was so cold up here in the mountains that she wondered whether she'd make it to the next village. And if she did get there, was there a coach that could take her around the Tartras?

At the end of the second long day's walking, Serel was on the verge of unstitching the jeweller's money from her bodice, returning to Poprad and spending some of it on a carriage which would take them to their next destination. She and the children were exhausted and Serel no longer cared whether or not anybody knew she'd sold her golden necklace. The air was somehow thinner here, and colder than it had been in Poprad. It was more of an effort to walk than it was near to her home far down in the valleys.

But if she did spend some money getting to Kraków, how much would she have left to take the children to Hamburg? And then to America? Did she dare spend some of it … the money for which her husband had died?

Yes, she did. She had to. She looked at her children, and knew that she couldn't be that cruel. She would see them safe in a warm home, and then she'd do something to get tickets on a steamer to America.

In her new determination, she felt an inner glow. But it didn't warm her for long. As the sun sunk beyond the distant mountains the air rapidly cooled. Serel was no longer thinking about the cook in the kitchen. The mistress's kindness didn't excuse the anger in the household below stairs. Why was it so? They were all Jews. She would never treat anybody the way that damn cook had treated her, may all her milk curdle. Yitzchok was nearly dropping with exhaustion; he'd been sharing the burden of carrying little baby Eva. Rosl just kept plodding on, bless her. But she looked ghost-white from tiredness.

Concerned that it would soon be dark, they stopped. Serel found a field of bluish-purple flowers she knew to be lucerne, where she spread three blankets on the ground. They ate sparingly that night. Baby Eva suckled greedily. Yitzchok and Rosl ate slices of tongue and beef which the maid had insisted they take with them, much to the cook's disgust. There was even a duck's leg in the package which Serel would eat the following night. The maid had even taken some money from the housekeeping with the mistress's permission and given Serel enough to buy food for at least the next couple of weeks. Things were much happier now, despite the anger she felt when she first started out.

They settled down and as the temperature fell they said their prayers communally and covered each other with blankets. There was a real nip in the air. Yitzchok looked with amusement as the last dying rays of the distant sun showed his breath flying out of his body. He kept puffing and puffing as transparent clouds flew upwards from his mouth. Serel sighed deeply. Perhaps tomorrow she might feel less tired.

In the middle of the night, she had no idea what time it was but she knew she had been asleep for a long while, she heard wolves baying. They were calling to each other from a distant hillside. She felt her blood go cold. In Roznava she would hurry inside the house and gather up all her children. Here, she was exposed. She looked around but she had no weapons. Cautiously, she crawled out of the blanket. The air was freezing. The moonlight enabled her to find a large stone. Then another. Soon she had a whole collection of them. Would it be enough? Wolves attacked in packs. If she hit one, she would hurt it. What happens if there were three, or five, or twenty? How could she defend her children? She got under the blanket but didn't lie down. Instead she put another around her shoulders and peered at the landscape. She stayed sitting up and awake until morning.

They had been on the road for three days since leaving Poprad. They hadn't tried to cross the High Tartras, but had travelled westwards along their border. She had no idea when they would be able to turn northwards again, and head for Kraków. On the road, they hardly saw anybody. Occasionally a farmer would wave to them. Sometimes somebody riding on a horse would ask them where they were headed. But there were very few towns, and no inns. Her plans to get a train or a carriage to carry them came to nothing. There was no such transport.

All there seemed to be in these damned interminable mountains were holiday resorts where hot water gushed out of the ground; there, she saw many rich people. But she couldn't stay there. So she continued to walk.

Serel didn't know how far she had walked but she did know that she had walked a long way. How far could it be before they could get back onto the Kraków road? How much longer could she and the children walk without collapsing? When would it all end?

It was on the fourth day, after a particularly bitter night, that baby Eva began to cough. At first it was an irritating little cough. A silly little noise, which made Yitzchok laugh. Even Serel thought it was amusing. The baby sometimes coughed, sometimes sneezed, sometimes both at once. But after the third and the fourth hour when little baby Eva continued to cough and sneeze, and cried because it was exhausting her body, Serel became worried. When Eva's temperature began to rise sharply, Serel became terrified. She increased her pace in the forlorn hope that soon, perhaps around the next bend, she might come to a town where there would be a doctor. Thank God she'd saved her money and could afford medicine … if only she could find it.

Often when babies coughed, a lotion or a medicine would cure them quickly. They would be wrapped up in the warmth of the house, a fire would be lit, the cough would go away. Everybody would smile. Only occasionally had she known of a baby whose cough didn't go away. Then everybody looked terribly concerned and the Rabbi came and said prayers and the baby's cold limp silent body was carried out of the room followed by the grieving parents and buried in the village's cemetery. This couldn't happen to her baby. Not baby Eva. She had always been so strong. She had taken to solid foods quickly. She always responded with a smile whenever Serel smiled at her. She made cooing sounds with her mouth. She was interested in everything around her.

Serel looked at her baby in terror. Her body had gone limp. Her face was flushed. Serel felt inside her clothes. Her body was burning. She undid the clothes and used some water from the flask to try to cool her little body but even though the water wasn't particularly cold, it made the baby howl. Serel didn't know what to do. She cried, and mumbled half-forgotten prayers. This was a curse; because she hadn't buried her husband; because the men of her village hadn't said mourning prayers over his memory; because she'd eaten food in a Christian house; because of the chain she'd sold and the amulet. Because … because.

And then baby Eva suddenly stopped howling. Her body became flaccid, as if there were no bones inside her. She just lay there, her eyes hollow and gaunt. Serel didn't know what to do. She tried to suckle her. The baby attached herself to her nipple but coughed and sneezed and moved her face away to breathe. Her breathing was in short pants.

Serel left the road, and went into a field so that her walking wouldn't hurt the baby, praying to God that the illness which had arrived so suddenly would pass as quickly. But it didn't. Baby Eva didn't even have the strength to cry. Instead she just lay there and slowly stopped moving.

Serel stared at her. At first, she didn't realise that her baby was dead. But when she picked up the little girl's hand and let it go, it seemed to fall towards the earth.

Serel lay the child in her lap, put her head in her hands and sobbed. She looked up into the sky and screamed 'Why?' There was no answer. Serel sat there for so long, that the temperature began to drop. So she stood, and carried baby Eva's body to the edge of the field, to a place where the last rays of God's sun shone before disappearing beyond the mountain and with a stick she'd found, did her best to open up a depression in the ground. She lay her baby in the depression, kissed her, told Yitzchok and Rosl, who were numb with shock and incomprehension, to kiss their baby sister goodbye. Then she covered the little girl's body with earth. Serel looked at the tiny mound, sat on the filthy ground and said whatever prayers she could remember.

Then, howling in agony and grief, she took Yitzchok and Rosl by their hands and led them out of the field. They all cried as they walked slowly into the darkness of the night.

CHAPTER SEVEN

MUNICH, NOVEMBER 1923

Reinholdt Stricher read and re-read the words printed in the textbook. He had tried to make sense of the same paragraph four times but the words joined the difficult engineering drawings with all the other concepts in the space above his head, and the ideas seemed to float into and out of the confusing diagram on the page. He blinked several times to clear his thoughts and try to study the pillars supporting the cantilevered bridge. The exam next week would surely demand his knowledge of different ways to measure the forces which one day he might encounter if ever he passed his degree and was constructing a bridge on marshy, sandy or rocky ground.

He couldn't concentrate because his mind was being continually drawn out of the apartment towards the noise of anger in the streets. But within the stuffy flat, claustrophobically warm from the hissing gas mantle which burned in the fireplace across the room, there was another distraction; the noise of his mother whimpering; well, at least she was quietly sobbing; only yesterday, she'd sounded like a she-wolf baying over the dead body of its mate. For two days he had comforted her, assuring her that everything would be alright. Only today had she smiled and thanked him, grasping him by the hand, assuring him that she was strong and that she needed no further comforting. Then, when she'd kissed his hand or his forehead, he would turn his back to continue his study, just in time to hear her burst into tears again. If this was how she reacted to her husband's disappearance, how would she be when ultimately she became a widow?

Three nights ago, they had waited until the early hours for Otto Stricher's return. He had gone to the Munich *Bierkeller* with Adolf Hitler, Hermann Göring and a huge contingent of SA troops and storm-troopers. They had heard that there was a large gathering of businessmen in the beer hall and that the leaders of the Bavarian government were to be their guests of honour. The businessmen wanted to work out ways of reinvesting Bavarian industry with life since the annihilation of the German mark. Everybody's savings had been wiped out because the French and the British were demanding such vicious reparations. Thirty-three billion dollars from Germany to pay for the damage it had caused in the war. Unbelievable! Especially as Germany had been stabbed in the back by the Jews and the communists and could easily have won the Great War.

Reinholdt put down his pen. It was no use. There was no way he would be able to concentrate. They had eaten cabbages again that night and the stench filled the apartment. Thank God his father still had a job at the textile mill owned by Abraham Engleman. If not for that, the family would be like all others in Munich; queuing up for soup and a crust of bread. Engleman's factory was still producing knitwear goods for the American and the Palestinian markets. Even though the factory was forced to accept a dramatically reduced production quota, Mr Engleman had kept Otto on as a labourer and a machinist; he was no longer factory foreman ... there were almost no staff left for him to supervise ... but at least there was a wage coming in. The family's money came home regularly but Otto had to bring it home in suitcases, and even when he did it was worth less on the Monday than it was on the Friday.

Reinholdt put his hands behind his neck and breathed in deeply. What a calamity! All because of the French. In January they had occupied the Ruhr to ensure that Germany met its financial commitments. The glorious German mark had fallen from 18 000 to the dollar to 160 000 by July. By August it was a million to the dollar and just recently it was four billion marks for one dollar. It was ludicrous. The Berlin government was even now contemplating printing a trillion mark note. What the hell was a trillion? There was no such number, surely. A trillion? A billion? A million? What did it all mean?

That was why Adolf Hitler decided the time was right to strike. Bavaria would break away from the government of Berlin. It would form its own true government to rival the arrogant, know-it-all Berliners and no longer be just a small provincial chamber. Hitler had organised for General Ludendorff to encourage the German army to back the revolt which they were confident would spread nationally. Then Hitler would be in charge. He would stop these obscene payments. He would put some strength back into the mark, and make it one German mark to one American dollar. He would take the Ruhr back from the French and throw up barriers to the rest of Europe; then he'd kick out the foreigners; the revolution was about to happen. It had all been due to start two days ago in the Munich beer hall.

Reinholdt's nose wrinkled at the persistent smell of cabbage. God Almighty, why did it smell so badly? It hung in the air. It clung to the curtains. It was even in his own jacket. He was never a smoker, unlike the other students at the Institute. Tobacco clung to their jackets and their hair. He found it objectionable. Yet now he was wearing his own obnoxious fumes. The fumes of poverty, of starvation, of cheap food. He couldn't even remember the last time he had eaten meat. A week, two weeks ago. Father had brought home some sausage. God, it tasted wonderful, even though there were no potatoes to go with it. So he'd been forced to eat the sausage with black bread. But nothing mattered while the delicious aroma of the sausage invaded every part of his being. Its tangy oiliness spread from his mouth into his nose into his chest and warmed his stomach, his very fingers trembling at the thought of that sausage. A Knackwurst. Spicy, full of rich pork. Beautiful white glistening globules of fat laying indulgently between a kaleidoscope of firm, hot meat, all held together in a transparent glove of sausage casing. His mouth was watering, just thinking about it.

His mother began to whimper again, crying in her bedroom. He should get up and comfort her but he couldn't bear another display. Enough suffering. But why no news? Why was it that the *putsch* had happened two days ago and the whole of Munich was talking about it, yet there was no news about his father? Everybody wondered what was happening, and yet Otto had disappeared. He looked at his watch. Nine o'clock. He could do with a good night's sleep. He was still tired from spending the early hours of the morning looking out the window of their apartment into the lightless passageway trying to see faces in the gloom, wondering what the noises of the night were.

When his father had left the apartment three nights ago, Reinholdt had ached to go out and join in the fray but his father had forbidden it. His father had commanded him to stay and protect his mother in case anything went wrong. That was the last thing his father said; Protect your mother.

He took off his shirt, poured water from the tap into a

bowl and shaved. He wasn't good in the morning. He shaved at night so that he was clean before going to bed. He washed the soap off the razor blade, patted his face dry with a towel, took off his trousers, left the kitchen and went to bed. Within minutes he was asleep.

He didn't know what time of the night it was when the door slammed. In his daze, he tried to understand what the voices were saying. He sat up and he was still dreamily asleep, lost in a confusion of images. And then distinctly he heard his father's voice, even though it was whispering. He breathed a sigh of relief. He shot out of bed, banged his knee against a side table and opened the bedroom door. Lotte was on her knees like a genuflecting worshipper, her arms around her husband's waist, her head buried in his stomach, sobbing. Otto prevented her from laying full length in front of him and kissing his feet like a penitent nun.

'Get up darling' he whispered. 'Get up. I'm safe. I'm alright. I'm back.'

He turned as Reinholdt entered the room. 'Reinnie. Reinnie, come here and hug your father. Lotte, get up. Get up. Kiss me like a wife.'

She stood painfully, her body frail and threw her arms around her husband and her son. They hugged and stood there in the centre of the room like a statue of the holy family. Lotte's body was shaking in paroxysms of tears. Reinholdt kissed his father's cheek, bending slightly. And Otto, strong yet obviously exhausted, held his wife and son in an iron grip, absorbing their love into his depleted body.

'Thank God,' he said repeatedly. 'Thank God.'

'What happened, father?' Reinholdt asked.

'Later,' he said. 'First let me comfort your mother.'

Lotte controlled her emotions although occasionally she sobbed. She smiled and continued to run her hands through Otto's bristling hair and over his cheeks. Reinholdt was desperate for information, aching to be told the circumstances behind the Beer Hall *putsch* and his father's disappearance, but Otto refused to continue until he was sure that Lotte's mind was comforted by his reappearance. Reinholdt had lived in a state of frustration for days. There was no talk on the street about Adolf Hitler's whereabouts. Everybody had a theory; killed, imprisoned, his body floating in the river, captured by the French, under arrest by the British, the communists had him, the Jews had him. Everybody had an idea. Nobody knew.

Eventually Otto sat on a couch drinking beer from his favourite stein, a beer which his wife had deliberately saved for a special occasion and which was opened with great ceremony. Lotte sat beside him, clinging to his arm. She would have got even closer if only she could. Reinholdt drew up a chair and sat close to his father, touching his knee. The time for tears was past. Now was the time for explanation.

'It was unbelievable. I've never known anything like it. So close. So near, and yet' ... He shook his head in continued disbelief. 'It was 8.30 on the evening of the 8th. We knew the politicians were inside the *bierkeller*. We knew that there was minimal police presence, and even if they were there in force, we were prepared to shoot it out. This was make or break. This was the beginning of the revolution to make Germany strong again.' He shook his head. 'But there were almost no police. A couple and when they saw the numbers of our troops,' he smiled, 'they just joined us. Unbelievable. They didn't even draw a gun, they just knew they'd lost, and they entered the *bierkeller* with us. Hitler was first. God that man's brave. He took out his pistol and fired a shot into the ceiling. Otto screamed "silence!".'

Lotte jumped at her husband's shout. She looked into his eyes. He was reliving every moment of his glory.

'I was four or five men behind. Göring and Hitler forced their way through the screaming crowd of businessmen and politicians in the *keller*. Everybody was frightened. Not us. We knew what we were doing. Everybody took their guns out. We were in charge. Von Kahr was speaking. He was standing on the podium and when he saw us coming towards him, he could have shat in his pants. You should have seen his jaw drop.'

'Who's von Kahr?' asked Lotte.

Reinholdt said, 'He's the State Commissioner, *mamma*. He's one of the top politicians in Munich.'

She nodded and turned to continue listening to her husband.

'Hitler jumped on to the podium and stood beside him. Von Kahr looked at the men of the SA. He knew he was beaten. He yielded to Adolf. Adolf stood there for a moment looking at the important businessmen and politicians and Jews and Communists. He was totally collected, almost calm. He knew exactly what he was doing. "The national revolution has begun," he shouted. "No one may leave the hall. Unless there is immediate quiet I shall have a machine gun posted in the gallery. The Bavarian and Reich governments have been removed and a professional national government formed. The barracks of the Reichswehr and police are occupied. The army and the police are marching on the city under the swastika banner!"'

Reinholdt looked at his father in astonishment. 'Really? Were they?'

'Nah,' said Otto dismissively. 'Of course not, but those morons didn't know that. Then Hitler ordered von Kahr and a couple of others into a back room along with the head of the police and the commander of the German army in Bavaria. He wanted to negotiate a surrender. Hitler said to them that they would join him in proclaiming a Nazi revolution and that he would make them part of the government. Our being the biggest party, we thought that they would just agree.' He shook his head in disbelief, 'but they didn't. Unbelievable. They wouldn't even talk to Adolf. Can you believe it? They wouldn't even acknowledge his presence. They just stared at each other silently. Cowardly bastards. By this time, Adolf was getting really furious, angry enough to piss in his pants, so he took out his pistol again and he waved it in their faces. He shouted at them. "I've got four shots in my pistol; three are for you. The last is for myself. I would rather die than fail." But they continued to look at him as if he was mad, refusing to talk to him. They just smiled that knowing smile of the elite as if Hitler was dirt under their feet.

'He ran out of the back room, back onto the podium and he shouted, "The government of the November criminals and the Reich President are declared to be removed. A new national government will be named this very day in Munich. A new German National Army will be formed immediately … the task of the provisional German National Government is to organise the march on that sinful Babel, Berlin, and save the German people! Tomorrow will find either a National Government in Germany or us dead!"

'Well, of course everybody thought that the *putsch* had been successful. Everybody thought the leaders had given in to Adolf's demands. You should have seen the applause. It was wild. Men were standing on chairs and tables, clapping and screaming. It was wonderful. A glorious moment. That was when General Ludendorff arrived. It was a good moment for Adolf. Ludendorff was brought forward and Hitler whispered into his ear.

Ludendorff went into the back and it took him only a few moments to convince the cowardly bastards to agree to the revolution, which they did. They knew the gun was at their head. They came out to the podium, all of them, and they pledged loyalty to Hitler and the new regime. I have never seen Hitler's face look like it. He was ...' Otto searched for the word. 'It was as if he was touched by God. Then choking back tears, he said "I am going to fulfil the vow I made to myself five years ago when I was a blind cripple in the military hospital – to know neither rest nor peace until the November criminals had been overthrown, until on the ruins of the wretched Germany of today there should have arisen once more a Germany of power and greatness, of freedom and splendour".

'Well,' said Otto, ignoring interruptions from Reinholdt for more details. 'You should have seen the crowd. We began to sing *Deutchsland über Alles*. It was the most triumphant moment of my life.'

He stopped talking, biting back tears. Reinholdt looked at his father closely. Tears of what? Of anger at the failure which was now apparent, or joy at the triumph in the few moments when it had all begun?

'Hitler called together a few of the leaders of the SA. Not me, unfortunately, I'm not high enough, but Göring and others and word spread of what he said. He said that tomorrow he would go to Berlin and declare himself dictator of Germany. He was like a hero from some opera by Wagner, a Lohengrin, a Tristan. He was talking about how this was the birth of the new Germany, the new Reich. Ah,' said Otto. 'If only. But then it all began to unravel. We assumed that the German army would go with us. The storm-troopers marched into the military compound but they held out against us in their barracks.

'When Hitler got word that the army had not moved with him, he couldn't believe it. So he left the beer hall and went there to try to negotiate with them. He was going to tell them that their leader, their own General Ludendorff, was one of us. If only he hadn't left the beer hall. That,' he said, talking directly to Reinholdt instead of to the floor, 'that was his big mistake. Kahr, Lossow and Seisser reneged on their agreement. They slipped out of the beer hall like cowards promising Ludendorff that they would remain faithful but they were planning to renege, to turn traitor. Hitler couldn't get the soldiers to surrender, no matter how much he begged and pleaded and commanded. Only a handful of troops were interested, so he came back to the beer hall but the crowd had already dispersed. Why should they stay? With Hitler and with the three top government people gone, the businessmen thought that it was all over, and they left. When Adolf got back, there was only a crowd of SA men.' Otto shook his head in disbelief.

'The planned march on Berlin the following day wasn't going to happen, because there was nobody to support it. Not even Munich was occupied. It was as if a balloon had exploded. All hot air and then nothing. I must say that Ernst Röhm managed to occupy army headquarters at the war ministry and his storm-troopers were very good.

'We sent out bands of SA men to round up political opponents and to break some Jewish windows and crack a couple of Jewish heads. Maybe kill a couple of communists, just to warn them off. But early yesterday morning Kahr said that his promise had been extorted from him by Adolf and he called our revolution senseless and purposeless. He said that we would have plunged Germany into an abyss and Bavaria with it.'

Reinholdt nodded. He had read the reports posted upon walls throughout the university.

'Everybody was abandoning Adolf by that stage. Adolf was absolutely frantic. I have never seen him like it. He just didn't know what to do. He was walking around headquarters like a lion in a cage. You couldn't talk to him without his screaming. I asked him if I could get him a coffee, and he bit my head off. How was I to know he didn't drink tea or coffee?

'The problem was that it was never in his mind that things would turn against him. But Ludendorff came good. He suggested that the entire SA march into the middle of Munich and take it over. By eleven o'clock yesterday morning, 3000 of us, Hitler, Göring, Ludendorff, me and others in the lead, marched towards the centre of Munich.'

'You were in that march?' said Reinholdt. 'I looked for you. I looked everywhere.'

Otto glared at Reinholdt as though he had unmasked a traitor. 'You left your mother? I ordered you not to leave your mother's side.'

'I'm sorry, father. It was only for an hour or so. I'd been to the university because things were quiet in town. I have exams next week.'

'Exams! What do you mean, exams, Reinholdt?' shouted Otto. 'Don't you understand yet, you stupid boy? There will be no more exams. It's all over. A new Germany is beginning. Sure, we've lost ground now but there's a new order in the world which is out there for the taking. A new start. Exams don't form any part of it. You should never have left your mother.'

Lotte interrupted. 'Otto, it's alright. Truly. I stayed with a neighbour while he left to go to the university. I didn't know he went to the demonstration. I would have stopped it. I thought you were at the university, Reinholdt.'

Reinholdt apologised. 'I had to see what was going on.'

Otto nodded, his mood relenting. 'Yes, I can imagine myself doing the same; but don't ever disobey my instructions again. You have no idea how dangerous the streets were yesterday. God forbid anything should happen to you or to your mother. Then I would be truly lost.'

Lotte put her arms around Otto's neck and kissed him.

'What about the shooting, father? As I was returning, I heard shooting. What happened?'

'We reached the centre of Munich. We were heading for the War Ministry. Röhm was there waiting for us but Seisser had ordered that a police blockade should be erected to stop us from going through. We came to a halt in front of it. There were 100 policemen, all fully armed. Adolf was magnificent. He stood right out in front on his own. He shouted to the police to surrender. He told them that the Nazi Party was now in control of Munich, that all other orders had been suspended. He gave them one minute to put down their arms and to yield. But they didn't. Somebody fired a shot into the air, then others fired from our side. Ulrich Graff, Adolf's bodyguard was one of the men killed,' said Otto shaking his head in disbelief. 'I've known Ulrich for ten years. We've drunk together. He has three children. He ran forward when the shooting started and jumped on Hitler knocking him to the ground. Sixteen of our men were killed. Sixteen! Can you believe those butchers. Mind you, we got three. Göring was hit in the groin. Even Adolf dislocated his shoulder. The last I saw of Adolf was when he was crawling along the sidewalk to get out of the line of fire. I heard a car pull away. I hope he got into it.'

'Hitler left you?'

'Of course,' snapped Otto. 'A leader can't afford to be killed in a mindless act of bravery. It doesn't matter how many of us died, the leader has to be safe so that Germany has a future.'

Stunned by the rebuke, Reinholdt looked down at the floor again.

'And where have you been for the last couple of days?' his wife asked.

'I've been staying in a cellar in the home of one of the comrades. I couldn't cross town to come here. It was impossible. Eventually when I was told that the streets were less dangerous, I took the risk, and here I am.'

'The police are everywhere, father,' said Reinholdt. 'The word is that they're looking for Adolf to arrest him. The last I heard they were going to all of Adolf's friends to find if he was staying there.'

Otto nodded sadly. 'Yes, so I've heard.'

'But are we safe?' asked Lotte. 'Will the police come here?'

'I don't know,' said her husband sadly. 'I just don't know.'

NEW YORK, PRESENT DAY

Sarah was concentrating so deeply on an email she was sending to one of her agents in the United Kingdom that she jumped when the telephone rang. Natalie on the switchboard said, 'It's your Mom.'

Sarah was immediately irritated by the reverse snobbery of her mother. She'd given Bertha her private line telephone number but her mother claimed she was always losing it and so she relied upon Sarah's business card to remember the telephone number for her daughter.

After the usual greetings and inquiries after health, Sarah asked 'So, what can I do for you, Mom?'

'That letter from the crazy doctor in South America.'

Sarah instantly forgot the email she was sending to Britain. 'What about it?'

'I've been thinking. There's something about it. But like I told you over lunch Sunday, that thing's got nothing to do with me or our family, darling. Listen to me when I tell you that. This *meshuggas* about how we came from South America ... such nonsense, so put it out of your mind. But one thing he said in his letter made me think of something. Y'know, it's odd how just one small thing can open up your memory. This doctor, he mentioned a woman called Annelise. You know, I'd forgotten the name all those years, and suddenly I see it there and something starts to niggle in the back of my mind. How often in America do you come across a woman called Annelise. So I'm reading his letter, and I'm thinking to myself, "I remember hearing that name ... ages ago". But from where. All night, I sit up in bed thinking ... now where did I hear that name? And then suddenly it hits me. Now I don't want you to get excited or anything ...'

'What is it?' asked Sarah, her interest in the letter reawakened.

'Well, before your *Bubba* Eva died, a couple of years before, she got a letter from Germany. It was a short letter in German. I could understand bits of it but it was signed by a woman called Annelise. Now there's got to be a million Annelises in Germany. Sol says it's a common name so it doesn't mean nothing. But I remember the effect that the letter had on your *Bubba*. She read it, must have been a dozen times and then she started to cry. I remember the shock I got seeing this woman who never ever cried, suddenly sitting on the couch sobbing. I remember thinking, my God, what's happened? I asked her about the letter and she told me it was just news about the old days from Germany. She said it was nothing to do with me, to forget it. But you can't forget something like that. So, I found the letter and I read it when she was out of the house. Like I said, it was from a woman called Annelise. Something about moving into a hostel, or hospital.'

'Have you still got the letter?'

'Yeah. After you left, on Tuesday, I remember the letter and I go looking for it in Mama's things. It was in the big cedar box with photos and documents and stuff. Family things. I knew I hadn't thrown it away after *Bubba* died. I've got it here. You want to pick it up next time you come over?'

'Could you fax it to me?'

'You think I know how to use the phone fax you bought? Not even Sol can use that and he's good with electrical things.'

Sarah smiled. 'I'll talk you through it Mom, while you do it.'

A few minutes later, Sarah was holding the faxed document in her hand. Some of the spidery writing was difficult to read but other parts were quite legible. She had a fairly good working knowledge of German but not sufficient to understand the idiomatic expressions which had been in use half a century before, and certainly not the conversational pleasantries used between intimates. She phoned down for the young man who was fluently bilingual in German and English and she had a transcription within half an hour.

The letter was a plea from one old friend to another. Much of it was mysterious. Sarah underlined key phrases.

'I'll never forget the love we shared as friends during the worst time in history for Jews.'

'You rose so high and yet never once did you forget me, even though my life was lived in the sewers while Hitler goosestepped above me.'

'I did things which neither God nor mankind will ever forgive but you found it in your heart, neither to condemn nor to judge as I have been condemned by those who knew me. That's why I have to move.'

'I know the man in your life was not what you wished but he has been so good to me. Understand him as he understood you.'

The last part of the letter had been written with obvious pain and a depth of emotion which seemed to scream from the ancient pages. Although she held a clean crisp modern fax, the old writing, faded after thirty years, still bore the hallmarks of the traumas of the woman who had written it. It was signed simply, 'Your loving and true friend, Annelise'.

And there was a postscript. It said that from that day onwards, she was going to use the name Annelise Liebemann, in order to hide from the crimes which she'd committed, and for which the Jews of the world would never understand, or forgive.

Sarah was mystified. Crimes? And crimes so great that she made herself sound like a war criminal. It was all so bewildering. Sarah was compelled out of curiosity and interest to follow it up immediately. There was an address contained in the letter, the address of the hostel to which Annelise told Sarah's grandmother Eva that she was moving, to live out the rest of her days.

Sarah turned to her computer and brought up the Internet web searcher she used. She immediately found the Munich telephone book and used its search engine to find the telephone number of the address contained in the letter. She hoped her conversational German was good enough as she checked the time and dialled the number.

The conversation she had with the manager of the hostel was stilted and formal. She was, she claimed, the American niece of Annelise Liebemann, a resident from many years back in the hostel. No, he said, there was no

Annelise Liebemann still resident in the hostel, but if she was now in her eighties or possibly nineties, then the hostel with all its steps would not be suitable. She would, said the manager, have been transferred to a hospital or an aged person's home.

Sarah begged him to look in the records and try to find where Annelise had gone after she'd left the hostel. She told him she knew the exact date she had moved there from the letter her grandmother had received – June 16, 1961 – but not the date on which she would have left. The manager grumbled but stopped his grumbling when Sarah assured him she'd send him a cheque for $US100 for his trouble. She took his details, put the phone down and waited for a fax to come through after the manager had retrieved the old files from the basement. It was a miracle he still held the old files. There was nothing on earth like German efficiency, Sarah thought. In America, the files would have been destroyed after seven years for reasons of space and economic rationalism. Space was real estate, and real estate was value.

Sarah found it hard to concentrate on her work. It was yet another distraction created by that damn letter from Dr Forenjo. But at the same time, it was further information about her family which, since the nightmare episode she'd suffered over the amulet in Slovakia two years back, had figured much larger in her mind.

It took three hours for the fax to arrive. When it did, it began with a long preamble about how much work the manager had had to do in order to find the records and how he trusted her as an honest American woman not to renege on the $100 but to send it immediately. And then the all important information. Annelise had left the hostel in July of 1986. Her next address for forwarding of mail was in Frankfurt. It was, according to the manager, a communal building for single elderly Jewish women whose husbands had been killed in concentration camps and who were now living alone. It was a charity run by American Jews.

Sarah again checked the time. It would be fairly late in the evening in Germany but she was keen to find out whether Annelise was still there. She phoned through to the number that she retrieved from the Internet. This time the information came much more quickly. Annelise had moved from the home into a hospital four years earlier. They were happy to give her long-lost relative the name of the hospital but reminded Sarah that Annelise would now be in her late eighties and might not remember anything or anybody. She had left the hostel because she had suffered a stroke and the right side of her body was paralysed.

Sarah had nearly come to the end of her search. Now she had to find out whether Annelise was still alive and if she was, whether she would be willing to talk to Sarah. She sent an email to her Swiss representative asking him to go to the hospital in Frankfurt, check on the condition of Annelise Liebemann and determine whether the old lady was alive and if so, would she consent to talk to Sarah by phone.

Sarah phoned her mother and told her that she'd managed to track down Annelise's last home. She could tell over the phone that her mother was trying hard to restrain her interest.

The following day, Sarah was still re-reading the letter she had written to Dr Forenjo. It had taken several days to write, in between the frantic schedule she set herself, but eventually she was able to free her mind from the immediacy of her work at The Institute to encapsulate and write all the relevant details, and the tone of the letter was precisely what she wanted to convey; interest, assistance, curiosity, possibility; but a specific denial that the Bertha or Bettina Kaplan was related to her. And she said nothing about finding the whereabouts of Annelise Liebemann.

In her letter to the South American doctor, she asked him whether, despite her denials about her own family involvement, he was able to shed any further light from the South American perspective on Eva and Bertha Arpel, saying that if she were to help him, she would need to know more.

Sarah looked at the construction of the sentences and wondered whether she was being too academic and removed. Dr Forenjo's letter was full of light and passion; hers was a response from a corporate executive. But she decided to keep it like it was; if there was a rebound, then she could hide behind the veil of corporate impartiality.

She told him there must be facts which he hadn't sent her … details like other letters, certificates, official documentation, exact dates, precise spelling of names. She reached for the mouse on her computer to hit the print button. Her hand stayed where it was. She looked at her diary. Her next appointment was in two hours. She had a report to write for the Finance Committee meeting for the following day, but most of it had already been done by her Vice-President, Treasury, and she would only have to check that it was okay and write a few introductory remarks.

She clicked the mouse point onto her desktop icon which gave her international times. It was 2.15 on a New York afternoon. There was no time difference between her city and Argentina thousands of miles south. She picked up the phone and dialled the international operator. Within minutes she was connected to the telephone of Dr Luis Forenjo. A man answered the phone, an elderly man.

'Do you speak English?' she asked slowly and distinctly.

'Yes,' he said quizzically with a strong Spanish accent.

'You wrote to me a week ago. My name is Sarah Kaplan. I'm Chief Executive Officer of the *Moishe, Vilma and Hermann Krantz Institute* …'

He prevented her from naming the rest of The Institute by interrupting, 'Yes, Miss Kaplan. Yes, I wrote to you. How are you?' Sarah could hear the excitement in his voice.

'I'm very good, thank you. How are things down there in Argentina?'

'One day you will come,' he told her, 'and see us for yourself.' She smiled. From him, it sounded like the archetypal remark of a grandparent. 'What can I do for you, my dear young lady?' he said. 'I hope you have some news for me following my letter to you.'

'No news, I'm afraid Dr Forenjo. Instead, I have more questions.'

'Oh. I thought I had answered all the questions you might ask by my very long and detailed letter.'

'It was a very good and particular letter, but you will understand that during this century tens of millions of people have migrated from all over the world and come to find a new home in America. Even though we're dealing with just a couple of months in 1950, I'm afraid the vast numbers of people still make the search quite long and tedious.'

'So, you are not the Sarah Kaplan?' he said, his voice carrying a note of disappointment and resignation.

'I'm afraid not. I've asked my mother, and she is absolutely convinced that she and her mother Eva came to America directly from Germany.'

'Ah,' he said. 'That is what I feared. But what about the real Miss Kaplan? The one whom I seek,' he asked.

'How do you know that the person you're looking for

is called Sarah Kaplan? How do you know it's not another Kaplan with a different forename; or maybe a different Bettina Arpel who didn't marry a Kaplan? How are you so sure?'

'But it is as I said in my letter. It is incontrovertible. I know these things from Ricardo's letters. I've traced the details. I know that Eva entered America with a daughter named Bettina. I followed the link to a hostel. From there I managed to trace her despite her change of name to the Americanised Bertha who became Kaplan when she married Solomon; they had a daughter Sarah. All these things are in the public record.'

Sarah found herself perspiring, despite the air-conditioning in the room. She herself was still waiting for a response from the Jewish agency which had once been responsible for the trustees of the now-defunct Betty Freyer Hostel. Obviously, Dr Forenjo had been searching for the information over a long period of time. Sarah had only been on the case for a matter of days.

'I'm phoning you to tell you that I'm tracing it through myself. I'm going to try to track down whoever this Bettina Arpel was. I don't think she is the one who became Bertha Kaplan. So many people changed their names when they left Europe to come to America. I think that's where you've gone wrong, Dr Forenjo. I can't find another Eva and Bettina who entered America in that time frame, so you may be right about your client's first wife and daughter but I think that's where the link breaks down. Those might be the names they are using, but they aren't my family. You claim to have traced them through to me and my family but as I said, when your Bertha grew up she may have changed her name or moved to another country or something. The point I'm making is that it's not me. However, I will, I promise, continue to check and let you know.'

There was a long silence on the other end of the line. 'Are you still there, doctor?'

'Yes,' he said sadly. 'My dear, how certain are you that your mother is correct?'

'Certain,' Sarah said immediately. 'I spoke to her a few days ago at great length. She is absolutely sure.'

Another prolonged silence. This time Sarah didn't interrupt.

'My friend and patient, Ricardo, took great pains to keep an accurate record of what was going on in his life, before his robust health began to give way. When Eva left him and sent back a letter saying that she would no longer keep in touch, that didn't stop him. As far as he could from such a distance as lies between our two countries, he followed Eva's activities with great interest. It became, I think, something of a passion. I have in his private documentation letters from inquiry agents in New York. They are over a period of many years. They report back on the activities of Eva Arpel when she is in America. These inquiry agents inform him of where she had moved, of the address that she and her daughter lived in for seven years. There's a report, a newspaper cutting of Bertha's *Bas Mitzvah* in the early 1960s. Further along, there are newspaper cuttings of Bertha's activities in Jewish youth groups. There's a photograph of her from a Jewish New York newspaper of Bertha as a fifteen year old in a singing competition in which she took a third prize. Later, there's a record of her marriage to a man called Solomon Kaplan. There's a record in 1973 of the birth of a daughter Sarah. A beautiful photograph indeed of the Kaplan family, Sol, Bertha and their daughter at a United Israel Appeal family day.'

Sarah felt her body suddenly go cold. 'But why didn't you write these things in your original letter? Why didn't you send copies of the photographs?'

Again there was an uncomfortable silence. 'I don't know. Perhaps when I sent the letter to you, I was on insecure ground. I didn't know you, or how you would react. Or how your mother would react. I was merely feeling out the situation. Perhaps I should have done, but I'm an old man, and I …'

She immediately regretted her tone. She must have sounded like a prosecutor. 'I'm sorry, I didn't mean to sound rude. Tell me, Doctor, is it possible for you to fax these photographs to me? Do you have access to a fax machine?'

'Certainly. I have one here right in my office.'

'Could you perhaps send me the photograph right now?'

'Of course.'

'When I've received it, I'll phone you back.'

Sarah gave him the fax number which led directly into her office. She bade him goodbye and waited anxiously. In less than a minute, the fax machine sprang to life and a grainy black-and-white photo, more dark than white, began to transmit slowly She held onto the sheet the moment it began to emerge, peering nervously as it recreated itself in her hands. It was a family group. A smiling father and mother and daughter. The images were hard to identify. Indeed, they were almost impossible to make out. It could be any family group. Even the words below, the caption Sol and Bertha Kaplan with daughter Sarah of Long Island at a recent UIA function, were barely legible.

Sarah looked at the photograph and sat down heavily in her chair. She realised that she wasn't breathing. She was gasping. It couldn't be! Yet, there, grainy and indistinct but obvious to anybody and everybody who knew it, who had seen it, was her amulet. Her mother was wearing it around her neck. It had caught the light of the photographer's flash gun. It was a point of brilliance in an otherwise indistinct photograph. It was an accusation that went to the very core of her mother's existence. Where had her mother come from? Germany as she'd always thought, or South America? And why Argentina, for God's sake. Thoughts raced around Sarah's mind. Why South America? How did *Bubba* Eva get there after the war? Sarah couldn't remember when she started to breathe again.

CHAPTER EIGHT

MUNICH, 1930

For the second time in a decade, Germany was in the process of disappearing before Eva Arpel's eyes. The first time that poverty had visited the city, with queues of men and women at soup tureens in the middle of the streets was when Eva was a girl of thirteen. She remembered the hollow eyes of the men and women; she remembered the anger which hung over the city like a malicious cloud; and she remembered that everybody seemed to be queuing for everything; she remembered Frau Büchbinder organising meals for the servants' families, and for the servants of their neighbours.

Now it was all happening again. Poverty was everywhere once more. But now she understood why. The first time had been because France and Britain had demanded huge amounts of money called reparations because of the Great War; that had led to the mark crashing and people losing their lifetimes' savings.

Then things had got back to normal, and times had been good. But now it was all happening again. And this time, it was because the stock market in America had crashed, and American investors were demanding that German companies pay them back the massive loans they'd made for the new Germany to build roads and bridges and buildings and expand their operations and things. Now even the largest of German corporations were going bankrupt. There was no work. And the men with hollow eyes were again on the streets, sitting like zombies on curbsides, waiting for … for … for anything.

Every time she left her basement home and walked up the iron railings to the back door which led out onto Salzburgstrasse, she felt that there was something in the air, some imperceptible and dangerous change. Imperceptible? Rubbish. There was nothing imperceptible about the change. It was vicious, fast and furious. And horrible. Munich had been such a city of fun and gaiety for as long as she could remember. Since her childhood, the theatres and restaurants and cinemas had been alive. Now everything was dark and cold. Now, suddenly, it was a city full of cheerless foreboding; long queues of freezing people, stretching around whole city blocks whenever somebody advertised a job; wagons in the middle of the road, giving soup to starving men, women and children. Even Herr Büchbinder's accountant was talking about dismissing staff who weren't integral to the running of his large house. It was horrible. Eva's mother Serel always seemed to be edgy and confused, talking about 'the old days'. Eva's father, Franz, was always trying to calm Serel down. Franz was Herr Büchbinder's chauffeur and handyman and was in a position to know what was going on because whenever he drove their employer around in his large Daimler Benz, he always talked to Herr Büchbinder about what was happening in the world. And when Franz came downstairs at night after bringing the master home, he'd recount all the details; yet despite his assurances, Serel was always scared and saying, 'What'll become of us if they get rid of us' … She had reason to be scared. As she grew older, Serel told Eva what had happened in Slovakia. It was a nightmare she didn't want to live again.

But Eva's father Franz was certain that they'd be alright, and that things would get back to normal soon. Because that was what he was told when he drove the master around from their house to one of Herr's Büchbinder's many shops. They had longer conversations when Herr Büchbinder was driven to Mürnburg or Frankfurt or Mannheim or Stuttgart when he went buying gold or other precious stones for his craftsmen to make jewellery.

But recently, Eva's father would assure Serel that everything was alright, then wait until Serel was asleep to tell Eva of the conversation he'd had with his employer. The father/daughter conversations were always private, always in an undertone. Yes, things were difficult but it was all because Germany had borrowed so much from America, and America had collapsed, its economy in ruins, its stock market valueless. All the loans which American banks had made to German firms to build new equipment or which had been made to the German government to build stadiums and railways and bridges, were now being called in and the money was being demanded back by banks who were seeing millions of people in America trying to take out their life savings. It was putting unbelievable pressure on the Reich's economy. Last year, before the American stock market crash, there were less than one million people without work throughout the whole of Germany. Now there were millions and millions suddenly unemployed, thrown on the scrap heap, out there on the streets looking for work. Families were starving, tenants were being evicted, and the government was impotent, dithering, making promises, but doing nothing.

Although Eva was twenty and had enjoyed the benefits of a fine education thanks to the goodness and generosity of Herr and Frau Büchbinder, Eva really didn't understand what was going on. She had never paid attention to these sorts of things in the *Gymnasium* she had attended. She was always more interested in singing.

Her voice had won her awards and she'd even sung on the radio. But because of the growing anti-Semitism in the country, and because the hated NSDAP were intimidating everyone who employed Jews, Jewish boys and girls were beginning to find it difficult to get into opera schools in Munich. Yet her mother had refused to allow her to go to Berlin where the Jews were so much more a part of the city's culture, and where the NSDAP was much weaker.

These many thoughts were going through her mind as Eva tucked her shopping bag under her arm and walked, eyes downcast, towards the provision shop on the corner of the street. Men were sitting around in huddles, some on the pavement, some in gutters, some on small wooden stools they had brought with them, knowing that they were going to spend their entire day waiting for night time to come. They were playing cards or just talking and smoking and drinking. They looked at her as she walked along the road. Some of them shouted obscene suggestions. She was shocked. It would never have happened last year. She hurried past them, anxious to do her shopping and return to the house.

Since breakfast, she had spent the morning cleaning the downstairs family living area. This morning Eva was working with Josephine and Hermione, girls who didn't live in the house but who came in to work at six o'clock every morning. They had been talking about their fear of losing their positions. Eva had assured them that while there must be some loss of work in the house, it would be among the gardeners and the handymen; maybe even one of her mother's kitchen staff. Eva had said that such a large house couldn't run on its own and it took at least four maids to clean and serve the family food, and an absolute minimum of three people in the kitchen to prepare the meals. That was the very least that a household the size of the Büchbinder's, especially one which entertained social and business people so frequently, could possibly afford.

Many things worried Eva as she walked towards the shops, feeling as if she were an errand boy. She had once harboured such exciting hopes … hope to be somebody famous, to be a singer, to be a somebody who acted in plays; even though she was the daughter of a Jewish cook and a Jewish chauffeur, she grew up with the passion that one day, her talent and energy would enable her to break away from a below-stairs life, and emerge into society to be something … somebody.

And what was she doing now? She was buying milk, bread, cabbages, onions and potatoes and then returning quickly because of the dangers in the streets. A week ago, these everyday food things had all been delivered to the house before six in the morning, but since then the provision shop and grocer had dismissed all of their errand boys on bicycles. Now families such as hers had to arrange for their own collection of food. It was unheard of. Even Herr Büchbinder had been surprised when Eva told him what she now had to do.

Their conversation had taken place the previous night, while her mother snored, asleep in the armchair in her parent's room. She was at the kitchen table, reading a novel when Herr Büchbinder knocked politely on the door and asked permission to enter his own kitchen. Such a gentleman! He had come down into the kitchen to talk to Serel and Eva, and reassure them that even though Germany was facing tough times, things would soon improve. Instead he talked to Eva alone, and she promised to pass on his assurances to her mother. He had told her that the League of Nations would set things to right very quickly and that this uncomfortable year would quickly be behind them. Then Germany would be back on the road to full employment and prosperity once again.

Eva had reached across and gripped his hand and kissed him. Then she stood, and curtsied. She knew that Herr Büchbinder liked to see her curtsy. She had curtsied for him ever since she was a tiny girl, growing up in his house. She had even performed little dance routines at night for some of his guests, but what Herr Büchbinder particularly loved was when she'd sing a Schumann *lieder* ... or maybe a part of an aria from Mozart. When she was eleven, one of the guests, an impresario visiting from Berlin, kissed her on the forehead when she'd finished, and told her that she had great talent and one day would be world famous. 'Perhaps one day, you'll sing Mozart or Bellini before the Crowned Heads of Europe. Who knows what's possible,' he had said, 'the operas of Puccini and Verdi could be in your grasp in only a handful of years.'

As a child, his words had formed part of her present and her future; whenever she helped her ruddy-faced mother in the steaming kitchen; whenever she helped her father clean one of Herr Büchbinder's cars, whenever children spat at her in school, calling her 'dirty kitchen Jew'; whenever she was denied entry to an opera school because she was Jewish, the important man's voice came into her head; 'one day, you will be a famous star'.

Eva mused on the past as she walked through her present. Where had the wonderful times gone? Suddenly the world was cold. She was twenty and there wasn't a man in sight that she was interested in. There were many young men of course from good Jewish families who wanted an affair with her. She knew she was very pretty. But who in Munich from a good Jewish family would marry the daughter of a below-stairs cook whose father was a chauffeur? She now realised that her father Franz, good man though he was, was quite simple. It had come as a shock when she realised that he wasn't capable of helping her with her school homework. He had never enjoyed the benefits of an education and it was only Herr Büchbinder's generosity in employing him that had given the family its security.

Her mother had lost her first husband twenty-seven years ago in some hideous pogrom in the old Austro-Hungarian empire. Serel had only just recently begun to talk about it. But Eva knew there was much anti-Semitism in those days and now with this maniac Adolf Hitler shouting and screaming, it was all starting up again. In Germany of all places! Germany! The most enlightened country in Europe. Eva could understand the anti-Semitism of Russia and the East. The people there were crude peasants, brainless dolts. But Germany? It was unthinkable. The Jews had been part of German society for hundreds of years. Doctors, lawyers, businessmen, community leaders, politicians. It was unthinkable, a temporary aberration.

In their discussion at the kitchen table, she had asked Herr Büchbinder about Adolf Hitler. She had read extracts in a copy of the *Volkischer Beobachter* of what Hitler was saying. He seemed to be gathering support from everywhere. He said the Jews were responsible for everything; the Jews and the Bolsheviks and the other socialists. She didn't understand. A man had thrust this horrible rag, this *Volkischer Beobachter*, this ugly little paper at her when she was walking near the station. He was dressed in a ghastly, warlike uniform, and he demanded money for the damn paper.

She tried to give it back to him, but he wouldn't take it. Instead, he shouted at her. 'What is it? You're a Jew? You don't want to spend money?'

She had gone bright red. People were looking at her. 'No. I'm not a Jew,' she said, taking far more money than he'd demanded out of her purse and giving it to the man, disappearing quickly into the crowd. Her heart was pounding as she frantically walked around the corner. She wanted to throw the vile thing away but it was too late. She'd touched it. It had already become a part of her. She read it secretly in her room. This Hitler was mad. He said the Jews had caused the Great War and had stabbed German soldiers in the back by making an obscene treaty with the Allies. He said that Germany could have won the Great War, had the Jews not profited by Germany's defeat. Only by Germany becoming a victim could International Bolshevism succeed; and through International Bolshevism would come world Jewish domination. He warned all of the German Folk to be wary; that the Jews were trying to take over the world.

Eva had talked to Herr Büchbinder about Hitler's claims. He had laughed and held her hand.

'My dear,' he said. 'With your beautiful, wonderful voice, you have no need to think of such men as Herr Hitler. He is like the scum that always rises to the top of your mother's soup when it's boiled. He attracts other scum and then you ladle him off and throw him away in the rubbish. God gave you beautiful legs on which to stand and a wonderful voice with which to sing. Thrill the world with the joy of your voice, drown out this man Hitler with the glory of your songs.'

But the singing lessons suddenly stopped. Her singing teacher, Herr Schonerer decided to emigrate to Australia. He predicted the end of Europe. He wished her luck. Since then, even though Herr Büchbinder was willing to pay extra for her lessons, she hadn't been able to find another teacher. The first question they always asked was, 'Are you a Jew?' When she admitted it, they said, 'It's too dangerous for me to teach you. I don't need trouble.'

Eva hurried back to the house with her shopping, and ran down the iron railings. She opened the door to the kitchen, her face immediately began to flush red with the warmth and the delicious steamy smell of cooking food. It was like an oven in there. Outside on the streets, it was so cold. It must be just above freezing. Inside the kitchen, the warmth was comforting. Eva closed the door behind her and saw her mother cooking lunch for the family. Herr Büchbinder was bringing home a client and so it was a special lunch in the formal dining room. Frau Büchbinder would be eating separately in the family dining room with the members of one of her charity committees. Several of the Büchbinder children were also in the house, just returned from skiing in Switzerland. Eva always enjoyed it when the house was full and there was lots of noise upstairs. It was comforting as she snuggled up in her room, under her blanket at night, listening to the laughter and raucous enjoyment of the family upstairs above her head.

As a little girl she remembered thinking that one day she would also live upstairs like them. She would marry somebody rich and become famous. Another dream, just like the dream of her becoming a world-famous actress, or an opera singer.

Some chance. She was twenty years old and still unmarried. Her mother was fretting, saying that Eva was too fussy, that there were plenty of boys in the Jewish community who would gladly marry her. Eva's father was understanding, and kept kissing her, saying, 'A girl as beautiful as you will attract bees like a jar of honey. Take your time in who you select.'

She loved her parents. And she loved her half-brother and half-sister, Yitzchok and Rosl, though God knows she didn't see them nearly enough. They had their own families and she enjoyed being auntie to their children. One day she would have her own family but she was still young, and because of her circumstances, she lived below stairs as a servant, not a very attractive environment to bring young men. And now with this man Hitler on the streets, with his gangs of thugs making life difficult for Jews, life was going to be getting even tougher.

But at least it was warm in the kitchen. At least she had a job. At least she lived with a wonderful family who laughed and cared for her and were generous. A family which enabled her to sing for them, and sometimes to put on a play and pretend it was a real theatre, even though she knew that it was only their living room, and the audience was the Büchbinder family and their friends and her own parents looking on in such pride and joy. Life wasn't so bad after all. Not in the security of the Büchbinder home.

Serel clicked off the radio. She felt humiliated and frightened. She had been listening to a programme in which a man called Joseph Goebbels was screaming to an audience about how the comrades-in-struggle had been knifed in the back by Jews and communists. According to the programme announcer, this man Goebbels was the Reich Propaganda Director of the National Socialists German Workers Party. He was speaking in a rally in Berlin and kept on using words and sentences to do with blood; blood flag, blood witness, blood martyrs, blood in the air, clouds the colour of blood, rivers running deep with blood and peoples' bloody corpses, slain for the good of the Reich. It was all too much for her. What was he talking about?

What really frightened her were not his words. No! She'd heard rabblerousers like him before. What really terrified her was the way in which the crowd that he was talking to kept on screaming in approval. From the sound of them there were thousands standing there, interrupting every sentence with their screams of '*Seig Heil*' and words like that. She'd asked Herr Büchbinder what '*Seig Heil*' meant. He'd explained patiently that '*heil*' was a word borrowed from the Society of Gymnasts in the middle of the last century, who said to each other '*Gut Heil!*' as a type of blessing … that it was a corruption of the word '*heilig*', meaning holy.

Serel had looked at him in amazement. 'Is Adolf Hitler holy?'

Büchbinder burst out laughing. 'He's a clown. A nasty little Austrian artisan. A failed painter. Look,' he said, taking out a cartoon which he'd picked up from a book store just the other day, and unfolded it onto the table, 'this is your Herr Hitler.'

The cartoon was the face of Adolf Hitler, but inside the black outline of his body were ribs and his windpipe; and at the bottom of the windpipe was a collection of golden coins. On top of the cartoon were the words, 'Adolf − Der Übermensch'.

Herr Büchbinder looked at the cartoon in admiration. 'This is by the great Helmut Herzfeld. Brilliant. Read the words …"Adolf − the Superman. Swallows gold, and speaks tin."' Herr Büchbinder burst out laughing. 'The German people aren't going to buy tin from a trumped up little demagogue like him, now are they? We're too sensible, too rational. The German people will soon see through him and his nonsense, and realise that he sounds like he's ingesting lots of their gold in the form of donations from large corporations and from rich private individuals sponsoring him, but the words coming out are tin, rubbish … valueless … wrong.'

When Herr Büchbinder disappeared up the stairs ten minutes later, Serel was already beginning to feel better. But not Eva. She had disappeared into her room the moment the broadcast had started.

Serel worried about her daughter; what would become of her if Herr Büchbinder was incorrect? Her employer's comforting words disappeared like steam from a kettle. Again, she was concerned. Serel was increasingly frightened of this hostility that seemed to be growing everywhere. As more people became unemployed, as German companies closed down because their products could not sell overseas and American banks were demanding the repayment of loans, the communists screamed on one corner and these followers of Adolf Hitler in their Brown Shirts and horrible spidery insignia screamed on an opposite corner. The air was full of hysterical voices.

Was it only last year that things had been so good? Munich had always been so quiet, except for the sound of music in the air. There were no raised voices. Brass bands played in parks, everywhere, children were laughing as they played in the street. Men doffed their hats as ladies passed them by. Politeness was in all the cafes. 'Good morning, may I help you to your seat?' 'Good evening, may I assist you?' Where was it all now? All gone. All because people, men, were sitting in the gutters talking about how their lives had collapsed. Everybody was searching for an answer. The communists provided one answer. Hitler and the National Socialists provided another.

It was all so different from when she had been born. As a child in Roznava, even as a married woman, the Jews had been forced to live separately. They had lived in their own *stetl*, a tiny village of 150 families like a pimple on the skin of the much larger Christian town. Daily, the Jews in the East were abused in their ghettos just because they were Jews. Her first husband, Nussan, may God Almighty rest his soul, had been murdered by people from the Christian village. Her baby, Eva, had died as she'd fled from the maniacs. Thank God she'd come to Germany instead of going to America. How would she have managed in a country where she couldn't speak the language; and had she not met Franz in the cafe … and if he'd not introduced her to the blessed Herr and Frau Büchbinder … ? How lucky she'd been.

Lucky? Yes, for so many years. But now what? She escaped Jew hatred in the land where she'd been born. But now it was happening in Germany of all places. Yet Germany was so very different. For one hundred years the Jews had been free to move around in society. They had been accepted. They were an important part of Germany. Sure, there were some trades and professions, some areas of life, which Jews found hard to follow because of the growing anti-Semitism. But not many. There were no real laws against the Jews like there were in the East. And now Serel was afraid it was going to change. That Jews would no longer be free to walk the streets without fear of abuse.

Not a week ago, Serel was abused when she was walking to the cinema with Franz. They were ambling down Salzburgstrasse and turned left intending to go to a movie house in the centre of the town. A crowd of Germans were standing there, neat looking men, dressed in jackets and trousers and shirts and ties; all were wearing hats and their shoes were polished; they weren't bums, but by their hungry faces, she could tell that they were unemployed. They were standing or sitting around the streets listlessly, wondering what had happened to their lives.

Arm in arm, Franz and Serel walked towards the group. One of the group had watched them turn out of Salzburgstrasse, where many wealthy families lived.

'Here come the Jews,' he had spat. The others looked at them in curiosity or anger. Serel gripped Franz's arm more tightly. 'Where are you going, Jews? To stab Germany in the back again?'

'Let me pass,' Franz had insisted, not backing off or cowering at all, but facing the bullies like a man. The Germans, however, had stood in their path.

'Find another street, Jew,' one of them said, spitting. 'Look at what you've done to us. You and your international conspiracy. You've caused our misery. I used to work in an insurance company. Twenty years. How am I going to pay for my family's food? Where am I going to find employment? Jew!'

Franz had tried to walk around the group who were straddling the road and the footpath, but they spread out even further to prevent them passing. There was a policeman on the other side of the road. The police were out on the streets in force these days. There always seemed to be demonstrations and riots. Shop windows broken; food stolen; looting like in Chicago.

Franz called across to him, 'We need your help.'

The group of men stopped their menacing, and watched the officer walk slowly towards him.

'What's the problem?' asked the man. He had a thick, peasant Bavarian accent. His face was florid and ruddy beneath his bushy moustache.

'My wife and I want to pass and these men are preventing us.'

The Bavarian policeman smiled. 'I don't see them preventing you. You're Jews. You're preventing these men from working. Now fuck off, both of you. Get back to where you came from, scum. Go to Russia or Palestine, or wherever your kind comes from. Get out of my sight, or I'll arrest you for causing a disturbance. Yids!' He spat and the globule hit Serel's chest.

Franz, furious, stood his ground. Through his body, Serel could feel his fear turning to anger and rising to the point where he'd hit the policeman. She forced him to turn around, to swallow his indignity.

'Come on. Let's go.' He resisted but she pulled him. 'Don't make trouble. We'll only get hurt.'

Slowly he turned around, retaining whatever dignity the policeman had tried to rob him of and walked back. He could hear the men laughing until he arrived at the corner of Salzburgstrasse. But before they had managed to turn into the street of his home, a stone whistled nearby and caught Serel's dress. She screamed in shock. The stone hadn't touched her, only her clothes. Franz looked back again; his body tensed. He was going to run back to the group and beat up the man who had dared to throw something at his wife; to thrash the policeman who'd dared to spit at her; but Serel prevented him. There were so many of them.

'We're going home now. Come,' she ordered. 'I'll change my dress and we'll find another way to go to the cinema.' But they spent that night indoors, listening to the radio. Cowering as they listened to Adolf Hitler.

Serel leaned back in the wooden chair, its slats pressing comfortingly into her shoulders. She had sat in this same chair for year upon year; ever since she'd been taken in by Herr and Frau Büchbinder. In the early days, when she was first married to Franz, she had worked in the scullery, but one *Shabbos*, the real cook had suddenly fallen ill, and Serel stepped into the breach at the last moment. Her *Goldene Yoich* with *Knaidlach*, chicken soup and matzo balls made the special way taught by her mother, followed by baked *Kreplach*, and then the most succulent goose the family had ever eaten, topped off with a honey *Lekach* cake confirmed her in a new position as second cook. It was only a matter of six months before the first cook's cancer forced Herr

Büchbinder to place her in a sanitarium in the Bavarian Alps, where the poor woman had died within the year.

The wooden seat, with its wooden slats became Serel's proprietary right. Now she sat and switched off the radio, thinking about the speech which this awful Joseph Goebbels had just made. She looked at the kitchen clock. It was already late. An hour later than Franz and Herr Büchbinder were supposed to be home. He had telephoned to say he was leaving one of his shops on the north side of the town and should be home in half an hour. Frau Büchbinder had told Serel to heat up the meal, to be ready for her husband's return. Serel and Franz were going out that night. They had arranged to meet a woman called Minke, now a widow, who had been friendly with Franz and his first wife. Minke and Serel had initially been distant but over the years had grown to be close.

Serel looked at the clock. Where was he? Perhaps he'd been held up in one of these interminable demonstrations. Perhaps Franz had had to drive all the way around the city to avoid groups of people on the street. She heard the upstairs doorbell ring. She sighed with relief and walked to the stove turning up the gas. She began to ladle off bits of fat that had settled on the soup as it cooled; and then a thought struck her.

Why would Herr Büchbinder ring his own doorbell, and surely, Franz should have parked the car in the garage by now. She should have heard the garage door open. She frowned and walked to the kitchen door, opened it and listened to the conversation at the top of the stairs.

One of the maids had called Frau Büchbinder to the open door. A voice in authority was saying something. She heard Frau Büchbinder shout, 'God in Heaven!'

There was a flurry of steps. People running. Serel's heart began to beat. She ran up the steps from the kitchen and opened the door which led to the hallway. One of the maids, Hermione, looking flushed and upset, was walking quickly down the stairs carrying the mistress's coat.

'What's wrong?' she asked.

'I can't stop now,' said Hermione.

Serel grabbed her arm. 'What's wrong?'

'Herr Büchbinder's car was attacked by a mob. He's in hospital.'

Blood drained from Serel's face. 'And Franz?'

'I don't know,' said Hermione and shook the grip free, running in to her mistress in the front salon.

Disregarding her station in life, and the protocol of the house, Serel ran into the front salon. 'Madam,' she said. 'What's happened? Is Franz hurt?'

Frau Büchbinder turned and saw the cook. 'My dear. My husband has been badly beaten. He's in hospital. I have no idea what's happened to Franz. You must come with me. One of the girls has called for a taxi. We go together. The wives. You and me.' She turned and addressed the maid. 'Hermione, instruct the parlour maid to turn everything off in the kitchen. Tell her cook and I are going to the hospital.' The maid curtsied and ran out, but Frau Büchbinder stopped her. 'Wait! Get Eva. Tell her to come as well. And when my children return from work, tell them exactly what's happened … don't alarm them unnecessarily … and tell them to come immediately to the hospital.'

Half an hour later, the three women entered St Kristoff's Hospital in Lindenstrasse. They were shown immediately to an upper floor. Franz was sitting outside a room. His face cut and bruised, with bandages on his knuckles as well as just below his lip and above his eye. His clothes were bloody and torn but he stood when he saw the three women running towards him. Frau

Büchbinder pushed her way into the room. Serel threw her arms around her husband, who winced in pain.

'What happened?' she said.

His voice was raspy. He had been hit in the throat. 'We didn't even get past the entrance to the shop. They started to throw rocks and stones and broke the windows. I bolted the door but they broke it down. There were hundreds of them. I saw the police on the other side of the road. They just stood and smiled. The men were wearing SA uniforms with swastikas on their armbands. They kept on screaming 'Filthy Jew! Kill the Jew!' They were going to kill us all. I grabbed Herr Büchbinder and pulled him out of the back door but there was a small group waiting for us. They beat me and just laid into the boss. I tried to defend him. I did my best.' He began to sob.

Eva put her arm around him. Serel kissed him on the forehead. The pain wasn't the problem. Just the memory. He cried into Eva's shoulder.

'I tried to stop them. There were so many. They wouldn't stop. They kept kicking him and kicking me. I just protected my body as they kicked and kicked but I was only wearing a chauffeur's uniform. Herr Büchbinder ... because of his clothes, his cigar, something. I don't know. They hated him. They wanted to kill him. They picked him up and kept pushing him against a wall, hitting him with batons and sticks, kicking him. It was terrible. I wanted to stand and help but every time I took my hands away from my face, they kicked me again. I just lay there and then I blacked out. I was unconscious.'

His words were coming out in short gasps. The pain of the memory was overwhelming. The two women held him tightly. After a few moments, Eva released her grip and walked to the hospital room door. She opened it slowly and saw Frau Büchbinder, her hands holding her husband's arm, her head resting on the blankets as though she was in some sort of devotional prayer. Something was lying in the bed swathed in white. It was the shape of a man but only barely recognisable. Bandages covered his entire head. Even his eyes were covered by gauze and bandage. A tube was in his nose. His upper body was bulky from its covering of dressings. Herr Büchbinder looked more like an Egyptian mummy than a human being. Eva recoiled in horror. She had never seen a sight as ghastly as this. She wanted to run from the room, but respect made her stay. She steeled herself, and walked slowly over to her mistress, laying a hand gently on the woman's shoulder.

A bored nurse was sitting at the foot of the bed reading a magazine. She had looked up as Eva walked through the door. When Eva touched her mistress, the nurse asked curtly, 'Are you family?'.

'I'm his daughter,' Eva lied.

Without looking up, Frau Büchbinder extended her hand and clasped Eva's for the comfort of human touch, something which she needed in her confusion.

'How is Herr Büchbinder?' Eva asked the nurse.

The woman was too curt and matter-of-fact to be a nurse. Eva couldn't understand her animosity. Nurses were supposed to be full of gentleness and concern. 'He's in a coma. We have no idea how long it will last. He has many broken bones in his ribs. None fortunately in his legs or arms. We think there's a blood clot in his brain which is why he's unconscious.'

'Why are his eyes covered?'

'He was kicked in the head. We're concerned that there might have been damage to the retina so we're not allowing any light to fall upon his face until our doctors have checked him when the swelling goes down. Unfortunately we can only check him when his wounds begin to subside. We've given him penicillin in case he's been infected by his wounds. That's all we can do at the moment. Just wait. Pray to your God that he heals.'

'My God?' asked Eva.

'The Jewish God looks after His own people, I believe,' the nurse said, and returned to her magazine.

CHAPTER NINE

NEW YORK, PRESENT DAY

Her staff knew that Sarah had a problem when she walked out with a few cursory goodbyes. They looked at the office clock. It had just gone four. Of all the people who worked for The Institute, Sarah was always the one to be found working in her office when the rest of the staff packed up and left for the day. Sometimes when a member of staff came back from a meeting after eight in the evening, she would still be in her office, furiously making phone calls or doing deals, cajoling a West Coast financier or an Australian Jewish community leader. Always wheeling and dealing. For her to leave at four o'clock with no appointments to go to was unheard of.

David was also surprised when Sarah's car pulled up in front of their brownstone house. He had been practicing some difficult pieces of a rarely played Lalo cello work which he would be recording the following week. A violinist and a pianist had joined him for their afternoon session. Sarah knew both of them intimately and kissed everybody as she walked into the front room. She was smiling radiantly as she promised everyone she wouldn't interrupt what was going on.

David knew that smile. It was a smile which masked a deeply buried difficulty or concern, something which she rarely made public, even to him. As quickly as possible, he wrapped up the rehearsal and bade everybody goodbye. Sarah was sitting at the kitchen table, cradling a cup of coffee. David kissed her on the forehead and poured himself a cup. He sat with her and reached over to hold her hand. He said nothing. He knew her as well as, perhaps better than, she knew herself. He would wait until she was ready. Any direct interrogation, 'What's the problem?' 'You look worried. What is it?' would have elicited a casual dismissal and so he lovingly and patiently waited until she began to explain.

She told him about the phone call. She pulled the facsimile of the photograph out of her briefcase. She laid the evidence before him. He nodded, absorbing the facts.

'Okay,' he said. 'Let's work through this. You've been brought up to believe that your grandfather Saul died in Berlin in 1950. He was so brutalised by his experiences in the concentration camps that he became a belated victim of the Nazis. You now have a photograph of your family taken in 1980 at a B'nai B'rith function. It was hidden in a security box in a bank in Buenos Aires, owned by this guy …'

She reminded him of the name.

'Ricardo Padrone. You've never heard of this guy before. He has never appeared in your life. Your mum knows nothing about him. Yet he claims in a letter to be your mother's father, your grandfather. The doctor who's the executor believes that you are the granddaughter. Your investigation of the database indicates that he may possibly have some connection to you because you can find no official record of Grandma Eva coming into America from Berlin.'

Sarah nodded.

'Before we start jumping to conclusions, what's the possibility that this guy in South America, this Padrone or whatever his name is, could be your grandfather, could be Saul? Could have divorced your grandmother instead of dying. Could have remarried and then gone to live in South America. Why not? Maybe Grandma Eva was too ashamed to say that she was divorced. Maybe she wanted to put her past behind her. Six million Jews died. Maybe she came here, and put about a story that instead of being a divorced woman, her husband had died as one of Hitler's victims so that she'd find it easier to get help or something,.'

Sarah nodded and sat back in the chair. 'That's the same conclusion that I came to.'

A silence descended on them.

'But?' said David.

'But I have to be sure.'

'I know you do.'

She smiled. He knew her so well. He knew that she was the last person on earth who would let a piece of evidence lie unexamined.

'Aren't you a little bit concerned about finding what's under the rock?'

'Of course I am,' said Sarah. 'I'm terrified that this guy Saul, a man I've always regarded as a Jewish martyr, changed his name because of something evil he'd done in the past. You know about the *Sonderkommandos*. Jews who assisted the Nazis in the concentration camps. That's what's been going through my mind all day, ever since I got this damn photograph. What if he was one of those? What if he ...'

David held up his hand. 'Sarah, you're fantasising. Lawyers don't deal in fantasy.'

'I'm not a lawyer, David. I'm a granddaughter.'

'Your grandfather died in your grandmother's arms in Berlin. You have no evidence to disprove that. Maybe this guy in South America was a nut case, a spaced-out lunatic, a stalker, a fantasist, somebody who saw your grandmother's picture in a newspaper, and took a distant fancy to her. Maybe he started to collect everything there was about her? Maybe he had fixed on a family and decided to persecute them. Maybe he was doing some sort of private research for reasons which are lost to history. Maybe he was building himself a life. There could be ten or a hundred or a thousand other bank security boxes which this guy kept, in which there are other photos of other families. Families that are also being plagued by doubt just because some weirdo in South America decides to keep a picture of a happy Jewish family.'

'Do you believe that, David?'

'I believe that your grandfather died in your grandmother's arms. I believe she came here from Berlin. Your mother married your father and you were born. You married me and we're a pretty lucky couple. I believe all that, because right now, except for a photograph which appeared in a newspaper in 1980, I've got no other reason to believe anything but what I've known for years. But the main thing I believe is that despite what went on fifty or a hundred years ago, you and me have got each other. And God knows you're lucky to have me and most of my friends insist that I'm lucky to have you.'

Sarah smiled. His gentle mockery was pricking the bubble of fear in which she had encased herself.

'Sarah, in the end, no matter what happened, nothing's going to affect us. Keep that in mind as you tread the rocky path you're about to embark upon. Now,' he continued. 'Let's take this whole shitheap one day at a time and step by step. Let's not go to pieces. Let's cautiously and carefully use all the phenomenal resources of massive computers and databases and all the brilliant contacts you've built since you began working for Josh. Let's try and establish the facts before we start looking down in the black void of fantasy and nightmares.'

Her body suddenly released its tension. She had known instinctively everything that he had already said. On the drive home, she had been through it in her mind a dozen times but coming from David it had the ring of authority which her own dichotomised mind desperately needed. It was wonderful and refreshing. It was like placing her two feet back on the floor. It was her coming down to earth. *Tachlis*. It was just what she needed.

'Have I ever told you just how sexy you are?' she asked. Her husband smiled.

'Not today.'

'I think we'd better redress that situation right now, don't you?'

David lay curled up on his side, breathing smoothly. He was in the half life between wake and sleep, when even the most minor disturbance brings the mind back to the reality of the afternoon. Sarah's almost imperceptible movement was just such a disturbance. He yawned and turned to look at Sarah's profile, her head resting on her arm, her eyes staring at him. He smiled. She reached over and stroked his cheek.

'You can always tell when something's the matter, can't you. I don't even have to say a word. Here I am, looking at you in love and admiration and somehow, instinctively, you know that something's going through my mind.'

He yawned again. 'I play your body like my cello and I read your mind like a book.'

She pulled his ear. 'Don't be so damned smug! There's a lot about me you don't know.'

'So what's on your mind?' he asked.

'Nothing in particular. I was just musing; you know, the way you do after great sex.'

'You muse. I sleep,' he said.

But she wouldn't let him. There were things she had to say. 'It's odd, isn't it, how life works out? Two years ago we were living together happily. No serious thoughts about marriage; no serious problems. You were a great cellist but not famous. I was a great lawyer but not famous. Suddenly you play at Carnegie and you're a superstar. And I defend a neo-Nazi who's denying the Holocaust ever happened and overnight I become one of the most hated people in the entire American Jewish community.'

'Jesus,' said David. 'I thought you'd put all that behind you.'

'I was just musing. But think about it. If I hadn't defended that bastard Frank Darman, trying to save the First Amendment just so pricks like him can continue to spout their vile nonsense, I'd never have come to the attention of Josh Krantz. If I hadn't come to his attention, I would never have gone to Slovakia with him. Without Josh, I'd never have got the job at The Institute, so I could help hundreds of people get back what had been stolen from them in wars and conflicts.'

David sighed as he listened. He knew her career path intimately. He was waiting for the denouement.

'And if I hadn't been the Director of The Institute, I'd never have got that damn letter from that damn doctor in Argentina, which has put a spoke in the security of my family history.'

David tried to suppress a yawn. 'He would have written to you anyway. He was on the verge of tracing you. Your letter just happened to coincide with the culmination of his investigation.'

'It's all so coincidental though, isn't it? She waited for a response. 'Darling?'

David tried to wake up again, and shrugged. 'Shit happens,' he said, yawning. 'Where are we going for dinner tonight?'

'I bought some salmon. I thought we'd do a barbecue.'

David nodded, closed his eyes and slowly fell back into a relaxing afternoon sleep.

KRUGERSDORP, SOUTH AFRICA, PRESENT DAY

The hall was overflowing with people. The air slowly warmed as the audience filed in – single men, couples, even entire families – so that by the time the marshals were telling people to stand quietly at the back because there were no seats left, the atmosphere was clammy and uncomfortable. Outside it had been bitterly cold, a freezing mid-July evening. When Frank Darman first entered the hall an hour earlier the air had been cold but the organisers assured him that, with the number of people they were expecting, it would warm up very quickly. Now he felt himself perspiring in his buttoned-down white shirt, jacket and waistcoat.

He looked at the audience in mild amusement. They looked like a cast of Hollywood hillbilly extras from some 1950s movie about the mid-west of America's farm belt. Women in pearls and twin-sets, farmers wearing boots, their ruddy faces looking like over-ripe cherries; most of them were wearing plaid shirts, dungarees, and jeans; farm clothes were everywhere, not one person displayed any knowledge of fashion.

Ringing the perimeter of the hall, standing to martial attention were members of the Afrikaner Resistance Movement, banned by the niggers in Jewberg and KipperTown, but proudly on display in this area which was the centre of white resistance to black rule. There were dozens of militaristic-looking men spread around the hall, standing at exits, leather holsters ready to be unzipped in case of trouble.

Not that there would be any trouble from the audience. They were here because they were terrified; because their lives had been thrown into the air and kicked around by niggers like Mandela and Mbeki, and others whose names were full of Ms and Bs and Ws and Zs that he couldn't even begin to pronounce.

It was his fourth speech that week. The crowds had been overflowing wherever he went. He was an international hero of the white resistance movement. He was a proud man and in a supreme irony, he owed it all to that bitch Jew lawyer who had turned his trial into a mockery. He bit his lip when he thought about her. Sarah Kaplan! He had known right from the beginning that it was a stupid idea to hire a Jewish lawyer, but the directors of the Institute for Historical Research, who were funding his trial, absolutely insisted. Their logic had seemed good at the time but it had all blown up in their faces. Go to a Jewish lawyer. Let her defend you against charges of racial vilification. Let her defend your right to say what history is too frightened to record; let her argue that the Holocaust never happened. She'd be bound to lose against the Jew professor lawyer from Harvard; then the matter would go to the Supreme Court in Washington, and a new application of law would be made. After a lot of searching, he'd found some hick Wall Street firm of Yids, and she'd been assigned to defend him. Not even a partner, mind. But some puppyshit Jew associate, still with mother's milk in her belly.

But at the time, none of that mattered. What mattered was to get the lawyer to lose the case in the lower court and get the decision heard on appeal in the Supreme Court, so that the Jews, who were trying to get a law forbidding Holocaust denial, would be beaten hands down. That was the logic. Whether he got fined, even jailed, wasn't an issue. The issue was to get before the Supreme Court. Of course, Frank Darman was doing it for a different reason. Publicity! But the Directors didn't know that. All they wanted were the issues of the case to be argued, so that the Institute for Historical Research would have bona fide credentials in the world's media.

But the bitch lawyer Sarah Kaplan had spiked his guns; she'd turned the whole thing round, and made him a laughing-stock. Against the odds, against this Jew professor lawyer, this Kaplan girl managed to get him off on a technicality. She had made a fool out of him despite weeks of sitting in a room with her talking about how the Holocaust didn't really happen. When she stood on her feet in an open court, the bitch had told everyone that he was scum, that he was a liar, that he was an idiot. But then she had said that it would be more dangerous to take away his freedoms to say these things than it would be to allow him to say them. She had scored points at his expense. And she'd carried the jury with her. The professor from Harvard had trotted out a menagerie of old Jews as witnesses, so-called survivors of the gas chambers, and they'd all told their stories. But instead of cross-examining them, instead of proving what they said was all lies, Sarah Kaplan hadn't uttered a single word. She'd said that she wouldn't add further to the suffering of these witnesses by trying to disprove 'the greatest and most carefully established fact in all of history … the existence of the Holocaust'. And then she'd turned around and defended the First Amendment right to free speech, even if what was said in his freedom to speak was 'an outright piece of anti-Semitic claptrap'.

And the moment he'd won the case, the directors had kicked him out of the Institute, dismissed him from his post as historical research director, thrown on the scrap heap by those limp dicks. As though it was his fault!

Well, fuck them. Frank Darman was a historian. He had a degree in History from Pat Buchanan University. He knew the truth about the Holocaust. It had taken him just a week after being fired from the Institute to start his own organisation, the Aryan Nations Confraternity of the Fourth Reich. Now he had branches in South Africa, mid-west America, Texas, Alabama. He was even thinking of setting one up in Austria. Germany was out of the question because of their stupid laws, the ones the Zionists wanted to introduce into America, making denying the Holocaust illegal. Not Germany, that's for sure. He would be arrested.

He listened carefully to what was being said by the guy at the lectern … he turned his attention back to the meeting. Soon as he was finished, he'd go back to his hotel, and have a shower. He hated feeling clammy and sweaty. Sometimes, he showered three times a day.

The fat guy who'd met him at the airport, Pete or Peet or Piet or something or other, with the heavy Afrikaaner accent Darman could hardly understand, was introducing him.

'Our inspiration and our leader, the man behind the movement for the white people to reassert their rights to overthrow those who would stand in our way. Brothers and sisters, I give you the hero of the white man, Frank Darman.'

Frank stood and walked towards the microphone. The local Afrikaner leader, Piet Van der Kloost threw his arms around him and gave him a bear hug. God, the man stank of sweat and body odour. Darman refused to wear one of their uniforms despite the fact that Van der Kloost had begged. No way he would let the press take shots of him in a neo-Nazi uniform. He was a genuine historical researcher, a purveyor of truth. If these guys wanted to wear uniforms and play at being soldiers, it was up to them. They didn't wear uniforms anywhere else.

Darman walked to the microphone, licked his lips and stood silently for a few moments. The audience, cheering at his feet, continued to shout and clap and whistle. His silence was a sign for them to shut up and sit down. And they did. Slowly at first, one and two; and then quite rapidly everybody stopped clapping and sat, waiting for Frank Darman to inspire them with confidence in their future.

Frank continued to look at them. Just look. And he stood. And stood. It was a technique that Adolf had used so successfully. Speakers today had forgotten that technique. The power of silence. Adolf knew it. Frank Darman knew it. And Frank knew other techniques which had made Adolf the greatest orator the world had ever known.

When Adolf began to speak, he had started off slowly, cautiously, convincingly and unemotionally … and quietly so that people had to strain to listen … just as Frank would soon start, when people were wondering what was happening, when they were hanging on his every breath. He had studied every available video still in existence regarding Hitler's political genius. He knew exactly how the master would have done it. Now, he was the master.

He clasped his hands behind his back, looking at different points in the audience. Eye contact. He rocked slowly on the balls of his feet, and then back on to his heels and then back again. He took out a handkerchief, a carefully studied action, and slowly wiped his lips. He turned and smiled at the people on the dais, people in uniforms, and their frumpy wives in flowery dresses who sat alongside them, glorying in their fifteen minutes of fame.

Then he turned back to the audience. Softly, so that people actually had to make an effort to hear, he began.

'I want to take you on a journey. I want you to come with me into the past.'

Speakers these days tended to start their speeches screaming and shouting as if to get attention. Crap. People paid attention when they had to study the words and they would study his words. Every single syllable he uttered.

'I want to take you to Auschwitz and Dachau and Bergen–Belsen. I want to take you to Sachsenhausen and to Treblinka and to Majdanek. I want you to look at them, not through the biased eyes of the Jewish-controlled media, but impartially, as intelligent, thinking adults. I want you to come with me in your minds to a time when Germany was in the ascendancy. Rich, strong, powerful, committed to peace. To the time after it had overcome the terrible privations of the First World War, a war it should never have lost, when its defeat had devastated its economy and people were starving … but from which it had recovered, and was now one of the richest and most efficient nations of Europe.

'To a time when it was being attacked on all sides in words and in deeds, when it stood alone against the industrial military might of Britain, the USA, Canada and France and Russia. I want you to put yourself into the mindset of the people who lived back then. For twenty years from 1918 to 1938, Germany had lived through some horrible times and some wonderful times. After the First World War, she was strangled by greedy hands strangling her throat in their bloodthirsty, greedy demands for reparations. Hyperinflation made everybody into a pauper. People who were lucky enough to have jobs were paid in wheelbarrows of money. But despite the hardships, Germany pulled out of the mire. And for years she prospered. She was the model of European industry. But again, only a few short years later, Germany was forced to live through the agonies of the Great Depression when Jewish capitalists, in league with world governments, tried to ruin Germany's economy yet again by artificially engineering the most devastating collapse of the financial system in the history of the world. Friends, the Great Depression was brought on due to the greed and avarice of the people who controlled the world finances; do I have to tell you to which nation those people belong?'

There was laughter in the hall.

'Did Germany collapse? No! Germany went on in the 1930s to become strong again, indeed the strongest and greatest nation in the whole of Europe.'

His voice began to rise. He had them in the palm of his hand. This was an aspect of history they just didn't know. He paused again, to make them concentrate.

'The First World War was started because of a Jewish conspiracy for International Bolshevik control. Germany was virtually alone to face the might of the whole world. Why did Germany lose? Because Jews and communists stabbed in the back the millions of German soldiers still fresh and eager to continue the war. And Germany paid billions and billions in reparations for the cost of a war it should never have been fighting.

'Now, Adolf Hitler's been called the greatest criminal in history. Let me rephrase that somewhat. Let me tell you that Adolf Hitler is the most misunderstood human being in history. Let me explain why. Hitler simply said "no!". No more reparations, no more communists. Germany for the Germans. And so the Germans elected him to be their *Reichschancellor*. But the Jews and the communists were working to undermine him.

'Do I need to tell you South Africans about how people work against you … not just the outside world, but people who might be your neighbours, who may once have been your friends? Now these people, the Jews in Berlin and Munich and Hamburg were German citizens. Or were they? Sure, they enjoyed all the benefits of the greatest nation in Europe, but they owed a greater loyalty to a land far away, a land in the mid-East, a land then called Palestine. These people, these Jews, had to be contained to protect Germany from what the enemy within, the fifth column, was doing. That's all. Nothing more. Nothing less. And that's why the camps were built. Simple. To contain them, so the German authorities could keep an eye on them.'

He allowed his voice to rise a couple of notches. He began to speak more quickly, with more emotional intensity. The audience, silent and concentrating, was sitting on the edge of their seats.

But then, for the next thirty seconds, he remained absolutely still; absolutely silent. Now they were really hanging on his next words, which he spat with vengeance into the microphone, 'These weren't death camps. These were concentration camps. Concentration!' he shouted, stabbing his finger in the air. 'Concentrating the enemy so you know what he's doing, and so he can't do evil things to you behind your back. And nobody knows more about concentration camps than the people of South Africa. It was the British that built the world's first ever concentration camp. Here!' he stabbed his finger towards the earth. 'Right here in South Africa! The British. And the Americans had concentration camps. Where do you think Adolf Hitler learned the concept? From the Americans and the British. From the great liars, the great distorters of history.'

He stopped shouting. His heart was pounding. People were straining for his next revelations.

'There's no proof that the Holocaust ever occurred.

There's not one single document to prove that the camps were used to kill people. People died. They died by their hundreds of thousands. Dirty people always die when they're confined in a space, because that's when typhus and rats abound. Concerned that there would be an epidemic which would kill even more people than had already died, the Germans decided to fumigate the Jews' clothes with Zyklon-B. Zyklon-B takes twenty-four hours before it's safe for a human being to re-enter a room. Twenty-four hours! And yet we have stories of *Sonderkommandos* who walked straight into so-called gas chambers and pulled out so-called dead bodies while the bodies were still warm; while there was still Zyklon-B floating around in the air. Lies! All lies, my friends.'

He could see people nodding in the audience. Fathers turning to children telling them to listen carefully.

'What do you do with hundreds of thousands of dead bodies? Do you burn them?' he asked sarcastically. 'One of America's greatest experts on executions, a brilliant engineer and scientist called Fred Leuchter has proven beyond any doubt that the gas chambers in Auschwitz could never have been used for the purposes that the Allies claim.'

And so he began to paint a picture of a world conspiracy to make the Holocaust into a reality, while scientific evidence proved that it couldn't have happened. He told them facts and figures which even their dumb faces and their slow wits could understand, so that by the time he'd spoken for another thirty minutes, giving a detailed and devastating analysis of why every single lie told about Adolf Hitler had been believed by the Western world, they now understood the enormity of the Jewish conspiracy. Nobody in his audience realised the way in which the Jews controlled the media, banking system, computers, international communications.

By the time he had finished, hundreds and hundreds of people were standing, cheering and shouting his name. They wouldn't let him go. He was a hero. He was their messiah. Darman was their future. He stood looking at a sea of screaming faces. Hands raised to the ceiling in exclamation of his brilliance.

Was this how Hitler felt at Nuremberg?

Sarah sipped her cup of coffee, and mused. David was busy reading a score he would have to perform later that week, and every spare moment was spent imprinting the formation of the notes in his mind.

But she needed to interrupt him.

'Guess who called today?'

He looked up, without responding.

'The Chicago Trib.'

'So?' he asked. Newspapers were always telephoning Sarah.

'They asked me to comment on Frank Darman, and his arrest in South Africa. Asked me whether I'd be interested in going over there and defending him a second time.'

David burst out laughing. 'I trust you gave them a "no comment".'

'Of course,' she said, and continued to drink her coffee.

CHAPTER TEN

BERLIN, 1930

Haupttruppführer Reinholdt Stricher stood in the freezing cold of the Tiergarten on Charlottenburger at the head of a phalanx of one hundred men. He was one of forty such Chief Troop Leaders in the long column of four thousand men, a column that stretched far behind and ahead towards the Chaussee. A review stand had been set up close to the Reichstag, contrary to the ordinances and the explicit instructions of the city authorities; no marches through the city, no parades in the streets, no uniforms, no swastikas; meetings to be held only in the Sports Stadium; but who gave a damn about what the city authorities and the police and the army said? Certainly nobody in his beloved organisation, the *Sturmabteilung*. The fickle Berliners had never liked Hitler, or the SA. And since the first performance of that damned play, the whole city had been talking of nothing but how corrupt the SA was. Everyone, it seemed, had turned against the SA because of that Jew-loving communist, Bertolt Brecht and the drama he'd written two years ago with that other piece of filth, Kurt Weill. Reinholdt had been to see *The Threepenny Opera*; according to the programme notes, it was something to do with an English play from the eighteenth century, *The Beggar's Opera*. It laughed at Berlin's *Ringvereine*, the sporting clubs from which most of the SA's new members were recruited; his own father had been a member of these men's clubs all his life; they were wonderful, they were for comradeship ... they were not to be the subject of ridicule from a communist Jew-lover like Brecht; sure, some of the *Ringvereine* dealt in drugs, some were criminals, but no intellect was required to be a member of the *Sturmabteilung*, the People's Army. Indeed, Reinholdt was probably one of the very few with a University education. Another was the glorious *Gauleiter* of Greater Berlin, Dr Joseph Goebbels. He'd arrived at Friedrichstrasse station on a cold day in November 1926 with one suitcase and burning ambition for the good of the party. Within just a matter of a couple of years had turned the SA into Berlin's most effective fighting force, more powerful than the police, the army, and a match for the Red Communists who were trying to take over the city ... then the country ... and then, with aid from the Jewish commune of bankers and financiers ... the world!

Reinholdt was intensely proud of his newfound standing in the People's Army. He was a leader of a force which would create a new Germany, sweep away the diseased remnants of the old, overturn the monstrous discrimination of the Versailles Treaty and its bloodsucking reparations; get Germany back on top.

Ahead of him in the far distance, astride a magnificent stallion, was the *Standartenführer* who controlled six of the troops; beyond the *Standartenführer*, somewhere much further in the distance and beyond the level of Reinholdt's sight, somewhere so far ahead that it would take ten minutes of marching to reach the presentation dais, was the *Stabschef*, the Chief of Staff of the SA, Otto Wagener.

Wagener would be standing there, pompous and incompetent, slapping his leg with a riding crop; Reinholdt was absolutely certain that Wagener would be all puffed up and full of self-importance as his men paraded before him.

'His men! What a laugh. The SA was so far beyond Wagener and the others who currently led it that they had no idea what was going on in the ranks … what the men who fought the pitched battles in the streets actually felt. Reinholdt knew all about Wagener and his pomposity from previous experience. He also knew about the shaky ground on which they stood, from asides he'd overheard spoken by party insiders and the current in-jokes that were going around. But he knew more than this. For the past few weeks, Reinholdt had enjoyed the patronage of a special friend, someone who really knew the inside workings of the SA; somebody who had been wounded three times in the Great War, and who had founded, even before Adolf Hitler joined, the National Socialist German Workers' Party.

Were it not for Reinholdt's special friend, Ernst Röhm, Hitler would never have won the support of the army in Bavaria; nor would Hitler have been able to organise the Beer Hall *Putsch* in Munich, in which Reinholdt's own father had participated. Had it not been for the Jews and communists who stabbed him in the back, Hitler would have been *Reichschancellor* and dictator seven years ago.

Reinholdt was sure that Wagener was being set up to be toppled from his position. That was why Adolf Hitler had begged Röhm to return from Bolivia where he was a military adviser to the government. Obviously, it was because the Führer wanted Röhm to lead the SA. Of course, only Reinholdt, and a handful of others knew that, and Reinholdt was sworn to secrecy. He'd been told all this by his father. Soon Reinholdt's special friend, Ernst Röhm, would lead the vast army of once unemployed, disempowered men; men who were now clearing the streets of communists and hoodlums. Soon, or so Reinholdt had been informed by Röhm himself, Adolf Hitler would organise for Röhm to lead the SA in order to build the hundreds of thousands of men still out of work into what was now becoming Germany's most powerful army.

And God knows how many men were out of work. What a turnaround! Two years ago, the money had been flowing, the country had been on top, people had wages ... the good times were here. Then the Jewish capitalists in America had organised the crash of the stock market on Wall Street as part of their evil scheme to control the world's finances; money began to disappear as quickly as jobs, and within a year, the SA was being besieged with requests from unemployed men to become members. Even if it was just for a good meal, and somewhere to sleep, they would soon become committed to the ideals of the People's Army.

And it was Ernst Röhm who would make them coalesce into the most important force in the history of the Reich. Reinholdt had first met Röhm when his father Otto had introduced them at a cocktail party to celebrate the soldier's return from active military duty in Bolivia in South America. Röhm had taken an immediate interest in the young man, much to his mother, Lotte's consternation; but since their meeting only a few months earlier, Reinholdt had gained rapid and convincing promotion through the ranks and now stood at the head of a hundred men ... even if it did mean pretending to be flattered by Röhm's attention and occasionally masturbating him when they were in private.

On the first occasion that Röhm had suggested such an act, Reinholdt had retreated in horror. For Reinholdt, a real woman's man, such a thing was an act against Nature.

But before he left the room, Röhm called out, 'Think carefully before you make such an escape, boy. It was your father who introduced us. It's your father who could suffer if you displease me.'

The first act had been the most difficult. Reinholdt had returned to his home and spent hours under the shower washing his hand a dozen times in the scalding water. He had retreated to his room. It was his father who broached the subject that night. Reinholdt didn't hold back a single detail. Why should he? He wasn't guilty. But his father's reaction staggered him.

'These are difficult times,' Otto told him. 'We're on the threshold of Germany becoming great again. Röhm and Hitler and Göring aren't like ordinary mortal men. They're the Gods of our country. If they ask you to worship them, then so be it. In the old days, people sacrificed their babies to Gods like these. What are you being asked to do?' demanded Otto. 'Fulfil a man's sexual fantasies, that's all.'

But performing the act of masturbation on him was as far as Reinholdt was willing to go, and he told Röhm so next time they were alone together. Röhm understood the limits, although there'd been some near misses in the past couple of weeks.

Reinholdt was a tall, strong, athletic and good-looking young man, the apple of his father's eye. Röhm insisted that the young man travel as his adjutant to Berlin. Neither his mother Lotte nor his father Otto was particularly happy about their son's move from Bavaria, but both were delighted that the legendary Röhm himself had taken such an interest in their son's career. Thank God Lotte didn't understand the full implications of Röhm's sexual orientation, or she'd have begged Otto to drag her beloved Reinholdt back to Bavaria. But Otto knew that Reinholdt was wise enough to look after himself. What did it matter if he used his hands to advance his career … just so long as Röhm didn't want him to open his mouth, or bend over.

In their journeys, and the time they spent together, Röhm loved most to talk about his instrumental part in the 1923 Beer Hall *Putsch*. Brave and gallant men had fallen, and the event was a landmark in German history; the moment which future generations would come to realise was the birth of the new Germany, a brave Germany, where Jews and communists and Slavs and similar characters of the underworld, began to be expelled from the Aryan face of the nation.

Young Reinholdt Stricher, well-educated and a twenty-seven-year-old man whose family would follow Adolf Hitler wherever he led them, stood smartly to attention as he sensed the march formation coming to order. Things were so different today. What a life. What a life! When he was a student, Germany had been through the greatest chaos in history. Hyperinflation, everybody was made impoverished overnight, thanks to the fucking Jews and the way they stabbed everybody in the back. And now they were at it again. Only seven years later, and the fucking Jews were at it again.

It had been an amazing few years. After the failed *putsch*, Germany slowly recovered and Reinholdt had qualified as an engineer. But then the German economy just went through the roof. Suddenly everybody was dancing and laughing and singing. Money was everywhere. His father had finally given up working for the Jew Engleman and had become a full-time member of Adolf Hitler's Nazi Party headquarters' staff. Unfortunately, because there were so many intelligent men serving Adolf, his father only had fairly menial clerical work to do but it didn't matter. Otto was at the centre of the universe and he had arranged for Reinholdt to gain ascendancy in the SA. He had only worked for a couple of years as an engineer, built a bridge or two, a road or two, and then like his father, he had given up civilian work to become part of the Nazi Army, the SA, leading Germany under the gun and the sword, into a new future. A future without Jews and communists and the scum which were weakening his Fatherland.

Reinholdt's hand still hurt from last night's battle with a mob of fifty communists, but it was nothing compared to the pride he felt as the orders rang out from one phalanx to the next, to be ready to march. Those ahead started to march, and when it came to his turn, Reinholdt shouted out the order to his men to raise their flags, hoist their standards and march with confidence and pride. Girls walking up and down the route of the march to inspect the brown-shirted soldiers of the people had dallied when they came to Reinholdt. He cut a tall and dashing figure and looked wonderful in his uniform. Some of the girls, the cheekier ones, stood still in admiration when they came to where he was standing stiffly at attention; when Reinholdt began to march ahead of his phalanx, so did a dozen girls along the roadside.

As his troops marched, bands along the way played rousing German music. They marched from one band to the next and when they came to the fifth band in line, the bandmaster struck up the wonderful *Horst-Wessel Liede*, written by the martyr himself. A cheer went up from the hundred men behind him. It was their favourite song. By now everyone knew the words; by now everyone began to sing, even some of the young girls on the pavement, even if the men and women, the Berliners, who lined the route curious to know what would happen next, looked on silently and with palpable hostility.

His troops were not even singing; they were shouting the words in pride to the thousands who had come to listen.

Die Fahn Hock! Die Reihe dict geschlossen!
SA marschiert mit ruhig festem Schritt …

The flags held high! The ranks closed tight together!
The SA march with firm and steady tread.

So what if Berliners hated him and the SA and Hitler?
Who gave a damn what they felt? What had the party
newspaper, *Volkischer Beobachter* said a couple of years
back? *Berlin was a despicable northern city which was a melting
pot of everything that is evil – prostitutes, drinking houses,
cinemas, Marxists, Jews, strippers, Negroes, dancing, and all the
vile offshoots of so-called 'modern art'.*

How true! Well, now the SA was firmly in control of
the streets of Berlin, despite the occasional interference of
the civil police, and ridiculous orders about not wearing
uniforms. Soon the Nazi Party would be in complete
control of Germany. Just a few months earlier, over six
million Germans had voted for the party, giving them
107 seats in the Reichstag. Not the Berliners, of course.
Stiff-necked, Jew communist scum of the earth. They'd
roundly ignored the Nazi candidature. Hitler had been
beyond himself with fury, vowing to teach Berlin a lesson
it would never forget.

One of the reasons he'd been taken to Berlin by Röhm
was because of the danger posed by this man Walter
Stennes, a deputy of the *Oberster SA-Führer*, who at the
end of August had the audacity to march into the *Gau*
Headquarters and threaten the *Gauleiter*, Joseph Goebbels.
Stennes demanded autonomy for himself and his men,
and Goebbels had been forced to call in the police. Hitler
had been under intolerable pressure to intervene and
accede to Stennes demands because the elections were so
close, but the bastard's days were numbered. Now Röhm
was here, men like Stennes and his communist-loving SA
faction would soon suffer from cracked heads.

As would other communists and their fellow-
travellers. Reinholdt and his comrades were here to

teach these mocking, sneering subhumans a lesson, as well as to get rid of the prostitutes and Negroes and Jews and other filth from the gutters of the streets. That was why the Berliners were so silent when the SA marched. Only a handful waved Nazi flags, or cheered or waved. Still, the girls of Berlin loved the SA, even if the old people hated them.

But right now, Reinholdt had other problems. This was a march; singing was not permitted. It was an undisciplined exhibition from the troops under his command, and Reinholdt should be angry; he should, by rights, turn and silence them. It wasn't what a march should be. But the spontaneous eruption of joy through song was such that it would be the mark of a small man to do so, and Reinholdt was anything but a small man.

He was loved by his troop. He was always the first into battles in the streets. He was always there when his men were beating the shit out of Jews and homosexuals and communists. He was the one that struck the first blow. He was the one whose baton broke the first window and the first skull. Unlike other troop leaders, he rarely stood in a staff car or sat on a horse to command his men. Instead, he ran down a road ahead of the troops shouting orders and screaming bloodcurdling threats to the homosexuals and communists and Slavs and Jews who dared stand in his way.

Last night had been something special. Berliners were so different to the Bavarians that he knew and loved so well. Indeed, Berlin was unique throughout the whole of Germany. It was well known that Adolf Hitler's hatred was spread between communists and Jews, and now Berliners because of their rejection of him. Two years earlier, the party had won only a handful of seats in the Reichstag. Throughout the whole of Germany in 1928 they'd only managed to gain less than a million votes.

But in the recent elections, their vote had shot up to nearly seven million, making Hitler and the Nazis the second biggest party in the Reichstag. Everywhere the Nazis were on the march, except fucking Red Berlin, home of Jews and Slavs and communists.

Well, these days, Reinholdt and his hundred men were teaching these fucking Yids a lesson. God, it felt good to smash a Jewish head or to see a filthy whining communist or socialist fall into the filth of the floor where they belonged, and beg not to be hurt. But best of all was the reaction of the Slavs. Reinholdt could tell a Slav a mile off. The broad cheekbones, flat nose, the sloping forehead, the filthy leering grin on their greasy faces. Poles, Czechs, Slovaks, Russians, Hungarians, Ukrainians; all filthy subhumans. He had seen the party films. He had read the party books. The party knew what it was doing.

He smiled when he thought of last night in the streets of Berlin's Kreuzberg. God, that had been something else. He smiled uncontrollably as he marched past the band, thinking about the glories of the previous night, the fear in the faces of the subhumans, the smell of urine in the air as men and women and children pissed themselves when they first caught sight of *Haupttruppführer* Reinholdt Stricher and his phalanx. And then the communists had come around the corner, daring the SA to fight them. Fight them, they had. Only a few SA men were in hospital, but reports early this morning told of twenty communists badly hurt and two had subsequently died. Wonderful!

And as he marched ahead of his troop, to his surprise, Reinholdt found his body swelling up in pride as he joined his troops and sang aloud and at the top of his voice of the glories of the martyred Horst Wessel; he sang his words to the cold and hostile sky; and everything was alright.

NEW YORK, PRESENT DAY

Everything wasn't alright for Sarah Kaplan. Against her wishes, and at David's insistence, Sarah went with him to see her mother and father on Thursday, a break in the traditional routine of the Sunday visit. Bertha speculated that it was either a marital or a health problem, and had made Sol's life miserable ever since her daughter had announced her intentions on the Wednesday. What Bertha didn't know, of course, was that the Swiss agent had reported back on the previous afternoon, and what he'd said had caused Sarah to make the visit.

There was none of the Sunday lunchtime threshold banter, none of the parody at the door about their lateness or the state of the meal. They were met by both Sol and Bertha, who had been waiting in the front room, peering out of the window at every passing car.

After an uncomfortable moment, they were inside seated opposite Sol and Bertha in the lounge, like unexpected guests. Sarah knew her mother well enough to know that right now she was holding her breath in anticipation of a disaster.

'Mom, there's nothing wrong. I just need to talk to you a bit more about Annelise.'

Sol broke the momentum of her thoughts. 'That's why you came out here?' he asked incredulously. 'How could you do this to us? We thought there was something seriously wrong.'

'I told you over the phone that I wanted to ask some questions.'

'Yeah, but … never mind. Mom's told you all about Annelise. What more does she know?'

'I've found her,' said Sarah.

Her mother looked at her in amazement. 'You found her? You mean, she's still alive?'

Sarah nodded. 'She's old and frail and she's had a stroke, but she's told my agent over there that she's never heard of *Bubba* Eva. That's why I need to know if there's anything, even the smallest thing, no matter how trivial, that you can remember about her.'

'What should I remember?' her mother asked. 'Before that letter that came for *Bubba* Eva, I'd never heard of her. And since then, who mentions her name? What should I know about her? And why should an old woman remember your grandma after all these years.'

'But is there anything else. Anything at all?'

Again Sol interrupted. 'What is this? You're on a mission to Mars or something. What do you have to know? Just leave it. Mom's told you everything there is to know about Annelise. More than that, she doesn't know.'

'I just … what can I say? I need to know.'

She sighed. She couldn't bring herself to say it. Coming to see her Mom had been a terrible mistake.

'So where'd you find her?' asked Bertha.

'I found her in a home for elderly people. Especially people who have had strokes or who are suffering from terminal illnesses. It's a sort of a hostel. She's been in there for a few years.'

Bertha nodded, wondering what was so important.

'So?' said Sol, beginning to become frustrated. 'What's this got to do with your Mom? What's this got to do with why you make a special trip here and scare the pants off us?'

'Dad, I didn't mean to frighten you, I swear. All I meant to do was to come up here and tell you what I've found. And to ask you again whether there's anything, anything at all, you remember about *Bubba* Eva that you haven't told me so far. Even the most innocent thing. Why wouldn't Annelise remember her? The Swiss agent told me that she still had most of her faculties. Her memory wasn't all that bad.'

'I don't understand why,' said Bertha. 'I mean, why the song and dance? Some madman from South America writes a letter and all of a sudden, you're on a witch-hunt. It just doesn't make sense.'

Sarah sighed. She knew that coming to see her mother and father was a mistake. But David had insisted. That very morning when she'd again objected to coming out here, he'd said 'You can't possibly follow this thing through and keep your Mom in the dark. If there are any family skeletons, not that for one minute I think there are, but if you find something and you haven't told your mother what you're doing, it will devastate her. This concerns her and Sol just as much as it concerns you.'

Logically, she knew that David was right but logic and Sol and Bertha weren't necessarily bedmates. Their reaction now that Sarah was in their house proved that.

'All I wanted to say was that I'm going to try to communicate with Annelise myself. To find out whether Eva went from Germany to South America after the war. That's all. Nothing more, I promise.'

'You think you ought to do this?' asked Bertha after a moment's reflection.

'Why not?'

'You think you should try to find out what happened fifty years ago? I mean, what's to be served? Why? Why do you need to know?'

'But surely you're interested as well, Mom. I mean, this concerns you as much as it concerns me and Dad and David.'

Bertha looked concerned, and then shrugged as though in nonchalance. 'What concerns me is that I had no father. What concerns me is that the Nazis murdered him. That a man who should have enjoyed his life, his family, was taken from us by barbarians, by monsters. That's what concerns me, Sarah, not what happened to a woman who was left alone with a child after the war. My mother was a wonderful woman. She slaved and struggled after the war to bring me up and make sure that I had everything. She never looked at another man after my father died. Now you want to find out stuff about her. I don't want you to. Leave it alone.'

So that was it. Sarah looked at her mother and glanced up to the picture on the mantlepiece of *Bubba* Eva taken when Sarah was seven years old, shortly before she died. What was her mother frightened of? And did *Bubba* Eva, a woman held up as the very paragon of the suffering which comes from virtue, have something to hide?

By one of those coincidences which are increasingly an aspect of modern living, the weekend newspapers carried an article about the Swiss government's new deal on reparations for people whose wartime bank accounts had suddenly been rediscovered. The article said that upon confirmation of the victim's identity before a new Tribunal, which was to be established from representatives of Swiss banks, the Swiss government, the Red Cross and the international Jewish organisations, new mandates would be issued forcing banks to disclose details of long-hidden accounts.

Josh phoned Sarah from Scotland in a state of excitement.

'You have to get over there, Sarah. We have to be on that commission. We've got just as much reason to be sitting in judgement on the banks as has B'nai B'rith and the World Zionist Congress and the Red Cross. Jesus, we've helped more people get more assets back in the last year than the whole load of them put together. You should be our representative. Get over there and start lobbying.'

He was of course absolutely right and she could tell from his tone that there was to be no argument.

'Josh, you've got no idea how much work I've got on my desk at the moment and how deep I am in discussions with Congress about funding.'

'Sarah,' he insisted. 'You've got three deputies that can keep discussions alive while you're over there. I'm asking you for a week, two at the most. It's a pivotal time. You go now or we lose it. Once the decision about membership of the commission is made, that's it. If we're not in, then we're locked out forever.'

And so, three days later, she found herself in Berne in negotiations with the responsible Swiss Minister's executive officer. When she presented her credentials and the work that she and Josh had done on behalf of Jewish refugees, the Minister's assistant listened closely, and assured her that he would give careful consideration to putting her Institute's name forward; but he warned her not to hold out too much hope.

'These things,' he told her, 'are highly political. If you come on board, we may have problems with the Zionists.' But he seemed to be a decent man and agreed to put her case vigorously. She believed him. He didn't look like the type of man who would dissemble, but the Swiss way of doing business and dealing with government gave her an entire week with little to do before he came back to her with the Minister's decision.

She had lunch with the Swiss agent and the conversation turned to Annelise. What was she like? How good were her faculties? What was her memory like? What was her attitude when Eva Arpel's name was mentioned?

'As I told you, Sarah,' the agent said. 'She had never heard of Eva Arpel. At least, that's what she said. Whether it was true or not, I don't know. I didn't want to press it too far. She's a very frail old lady. Why don't you go and see her yourself?' he said. 'It's only an hour's flight. You have time. A week. Frankfurt … It's not the most beautiful of cities but if you've never been there, it's worth a visit.'

The following morning she left Berne and flew to Frankfurt. Her secretary had booked her in to a hotel; once she'd unpacked, she took a taxi to the Marta and Walter Eisenstein Home in a distant suburb. When she entered the building, Sarah found that there were no receptionists, nor was there even a proper entry hall. It was a large 1920s or 30s building, amorphous and anonymous alongside all the regimented blocks in the long, tree-lined street. She walked through the tiny vestibule and immediately took in the smell of age, the heavy cloying, slightly astringent smell which she remembered from the hospital where her grandmother Eva had been taken on the day that she was carried out of the house on a stretcher. Sarah had been, what? Nine or ten? She'd been to hospitals since, of course, but never to one which specialised in geriatric medicine. Yet the smell of old age was still in her memory. She shuddered.

Sarah waited in the entry corridor until somebody eventually came towards her and asked how they could help her. She used her best German and easily made herself understood. Everybody would know she was an American, but her conversational German was certainly good enough.

'Do you have an appointment with Fräulein Liebemann?'

Sarah shook her head. 'No, but I believe that my grandmother was her friend.'

'Ah,' said the nurse. 'Alright, follow me.'

The nurse checked her over again before leading the way. Tall, young, attractive, carrying nothing but a small attaché case. What harm could there be from such a young woman, especially one who was obviously Jewish? They walked down a long corridor, then up a flight of stairs. The room almost directly opposite the top of the stairs was closed. The nurse knocked on the door, put her head around and said loudly, 'Annelise, darling. A visitor for you' … There was a mumble from inside the room, following which the nurse said, 'I don't know who she is. Just a visitor.'

The nurse, too busy to engage in conversation, opened the door and let Sarah walk in. The woman in front of her sat in a wheelchair; she was wizened and stared vacantly in her direction through eyes whose lustre was dulled by age. She was sitting positioned so that her chair was close to the window. Her view had been of the park opposite. It was how she spent her days … staring into the park in case anything caught her interest. The old lady said nothing to Sarah as she walked in, scrutinising her instead.

Sarah walked into the middle of the room and said, 'Fräulein Liebemann, my name is Sarah Kaplan.'

The old lady knew immediately that her German was tainted by an American accent. 'Yes?' she said, her voice dry and croaky and low; unnaturally low, the voice of a man. From the skew in her face, she'd suffered a stroke some time ago and had lost the power over the muscles in her cheek, her neck, her arm and probably her legs on the right side of her body. Her right arm was bent and seemed to be resting on her lap as though it didn't belong to her.

'I've just come from Switzerland. I was in Berne. I hope you don't mind that I came. You were visited by a colleague of mine who asked you some questions about my grandmother. Eva Arpel. Can you understand what I'm saying? Do you remember him coming to see you? It would have been a week ago.'

'Yes,' said the woman frowning. Sarah noticed her hands. They gave the impression of being pale old spiders, gnarled and bent, lying in her lap. But when Sarah looked more closely, she saw that the old woman's fingers were more like the claws of a bird of prey, the joints swollen bumps, obviously painful. Fräulein Liebemann was wrapped in a dun coloured hospital blanket and beneath the blanket was a sky-blue cardigan and beneath that, some other item of clothing, insulating her from the cold which old people felt, regardless of the radiator pumping out overpowering heat into the room.

'I'm the granddaughter of Eva Arpel. My name is Sarah Kaplan. I live in America. I'm here to find out about my grandmother.'

Fräulein Liebemann frowned and shook her head. 'I'm sorry. I don't know you.'

'My grandmother was Eva Arpel. Do you not remember her?'

Her eyes, uncertain and timid, suddenly opened fractionally wider. A chord had been struck.

'I don't know who this is.'

'My grandmother knew you. You wrote a letter to her many years ago. Do you remember writing the letter? Fräulein Liebemann, my grandmother is dead. She passed away in 1975. If you do remember anything about her, then it's important for me that you tell me how you knew her. I swear to you that I only want to know for my own satisfaction, not for any other reason. It's just that I've come across information about my late grandmother which I need to clarify. Do you understand what I'm saying to you?'

The old woman shook her head. 'I don't know her,' she croaked.

A weight of sadness fell on Sarah's shoulders. As an attorney used to cross-examinations, Sarah's instincts told her that either the old woman was lying, or that age had dulled her thinking and affected her brain. Either way Sarah wasn't willing to distress an elderly sick lady. It was the end of that line of enquiry. Now, if there was anything to find out, she'd have to pursue the South American link to this enigmatic Dr Forenjo and his even more enigmatic client, Ricardo Padrone.

'I'm sorry I have disturbed your peace, Fräulein. I'll leave now. Thank you for seeing me.'

Sarah turned and walked towards the door. An instinct, an imperceptible sound made her pause.

It was barely audible. Indeed, Sarah was almost into the corridor when she heard the words, '1975? So she died in 1975. So long ago. I was in some hospital or hotel in Bonn, I seem to remember. No, I was in Berlin in 1975. I didn't know, or I would have written … sent flowers.'

Sarah turned and looked at her. The old woman was staring down at the blanket covering her legs, looking at her useless arm. Quietly Sarah returned to the room and sat on the bed.

The old woman continued to stare down at her blanket, thinking. Then, she looked upwards, but not at Sarah. Instead she stared first at the park, and then upwards into the dull metal grey of the sky.

A smile appeared on her lips. 'Tell me, child,' she whispered, 'have you ever made love to a Negro?'

Shocked, Sarah tried to shake her head, but couldn't. Neither could she bring herself to say 'no'. A question like this from such an old person.

Annelise sensed that the response was negative. 'I have,' she said in an almost asthmatic wheeze. 'I made love to a Negro once when I was working in Berlin. I took him home. He told me what a dyke was. He was beautiful. And such a lover. I was sore for weeks afterwards.' She laughed, the fairytale cackle of a Grimm's witch. Sarah didn't know whether to laugh or stay silent. It was obvious that the old woman's long-term memory was in fine working order.

She continued, 'Adolf would have been furious if he'd known. I bet Adolf never made love to a Negress.' Again, the old woman laughed as she stared out of the window at the cold bare park beyond.

And then the old woman turned from the window and looked up at Sarah's beautiful face. She reached up with her good hand, the hand still working after the stroke, and touched Sarah's cheek. Sarah felt as if she had been touched by parchment. She was mystified by the old woman. There was something in her eyes, some ancient pain but beyond the pain there was a story.

The old lady looked closely at Sarah, and then her attention wandered down to the amulet which hung between Sarah's breasts. Tentatively, like a grandmother touching her newborn grandchild, Annelise fondled the gold medallion. She held it in her hand and nodded. 'So, you have her amulet. She was so proud of it. But it nearly brought her undone, you know.' Annelise took the amulet in her hands, and examined its intricacy, the crude yet delicate markings. 'This is old, you know. There was much pain which went into making this. What happened …?' asked the old lady rhetorically … 'ah! yes. The father she never knew made it. But I seem to remember he was killed for it.'

Sarah was about to correct her, telling Annelise that the amulet dated back to the time of the Hittites … that the story of it having been made by Nussan, Sarah's great grandfather, was a lie; that he'd found it in an ancient grave and had been killed for it during a pogrom in the end of the last century which had caused the family to migrate from Carpathia to Germany and then to America. But she remained silent, breathlessly waiting for the old lady to remember more.

'How much do you know about the war?' Annelise asked after letting the amulet fall back on Sarah's chest. 'What do you really know about your grandmother?'

'Almost nothing,' said Sarah in a whisper, frightened that her words might destroy the moment. 'I know that she married my grandfather Saul and that he died in 1950 from ill health caused by his time in Sachsenhausen Concentration Camp. I know that she came straight from Germany to America in 1950 with my mother Bertha, who was only then a little girl. But I know nothing more.'

'She was a wonderful woman, your *Bubba*. She was my friend. She was born in Munich. Did you know that?'

Sarah shook her head. 'There's so much I don't know.'

Annelise's eyes began to water and a tear ran down her cheek. Not a tear of pain or sorry, a tear of old age. With her good hand, she used a paper handkerchief to wipe her eyes.

'I'm tired,' she said.

'Perhaps I could come back tomorrow?' asked Sarah.

Annelise smiled a crooked smile. 'Tomorrow I will be tired as well. I'm old. I'm always tired. Your grandmother was always tired in the early days, even though she was young. She came to Berlin out of fear of the Nazis, you know. She came from Munich … did I tell you that?'

MUNICH, 1930

Serel held her cup of coffee motionless, her mouth gaping, as she listened in astonishment to Eva explaining again what was still incomprehensible.

'You're going to live in Berlin?'

Eva nodded.

'But …'

'I have to leave. We have to leave. Our family. We must get away from the madness in this city. Can't you understand? We can't stay here another moment. The streets are too frightening. You and father must come with me. Now that he's recovered, we'll all travel to Berlin. Things are different there.'

'But it's too cold to travel. You'll freeze.' Her mind still hadn't encompassed the enormity of the news her daughter had just delivered. 'You're going to Berlin? Why?'

Eva sighed. 'Mama, Munich is dangerous. The crowds in the streets hate us. Everywhere we go, they spit at Jews and throw things and beat us up.' As she spoke, reliving the nightmare her father and Herr Büchbinder had suffered, her voice became increasingly tense.

Serel shook her head. 'But things are no different in Berlin. Jews are beaten up there all the while. Just like here. Everywhere. But this madness won't last. It's not like Ruthenia or Carpathia or Lithuania. The Germans aren't animals. They're educated. Intelligent. Jew's have been free citizens here for ages. This isn't like the Dark Ages. This isn't like back home, in the East. We're Germans as well as Jews. We're not *stetl* peasants. We don't speak Yiddish here. And the German people are sensible. Once things settle down, everything will return to normal.'

'Mother,' shouted Eva, fear and exasperation in her voice. 'Herr Büchbinder is still in hospital, and the longer he stays, the less chance there is that he'll ever come out. Face it, Mama. Open your eyes, even if he can't. Thanks to those madmen, he's had a stroke, and can't walk and he might even be blind. How is he going to run the shops? How is Frau Büchbinder going to be able to maintain this house? Why should she, anyway? There's no more clients to entertain. Germans aren't buying jewellery from Jewish shopkeepers any more. Nobody buys from Jews. And the Jews are too frightened to spend money. Can't you see what's going to happen? Look around you, for God's sake.'

Serel still looked dumbstruck. If only Franz were here, he'd talk sense into her. But, despite the fact that he should be resting from his injuries, he was driving Frau Büchbinder from shop to shop with their accountant, working out which of their stores could run themselves, and which had to be closed to conserve money. Serel had only heard the gossip which drifted down from above stairs; she knew that with Herr Büchbinder so critically ill, things would be different; they'd have to be. But what was Eva saying? That Frau Büchbinder would be sacking people? Nonsense. Even through the worst of things nobody in the household was ever sacked. Sacked? It was too silly. They wouldn't be sacked. Sure, there was unemployment, but not in a Jewish household. Where would the staff go? What would they do with so much misery on the streets? And who would drive Frau Büchbinder around if Franz were to go to Berlin. It was crazy. Unthinkable.

Serel sat back in her cook's chair with its comfortable and familiar slats and looked at her unfamiliar daughter. It had been twenty years since she'd been born; twenty! Yet even today, even after … what … twenty-seven years after the first Eva died of a fever in a field outside Poprad, even now Serel still thought of her as 'Baby Eva'. As if the first Eva, buried under the ground in some cold and hostile field in Ruthenia was somehow still to be counted. The pain of losing her baby, alone with no husband to share in the grief, had been so all-encompassing, so overwhelming, she'd hardly been able to breathe. But then she somehow arrived in Munich, and she'd met Franz, and the pain of Nussan and her first Eva became less intense, less raw. God, how time and pain disappeared when life changed. The pain was still there. Every year, without fail, on her birthday and on the day she'd died, Serel would go to *shul* and pray. She'd stopped praying for Nussan when she'd married Franz. It was wrong of her. Nussan was still the father of two of their children. Franz had tried to get her to continue to remember Nussan, if only for the sake of Yitzchok and Rosl. Her new husband, God bless him, had offered to say prayers, even though he'd never met her first husband; but Nussan could be prayed for by his own family back in Ruthenia, if any of them were still alive. And Serel knew that their son, Yitzchok, would go to *shul* once a year and say prayers for his real father. Were Nussan's family still alive? Sari and Rivkele and Hannele and Feige Estele and Boris and Yossele? Were any of Nussan's family still living in the old *stetl*? All hers had died in the madness of the pogroms which had rocked the area in the years following Serel's departure. Despite a bit of anti-Semitism in the streets of Munich, getting out of Ruthenia and the Ukraine and Eastern Europe had been the right thing to do.

Now little Eva wanted to go to Berlin? Where would it all end?

Not even Franz had managed to dissuade her, and she was the apple of his eye. It was all going wrong. For two days, the household below stairs had been in uproar. Shouting, screaming, pleading; all to no avail. She was stubborn and wilful and would do only what she wanted.

Serel began to cry again. She'd been in tears every night and every morning since Franz had been beaten up by the madmen. What was happening to her? Everything was going wrong. Even the cooking was too much. Once, she'd found relief in her pots and pans; now she couldn't be bothered. Poor Frau Büchbinder had eaten cold dinner twice. And had she complained, even when she'd come back from the hospital, cold and tired and worried, and all that greeted her was a plate of cold roast beef and potatoes and cabbage? No, she'd not said a word. She was a lady. She understood the problems that Serel and Franz were having with the wilful Eva.

But there was only so much that a woman could do. Her first husband was killed by madmen. Her second husband was beaten up by madmen. Her boss, one of the kindest men she had ever known, who had taken her in and saved her life all those years back, was in hospital, seriously ill, beaten up by madmen. And now her daughter wanted to leave home and go out, unprotected, into the company of madmen.

Why? Just because there were more Jews in Berlin? Just because of the opera and the ballet and the film and the plays and because all writers seemed to live in Berlin. Sure, it was a big centre of Jewish culture. That she knew. But the SA was there as well. According to the newspapers and the radio, they were beating up Jews on the streets of Berlin. Was a beating in Berlin different from a beating in Munich?

One day soon, all the madness would stop; of that Serel was certain. These people were Germans. Intelligent, sensible. Not like the evil Ukrainians and the Slovaks and the Ruthenians, God damn all their soulless hearts. But would Frau Büchbinder allow Eva back into her household as a servant if she left just when things were starting to get grim? She was running out. This was a time for loyalty. Herr and Frau Büchbinder had been loyal to her and her family, and now she should remain loyal to them. Serel had no intention of running away. Who would cook for Frau Büchbinder if Serel suddenly upped and went to live in Berlin?

Eva stood and put her arm around her mother's shoulder. 'Don't cry. Come with me. You and Papa. If things get worse we can even leave Berlin and go and live in Paris. Maybe even Palestine. Everybody is talking about going to Palestine. Yitzchok and Rosl will listen to me. They'll take their families when they understand what's happening. They'll leave. We'll all be together in a new country, where it's safe.'

'Enough!' said her mother, shouting and raising both her hands in finality. 'Enough! You're my daughter. You will stay here. You will stay in this house. You will not go. How can you think of leaving the Büchbinders when poor Herr Büchbinder is in hospital? How could you even contemplate it?'

Eva sat down in shock. It was always her father who raised his voice, never her mother. For two days, her father had been shouting; now Serel! Never had Eva known Serel to raise her voice.

'Mama, I'm going to save my life,' she said quietly, 'I want you to leave here so you'll save your life as well. I want to save Papa's life. I've also begged Yitzchok and Rosl to join us. They've promised to think about it. This is no place for Jews. We must go to Berlin, all of us. Now! And if things get bad there, we'll go to Palestine. You have to believe me.'

Serel shook her head. It infuriated Eva. 'Does somebody have to die to prove I'm right!' Eva screamed. Serel looked at her in shock. Then in disgust. How dare she shout at her mother. Serel clamped her jaw tightly. Eva had never seen such anger in her mother's eyes.

An hour later, Eva's meagre bag of possessions was packed and in the hall waiting for a taxi to take her to the station. Her father adamantly refused to drive his daughter, despite Frau Büchbinder's plea which turned into an instruction which turned into a command when she saw the intransigence in Franz's face. It was the first time he had ever disobeyed his employer.

Eva sat on her solitary suitcase waiting for the rap on the door. Frau Büchbinder came out of the library and looked at her sadly. Normally Eva left by the back door but this time Frau Büchbinder had particularly asked her to come up and say goodbye before she left. She walked over to where the young woman was sitting. Eva stood immediately and smiled. It was a nervous smile, unsure of what her employer would say about her desertion. Frau Büchbinder opened her arms and kissed Eva on both cheeks.

'I've known you since you were born. This is your house. This always will be your house as long as Almighty God gives us strength to maintain it. I believe you're wrong in going to Berlin. This madness will come to an end soon but if it's your considered wish then I support you. I know your parents are angry but they're good people. They see your going as being self-serving. I don't. I see a young woman who's terrified, with great justification. I see a brilliantly talented young woman whose voice and singing career are constrained from developing their full potential because of the hideous anti-Semitism in this city. But Munich is an old and decent place and will soon recover from this insanity. That is when you must come back. Come back as a great diva or as a wonderful actress. You must always know that this is your home, and wherever your talents lead you, this is where you must return if ever you are in need.'

Tears streamed down Eva's cheeks. She sobbed into Frau Büchbinder's shoulder. There was a knock on the door. Frau Büchbinder walked over and opened it. The taxi driver doffed his cap. Eva picked up her case and walked out of the door and down the steps. The taxi-driver held open the door for her to enter. She sat down on the cold leather seats. There was a heavy smell of cigarettes in the cab's confined air, the windows closed against the chill of the day. The driver walked around and sat in his seat but before he could start the engine, a woman walked out of the lane beside the house and then ran in front of the taxi to prevent it from moving.

It was Serel. Her face was flushed from crying. She walked around to Eva's side of the car. Frowning, terrified of another tirade, Eva grasped the metal tongue and pulled down the window. Wordlessly mother and daughter looked at each other. Serel lifted her hands inside the cab. In the palm of her left hand was her amulet. Serel had sold the gold chain years earlier in Poprad in order to pay for food and clothing and travel to Germany, but the gold amulet remained, suspended on a leather thong. She slipped the thong over Eva's head and pushed the amulet inside her bodice. Neither woman spoke to each other. Instead, Serel's eyes brimmed with tears. She turned and walked quickly back down the lane.

The taxi drove Eva to the station and she boarded the train to Berlin.

BERLIN, 1930

A ripple seemed to pass through the crowd in the Tiergarten as men and women stamped their feet on the freezing ground in an effort to restore circulation. Some of the people on the periphery drifted away during the speaker's invective, while others crossing the park were attracted to the growing mass, curious to see what the commotion was all about this time.

On a high platform, the thin reedy voice of the thirty-three-year-old self-appointed *Gauleiter* of Berlin, Dr Joseph Goebbels was screaming vituperatively at the crowd. His voice, high-pitched at the best of times, was accentuated into the realms of the almost feminine by the poor quality of the loudspeakers and the microphone. He sounded so much better in an assembly hall or a beer cellar. There, his voice resonated with power as it rebounded sternly off the walls. But in this open park, his voice floated ethereally on the wind. Not that its timbre concerned those who had been listening for the past fifteen minutes, curious to hear what he was saying.

'Fully half the lawyers and half the doctors in Berlin are Jews. What room does that leave for decent Germans to practise in these professions of the wealthy classes? The whole press in Berlin, and indeed all the newspapers in the whole of Germany itself and in most of the rest of the world, is in the hands of the Jews. We're controlled, manipulated in every way by these vermin.'

Every time he stressed the words of hate and ridicule, there were uncomfortable murmurings in the crowd. These grumbles of dissent did not come from the converted. Many who stood listening were the enemy, the vermin which *Gauleiter* Goebbels was speaking about.

Haupttruppführer Reinholdt Stricher concentrated with increasing vigilance on the dynamics within the audience. He and one hundred men were scattered all around the park, and knew precisely what to do in case of trouble. This was their fifth rally that week and for months now, they'd been preventing troublemakers from disrupting these rallies. This particular rally was better attended than on previous days, where Goebbels had only managed to attract less than one hundred people. Today, perhaps because he had chosen a sunny day despite the freezing temperature, more people were willing to stand and listen during their lunchtime to the message of the SA, the message of the Nazis.

'Every banking institution,' the *Gauleiter* shouted, 'is controlled by a Jewish hand somewhere in the background. Never in the foreground, you understand.

In the old days they liked to get their hands dirty on marks and pfennigs and guilders and pound notes and for most of this century, the US dollar. They loved getting their grubby little hands all covered with the smell of money. Nowadays, of course, they're too rich and too important. So they have ordinary people like you counting their money for them while they sit in the background massaging their *schmaltz*-filled bellies, smoking on their fat cigars.'

Before he could say anything else, there was a sudden and very obvious disturbance in the crowd. Ten young men, all separated from each other, began as one to shout and heckle. Goebbels listened for a moment to what they were saying. It was a mistake. He should have just kept talking and let Reinholdt and his men see to the troublemakers; but with the deafening silence from the podium, the young men's voices sounded righteous when they were raised in anger.

'Liar!'

'You're scum, Goebbels.'

'Where's your proof, Goebbels? Prove what you're saying.'

The voices rose and shouted louder and louder in increasing fury against the *Gauleiter*.

But Reinholdt Stricher was much quicker on the uptake than *Gauleiter* Goebbels. He and twenty of his men pushed their way into the crowd like an arrowhead piercing human flesh, pushing, forcing, angrily demanding until they had two, then three, then eight, then all ten of the angry young men in their sights. The SA men weren't allowed to wear uniforms. Instead, they wore their own uniforms; a white shirt with a brown rubber band around one of the upper buttons, but everybody knew that they were the strong arm of Goebbels and the Nazi Party.

Reinholdt grabbed one of the young men by the hair and pulled him backwards towards the ground, kneeing him in the back of the head as he did so. The young man, expecting trouble, didn't think it was coming from behind. He should have realised he and his colleagues were surrounded, but it was too late. Suddenly, he found himself lying on the ground, staring up at a tall athletic blond young German who was standing, snarling over him. He tried to defend himself but couldn't. Reinholdt kicked him viciously in the ribs and then immediately moved his heel to kick the young man just below the diaphragm in the solar plexus.

Reinholdt knew that his prey was immobile and stood on tiptoe to find out what the rest of his men were doing. Over the top of the crowd, he could see movement and hear screams of frightened women trying to back away from the violence. Everything in and around the audience was suddenly a sea of anger. It was exactly what he wanted.

Reinholdt bent down and grasped the young man by his jacket, the youth's mouth distended like a landed fish, panicking that he couldn't breathe, trying to suck air into his body. The SA man pulled the youth to his feet, put him in a headlock and frogmarched him through the crowd, which instantly gave way in fear for their own safety. The anger which had developed out of nowhere had made people walk quickly away. Berliners were getting used to moving quickly to get away from demonstrations. People were being beaten up on the streets every hour of the day. Berlin wasn't a safe place to be, unless you were one of the men of strength.

Reinholdt half-walked, half-ran across the open ground with the young man's head tucked forcefully under his arm. The man tripped and then struggled, trying to keep up with Reinholdt's quickening pace. He took him behind a large oak tree where ten men were already standing, waiting to play their part in teaching troublemakers a lesson. In the distance, Reinholdt saw the contingent of the Berlin police waiting on the sidelines in case of trouble but he knew there would be no intervention. The last thing the Berlin police wanted was to engage with Reinholdt and his SA troops. So long as the SA didn't break the law too badly ... so long as they only attacked Jews and communists and foreigners ... and so long as they didn't attract too much attention by wearing uniforms, they could do more or less what they wanted.

He threw the man on the ground and snapped, 'Guard him'.

Reinholdt turned and walked back around the massive trunk of the old oak tree to supervise what was going on. *Gauleiter* Goebbels was continuing to address the rapidly diminishing crowd, exulting them, begging them to stay and listen to the truth. A procession of twenty SA men and nine bloody-faced agitators were coming towards him.

'Behind the tree,' barked Reinholdt.

Several of the captives showed spirit and tried desperately to punch their SA captors. They knew the danger they were in, and were desperate to escape. But it was futile. Now they were free from the crush of the crowd, the SA men got out their batons and, in full view of both the police and the horrified audience, beat the agitators over the head or in the balls. That always stopped them from struggling, Reinholdt had told his men. Within seconds they had concentrated the ten agitators, corralled them into the human pen formed by the SA. There were thirty SA men altogether surrounding the ten petrified agitators. Reinholdt had twenty guarding the periphery with ten in the centre to mete out punishment. He had expected more Jews and communists to be at the rally. They were beginning to mobilise now. They were fighting back. He was disappointed that there were so few. He had hoped for a good meaty battle, one that would appear on the front page of *Der Angriff*. But there was no opposition at this rally, just young kids trying to show how brave they were. Several times, his face had been on the front page of the party's newspaper, the handsome, strong youth of German Aryanism.

He looked at them. They were all lying on the ground. Some were holding their crotches, whimpering in agony. Others were nursing their bruised and bloody faces, still others trying to restore their breathing, massaging their chests and diaphragms. Kicking a man just above the stomach with the heel of your shoe, or if he was still standing, punching him with your fist, ensuring that the boot went right into the rib cage. It was a technique that Ernst Röhm had taught him. Hit a man in the solar plexus hard the first time and there's nothing he can do for five minutes while he's still struggling for breath; sometimes they even blacked out. And it worked every time. The *Haupttruppführer* looked down in contempt at the enemy grovelling on the ground at his knees. Not one of the young men in his troop had been hurt. It was a disappointment; unlike on other occasions when someone had got hurt, this rally wouldn't even rank as a paragraph in the SA's newspaper.

'So, which of you are Jews? Which communists? Which homosexuals? There are no Slavs here. I can see that by looking at your disgusting faces.'

They all looked up at him with contempt. He looked back at them carefully, like a ringmaster in a circus, determining which one would be first for their amusement. Which was which? Which the Jew, which the communist, which the faggot? It was easy to be fooled, even for someone experienced in sniffing out the enemy within. Homosexuals weren't always weak and effeminate. Communists could look like Nazis if they dressed in the uniform. But you could always tell a Jew. Evil, grasping, hook-nosed. You could always tell a Jew.

There was a Jew sitting in the middle, clutching his chest. *Haupttruppführer* Stricher walked over and lifted him bodily off the ground by the lapels of his jacket until he was forced to stand on tiptoe.

'Jew?' he spat in his face.

The man shook his head in fear. There was something in his pocket which was jingling as Reinholdt moved the man's jacket. He put his hand inside and pulled out a fob watch. It was smashed in the violence of the kicking that he himself had given the man earlier. He opened the fob watch and read the words contemptuously. *To our dearest Herschel. Mazeltov on your barmitzvah. Love Mama and Papa.*

Reinholdt put it in his pocket. It was broken but it was an interesting souvenir, a metaphor for the future; how the master race would subjugate the space and time of subhumans and Jews. He released his grip on the little man who tried to back away.

'Why do you hide the fact that you're a Jew?' said Reinholdt contemptuously.

The man didn't answer so Reinholdt flicked his baton and hit him again in the crotch. The man screamed in agony and doubled up. Reinholdt brought the baton thumping down on the man's spine. He pitched forward into the leaves and roots of the tree, semi-conscious. The other captives were looking in terror, knowing that this would soon be their fate.

Reinholdt looked in intense pleasure at the fear in their faces. He snapped his fingers and two SA men brought out cutthroat razors from their pockets. The captives looked wide-eyed in shock at the blades which the men opened with slow and terrifying menace. One of them screamed … just like a woman!

'That's murder! You can't just murder us,' shouted one of the men in hysteria, a dark stain suddenly appearing as he pissed into his pants while he sat on the ground.

'That's what we do to communists. Why should we send you back to Russia when we can finish you off here,' he said. 'Alright. Start with him,' said Reinholdt, pointing to the man who had spoken out.

Two SA men picked him up while the one with the cutthroat walked across the circle and savagely pulled the young man's hair, cropping it to the roots. He pulled so hard that some hair came out in clumps. The communist screamed in agony while the rest of his head was shaved almost to his scalp.

It took the SA men only minutes to shave the heads of their victims. Their hair lay on the ground in various colours, some long, some curly, blowing this way and that in the cold blasts of wind that whipped around the oak tree. The hair looked like fallen tresses from a willow tree in autumn, seeming strangely out of place against the hard-packed earth and the exposed roots which reached like fingers out of the dead ground. The shaven men lay there, covering their bald heads in shame, as though their private parts had been revealed. They felt the exposure of sudden public nudity. And the SA men laughed hysterically at the agony their victims were feeling. Some time ago, Reinholdt and other groups used to force off their victims pants, and cut off their balls, but they'd been arrests, and the outrage it had caused amongst Berliners had reacted against new membership figures; so the instruction was to humiliate, not emasculate. A pity, thought Reinholdt.

There were no parting words, no final shots. Instead each of the SA men came over and kicked one or more victims hard and mercilessly with their tough leather boots. The men on the ground didn't respond. Instead their battered bodies just absorbed the anger in the boot as another indignity.

The SA troop formed up a line at *Haupttruppführer* Reinholdt Stricher's orders and walked around the oak tree like Reichswehr soldiers. There were only fifty or so people left listening to *Gauleiter* Goebbels. In the few minutes it had taken the SA men to dehumanise their victims and leave them crying and bleeding on the ground, most of the crowd had drifted away despite Goebbels' imprecations. And so his men marched towards their leader, and began to sing the Horst Wessel song.

Goebbels stopped speaking in mid-sentence, turning at the sudden interruption. He smiled. He raised his right hand in salute. *Haupttruppführer* Reinholdt Stricher raised his, beaming in pride. The people still standing in the audience, still listening to Goebbels, the committed Nazis, raised their hands and began to sing the song. And the police in the far distance continued to look indifferently at what was going on.

It was the most famous street in the world. More famous even than the Champs Elysées. The Unter den Linden, wide, fashionable, busy, was the focus of Eva's childhood dreams. She'd read about it in picture books as a toddler, and in romance books as a young teenager; she'd even begun dreaming about it when she was preparing to tell her parents that she was leaving the violence of Munich to live a more peaceful life in Berlin.

Now she was living only a block away from it; but the dream had disappeared in the harsh winter of her reality. Her rundown, airless dark room was only a street or two behind the Hotel Adlon, the most wonderful and glamorous hotel in the world; yet it could have been a million miles away. Just behind the charismatic main roads of central Berlin with their exquisite boutiques and fabulous cafes there was the real Berlin. Crowded tenement blocks, narrow lightless alleys with washing constantly strung between the buildings, and the smells of cabbage and rancid fat.

Yet despite it all, despite the crippling unemployment of Berlin, despite the angry and disaffected crowds of grey men gathered on every street corner, despite the burning braziers smoking with coke and horse chestnuts, the Unter den Linden always ran straight and true, bristling with tall, imperious linden trees standing like soldiers for the never-ending procession of cars. The automobiles carried elegantly dressed men and women whose occupation, it seemed, was to waltz up and down the steps of the Hotel Adlon for purposes which Eva could never seem to understand. How could so many elegant people afford to use such an expensive hotel when there was so much poverty just around the corner?

Eva often stood on the opposite side of the road for hours on end, close to the Brandenburg Gate, watching the comings and goings of the people who made the Hotel Adlon just that … the Hotel Adlon!

That's all Eva did. She just stood there watching! Looking at the tall, well-fed women in their furs and silks alighting from chauffeur-driven cars, glancing neither to the right or left (as if they didn't want to see what was happening around them) and walking up the white marble steps, to be swallowed by golden doors, magically opened in a perfection of timing by men dressed as though they were performers in a comic opera. What was it like, she wondered, to enter the Adlon's luxury and mystique?

One day, the urge to know had overcome her reticence. She had dared to walk up the steps herself. She was given strange looks by the doormen, but regardless, wearing a confidence on the outside which she didn't have on the inside, she waltzed though the doors as though she'd been born to it and entered a world of walnut panelling and white marble and veined travertine, and deep burgundy leather armchairs and red carpets and tasselled velvet seats. From the moment she entered the perfumed and strangely hushed lobby, all the noises of the outside world seemingly swallowed by the thick carpets, she knew that this was the world of which she wanted to be a part.

She'd just stood there, dumbstruck, feeling like a waif, looking upwards in awe at the majestic crystal chandeliers, watching the sculptured staircases sweep upwards, listening to the oiled music of the lift cage. The men sitting in the lobby were nothing like the huddled men on the streets outside. These men wore bright yellow waistcoats and red-silk neckties and carried Prussian blue handkerchiefs in their top pockets. Their gold fob watches alone would have paid for a year's food just beyond the hotel's doors. Yet these peacocks were sitting confidently in gilt chairs sipping coffee from porcelain cups and eating petit fours and talking to their sumptuous ladies about subjects which were removed from Eva's day-to-day existence.

That's all she did. Just stood there in the hotel's vestibule, breathing in the perfume of the waxed woods and listening to their refined laughter and luxuriating in the elegance of the hotel. And suddenly she was approached by some stiff officious little man in a winged collar, asking her what her business was. She'd told him that she was just looking; he'd snapped his fingers. Two porters were suddenly standing by her side, escorting her back to the streets from where she'd come. She left silently, too embarrassed to make a fuss, or to object to their horrible treatment. But she vowed that one day she'd be back, dressed in ermine and silks, flicking her fingers, and having the porters and the hideous little under-manager come running to do the rich lady's bidding.

She lived so near, but it was totally out of reach. One block. That's all. She was living in the Berlin Mitte district, in a room which she shared with another two girls; it was all she could afford. When she first came to Berlin, she'd lived in a cheap hotel. She'd contacted the Jewish community, but had been told to go back to Munich, to the security of her family. They'd told her that Berlin was no place for a young Jewish girl on her own. It was too dangerous, with gangs of armed thugs roaming the streets looking for Jews to bash up, drugs and prostitution were everywhere, nightclubs where decent girls could lose their honour, men constantly on the prowl for victims … no, they told her, go back to your parents and the security of where you used to live.

She'd ignored them, of course. For the past month, Eva had spent every available moment she had looking for work; but everywhere she'd gone, she was told that there were no jobs available. When her money began to get low, she'd moved out, and found even cheaper lodgings with an elderly gentleman; he made her shudder, just looking at him. He looked decrepit, disreputable. He was unshaven most of the time, and he smelled unwashed. He was nothing like the elderly men who came to the Büchbinder's house. And then, completely out of the blue one day, he'd run his hand over her bottom as she was climbing the stairs past him. She'd screamed and pushed him against the wall; but that seemed to egg him on. He'd offered her money to go with him into his room. She'd been horrified, and told him to go to hell. He'd looked at her strangely; the lust in his eyes suddenly disappeared; suddenly he seemed to be scrutinising her eyes, trying to get inside her soul. 'Are you a Jewess?' he'd asked.

Eva had been horribly afraid. She denied it vehemently. She ran down the stairs and out into the street. She sat in a cafe for an hour, smoking, drinking coffee, shaking, not daring to return. When she did, there was nobody on the stairs. She ran to her room intending to pack and get out, but she screamed when she opened the door. The old man was peering into her suitcase, its contents spilled on the bed. He pulled out a Hebrew prayer book and held it up triumphantly.

'Jew!' he shouted. 'You're a Jew.'

Furious beyond words, Eva stormed over and snatched the prayer book out of his skinny, livery hand. She was taller, and stronger than him, but he had the vengeance by calling the *Sturmabteilung*. And one thing she knew for certain was that the SA would beat her, and probably rape her. She had to escape. The old man leered at her, knowing that she was fully in his control. He said that if she knew what was good for her, she'd do exactly what he wanted. He reached out to put his hand on her breast, but Eva knocked it away. His arm was as light as a feather. She was used to the physical presence of her strong father and her brother Yitzchok. They were men. But this old man; he was like paper. Confidence flooded into her. Instead of packing straight away, Eva had walked over to the door, and closed it quietly. Smiling, she looked at the confused old man who stood frowning in the middle of the room. She walked over towards him. She sashayed in a sultry, somewhat seductive way. She was no longer terrified, because she knew that he could do nothing against her.

His face was a mask of confusion. Violent one minute, seductive the next. What was going on? He licked his lips. Eva closed the gap between them. She reached up, and ran her fingers through his whispy white hair. A smile appeared on his face; his eyes widened.

'You win. I'll give you what you want if you don't tell the police. Now, take off your pants,' she said, her voice deep and breathy. She tried to sound like Marlene Dietrich in the film she'd just made, *The Blue Angel*.

The old landlord struggled to remove his pants, but the button on his braces wouldn't obey the commands of his trembling fingers. Instead, he almost tore his trousers off his body. They he nearly ripped off his shirt. He stood there in his sweat-stained long underwear, once white but now the colour of his rheumy milk eyes and tried to look seductive. But the sight of him repelled her so much that Eva no longer wanted to play the game. Instead she felt disgusted with him. She was going to get him to strip naked, and then just pack her bags, take his clothes, and throw them out onto the street. But he looked so pathetic that the game just wasn't worth it.

'Put your clothes back on, old fool,' she said, and started to pack her valise.

The old man suddenly understood her game, and started to shout. 'Jew! Slut! Whore!' His words filled the room. Soon, they would leak out into the street. She had to quieten him. He continued to shout. She kicked him in his crotch. Hard. It felt wonderful. He didn't say anything else. All he did was emit a sigh, fall on the floor, and gasp for air.

It took her less than a minute to empty the drawers in her room, throw her few possessions into her bag, and walk out. She took one last look at the man, lying on the floor, still gasping, still moaning. His eyes wouldn't focus, otherwise no doubt he'd look at her in hatred. Oh well! She was better off out of there.

But the walk in the freezing streets of Berlin with no money and nowhere to rest her head was an unnerving experience.

She'd stopped at a mobile canteen, and bought a cup of tea. There was another young woman standing there. They smiled at each other. The other woman noticed the valise. They began to talk. The young woman was an actress, working odd roles as an extra at UFA's Babelsberg studios on the south-western edge of Berlin.

Eva's eyes widened in excitement, but the young woman, Gerte, immediately dissuaded her. 'Without any acting experience, you don't stand a chance. In the old days, maybe. Or if a director falls in love with you. That's how Dietrich got her part in *The Blue Angel*. Josef von Sternberg fell in love with her, and suddenly she's the toast of Berlin.'

Eva frowned in astonishment. 'I don't know about love, but I do know that Dietrich had lots of acting experience. She played in *Duel on the Lido* and *From Mouth to Mouth*. I saw her myself in the cinema in Munich in *Cafe Elektric* and *The Ship of Lost Souls*.'

Gerte nodded appreciatively. 'You certainly know your theatre and movies. You're quite right, but Marlene had no acting experience in talkies until von Sternberg came over from Hollywood to work for Emil Jannings. The minute he saw Marlene on stage, it was love at first sight, and he wanted her for his film. Now it's playing everywhere.'

Eva sighed. 'Tell me,' she said, draining the last of her tea. 'Do you know of anywhere cheap for me to stay the night. I was nearly raped by my last landlord, and I'm fast running out of money.'

And that was how Eva, Gerte Sternburg and Annelise Liebemann began to share a room in the centre of Berlin, in a district so packed with squalid apartment blocks that the sun never managed to penetrate the ground between them to shine on the pavement, which was always thick with dirt and greasy underfoot; and their room was a basement one which was not only damp, but also housed entire colonies of cockroaches.

It wasn't until the third day that Eva had lived in the apartment at No 34, Potsdamerplatz, that Annelise admitted she worked as a waitress and a hostess in a cabaret called The German Sausage. She told Eva that the management was always looking for attractive girls with good legs to serve food and drinks and to smoke and talk with the customers. As politely as she could, Eva told her that she was still keen to get work as a singer or dancer in the serious theatre, and that as soon as she had the money to buy clothes and lessons, that's precisely where she would make her life.

Annelise nodded sagely, and advised her to get new papers, changing her religion from Jewish to Lutheran. She said it in such a matter-of-fact manner that at first, Eva didn't fully understand the import of what she was saying, or that for the second time in a day, her Jewish identity had been uncovered.

'You're not the first Jew to try to hide the fact, you know,' Annelise told her. 'I was born Jewish too. In Mannheim. When I came here last year, I was caught up in a riot in the streets. Someone stole my bag with all my papers, my money. I thought, now's as good a time as any to overcome a problem. So I went to the authorities, and told them that all my papers had been stolen. I gave them the name of a girl in Mannheim who died last year. She was the daughter of one of my father's employees. Tuberculosis. I took a risk, but it paid off. Her name was Annelise. The next day, I had a new identity, and suddenly I was Christian. You've got no idea how much easier it makes life.'

'But … I don't understand. If you can get a job as a Christian, why are you working … I mean, there's nothing wrong with working in a cabaret, but…'

'Christian or Jew, times are tough. You get work when you can. I'm a qualified dress designer. I worked in my father's factory, until it was burned to the ground. No guesses who burnt it, the bastards. But there's no work for dress designers these days. Not for the likes of me, without a famous name that wealthy ladies would patronise. So I'm a waitress to pay the rent. I eat well. Soon I'll have enough to move out of this dump. There's plenty of beautiful apartments going vacant in Berlin right now. People without work can't afford the rents. I'm in work. And all from serving people food and drinks and telling fat old men that they're cute and sexy and they turn me on. What's the harm? Doesn't hurt them; doesn't hurt me.'

CHAPTER ELEVEN

FRANKFURT, PRESENT DAY

Sarah waited breathlessly for Annelise to continue but realised that the elderly lady had fallen asleep. A nurse came in and looked at what was happening. She smiled. 'I think perhaps you'd better leave.'

'How serious is her condition?' whispered Sarah.

The nurse shrugged. 'Very serious. Her heart is weak. She could die at any minute but then we've been saying that for four years. She's a survivor, this old one. She was brought in here after she'd had a stroke. We gave her rehabilitation and now she communicates well. But stroke victims of her age, especially those without relatives and regular visitors, usually don't last as long as she has. They seem to give up. Like I say, she's a survivor. Somehow she seems just to go on and on. God bless her.'

'Can I come back tomorrow?' asked Sarah.

'You can come back whenever you want. Nobody ever visits her. Provided you don't tire her out, it should be alright.'

That night, Sarah explored the cultural life of Frankfurt and immediately retreated to the security of a good restaurant, and then to her hotel. She phoned David, then Josh, reported in and slept. The following morning she jogged in a nearby park and showered, dressed and went back to the hostel.

Annelise seemed to be a different woman, almost as if she was anticipating Sarah's visit.

'Why did you go?' she asked tetchily, the moment that Sarah walked into the room. 'Why did you leave?'

'I'm sorry,' said Sarah, not expecting to be castigated. 'You were asleep.'

'Ach,' said Annelise with a dismissive wave of her hand. 'I always sleep. Just make a noise, cough or something, and I'll wake up. Anyway, I don't sleep. I think with my eyes closed. I haven't slept since the war. Not properly.'

Sarah sat down and gave the old lady the present she'd bought. Handtowels perfumed with eau de Cologne to refresh her, and a huge box of chocolates.

Annelise was ecstatic when she saw the glittering wrapping. She hadn't had a present in more years than she could remember. Perhaps the last present was from Eva so long ago. And now a present from the granddaughter. 'What goes around, comes around,' she mumbled to herself, but Sarah failed to hear what she said.

'You'd better hide it in my cabinet,' said Annelise. 'If the doctor finds it, he'll take it away. It's not healthy for me.'

She burst out laughing, more a cackle than a laugh. 'At my age! They're still trying to keep me alive, can you believe it? But I'll outlive them all, especially now you're here, I've got a reason to get up in the morning. You know, there's so much I have bottled up inside me. So much I could tell you.'

'How well did you know my grandmother in those early days in Berlin?'

'Not as well as during the war. In the early days, I helped her out. I got her a job.'

'Where were you working?'

'In a cabaret. I helped your grandmummy get a job in my cabaret.'

'My grandmother worked in a cabaret?' said Sarah, the shock in her voice sounding like condemnation.

'You sound as if you don't approve.'

'Well, it's not … I mean … I only ever knew her when I was a little girl, but … I never once imagined that she'd worked in a cabaret.'

'It wasn't that kind of a place,' said Annelise. 'There's so much young people like you don't know about the war…'

BERLIN, 1930

It was four months before Eva was sufficiently desperate to begin working in Annelise's cabaret, The German Sausage. During those demoralising, terrifying months, Eva applied for work at the back doors of countless shops, factories, houses, and offices. Only occasionally was she admitted to the interior of a potential employer's establishment; then just to be told not to be ridiculous in thinking that somebody without any experience in that particular line of work would even be considered for a salaried position when there were hundreds of thousands of highly qualified people … proper Berliners … out of work and walking the streets.

She even approached the *Staats Oper*, the *Neuen Königlichen Operntheater* and all fifteen of Berlin's theatres to see if they needed anybody to sweep the floors or make tea and sandwiches for the staff. Despite warm letters of introduction from her drama and opera teachers in Munich, nobody would give her work.

And despite spending every mark and every pfennig as though it was made of gold, despite eating only one meal of bread and oatmeal a day, her money eventually ran out. Gerte, who herself hadn't worked in any film part for six weeks and was worried about her own ability to pay her rent, looked at Eva in distress, and begged her to go and see Annelise, now living in a respectable apartment in

Bismarkstrasse, once the home of the chief clerk of a prosperous import and export agent. The apartment had four rooms. Annelise had begged her two flatmates to join her free of charge until they got on their feet, but neither felt able to accept Annelise's generosity. They had met many times since Annelise's move; each time, she had tried to persuade them both to join her in working at the cabaret. Gerte said that she could never, ever bring herself to go to one of those places, let alone work in one. Eva said the same thing at the beginning, but hunger overcame her condemnation.

Eva never agreed to work there. Not as such. But late one evening, well after two in the morning, Annelise was leaving the cabaret's back door with another of the waitresses when a figure emerged from the shadows across the street.

'Coffee?' asked the familiar voice.

The two women looked at each other for a moment. Annelise walked over and threw her arms around Eva. She told her, 'The coffee's free inside. Come, it's not so bad. A bit smoky. It's been a big night. But there's no customers left, and the coffee's not only free but strong. So's the fried potatoes and cabbage and sausage and there might even be some steak left over. Not kosher, but what the hell. You look starving.'

Eva followed Annelise inside. The atmosphere was blue with cigar and cigarette smoke. Eva began to cough, and blink; her eye's were watering.

'You get used to it. Trust me.'

It was the first decent meal that Eva had eaten in weeks. It was the first unkosher meat she had ever eaten. She was surprised. It didn't taste all that different from the meat her mother made, and there was no flash of lightning, no clap of thunder from a furious God. Indeed, nothing happened except that her mouth seemed to take on a life of its own. Suddenly she was starving. The more she ate, the hungrier she realised she was.

And the meat was delicious. There was an all-enveloping richness about its taste which made it the most glorious food she had ever eaten. Her feeling of perpetual hunger, her feeling of drifting in the winds of Berlin's cold and hostile environment was suddenly ended. The room was bright and warm, the food was hot and unbelievably good. The cook, who had come to sit with them, smiled in amusement as the skinny young girl finished one sausage, then another, then a third, mopping up the gravy with black bread, then ate a potato cake, then sauerkraut and then, shyly admitting she had room for one more sausage, ate the biggest one which the cook had gone off to find.

The cook returned after Eva had finished eating, and sat down with the two younger women. 'What the hell is wrong with this girl?' she asked Annelise. 'You bring her back from the grave? She looks starving.'

Annelise explained her story, omitting only the fact that she was Jewish.

'So,' said the cook, a big busty Berlin fraülein who looked more like a man than a woman. 'You're coming to work in our fine establishment. Ignore the customers and it's not a bad place. The work is regular. The place is always full. You get free food and even though the wages are shit, the tips are great. Remember kid,' said the woman, 'the more tips you get, the better off I am, so work the tables real hard. Do what the customers want, ask no questions, and we'll all make money.'

Eva didn't understand. Annelise explained, 'Marta gets 10 per cent of the combined tips. We get 30 per cent to keep for ourselves. The management gets the other 60 per cent which they split with the band and the cabaret artists. Some sticks to the boss' fingers, but that's life.'

'Is there that much to go around?' Eva asked. She had tipped waitresses in tearooms when she lived in Munich. She usually gave only a small amount of change.

Marta burst out laughing. 'Play your cards right girl and you won't even look at your wage packet at the end of the week. Some of the men here tip big just to look big. God knows why. They can have any girl, just flicking their fingers.'

Eva thought she understood but closed her mind to the subtext of what was being said. She would be a waitress. That was all. She would work for wages. She would do no more than her job but she had to have a regular income. Then she would be able to get out of the room in which she and Gerte were living. When Gerte worked weeks ago she had given money to Eva to buy food. Now it was Eva's turn to look after her friend, until she could get back on to her feet. There was talk of a new film, the third director had even mentioned Gerte for a small speaking part. That could mean enough money for her to live for months.

Marta leaned back in the chair and yawned, scratching under her armpit. 'Well, I'm going home. Leave the dishes. The morning crew will do them. You look all in, both of you. Go.'

Annelise stood and kissed Marta on the forehead. Marta stuck her hand up Annelise's skirt and stroked her bottom; with her other hand, she fondled Annelise's breasts. What was surprising was that Annelise allowed her. She wasn't a lesbian. Of that Eva was certain … they'd slept together in the same bed night after night, and Annelise had never even tried to touch her. Yet she let this fat, mannish-looking woman fondle her.

Eva chose to turn around and ignore it. What really shocked her was that Annelise wasn't objecting. Outside, they walked arm in arm to the S-Bahn.

'Don't go home tonight. Come back with me.'

Eva shook her head. 'No. I'll go back to my own bed.'

'Don't,' insisted Annelise. 'Come with me. There's things we have to talk about. I've got another bed in my apartment. We'll go to sleep and in the morning we'll go down to Cafe Otto and I'll treat you to steaming hot coffee and bread and pastries. You're going to need clothes for tomorrow night. You can't wear what you're wearing. People would just laugh. I'll lend you something from my wardrobe. They're nice clothes. Nothing to be ashamed of. But the men will want to see you in an evening gown. They'll want to see a bit of tit and some stocking top.'

Eva's body shrank from that of her friend. The enormity of what she was doing began to sink in as she listened and grasped what was expected of her. Annelise put out her arm and hugged her around the shoulders. 'Listen, these are not easy days. It's a bitch of a world. What you have to do is to survive. You don't have to sleep with the customers, though you'll make a lot more money if you do. But you can get by on what you earn as a waitress. You don't have to do anything you don't want to. Believe me. I don't.'

Eva looked at her.

'I'm serious,' said Annelise. 'I don't sleep with the customers. Lots of them want me. Many of them put their hand on my knee and in my dress, and I handle it but I never go upstairs with them. I never go back to a hotel. Most of the girls do and they earn a lot of money. I won't. The management doesn't like my attitude, but fuck them. I'm not here to be a whore. I'm here to survive. Understand?'

Eva nodded slowly. She thought she understood. 'But what about … that woman back there … the cook … you let her' … The words faded away into the cold night air.

'Marta? She's just an old dyke. Completely harmless.'

'Dyke? What's that?' asked Eva.

'It means lesbian. I learned the word from an American Negro who was here a month or two ago. He said it came from some old British queen called Boadicea or Bourdicca or something. God, he was nice. He'd been to university in America, and was working for some organisation to do with equality or something. He was in Berlin to study Hitler and Nazism. He said we're in more trouble than we realise. His name was Clyde. We spent the whole evening together in the club. Cost him a fortune. Now he was one man who I did take home. We spent more than the evening together, I can tell you … and before you ask, everything they say about black men's private parts is absolutely true. I could hardly walk the next morning.'

Eva burst out laughing, and hugged her friend. But she wondered what her mother Serel and her father Franz would think of her, and what she was planning to do. Maybe the whole thing was wrong. Maybe she should just get on the next train and go back to Munich and beg forgiveness from her parents and work again for Frau Büchbinder. But she didn't even have money for the train fare. She couldn't even go home.

The chubby Austrian midget hardly reached Eva's thigh. He was so small in fact, with such rotund little legs and arms which he was incapable of folding by his side because of the roundness of his body, that Eva wondered how the poor little thing managed to walk. He was dressed in an alpine hat, *lederhosen* and leather boots which would have fitted a four year old. He was the funniest part of the show. He was the compere and he had been on and off the stage all night; one minute he was marching around the stage in a parody of the Nazi goosestep, another he was shooting his hand high into the air screaming out '*Seig Heil and long live midgets!*'; then he suddenly turned his back on the audience, bent down and farted. But worst of all was his constant running onto the stage when proper performers were singing or dancing or juggling. He interrupted their acts to the hilarity of the audience and to the constant anger and frustration of the performers with his lampoon of Nazism. Without him the show would have been next to nothing, a collection of talentless no-hopers. How much joy could there be in cheap singers, out-of-tune bands, acrobats who kept dropping clubs and rings, and beautiful girls who, beneath their make-up and wigs, were dreadful looking women in their mid-forties with saggy breasts and cackling laughs and breath which smelled of turpentine.

But because of the compere, the whole show had an extraordinary vivacity. Eva had never been to a cabaret before. Her only experience of theatre was the ponderous and terribly serious plays of the Munich artistic community, as well as the Munich opera house and the ballet. But that was all high art, far from the comedic, raucous, crude, bellicose, belligerent and often offensive performances of people who would never have been considered a part of serious culture. The people who performed in cabaret made fun of themselves if they were beyond real performances, or were made fun of by the audience and the compere if they tried to undertake a real performance. The ones which Eva like the best were the old hands who really played up to the raucousness of the audience. They would shout insults, swear at the diners, expose their private parts, and sometimes even turn round, expose their buttocks, and fart. She'd never seen anything like it in her life.

Yet most of the audience loved it. They shouted and clapped and screamed and hollered and demanded more and stood on their chairs and threw coins on the stage.

And the more the little midget appeared, the more money left their pockets, flying through the air towards the performers like slow-motion missiles. The ruder he was to the audience, the more they loved and adored him. He was what every mother and father feared for their child – a freak of nature. Yet the more she watched him, the more Eva could perceive a certain dignity behind his vulgarity. They were laughing at him but he was laughing at them and the cruder he was, the more he bent over and exposed himself and farted and threw things at the audience, the more they appreciated his good nature and participation in the fun at his own expense. Most of the audience, that is. All except for one table of clean-cut young men in white shirts, sitting emotionless and stolid. Ah well, Eva thought, you can't please everyone.

Eva suddenly felt a tug on her arm and turned around in surprise. It was the boss, Klaus Gruber. 'I don't pay you to stand and look at the performers. There's people over there without drinks. See to it.'

She apologised and sashayed between the tables. There were very few women in the audience of the cabaret that night. It was her first night and Eva had no idea whether women sometimes attended with men – whether this was a normal or abnormal night. But there were a dozen or more women like her, dressed in sexy evening clothes, bending provocatively, touching the diner's shoulders or legs or even between their legs and smiling suggestively. And she was expected to do that! She would touch their shoulders, and maybe their arms, but not their legs … and certainly nowhere else.

The table Herr Gruber ordered her to serve had four military men seated at it, each watching the show, each roaring loudly at the performers, laughing hilariously, their florid faces turning redder and redder as the evening progressed and the jokes and performers became increasingly coarse. She had served five tables during the night and it was only ten o'clock. Her job was a constant parade from bar to kitchen to tables. One thing that Annelise said was correct. As the room got smokier, she noticed the fug in the atmosphere less and less. Her throat felt dry but it went with the job. She had only rarely smoked and never in her own home in Munich. Her mother had never allowed it in the kitchen and as her family in the basement of Frau Büchbinder's mansion lived so close to the kitchen, smoking had never really been a part of the family's habit. But she'd tried it at friend's houses, and since she'd been in Berlin, she'd found she was smoking more and more.

Eva arrived at the table and bent over one of the officers. She put her arm on his shoulder as she had been shown by Herr Gruber and asked as seductively as she was able, 'Can I get you gentlemen some drinks?' The table was already littered with beer steins and glasses, as well as overflowing ashtrays. Fortunately, other people had to clear up dirty glasses and table litter.

Two of the officers totally ignored her, appearing to dismiss her with a curt wave of the hand. One of them, sitting next to the man whose shoulder she was touching, turned and looked up at her. She hadn't served that table during the evening. It was Annelise's table and Annelise was busy fetching food to another station.

The man who looked at her wore a Reichswehr uniform. He had braids on his shoulders and on his chest were stripes indicating he had fought in battles. He must be in his fifties or something like that; maybe even in his early sixties. He certainly looked important. Perhaps a captain. Maybe even higher. Eva had no knowledge of army ranks.

'And who are you?' asked the Reichswehr officer.

'My name is Eva.'

'Well, you're a dark-haired, dark-eyed beauty for sure,' he said. 'where do you come from, my love?'

'Munich sir,' she said.

'Ah,' said the Reichswehr officer knowingly. 'Home of the madman. That's where the little Austrian's set up his headquarters.'

'Can I get you a drink or perhaps some food? You gentlemen look hungry. What about some nice sausage or pork? There's some delicious food prepared fresh in the kitchens tonight.'

She prayed she didn't sound as if she was merely parroting what she had been taught. It was important that she extract money from these army officers and that they didn't occupy a table just drinking cheap beer. She got a cut of every bottle of champagne that was ordered from her tables.

'You can bring me some bratwurst, hot and spicy,' he said. He turned to the others. 'Take your eyes off the stage for a minute. This young lady wants to take your orders.' They seemed to defer to this officer. She wished she knew their insignia. She must learn these things, so that she would know who to address in future, whose shoulders to touch. Each of the men ordered plates of beans and sausage, cabbage and sauerkraut.

'And to wash that down we have some excellent champagne brought all the way from France,' she said. 'Can I open a bottle for you?'

The officer burst out laughing. 'It might have come from France originally but I bet it was strained through somebody's kidneys first. No. Beer. Lots of it. Tonight we're celebrating.'

'Certainly,' she said and turned to walk away. But before she could leave, the German officer reached out and gripped her by the arm.

'When you come back with the food, why don't you sit with us? You'll enjoy our company.'

'Certainly,' she said smiling and extricated her arm from his grip.

When she returned with the food she found another chair had been placed at the table, strategically beside the Reichswehr officer. 'And you are?' he asked when she sat.

'My name is Eva.'

'You've told me that already, lovely Eva. But do you have another name apart from Eva?' he asked

'Eva Schmidt,' she said.

'And is there a Herr Schmidt?'

'Of course,' she said. 'My father.'

The officer burst out laughing. So far it was going well. Precisely as the boss had told her; as he had taught her. Herr Gruber really understood the dynamics of the situation she now found herself in.

'And how long have you worked in this cabaret?'

'Tonight is my first night,' she answered truthfully.

'Your first night! I'll bet that's what you say every night when customers ask.'

'No sir,' she said, shaking her head. 'Truly, tonight is my first night. I'm trying to become a singer in the Berlin opera but I haven't the money for lessons.'

The other men at the table who had been watching the cabaret intently turned and began to listen to the exchange between their senior officer and the waitress. 'You should be swimming in money with your face and your eyes.' He ran his hand over her breasts, 'and your body.'

'Surely sir,' she said coyly. 'You're going to need two hands to eat your sausage.' She took his hand firmly from her breasts, and placed it on his knife. She turned, and sat watching the cabaret; she'd been warned and told what to expect, but even so, when it did happen, Eva felt great discomfort in what the officer had just done. Knowing about it in advance didn't make the offence of this old stranger feeling her body any easier … it was something which she'd never allowed anybody to do … well, very few.

She heard the men whispering about her. She saw them nudging each other. At the moment, they were concentrating on their food and their beer. One of them asked the captain's permission to instruct the hostess Eva to fetch more beer. The captain gave a curt nod, and the man sitting next to her said, 'Get us more beers, darling.'

She returned a few minutes later with their glass beer steins overflowing, the white creamy foam running down the side of the glass and onto the tray she was using. She placed the four glasses in front of the men who picked them up as though it was a ballet movement and gulped the liquid.

The army captain finished his food at the same time as he finished his beer. He pushed the plate away and wiped the foam from his mouth with the back of his hand. Then, assuming that he had the right to do so, he put his arm around Eva's shoulder and pulled her to him so that together they were watching the cabaret. She was sitting just in front of him, her shoulder touching his chest, his arms gripping her. A sense of overwhelming capture suffused her body. She was offended by his presumption, as well as his smells of stale perspiration and tobacco.

Within seconds, she felt his other arm creeping around the front and resting on her stomach. Her heart was pounding. This was the moment she had been dreading. Only a small downward movement of his hand, and he'd be touching her … her …

The boss had told her what to do. He had said to amuse the guests and encourage them to buy drinks. More amusement meant more drinks and more food. If she didn't want to go all the way, she was stupid, but that was up to her. There were plenty who did; women who lived well in beautiful apartments and some of whom even had servants; women who earned good money just for doing what wives did for free. But whatever she decided, he had told Eva bluntly that there were fifty beautiful women out there for every job he had, and that under no circumstances was she to cause problems. He'd taught her how to suggest to a gentleman that while she stays around serving him with food and drink, she'll find him another girl to look after his 'other' needs; Eva was to arrange for one of the other girls to go over and sit with the customer. But this army man obviously wanted her. His hand moved from her stomach up and started to feel and massage her breasts. She turned, putting her hand on his to stop any movement.

'Darling, I don't, but there's plenty who do. Let me go and introduce one of the most beautiful girls here to you, a real charmer, doesn't even care about the money, if you see what I mean. She loves sex. I'll bet she'll do a lot more than your wife does, if you take my meaning.'

She hated saying the words but it was her way of extricating herself. The one thing she kept thinking about was the money at the end of the week. It was all worth it because on Saturday night, Eva would have enough to pay back the money she'd borrowed from Annelise and Gerte, and the three of them would all live together again in Annelise's new clean apartment.

The captain leaned forward and whispered in her ear. 'I don't want any other girl. I want you.'

He forced his hand against her pressure and started pinching her breasts. He pinched her nipple and she felt a surge of pain shoot through her body. Pain and anger. She turned to him, her voice somewhat more confident. 'Darling, please stop that. I'm only a waitress. There's plenty of girls here who want you to do it to them. They love it. Let me bring one over.'

'I said I want you,' snapped the captain.

'I'm sorry,' she said, forcing herself away from him and turning. 'I'm not a whore. I'm a waitress.' There was an edge in her voice, an edge of steel and indignation. But the captain laughed.

'All waitresses are whores. All whores are waitresses. Now, shut up and come here. I fancy you. I like dark girls, especially ones with flashing eyes and you've got a great body. Now, do your job and come back and give me a cuddle.'

She didn't know what to do in this situation. She was confused. She remained seated, hoping that he would soon come to his senses. She couldn't afford to cause trouble. She had been warned by Herr Gruber. Any problems and she was out. So, she sat. The captain took her continued presence as a sign of assent.

'That's better,' he said and pulled her crudely towards him. He put his hand back on her breast; this time she didn't resist. She couldn't. She was too scared he would report her. She would be sacked immediately. She would be finished.

And then he moved his hand down into her lap and hitched up her skirt. He felt her stockings and moved his hand up towards the inside of her thighs. She bit her lip; she looked at the other soldiers who were grinning at the agony on her face. How dare they! How dare they!

She stood abruptly and knocked the chair backward. 'Don't! You have no right to touch me.'

The captain was shocked. He looked up at her face. 'I have every right to touch you. That's why I'm here; that's why you're here. Now, shut up and sit down.'

'I told you I'll get you another girl. I told you I don't do this sort of thing. Why can't you listen?'

The captain stood. He was taller than her. He was menacing. She felt herself cowering in fear. People who were laughing at the cabaret turned suddenly, distracted by a new performance; customers at other tables were looking at the interchange.

He was wavering in his drunkenness, weaving backwards and forwards; but when he spoke, it was as an army commander: 'Now listen to me, slut. Your job is to amuse the customers. I'm a customer. You'll do what you're told, when you're told. Sit down, shut up and do your job.'

Slowly Eva turned away from him and began to walk away. But he grabbed her by the arm, pinching her muscles painfully and spun her around. He was angry. He was going to hit her.

'Listen slut!' he shouted. 'When I give an order, I expect it to be followed.'

Now the entire room suddenly became quiet. Even the cabaret and band had stopped their performances and were looking. It happened often and the bandmaster knew what to do. He struck up a loud tune to drown out the noise – a comic tune to make people laugh. And laugh they did. The room erupted into raucous hilarity. But there was none between Eva and the captain. She looked at him in fear and hatred. He looked at her in disgust and anger. Quickly he grabbed her by the hair and pushed her down on his seat. He reached down and picked up her fallen chair and banged it solidly on the floor. She knew then that she had lost.

She watched the cabaret which restarted immediately the band struck up their new song. There were jugglers on stage, and they were throwing clubs and balls and hoops to each other, one man riding in circles on the small stage on a unicycle.

Eva's heart was pounding. Her throat constricted in fear. She glanced across to the bar where Herr Gruber continued to look at her in anger and annoyance. Annelise stood and started to walk towards the table but Herr Gruber had stopped her, telling her to get back to her customer and to leave the new girl alone to face the vicissitudes of the business. Herr Gruber was frowning at Eva and put his finger to his lips to tell her to be quiet and do what she was told.

The captain was emboldened. The woman had sat down and was now subject to his will. He smiled at her.

'Come,' he said trying to restore the atmosphere to what it had been. 'I'm not so bad. I have money and position. What more does a girl like you want? If you treat me right, this could be very valuable for you.'

He put his hand again on her knee. She smiled but there was no joy in her forced smile. It was a smile forced from a slave. He moved his hand again up her dress, forcing apart her legs. His hand climbed higher and higher. He was testing her, like a schoolyard bully. His hand went beyond her stocking tops to her naked flesh. She started to recite a barely remembered prayer in Hebrew.

'Heavenly Father … again we beseech thee … our trial and tribulation … Sorrow and pain … and that thy shall make it short lived…'

His hand began to massage the gusset of her knickers, his fingers pushing the material into the lips of her vagina. A shock ran through her body as though she'd just been electrocuted. She sprang away from him, standing. She said nothing, but stared down at him in incomprehension. The captain reacted in fury.

'Sit down!' he screamed. Again, everybody turned in shock. Out of the corner of her eye, she saw a man at the next table stand. She was swaying and clutched a chair for stability to stop herself from shaking uncontrollably. She felt she was going to throw up, or even to faint in the suddenly smoky atmosphere. The room became heavy and claustrophobic, as though the walls were closing in on her. She tried to breathe but the smell of the cigarettes and the cigars was suddenly overwhelming. Her throat was constricting. Then suddenly she was light-headed. She tried to focus on what was going on around her, but the captain wouldn't keep still. His body kept weaving in front of her, like the air in front of a fire. She could hear him shouting, but from a distance. From another direction she heard somebody clattering through tables towards her. She turned and vaguely recognised Annelise. And then she heard another voice. Above the music. Above the laughter. A young man's voice, strong and confident. She began to focus on what he was saying. She didn't understand what was happening.

'I said, sit down.'

It was the captain's voice. Then the young man spoke.

'And I said, leave this young woman alone, you filthy old bastard. Just sit down and control yourself. She obviously doesn't want to be with you. Haven't you learned yet?'

The three other military men at the table stood and confronted this tall young man in a white shirt. There was something odd about his top button. It had a brown rubber band around it.

'You think I'm frightened of you army morons?' he said. 'Why don't you get out of here? Come on. You've had your fun. Leave this girl alone.'

'And I told you that you're a fool. An interfering fool. Look at how many we are. You're outnumbered, idiot. Now be a good boy and sit down or we'll teach you a lesson, you stupid young puppy. What are you, SA? A ruffian, a filthy street-fighter. Fancy taking on four tough army men on your own, do you? Try us, sonny. We're a bit different from defenceless Slavs and homosexuals and Jews.'

'Alright, you old bastards. You army bastards. I'll take you on,' sneered the young man. He turned to the table from where he had stood. It was a large table, a big party of men. The six other young men stood. Each one was tall and strong. They pushed their way through the spaces between the tables and stood beside their comrade. The expressions of confidence on the faces of the army men suddenly disappeared. Seven young SA men were a very different proposition to a young thug all on his own.

Suddenly Klaus Gruber pushed his way through the crowd, shouting, 'Gentlemen. Gentlemen,' His voice was that of a man pleading for reason and understanding. 'Gentlemen, please. This is a house of enjoyment. If you have a problem, go outside and sort it out. I have customers here who want to enjoy the cabaret. Now, sit down and continue to enjoy. You, sir,' he said talking to the captain. 'You've been insulted by one of my waitresses. For this I apologise. Your meal is on the house tonight, so are the meals of all your friends. All you have to do is pay for your drinks. It's my way of saying I'm sorry. Now sit down gentlemen.

'And you,' he said turning to the seven SA men. 'You young gentlemen, you're here for a good time. I have plenty of girls who will show you how to have a good time. Sit down as well. There's no need to fight. There's enough fighting on the streets. Here there's no fighting. Here there's only fun.'

No matter what he said, he couldn't decrease the hostility which had been sparked between the two groups. The tall blond young man who had first confronted the captain spoke. 'We'll sit down when this old bastard apologises to this young lady.'

'Apologies are not necessary,' said Herr Gruber. 'No

apologies. No problems. This young lady doesn't want an apology. It's her job. It was fun. She was just having a bit of fun.'

Other people in the cabaret audience began to shout.

'Sit down.'

'Shut up. We want to see the show.'

'Just behave yourselves.'

'He apologises,' said the blond young man stabbing his finger towards the army captain, 'Or we'll kick his head in.'

This time Klaus Gruber knew well enough to remain quiet. This could really get out of hand. The four army men showed no sign of apologising. Klaus Gruber changed his tone. He looked at one group; then the other and made a quick, economic appraisal. Army men spent up big, but these madmen in the SA could marshal a thousand other thugs and trash his cabaret overnight, and then he'd have no income. He turned to the army captain.

'Alright, you four. Out! I don't want any trouble. Leave now.'

The captain turned to Gruber in astonishment. 'I haven't finished my meal.'

'Yes you have. Come on, out. This place is closed to you.'

'You're siding with this street ruffian, against an officer of the Reichswehr?'

'That's right,' said Klaus. 'Any time. These guys know how to fight. All your lot did was lose us the Great War. Now get out and don't come back.' Five tall and burly men dressed in dinner jackets knew that now was the moment for them to intervene; they pushed their way through the crowd and encircled the four army officers. It was now twelve thugs against the four of them. They knew when to retreat.

The captain picked up his hat from beneath the table and placed it arrogantly on his head. 'Never again will any officers of my regiment patronise this fleapit. Not only that, I'll ensure you are reported to the authorities.'

Klaus Gruber laughed. 'Do you seriously think I want army officers? Bastards, the lot of you. Now get out!' It was said more for the benefit of the SA men than for any other reason.

The four men turned on their heels and walked around the tables to the exit. Then Klaus turned to Eva. 'You, pack your bags and get out.'

She looked at him in horror. 'But … But he …'

'Get out. Now!'

He turned on his heels and walked back to the bar. Eva sat down on the chair with a thud. This was the worst of all circumstances. What was she going to do now? Even when the captain was messing around with her, the one thought that kept her going was money at the end of the week. Now she had worked in this hell hole for a whole night and had nothing to show for it.

The tall young man sat down beside her. 'My name is Reinholdt Stricher. I'm sorry you were fired. Do you want me to change his mind? There's enough of us to persuade him. His gorillas don't worry me. They look all puff and wind.'

She looked at him in incomprehension.

'I've lost my job. I've been trying to get a job for four months. This was my first job. My first day. And I've been fired.' She shook her head.

Reinholdt reached over and gently held her hand. 'What's your name?'

'Eva.'

'Eva what?'

In her muddled mind, she had to try to remember her created name. 'Eva Schmidt,' she told him. Her mind wasn't working properly. She was thinking about Annelise and how she was going to pay her back for the make-up she had borrowed, for the food she had eaten. She had no money in her purse, not even enough to get home on the S-Bahn. This was terrible. What in God's name was she going to do?

'Come, Eva Schmidt,' said the young man. 'We're going to get out of here and I'm going to take you for a proper meal. Not the shit this place serves.'

She shook her head. 'No. Leave me alone. I have to have time to think.'

'And I said, you're coming with me. I'm not like that disgusting army captain. I'm an educated man. I've been to university. I deal with women with great respect. I love my mother and father. I come from a good family. You have no need to fear me but you're a girl who needs help. Come with me. I'll buy you a meal.'

'Leave me alone. Please! You don't understand. I have no money. I can't even get home. I can't pay for food,' she said.

He laughed. 'You're in a daze. I said I'd buy you a meal. Anyway, a German gentleman doesn't accept money from a woman. Now come. Stop being silly. They don't want you here and this isn't the place for you, anyway.'

She followed him to the cloakroom like an automaton. There he grabbed his coat and she took hers. She looked around for Annelise, but her friend deliberately avoided her eyes, for the sake of her own job.

Even though it was March there was still a chill wind in the city. They emerged from the basement cellar into the fresh air. The cold night awoke her senses. She breathed in and she smelled the petrol of motor cars. It smelled wonderful compared to the dense fug of cigars and cigarettes downstairs. The air was clean and pure in comparison. He walked slightly ahead of her. She would never, not for the rest of her life, understand why she followed him from the basement.

CHAPTER TWELVE

FRANKFURT, PRESENT DAY

'It was a lovely nightclub,' Annelise told Sarah. 'Elegant, sophisticated, full of beautiful men and women. Ahh,' she said, 'not like today with the *boom boom* music and the wild dancing. In those days it was all elegance.' The old woman stole a glance at Sarah.

'What did my grandmother do there?'

'She was a waitress. She greeted customers at the door. She sang.'

'Did she have a good voice?' asked Sarah.

Annelise turned in surprise. 'You didn't know your grandmother had a good voice?'

Sarah shook her head. 'I've told you that I know so little about her. That's why whatever you tell me is important.'

'So you didn't know she was a singer?'

Sarah laughed. 'No. I had no idea. What did she sing? What kind of songs?'

'Songs. Nice songs. Not often. I mean, she wasn't that good. But she was a waitress for most of that time.'

Sarah realised that Annelise was studying her face as if trying to discern her reaction. 'So, did my grandmother like working in the nightclub?'

'Oh, she loved it,' said Annelise. 'So did I. It was a very warm environment. Very comforting, compared to what was going on outside. We lived in a world of fantasy, of colour, of light. Outside on the streets, it was frightening.

But inside in the nightclub, with the music and the cabaret artists … every night was magical.'

BERLIN, 1930

Eva and the SA officer walked through the hostile and convoluted streets of the freezing Tiergarten and onto Bellevuestrasse before crossing the Potsdamer Platz. As they were negotiating the traffic, they were forced to run into Leipzigerstrasse to escape a drunk in a car who was weaving all over the road; this was the street where Reinholdt lived in an apartment paid for out of the funds allocated to Ernst Röhm.

They had walked in silence for most of the journey from the cabaret to the restaurant, and from the restaurant to his home. It was the early hours of the morning, but Berlin still wore the mantle of antagonism. The long moments of the city's silence were punctuated by angry shouts, threats, even the occasional jarring gunshot, echoing between the dark buildings. The streets, shining with the slick of rain, ran into the distant nowhere. Eva had never felt more exposed, more alone. They had eaten their meals in an almost surreal stillness, their conversation constrained by discomfort, embarrassment; he asked the occasional question, she gave a half-hearted answer; there were apologies, she again offered him thanks and Reinholdt attempted to assure Eva of his sincerity in wanting to help.

But she could be nothing but distant from him, despite his rescue of her. She knew she was being remote and she intended to maintain that mood which he took for aloofness. This young man was full of confidence and concern for her well being, but she wasn't a fool. She knew he was only trying to get her into his bed. He was a member of the SA. Eva knew all about the SA. They had beaten Herr Büchbinder into a cripple; they castrated and shaved the heads of Jews and homosexuals; they boasted that when they came to power, they would sterilise all cripples; they would expel all Jews to Palestine … oh yes, Eva knew all about the SA and what they were capable of doing. She had stolen surreptitious glances of the young man opposite her as he ate his dinner. He was good-looking, strong, even kind; but she knew that inside his shirt and trousers was the naked body of a member of the Nazi Party, the very person from whom she'd tried to escape by leaving Munich.

Over dinner, they hardly mentioned his political affiliations. They spoke more about her. Why had she ended up living in Berlin when she was born in the world's greatest city, Munich? Why was she living in such a hellhole in an alleyway off the Behrenstrasse and why did a girl who was destined to be an opera singer or a great theatre or film actress or something else creative, end up working as a waitress in a cheap cabaret?

He believed her when she said he had found her there on her first night. She showed all the reserve of an ingenue, a young woman totally out of her depth in a heartless society which ate attractive young women and spat them out without a thought. The night air in the streets was freezing, but the food in the restaurant was good and not swimming in grease as it did in the cabaret. He had plied her with schnapps and a fruity white wine and she was feeling light-hearted as well as a little bit drunk, but despite her fluffy head, as they walked towards Reinholdt's apartment, she knew with an absolute certainty that she was entering the den of a lion and that as soon as the door was closed, he would force himself upon her.

If only she had an alternative. She had no money to catch a taxi home and even if she did manage to walk the long distance to Annelise's apartment, would her friend allow her to come in? And she couldn't bear to go home to the dark alleyway, the cockroaches in her sink, the smell of cabbages; in her mind, she'd already said goodbye to them; if she had to return, she knew that she'd consider suicide. But how could she return, tonight of all nights, to Annelise? She had jeopardised her best friend's security when she refused to allow that filthy old sweaty smelly army swine to let his hands play over her body.

And now, by circumstances which she simply couldn't understand, Eva was in Reinholdt's thrall. Even though he gave all the outward appearances of being a gentleman, he was still SA. He beat up Jews and he was possibly a killer. This was not the place for her. Four times during the evening, she had thanked him, stood and tried to walk out but on each occasion he implored her to stay, asking her what money she had and how she was going to live. And each time, his words made sense, and an instinct for survival held her back. Each time she tried to leave, rationality overcame fear.

They arrived at the front steps of his apartment. He pointed to the third-floor window. It was not a luxurious building but compared to where she had recently been living, it was a palace. Reinholdt tapped on the glass door and an elderly man, half asleep behind the desk, shook himself to attention and walked over to open it.

'Good evening, sir. Madam,' he said obsequiously.

'Hans,' said Reinholdt acknowledging his presence and headed for the red-carpeted stairs. The higher they ascended, the quieter the house became. On one of the floors, the middle floor, there was a smell of baked meats, even at this hour of the morning. When they ascended to the third floor where Reinholdt had his apartment, there was neither noise nor smell. Everything seemed to be absorbed by the feeling of solidarity, of completeness, of wealth. Eva was transported back a lifetime to the upper floors of the Büchbinder household in Munich; there, the hallways were carpeted in thick piles, and everything was perfumed, opulent. She bit her lip, so she didn't compare the wonderful Büchbinders to the SA man who was leading her into his apartment. She'd wanted to escape from him all night, but she couldn't. If she did object to his attentions, he might suspect her … might even investigate her … might discover her true secret. Then she'd be beaten and possibly killed. She was trapped in a spider's web.

He took out a key and opened the front door, flicking on a light. It was a bachelor's apartment. Of that, there was no doubt. Even from the entrance foyer, she could see down one of the corridors; there were two rooms which led off it, one with the door closed, the other where the door was just ajar but was full of clothes and sports equipment and newspapers left untidily around without any consideration for the presence of other people.

He turned to look at her. She looked like a scared rabbit, standing in the doorway. 'Eva,' he said. 'It's not my intention to make love to you, to molest you, to offend you. For the whole of the night, you've made me feel like a man about to rape you. I don't know why. I don't know what I've done to give you that impression.' Then he corrected himself. 'Yes, I do. You're a decent German woman who has had a terrifying experience, to which you should never have been subjected. I want you to know that not all Germans are like that army bastard. That's why Ernst Röhm and my men in the SA and Adolf Hitler and the NSDAP are working so hard to clear up the mess that Germany has become. You can be a part of that movement. You should be part of it.'

Her face registered shock.

'But now you're tired. You look terrible, if you'll forgive my saying so. You need a good night's sleep.

I have no women's clothes here but you can sleep in my bed and I'll sleep here on the sofa. Or if you would feel more comfortable, I'll clear the second bedroom and make a new bed.'

She looked at him, her eyes questioning his motives. He smiled and walked down the corridor, fiddling with the lock of the half – open door. He returned and held her hand.

'Here,' he said, placing a key inside her palm. 'Lock the door and open it only when you're ready. In the morning, when you're dressed, we'll have breakfast then I'll give you some money and you can go and buy proper clothes.'

He looked at her and realised she was wearing an evening gown. 'On second thoughts, I'll get Hans' wife to go out and buy some things. I don't think it would be a good idea for you to walk the streets dressed like that.'

She smiled. It was the first smile for days – since she had agreed to work at the cabaret. Why was he being so nice?

'You're being very kind,' she said softly. 'Why are you like this? Isn't it the nature of men to take advantage of women who find themselves in a position like mine?'

Reinholdt smiled. 'Like I said, I could easily rape you and throw you out, or ply you with alcohol and make you an easy target, but I'm not like that. I come from a good background, a good German home. I was taught to respect Germans, especially German women. You'd like my mother if you ever meet her. Her name is Lotte. She's how everybody envisages a Bavarian *hausfrau*. She's chubby with red cheeks and she's always cooking, cooking, cooking in the kitchen. My house always smells of apple pie and cabbage and roast meats and freshly baked bread. None of this bread bought from the shops.'

Eva felt herself smiling again at the memory of her own mother and the smells from her own kitchen. So similar to this Lotte person, except her mother was a Jew, and Lotte almost certainly hated Jews with a vengeance.

No! She wouldn't sleep here for the night. The dangers were too great. It was one thing flitting around a nightclub as a hostess, pretending to be a Christian but sleeping in the same house as a Nazi? No, it was too dangerous. Her life was in danger.

She shook her head. 'Thank you for your kindness, but I'll go now. I really appreciate your buying me that meal but it's wrong for me to stay here.'

He looked offended. 'I don't understand. You work in a cabaret with girls who are whores. I believe you when you say that you're not one yourself but you're on your way to becoming one, and yet when I rescue you, you treat me as if I have no value.'

'You don't have any value,' she said. 'You're a man. You did a nice thing. I thanked you. Now I must go.' She turned and opened the door.

'Go if you must,' he said, 'but how will you get home? It's two o'clock in the morning. You have no money for a taxi. Public transport doesn't run at this time of night. You're dressed in an evening gown. So, you get home. Good. What about tomorrow? You've told me that you have got nothing in the bank, that you spent all the money you brought from Munich. What will you do? There's no jobs out there for girls like you.'

Her mind instinctively reached out to the amulet. She could sell it. It would end all her problems. The price of gold was sky high. But she never felt it belonged to her. Even though her mother had given it to her, it was a family heirloom. It had belonged to Nussan, her mother's first husband. It had come down to her in the bitterness of a pogrom. How could she possibly sell it for her own comfort when it was her mother's last link to a life which had disappeared forever?

Eva looked at the young man. She was caught in the middle; halfway between his apartment and the corridor, in a no-man's-land. She was neither in nor out. Every instinct told her to leave, except the instinct of self-preservation. She turned and looked at him. He wasn't bad looking. He was straight of shoulder, taller than she was, older than her but not so much older, not like the dirty old men in the cabaret. But how could she trust a man like him, a man who marshalled forces against her people, who beat up Jews, who put them into terror of their lives? No, it was impossible.

But what option did she have? She thought about the journey home. Her cold and friendless room. The smells of poverty. Waking up exhausted in the morning with no coffee, no bread, nothing. She turned and walked back into his apartment. She looked at his face carefully. There was no condescending smile on his face, no sign of victory. Instead he nodded encouragingly. It was a face of friendship.

Yes! She would sleep the night here. She would allow him to buy her clothes and then, when he was out on his marches or beating up homosexuals and Jews, she would slip away into the streets. She would steal money from him. She would buy herself a ticket back to Munich. She would beg forgiveness of her mother and father and Frau Büchbinder and she would thank Almighty God that through His mysterious ways and through the agency of a man who hated her kind, she had been saved from disgrace and starvation.

It was the metallic clanking of a tram's wheels on the distant Wilhelmstrasse which woke her. She had slept beautifully all night, one of the longest and most refreshing sleeps she had enjoyed since she left Munich. Her body, for some reason, felt marvellous. Her hair was clean and fresh from the shower she had taken the previous night. Her skin felt completely renewed. Her mind was alert. Suddenly she felt like she used to feel in the old days.

It took her a moment to realise where she was. She looked around the strange room with its posters advertising movies and plays and smiled. It was a pleasant room, and remained so until she looked on another wall; until she saw a huge swastika on the wall above the dressing table, with its evil black spidery legs crawling around a white circle, embedded in a large red canvas. Immediately she felt ill. She sat up and looked at the pyjamas she was wearing. They were his pyjamas. Reinholdt's. Last night she had been so tired, she would have worn anything, slept anywhere, just so long as she could sleep. Now she felt uncomfortable in herself and of herself.

She got out of bed and walked to the door. It was firmly locked. She had taken the key out of the lock and placed it on the credenza. It was a deliberate action before she got into bed; once in Munich, she'd seen a film in which a man had placed a newspaper under a door and poked out the key of a door locked from the inside, so that he opened it and had his way with the heroine. She wouldn't allow that to happen to her.

Eva slipped the key into the lock and turned it carefully, listening all the while to the sound of the apartment. But there was silence outside. The only noise was the voice of the street. Vendors and hawkers and motor cars plying their way up and down. She walked cautiously into the corridor and listened. There wasn't a sound.

'Hello,' she whispered. Again, no sound. 'Hello,' she said louder.

'Yes,' shouted a voice from the kitchen. A woman's voice. She felt immediately safer, though she had no reason to enjoy the feeling. 'Come here, fräulein. In the kitchen. I'm instructed to make you eggs and bacon and coffee. Fräulein, where are you?' shouted the voice. It was an old woman's voice.

Quizzically, Eva walked along the corridor and into the salon, following the smell of coffee towards the kitchen. The apartment was much larger than she had anticipated when she'd seen it the previous night. All she had really done was go from the front door to the bathroom to her bedroom. It was an apartment with plenty of daylight, and with comfortable looking leather armchairs, a radio set on the mantlepiece, reproductions of heroic art on the walls, more posters of the swastika, and a huge photograph of a line of men with torches marching into a distant night.

She heard eggs being cracked into a frying pan. 'Fräulein!' shouted the woman. 'Come into the kitchen please. I'm making you eggs and toast, bacon and coffee. Yes?'

Eva was about to say, 'No bacon,' but bit the words back. Until she was free of this place, she couldn't afford even the faintest hint of suspicion of her Jewishness. Herr Büchbinder had once told her how the Spaniards, at the time of Ferdinand and Isabella, used to catch Marano Jews pretending to be Christians. They would invite them to a meal and look on their faces when they ate pork. Even the slightest grimace, the merest hint of distress would be enough for the guest to be sent to the torture chamber.

'Smells lovely,' said Eva, entering the kitchen through the open archway. The woman standing in front of the gas stove was stout and florid. With a frying pan in one hand, and a spatula in the other, the old woman turned to greet the guest, and did a pretend curtsy. 'So, you're up, my dear fräulein.'

Eva remembered that Reinholdt had mentioned his mother Lotte. Perhaps this was her.

'My name is Eva,' she said.

'And I am Frau Hochstetter. I am the wife of Hans the porter. I'm friendly with Herr Stricher. And I do much for him. Sometimes I cook extra for my man, and I give it to Herr Stricher for when he comes home from his work. He's told me that I must take your measurements and go into the shops and buy you clothes. You need personal items as well as clothes for the street?' Eva nodded. 'He's given me enough money to buy you several outfits.'

Eva sat at the kitchen table. 'Is he normally this generous?' she asked.

Frau Hochstetter shrugged. 'Not for me to say.'

'Does he often bring women home?'

'I mind my business. I do what I'm told.'

Eva sat at the table silently watching the old woman busy herself with the cooking. The smells coming from her frying pan were delicious. They excited her mind and made her feel terribly guilty, a kind of vicarious feeling which she both enjoyed and dreaded at the same time.

Frau Hochstetter took a plate from inside the oven and wiped it with her floral apron. Holding the hot plate with a cloth, Frau Hochstetter scooped some fried bread from the frying pan onto the plate, followed by sliding two perfectly cooked fried eggs on top. She then forked four curling slices of crisp bacon beside the eggs with slices of bratwurst and knackwurst. She poured a cup of coffee and carried everything over to Eva.

Eva had rarely experienced the sensation of being waited on. It was novel and exciting. 'Thank you,' she said politely.

'Eat. You look like you need fattening up, my girl. Now, tell me your size and I'll go into Ka-De-We to buy you what you need.'

Eva had seen the department store many times but had never dared to go in. The merchandise was so expensive compared to how much she had left in her purse.

'Please don't go to too much trouble.'

Frau Hochstetter laughed. 'And how are you going into the streets again? In Herr Stricher's pyjamas? I'll be back in an hour. Don't bother to clear up. I'll do it when I get back. Have a bath. I brought up some lavender bath salts for you. Naturally Herr Stricher doesn't use them.'

Eva told her what her dress size was and with that, the woman left. She finished her eggs and fried bread and drank her coffee. The bacon and sausages stared at her temptingly. She wasn't so much hungry as guilty. All she had to do was to eat them, but it was another bit of treachery. Another step on the path of turning her back on her former self. But what to do? If she put them into the rubbish, Frau Hochstetter would see and perhaps report it to Reinholdt.

What if she was to flush them down the toilet? But what if they wouldn't flush? She picked up a piece of bacon in her hand. It was stiff and already lukewarm. She nibbled the end, just for a taste. She had already eaten unkosher meat. The sky didn't open up. She didn't fall into a huge hellish hole in the ground. The bacon tasted salty but the fat was delicious. She ate a bit more and then pushed the entire strip into her mouth. Then the next strip and before she had even realised it, she finished the sausages as well. She drained the rest of her coffee and then poured herself another cup from the percolator on the stove.

What a mess. What a paradox. She couldn't have found a more ideal situation for herself. Everything was here.

Cleanliness, luxury, food, warmth, wealth. She could ask for no more. And Reinholdt seemed such a gentleman that it appeared he wanted nothing from her, not even her body.

Yet!

Yet, he was a member of the SA. He was a man who went out day and night to beat the skulls of her own people. There had been dozens of Jewish deaths on the streets of Berlin, windows smashed, houses torched, synagogues defiled. She knew about them all. They were all the work of the SA. Even the vile Adolf Hitler had made a public plea to the SA to control itself and to abide by the democratic processes, to desist from street-fighting. But they didn't obey Hitler. Instead they had gone on and on, fighting like animals, fighting people who were defenceless, unorganised, weak.

She was living in the home of, and accepting benefits from a man whose mission in life was to cause great damage to her people. Everywhere she looked in the apartment were the symbols she hated and feared the most. The swastika, the armbands, the pennants, the flags, the photographs of hatred. Hatred against her, against her parents, against the rabbis and the thousands of years of Jewish culture.

Everything told her to get out now. But she was trapped.

She left the plate where it was on the table and walked out of the kitchen to the bathroom, determining to have a look around the apartment while the bath was filling. She turned on the bath taps and tipped in lavender bath salts as she had been instructed. Then she went into Reinholdt's bedroom. His bed had been made and looked fresh and innocent, the sheets and blankets folded creaselessly, with military precision. His shelves were full of knick-knacks and mementoes of his time with the SA and growing up as a child and then a young man in Bavaria. It was the room of a single man, exhibiting his tendencies, his likes and foibles, his habits, his personality.

Around the room were photographs; Reinholdt with some colleagues, Reinholdt with an older, fat man, arm around the younger man's shoulders; Reinholdt leading a line of troops. On the fireplace opposite his bed were more photographs; these were not of Reinholdt in uniform, but of a family. One of them showed a rotund and amiable looking couple. His mother and father, no doubt. She recognised Lotte from Reinholdt's description. She smiled. She could be her own mother, Serel, except for the colour of the hair; Lotte's was fair, Serel's, now grey, had once been jet-black, darker even than Eva's. But there the similarities between their families ended. Franz, her father, was lean and tall; Reinholdt's father was short and somewhat stocky. And what was the father wearing on his arm? It was a photograph taken at a distance in some alpine location but, God Almighty, even the father was wearing an armband with the evil swastika on it. Yes, she determined, as soon as Frau Hochstetter returned, she would dress, excuse herself, take whatever she could steal and sell so that she could survive, and disappear onto the cold and heartless streets of Berlin.

The garments were sumptuous; not even when she went shopping in Munich with her mother did she buy such beautiful clothes. Reinholdt must have spent a fortune. But why? She asked Frau Hochstetter as she was modelling the third complete outfit.

'Why are you always asking "why"? Can't you accept that Herr Stricher is a decent young gentleman who is concerned for a young woman like you.'

Eva smiled. 'I'd like to, but I think this is all a … I mean, I don't know …'

'You think he's doing this because he wants to make love to you. Stupid girl. He's a tall, handsome young man. The girls fall over themselves to be with him. He has no shortage of girls. Why you? I don't know? Who can say what turns a young man's head?'

Eva returned to the room in which she had slept the previous night. It still wore the scent of lavender from her bath. She took off the jumper and the skirt and looked at herself in her new silk underwear. She'd never looked as lovely. In Munich, she'd only been able to afford woollen undergarments. Even when she could afford silk stockings, they'd been anchored to a ghastly corset made of the coarsest linen. She'd seen Frau Büchbinder's undergarments, of course. They were pure silk. She'd often held up her employer's slips and petticoats and nightdresses to her face, just to luxuriate for a moment or two in their softness, their slinkiness. Now she was wearing them.

Eva's fingers traced the outline of the seams in her brassiere and underpants. Then she ran her entire hand over the front of her breasts and her knickers, thrilling to the eroticism of the silk, the excitement of the shocking blue which Frau Hochstetter had purchased. She'd never worn coloured underwear; even when she'd seen it displayed in Munich department stores, something – upbringing, denial, guilt – had stopped her from buying … not that she could afford it.

The more she ran her hands over her silky body, the more erotic the feeling became. Her nipples hardened, and she felt a flush of excitement spreading from between her legs. She looked at her face. It was reddening. Guilt or passion?

She heard noises outside her bedroom door. A man's voice. She was suddenly terrified. She raced to the bed, and put on the top and skirt, got into her shoes, and straightened her clothes before unlocking the door, and emerging. Her heart raced when she came face to face with Reinholdt, walking down the corridor to his bedroom. Why was he back so early?

He stopped and looked at her. 'My, don't you look different? Quite the beauty. Excuse me, I have to freshen up; go to the lounge room, and we'll have coffee. Frau Hochstetter, could you make some for me and my guest please.'

The old woman turned and disappeared down the corridor without saying a word.

Eva walked into the lounge room, and sat. She busied herself reading a newspaper; it was *Der Angriff*. She scanned the headlines. *Our bloody Martyrs battle for the life of Germany*. The photos showed a swastika in the background with a picture of a man in an SA uniform, his face bruised and battered. Other men were standing around, some with hatred in their faces, others looking at the battered man in anguish. She didn't bother to read the story. The very name of the newspaper, 'The Attack' said it all. This was the work of that hideous cripple who had the audacity to call himself Berlin's *Gauleiter*, Herr Dr Goebbels. All she did was look at the motto underneath the screaming masthead: *For the Oppressed against the Exploiters*, and she knew exactly who this dreadful Goebbels man meant by the exploiters. It was unbelievable. Here she was, hated by everybody, living in poverty, forced to work in a filthy cheap cabaret just to earn enough to eat and she was classified by Dr Goebbels as an exploiter. And the man who had saved her, bought clothes for her, had given her a comfortable bed to sleep in and a luxurious lavender water bath; and in whose apartment she was living; who even had a cook and a housekeeper … such a man was classified as one of the oppressed.

Sure, there were millions of Germans out of work, but it wasn't because of Jews, their synagogues, their holy books or the other things that Goebbels ranted and raved about on street corners and on the radio and in newspapers. The Depression was world-wide. It had been caused by the collapse of the stock market in America. And her people were being blamed. It was all so monstrously unfair.

She put down the newspaper when she heard Reinholdt returning from his bedroom. He had changed his shirt and was wearing slacks and a knit top. He looked strong, potent and disarmingly attractive. He sat down and smiled at her. As he entered the lounge room so did Frau Hochstetter, placing a tray on the coffee table. It contained a silver coffee pot, porcelain cups and saucers, a plate of biscuits, some apple strudel which Eva was sure she had made fresh that morning and slices of black bread and butter. It was the sort of thing that she, as an upstairs maid, had served Frau Büchbinder when life had been normal. How normal was it that she was being served in this way in the middle of a spider's web?

'And what are your plans for today?' he asked as he sat, the very model of a proprietor, a young man confident in and with himself. He had a strong masculine voice, a commanding voice, but it was his muscles, his strength, which was so predominant. He could have been an athlete. His knit top clung to his body. His arms protruded, fit and with bulging muscles, from the short sleeves of his top. She couldn't see his legs but she was sure that they too were strong and muscular.

'I was thinking of going to see a girlfriend,' she said innocently.

'And what about work? I assume that you don't want to stay here for the rest of your life. Without work you won't be able to find an apartment or pay the rent, or buy food and clothes.'

She bridled at his intrusion. 'I'll pay you back every mark you've spent on me. You've been very generous. Truly. But I can't accept your generosity. I don't know when I'll be able to repay you but …'

He held up his hand to stop her.

'Why are you talking about repayment?' he asked. 'Have I asked you for one thing in return?'

'No,' replied Eva, 'but you must understand that I feel somewhat compromised.'

'I would have thought that where you were last night would have compromised you even more.'

'I was there because I was starving. Why were you there, if you have such a feeling of respect for German womanhood? Why were you in a place like that?'

'A fair question,' he said nodding. 'One of the men in my troop, Günter, was celebrating his twenty-first birthday. I agreed to go along and join my men in their celebration. To forbid them going into places where they would naturally go without my knowledge or consent is merely to compound their guilt. Rather I decided that I should go with them and prevent them from shaming their German manhood.'

Eva didn't believe him. Her face registered her cynicism.

'Do you think I need to go there for the satisfaction of my bodily needs? There's no shortage of women in my life.'

She looked at him and knew that he was telling the truth. Why would a man as handsome and virile as Reinholdt need to frequent a place like the cabaret in order to buy the favours of women?

'Why are you taking such an interest in me?' Eva asked.

'I've already told you. Last night.' he said. 'Even if you ask further and go deeper into my motives, you'll find precisely the same answer.'

'And you have no interest in my body?' She was surprised that she had even asked the question. It was so bold, so completely out of her normal way of speaking.

Reinholdt smiled. 'You're a beautiful woman. You looked stunning last night in that red ballgown. I'm not immune to your beauty. I just don't need it. When I have a need of a woman, I have an address book with sufficient eager women who will happily give me their favours. Even married women whose husbands are unemployed and out on the street and where the physical side of marriage has evaporated, even these women are throwing themselves at me in the hope that I might favour them with a dress or silk stockings or something like that. Yet to take advantage of them makes me feel guilty. I buy them presents, but never demand anything in return. If they want to give me their affections, I'm certainly not going to reject them.'

Eva looked at him in curiosity. There was a disarming streak of honesty, of gentleness, of consideration about him; yet from everything she knew about the SA, he must be a vicious thug when he was out on the street. He must be beating up old men and women, throwing bricks through the windows of shops which had a Jewish name outside it, ransacking the holiest places of synagogues and spilling the scrolls of the *Sefer Torahs* onto the floor, to be trampled to shreds by the thugs under his command.

How could a man be so different, have two such completely opposite sides to his life? How was it possible?

'Where are you going to look for a job? There's lots of unemployment. Jobs are hard to come by,' he asked.

'You think I don't know that,' she said. 'I've been pounding the pavements for months.'

'Last night you said to me that you were keen to become an opera singer. How good is your voice?'

She nodded. She said nothing. She knew her voice needed a lot of training but her teacher had told her she had a great natural talent.

'I have friends who work in the opera. One of them has a son in my battalion. He is …' Reinholdt struggled for the word. 'he does things to teach singers how to sing or teach them the opera or something …'

'*Repetiteur,*' said Eva.

'That's it,' said Reinholdt, impressed that she would know such a word. 'That's what he does. I was having dinner with him a couple of weeks ago. I'll phone him if you want and ask him to give you an audition.'

She stared at him in astonishment. After four months, Eva had only managed to talk to people at the stage door of the Staatsoper. By luck, she had once managed to speak to an administrative assistant who was walking through the stage door at the time and who took time to listen to her pleas; but he told her she stood no chance without formal training. She hadn't yet managed to show her letter of introduction from her opera coach in Munich to anybody.

Now, suddenly, thanks to a man she'd only just met, she was flying up into the stratosphere to be introduced to one of the most important people in the operatic hierarchy. The *repetiteur* was a man with the ear of the conductor, the artistic director, the management. It was unbelievable. She knew how important contacts were, especially in an artistic community. She didn't think for one moment, not for one single second, that a man like Reinholdt would know anybody in opera. She realised her jaw was gaping. Reinholdt was smiling at her.

'Shall I invite him and his wife to dinner tomorrow night? I find these social occasions important for this type of professional contact. Frau Hochstetter cooks a wonderful roast ham, with saurbrauten.'

Eva nodded dumbly. Her heart was screaming yes. Her mind was telling her to be cautious. Not to be so stupid. She was moving deeper and deeper into the lion's den or was it, as she first suspected, a spider's web? Was he going to suck the life force out of her, and wrap her up in silken threads until she was incapable of movement? And when he did, as seemed inevitable, would he then cast her out as so much refuse?

'You're amazing,' she said. 'You don't know me. You have no idea of my talent or background. Yet you buy me clothes. You offer me meetings with people I haven't a hope in hell of getting to see, just with a snap of your fingers. Yet you claim you don't want anything from me. Nobody is that good, Reinholdt. You must want something from me. I must know the price I have to pay.'

He looked at her wordlessly, and sipped his coffee. He shook his head in sorrow, stood and walked out of the apartment. Eva sat there, staring through the window to the beech trees, swaying in the afternoon breeze across the road. What was happening to her? What did he want from her?

CHAPTER THIRTEEN

FRANKFURT, PRESENT DAY

Annelise steadied a glass of water with her useless hand. That was all it was good for after the stroke: a counterbalance for her good hand. Thank God, she had still got one good side of her body left, even though the other side was withering like some sort of divine joke for the crimes she'd committed throughout her life, the sins of her life weighing heavily on her.

Her voice was dry from talking to Eva's granddaughter, Sarah. There was much about Sarah's face that reminded her so much of her old friend. Just as beautiful, just as self-confident, just as elegant. And the amulet, of course, cemented the connection. At times, it was as though Annelise had been catapulted back half a century, and was a young woman again, talking to her friend Eva.

A nurse brought in a tray of morning tea with a precisely cut square of a yellow concoction that Sarah guessed was a sponge cake.

'Shall I help you eat?' asked Sarah.

The old woman smiled in gratitude and shook her head, putting the glass down and immediately picking up the cup of tea. It was odd how routine became so important when one was confined to a bed or a room with nothing to do all day. The routine of waking, breakfasting, being washed, being toileted and then sitting in a wheelchair overlooking a park; the routine of the buses which arrived at regular intervals, the routine of watching the same men who walked with the same briefcases down the road to the same work at the same time every morning.

Annelise put down the cup and wiped her mouth. It was so wonderful to have this young woman here to break the routine, even though she knew that she must keep to her routine and not lose it because the young woman would be gone in one or two days and her moment of excitement would be over forever.

But there was sadness to Sarah's visit. She was such an honest, open young woman. How could she tell her the truth about her grandmother? No, she must alter some of the reality, so that Sarah went away with a good impression, and the truth would die whenever God stopped Annelise's heart. What good would it do to tell this child the truth, Annelise wondered. But there was so much of Eva in her face, so much … life. So much goodness.

Sarah waited impatiently for the old woman to settle again. 'What about friends? Men? Did she have men friends?'

Annelise's smile was lopsided from the stroke, a grin crawling halfway up her cheeks. 'Oh yes, one in particular.'

'Really?' said Sarah enthusiastically, keen for all the personal gossip about her grandmother. She was learning so much about a closed off section of family history that she never knew before. Her grandmother was now flesh and blood, a real woman instead of just an ancient photograph on a mantelpiece and a vague memory from her childhood.

'Tell me about this man. Tell me all about him.'

Annelise sighed. What did the Americans call this moment? She tried to recall from the Hollywood movies she'd seen on the hospital's television; but of course the words were all in translation. Yes, it was called 'crunch time', or something like that. What should she tell Sarah about the man in Eva's life? Better to say nothing about the truth.

'His name was Reinholdt. He was a lovely young man. He was an artist, a musician.' The lies came easier now she'd started.

Reinholdt? Ricardo? Suddenly her mind was catapulted back to New York and the letter from Dr Forenjo, executor for a man he believed was Sarah's grandfather. Could they be one and the same?

'Jewish?' asked Sarah.

She shook her head imperceptibly. 'In those days, being a Jew was being cursed.'

'He wasn't Jewish!' Sarah exclaimed. 'But what about the danger to him? I thought that non-Jews weren't allowed to be with Jews.'

'Later maybe. In the early days it wasn't so bad. Anyway, he protected her from the worst that happened and he helped her with her singing career.'

'How?' asked Sarah. 'I mean, how far did her singing career develop? I can't wait to tell my mother. My grandmother, a singer! It's unbelievable.'

BERLIN, 1930

The *repetiteur* of the Berlin State Opera, a thin angular academic gentleman, had been staring at Eva's chest with great interest for most of the night. She was wearing Annelise's low-cut red evening dress, and continued to feel guilty for not having returned it. But life had taken such an extraordinary turn of events that her social responsibilities to her friends had become secondary to what was happening right now. As she was dressing and preparing for the arrival of Reinholdt's guests, Eva had felt herself flushing with embarrassment at her inconsiderate behaviour, and determined to go over with the dress to Annelise's apartment the following morning.

Over dessert, the *repetiteur* plucked up courage to mention his fascination with the jewel. He surprised himself with his own diffidence. With his singers, he was like a dictator; a raised eyebrow could send a tenor's confidence crashing. But with women … certainly in the thirty years of his marriage … and especially young women in a social situation … he continued to feel as awkward as he'd felt in his teenage years.

'Before you sing for me, my dear, I hope you will forgive this personal intrusion, but I'm fascinated by your jewel. I've never seen such markings.'

Sitting at the opposite side of the table, Eva put her hand to the amulet and felt its solidity, its smoothness. She ran her hands over the images on both sides, indentations with which she had been fascinated since she was a little girl, markings which her mother had refused to discuss with her, despite persistent questioning. Indeed, for Eva, the amulet was always associated with her mother's sorrow.

'May I?' asked the *repetiteur*.

Eva smiled and nodded, taking off the amulet and soothing back her chestnut curls. She handed it over the table. Now the time for the story she'd prepared this afternoon. 'It was purchased by my mother's first husband. He bought it from a Jew; a tradesman,' she said.

'These markings don't look Jewish,' said Herr Helldorp. 'Normally the Jews put their markings on things. The hexagram and their Jewish writing. This doesn't look Jewish to me.'

Eva shrugged nonchalantly. She hadn't thought of that when she made up the story. She had no intention of allowing Reinholdt to know about the amulet. She planned to retrieve it and hide it, but Annelise had brought it around to the apartment unexpectedly just that afternoon. She had handed the amulet and some other possessions over to Eva in Reinholdt's presence, making some caustic remarks about how lucky she had been to fall in with a young gentleman such as Herr Stricher. Eva was mortified when her friend suddenly appeared at the apartment. Eva had phoned Annelise that morning, leaving a message with her housekeeper, telling her where she was now staying, begging her to phone so that she could explain things; she'd said that as soon as she had some money, she'd pay Annelise back what she owed; as well as returning her dress.

But the message Eva left was mangled by the woman; she intended to go around and pick up her things, not for Annelise to intrude upon her privacy. The last thing she wanted Annelise and Gerte to know was that she was living with an SA man. It was all too much. They would misunderstand. They would condemn her. They would never believe that she was only staying here for a couple more days until she had a permanent position, and then she would move into an apartment of her own. Nor would they believe that she wasn't sleeping with him.

So she had been forced to make up the story about the amulet as quickly as she could. Reinholdt hadn't thought to question her story, but now she was trapped into a lie.

'Maybe it's not Jewish,' she said. 'I don't know. Apparently he bought it from a Jewish merchant. He paid a good price for it. My mother gave it to me when I left Munich.'

'I think it's very old,' said Herr Helldorp. 'You should get it valued. With the mark crashing, things like this suddenly have an entirely new value. If you could get American dollars for it, you could buy up half of Germany.'

Eva held out her hand. He placed the amulet back into her palm but before she could put it on, Reinholdt held her hand and took it from her. 'This leather strap is completely wrong. What you need for this is a gold chain. Gold chains are often easy to come by, depending on where you shop,' he said. There was a smirk on his face, an evil grin, contemptuous of those Jewish shops which he and his men regularly raided. He never came home with the spoils of theft. He was above that, as far as she knew. Nor did he ever discuss his work with her, even though she had asked him about it for the last two nights, in the brief moments when they saw each other. He said it wasn't the sort of thing that he wanted to discuss. He placed the amulet back in her hand.

'Now,' said Herr Helldorp, 'as to your singing. You will appreciate that we have no shortage of would-be divas wanting to find work with us. We are also fortunate still to have a full house every night. Despite the millions of unemployed, opera has never been more popular. I can't explain it. I would have thought we would be playing to empty houses but somehow people find the money for tickets and the government is still very generous in its subsidies. The Roman emperors' concept of bread and circuses, no doubt, feeding the poor with what entertains them until a brave new government will arise and sweep them away. But I mustn't begin to talk about my political philosophies. Now isn't the time.

'As I was saying, Fräulein, we at the opera have singers from France, Italy, Switzerland and all over Europe applying to us for positions as resident performers. So, for me to recommend you, your voice has to be extraordinary, despite your friendship with Herr Stricher.'

'Of course,' said Eva.

'May I?' said Herr Helldorp, standing and walking towards the piano. 'Come, my dear. Stand beside me. Now, what aria are you going to sing?'

'*Vissi d'arte*, from Tosca?'

He was impressed. It was a difficult piece, requiring a great understanding of emotion, as well as producing considerable strain in the upper registers of a soprano's voice. But it was a performance favourite which always brought the house down, especially when Elizabeth Schwarzkopf sang it.

'Well,' he said, 'that's a real test.' He opened his briefcase and sorted though innumerable pieces of sheet music. Eventually, he found it and opened it on the stand above the keyboard. He played a middle C and enabled Eva to warm up her throat. He played the same note again, and turned to Reinholdt. 'This piano is badly out of tune, my friend. I'll send a man from the opera around tomorrow to tune it for you. Meantime, my dear, you must do your best.'

He began the opening chords. She cleared her throat, breathed deeply and began to sing a song that she hadn't sung before an audience in nearly three years, although she'd practised it all morning and afternoon. She both heard and felt her voice filling the room. But as it expanded outwards, she knew immediately that it wasn't quite right. Her voice should have been stronger and richer. It was lack of practise; in the intervening time since she was singing regularly, her chords had lost their tone, her chest its breath. She listened carefully to the notes Herr Helldorp was playing and rose to the triumphal crescendos, fell to the subtle melodic interludes. It was only after about twenty bars that she began to relax into the role; that she started to notice things around her, like Reinholdt watching in fascination, and Frau Helldorp listening with a smile on her face, a cup of coffee poised mid-way to her mouth. Now she felt confident, as she used to feel in the music room in Munich when she sang for Herr Büchbinder and his guests. Now she was pleased with the way her chest rose and fell to the voice of the piano. And at the very end, Eva allowed the final notes to remain in the room long after the last word of the aria had been enunciated.

As she slowly lowered her arms to her side from their dramatic pose, Eva looked at Reinholdt. His face was a vision of ecstasy. He was nothing short of stunned. He had only ever trusted her word that she was a good singer but he never expected anything like this. Hers was a voice of genius, a voice the like of which he had only ever experienced on concert platforms or in opera.

Eva looked from Reinholdt to Herr Helldorp. He folded his hands thoughtfully and ponderously, pursed his lips and remained looking at the keyboard, stunningly indifferent to her concern, he turned to Reinholdt.

'A lot of work is needed. She was struggling in certain high registers and in the lower registers her voice developed a tremble. These must be corrected.'

Eva felt crushed, as if she had come last in an important race. Herr Helldorp turned to her and grasped her hand. 'But there was great power there. A nascent talent which is crude and raw at the moment but with work, one which can flower. You have the makings of an extraordinary voice my dear, for one who has been trained by a barbarian.'

She looked at him in shock. 'A barbarian?'

'A moron, then. A looker-on; a man who stands in the demi-light of the periphery. Who was this man who taught you?' he asked.

She was suddenly trapped. He was a Jewish teacher who'd left Munich two years previously to go to live in Palestine to escape the Nazis. If Eva gave his name, Herr Helldorp would know instantly that he was Jewish; and that might give her identity away.

'His name is Schneider.' She'd chosen a typically Germanic name.

Herr Helldorp shrugged. 'Never heard of him. As I thought. He's probably a nothing. I've known dozens of men like him. They're all the same; failed tenors or baritones, men of no academic training, teaching pretty little children how to sing a few works of Schubertian *liede*. You're way beyond a man such as him, even at present. Even with your voice untrained, he wouldn't know how to mould a talent like yours. You have an edge to your voice which needs smoothing. Your diaphragm needs strengthening, which exercises will provide. But most importantly my dear, you have an extraordinary clarity and tone. This is something which God gave you. Not some upstart teacher in Munich. With your permission,' he said again turning to Reinholdt, 'I'll take this young lady into the opera with me tomorrow. She will start in the chorus and I'll give her training. I have assistants who will work with each part of her body and voice. One day, with hard work and application, we might even turn this young woman into something outstanding. Another Schwarzkopf.'

Reinholdt stood, grinning ear to ear. Again good fortune had stayed with him. He'd taken a gamble. This could have been a moment of embarrassment in front of an important man; but something about this young woman, something about her innocence, her beauty, her obvious talents, attracted him and together he knew they would do some extraordinary things.

Eva was still in a state of shock.

'Eight-thirty tomorrow morning at the Berlin Opera. You will, of course, be using the stage door,' said Herr Helldorp.

'I don't know what to say,' she gasped.

Herr Helldorp smiled. 'From now on you will say nothing. You will sing. Only sing. The more you practise, the better your voice. There are years of experience which you should have had by your age … these will need to be made up in the next six months. But you'll do it, my dear. With your connections' … He turned and glanced at Reinholdt, '… and with my assistance, you'll have a lifetime's experience of opera before Christmas. It'll be gruelling, but stay the course, and you'll succeed.'

'Will I be paid?' she asked.

He burst out laughing. 'I'm not the one with whom you must discuss your wages. As *repetiteur*, I'm not part of management. But that mustn't concern you. My word is powerful when it comes to the selection of new singers. Let's just say that if I recommend you, you'll be paid.'

'How much?' she asked again.

He was surprised by the tone of the question. 'Is this an issue?' he asked. 'You're being offered an opportunity which thousands of young men and women would kill for; to sing at the Berlin State Opera. You're an unknown. You have no history and you're worried about money!'

Reinholdt walked over and stood by her side. 'My dear Herr Helldorp, I think you have to understand that Fräulein Schmidt has been unemployed for a long time and is desperate for an income. Of course she's grateful to you, immensely grateful. Who wouldn't be? But please, Eva,' he said turning to her, putting his arm around her bare shoulders, 'allow me to negotiate your salary. You just concentrate on learning and singing and becoming a great diva.'

She flushed at the gentle rebuke and turned to Herr Helldorp. 'Forgive me. I've had a very bad time recently. This is the first bit of truly great fortune which I have enjoyed. All thanks to Herr Stricher. But in your opinion, sir, how far do you think I can go?'

He shrugged. He closed the piano's lid and stood. Even standing he was a head shorter than Reinholdt. 'It's impossible to say,' he answered curtly. 'If you wanted,

I could make you wild and absurd promises, but they would only raise up your expectations. Still, you do have a very powerful and rich voice. There's no reason why you shouldn't rise to the top, but only your talent will take you any further than you are today. No amount of teaching and techniques can assist you if you're not willing to put in the practise. How far? Well, I will say this. Work hard, eat well, plenty of exercise, unbelievable amounts of practise, and you could be singing Brunnhilde in Bayreuth in four or five years.'

Reinholdt felt his chest swell in pride.

Herr Helldorp's wife looked at her watch. 'Come,' she said. 'It's getting late and we have an early start in the morning and this young lady has to get a good night's sleep if she is to sing for you. So, my dear young people. I thank you for a wonderful dinner and again, Herr Stricher, our thanks for ensuring that our headstrong son continues to remain well and doesn't get into too much trouble.'

Eva and Reinholdt saw their guests to the door. They walked back into the lounge room. Reinholdt yawned. It was nearly eleven. He was tired. He had had several late nights recently and wanted a good night's sleep.

'Well,' he said. 'You certainly made an impression.'

'I don't know what to say,' said Eva, still in a state of shock, sitting at the dinner table and with her fingers picking up sultanas which had dropped onto the plate from the remnants of the apple strudel. 'I don't think you'll ever know how grateful I am to you. A break like this, well, I just couldn't have done it on my own.'

'Contacts,' said Reinholdt. 'That's what it's all about.' He yawned again. 'Anyway, leave the dishes. Frau Hochstetter will clear up in the morning. Good night,' he said. He kissed her on the top of the head and walked down the corridor.

She looked at the mantlepiece and saw the pictures of him in his SA uniform. She saw the swastika on the pennant above the fireplace. She was so confused. He was everything she had ever hoped to meet. Articulate, intelligent, gentle, generous, funny, perceptive. He had done more for her than any other human being except her mother and father. Nobody had shown her this kindness and yet he had still made no move towards her, no overtures of romance. He had been the model of German chivalry.

After three days, she was convinced that he wasn't playing a game with her. Only two nights earlier, she clearly heard the voice of a young woman, giggling somewhere in the apartment. Even a cursory ear at her locked door told her that the noise was coming from his bedroom. So it certainly wasn't sex he was after.

If not sex, then what was it? Why her? She was alone with him in his apartment. He had told her she could stay as long as necessary, until she had enough money of her own. And from the looks of it, that would be soon.

Not that they had spent much time together. By the time she got up in the morning he had often gone to work. He returned late and then spent time writing letters, listening to the radio, reading newspapers. Often at night, he went out. It was ten or eleven o'clock when he left, and he didn't come back until the early hours. And he was gone again when she was awake. She had only seen him four or five times during the few days she had lived in his apartment. He had been courteous, even charming but never once had he touched her. His kiss tonight, a friendly almost brotherly kiss, and putting his arm around her, were the first occasions that he had put his hand on her since they first met in the cabaret.

Perhaps he didn't find her attractive. Perhaps he preferred fair-haired, blue-eyed girls. She was the very opposite: coal–black eyes, chestnut hair. Maybe she was like an exhibit in the zoo, strange and mysterious, yet unappealing when he saw her too close. But if that was the case, why hadn't he kicked her out?

Emotions swept through her body. Emotions she couldn't explain or understand. She was wearing the same red gown as when he had first met her. She had wanted to give it back to Annelise but Reinholdt had sent it to the nearby laundry who had the machinery for waterless cleaning with chemical solvents, so that it would be ready for that night's dinner. She would return it tomorrow. He seemed absorbed with her over the dinner table, laughing and joking and occasionally reaching out as though to touch her. But then just as suddenly, he withdrew his hand.

The first time he'd touched her was when he took the amulet from her hands, the second when he stood and walked over to the piano and put his arm around her shoulder. But then she was in a daze. She didn't realise what was happening. Now he kissed her like Yitzchok kissed her. A brotherly friendly kiss, not the kiss of a lover.

Did she really repel him? Maybe she did. But why? Other men found her attractive; she'd had no shortage of suitors when she lived in Munich, even if they were all poor and without assets. And in Berlin, men were always staring at her. Even the owner of the cabaret had suggested that he 'road test' her; she knew exactly what he meant, and rejected his disgusting suggestion.

Eva found herself walking down the corridor to her room. His room was two doors further down, the bathroom in between them. His door was firmly closed. It was dark at his end of the corridor. She stood outside her room, her heart pounding. Her mind was a confusion of thoughts. She walked towards the bathroom to brush her teeth and wash her face and hands. She stood outside the door. Something stopped her from going in.

That same impulse made her walk towards his door. She had only been in his room once, the first day. She had never been in since. She reached down and grasped the handle. Her heart was thumping, a rush of noise in her ears. It was cool to the touch. It was made of porcelain, just like her doorhandle. She turned it gently. It opened without resistance. The room was in darkness but she knew he was there. She could smell his presence, a strong masculine smell. The curtains were drawn against the streetlights. She heard him breathing. She heard him rustle in his bed.

She knew he could see her shrouded by the light of the doorway although she could hardly see him. She entered his room and closed the door behind her. He didn't say a word. Neither did she. She wanted to ask him why he found her unattractive. She wanted to ask him why a man as lovely and considerate as he was beating up Jews during the day.

She walked over to his bed in the pitch dark. She heard him pull the sheets and blankets back. She felt his warmth, even from a distance. She unzipped her dress and let it slip to the floor. With trembling hands she released herself from the rest of her undergarments. She hesitated momentarily before she took off her underpants and got into bed beside him.

Annelise looked gaunt. It was the middle of the afternoon, but she was still recovering from the previous evening at the cabaret, and the party afterwards which had begun to break up as decent people, those lucky enough to have ordinary jobs, were catching the trams and buses to where they worked.

She had crawled into bed after eating some oatmeal to keep her going so she wouldn't wake up with hunger pangs in the middle of the day; if she could sleep through the day, and only wake up in the early evening, then she could function for another night.

The only good thing about what she had been forced to go through was the money in her pocket. Enough to pay the rent for two months and buy food and clothes. It had been a once-in-a-lifetime event, something which she'd sworn in the taxi home that she'd never, ever do again. A group of elderly American executives from a company called International Combines or something were in town, intent on having a good time after trying to negotiate some deal or other with the German government. For reasons which Annelise still couldn't understand, despite their American dollars, they hadn't chosen to go to one of the fashionable nightclubs, but instead had decided to come into the rather run-down and sordid cabaret in which she worked. Apparently the owner knew the taxi-driver, and he'd recommended it to them as a place where they could get laid, or something.

The moment they walked in from the street, and stood at the landing on the top of the stairs, the owner had been fawning all over them, recognising money when he saw it, and ensuring that the prettiest and most willing girls were made available to the men for the whole night. Annelise had been one of them, agreeing to go along with it just to make up the numbers, making it clear to him that she didn't intend to have sex, American dollars or not.

A party in private rooms had been arranged, which had ended up as an orgy. Annelise had taken part. Even twelve hours later, she still didn't understand herself. For the first time in her life, Annelise had not only taken off all her clothes at the behest of a fat and unattractive American from Minnesota, but had done things to him which she'd vowed she would never do. She hadn't gone all the way; of that, she could at least differentiate herself from the other girls in order to retain some sense of dignity; but what she had done was what the other girls assured her wasn't so bad. She'd closed her eyes, and quickly came to realise that, despite his moaning and groaning, it was as bad as she'd feared.

When she returned home, she'd spent an hour in the bath, rinsing her mouth with salt water, brushing her teeth, washing her hair, scrubbing her nails; finally, at about nine in the morning, she fell into bed, and cried.

Eva's loud knocking on the door had awoken her from a deep slumber. It was three-thirty in the afternoon. She needed at least another four hours sleep so that she wouldn't look like a bedraggled hag for work that evening.

Annelise padded to the door of her apartment painfully and somewhat ponderously, with the gait of an old woman, and shouted huskily, 'Who is it?' Her voice sounded dry and rasping from all the smoke in the room where the orgy had been held.

'Me. Eva. Open up. What's the matter with you? I've been knocking for half an hour.'

Annelise unlatched the three locks on the door and squinted into the hallway. Eva was standing there, surrounded by soft afternoon light, looking glorious. She was wearing an expensive coat and pearls. Her hair was freshly done. She was carefully made up, an expert job obviously done in a salon or a department store. Annelise hadn't seen her looking this good – ever. Her clothes, patent high-heel shoes, an attractive Prussian blue silk dress, made her look like a model from the pages of a fashion magazine. Walking through the streets, she would be a symbol of decadence, of hatred. What the hell was going on? Eva breezed past her into the apartment.

'Darling,' said Eva. 'You look terrible. Are you ill?'

Annelise shook her head and swallowed. 'Make me a cup of coffee,' she mumbled huskily.

Eva waltzed into the kitchen and busied herself clearing pots, moving pans, putting away dry dishes and filling the percolator with coffee and water. She lit the gas flame with a safety match. Coffee would be ready in five minutes.

She walked back in and found Annelise curled up in a chair, her eyes heavy, as if falling asleep. 'It's the middle of the afternoon. What in God's name is wrong? Are you sure you're not ill?'

Annelise shook her head. 'It was a bitch of a night. I didn't get in until past seven this morning. What do you want? Why are you so happy and breezy, and where did you get the clothes? Is your young gentleman paying for everything?'

Although her voice was croaking, she couldn't mask the contempt. And then she suddenly felt an overwhelming sense of guilt. How could she possibly moralise after last night? She smiled at Eva and stood up, her legs feeling shaky. She walked over to where Eva was standing, and threw her arms around her.

'I'm sorry. I had no right to say what I just said. You look fabulous. You're a lucky girl. So, tell me about him.'

'What's to tell?' said Eva. 'He's kind, considerate, loving.'

'And generous,' said Annelise. 'Those clothes must have cost a fortune. How come he's so rich?'

'He isn't. He comes from ordinary parents and ordinary family. But the guy he works for, Ernst Röhm, gets lots of money from German industrialists and he spends it very freely on people that he's fond of, and that are part of the movement. He's set up a lot of young men in apartments and given them spending money. Their job is to go out and recruit new people.'

'New people for what?' asked Annelise quizzically. 'Röhm? He's the SA. He's the bastard that's killing people on the streets. I don't understand. What's your man got to do with Röhm?'

Eva bit her lip. Softly, like admitting guilt, she said, 'Reinholdt is in the SA. You were in the apartment. You must have seen the swastikas.'

'I thought it was a joke. It didn't occur to me … I wasn't there more than a minute … I just thought … I mean … I thought he was making fun of the thugs. You're living with a Nazi thug? He knows you're Jewish?'

Eva shook her head slowly, in guilt. 'I call myself Schmidt.'

Fully awake, Annelise stared at her friend in horror. 'You're mad,' said Annelise. 'All he has to do is examine your background, look at your papers. He'll kill you. These men are killers,' she began to shout. 'You think they're playing toy soldiers. These bastards go out onto the streets every night and beat up anybody that stands in their way. They break shop windows, steal, fight with the police. They're scaring the shit out of the whole of Berlin and you're living with one of them. Are you mental?'

'That's what I came to talk to you about. Reinholdt isn't like that. He's different. He must be in another branch or division or something. He's so kind to me. He's got me a position in the opera. It's what I've always wanted to do. I auditioned last week for Herr Helldorp, the *repetiteur*. I'm now singing full-time in the chorus and I'm having private voice training and acting instruction without any cost to me from some of the best voice trainers in Germany. Without cost, Annelise! They're talking about me being able to sing a minor solo role next season. Do you know what that means? In two years time, I could be Aida or Violetta.'

'In two years time you could be dead, you fool,' Annelise screamed. 'This man is a killer. He's a fucking killer. Of Jews.'

'He isn't!' shouted Eva back, her face reddening in the embarrassment of the confrontation.

'Then why are you here? What do you want? Permission to fuck him? Approval from me so that you can have his Nazi bastard baby?'

She heard the noise of the coffee percolator bubbling and fuming; Eva retreated quickly into the kitchen, away from Annelise's indignation and fury. A minute later, she returned with two cups of black coffee. They sat down, both keen for the anger between them to dissipate. Neither wanted to fight. Their once-intimate friendship had diminished into an unwelcome coldness since Eva had left the apartment, and both were keen to revitalise it.

'What I want is papers. Papers like yours. Papers which say I'm a Christian.'

'You're a fool,' said Annelise. 'You're blind. You're incapable of seeing the danger you're in. Your mind has been clouded as you've been swept along by your sudden good fortune. Your stomach is full, your body is clothed, you sleep at night in clean sheets. Wonderful … but remember Eva, that you're sleeping with a killer.'

'I'm not!' Eva yelled.

Annelise was shocked by Eva's vehemence. And then something struck her with the violence of a punch. Annelise scrutinised Eva's face. Softly, as though what she was saying was an incantation to the devil, she whispered, 'God Almighty, you're in love with him, aren't you?'

Eva remained silent.

'Aren't you!' Annelise shouted.

Eva nodded silently.

'He's killing our people. He's killing Jews. He's killing communists. Anybody that's old, or crippled, or mental.

Or who's queer. Haven't you read the papers? Don't you know what these bastards are doing in the street, or are you closing your eyes to it for the sake of your own convenience?'

Tears welled up in Eva's eyes. She nodded. 'I don't know what to do,' she said softly. 'My life has never been so wonderful. I think he actually likes me very much. He could have any woman he wants. Any woman in Berlin. Yet he wants me. He's handsome and strong and he's intelligent. He's everything. I love him.' Eva sobbed.

'You only love him because he's an answer to your problems. Because he's sheltering you, clothing you. You're shutting your eyes to the fact that he's a Nazi,' Annelise shouted, this time louder. She had no intention of going soft on her friend just because she was riven by emotions. This was life and death. Eva's, and everybody with whom Eva was associated.

'He's not like the other Nazis,' Eva said softly, sobbing into her hands.

'You're not looking at the truth.'

'And you? Aren't you closing your eyes to what you've become?' said Eva. Annelise remained silent. 'Aren't you a whore? Aren't you sleeping with Nazis and dirty old men and adulterers. Can you write to your mother and father in Mannheim and tell them honestly what you're doing? We all lead a double life. All of us. There's no room for truth in Germany any more. Anybody who tells the truth gets beaten up. So what can we do? All we have left to us is the right to survive. That's all I'm trying to do. Survive.'

The moment she'd said it, Eva saw the hurt in her friend's face. But why should she let up about the sort of things Annelise did to survive? Annelise had said horrible things about her. Now she should be confronted with the truth. Eva dabbed her eyes with a handkerchief. 'We can go along with it and live comfortably or walk in peril in the streets, like Jews throughout history, always being on the outside. I know what I'd rather do. I'd rather live a lie and live on the inside of society where it's warm, and where I'm fed and clothed, and where I don't have to sleep with cockroaches and lizards. And where I don't have to put up with filthy old men who put their hands on my breasts and make me feel dirty. I'm sorry that the Nazis are so evil. I'm sorry they're telling these lies about us. But I'm one woman, Annelise. I can't stand up to the whole world.'

Annelise sighed. The coffee was clearing her head. She nodded slowly. 'Just keep your eyes open all the while, for God's sake. Use him. Let him do things for you, not to you. Let him introduce you to important people. Let him give you money and clothes but all the time, remember who you are and where you've come from. The higher up the ladder you climb, the more dangerous the step and the more perilous the fall. Because if you make one slip-up, everything will come out, and God help you then. And God help me and all your friends.'

'You?'

'Of course me. And all the other Jews and communists who are hiding from the Nazis. What you're doing is putting not only yourself at risk, but everyone else. If you're caught, you don't think they'll stop at you, do you? They'll trace each and every one of your friends and family.'

'But…'

Annelise shook her head in sadness at the naivety of her friend. 'What you'll need is rock-solid identification. The sort which will pass all sorts of scrutiny.'

'The papers. How will I get the papers?' asked Eva.

Annelise smiled. 'The circles I move in aren't quite as glorious as yours. There's sharks and criminals who breeze into and out of the cabaret. I can get you papers easily.'

Eva sighed in relief. 'Thank God,' she said. 'With papers I can talk my way out of any situation.'

Annelise shrugged. 'Papers are papers. Nothing more. Even people with the right papers are being arrested and hauled off the streets.'

'But papers will stop questions being asked if a policeman or an SA man reads them. He'll see I'm a good German Lutheran *hausfrau* or something. He'll leave me alone.'

'Do you look like a Lutheran *hausfrau*, Eva?' asked Annelise. 'Look at you. You're beautiful. Dark-haired, flashing eyes, dark skin. You're the archetypal semite. You're like Judith or Rebecca or Leah in the Bible. You could fool a Rabbi for ten seconds and a Nazi for ten minutes, but no more. You're playing a game of life and death, you idiot.'

Eva ignored her friend. She wasn't interested. All she wanted was the papers. 'Will you get me the papers?'

'Yes,' said Annelise in resignation. 'What name?'

'Schmidt. It's the name I'm already using. Eva Schmidt.'

'Couldn't you think up anything more imaginative than Schmidt?'

Eva shrugged.

'Okay, Schmidt it is. How about you're the daughter of Wilhelm and Trude Schmidt of Munich?'

Eva nodded and smiled gratefully.

'Money? It'll cost plenty.'

'Don't let money worry you. Reinholdt gives me lots to buy clothes and underwear and food and stuff. So long as I show off in a couple of new outfits, he'll never notice the difference.'

Annelise shrugged indifferently.

'And that means that there's plenty for you and Gerte. I've got enough so that you don't have to work in that damned nightclub anymore. And I can support Gerte until she finds more work in the movies. I've got my own income starting soon from the opera, and with what Reinholdt gives me, there's more than enough to go around.'

Annelise looked at her strangely. Every instinct told her to reject the offer, but she'd do anything to get out of that place. She remained silent.

A frown crossed Eva's forehead. 'Do you really think they could ever trace me with false papers?' she asked plaintively.

'Of course they could; and then you're in deep shit. They can trace you and anybody else they please. Give them reason and they'll certainly trace you. Then you'll be dead. That's the game you're playing, Eva.'

Her friend's mood sagged with the enormity of the way in which her life had suddenly dichotomised; outside of Annelise, Eva's life was suddenly rich and happy; but the moment she came into her friend's umbra, she was confronted with the enormity of the risks she was taking, risks which she hourly denied to herself. And all Eva wanted to do was to make life easier for herself.

'Look, Eva darling,' Annelise said gently. 'It's not too late. Why not come back here and live with Gerte and me. Life won't be so comfortable, but now you've got a job singing ...'

'How quickly would I lose that job if I left Reinholdt?'

'You told me you're a good singer. You told me they think highly of you. Why should they worry who you're living with?'

'Elizabeth Schwarzkopf supports the Nazis. Herbert von Karajan supports the Nazis. Many Berlin musicians and people in the opera support them. I wouldn't last a minute if Reinholdt said I should be dropped.'

'But there are huge numbers of Jews who play in the Berlin Philharmonic and the opera and places like that.'

'Many have already left, and those that haven't are thinking about leaving. Some have even been replaced or kicked out because of pressure from *Gauleiter* Goebbels and the SA. And it'll just get worse. You've no idea how much pressure these Nazis put on businesses and the opera and the music establishment. You'd think they were the government. Anybody who doesn't support them soon finds out about it. Performances disrupted by men standing up and booing when a Jewish performer comes on stage; film sets disrupted by strange breakdowns, by klieg lights being pushed over; it's everywhere.

'The film industry's probably feeling the pressure more than most. All the great Jewish directors and producers and cameramen are thinking about leaving to go to Hollywood. They've seen the writing on the wall. They think the Nazis are going to win at the next elections.

'There's every chance they will. Then it won't just be shouting and screaming. Then it'll get truly murderous,' said Annelise.

Eva shook her head. 'The Germans will never vote in the Nazis. Sure, they're strong at the moment but they'll never allow them to govern. It just couldn't happen and as soon as the money thing settles down in America, the world will get back to normal. Then Reinholdt will get a job teaching in university or as an engineer. He'll build bridges and railways. He'll stop all this SA nonsense. He'll come to his senses.'

'Sure,' said Annelise. 'Maybe he'll convert to Judaism and marry you. Who knows?'

CHAPTER FOURTEEN

FRANKFURT, PRESENT DAY

Sarah waited until Annelise had recovered from a bout of coughing before she continued to ask her questions. Terrified of straining the old lady, Sarah was even more terrified of not being able to extract any further information from her, especially about this mysterious South American, Ricardo Padrone.

Annelise looked pale. Gaunt. She lay back on her pillow, wearing the signs of age and infirmity as her body seemed to make hardly any impression on the bed. Perhaps she should go, leave the old lady to continue to recover from the strains of telling the history of Sarah's grandmother.

In just a few hours, she'd learned more about her origins than in all the days of her adult life. Sarah had never been particularly interested in her family history. Her lack of interest originated with her grandmother's continual response.

'Don't ask. You don't want to know.'

'What happened to Grandpa?' 'Don't ask, *bubeleh*. You don't want to know.'

'What happened in the war, Grandma?' 'Don't ask *bubeleh*. You don't want to know.'

Even when she asked her own mother about her family origins, her mother brought up the same diet of maternal indifference to family history and gave Sarah the same response. 'You've got no idea how hard times were back then. When I was a little girl, my mother could hardly speak the language. Right from the beginning, I felt like a stranger; in school with no father and a mother for whom I had to translate what the teachers said to me. You've got no idea how difficult things were, Sarah. Don't ask. Thank God you're living in a world like we are today.'

And so, Sarah's natural curiosity about her origins was constrained by both lack of information and willingness to share. Up until the time she went to Slovakia with Josh Krantz. Then she was told by an archaeologist that the amulet she wore so proudly was not just a family heirloom but a piece of Bronze Age jewellery dug up from a grave by her grandfather Nussan, which had caused his death in a pogrom.

Annelise coughed again but opened her eyes and smiled. Sarah smiled back and reached over to hold her hand.

'Do you want that I should go?' asked Sarah.

The old lady shook her head. 'No, because we're coming to the important bit now, about your grandmother and me. The part where the Nazis begin to take over Germany. I suppose you know about that period from reading about it in history?'

Sarah nodded.

Annelise shook her head in mock contempt. 'Then let me tell you. You know nothing. You couldn't begin to understand the nightmare of the streets, the fear in everybody's mind. Things happened that were straight out of a horror story, but they happened to us and to your grandmother. May God rest her soul.'

BERLIN, 1933

The days were passing with unnerving, indeed stupendous rapidity. For Eva, the days were performing like an operetta by Franz Lehár, she the heroine; different ballgowns, nightly social events where handsome young men clicked their heels and nodded to her as she walked towards the buffet, Reinholdt sweeping her off her chair and onto a dance floor, parties at which jovial elderly men in uniform were surrounded by young acolytes who burst out laughing uproariously at every second or third remark. Such happiness. Such frivolity.

Such an unbelievable contrast with what was happening in the streets of Berlin. As Eva and Reinholdt drove from party to party, being swept up into the rarefied echelons of Berlin's military and political life, the dark and frightening streets were littered with broken bones, crushed skulls, fractured windows, signs daubed in hate and anger and the gutters littered with blood-stained leaflets proclaiming who the hidden enemy really was.

Occasionally Eva still stooped to pick up the leaflets from the gutter. She was increasingly mortified that she was identified as one of the hidden enemy, one of the people who was gnawing away at the very innards of the German Republic.

From early on in their relationship, Eva had forced Reinholdt into an agreement. She begged him not to talk about his work or the Jewish, communist conspiracy when they were at home together. She pleaded with him that even though she realised how important it was, she wasn't a political woman. She was a singer and as a singer, she had to focus her mind entirely upon eighteenth and nineteenth century music, manners, and mores. Even thinking about Adolf Hitler and the SA and the Nazis and the Jews and the communists, she pleaded, would distract her.

Unhappily, Reinholdt had agreed. He was disappointed. She could have been his star pupil if ever she grew so prestigious, a famous diva; then she would be the prime example of the new Germany, the Fascist Germany, Nazi

Germany. She could hold her head up in international circles as the very best that the German state had to offer. She had done her best to smile apologetically, to beg him to understand her complete and total lack of interest in politics. She even paid him the ultimate compliment of subsuming her identity within his, to show him her gratitude and love. She was no longer Eva Schmidt. She was Eva Stricher, married in all respects other than a wedding. And this time, he'd willingly paid for her new set of papers.

He had even once asked her seriously whether she had sympathies towards Jews or homosexuals or communists. She laughed dismissively and refrained from commenting. It was the most honest answer she had ever given him on the subject. But he insisted. He drew her out. He was insulted by his partner's lack of understanding of the inner political philosophies which coursed around his mind.

'I neither like nor dislike them. I neither approve nor condemn them. I have no feelings one way or the other. Once I was Eva Schmidt; now I'm Eva Stricher. That's all I am. All I want to be is your lover and a great singer. Outside of that, I have no life, nor do I want a life.'

And they had grown together, closer and closer. He seeking companionship and fulfilment in her; she, from him, security and entree into an otherwise menacing and forbidden society.

One Sunday night in the middle of winter, the weather had been freezing cold. Slush lay in the streets and the bulbous clouds hanging menacingly over the city, dark and grey, were full of snow and ice waiting to blanket Berlin. It was already dark when they left their apartment and drove along the crowded, cheerless streets to the home of a Wehrmacht general, a man who was sympathetic to the growing importance of the SA as a domestic army of law and order. The general was cultivating ties between the army, the government, and the more intellectual of the organisation's leaders. He had arranged a typical Berlin party and even though Reinholdt was wearing civilian clothes, as the local ordinances had banned the wearing of the SA uniform, most of the other men were dressed magnificently in the various ranks of the German armed forces. There were naval men in their gleaming tunics, army men wearing the colours of the earth and members of the Luftwaffe looking like the sky, stunning in their braids and medals.

As always, Eva stayed close to Reinholdt. She never felt a part of an occasion such as this until she had had a couple of drinks and relaxed into the night. But even so, she never drank so much that her tongue was left unguarded. Over supper, standing holding his plate and relaxing near one of the columns in the ballroom of the house, Reinholdt was speaking to a colonel in an infantry division, a man whose charming and good-natured conversation made Eva feel instantly at ease. He was fascinated by her desire to become part of the opera and confessed his love for dramatic music.

'My mother was an opera singer,' he said. 'Well, she was in the chorus of the Prague State Opera before she married my father and moved to Germany.'

'Ah,' said Eva. 'A soprano? Contralto?'

'She used to be a soprano but unfortunately with age her voice has deepened. She no longer sings except on private family occasions.'

'Your mother was from Prague?' Reinholdt said, a stiffness overcoming his body. 'She's a Slav?'

'A Bohemian,' corrected the colonel. It was as if he knew that the question would arrive, as though he had deliberately introduced the issue for Reinholdt's reaction. 'And you might also be interested in the fact that she's a Jew,' he said. For much of their conversation, the colonel's eyes had darted to the rubber band wrapped around one of the upper buttons of Reinholdt's dress shirt, the only way in which SA men were able to signify their membership of the organisation. 'Of course, you may have a problem with that, Herr Stricher, but that's your problem, not mine.'

'Germany has a problem with that, Herr Oberst. If your mother is a Jew, then by definition, you are a Jew.'

'You make it sound like a disease, Herr Stricher.'

'It is a disease. It's a cancer which is eating away at the body of Germany. The Jews must be eradicated. They must be shipped to another land, expelled from Germany.'

The colonel shook his head in sorrow. 'I've read your leaflets. They're pathetic. They say more about you and people like you, Herr Stricher, than they say about me and my religion. Jews have had a long and generally very happy relationship with Germany which goes back a thousand years. Luther tried to squash us and failed. Tinpot dictators in principalities all over Prussia and Bavaria and other parts of the Austro-Hungarian empire have tried to finish us off, but failed. Why do you think that the rabble that you lead has any chance of success?'

Reinholdt bridled. 'This is a cocktail party. I have no intention of embarrassing my host by taking this matter further. Nor do I intend to sully myself or my companion by remaining in your company.' Reinholdt nodded curtly, dismissively, and turned.

'Come Eva,' he said. But she didn't. For an instant, she delayed, looking in astonishment at the Jewish colonel. It lasted only for a fraction of a moment, but long enough for him to smile at her, a gentle understanding smile. She flushed in embarrassment and turned to walk away. But before she did, she delayed another instant. She looked at Reinholdt. He was already halfway across the room when the colonel whispered in her ear, 'There seems to be a depth of empathy in you which isn't present in your companion. Don't be fooled by the rhetoric, my dear. Listen to your heart.'

Again he smiled and nodded in encouragement. Did he know? Was he going to be the agent of her undoing? Eva blanched and turned away from him, her body stiff with anguish; she walked rapidly away from her conscience.

Later that night, they were in bed. Reinholdt was almost asleep. He always slept quickly after they had made love. Normally Eva was an enthusiastic participant. Tonight she had merely been a vehicle for his orgasm, a convenient receptacle for his desires, his frustrations, his fears, his triumphs. She heard him breathing regularly, with increasing depth. She wanted to talk to him about tonight. She wanted to ask him why he had such a hatred towards Jews when Herr Oberst at the cocktail party was probably one of the few Jews he had ever known. She didn't understand. For months she had closed her eyes to the reality that was her lover; she was singing in the chorus of the Berlin State Opera thanks to him; she was warm when the streets were freezing, thanks to him; her belly was full when the starving had aching bodies and rumbling stomachs; she was lying beside a man who she knew genuinely loved her, whom she genuinely loved, except …

Except … why did he hate her people so much? It was at that moment that an overwhelming feeling of shame swept through her body. It began in her heart. It flushed her face. It made her feet and legs leaden with remorse. She was lying beside a man who hated everything about her except the mask which she showed him. She was nothing more than veneer, a figurine, a pretty oil painting, a representation of what he wanted. There was nothing about reality in their relationship. She had become a *golem*, a soulless thing, a creation like Dr Frankenstein's monster, made in desperation, living in fear of undoing. Where was the true Eva? How deeply had she allowed the true Eva to be buried? Just for convenience. Just for food and warmth and safety. How could she look at herself in the mirror? And when she did, whose face did she see? She hardly slept that night. In the early hours of the morning, she drifted into a troubled series of dreams from which she emerged before the sun had arisen.

Over breakfast, she said to Reinholdt, 'I'm going to Munich today.'

He looked at her in surprise. 'Aren't you in the middle of a rehearsal?'

'I had a telephone call yesterday from a friend who's sick. I promised to visit her.'

'Why didn't you tell me?'

'I'm sorry. I forgot. I've only just made up my mind anyway. I want to go back to Munich to see her and to see other people. I'll be back in a couple of days.'

Reinholdt shrugged and went back to reading *Der Angriff*.

Eva packed only a dozen or so things for the journey, leaving behind almost all of the clothes that Reinholdt had bought her hanging in her wardrobe. When she had begun living with him, when she came in off the cold and lonely streets with just a suitcase, she had brought almost nothing to the relationship. When she first arrived in Berlin, in an effort to survive, Eva had been forced to sell most of the things she'd taken from Munich. Her remaining clothes had been so dowdy and lifeless that she had tossed them out as soon as her wardrobe began to fill with silk underwear, stockings, beautiful tops and skirts as well as leather shoes and ballgowns. There was almost nothing left of the old Eva. Pragmatically, on leaving, she chose the most conservative of all the garments. She couldn't go to Munich naked.

She closed the door on the apartment and on her life of falsehood and walked down the stairs to the street to catch a taxi. Reinholdt had already gone to his office. He had kissed her, given her money for the journey and enough to tide her over while she was in Munich. She kissed him back and thanked him for everything he'd done for her. He was in a rush and so he didn't think about the remark. It was the last time she intended to see him.

As she arrived at the street, Eva didn't even look back towards the apartment. She felt no nostalgia, no fondness. She had no feelings towards it. It was a necessary part of her life. It was now over. There was relief and shame. But mainly a turning of her back, a finalisation of the life she'd been forced to live. For the first time since she had moved to Berlin, she felt something approaching a sense of pride, a sense of self. She was discarding the mask, the career, the lover, the life and going back to her reality.

A taxi pulled up. She got into the cab and drove to the train station. It was as crowded as when she'd stepped off the Munich train into the bustle of Banhoffstrasse, but now she was leaving the city, there seemed to be more people, more depression, than there had been when she arrived. Then she had been full of hope in her flight from Berlin; now she was leaving, she was full of pride at her decision.

These days, her life often seemed to be riven by conflicting emotions. Now, though, her emotions were quite clear. There was no sadness at leaving the city. Now she was full of emotions of self-respect. When she left her home, she had escaped the beatings and brutality of Munich. She had hoped to find security in Berlin. But what she'd found was security within a milieu of evil. It wasn't for her. She needed her family, and now she was returning to Frau Büchbinder's house, to her parents downstairs and to all the dangers that she knew Munich was suffering. She was leaving behind her career as an opera singer; she was leaving a man who truly loved her.

But now she would again be Eva Arpel; she would no longer be Eva Schmidt or Eva Stricher; now again she would be a real person, herself, the woman of whom she was most proud. And when she was secure again as herself, she'd get Annelise and Gerte out of the city, and they'd all emigrate … she and her family and her friends. And they'd go and live in Palestine. Or somewhere.

He missed her. He missed her at breakfast. He missed her delightful irreverent humour, her intelligence, her beauty. Even in the morning, she was beautiful. Most people looked dreadful in the morning, but not Eva. Her eyes were always bright, her skin glowing and pink from a good night's sleep. They made love every night except when she had a period. She was squeamish about that. He wasn't. Sometimes they made love in the morning. She would languidly stretch her warm naked body against him, lifting her leg so that it covered his groin. She was still half asleep but the heat of her body and the ease of her availability excited him. He would feel himself becoming erect and then without any resistance or complaint or regret, she would allow him to slip into her and she would moan as she felt his orgasm. Sometimes she fell asleep again underneath, or on top of his body. She was like a big, cuddly pet at these moments, the ideal uncomplaining, ultimate indulgence.

As Reinholdt Stricher sat in his office listening to Ernst Röhm and Julius Lippert and the other senior members of the SA talk about the forthcoming plans, his mind kept drifting back to his wife in all but name, his Eva. She wouldn't marry him, the idiot. She would have total security in him, in the new Reich, in the future. She wouldn't even introduce him to her family. She was too ashamed of the fact that she was no longer a virgin and that she was living with a man. He smiled. Her parents must be ogres in this day and age to be critical of a daughter who wasn't a virgin in her twenties. Unbelievable!

'Are you listening to me, Stricher?' demanded the rasping voice.

Reinholdt looked up in surprise. Röhm had asked him a pointed question.

'I'm sorry, Herr *Stabschef*. My mind was elsewhere,' Reinholdt said to the Chief of Staff of the SA.

'Your mind cannot afford to be elsewhere, Stricher. This is not kindergarten. We're dealing with issues of life and death. For God's sake, pay attention. Now, I was talking about clearing up the Jews and the communists who live in the north of Berlin. I can give you six thousand men. I asked whether you would have a battle plan ready by tonight. Streets; apartment buildings; houses; escape routes for the fucking Jews. Well?'

Reinholdt nodded. 'Of course, Herr *Stabschef*. It would be my privilege.'

'Never mind about privilege, Stricher. Get your act together or I'll take you off the command. There's plenty of other young men who would happily replace you.'

Stung by the rebuke, Stricher looked down at the floor. The others felt for him. He was one of the more popular of the young commanders. And unlike most, who were uneducated and unemployed, they looked to him as the intellectual of the group because he had a university education. If only he hadn't been thinking of Eva.

The meeting continued for another hour and then broke up. Reinholdt spent the rest of that day with his men as well as most of the following day, drawing up plans of attack; how many men would enter which streets, who would enter the houses first; what to do if they met armed resistance; how they would gather and beat the enemy to a pulp, how they would fend off police provocation if any arose; what to do if the army intervened; how to deal with Jewish resistance groups, if any; whether there were any members left of the Communist KPD or the Red Front Line Fighters League in that area.

By four o'clock that afternoon he had a fully comprehensive plan. They met again in Röhm's office. Just the commanders. Reinholdt had agreed to present the entirety of the SA's battle plan on behalf of all the other leaders. He was the best presenter in headquarters. He could remember and marshal the facts. They happily allowed him the privilege. By the end of the presentation, Röhm had forgotten the tiff of the previous day. He beamed at his young protégé.

'Brilliant,' he said. 'Absolutely brilliant, Reinholdt. Good, so 0800 hours tomorrow, we begin.'

It was a particularly cold morning for March. Indeed, much of winter 1933 had been freezing; colder than most could remember. Steam was on the breaths of the men and the horses; exhaust was visible coming out of the cars as they sat angry, waiting to roar into action. The men were in shirts and coats and caps; no one wore uniform; even the rubber bands were missing.

They gathered in the streets surrounding the northern area. They closed off through traffic with barricades. Angry motorists who used their horns to complain about the unofficial diversions were dragged from their cars by men called SA Traffic Police and had the realities of life explained to them. Grasping their groins, their eyes watering, they got back into their cars and sat still, trying to catch their breath. Traffic became quiet around the area, unnaturally quiet.

At 8.15 Reinholdt looked at his watch and gave the order to move. A thousand men behind him slowly walked into the area inhabited by Jews. It was so easy to tell their houses. They all had these signs on the door posts, *Magen Davids*. Some mystical symbol identifying Jews to other Jews. It would make things much easier. His men fanned out and walked down the length of seven of the roads and stood on each of their sides. Another thousand entered, then another thousand, until five thousand of his men were in position. It was a huge number, but the size of the area seemed to swallow them up.

Sub-commanders gave him reports, sending couriers riding around the district on motor bikes. Against his wishes, Röhm had ordered him to view the whole operation from an open staff car. Röhm had seen the effect on the troops when Hitler had done the same thing. Strangely, it made Reinholdt feel proud, his groin stirring but not for the reason that the recalcitrant drivers were now massaging their groins.

Eight-thirty. Time when Jews would start to emerge and walk to work. He took out a pistol and fired a single shot into the air. It reverberated up and down the unnaturally quiet streets. The Jews, of course, knew what was happening. Curtains had been flapping for the last hour. The residents were well aware that something was going on and many had phoned the police … only to be told that no police were able to be spared to come to their aid.

Reinholdt didn't give a damn that the residents knew what was going to happen. They were trapped like rabbits in burrows. He watched his men run into nominated Jewish houses, identified by the signpost of their door lintels. He watched until the first Jews were pulled out into the streets. Men, women, children; it didn't matter. They were all fodder for his cannons. A screaming began. Hysterical, guttural shouts of anger. He saw women in dresses thrown into gutters, pulled up by the hair, truncheons smashing down on shoulders. Men dressed in their business suits set upon by his troops. Wealthy businessmen dressed in their silks and fineries and their gold watch fobs showing proudly, being beaten up by young unemployed Germans who had been thrown out of work because of the Jews of America and capitalism. It was just reward.

He turned to his driver. 'Move,' he said. The driver knew where to go. The car weaved in and out of the writhing mass of his troops, as they beat the shit out of the residents. He turned right into a nearby street, fewer of his men were there, but those that were carrying out his orders were just as ruthless. The whole area was alive with beatings. And then he heard the band. Röhm had ordered the *Horst Wessel* be played in the streets loudly over the noise of Jewish tears. Wonderful. He stood in the back of the car like Hitler driving along, gripping the handrail; but unlike those occasions when the Führer drove through the throng, here were no adoring crowds; but this was just as much a Nazi Party rally ... an SA rally. There were no shining faces, eyes wide in excitement, seeing their leader, arms raised high in the Nazi salute, screaming out '*Seig Heil.*' There was nothing like that for him. Just occasional grins from his troops as they straightened up and adjusted their clothing over the moaning forms of their victims. The occasional wave. He even merited a salute from one young eager man. He didn't know how Hitler felt; but Reinholdt felt good. He felt so damned good.

MUNICH, 1933

The house was the same, but different. It was as if somehow the spirit of the house was gone, and all that was left was bricks and mortar; as if the house had died. The life and vitality which had once made the house so welcoming had gone from it. Had left its windows, its paintwork, it's facias and facades.

Eva stood beside her suitcases on the street, looking up at the house where she had been born; where she had grown into maturity, into womanhood. Where had the house in which she had been a maid from the day she left school disappeared? The house where Herr and Frau Büchbinder had loved her like a daughter, had brought her into dinner parties and asked her to perform complex Schubertian *lieder* or Mozart arias. The house where she had first thrilled to the seduction of applause, had seen faces light up with genuine affection at her resonant voice. It was the house to which she had thrilled to bring friends, admitting that while she lived downstairs in a comfortable basement apartment, the real household lived upstairs among a family which was the scion of Munich's large Jewish community. Pride by association.

When she left Munich to live in Berlin, she had harboured a deeply buried secret desire; to return to the house as an equal with the Büchbinders and their children, as a famous opera singer or successful screen actress. She was so talented in both areas. Her beautiful lithe body and pretty face could have enraptured German audiences in the movies ... and her extraordinary voice would have thrilled those whose tastes were more refined. But in the end she had chosen opera. It was fortune, or ... what was that American word? ... serendipity.

She picked up the case and walked up the stairs to the house. There was dust in the corners of the granite risers. Frau Büchbinder would normally never allow dust to gather. The windows in the front rooms were dirty. Something was wrong. Something was out of order. She knocked on the door, too frightened to go around the side of the house and down into her own parent's domain. And then she noticed with a sense of deep shock that the mezzuzah, the little box containing Jewish prayers which adorned the doorpost of every Jewish home throughout the world, was missing. Its place had been taken by fresh paint. The house's Jewish identity was no more. But what about the injunction from Chapter 6 of the Book of Deuteronomy?

'And thou shalt bind these words for a sign upon
thine hand, and they shall be for frontlets between
thine eyes. And thou shalt write them upon the door
posts of thy house, and upon thy gates.'

And then it struck her with an awful clarity. The house was hiding from the rest of Munich. The people inside, once fiercely proud of their heritage, were trying to remain inconspicuous, hiding from those around them … just as she had hidden from herself in Berlin. Well, not any more!

If only she'd called her mother and father before coming, the shock wouldn't have been as great. Her whole childhood, the security of her youth, her memories, were undercut, devalued. At least she would have been prepared if she'd told somebody in advance that she was returning. But she hadn't. And why hadn't she telephoned her mother to say she was coming home? Because it was an on-the-spot decision. And before she saw her mother and father, she wanted to talk to Frau

Büchbinder to see if it was alright to come home. It was odd. She phoned her mother less these days. There was a disappointment she could hear in her mother's voice. She felt closer at the moment to Frau Büchbinder.

She knocked on the door a second time. Again, this was odd. Normally the door was opened almost straight away by one of the upstairs maids. She heard a scuffling of feet. An elderly woman in a black dress opened the door just enough for her face and neck to appear, disembodied. She left the door securely fastened on the chain. Eva didn't recognise her. For a moment she thought she might have gone to the wrong house, but that was nonsense.

'Yes?' demanded the woman.

'Who are you?' asked Eva.

'Who are you?' snapped the woman.

'Is this the Büchbinder house?'

'Who are you? What do you want?'

'I'm Eva Arpel. I live here. Is Frau Büchbinder here?'

'Serel's daughter?'

'Yes,' said Eva. 'What's going on?'

'How do I know you're really Eva?'

'This is my home. Let me in,' she said in rising anger.

The old woman opened the door fractionally more to scrutinise her, and looked beyond her to the street. Satisfied that there was nobody standing behind Eva, the old woman softened. 'I'm sorry,' she said, closing the door. Eva heard the chain being slipped off the latch and the door re-opened wide. 'Come in quickly,' said the woman urgently. Eva walked into the hall. At least this was familiar, though again it seemed to be lifeless, without activity. The woman slipped the chain across again and bolted it in three places. The bolts were new.

'Do you want to come and see your mother?' the woman asked with as much urgency in her voice.

'Who are you?'

'I'm Frau Blumberg. I'm Frau Büchbinder's companion. Go downstairs to the kitchen. Your mother is there now. She's making lunch.'

'But I came to see Frau Büchbinder first. I don't understand. You're her companion?'

'Yes. I look after her and I direct the nurse who looks after Herr Büchbinder.'

'How is he? Is he still bedridden?'

'Yes,' said Frau Blumberg.

'Before I go downstairs, I wanted to talk to Frau Büchbinder. You don't understand. This is my home. My family lives here.'

'I know who you are,' she said impassively. Then she shrugged, and said, 'Very well.' She nodded curtly and told Eva, 'I'll see if Frau Büchbinder will receive you. Stay here.' The woman disappeared into the second reception room. Eva heard a muttering of voices in the distance. Frau Büchbinder came to the door. Eva was shocked. She had become an old woman. Her hair was greyer and less sculptured. It could almost be defined as messy. Her clothes were frumpy and inelegant. Her face seemed to be sagging as though the cares of her life were pulling her downwards.

'Eva!' said Frau Büchbinder. 'Eva, my love. My darling girl. Oh how good to see you. How wonderful. We didn't know you were coming home. You should have phoned. Does your mother know? She didn't say anything this morning.'

Frau Büchbinder walked towards her slowly. Her energy seemed to have deserted her. She threw her arms around Eva and kissed her on the cheeks. They hugged, old woman and young woman. Frau Büchbinder gripped her by the shoulders.

'You look fabulous. Fantastic. Ah, you look like …' She searched for the words. 'Wonderful! These clothes.

They're so good. You've done well for yourself. How is your health? Tell me everything. Your mother said you were working in the opera. Are you singing? Where do you live in Berlin? Do you see any of the Berlin Jewish community? What's it like there? Here, it's terrible. You wouldn't believe it. There's death everywhere. People being beaten up by the Nazis right in front of the eyes of policemen. Worse than when you left. A thousand times worse. How is Berlin?'

Questions tumbled like water over a cataract.

'Frau Büchbinder, is it alright for me to return here to live?'

The old woman's face glowed in joy. 'Oh, my dear, dear girl. This is your home. This is like the old days. How wonderful to have you back. You must tell us the stories of your life in Berlin. Your mother didn't say you were returning. I don't understand.'

'I haven't told her.'

The old woman looked shocked. 'What?'

'I wanted to find out from you whether I could return.'

'But I told you when you left. I said to you, this is your home.'

'Does my mother want me to return?'

'More than anything.'

She reached up again and kissed Eva. She took her by the hand and led her to the door below the stairs which led down to the kitchen. Together they stood on the landing. Frau Buchbinder let go of Eva's hand and grasped the rail with both hands, lowering herself cautiously from step to step.

'Serel,' she said when the kitchen came into full view. 'I have a surprise guest. Can you cook enough to fill another plate?'

Eva heard her mother's voice. 'Of course, Madam,' she said. 'Who's the guest?'

Frau Büchbinder masked her smile. Eva walked down and stood beside her.

'Hello Mother,' she said quietly.

Her mother looked up, her face a confusion of emotions. And then she began to cry.

They wheeled Herr Büchbinder into the dining room from his adjoining bedroom, the former first reception hall which had been converted into the room in which he would remain for what years he had left in his life. Eva was shocked when she saw him. His once sturdy and wiry gray hair was now thin and wispy, white in places, a dull lifeless almost sick grey in others. The pallor of his face was as deathly as parts of his hair. The last time she had seen Herr Büchbinder in this house he was a robust handsome man with a straight back, broad shoulders, strong legs, and receding hair … he used to comb parts of his hair and position them strategically with pomade so that they hid his emerging scalp. Now, she had hardly recognised him. When she'd last seen him, a day or two before she left for Berlin, he was a cadaverous form covered in bandages lying in a hospital bed.

But the man now being wheeled by the nurse into the dining room was little more than a mockery of the man she had known since her birth. Herr Büchbinder was dressed in a blue suit but his body seemed to have shrunk inside it. It looked as if he needed pumping up in order to fill out his clothes. His hands were mottled and spidery, his eyes hollow, his face unsmiling. Even his neck, once thick and almost bursting out of his stiff white collars, was wizened and knotted, a series of chords held in place by his parchment skin. There was a withering gap between his skin and the shirt collar.

Eva realised her face was registering shock when he was wheeled in by the nurse but she tried to control her emotions. Frau Büchbinder, who had changed into a black beaded dress for dinner, walked over to her husband and, bending down, kissed him on the top of the head.

'See who is here, Wilhelm, my dear. See, it's little Eva. She's come home. Now the house is full again.'

His eyes moved slowly towards her; but not his head! His head stayed motionless, lolling on the pillow supporting it. There was something demonic in the act, and she averted her gaze. His eyes were moving, yet his body was immobile in the wheelchair. A speckle of dribble appeared in the corner of his mouth as he tried to move his lips. A noise was emitted, indefinable. Eva realised that she was shrinking back from the horror before her.

'Come over Eva, and stroke Herr Büchbinder's hand. He likes being touched.'

She looked at him again, and tried to visualise the man who had boasted of her to all his friends when she was a little girl; a man whom she'd always seen as strong and robust. She walked over, unable to take her eyes off his face, trying to recognise something within him that was associated with her memory of the past. There was almost nothing. All there was in his face was death. Death and helplessness. Eva bent down and grasped his hand. It was warm but dry, crackly like a winter leaf. She squeezed his palm.

'How nice to see you again, Herr Büchbinder.'

His eyes looked intently into hers, his mouth tried to smile but it was crooked, as though a drawstring was forcing it into obscene shapes. Again, another moan or noise or some kind of animal or feral communication. She wasn't sure.

'Unfortunately he finds it hard to move since the stroke caused by the blows on the head. The doctors say he's had a massive blood clot and he has lost all use of the left side of his body. His right side is of little use either because his limbs were so badly broken the nerves were severed.'

She thought she could see him nodding his head. And when she looked closely, she could see that there was life, especially when she came to look deeply into his eyes. She saw recognition. She knelt down beside his chair and put both hands on his arm.

'Herr Büchbinder, it's your Eva. Remember when you used to enjoy my singing to you?'

His eyes blinked. More dribble. She looked up at the nurse. 'A cloth please.'

The nurse passed down a cloth and Eva dried the saliva. The other women in the room looked in surprise … and then in admiration. Most people recoiled but Frau Büchbinder had been confident of Eva's reaction to her husband's fate.

'Would you like me to sing for you again, Herr Büchbinder? Just blink if you'd like me to sing.'

His mouth seemed to be wanting to purse again into a smile. Slowly, almost painfully he closed his eyes and opened them again.

'Shall I sing before dinner or after dinner? Would you like me to sing Schubert *Lieder*? I know some lovely French songs. I know Italian songs now. What about an aria from Mozart? Say something from *The Magic Flute*. Do you remember *Pappagena*. You took me to see *The Magic Flute* when I was seven or eight. Do you remember?'

Again he tried to blink.

'I'll sing you an aria after dinner. Yes?'

She reached up and kissed him on the side of his face. She heard her mother beginning to sob.

'So,' said Frau Büchbinder. 'time for dinner. Serel, perhaps you'll instruct Lucy to serve tonight while you sit with us.'

'Thank you, Frau Büchbinder' said Serel, bowing slightly.

It was a true family get-together. Herr Büchbinder sat in his usual place but not in his usual carver, which had been moved over to the side of the room. The bib was tied securely around his neck and its two opposite corners were placed under weights on the table so there appeared to be a little tent shielding his clothes from any food that might spill from his inoperative mouth. Frau Büchbinder sat to his left. Normally she was at the foot of the table opposite him but on this occasion, she had given Eva pride of place, not only because Eva had returned home but because she was a woman of stature, a one-time household maid who was now singing with the great Berlin Opera. Eva's fear, that her mother might have recognised her picture in the paper, never materialised. And communications were so dominated by the Nazi machine that opera was sidelined by propaganda.

She looked around the table. Beside Eva sat Serel and then the various children of the Büchbinder family. Further up the table towards Herr Büchbinder sat Eva's father Franz but there was one place which had been laid yet was unoccupied, indeed the occupant conspicuous in his absence. It was an unspoken absence, a horror which Eva had been told in whispered conversation in the kitchen and from which she was still trying to recover. A horror which was the first thing her father had confided in her after they'd hugged and kissed ... joy subsumed within pain.

Samuel, one of the sons of the Büchbinder family, had disappeared off the streets early one afternoon. Despite massive investigations by the family and total indifference by the police to whom his disappearance was reported, his whereabouts were still unknown. It was assumed that he, like many other Jews and communists and anybody who disagreed with the contemptible Nazis, had been sucked up out of the safety of their environment and deposited into a large internment camp which had been built just outside Munich in an upper Bavarian town called Dachau. Apparently, there was an ammunitions factory on the outskirts of the small town, a town of no more than eight thousand inhabitants. This munitions establishment had been converted by the National Socialists into an armed and heavily fortified encampment, where illegally detained people were placed under guard for what the Nazis were calling 'protective custody.' The Munich authorities knew all about it, but chose to close their eyes.

The camp was supposed to be for political offenders but any clergy or Jews or homosexuals or criminals or Gypsies or even handicapped people were disappearing at an alarming rate off the streets of Munich and other Bavarian cities, and were thought to have been transported into this camp. Protests by Jewish leaders were met with scorn and derision from the Munich Chief of Police, and with violence and aggression when the comments were made known to Nazi headquarters.

Frau Büchbinder had made it very clear that a place would be laid for Samuel until the day he arrived home. She wouldn't even contemplate giving up her search for her beloved youngest son.

But what his disappearance had done was to make the family cringe in fear of going out onto the streets. Only rarely now did any family member go outdoors. The young men, of course, went to their offices accompanied by bodyguards. Frau Büchbinder thanked God every day that the children had not gone into the family business as her husband had wanted but instead had embarked on careers of their own. This to some extent had maintained the family income when all of the jewellery shops had been forced to close.

Her other two children, one a man of twenty-eight, the other twenty-six, were a lawyer and a doctor of medicine. It was primarily their income which was supporting the family.

The dinner was a desultory affair. The food, delicious as it was, was no match for the mood of the dining room. Eva had spent innumerable nights serving the family dinners in the old days. There was tolerance around the table when it was just the family. Laughter and hilarity on their own, courtesy and solemnity when the Büchbinders were entertaining friends or clients or members of the Munich Jewish community. Eva's overwhelming memory was of Herr Büchbinder's stentorian laugh. It used to stop all conversations as he would pull down his waistcoat to try to control his expanding stomach, his face florid with good humour, his eyes twinkling with abandon. At times he would call Eva over to his side and kiss her hand, saying, 'She may just be serving you, but this wonderful, beautiful girl … she's just like a daughter to me. I've known this girl since she was a baby. She even wee-wee'd on one of my best suits and I still can't get the stain out,' and the company would laugh and Eva would laugh because even though she was a servant, she was family.

But the laughter had all gone. It had evaporated. A bubble had burst.

They ate a first course of liver pâté. Herr Büchbinder was served soup. The nurse brought the spoon to his mouth carefully using a cloth to catch the drips. She put the edge of the spoon to his lips which he painfully opened. He swallowed the spoonful. Some of it went down his throat, much cascaded outwards mixed with saliva.

Eva turned her head in disgust, and then she felt fury at herself for these unworthy feelings towards a man whose life had been ended while he was still alive. She bit her lip to stop herself from crying. She smiled at Frau Büchbinder who reached over and grasped her hand.

'Nothing will be as it was. We must try to make the most of what we have. One day perhaps I will understand what has happened to my family. But not now. Now, I must just have the strength to keep going. If it wasn't for your mother and father, for my dear Serel and Franz, I don't know what I would have …'

Her lower lip began to quiver and she looked down at her plate of pâté.

'Tell us all about the opera in Berlin,' said Serel. 'How glorious is it to sing on stage? Why have you told us nothing? You never write. You call but you don't tell me what you're doing.'

Her husband reached across and grasped her arm to restrain Serel from being a Jewish mother and scolding the daughter for transgressions. For ten minutes, Eva regaled them with tales from the Berlin Opera. How she had been an Egyptian goddess in *Aida*, a gay Parisienne in *La Boheme*, a Hebrew slave in *Nabucco* and a member of a Catholic congregation in *Tosca*.

'I play so many roles that sometimes it's hard to remember who I am and what I'm doing,' she said.

'And the Nazis?' asked her father. 'How bad are they in Berlin? Are they as bad as they are here?'

Eva shrugged her shoulders. 'There's some trouble that you see on the streets. Occasionally, bad things happen. Windows broken in synagogues, Jewish shop-keepers having the Star of David daubed on their windows with the word, 'Jude' written inside. But the Berliners hate the Nazis. They won't have anything to do with them.'

'You have that madman Goebbels there, don't you?' asked her father.

'Yes. He's called himself the *Gauleiter*. Regional leader! Can you believe it? This trumped up peacock of a man comes to Berlin, of all places, and stands there in front of a couple of hundred people and says 'I'm the boss of Berlin'. Imagine! I once went to one of his rallies. He's a good speaker. People were booing and hissing at him. That's why I'm confident this whole thing with the Nazis will blow over soon. I don't think it will last.'

Frau Büchbinder looked at her. Her eyes were heavy with tears. 'Do you know that, or is it just a guess? Have you any idea whether this damn camp at Dachau will be closed soon by the proper government? What do you think will happen?'

'I'm sure things will be well.'

'Do you have any friends in Berlin who know? We have nobody. We're cut off. We know nothing here.'

Eva swallowed. Frau Büchbinder was obviously desperate for information about her son Samuel, whether he was still alive and if so, was he in this Dachau camp? And if he was in the camp, when would he be released?

Hesitantly, she said, 'I have a friend in Berlin. Somebody who knows about these things. I could phone and ask him what he knows about this camp.'

Frau Büchbinder looked at her. Her eyes were imploring. 'Would you? Any information. Anything at all. I don't sleep at night worrying about him. Is he eating? Is he well? Is he cold? I think it would be easier if I knew that he was dead, then I could stop worrying for him and grieve. But ...'

The tears began to run down her cheek. Her daughter stood and walked over to her, putting her arms around her shoulder and kissing her. The maid brought the next course.

Eva looked at the telephone. It was in Herr Büchbinder's study. The door was closed by her request. She had only ever once sat in the chair in this study and that was just for a bit of fun. It was his private domain. All she had ever done was to clean it. Now, she was using it as though she were a member of the family. And she was. The tables had turned. By a stroke of fortune … or malice … Eva was the one with power and knowledge. She held the cards. She had the connections. Nobody had dared ask her who her friend was, nor of his possible connection with Adolf Hitler and the Nazi Party and this camp in Dachau. They had just accepted that she had the knowledge.

She picked up the phone. It felt cold and strange in her hand, like the metallic instruments of a surgeon. She held it to her ear and heard the distant echoing silence. An operator's voice suddenly interrupted the echo and asked, 'May I help you?'

'Please connect me to the following number in Berlin.' Eva gave the telephone number of the apartment she had shared with Reinholdt until that morning. She prayed he wouldn't be home. She prayed she would have to report her failure. She listened to the connection being made. The Munich operator telephoned the operator in Nuremberg who phoned the operator in Frankfurt who was connected to the operator in Köln who spoke to the operator in Berlin. The operator in Berlin repeated the number which Eva had given. It rang four times. A voice, echoing in the distance, answered, a voice which Eva recognised immediately as Reinholdt's.

'Yes. Hello?' he asked.

'Go ahead caller,' said the Berlin operator.

The connection strengthened as the Berlin operator disconnected herself from the line.

'Hello,' said Reinholdt again, this time his voice stronger, clearer. 'Who's there?'

Eva remained silent.

'Hello. Who is this?' said Reinholdt.

She wanted to speak. She wanted to ask him about Dachau, about helping her friends, about Samuel and his incarceration. She wanted to tell him about what his friends in the SA had done to Herr Büchbinder, about how they had made him, a vigorous and respectable man, into a dribbling cripple. She wanted to shout at him and ask him why he had done these things.

'Hello!' he shouted.

Eva remained silent. It would be so easy on the phone. She knew what she wanted to tell him. That she was a Jew and that she was proud of being a Jew, and that no matter what he did, she would never change.

'Answer me!' Reinholdt shouted. 'Is this a joke? Who are you?'

Eva replaced the phone to the cradle. If she were to tell him the truth, he would seek her out for the damage she had done to him. He would ensure that she would be the next to die, as would her mother and father and all the rest of the Büchbinders. How could she allow evil like this to enter the house which was her home? The house in which she had grown. She took out a handkerchief and wiped her mouth, then her forehead. She was sweating despite the cold of the study. Her heart was pounding, the noise rushing through her ears. What was she to tell Frau Büchbinder? What could she possibly tell her mother and father? What on earth could she do now?

She had drunk with the enemy. She had eaten with the enemy. She had kept house for the enemy. She had sung for the enemy. She had slept with the enemy. And now she was part of the enemy. As much a part as Reinholdt and all the other men with whom he associated were. Her only hope for her survival and that of her family was to continue. Did she want to end up like Samuel? Did she want her father to end up like Herr Büchbinder? Nobody deserved this fate. Perhaps, just perhaps, she could protect herself and her parents by continuing to make love to and satisfy the enemy.

CHAPTER FIFTEEN

FRANKFURT, PRESENT DAY

When the doctor arrived to give Annelise her routine examination, Sarah was asked to leave the room. She went downstairs to find a coffee shop. The street was an ordinary Frankfurt suburban street. She had never been to Frankfurt before but she imagined that all the streets around this suburb looked the same. Elegant turn-of-the-century houses, their unified facades interrupted by utilitarian 1950s, '60s and '70s examples of architectural dreariness. What impressed Sarah was that the houses were shielded from the road by a wide pavement, and then a phalanx of trees before the roadway started. They were interesting leafy poplars and absorbed much of the traffic noise as well as the exhaust stench of modern life. Now why didn't New York figure out the importance of the motor vehicle when it was building itself in the 1920s and '30s, she wondered?

Thinking of New York, she immediately thought of David. She looked at her watch. It would be very late at night but she ached to talk to him. She took out her mobile phone and stabbed a long series of numbers.

'Why are you smiling?' the old lady asked.

'I've just spoken to my husband. He sends you his love and asked whether he could visit you one day. He'll be in Germany in a couple of months time for a concert. He could drop by and see how you are.'

The old lady smiled. 'A couple of months. That's a long time for somebody of my age. Tell me about him. Tell me about Eva's grandson-in-law. Is he the type of man your grandmummy would have approved of? Is he Jewish?' asked Annelise.

The old woman looked exhausted. The doctor had prodded and poked in all the wrong places. Even the act of sounding her chest for fluid was an agony. Coughing these days exhausted her. She listened and smiled while Sarah explained all about David, where they'd met, her love for him, her love for his work as a concert cellist, the way in which she revelled at his ability to produce deep sensuous music from the instrument.

'Your grandmother's voice was a beautiful instrument,' Annelise said interrupting. 'It was what made her well known.'

'Did she sing on radio? Did she sing popular German songs outside of the club?'

Annelise tried to remember what lies she'd told Sarah so as not to hurt her with the truth.

'All that,' she said with a dismissive wave of her good hand. 'All that.'

'Tell me about her society; about the people she knew. Before the war, say when Hitler began his rise. Say in 1933, with Von Pappen and Hindenburg; Goebbels and Göring. I know the history from books, but you're right. I know nothing about what life was like in those days. Were people frightened all the time, or did they sometimes laugh? Were the Jews treated horribly when Hitler first came to power? What happened when an SA man or an SS man met a Jew in the street? How bad were they? I mean, I know they were bad,' she said correcting herself. 'But what was it like, living an ordinary life for a Jew? How frightened were people?' She stilled her curiosity. She was repeating herself.

Annelise lay back in the pillow. Even breathing was difficult. Talking wasn't easy. But worst than these was the story she had to tell. How could she tell this beautiful child, this innocent granddaughter, about the realities of life in Berlin when Hitler had just come to power and when the SA was terrorising everybody's life.

BERLIN, 1934

Frau Eva Stricher closed the window in order to shut out the noise of people shouting in the street below. She wondered how Reinholdt's father, Herr Stricher would manage to get through the crowds. Funny. She still called him 'Herr' after three years. And she would go on calling him that until she became a proper Frau, until she was properly married. Then she would call him by the title he wanted, Papa.

The noise of the crowds had distracted her from her singing. Closing the window made it much easier. Crowds! There always seemed to be crowds in Berlin these days. People marching backwards and forwards, people carrying banners, people running away from the sounds of shouting, people running towards the sounds of shouting; demonstrations everywhere about this or that … running, always running so that they could join in or escape whatever was going on. You couldn't even shop without forcing your way through the crowds. Although in some shops, there were no customers at all. Some shops had the word, Jude, daubed inside a hideously crude Star of David painted in white poster paint all across the window. On occasion, the SA men stood as a gang in front of a shop owned by a Jew, and aggressively turned away anyone trying to enter, shouting that the Jews were the cause of Germany's problems, and that anybody who helped Jews make profits was a traitor to the German Reich. Naturally, very few Berliners had the guts to push past a gang of strong young men, and patronise the emporium.

When would it all end? There was so much hatred on the crowded streets, so much noise and violence. But to her shame, she was immune to it. She had willingly conspired to metamorphose and she was now playing a role which saw her happy, loved, comfortable, and enriched. She walked back from the window and glanced at herself in the mirror. Her eyebrows were a little bit too full. They needed plucking. She would get her beautician to do it tomorrow; after her massage. Another thing to worry about! If only she had known that Reinholdt's father would be visiting today she would have organised for her eyebrows to be done yesterday. Why couldn't men organise themselves better? Her days were beautifully organised. Reinholdt's life had never been more thoroughly prepared.

She heard a car horn and shouting in the street. She returned to the window and looked down. Eva saw an open car, its long bonnet bedecked by two flags now drooping because the car was stationary after failing to manoeuvre its way through a crush of people standing on the kerbside. The chauffeur, dressed in the black of an SS military man of some minor rank, was standing on the running board of the car shouting for people to get out of the way. They were treating him with the contempt that only Berliners seemed to be expressing these days for the Nazis. Everywhere else, they were lauded, praised, loved.

She looked closely at the man who was sitting in the back of the car staring with benign indifference. He was middle-aged, bordering on elderly. He was fat, his uniform manfully trying, but failing, to hide the flabby excesses of his body. His cap with its shining peak and aggressive golden insignia was placed beside him on the seat. It was Reinholdt's father, Otto. She had met him many times before. On the earlier occasions when he had visited she had been in fear of him. But lately, he'd been taking a fatherly interest in her, and she'd allowed herself the luxury of forgetting for a moment that he was a senior officer in the SS.

Otto's bushy moustache, clipped at the wings to ape Adolf Hitler's, the skulls which he wore on both lapels, shining gold metallic emblems of his disdain for all around him, the forked lightning SS badges which he wore on his breast pocket, were all symbols that she hated. Yet Otto had become a second father to her, a typically Bavarian father, all joy and laughter and good nature when he was with Reinholdt and his son's 'beautiful little girl'.

She ran into the corridor shouting out, 'Reinnie, Reinnie, your papa's here.' She opened the door of their bedroom. Reinholdt was sitting at his desk writing a letter. She walked over and kissed him on the neck. 'Your father's here,' she said again.

'Good,' he said, patting her on the hand. 'Tell Kirsten to put the coffee on. I'll be right out.'

She kissed him again. By the time she had given instructions to their maid, there was a knock on the door. Eva ran and opened it, curtseying in a skittish way which she knew he would laugh at.

'I'm so pleased to see the Herr *Obersturmbannführer*. Please enter my humble home,' she said, wafting her hand in a balletic movement.

Otto burst out laughing. 'And I'm delighted to see the brilliant diva, our very own Brunnhilde of the Valkyries.'

She closed the door and kissed him on the cheek.

'Ah Eva,' he said as he walked linking his arm through hers. They entered the lounge room. 'I don't see you nearly enough. All I do is hear about you and what they're saying. You'll be one of the Reich's greatest sopranos one day.'

'If I'm lucky,' she said.

'Luck has nothing to do with it, my dear,' he said, kissing her on the cheek. 'From what everybody tells me, you have brilliant talent.'

'You have a brilliant son who has introduced me to the right people.'

'And he,' Otto said, 'is lucky to have you. You've done amazing things for him. He even writes to us regularly.'

Again Otto burst out laughing. Reinholdt entered the room, stood stiffly to attention and gave a salute, saying '*Heil Hitler*'; he smiled and ran towards his father's outstretched arms. They embraced. Eva walked over, and the two men opened their arms to include her. The maid came out and served coffees.

'What brings you to Berlin again so soon?' asked Reinholdt.

'I came to see you.'

'About?'

Otto sipped the coffee. 'Something I can't discuss in front of Eva. I'm very sorry. I love you dearly as a daughter, but this is a matter which can't be talked about openly.'

'Eva is my wife in all but ceremony, Father. For God's sake, we're getting married next year. I have no secrets from her, nor she from me.'

'This isn't a matter of family secrets, Reinholdt,' said Otto more sternly. 'This is a matter of national security.'

Eva stood. 'I'll go and write some letters,' she said.

But before she could leave the room, Reinholdt held her by the hand. 'Does this involve my position in the SA, Father?'

Otto remained motionless.

'I thought so,' said Reinholdt. 'Then Eva stays.' His voice gave testament to Eva's position in his life, as well as her importance to him.

'I'm afraid she doesn't. I mean no disrespect to Eva. I welcome her into my family as does your mother. But these are not matters which can be discussed openly.'

It was a stand-off between father and son. Eva flushed in embarrassment.

'Reinholdt, please. Let me just go and write some letters. I've got plenty to do.' She stood and began to walk towards the door.

'No,' he said sharply. 'I'm sorry Father, and Eva, I'm sorry. I don't want to embarrass you but it's important to me that you stay. There were never secrets between you and mother. There will be no secrets between me and my wife.'

Eva bit the inside of her lip.

'These are State secrets, Reinholdt. These are matters of the greatest importance,' implored his father.

'Even so,' said the younger man.

'Why are you making such a fuss, Reinholdt?' said Eva. 'It's really not important to me that I stay.'

'Maybe not,' he responded, perhaps too quickly. 'But it's important to me. I discuss every aspect of my work with you. This is no different.' He turned to his father. 'If it involves me, Father, then it involves Eva.'

'It goes far beyond your personal circumstances, Reinholdt. These are things which I overheard in a party discussion and which I pass on to you because of my love for you as my son. These are matters which concern the Führer and the future of Germany.'

'Eva learned many years ago to keep her mouth shut. We have party meetings in here, discussing strategy. It's impossible for her not to overhear things. Everybody knows about it. Everybody trusts her.'

His father sighed. He looked at Eva. 'What I'm about to say concerns matters of life and death. Matters known only to the smallest number of people. I put you on your honour as a German Christian woman not to divulge what I'm about to tell you.'

'Of course,' she said.

Otto assured himself that the maid wasn't listening. Then in a low voice he continued, 'As you know' … His voice was barely above a whisper '… I'm deputy for Administrative Affairs under Himmler. Things are soon going to happen which will dramatically affect the life of everybody in the SA.'

Eva looked at Reinholdt in concern. His face was impassive, immobile. He was listening intently to his father.

'Röhm has got completely out of hand. He's trying to create a second force in the Reich. Hitler is Führer. Hitler is *Reichschancellor*, yet Röhm seems to believe that he, and he alone, should maintain absolute power through his personal army. And the next step is too awful even to contemplate. It's unforgivable; it's almost as if Röhm wants to be Führer.' Otto breathed deeply. He was building up to something; something he found difficult to say. 'The Führer thought that the restrictions he had placed on Röhm and the SA last year would have been enough to make him understand his position in the hierarchy. But it's not. The insubordination from Röhm and the SA leadership has now become intolerable.'

Reinholdt shook his head as if in disagreement, but Otto held up his hand. 'Röhm has four and a half million men under his command. Men trained by the Reichswehr. Soldiers from the Great War. It's a damned army, Reinholdt, an army of civilians, armed and dangerous. Don't you understand the position the Führer finds himself in?'

'We're Germans,' said Reinholdt. 'One people, one state, one leader. We have no alternative …'

'You know nothing,' said his father dismissively. 'You're blinded by your faith in Röhm and the others. Why do you think Goebbels has turned his back on the SA? Why do you think he's in Berlin now organising propaganda?'

Otto remained silent. The reality began to filter into Reinholdt's mind.

'Are you saying there's going to be a move against us? Is that why you're here?'

Instead of answering his son's question, Otto said, 'Röhm has always had plans for a powerful civilian militia. He wants a two-component army, a small elite of officers and men conducting offensive warfare on the borders and a huge manned defensive militia. Hitler completely disagrees. In February Röhm wrote the most alarming position paper for the Führer. He demanded … you hear that Reinholdt? He demanded of the Führer, of the *Reichschancellor*, that the army – the German Army, be merged into the SA and that the standing army is reduced to a military training organisation for use by his SA forces. It's unbelievable. It will undermine everything Hitler is trying to do. It damages the very standing of our Reichswehr.

'And there's something else you don't know. Something only a handful of us in party headquarters are aware of. And this is the reason I'm here to tell you. Two senior men from the SA have warned Hitler about Röhm's private intentions. They came to see Himmler and Hitler some time ago. What they said frightened the pants off us.

'Anyway, as a result of all of this, Hitler now knows positively that he can't rein in the SA any longer. Göring, Goebbels, Frick, Himmler and Heydrich have been pressuring Hitler towards immediate, devastating action, like cutting off the head of the poppy. We can't move against the whole of the SA. They're our people. There are millions of them. It would be a hideous civil war. But there are things which we have to do.'

'What are you planning to do?' interrupted Reinholdt.

'It's not me, Reinholdt,' insisted his father. 'These are plans at the very top. There are black lists prepared for us by the Gestapo and the SS. They've identified SA candidates who are to be eliminated.'

Eva went numb and cold. 'Is Reinholdt …'

'No,' said Otto reassuringly. 'Even though he's very important, he's far too junior to be one of those selected for elimination. Thank God. It's only the leaders of the SA. And at the same time as we're doing surgery to the SA, we're also going to be clearing up a long-term problem we've had with the Vice Chancellor of Germany, Von Pappen and all those weak-kneed idiots around him.'

'Von Pappen? But …'

'The time for fun and games is over. Germany has arisen and it's marching solidly forward. Anybody who tries to prevent our forward thrust will be hacked out of the marching body. Any internal dissent from aliens or weak-kneed socialists or communists or Jews or Serbs or other subhumans will be eliminated. Anybody who doesn't march with us is against us. Within three years, Germany will become the leader of Europe. France is finished. Belgium and the Low Countries have got no strength. Russia and those Slavic countries which protect it on its borders are vast but full of subhumans who won't dare to resist us. Our master race will very quickly eliminate them so that we can expand towards the east to gain more living space for the German people. Italy under Mussolini and Spain under Franco are the only countries in Europe with whom we'll deal on anything like an equal basis, although … No, I mustn't say anything else in that regard. Once we incorporate the Germans now forced to live in Czechoslovakia and other alien territory back into Germany, we'll be the greatest country in the world.'

'You're talking war,' said Reinholdt.

'There won't be a war. There needs to be no war. A war is when you have two sides fighting each other. Once the might of the German people is fully understood, countries like Austria, Czechoslovakia, Poland, Hungary, and the Ukraine will welcome us with open arms. They'll want to be part of our federation, especially when the German population in the Sudetanland and other German enclaves put pressure on their governments.'

Otto looked smugly at the two of them. Eva knew him well enough to realise there was something he was dying to say but that propriety and secrecy was preventing him. He was just a big child really, unable to hold a secret.

'Is there something the Herr *Obersturmbannführer* is trying to keep a secret?'

Otto turned to Reinholdt. 'God, I love this woman. She is so smart. It's about England. The Führer is working on a way of making England into our ally.'

'You're saying that England, that the Monarchy and the government would be willing to become Fascist?' asked Reinholdt in amazement.

Otto shrugged. 'Who knows? But we have it on very good authority that the Prince of Wales is strongly inclined towards us. When he becomes King the situation will be very good for us. Our Ambassador informs us that he holds enormous power and can deliver England into a détente with the Führer.'

Eva shook her head. 'But Ramsay MacDonald, their Prime Minister. He's a socialist. He's …'

'He's gutless,' said Otto. 'A woman. No, he won't last. Oswald Mosley will take over, provided that buffoon Baldwin doesn't stand too tall. It's a complicated situation. I don't want to bother you children with it.'

But Eva insisted. 'England? Fascist?'

Otto smiled the smile of a tolerant father. 'Hitler has had some very pleasant correspondence with the Prince, who applauds the Führer's firm policies towards the economy and towards his internationalism. There will be no war, my darling girl, but there will be no enemies tolerated within the borders of our new nation. Only through strength can we experience growth and to be strong we have to excise everyone who is different, everyone who doesn't think like us, everyone who isn't one of us.'

Eva sat in a state of confusion and anxiety. She'd always thought of this Nazi thing as a local difficulty, as a particularly German problem. But if the rest of the world became Nazi, where could the Jews hide? The daily lie she was living bothered her less and less as it became increasingly the truth of her life with Reinholdt. But every now and again, she came face to face with the reality her life had become. Now was such an occasion. Everything she and Reinholdt did was fine; because of her home life, her singing career, her friendships, her place in Berlin society, Eva had developed the facility to close her eyes to her lover's work with increasing ease. Whenever he tried to discuss his work with her, she smiled, and turned off her inner ear, instead thinking through the melody of an aria while nodding and smiling at him.

Reinholdt was her love, her lover, her security … but every now and then, reality broke through the carapace she had constructed around herself, especially when she was suddenly confronted by men like Otto Stricher, the archetype of the Nazi. And it was at these moments that she woke up from her dream in a sweat, wondering who she was.

Hearing what Reinholdt and those men like him in the SA and the Nazi Party were doing to Jews, especially coming from the mouth of a man as kindly and gentle as Otto was to his friends and family, was hideously confronting for her. It brought to the surface the life which she was burying every day.

'So what's going to happen, Father? When is it going to happen? How do I protect myself?'

Otto nodded, glad that he would have no further arguments from his son about the reality of what was to be. 'Next week,' he said, lowering his voice to a softer register so that even Eva, sitting opposite him, had to sit forward to hear. 'Hitler has summoned the SA leadership to a meeting at Bad Wiessee. Have you been invited?'

Reinholdt shook his head.

'Thank God. Whatever happens, don't go. More than that, I can't say anything.'

'They're going to be murdered,' said Reinholdt.

'You don't have to be a genius to work out what will take place.'

Reinholdt gulped. 'But there will be chaos. Millions of men ...'

'There will be no chaos. The leadership of the SS will move in to take control. The SA will be merged into the SS.'

'The SS?' Reinholdt said incredulously. 'What are you talking about? It's a small division of the SA. A couple of hundred thousand at the most.'

'The SS is to be moved out of the SA and will become completely autonomous. Himmler will take total charge. The SS will no longer be subject to the normal laws of Germany but will act directly under the will of the Führer carried out by Heinrich Himmler.'

'Father,' said Reinholdt still incredulous, 'the SA is millions and millions of men. The SS is a handful. Under what circumstances will the men of the SA accept leadership from the SS? The men will never agree.'

'They will have no alternative,' snapped his father. 'These aren't games we're playing, boy. There will be massacres everywhere. It's not just Von Pappen and other conservatives in the government we're after. It's not just Röhm and the SA leadership. We're going to silence General von Schleicher, Catholic activists, journalists, left-wingers, anybody who's against us.'

'But you're talking about mass murder,' said Eva in horror.

Otto shook his head and smiled at her. 'No. We'll enact laws legalising the massacre as a response to a state of emergency. It will be deemed as legalised killing by the Reich in order to protect itself. It's what every civilised country does already. Getting rid of troublemakers and people who would act treasonously.'

'Father,' insisted Reinholdt, still horrified by the news. 'You're talking about Ernst Röhm, Hitler's closest friend and ally. He was there in Munich at the *putsch*. He's been Hitler's most loyal supporter ever since…'

'Times change. The Führer knows where he's going. How else could he have become Chancellor. His is the clearest vision for Germany's future we've ever had. Do you think he became Chancellor because of the will of the people? Our vote was falling. If democracy had its way, we'd have been finished at the last election. How can you leave the decision about the government and the future of Germany to stupid people out there on the streets.

'Hitler had to engineer his way in, throw democracy aside, all for the good of Germany. It was the only way. The German people demand to be led. They're like children and they can be manipulated one way or the other by seductive voices like Röhm's and conservative voices like Von Pappen. These voices have to be silenced.'

He sat back in his chair, his anger suddenly spent.

'How can Reinholdt protect himself?' asked Eva quietly.

Otto smiled at her again and nodded. 'You see,' he said to his son. 'She understands. You don't. You're thinking of loyalty. You're thinking of friendship. You're even thinking of contacting Röhm and warning him. It was a risk I had to take in order to save your life; thank goodness I agreed to allow Eva to remain in the room. I should have known that she would make you see reason, make you understand. Let me warn you, Reinholdt. If you tell Röhm or somebody in the SA and Röhm gets to hear of the move against him, all that will happen is that the move will be brought forward. A lot more people will be killed. You will be one of them. As my son, it will also mean that I will be killed because you don't have to be a genius to realise that it was me who warned you. Your mother would also be killed in the vengeance of the party against traitors. There are no circumstances which would have forced me to tell you what I've just told you, to betray my leader, were it not for the fact that you were my son and that I love you dearly. Your mother knows nothing of this. My life, Eva's life, your mother's life, are in your hands. If you betray me as I have betrayed Himmler and the Führer by telling you the deepest party secrets, then nothing will change except our deaths will be added to the list.'

'What is Reinholdt to do?' asked Eva again.

'He is to write a letter to me. I'll make sure it gets to Himmler's desk. In the letter Reinholdt must express his gravest reservations about the activities of Röhm and the SA leadership. In the letter, he will tell me that

Adolf Hitler must be warned about the growing threat which comes from the SA leadership. That only because you're an insider, albeit a junior one, do you have these insights. You must warn me and beg me to tell Himmler and beg Himmler to tell Hitler that unless Röhm is brought under control immediately and even absorbed into the SS, Germany and the future of the Reich is in grave peril. That will establish your suitability for senior rank in the SS in Himmler's mind. Hopefully it will distance you from the SA leadership.'

Reinholdt shook his head. 'Himmler's not a fool. Whatever happens after, he will always view me as a traitor, as a turncoat. He'll read the letter and think to himself, "he's doing this to save his own life. How quickly will he turn and stab the SS in the back?"'

Otto responded, 'That's not how Himmler thinks. I've worked with him for three years. I know how he thinks. He suspects everybody and everybody's motives. He pins a medal on your chest and works out where to stab you in the back at precisely the same time. I have no illusions about Himmler. I know precisely what will happen. He'll see your letter as a way of continuing the pressure on Hitler to act against the SA. It's another cog in a fast spinning wheel. If you're lucky, he'll invite you in after the destruction of the SA leadership. You'll have coffee with him and he'll ask your views on the SA. I'll brief you intimately before that meeting. If he doesn't invite you for coffee, then I'll organise for you to come and visit me and I'll introduce you to him. Either way, you'll sit with him and you'll impress him.'

Reinholdt nodded. Eva felt a sense of profound relief. She thanked God that the SA was going to be brought under some control. She knew of the SS. It was a small division of the SA but according to Otto seemed to have much higher and more worthwhile objectives. But how could such a small group of a couple of hundred thousand men possibly take over the largest single entity in the whole of Germany – the SA?

Like so much, she would close her eyes to the reality that she knew was all around her and thank the Hebrew God for the paradox of giving her so much safety, so much security, yet allowing her to live in the home of a man whose mission it was to cripple the Hebrew God and His people in the state of Germany.

CHAPTER SIXTEEN

FRANKFURT, PRESENT DAY

Sarah was confused. 'So she was an opera singer? But two days ago, you told me that she just sang a few songs in a cabaret.'

Annelise couldn't remember what she'd told her two days ago, let alone two minutes ago. She remembered with crystal clarity everything which had happened during the war, the faces, the words, the nuances, even the smells of Berlin, but she couldn't remember a word about what she'd told Sarah about her grandmother since she'd first visited.

She sighed. 'Well, if I told you that, then I lied.'

Sarah was shocked. Her face reflected her surprise. 'So, how much more that you've told me is a lie?'

The old lady shrugged her shoulders and wiped her face with one of the perfumed handtowels that Sarah had brought for her on her second visit.

'In the beginning,' she said slowly, 'when you first came here, I didn't know you. Maybe there wasn't the trust there should be. I don't know what I told you then. But in the last visits, I realised that you really are Eva's granddaughter, not just in words, but I see the same gentleness and intelligence, so from now everything will be the truth.'

'But what wasn't true? What have you told me that I should disbelieve? Was her work in the cabaret not just as a waitress? Was she doing something ... different?'

Annelise desperately tried to remember what she'd already told Sarah but couldn't. 'She was a waitress, nothing more. That I promise you. Not a very good one.' The old lady laughed, wheezing. 'She was nearly fired for dropping a tray of drinks on a soldier. But she did more than sing songs in the cabaret, this is true. She was an opera singer.'

Sarah sat back in her chair in stunned silence. Her grandmother an opera singer? In Berlin? In the 1930s?

'But how could a Jew sing opera? Surely the Nazis would have stopped her.'

Annelise shook her head. 'Many Jewish artists were stopped but some, the Nazis ignored their religion until late in the day. For years, your grandma sang for the people of Berlin, not for the Nazis.'

'But there must have been Nazis in the audience.' Sarah recognised her tone was condemnatory, the moral rectitude which time and hindsight afford.

'Sure, there were Nazis in the audience, and Jews and Catholics. It was only on the streets that the Nazis were evil. The rest of us just got on with life as best we could.'

BERLIN, 1934

Eva Stricher alighted from the taxi and walked towards the stage door of the Berlin State Opera House. She was suffused by emotions which were at once exultant, triumphant, and yet full of trepidation. One final dress rehearsal and tonight she would be alone on the stage, convincing a huge audience that she wasn't Eva Stricher, but was indeed another diva, the wild and insanely jealous Floria Tosca.

Tonight, she would be singing opera's most dramatic role before Berlin's most glittering assembly. She had risen from the nadir of being a waitress slut in a cabaret, to a very nervous member of the chorus, to become the understudy of an utter harridan who screamed and shouted at the merest inconvenience, to minor solo roles stepping just beyond the fringe of her companions in the chorus; and now for the first time in her life, Eva was destined to sing one of the most famous and important roles in the entire pantheon of opera. And in her sudden rise, she had become the darling of Berlin's sophisticated night life. Thanks to Reinholdt's advice and contacts, she had risen to the very pinnacle of the mountain. Before, Eva had stood alone and isolated, staring from the periphery into a hostile and unwelcoming environment; today she teetered on the brink of the very top. But for how long would she stay there? One false move, one unsteady note, and, regardless of Reinholdt's position and his contacts, the Berlin audience would send her plummeting down the precipice.

Currently she was standing on the shoulders of the entire corpus of the men of influence. She knew that; she wasn't a fool. But she also knew that she had enormous talent. No amount of pressure could have been brought to bear on Maestro Furtwängler to allow her to sing the lead role in an opera he was conducting unless he considered she was ready and able. And he had been nothing but encouraging and helpful.

But she wasn't a fool. Once you were at the top, the only way was down; and then the road became very slippery, the plummet very fast.

And there was no hiding from this audience; no fooling them; the entire audience would be singing along in their minds with her tonight. Everybody there would know the arias and choruses of opera's most famous work. As she sang in the upper registers, the audience would have an intimate appreciation of what her voice should be doing.

She'd come so far in so short a time. She knew that it was an impossibility but her greatest wish would be for her mother and father to be present in the audience tonight. They would have been so intensely proud. But they didn't even know that the Eva Stricher taking the role of Tosca was their very own daughter, Eva Arpel. She was desperate to know how her parents were. Only the occasional telephone call, reassuring them that everything with their daughter was well, had saved her sanity. She desperately needed connection with the past, with the reality of who she actually was, rather than the role she was playing for the sake of her very life.

As she walked up the steps towards the stage door, she felt between her breasts and found the amulet, suspended on its heavy gold chain. The amulet was an anchor, her one way of remembering that her entire life was a dangerous charade, that no matter how huge his professed love or his devotion to her, Reinholdt would have no choice but to expel her and force her to suffer the consequences if he found out the truth about her Jewishness.

At the top of the stairs she smiled at the stage-door porter, Ulrich, sitting in his chair reading the paper.

'Good morning, diva,' he said in mock seriousness. Today she was entitled to be called diva, not simply Frau Stricher.

'Good morning, Ulrich.'

He folded the paper. She always spent a few moments talking to him before she entered the building.

'So, Madam. You are all prepared for tonight? Thank you for the tickets, by the way. My wife and I are greatly looking forward to your debut.'

'I'll look for you in the audience,' she responded.

'Terrible news,' he said pointing to the headlines in the paper. 'Who would have thought Ernst Röhm and all those SA men were traitors?'

He remained silent, keen for her to tell him that her man, *Sturmbannführer* Stricher hadn't been caught up in the massacre. But she kept her own counsel and said, 'Terrible news. Who would have believed it?'

She walked inside the building and smelled the comforting aroma of props and flats and make-up and dust, which created the very essence of an opera house. From their seats in the audience, witnesses to an opera only ever view the perfection of the drama. Beautiful singing, wonderful costumes, breathtaking sets, all moving seamlessly from one act to another until the final crescendo.

If only they could see the reality of life back here. Gigantic solid rectangles of canvas mounted on criss-crossing frames of splintering wood held crudely painted scenes of staircases or windows or fireplaces with blazing logs or night-time skies with ducks flying across an eternal moon. They were placed like massive medieval tapestries one in front of the other, flat against a back wall. On another wall were an equal number of similar backdrops and scenes but to this compressed collection were added huge rolls of curtains or carpets, as well as stage pieces such as staircases, balconies, doorways, architraves and the hundred other requirements for a hundred operas which the Berlin State Company staged regularly. Each was code-marked with its own symbol painted for identification on the back. *Aida 1–3. Valkyrie 3–1. Giovanni 2–2* and so on, with Germanic precision.

There were cables snaking all over the floor; men with saws and hammers shaping or fixing or moulding wood on trellises, taking up a quarter of the front of the stage area; there were men scaling up and down ladders like monkeys, adding last-minute touches of paint to a prop or a flat which, close-up, looked crude and harsh, yet from a distance to any member of the audience looked like a work from the skilful master painter Cavaradossi, trying to convince his beloved Tosca that the face she saw in the painting was merely a figment of her jealousy.

Eva stepped from the rear stage entry to the middle of the stage, where she was greeted by chorus and other members of the cast. They looked at her with serious intent and kissed her on the cheeks.

'How are you, my dear?' asked a contralto with concern. The tenor playing Cavaradossi in that night's performance stepped over to her and put his arm around her shoulder. 'How are things at home?' he asked.

To each question, she just nodded and said, 'Fine. Everything is good, thank you.'

There were more questions from people she knew well in the chorus, from stagehands, even from musicians with whom she'd sung for three years. Everyone knew that her lover was a senior man in the SA. Everyone had read the headlines in the morning paper. Everyone was concerned for her well being. With him arrested or executed, how long before she was expelled from the Opera? She was talented – sure – but experienced sopranos in the chorus wondered whether there might be a sudden vacancy for a diva's role for which they could apply.

She went over to the table containing orange juice, water, coffee and biscuits and helped herself. The coffee was hot and strong. Just what she needed. Why should she tell them that her Reinholdt not only had survived the coup of the previous day but had been assured by Himmler himself of an equivalent position in the SS? Himmler had told him that it was just a matter of changing uniforms … and saluting a different leader. Reinholdt, pragmatic to the end, had assured Himmler of his total loyalty as well as the loyalty of the ten thousand men under his immediate command. Reinholdt had recounted the moment of truth to Eva when he had told Himmler of his loyalty.

'And how can you guarantee the loyalty of ten thousand men?' Himmler had asked quizzically.

'Anyone who is disloyal will be shot,' Reinholdt had replied cold-heartedly.

Himmler asked no further questions, just nodded in appreciation. 'As will you be, Stricher,' he said softly.

Recounting the interview, Reinholdt knew with absolute certainty that he had managed to save his own skin, and those of the people he loved most in the world. But at what cost? he asked Eva. At the cost of denying his own people, at being a turncoat and a traitor. Eva, for the umpteenth time, had been forced to bite back her anguish.

She was even biting the inside of her lip, thinking about the way in which the SA had been brought to its knees and her Reinnie had managed to save his own neck, when the production director walked on to the stage with a clipboard and a stopwatch in his hand.

'Gentlemen,' he shouted to the crew. 'The full dress rehearsal starts in one hour. Every performer, please, to costume and make-up. Gentlemen of the stage crew, your work will be finished and all equipment cleared away by 11.30 at the latest. Thank you very much.'

Even Eva's dresser skirted around the question of whether her lover had been one of the unnamed 'hundred fellow traitors' the newspapers said had been arrested and shot. After evading the point for half an hour and asking all sorts of questions on the periphery of the issue, Eva turned to her dresser. 'Helga, I'm having supper with Reinholdt and some important people tonight, after my debut. People in the senior hierarchy of the SS. I'll need to be out of here as early as possible after the performance, so could you perhaps stay behind and help me?'

Helga beamed a smile. 'Of course Eva. I'd be delighted.'

It was the best method of communicating to the whole of the cast and crew, outside of the public address system, that Eva and her Reinholdt were safe from persecution by Adolf Hitler. By the time she got on stage for the final dress rehearsal, everybody would know that Eva was still a figure to be reckoned with in the Berlin Opera.

Wilhelm Furtwängler raised his baton. There was silence in the orchestra pit. There was silence on stage. Nobody amongst the seven hundred and fifty people in the audience dared breathe. The applause diminished to the joy of anticipation. The last cheer was absorbed by the walls of the Opera after Furtwängler had walked to the conductor's rostrum and taken his bow. When he turned his back on the audience, and addressed himself to the orchestra and the music, it marked the beginning of Puccini's most beloved of operas. Maestro Furtwängler lowered his arms and the orchestra took up the introductory bars of the overture to *Tosca*. Behind the curtain there was an empty stage. The curtain wouldn't be raised for some moments, not until the last strains of the overture had drifted over the audience and into the reckoning of history.

And as the overture died, Angelotti, a man described as a revolutionary, would come running on to the stage, desperately seeking the key to the vault of the empty church of Sant'Andrea della Valle in Rome. It was June 7, 1800 and the armies of Napoleon were spreading their revolutionary message throughout Europe. The Italians however had pushed back the Humanists and once again the Monarchists were in charge. This was the context in which Puccini had staged his opus; in the background of the stage was the painting of the Madonna which would be the beginning of the conflict between Tosca and her painter-lover.

Eva looked from the wings out into the audience. Normally a diva would wait in her dressing-room until she was called ten minutes before she was due to appear. But tonight, Eva had insisted on coming from the dressing-room and up to the stage in order to breathe in the atmosphere of the event, as though she could absorb its full power to give her greater authority, to give her Tosca a finer voice with more conviction.

She saw the curtain rise. There was a ripple of applause from the audience. It was a new set design, a bold and imaginative re-creation of the church. The audience, used to the glamour of Italian Baroque settings, was disappointed with the stark lines inspired by Albert Speer, Hitler's architect, who had done some sketches for his friend, the opera's designer. The church was monolithic and sparse and what applause there was very quickly diminished as Angelotti ran onto the stage to increasingly frantic music, as he searched everywhere for the key. Finally he found it and let himself into the vault before the old sacristan, muttering to himself as he shuffled into the church, began the grudging job of tidying and arranging and taking care of chores. The moment Cavaradossi appeared and the glorious singing began, the audience settled back to enjoy a work which, since its premiere just thirty-four years earlier, had quickly become one of the most beloved of operas in the repertoire.

Eva searched the front rows for Reinholdt. He was sitting there, resplendent in his black uniform with its medals from battles he had fought on the street. She felt a thrill of joy as he searched the stage for the first glimpse of her. Beside him sat other colleagues, men who had worn brown uniforms until yesterday and were now handsome in their shining black garb of authority.

She turned her attention from the audience to the performers. She had sung in three *Toscas* but always as a member of the chorus, appearing for the first time out of the wings of the stage to assemble as an ecclesiastical congregation at the end of Act One, when the evil police captain Scarpia was sending Tosca on her way in order to entrap Cavaradossi. The final moments of Act One *Va Tosca* when they sang the Angelus and the entire chorus, soloists and orchestra rose to an overpowering crescendo was one of the greatest moments in the entire history of dramatic music. But she had never in her life been anything but a voice in that chorus.

Now she was to sing the sumptuous arias which made *Tosca* into Puccini's finest dramatic work. She would walk across a near-empty stage and sing the ethereal and magnificent *Vissi d'arte*; she would stab the Machiavellian Scarpia in the back with a dagger and shout to the audience, 'This is Tosca's kiss'. In the third act, she would sing her love to Cavaradossi as he was led up the castle steps to be shot by a firing squad which Tosca had been tricked to believe would be firing blanks. Until the final moment when she clutched her dead lover in her arms, she truly believed that she would escape with her lover to revel in a life of joy and passion. And then, in the final breath of the opera, she would find herself totally alone on the battlements, spot-lit, visible to all, aware that the entire procession of the musical drama was on her shoulders alone. And she would sing of her love and her grief and then she would fling herself off the roof of the Castel Sant'Angelo. And then she would arise from the unseen mattress and walk hurriedly around the flats and props and hurry over the cables to the distant applause of the audience for a curtain call.

Applause? Would there be applause? Would they like her? Would they compare her to other great divas with whom they were intimately familiar? Wilhelm Furtwängler had told her she had an excellent voice, one which would be much prized in the future. In the future? But what about now? Now was her future. Now was the moment that she had been waiting for ever since she was a little girl performing *leide* in front of Herr and Frau Büchbinder's guests, bowing to their polite applause. She had known applause since she had become a proper opera singer. She had revelled in it as a member of the chorus and then more so when there were appreciative and increasingly loud hand claps and the occasional whistle and yell of 'Bravo' from the audience as she had bowed for minor solo roles which she had performed. But nothing like this.

Suddenly she and Cavaradossi and Scarpia would be alone at the front of the stage, standing before the cast, identified for everyone to see as the three singers who carried the entire weight of the work on their shoulders. And they, being gentlemen, would allow her to step one pace in front of them, and they would clap as she took a bow. She could hear the applause of the audience now. She could hear Reinholdt and his colleagues in the SS standing and screaming 'Bravo! Bravo!' She would glance down into the orchestra pit and see Furtwängler smiling up at her before he quickly disappeared into the bowels of the pit and then up the steps into the wings to walk onto the stage and to hold her hand and bow with her. She could hear it all so clearly. All she had to do was perform as she had performed at this morning's full dress rehearsal. Her voice had been clear and sharp, beautifully melodic in the high registers. Even the cleaners who were sitting in the audience waiting for the performance to finish before they continued, had applauded and shouted 'Bravo' when she finished one aria after another.

She swallowed and cleared her voice, closing her mouth tightly so that no sound came out but practising the notes of the arias in her mind. Most singers performed last minute rehearsals in their dressing-rooms, warming up their voices, practising scales so that their vocal chords were in fine mettle when they walked on to the stage. There were no second chances. The moment a soloist – soprano, contralto, tenor or baritone – walked on, the performance had to be perfect from the very first note. An inadequate opening aria would set the audience against the singer. There would be shuffling in their seats, polite coughs, maybe the occasional nudge or comment whispered into the ear of a companion. The audience didn't realise that singers knew what was going on, that there was a very potent intercourse between audience and singer. Opera singers knew from the very opening bars whether the audience liked their voices and if they didn't, if the opening bars were inadequate, then it was a devil's own job to get the audience back.

'Start off well and they'll shout "bravo" all night,' Furtwängler had told her. 'Start out badly and it can take the whole opera before they forgive you.'

She cursed herself for her arrogance and stupidity at not having stayed in her dressing-room to practise her scales. Why did she think she was any different from any other singer who had trodden the boards before her? Now she was worried. She should have been practising. Instead, her youthful and naive arrogance told her that she could do anything she wanted. She walked quickly away from the stage and into a corridor. The moment that the sound of the singers disappeared she began to practise her scales, up and down, up and down, high to low. She sang the opening lines of the first aria. It was slightly discordant. She sang it again and then again and her confidence returned as her voice warmed. She turned and walked back to the stage, ready to make her entrance.

The shouts and applause were still ringing in her ear as she did up the zipper on her trousers and pinned Reinholdt's rose firmly on to her breast pocket. She was alone for the first time since the morning. Totally and completely alone. She had even dismissed Helga after her dresser had helped her remove her costume and laid out her evening wear, a new black silk ensemble of trousers, top and waistcoat which Reinholdt had surprised her with when he came backstage after the performance.

She was amazed at how quiet solitude was. From the very early morning when she had entered the State Opera, she had been surrounded by the communion of people. Encouragement, warnings, concerns, the shouts of tradesmen, the banging of hammers and the rasping of saws, discordancies of the orchestra tuning up, the chatter of her dresser, her own voice in her mind and then in her ears as she practised her role ... and then finally walking on to the stage and berating Cavaradossi for daring to have another woman's face as the Madonna.

The moment she had overcome those first slightly tremulous notes, the moment she had launched into the full register of her voice, she knew she had the audience with her. Their silence, listening to every cadence in her voice, was overwhelming. They even interrupted the drama by applauding her at the end of an aria. She had been forced to walk to the front of the stage and bow, something which Furtwängler detested, but which the audience had demanded. And it was as infectious as measles. From the end of the first Act, the audience was waiting for every high-flying moment of her appearance, cheering her as though she was a ... a what? A film star?

Fifteen curtain calls. Fifteen! Not even the greatest divas at the Berlin Opera had enjoyed fifteen curtain calls. But they wouldn't let her go. And nor was she so lacking in confidence to think that it was Reinholdt alone leading the charge. Sure, he could have caused one or maybe two curtain calls; but the demands for her continual reappearance came from every section of the hall. She looked at Reinholdt sitting and beaming in pleasure as his colleagues stood around him and the entire audience was on their feet, shouting and clapping and screaming 'Bravo!' 'Encore!' and then Furtwängler instructed the curtain to remain down.

After that, it was a melee. First her operatic colleagues, both soloists and chorus, crowded around, congratulating, kissing, marvelling, exulting. Then the management had come out and kissed her and congratulated her. She was in a daze. She was beside herself. She hardly heard any of the words, just the voices. And then the voices suddenly stopped because Maestro Furtwängler appeared again at the side of the stage and walked towards her. He had returned from congratulating the orchestra; normally after appearing onstage, he would return to the orchestra pit and not be seen again until the following day. This was a rare appearance indeed. It could have been one of the Crown Heads of Europe the way the crowds parted. He walked through the aisle which the cast and crew had made for him, his eyes fixing on Eva as he drew closer and closer. He was taller than she was, straight and handsome, aesthetic and intellectual. He held out his hand. She placed hers in his and he kissed hers in an ennobling way.

'The audience has said it all, my dear. Your performance tonight was excellent. There are things which we must talk about in regard to your timing but that's for the morning. Tonight is your night and I don't want to spoil it. As a debut it was magnificent and you may think of me as crotchety and harsh but there's something that I have to tell you in front of all of your friends and admirers. And it has to be said now, whilst you are feeling triumphant.

'You must understand, Eva, that even though you feel that you are there right at this very minute, you're not yet at the top of the ladder. With hard work, you'll get there. Your voice has all the potential for being one of the greatest on the stage. But your inexperience showed tonight and if you are to go beyond Berlin to Paris, Milan and even Rome, then you have much to learn. I don't wish to dampen your excitement because tonight's debut was a triumph, but I must tell you this, Eva. Don't think that because of the audience, you have ended your journey. The next stage of the journey is the most difficult of all. It's where humility has to condition your every success. Where experience has to be your teacher. And where you must learn from the many mistakes which you will continue to make. Tonight's audience willed you to succeed. Audiences in La Scala and the Metropolitan will be in love with another soprano and will be willing you to fail. In order to triumph, you must exceed even your own expectations.'

He picked her hand up and kissed it again.

'Now go, Eva. Enjoy the glory of your successes. And in the morning, we'll talk again. Because tomorrow night you have another performance and tomorrow night's audience will expect as much of you as tonight's audience. There's no resting on laurels when you're a star. Each night's performance is a new experience for the people out there ... the only people who matter.'

Ever since she'd returned to her dressing-room, she'd been musing over his words. She would think about them again overnight, but not now. Now she was entitled to revel in her glory; now she'd earned the warmth of the love and regard which was going to be heaped upon her.

She put mascara on her eyelashes, checked her lipstick and turned towards the door. It was then that she saw the telephone, sitting accusingly on her dressing-room table.

She looked at the clock. It was 11.30. Dare she? Yes, she would. She picked up the phone and dialled the operator. She gave the number in Munich. Eventually, a sleeping voice answered the phone after ten rings.

'Mother, it's Eva.'

'What's the matter?' asked her mother in consternation. 'Why are you ringing so late? Are you alright? Is there a problem?' Her voice rose in a crescendo of concern.

'I'm fine. I've just come off ... I've been singing ... I just wanted to talk to you.'

'What's the matter. You don't ring unless something's the matter.'

'Mother, I want to come home and see you. There are things which I have to explain to you and Father; things about me which you don't know.'

'Don't come to Munich! Do you hear me, Eva? You mustn't. It's too dangerous. Especially now. The streets are very bad. Since Hitler became Chancellor, the Nazi's are doing terrible things. They're openly arresting Jews. We stay in the house. You remember this camp they've built at Dachau, just outside Munich. The one where they took Samuel Büchbinder. Well, since last year, they've increased their arrests of priests and Jews and Gypsies and cripples and Slavs and are throwing them in there. Anybody they don't like they take into protective custody. Anybody who says anything against Hitler disappears off the street. They say they've got 10 000 people locked up in there. Some come out and the things they've said about what goes on is just horrible. Beatings. Starvation. God knows how many people have actually died in there. The Nazis don't care. Don't come, Eva. I'm glad about the opera. I'm glad what's happening. We'll ...'

Her mother stopped speaking. How could Eva tell her mother that she knew all about Dachau; that Reinholdt had told her everything; that for once, she'd listened mute and acquiescent, nodding as he explained the purpose of the camp, and how locking up Germany's enemy within would make everything so much safer for the future of the Reich. Eva waited for her mother to continue, 'You'll what, Mother? What is it you'll do …?'

'Nothing,' said Serel.

'What?' asked Eva again.

She deeply regretted not having phoned more often, but how could she? There were people around her all the while. She was never free. She could never allow her real life to intervene into the lie she lived. No. That was an excuse. She was too scared to phone in case …

'What is it, Mother? What's happening?' she shouted, her mind beginning its path towards a state of panic.

'Your Father and I are thinking of going to Palestine.'

'Mother, this will all be over soon. I know these things. It's only temporary. Listen, it was in the papers yesterday … Hitler's been forced to stop the SA from doing things. Germany will settle down now. Röhm and his gang have been killed. Hundreds have been arrested. Things will soon get back to normal.'

'Ach!' shouted her mother disdainfully. 'When you left Munich you told us we should all go to Palestine. Now you're telling me that everything will be alright. You think a few German madmen being murdered will be the end of it. This is just the beginning.'

'Let me come and see you.'

'No,' said Serel immediately. 'No. Don't. Stay in Berlin. It's safer. We'll come and see you.'

Eva froze. 'I'll phone you again, Mother.'

'Alright,' said Serel.

'How's Father?'

'He's asleep. Now he's the man of the house he looks after everything. Frau Büchbinder isn't well. Remember she caught pneumonia last winter? Well, she hasn't got over it properly. She's coughing all the time. She's much thinner. You wouldn't recognise her. She asks about you always.'

'And Yitzchok and Rosl?' Her mother remained silent. 'Mother?'

'They're fine.'

Her voice belied reality. Panic was beginning to set in and Eva demanded, 'Mother, tell me the truth'.

In a whisper which Eva had to strain to hear, Serel said, 'Yitzchok is in Dachau. They took him last month.'

Eva suddenly went numb. She whispered, 'Have you seen him?'

Again silence.

'Don't come to Munich, Eva. Stay where you are. One thing I have to say … all those years ago … when you left the house … when I came out and you were in the taxi waiting to go to the station … you made the right move. You were right. We should have got out of Munich then. We stayed. We were wrong. You're safer there. Look at you. Berlin is safe. Safer than here, anyway.'

'Can you come to Berlin? I'll find you an apartment, something.'

'And leave Frau Büchbinder?'

'But you said you were going to Palestine. You'll be leaving her anyway.'

There was a silence. Neither woman spoke. Then, softly her mother said, 'How could you think that we'd leave here without her. We're taking Frau Büchbinder to Palestine with us. And she's trying to get her children out. Rosl and the children are coming with us, and Yitzchok and his family when we can arrange for his freedom. You must come with us. You must.'

Another silence.

'Before you go to Palestine, come here. Leave Frau Büchbinder, Mother. In these days, you must only think of yourselves.'

'You're a silly girl Eva. You always were silly and headstrong. Without us, she'll die. Phone me again in a week.'

Her mother put the phone down. Eva's night of operatic triumph had evaporated. She was encased in a tomb of silence and guilt. Outside her room and down the corridor in a reception area, Reinholdt and ten of his colleagues in the SS were waiting to take her to a prearranged supper. They would be eating with other members of the cast and even Furtwängler had said that he may drop around if he wasn't too tired. How could she go with them? How could she be a part of it? Everything in the lie which was her life was perfection. Everything she'd always wanted. So long as she closed her eyes on her past. But her past was now a part of her future. How could she close her eyes on her own parents? Her brother? Her sister? How could she ignore their plight?

But what could she do about it? Her hands were shaking. She breathed deeply to control her emotions. She stood and walked to the door. She looked at her image in the mirror and beamed a smile. She had to regain the role of Eva. She had to be what she had become, and so she spent a minute practising her smile.

'Hello, thank you so much for coming.'

'Yes, I was pleased with the performance.'

'I'm so happy.'

'Wasn't Furtwängler marvellous?'

She was mouthing phatic expressions, mere pleasantries. Did the people she was about to meet have any conception of the damage they were doing? Did they know anything about what she and her mother had just been speaking? What did they know, and what would they do if they ever came face to face with the truth?

She grasped the door handle and looked one more time in the mirror. She smiled at her image, practising a beaming and innocent look. She had a pleasing image. An image of calm and control. Her image was in command of her environment and her society. She smiled at her image.

'Hello, I'm Eva Stricher,' she told herself. 'I'm an opera singer. I'm a diva.' And then she opened the door and walked out of her dressing-room.

CHAPTER SEVENTEEN

BERLIN, SEPTEMBER 1941

The war was going exceptionally well and Germany was suffused with a feeling of pride in the achievements of its God come to Earth. Everything the Führer did was a new and phenomenally successful adventure in expansion for the Master Race of the Third Reich, yet devastating for those who stood in the path of Aryan progress. Now all Germany, every German citizen, was convinced of the absolute truth that there was nothing on Earth which could stop them; no force, no army, no government which was strong enough to contain the Reich's expansive thrusts into alien territory.

And this was especially true since the armies of the Reich had invaded the Soviet Union in June. Throughout central Germany, and including the newly conquered lands of greater Germany, which included the former Poland, Czechoslovakia and France, generals, colonels, leaders of political and police units, ideological advisers, wealthy businessmen, stars of German film and radio, journalists, and intellectuals could be found on any night dining on the very best of food and wine, at the very finest restaurants or being served delicious meals by newly acquired slave-servants in their own homes. Germany was flushed with money. The Reichsbank seemed to have an endless supply coming to it from Switzerland, as well as from industries and contributors in the newly conquered territories.

But the good news wasn't only financial and territorial. Businesses such as IG Farben, Volkswagen and Krupp, whose labour costs had fallen dramatically because of the generosity of the slave labour programme, now enjoyed astronomical production figures and massively increased profitability because of the insatiable needs of the war machine. Adolf Hitler had already won the most difficult war … that for the hearts and minds of the sceptics and enemies who had originally opposed his rise to the Chancellorship. His success was all the convincing his one-time opponents needed; now everybody was goosestepping to the strains of the *Horst Wessel*.

The Führer had performed miracles and he was always the first toast at every dinner party in every part of the greater German empire.

At a table laden with food, surrounded by some members of the hierarchy of Berlin's Nazi Party, including the leaders of its political, police and military elite, *SS Gruppenführer* Reinholdt Stricher stood and raised his Bohemian lead crystal wineglass of rich red claret and said, 'Friends, ladies and gentlemen, comrades, would you please stand and join me in a toast to the Führer'. There was a shuffling of chairs, the rustling of skirts, straightening of uniforms. Everybody stood and raised their glass and shouted as one, 'The Führer '.

Eva smiled as broadly as everybody else, but she mentioned the name only in an undertone. She had even taken to biting her tongue to remember the pain which her people were suffering and her guilt at the pleasure she was enjoying. She stood as tall as the others, raised her glass as high as everybody else, but each time she drank a toast such as this – and these dinner parties were becoming increasingly frequent as Reinholdt's position within the SS hierarchy in Berlin become increasingly important – her confused thoughts flooded back to those divine times when she was growing up in the Büchbinder house. And her memories always settled on the joy and serenity of the *Seder* nights of the Jewish Passover, at which Jews remembered the suffering of the Hebrew slaves in Egyptian captivity; they would eat eggs in a salt-water soup to remember the tears shed by the Hebrew slaves; they would eat bitter herbs to remember the bitterness of the work; and they would eat *matzos* to remember the haste with which the Jews had to leave the evils of captivity to escape to the freedom of their own God-given land, all those millenia ago.

Nothing, it seemed, changed with the passage of time. Once again, the Jews were slaves of evil taskmasters; once more, they were being beaten, murdered, and bent and bloodied by the whips and brutality of a supposed master race. And like Moses, Eva was a hidden Jew, living in the palace of the Pharaoh, enjoying all the privileges of power while her people were being destroyed … but she was no Moses; she would never rise up and throw off her golden robes and precious perfumes in order to join her people; she was too afraid.

She was the consort of one of the Egyptian slave masters, while her people's backs were being broken by taskmasters in concentration camps or were hiding like sewer rats beneath the streets of Berlin like U-boats in the sea, terrified of showing their faces and suffering the inevitability of transportation.

After the toast, the company sat and the food was served by their three maids. The first course was a vichysoisse, a recipe which their German-French cook had brought with her from Alsace. Eva's guests were talking animatedly as it was being served, the many different conversations being about the war, or the British bombing, or the latest film from UFA – people in Berlin still couldn't get used to the new name Goebbels had invented a couple of years back. UFi! What sort of a name for a film studio was UFi?

The man sitting next to Eva was Ernst Hiemer, editor of *Der Sturmer*. Since he had arrived half an hour earlier he had been talking to Eva in the reception room about a project on which he was currently working. Though she was passionately disinterested, she smiled and nodded animatedly as he explained, 'Three years ago I wrote a book for older schoolchildren called *The Poisonous Mushroom*. It was an allegorical tale about a mother, in a walk through the forest, telling her son Franz that there are good people and bad people in the world, just as there are good and poisonous mushrooms. It was a simple metaphor to explain how a poison like Judaism can spring up even in the most lush and fertile of environments like the German intellectual enlightenment. I'm currently revising it in light of the recent findings which have been conducted on Jews as proof of their inherent evil.'

She nodded. There was so much she wanted to say, so much which caution prevented her from saying. And she had made the mistake the last time she had had this type of conversation of asking the proponent of Nazi ideology to explain just what it was in Judaism that was so threatening to the Nazi State. Her question had sounded innocent enough but it was received badly and Reinholdt had been forced to intervene laughingly to explain that his wife, while a brilliant opera singer, had neither head nor heart for politics and must be excused if her words seemed to indicate a less than patriotic attitude towards the threat posed to the fascist nation by the Jews. That night he had been stern in his warnings of the dangers of what she was saying.

She looked over at Reinholdt who, despite being at the opposite end of the table, had a marvellous ability to tune in to a conversation far away and listen intently, not only to the words but also the manner in which they were spoken. She smiled at him and he raised his glass.

'This is very fascinating,' she said to Ernst Hiemer. 'As I'm sure you would appreciate, being an opera singer, I know little about politics, and even less about Jews. But what does concern me, Herr Doctor, is that Jews seem to have contributed so much to the world of science and art. It's something which I have always found hard to understand if they are as evil as you say.'

He nodded thoughtfully. 'Your point is well made, Frau Stricher. It's something which many of us have wondered about. How can there be so many works through the ages that have been written by the Jewish race and which appear to have stood the test of time? But the explanation is really quite simple, if you stop and think about it for a moment. The works are, without exception, decadent and easily dismissed. They have become part of the Western tradition because Jewish financiers have spent fortunes buying them and popularising them to artificially elevate the creators to a status which their talent simply doesn't fit.'

'Ah,' said Eva, warmly, raising her glass to toast the genius of the man sitting beside her. 'That's a good point. Something which I hadn't thought of.'

Warming to his theme, Herr Hiemer continued. 'You see, we've burned many millions of different books written by Jews for Jews. Indeed, you, I'm sure would remember May 1933 when the German Students' Corporation organised for the burning of Jewish books throughout all Germany's universities. I was in Berlin when Herr Dr Goebbels' speech was transmitted on radio throughout the city. Students, doctors, professors in academic robes joined with us to burn the works of Marx, Bloch, Freud, Hirschfeld, Heinrich Heine, Mann, Glaeser, Brecht, Hemingway and many others. All filth and trash. They shouted "No to decadence and moral corruption! Yes to decency and morality in family and state!" All these Jews or Jew sympathisers were guilty of membership of an intellectual underclass and of committing political treason, as well as activities alien to the *Volk*.

'Try to understand, my dear Frau, that superficially these works may sound intelligent. They may read well. But below the surface is a much more dangerous message. Nobody is denying the native cunning or intelligence of the Jew but what is the purpose, Frau Stricher, of Jews writing so much? Only other Jews would be interested in reading their words, which leads you then to the obvious conclusion that below the surface is this deeply hidden message. We're working on it at the moment to try to decode that message but it's obvious that it's to do with universal control.

'There has been, since the time of their expulsion from Judea in 70 AD, a universal policy by the Jews to gain control and ultimate power of world government. This is an established fact. It's beyond question. The Crusaders knew about it. The Popes knew about it. The Spanish monarchy under Ferdinand and Isabella knew about it. King Edward I of England knew all about the conspiracy when he expelled the bloodsuckers. He was particularly brilliant. First he borrowed all their money; then he expelled the lot of them in 1290. Catherine the Great of Russia knew about it. And they all adopted similar policies. To ensure that there was no domination by the Jews of their countries, all these great rulers enforced mass expulsions. As we are doing, making Berlin and other cities *Judenrein*. Jew-free. Throughout history, Jews have been forced to wear hats and badges to identify themselves as a way of warning the indigenous populace. Indeed, at the beginning of September, the Führer issued orders that all German Jews must wear yellow stars with the word Jude written clearly inside to identify them. The poisonous mushroom, my dear Frau Stricher. The poison mushroom!'

Reinholdt's voice at the opposite end of the table was suddenly raised slightly as he explained a point to Gunther Bauer, a Luftwaffe officer and one of his closest friends. He and Gunther had been in university together in Munich. They had shared women, shared drinks, and shared experiences for years in their student days. But whereas Reinholdt had joined the SA at his father's behest, Gunther, coming from a family of military men, had decided instead to follow the tradition of his Colonel father and General grandfather and join the forces. But his engineering knowledge and love of flying inclined him away from the Wehrmacht and into the air force. And he had not once regretted the move. He was a natural flier, at his happiest when he was in the air. Or when he was dining with Eva and Reinholdt.

Yet, during the past few months when he had been back from active duty on the Front, his attitude towards Reinholdt had changed. Mysteriously. Eva had been the first to notice the growing distance between Gunther and Reinholdt and it worried her, but she kept her peace.

As often happened in the intercourse of dinner parties, the conversation around the table hushed so that a person making a dominant or vital point, could be listened to by everybody. Eva looked up in concern, and in gratitude that the insufferable, evil, and ignorant bore beside her was forced to follow her gaze.

'You may think we're moving way too far, too fast, Gunther, but let me assure you that the Führer knows precisely what he's doing,' said Reinholdt. Eva knew from the tone of his voice that he was trying to truncate a conversation. She wondered how she could help him.

But the young air force officer suddenly realised that he was being listened to by everybody at the table. He also knew that one of those listening was in the political wing of the SS and that his words would undoubtedly be reported. But there were things he had to say and the claret gave him the confidence.

'That may be the case, Reinholdt, but these damn people of yours. The SS. The mass murderers who go in after the German army's advance. I mean, this is the most uncivilised form of warfare in all of history.'

A chill came over the table. Dr Hiemer shifted his attention from his beautiful hostess and concentrated on the opposite end where the young air officer was speaking. He listened with interest.

'I know this is going to sound traitorous and unpatriotic but for God's sake, we're all human beings around this table. The Reich has made marvellous military and territorial gains. The Führer is a genius. Nobody in their right mind could deny this but surely with victory comes magnanimity. Every invading army through history has learned that unless it makes an honourable peace with those it has conquered, then they will rise up and ultimately destroy their conquerors. Alexander the Great knew it. Saladin knew it. The Führer is no less a commander than these great men. Greater, in fact. But why does he send in the SS *Einsatzgrupen* after the German army's conquered enemy territory? Do you know what they do?' he said raising his voice, emotion now overtaking the reason which the claret had afforded him.

Desperately, Reinholdt tried to silence the young man before it was too late, 'Gunther, there are ladies present.' He burst out laughing. 'Surely we don't want to talk military matters when …'

But Gunther wasn't to be stopped. His disgust took

control of his sense of preservation. 'I'll tell you what they do. They follow in the path of the Panzers and the foot soldiers and the combat troops and they round up Jews and Slavs and anybody else who's on their list. And they take them into fields and they mow down innocent civilians with machine guns mounted on motorcycles. They don't even bother to bury the bodies any more. There's too much work for them to do.

'This isn't why I joined the air force, Reinholdt. Not to be part of a mass killing machine. What would my grandfather, the General, have said if he'd seen what was going on? How can I look my father in the eyes?'

He looked down disconsolately at the table and realised from the silence that people were staring at him in shock.

'I'm sorry. I know this isn't the time or place to discuss these matters. But I've just come back from a Luftwaffe conference where these matters were being discussed and I found it very difficult to comprehend that a nation like Germany, a nation which produced Goethe and Beethoven and Bach, could do such a thing. It's against all the protocols of armed warfare. It's against the Geneva Convention.'

Now he had gone too far. Reinholdt looked down the table in sadness as Dr Hiemer smiled and said, 'Need I remind the young man that the Greater Germany Reich also produced such degenerates as Schoenberg, Mendelssohn and Mann whose so-called art is incomprehensible and effete. Certainly we have produced the world's very finest artists, writers and intellectuals, but all without exception have been Aryan. Not one has owed his origins to membership of the Semitic or Slavic races.

'I might also point out that the Third Reich isn't a signatory to the Geneva Convention. Need I also remind the young man that when the second agreement of the

Geneva Convention was signed in 1907, it forbade many other things which are now generally accepted as perfectly legitimate means for a country to express itself in times of war.'

'No country,' insisted Gunther, 'can surely accept the deliberate mass murder of enemies. Of course civilians are killed in wars; that's an unavoidable consequence. But the deliberate killing of tens of thousands of unarmed men and women and children by armed thugs?' He shook his head sadly.

Hiemer took off his glasses and cleaned them with his napkin. It was a deliberate ploy he had used as a teacher when students needed to be put in place. It enabled the attention of everybody to be concentrated on him and away from the indignation of the air force officer, who might soon turn the other dinner guests' heads to his point of view. Replacing his glasses on his nose, he looked more carefully at the young man.

'My friend,' he said patiently. 'This year alone, over 2000 Jews have been killed in Romania. One hundred thousand Jews have been rounded up and sent to Kommandant Hoss in Auschwitz Concentration Camp. We've occupied Bulgaria with the consequent need to quell disturbances amongst the population. German Jews are now doing forced labour for our war machine. We've invaded Yugoslavia. We've made mass round-ups of Jews in Paris. Marshal Pétain has delivered France to us with hardly a loss on our side. We've invaded the Soviet Union. We've established ghettos all over eastern Europe to rein in the Jews so that we can concentrate them and know where they are. We've established another concentration camp near Lublin in Poland called Majdanek. Four thousand Jews were killed in a pogrom conducted by Lithuanians at Kovno. Seventy thousand Jews died on a forced march in Romania. Twenty thousand Jews were rounded up by the Hungarian army. And best of all, and may I say that this is only for your ears and not to be broadcast more widely, we're testing a new kind of gas called Zyklon-B at a newly built extension to Auschwitz called Birkenau as a method of dealing with the Jewish problem in a more cost-effective manner.'

Gunther, sobering up rapidly, looked coldly at the SS man and said, 'Your point?'

'My point is that there are things which are happening throughout Europe which are unstoppable and which are being conducted for the better good of Germany and the German people. You can't make an omelette without cracking eggs. You can't build a thousand year Reich by bowing and scraping to all the forces of morality which might threaten to weaken the resolve of the Führer. The time for conventional armies and conventional warfare will shortly be at an end. Political decisions will hold sway. New remedies are called for to deal with the problems which face the German nation as it expands throughout Europe and conquers the territory it needs to give it living space. We can't have a world governed by German people, yet which is subverted by Fifth columnists, internationalists, subhumans, homosexuals, Jews, Slavs, communists and other filth and excrescences which seep through the body of a nation and which weaken its strength. Your attitude, my dear young man, leaves me perplexed. Were we not at a dinner party hosted by my gracious colleague, *GruppenFührer* Stricher and his beautiful and talented wife, I would discuss these matters with you, shall we say, more intensely. However, I will defer to our circumstances and allow you to reflect upon my words. I'm in a particularly good frame of mind as the vichysoisse is my favourite soup and I know that we have a fine meal of roast pork, so I shall do nothing to interrupt my digestion or that of my fellow diners, other than to say that you should reflect very carefully on your words before you say them again. The next time you say them, my dear young man, you may find the consequences far less pleasant than what is about to arrive at the table.'

Realising that Gunther had imperilled himself gravely, Reinholdt said, 'I fear my friend has had far too much to drink'. He reached over and grasped him around the neck, shaking his head like school boys tousle each other. 'He doesn't mean these things, Ernst. It was the claret speaking. Not Gunther. Gunther is a good patriotic German, aren't you? Eh?'

He grasped Gunther's hair and pulled it tightly. There was no doubting the escape route that Reinholdt was trying to provide. Gunther smiled weakly. 'Forgive me. I've had far too much to drink and I'm exhausted from the conference. I said things I shouldn't have said.'

'Of course,' said Reinholdt. 'Now, let's have the table cleared so that we can get on with the next course.'

Relieved, the guests smiled and turned to each other to talk about anything other than politics or the war. Eva finished her soup, feeling sick to her stomach. If ever she opened her mouth to the truths she was thinking, she could expect far worse treatment than had just been meted out to the Luftwaffe officer.

The dinner party came to an end. Gunther was one of the first to leave, kissing Eva's hand and thanking her for a delightful dinner. He also apologised for forgetting himself temporarily. All the others left within a ten-minute period, except for Ernst Hiemer who dawdled over a cigar beside the fireplace in the lounge room. Reinholdt saw the last but one of his guests to the door and walked back to the lounge. He knew he would have to confront the situation sooner rather than later, but he didn't get a chance. Hiemer accosted him the moment he entered the room.

'It surprises me Reinholdt, that a man such as you would have had a traitorous Luftwaffe officer in your midst.'

'His thoughts came as a complete surprise to me as well, Ernst. I've always thought he was a loyal soldier, a patriot. But you never can tell in this day and age, can you? Anyway, bearing in mind he's a Luftwaffe officer, it might be best if we were to forget what happened? Put it down to the wine?'

Heimer looked at him as if he was mad. It spoke more eloquently than any words might, that a death sentence had just been pronounced upon Gunther, and nothing could prevent it. 'All the more reason to show him the error of his ways, my dear Reinholdt. Allow that sort of treason to spread within the officer ranks, and you'll soon have a mutiny.'

Reinholdt said, 'I'll give you his name and details so that you can follow him up later.'

'Later? I will be doing it tonight.'

'As you wish.'

'Why didn't you support me at the table?' Ernst asked as Reinholdt walked towards his writing desk to jot down Gunther's full name and unit number.

'I'm a host. It was my duty to ensure that my guests enjoy themselves. Any SS or party matters can be attended to afterwards.'

'Your duty as an SS officer surely supersedes your duty as a host. That man was uttering treason. Your guests will now believe that you aren't as staunch a party member as they might have expected. This might count against you in the long run.'

'My guests know my loyalty to the Führer and to the cause. But one thing Gunther said was right.'

Ernst Hiemer looked at him in surprise.

'We're a civilised nation. How can a nation who produced Goethe, Beethoven and Haydn' ... He tore the note from the pad and walked over, handing it to Hiemer; but he remained silent, realising the danger of what he was saying.

'Your point?'

'My point is that even in the most adverse and traitorous of circumstances, even during a bombing raid, no true German patriot would ever interrupt a fine meal.'

Hiemer looked at him closely and then burst out laughing. Reinholdt escorted the political theorist to the door. He clicked his heels, saluted and said '*Heil Hitler*'.

Reinholdt replied with as much gusto. Only when the door was closed did his smile drop and his jaw set. Eva was at the top of the stairs and came down quickly.

'Well?' she asked.

'The stupid fool. How could he have put me in a position like that? Especially with Hiemer here tonight.'

'He didn't realise. He was drunk,' said Eva urgently.

'No matter what, you don't make remarks like that in front of a friend of Heinrich Himmler. If I hadn't given him over, then you and I would find ourselves in Kurfurstenstrasse being tortured in one of the basements.'

'But what's going to happen to Gunther?' Eva asked urgently.

Reinholdt shook his head.

'What do you mean?'

'What do you think I mean, Eva? He spoke out against the SS. He's dead.'

'Not Gunther! No! He's your closest friend! I adore him. He has a wife and young family,' she shouted in horror.

'There's no saving him. The best I can do is to phone him and tell him to commit suicide.' He paused. 'No, I can't even do that in case he tries to escape. Ernst will know immediately that I've tipped him off. He's brought about his own destruction.'

'But he's your best friend.'

'There's nothing we can do.'

'But surely …'

'There's nothing we can do!' Reinholdt shouted.

Softly, she said, 'I'll go tomorrow to Bonn and comfort his wife.'

'You'll do no such thing. Anyway, by tomorrow, she and the children will be … who knows?'

Eva nodded. She knew that by morning, their friend would be dead, and his family shot. Eva felt tears welling up in her eyes.

'Let's go to bed. This is a night I want to forget,' said Reinholdt. He walked upstairs. She delayed a moment but then followed in his footsteps.

CHAPTER EIGHTEEN

FRANKFURT, PRESENT DAY

When Sarah returned from her unexpected meeting with the Swiss Minister for the Interior, the deterioration in Annelise's condition shocked her. It was as if she was getting frailer before Sarah's eyes. The meeting with the Swiss Minister had lasted only two hours. It was cordiality itself. It appeared as though The Krantz Institute would, after all, be granted a seat on the Tribunal investigating the disposal of Swiss-held assets. The decision had come much quicker than Sarah believed possible and even though it was still to be ratified, it had the Minister's support.

After the meeting, the official to whom she had first addressed her application explained why.

'If I might ask that what I am about to say to you is held in complete confidence, Sarah,' he said to her as he walked her to the waiting taxi outside his office building. 'The minister's pleasure at your application solves a very big problem for him. We have two competing applications from American Jewish organisations, both of whom are fiercely competitive and the Minister was terrified of internecine warfare. With your representation, the hostility between one group and the other will disappear by eliminating one of the applicants and we'll be able to get on with the work of returning stolen assets to their rightful owners.'

As she was shaking his hand, Sarah began to ask a question but he smiled.

'Of course I'm not going to tell you which are the two organisations. But let's just say that the League of Zionist Women will not be opening bottles of champagne next week.'

He kissed her on the hand as she got into the taxi. She would enjoy working with him. Her work in Switzerland was done. She could now fly home and report the good news to Josh. But she owed herself one day extra in Frankfurt.

She had already spent two full days with Annelise. Two days in which she had found out a surprising amount about her grandmother Eva's life. And yet … And yet there were so many inconsistencies in Annelise's tale. Sarah liked to believe that these were due to the old woman's frailty and loss of faculties but in her heart, Sarah knew that it was nothing to do with that. Her short-term memory was shot to hell but her long-term memory was so pinpoint accurate that Annelise could describe with phenomenal accuracy the deficiencies of the uniform of a particular SS lieutenant or the smell of the salted butter that she yearned for when the rationing began in Germany at the beginning of the war. Her description of wartime margarine as tasting like an oil slick on the tongue which didn't disappear with the change in tide, still sang in Sarah's mind as poetry.

When she arrived back in the Frankfurt nursing home, the nurses no longer questioned her presence, but smiled and wished her a good afternoon. 'Yes,' they said, 'of course you can see Frau Liebemann,' but in the twenty-four hours she'd been gone, the Frau Liebemann that she returned to seemed older.

'I thought you'd deserted me,' the old woman wheezed. 'I thought you'd gone.'

'I told you I had to go to Switzerland.'

'Did you? Oh. So many things have come back to me. During the night I woke in a sweat. I thought I was ill but then I realised I wasn't. I was remembering things long forgotten. You know the winter of 1942 was very cold,' she continued as though Sarah hadn't even been absent for the past day. 'It was very cold. I was living in a basement. The smell was … it was like being in a toilet. Your grandmother was very kind to me. She brought me things.'

'So you stayed friendly with my grandmother,' Sarah said, taking off her coat and sitting down on the bed. 'I had the feeling that your friendship was only before the war. You knew each other during the war?'

'Even when she was up there in the high society of Berlin,' said Annelise, pointing to the ceiling with her bony finger, 'she never forgot me. She would smuggle me food, look after me, give me money, papers.'

'Where did she get the papers from? I mean, how did she have papers, but you didn't? She was in high society. What, during the war?'

'There was … I don't know … I've forgotten so much. How? I don't know. You don't ask "how" in wartime. If you know people, you're lucky. You use them. Eva knew people. I didn't. She helped me.'

The old woman looked gaunt but Sarah felt a need to press her, as though she was trying to beat some hidden clock. 'Why were you living in such bad conditions in a basement, yet my grandmother had food. Was it this man who looked after her?'

'What man? What did I tell you?'

'You said that there was a non-Jewish man that protected her.'

'Yes,' said Annelise. 'And he protected me in the end.'

BERLIN, NOVEMBER 1942

Annelise apologised for the third time that afternoon about the state of her apartment, though only the most generous of guests would have called it an apartment. It was a room off a basement underneath a mansion in the fashionable Prinzregenstrasse, a room which had once been used to house coal for the family's fires. A small electric light bulb lit the airless, windowless room and only the fragrant smell of tea brightened the dampness of the atmosphere. Even the tea had been provided by Eva, as well as the loaves of fresh bread, meats and butter, obtainable only by senior SS men.

The once-Christian, once-confident, once-secure Annelise was now a Jew again. Her false identity papers had been examined in a routine street search by a zealous SS man. She was thrown into the back of a truck, and driven with a dozen other illegals to SS Headquarters. Only luck and confusion in the collection yard behind the headquarters building had allowed her to slip into an alleyway and escape back into the streets. Two months ago, she had gone to ground and was now moving from basement to basement, room to room, tram to tram, bus to bus, underground station to underground station, to travel for an eternity like the *Flying Dutchman*, avoiding the constant searches of buildings by the Nazis.

People like her called themselves U-boats; subterranean Jews who desperately hid from prying eyes and almost every Berliner who rushed to report anything unusual to the SS. The mission of every U-boat was to avoid deportation to the East. Tens of thousands of Berlin Jews had already been deported to concentration camps in Poland and other places. Since late 1941, Gestapo men had begun systematically arriving at Jewish homes, ordering the occupants to be outside on the pavement within fifteen minutes, allowed to take only one suitcase for the entire family. British pilots had already destroyed thousands of German homes in their bombing raids, before these were halted because the air defences around the capital were proving too costly to the Allied war planes. But their work had been done in large measure. Berlin, once the most beautiful city in all of Germany, had been hideously scarred and much of it had been destroyed, district by district, building by building.

Three huge hideous flak towers now dominated the centre of the city. One in the zoological gardens near the Kaiser Wilhelm Memorial Church, another in the Humbolthain Park three kilometres north of the Unter den Linden, and the third in Friedrichshain Park near the Alexanderplatz. Hitler's architect, Albert Speer, had designed them to be the first buildings in Hitler's new city of Germania and they were erected to remind people of the medieval fortresses of the Crusader times when Germany's Teutonic knights were at the zenith of their powers. From a pragmatic point of view, they were ideal protection for the elite against the British bombers. They were built with reinforced concrete, and were bomb-proof and shellproof. The fortresses all had their own water and electricity supplies, their own hospitals and enough food and ammunition for a year-long siege.

But it was the eight 128-millimetre guns mounted in towers on the top of each flak tower, as well as four more gun positions housing 12 multi-barrelled 20 millimetre quick-fire *pompoms* and 37-millimetre cannons which caused devastation to the British flyers. It was these which forced the British High Command to order a halt to the bombing of Berlin.

But despite the air defences, the British air force had caused massive loss of housing and accommodation in the capital. Added to that was the arrival of tens of thousands of Jews from small towns and villages all over Germany, where they felt isolated and exposed. They arrived like lemmings into the capital, seeking the comfort of their co-religionists. The situation for Jews was horrendous. These starving newcomer families, not allowed to work and with next to no charity to rely upon, caused massive over-crowding in the increasingly accommodation-desperate city.

As Jewish families were evacuated from their homes by the collection units of the SS, they were rounded up and sent to the synagogue on Levetzowstrasse, still in ruins from its destruction on the notorious *Krystallnacht*. Despite the freezing cold, the families were forced to remain there, exposed to the bitter elements, for three days before being marched in procession through the city to the train station at Grunewald, where they were taken to ghettos in eastern Poland, Bellorussia, Lithuania and into Russia itself.

'Do you want me to be like them?' asked Annelise of her friend Eva. 'You say I should come out of this rat hole. Come and live with you. Do you know the madness of that? You're lucky. You're protected by your SS husband. If I was to try to find accommodation, even with you, some bastard would turn me in to the SS and then I would join all the other Jews in some ghetto. This place is bad enough, but in the ghettos, there'd be ten people in a room this size and God only knows what would happen to me in the concentration camps. Who would look after me then? And in the ghettos? What happens there? It's said the SS work people to death. Literally until they drop down dead. Eighteen hours a day until they die and then they throw them in the gutter to rot away. And you know about the killing troops, don't you?'

Eva shook her head as she sipped her tea. How could she possibly tell her best friend that she knew all about the killing troops and much, much more; stuff they were doing to the Jews in the East which was simply too hideous to believe.

'Annelise, you saved my life when I first came to Berlin all those years ago. For God's sake, let me help you.'

'You've given me enough help, Eva. Any more would endanger you.'

'Reinholdt doesn't know what I'm up to. He thinks I'm meeting with my opera friends for lunch.'

'Don't be a fool, Eva. You have no idea what it's like on the street. Children are telling the SS about what their parents say. Brothers against sisters. And there's no such thing as a neighbour any more.' She laughed. Her laugh was hollow, completely empty, devoid of life. 'If somebody sees that you've got an extra bit of bread on your table, they report you to the SS, without even thinking about it. It's a nightmare out there. You have no idea how bad it is. It's a daily horror.'

'That's why you should come and stay with me.'

She laughed. 'Your husband would just love that. Think straight, darling. Since I've lost my papers, I'm nameless. How would you introduce me? He's an SS man. By nature, he's suspicious. If he begins to investigate me, then I'll instantly be transported to the East, and you'll follow within hours.'

'Reinholdt won't. You don't know him like I do. He just pays lip service to the Nazis. He hasn't got his heart in what he's doing.'

'How do you know, Eva?'

She remained silent. In all honesty, she didn't know what her husband thought when he got to his office. He talked to her at night about marshalling resources like trains, trucks and diesel fuel in order to transport Jews from here to there, and there to somewhere else. But never once had he told her that he genuinely knew what was going on in these concentration camps. Of course, at their dinner parties and their social get-togethers with the hierarchy there was talk. Some of the scum even loved to tell her what was happening. But Reinholdt never admitted to being anything more than a glorified clerk; in charge of thousands of men, yes, but only in an administrative capacity. And Eva chose to believe him, because to believe he knew all about the camps and the deaths was more than she could abide.

Yet, how could he not know? Everybody in Berlin knew. Some said that American newspapers were now carrying stories about Jews being gassed.

And now that things were going so badly for the Germans in Russia, thousands upon thousands of injured German soldiers on crutches or with bandaged stumps where their limbs were missing, were wandering the streets of the city in anger and humiliation. There was increasing discontent. People more and more believed it was the Jews yet again who were responsible for Germany's defeat. Just as in the First World War it had been a Jewish conspiracy which forced Germany's surrender and its humiliation at the Versailles Conference, so now Jewish intrigue had upset Germany's plans. The situation for Jews was catastrophic. How long could she herself hope to survive?

'If you won't come and live with us, what can I do for you?' she asked. Annelise looked gaunt and ill. Weeks of living underground had made her skin sallow and dimmed her eyes. She only ever came out at night when the city was crowded with people, when she could walk like any beggar along the footpaths and find a tram to catch or a train to jump on to. It would take her in an obscene dance of hope and fear around the city, like riding through Dante's levels of hell. She would be going nowhere, a nameless woman, stateless, purposeless.

'I need a passport. I need papers. I need to get out.'

'Of course,' said Eva. 'You'll need money.'

Annelise nodded. 'It costs about 30 000 marks. A fucking fortune. There's a man on Xantnerstrasse who's an expert forger. He's a Jew.'

Eva blinked in surprise. Thirty thousand marks was indeed a fortune.

'Of course I'll get it for you. I can have it in a week.'

Annelise sighed in relief. 'Thank you' hardly seemed adequate. 'With that I can get a passport, food ration card, post office identification, police identity papers. And best of all, I can claim to be a *bombenscheine*, certifying that my original papers were lost in an air raid. Then I'll be able to get an apartment and a job, and I can live like a human being again. Can you really help me?'

'Of course,' said Eva. She put down her cup of tea and moved towards her friend who was sitting on the remnants of a couch, whose stuffing was sagging and whose springs now showed beneath the transparent skin of cloth. She put her arms around Annelise and drew her friend towards her. The young woman stank of perspiration and body odours. The relief made her unwind and she began to sob. Eva held her to her bosom. The words came out fitfully.

'You've no idea what it's like … haven't been able to wash … haven't seen a bar of soap. I'm starving. I'm so scared all the while. Everybody is my enemy.'

'I just thank God that you got a message to me, so that I could come and see you.'

Annelise lifted her face from Eva's bosom and looked at her. 'It took me a week to pluck up the courage to send you a message. I didn't know whether you were still a Jew or whether in your heart you'd become an SS Nazi.'

Eva was shocked. 'How could you think … ?'

'How could I not think, Eva. You're living in luxury. You dance every night. You eat good food. You smell of perfume. Why shouldn't I think that life was so easy for you that you would become one of them?'

Eva's participation in the dialogue came to an end at that moment. She still spoke, exchanged pleasantries, promised even more assistance and assured Annelise that she would see her soon; but it wasn't Eva that was speaking. The woman who continued the conversation was the Eva who lived with Reinholdt ... the Eva who was the other face. The real Eva ... the one who was shocked and hurt that Annelise had thought she might have become a Nazi ... that Eva was cringing from her accuser; that Eva was a little child, hurt and offended, and scared of herself; scared of how far she must have fallen to become as she had become. In the eyes of her friend; in the eyes of her parents and the Büchbinders and the Jewish community and ... and herself.

For the entire journey home, checking behind her to make sure she wasn't followed, Eva felt a sense of emptiness and desolation. As if her whole life had become inextricably entwined with the evil which was around her. Was she saving herself by clambering on the mangled corpses of her people? She played over Annelise's words in her mind.

No! Annelise was wrong! Surely to God she was wrong. Maybe Eva had become one of them in her body but never, ever, would she become one of them in her heart. That alone gave her back to herself. That alone gave her some semblance of the confidence, the self-possession, that she would need to go on.

DECEMBER, 1942

Three black Mercedes slid to a halt, sliding in the slush of the gutters outside the tenement block in the Strelitz district just outside central Berlin. It was a once-elegant part of town, now scarred by rubble and neglect. As the three cars skidded against the frozen sleet, men and women who had been scurrying along the footpath trying to avoid the bitter winds, looked in concern as SS officers in their long black leather overcoats and black hats jumped out of the cars. Even patriotic Germans with nothing to hide turned to avoid the stares of the SS men who ran into the tenement block and up the stairs.

Annelise Liebemann had no idea that the eight men were coming for her. She was sitting in front of her gas fire cooking a piece of toast on a fork, thanking God for her new-found fortune, when the entire small apartment reverberated to the imperious thumping of men pounding on her front door. Her body froze in sudden fear and panic. Even though she had papers identifying her as Liselotte Pfitzner, she lived every moment of her life these days with the fear of exposure. She had more confidence now than she had enjoyed for months, now that she had a passport and identification papers in her handbag. In the last month she had gained a job in a factory making soldiers' boots. Eva had helped her find this apartment and was paying the rent, and food was no longer a problem thanks to Eva's careless over-ordering for her own needs. She thought she was set up until the war ended. She was wrong.

She stood on shaking knees and heard the voice outside. 'Gestapo. Open the door immediately.'

A feeling of nausea suddenly made her want to gag. She became dizzy. Her nightmare was outside the door, just when she was beginning to see daylight again. Slowly, terrified, Annelise stumbled over and undid the latches. Opening the door a fraction, it was suddenly pushed open aggressively by a tall thin man wearing the black leather overcoat uniform of the most feared police unit in Germany, the Gestapo. The man pushed her aside and walked into the apartment followed by four others, all wearing identical clothes. Annelise nearly fainted but she knew her only way to save herself was by braving it out.

'What do you want? How dare you force your way in here like this!'

'Silence,' barked the man in charge. 'Your papers!'

'Who the hell are you? You show me your papers!' But her voice lacked any conviction.

She was trying to be brave, as brave as she had seen German citizens in the street when confronted by these official thugs throwing their weight around. But these were German citizens with nothing to hide. The officer looked at her in contempt.

'I'll tear your apartment to pieces unless you show me your papers immediately, Fräulein.'

'They're in my bag.' Her voice was quivering in fear but she knew that any sign of weakness would expose her to her greatest danger. Before she went to fetch her papers, she tried to brave out the situation for another moment, anything to give her time to think. 'Why are you here? Please tell me why you have burst into my apartment.'

'We arrested a forger two days ago. A Jewish forger. We have a list of the people for whom he has made identification papers. Your name is on that list.'

Annelise looked at the Gestapo officer, trying to comprehend the enormity of his words. Then she fainted.

She had no idea how long she was unconscious, but the next thing she remembered she was being manhandled downstairs, her feet scraping painfully over the stone steps, as two men carried her prostrate form down towards street level. She looked up and saw doors open to reveal frightened and curious people, but then the doors closed the moment the residents saw what was going on.

She allowed the men to pull her downstairs, not having the strength to struggle. The SS men were confronted on the ground floor by the owner of the building, her landlady, blocking their path at the bottom of the stairs.

'Where are you taking her? Her rent is only paid until the end of the week.'

'Out of my way!' commanded the SS Gestapo officer.

'Will she be back? Can I let her room? There's plenty of people want it. I can't afford to have her room vacant. What's the crime?'

'Silence!' he barked and pushed passed her.

Annelise struggled to walk as quickly as the SS men who held her firmly under her armpits; they were dragging her towards the front door of the apartment block. People had gathered on the sidewalk to look at the drama. There was relief on their faces that the Gestapo weren't after them. The people looked at her in curiosity. And then the freezing air hit her. A bitterness in the street from which her gas fire had protected her. All she was wearing was a dress and a cardigan. Suddenly she was freezing. She shivered through the cold and also through fear. The cup of tea she'd drunk half an hour ago suddenly erupted from her stomach, and spilled over the path ahead. But the SS men didn't care. They bundled her into the middle one of the three cars of the motorcade and drove off towards SS Headquarters in Burgstrasse. She whimpered in the pain of their grip, and tried to shuffle on the seat, tried to clean up the vomit on the front of her dress, but the men on either side of her were like marble statues, cold and unmoving.

The windows of the car were too dark for her to see out but she knew where she was going. She also knew that she would be tortured and she would die. She sighed. All the expense; all the danger; just for nothing. She prayed that she would never reveal the name of

Eva Stricher, even under the most extreme of torture …
but she didn't trust herself. She must find a way to kill
herself before the torture. Perhaps a knife on a desk;
perhaps pulling a gun from a holster.

The cars skidded on the sleet-slicked roads, their horns
screaming to warn everybody to get out of their way.
Buildings which she used to walk past in innocence and
impunity, buildings which she knew from their gaudy
windows, were suddenly flashing past her eyes. Peoples'
faces became a sea of confusion. She shook her head to
try to clarify the confusion, but all she could do was close
her eyes, and try not to be sick again. What remained of
the rest of her life was going so quickly. But it didn't
matter. She would be better off dead than living the life
she had lived. She could accept her death sentence if it
was quick and immediate; but not transportation to a
ghetto or a concentration camp; not torture. Please God,
she thought, let me die. That's all I want to do. Just die.

Eventually the convoy drove through the arched
portico leading into the garage area of the SS
headquarters building. More shuffling of feet, more
opening and closing of doors, more shouting and
screaming. More freezing cold atmosphere. And then she
was pushed crudely through a door and into a cold urine-
stinking corridor. She fell on the floor into a maze of
feet, but was pulled up aggressively by her hair. She
screamed in pain. More feet. More pushing. She tried to
keep upright but it was hard. Especially as the men were
wearing jackboots and she was wearing carpet slippers.

They frogmarched her downstairs into a cellar area,
then along more dimly lit corridors. Their footsteps
echoed along the green-tiled walls as they forced her to
sink lower and lower into the building, descending
staircases and walking along corridors in the cold and
damp dungeon. The muffled noises which she had heard

vaguely and from a distance above the footsteps became louder and more insistent. There were screams of men in agony. There were noises of dogs barking and howling. It was like descending into a pit of death. Her knees gave way and she fell down again. Her knees were bleeding and the skin was torn in six places, but nobody cared. All they wanted was for her to keep up with their goosestepping, with their insistent march.

Fear prevented her from walking. She fell. She lost count of the number of times she'd fallen. They picked her up again and dragged her by her neck, and beneath her armpits. If only they'd slow down, she could keep up with them. She lost both of her carpet slippers and she felt the pain of the rough floor digging into the skin of her feet.

Did these corridors never end? Please God, let them just put a bullet in my head and that's the end of it, she thought. The forger had suggested she buy a cyanide tooth. One quick bite, a crack, bitterness, and all the suffering would be over. But she was too confident. She thought she could survive. All that money. Poor Eva. Please God, in the torture she wouldn't mention Eva's name, please God. *Baruch ata adonai*. If only she could remember the prayers. Where were her mother and father? Where was her brother who used to spring to her defence when boys pulled her pigtails? Where was the huge fire in the lounge room where the family gathered on cold winter nights, and toasted buns and drank chocolate milk? Where was her first lover who'd been so gentle when she was so nervous, and who had kissed her on the neck and the lips and the breasts and told her that she was the most beautiful girl he'd ever known?

And then they seemed to have arrived somewhere. They threw her against a wall. She sprawled over a bench, hitting her head on the wall, and feeling the shock reverberate through her body. Somebody with a large key opened a gated doorway. She looked up, her vision obscured by the dimness of the corridor and the stars from the bang on the head. He had turned on the light in the room. Two of the uniform officers pulled her hair and literally dragged her off the bench. She screamed again in pain. Her head felt on fire. They threw her into a room. There was water on the floor. She slipped and sprawled and fell. The water smelled of shit. It was too horrible. Suddenly, what little remained in her stomach from the food she had eaten not half an hour ago came up again in a gorge and sprayed all over the wet floor. A man filled a bucket with water from a tap and threw it over her. It was freezing but the shock brought her to her senses. She was wet all over. Her face, her hair, her chest; water was dribbling from her nose. She whimpered again. She was cold. So cold. She'd never been so cold in all her life.

The four SS men looked at her and laughed. She had never felt as naked and humiliated. She was wearing a dress whose wetness clung to her body, and ridiculously she covered her breasts.

'Sit,' said one of the men. She struggled to obey. It was a wooden chair. There were four chairs opposite her. Between them was an old table whose lacquer had peeled off decades ago.

'You are Annelise Liebemann. A Jew. Your papers say you are Liselotte Pfitzner. This is a lie. Do you admit buying the papers from the forger, Pieter Baruch, another Jew?'

What was the point of denial, of lying. Get it over with. Tell the truth. Avoid the torture. Be shot. End of life; end of pain.

'Yes,' she said.

'Good,' said the man. 'Now, who else do you know who has false papers?'

'Nobody,' she said.

The officer sitting in front of her, the man who had first burst into her apartment, smiled. It was a gentle smile. There was no cruelty there. Just the smile of a father. She was mystified. The man standing beside him took out a rubber truncheon from his belt. He walked over behind her. She turned and looked at him in fear, knowing that any minute her body would be racked by pain.

'Nobody,' she said. 'I know nobody. I just bought …'

The pain was so great that her body seemed to rocket forwards out of the chair, her head projecting downwards to hit the desk, her face transfixed in shock. He had brought the truncheon down in the middle of her back. She had no wind, no breath. Her head lay on the desk. Her mouth open like a fish on a beach, desperately trying to breathe. She made gurgling noises in her throat. And then she fainted. More wet. More shock. When consciousness returned, her back was no longer painful. It was numb. She remembered what had happened. Her breathing was painful. She could hardly move her shoulder but the pain, mercifully, was gone. But then slowly it started to return – a crippling, awful pain, as though the gas fire was right next to her skin. She screamed, but her voice was lower than before. And her throat felt as if it had been punched. She swallowed. It was painful. And the pain in her back was excruciating. Her mouth tasted of something she couldn't at first recognise. Then she realised that it was the taste of blood.

She let out a moan and tried to put her hand behind her back to touch the pain, to rub it, to make it go away.

'Now, we'll begin again. Fräulein Liebemann, who else do you know who has acquired identification from this man or from any other person? Don't think we don't know about people like you. You call yourself U-boats.

You hide from us, but there is no hiding. Now, answer my question and the pain will stop. Who else have you been consorting with that has false documentation?'

She shook her head. She tried to say 'nobody' but the words wouldn't come. The fatherly Gestapo officer looked upwards to the man standing behind her. There was an imperceptible nod of his head and then a pain radiated throughout her very being, a pain which made the previous pain dull into insignificance. She didn't faint this time. Instead she arched her back and screamed at the ceiling. She stood and her chair fell backwards into the filthy cesspool on the floor. She walked around the room, not knowing where to put herself. She wanted to cry but the sound wouldn't come. She couldn't breathe again. She fell against the wall and then slid onto the floor. If only she could scream, but there was no breath in her body. And then suddenly air flooded into her lungs and she screamed at the top of her voice. Her legs flailing in agony as she lay in the water and shit on the floor, making paddling motions. Seaside. But not the seaside. No warmth and fun. Just horror. Horror. She screamed and screamed until there was no more screaming from her voice. Just an open mouth, and loud breathing noises. She had no more voice. Her vision was fading, not because she was fainting, but because the assaults on her body had made her eyes blur.

Another man walked around and lifted her aggressively into a standing position on the chair. She was sobbing and screaming at the same time, but the noises which came out of her mouth were like those of an old dog. She didn't know what to do with herself. She knew she wanted to die.

And then the true horror began. The man behind her stripped her cardigan off with a knife, cutting it in two from the back and pulling the two halves off her arms.

He ripped open her dress and pulled it roughly off her body. She stood there in only her underclothes. They were wet from the floor. They stank. She screamed again in the cold and wet and misery of her life.

And then two of the Gestapo men came forward and forced her body to bend like a jackknife over the table. One of the other men pulled down her underpants and then pulled her hair roughly backwards so that her head was close to the Gestapo officer who was sitting comfortably opposite her in his chair, like a father watching the performing antics of his favourite child.

In a warm and comforting voice, he told her, 'The three men behind you will rape you in your anus if you don't tell us immediately what we want to know. When they've finished with their particular brand of pleasure, which you will find an unendurable torture, your nightmare won't be over. It will just be beginning. It will continue until you tell us everything we want to know. I myself have no interest in raping you, but they do. All of them have syphilis, by the way.

'Oh, and one more little detail, my dear Fräulein. I should also inform you that it's not just these three officers in this room who wish to visit the pleasures of your backside. Outside there are at least another ten who would be interested in joining in the fun. As a result of the rape, your anus will be horribly torn, and within a couple of hours, you will develop an infection which will spread through your body and kill you painfully in a week or so. None of this will happen if you tell me what I want to know. Now, Fräulein Liebemann, don't you think it's worth your telling me what I want to know?'

He spoke so calmly, so gently. He spoke like her father. She heard herself speak. Her voice was a million miles away. It said, 'Yes'.

'Will you tell me all their names?'

'Yes.'

Who was speaking? Could it be her?

'Now there's another thing, Fräulein Liebemann,' he said gently. 'It's not just these names we're interested in. There are, according to our estimates, about ten thousand Jews who are living as U-boats. It's difficult to tell a Jew from a non-Jew when they dress like an Aryan. When they put dye in their hair; when they have false identification papers. We need somebody who can help us to identify them, move among them, pretend to be one of them, but actually report their names and locations to us. Dear Fräulein, will you help us? My friends behind you have got very large penises and I'm sure they would like to put them inside you right now. Why don't the two of us spoil their fun. Eh? Why don't you just agree, and I'll forbid them to touch you? So will you help us?'

She nodded.

'I'm sorry,' he said gently. 'I don't think I heard.'

The same voice, a thousand miles away, said 'Yes.'

'Good,' said the officer. 'Now, let's take you into a nice suite of rooms we have upstairs. Wash you. Dress you. Get a doctor to give you some morphine for your pain and then you'll write a list for us.'

'Yes,' she said. This time the voice was much closer.

'And it goes without saying my dear Fräulein, that if any of the information on those lists is false, my colleagues' erections will be much bigger and much harder the next time around. I'm sure you understand me.'

Two weeks later, Annelise was walking along the streets of Kurfurstendamm with her minder, another Jew who had been turned and who had been a headhunter for the past eight months. She knew him as Rudy Goldfarb. They were both dressed to look like Aryans. They walked arm in arm in innocence, as though they were lovers.

They entered a cafe on the Kurfurstendamm, somewhere Annelise had been many times while she was a U-boat, a place where she could sit, just to get out of the cold. She looked around the cafe. Inside were thirty tables, most occupied by the usual patrons. She walked with Rudy to an empty table and looked towards the back of the cafe where there was less light, where people could hide their identities. She noticed a young woman, aged about nineteen or twenty, sitting with her back to the window, sipping a coffee. She had that feral hunted look of the U-boat, that feeling that she was there, but not there, ready at a moment to dash if there was the slightest disturbance in the environment; a car door slamming too loudly, someone barking a distant order, a barely heard police whistle … any alert would make her run like a startled fawn.

It was the first time that Annelise had acted as an SS informant, as a headhunter. The *hauptführer* had told her that they had at least ten Jews who were assisting them in their efforts to make Berlin *Judenrein*. She was their latest acquisition. Only a very few were selected for the task, those who looked Aryan, those who could blend, those who could be trusted by both sides. Those who didn't have a large nose and other Jewish characteristics which would immediately identify them. It wasn't just the fear which had allowed her to live in the last two weeks in the knowledge that she was to become a traitor to her own people. No, if it were just fear, then she would have resigned herself to attempting to escape. But slowly, through Nazi indoctrination, she began to realise that the people into whom she had been born were not a people at all. Though she didn't believe much of what she was told about her people, some of it was true. Hadn't she herself escaped from home when she was nineteen? Didn't she feel a complete distance from the path of

Judaism, even before the Nazis gained power? Didn't she hate the rabbis and all they stood for, and the elitism amongst the Jews? All she ever wanted to be when she was a girl was a German like the other German girls she knew … but there was always this distance, this gap, between her and the other children in her classes. Well, perhaps, she wasn't becoming traitor. Perhaps there was enough truth in what the Germans were saying about the Jews. Perhaps she was one of a new breed.

She whispered in Rudy's ear, 'The girl at the table at the back'.

'You're sure?'

Annelise nodded. Rudy stood and walked out of the door of the cafe. He turned right and entered a car parked one hundred metres away. He told the group leader about the girl in the cafe sitting alone at a table near the back, wearing a red beret and an old grey woollen coat.

Two men were despatched to the back alley behind the cafe. When they were in place, two men walked in through the front door. There was an immediate cessation of conversation. Everybody looked at the two Gestapo men who had just walked in, easily identifiable by their black leather overcoats. Annelise looked at the girl at the table. Her heart dropped as the girl turned to face her and she saw her full face for the first time. It was a girl called Magda. A girl with whom Annelise had once shared a bed in a rundown tenement. Magda looked at Annelise and recognised her but then she looked at the two SS men walking down the body of the cafe towards her. She leapt from her chair and ran to the back door, pulling it open. But before she could exit from the cafe the burly forms of two other SS officers stopped her.

She screamed. They grabbed her by the arms and pulled her back into the cafe, marching her between the tables. Magda looked down at Annelise sitting there, sipping a coffee and a look of surprise came over her face. It was the last time Annelise saw her. She paid for her coffee with a few coins and left the cafe and the hubbub a few minutes after Magda had been spirited away.

The street was freezing cold but Annelise felt empty inside. Empty. Nothing. No guilt, no pain, no sympathy, no understanding, no compassion, no reason. It had been easier than she thought. Rudy was standing beside the car smiling at her. She walked towards him. She smiled back.

If only she could save Eva. If only somehow she could keep quiet about Eva.

CHAPTER NINETEEN

FRANKFURT, PRESENT DAY

Sarah lay on the bed composing her thoughts, working out what she would tell David, how she would address the problem of informing her family about the new Eva, a mother and grandmother whom nobody knew.

And what right did she have to distress her mother and father because of her investigations? These were matters long ago buried in the hideousness of Jewish history. She, Sarah, had a yearning to know, an almost inexhaustible desire to find out the truth that was her life; to determine from where she came, how she was composed, what influences created her.

Not that she had always had this desire to know. Years before, after the trial of the hideous Frank Darman, she had been asked by the *New York Times* to write an OpEd piece on the conflict between free speech and hurting innocent victims with what was said.

Then she had told American Jews to close their eyes on the traditions and histories of Europe's Judaism, to turn away from it, to forget the old times, the old country, the old memories, to eschew the *stetls* and the Yiddish culture. And to look forward into the future, a future in which Jews could be free to be Jews in enlightened lands like Israel, America, Canada and England.

When she thought now of the monumental arrogance of that OpEd article, she cringed in embarrassment. How could she have been so self-righteous, even so indulgent.

But the article had served a purpose. Because of it, Josh Krantz had contacted her and talked her into getting his grandparent's property back from the Slovakian government; it had led to her finding out the truth about her amulet, that it wasn't a piece of gold jewellery created by her great-grandfather Nussan shortly before his death. That had reignited her curiosity about herself, and now she was faced with the prospect of yet another epiphany: finding out that the blessed and sacred memory of her grandmother was all wrong; that the woman who had been held up as a model of self-sacrifice and propriety, had been working in a cabaret which sounded as if it doubled as a brothel; that this upright Jewish woman had lived in a promiscuous relationship with a Christian who had protected her from the dangers of the street. But was this man a Nazi? Did he wear a swastika armband and goosestep? Was he part of the crowd that screamed their adulation for Adolf Hitler?

Annelise's story was all over the place. One minute, Eva was a goddess, the next minute she was somebody who was compromised, a virtual turncoat to her own religion.

And how could Sarah possibly moralise about how Eva should have behaved in the 1930s, a time of the greatest terror the Jewish people had ever known. How would Sarah have reacted under the same circumstances? It was all very well being moralistic when you had the US Constitution to protect you. But Eva? Germany? And if she was so well protected, if she could supply Annelise with food and comfort and money, then where was she getting it from? Just how high was the society in which her grandmother moved? Today, she would go and see Annelise again and try and work out some of the answers. But in the meantime, she had to compose herself and share her knowledge with David. He would know how to tell Bertha and

Sol. She reached over to the bedside table and picked up the phone.

BERLIN, FEBRUARY 10, 1943

The flush of morphine was evident both in his face and in his voice. His actions were quick-fire, his body occasionally jerking like a marionette. But it was his eyes which gave the most honest account of his condition; they were the eyes of a scavenging dog, alive with the drug as they reconnoitred the room to pierce the faces of those who walked in through the door.

In his burning white and gold uniform, he was a fat and preposterous Lohengrin or, as a Nazi political philosopher liked to call him in very private conversations, a medieval illuminated manuscript.

He was standing in the centre of the room, his left chest ablaze with decorations, his shoulders heavy with epaulettes, his boots polished to a mirror shine. Indeed, his boots were the only part of his florid and corpulent body which were dark. Even his once jet hair was now greying as a result of the titanic tensions of the war effort. Everybody who knew anything knew that *Reichsmarschal* Hermann Göring, obese to the point of obscenity and absurdity, was a waning light in the Führer's government. Even he, a perpetual joker and parodist, knew that unless he could pull a rabbit out of the hat and reverse the disasters of the past year, his days as *Reichsmarschal* were numbered, as were the days of the thousand year Reich.

Himmler now viewed him with utter contempt, denigrating him openly to the highest echelons of the SS, as well as those close to him in the government. Himmler ridiculed Göring's constant parade of young women in and out of his widowed life and the fabulous and widely plundered art treasures which were so thick on the walls of his palatial villas that humorists no longer talked about paintings being hung on the walls but the walls being supported by the genius of the world of art. And then, of course, there was the re-addiction to morphine which was again destroying everything that he had fought to become, despite the fact that he had suffered unbearable deprivations to give it up years before.

'In fact,' Heinrich Himmler had once said in a moment of unusual frankness to his startled underling, Reinholdt Stricher 'Göring is becoming a figure of idiocy and one who will soon need to be expunged from the party hierarchy. His Luftwaffe's monumental errors in attacking Britain and his obscene promises to resupply the German army in Stalingrad have been responsible for the greatest catastrophes that Germany has faced since the Great War'. It was a remark which resonated through Reinholdt's mind as he tried to determine where he should be standing on the political football field.

Germany was on the back foot. The premature, orgasmic explosion out of the constraints of the Versailles Peace Treaty, capturing Poland, Hungary, Austria, the Ukraine, France, and the Low Countries, were all now in danger of being consigned to a temporary footnote in history due to the unforeseen and merciless resistance of the enemy. Everywhere German troops were straining to maintain borders to which Hitler's genius had expanded the German Reich.

But these matters didn't concern Reinholdt Stricher and his wife Eva, Germany's most celebrated diva. *Gruppenführer* Reinholdt Stricher and his stunning and far more famous wife were guests at the party held at one of Göring's less pretentious residences in the Schorfheide. The Villa Karinhall was named after his late wife Karin von Kantzow over whom the *Reichsmarschal* still cried whenever he saw her picture, even though they had only been married ten years and she had died twelve years earlier.

It was a crisp clean night. There was hardly a noise in the area surrounding the *Reichsmarschal*'s villa. All the noise, indeed, was coming from a chamber orchestra which was playing in the entrance hall and whose music seeped upstairs and into every corner of every room. Not even an animal dared to stir outside in the area patrolled by a hundred bulky and heavily armed security men from the Luftwaffe.

Senior officers in Wehrmacht or Luftwaffe uniform were wandering everywhere around the mansion. The ranks on their shoulders or breasts told of their relative importance and their place in the hierarchy. Attractive German maidens with pigtails and dressed in Bavarian costumes, carried trays of canapés and drinks in a never-ending procession from the villa's kitchens. And the pivotal point around which the entire drama revolved was the obscene bulk of the *Reichsmarschal* Hermann Göring.

The moment Reinholdt and Eva entered the villa and had their coats removed by butlers, they spotted him in one of the vast antechambers. Although he was surrounded by dozens of people, his uniform, indeed his very presence, determined precisely the epicentre of the night.

Picking up champagne and canapés from trays, Reinholdt and Eva walked side by side into the antechamber where their host was speaking effusively about the speech he had made a few months earlier rallying the German people against the foul and inhuman tactics used against the army in Russia.

Reinholdt had only met Göring on half-a-dozen occasions and had been surprised when an invitation to this party was delivered personally to his home by one of the *Reichsmarschal*'s aides. From the envelope which carried the seal of the Office of the *Reichsmarschal* and the legend, *Strictly private and confidential. Eyes of addressee only!* Reinholdt knew that the letter spelled trouble.

That alone told Reinholdt to keep the receipt of the invitation very much to himself. If it was formal then it would have been sent to Reinholdt via his boss's office. It was obvious that Göring wanted Himmler to know nothing about the invitation.

As the music engulfed them, Reinholdt whispered into Eva's ear, 'Remember. Keep your mouth shut. Say nothing. Just nod and be pleasant.'

She looked at him with a moment of anger. 'Do you think I'm a fool? Do you think I don't know how to behave myself at these damned parties. It's like a minefield.'

'Just remember,' he whispered, 'that if you inadvertently explode a mine I'll die beside you.'

Göring talked effusively and with loud ebullience to all around him. Despite his morphine-generated ardour, he instantly knew that someone new had entered the room. He looked from his audience to determine who the new couple was, and whether they were worthy of being admitted to his presence. When he saw that it was the famous diva Eva Stricher, he beamed an especially generous smile and waved to her.

'My dear Eva,' he shouted above the heads of those listening, 'Come. Come over here and give me a kiss.'

She smiled at him and Göring's personal acolytes parted the ways so that she could walk with her husband straight over to their host. She reached up and kissed him on the cheek. He kissed her fondly, even though they had only met four or five times before.

'Thank you so much for your invitation, Herr *Reichsmarschal*,' she said.

'Ach. I'm so pleased that you could make it at such short notice. I particularly wanted to talk to you about your role of Elsa in *Lohengrin*. A very interesting interpretation.'

She was genuinely surprised. 'I wasn't aware that the *Reichsmarschal* was in the audience. And I certainly wasn't aware that the *Reichsmarschal* enjoyed opera.'

'Wagner perhaps. A bit of Beethoven, but Mozart and the others are all a bit thin and prissy. I like a good Wagner tune. And yes, I was there for half an hour or so, just to hear you. I just didn't want my presence to be too widely known, so I was in the Royal Box with the curtains; after what I've said so publicly about the effeteness of culture, I don't want too many people to know I've visited the opera. Anyway, we'll talk more about that later.' He looked at his watch. 'Ah, time for dinner. Tell me, with the permission of your husband, will you allow me to escort you in to the dining hall?'

She smiled. 'I would be gratified,' she said.

Reinholdt placed himself behind her and the thirty guests who had been honoured with an invitation to dinner. The majority of invitees had only been admitted to the cocktails and canapés before and after. The honour party walked behind the *Reichsmarschal* along the corridor into a baronial dining hall whose oak panels soared to the ceiling, the space above the table intercepted by fifty flags representing the ancient principalities from Germany's history. The table was set in a way which not even Eva, with all her experience of German high society, had anticipated. It was literally sagging with the weight of the food. A whole boar, placed on the biggest silver salver she had ever seen was the centrepiece of the table. It was surrounded by a ring of pheasants, duck and goose. Around the rim were smaller salvers each containing a dozen smaller birds such as ptarmigan, quail, woodcocks and squab. The thirty guests' places were laid so that they genuflected to the baronial chair of the *Reichsmarschal* himself, placed on a podium. Even his personal eating area at the banquet table was similarly raised so that his plate was higher than everybody else's.

He walked with Eva around the table and two servants pulled his throne aside so that his huge bulk could stand comfortably on the platform and fall back into its velvet cushions. He motioned to Eva to sit on his right, Reinholdt to his left, and the other guests found their seats according to their place cards. Immediately everybody was seated, servants descended like locusts and placed napkins on laps, filled glasses with red and white wine as well as champagne for the introductory course of soup.

In all the noise and clatter, Göring leaned forward and whispered into Reinholdt's ear, 'I assume you've said nothing about the invitation I sent you?'

'Of course not, Herr *Reichsmarschal*,' said Reinholdt.

'Not to Himmler?'

'Especially not to him.'

'Good,' he said. 'I need to discuss something with you in private. I've been checking your records. You're an engineer by training.'

'Yes, Herr *Reichsmarschal*.'

'How much engineering do you remember from your days in university?'

Reinholdt delayed answering for a moment, trying to determine what to say. To tell a lie would potentially gain him advancement but could be his undoing; to tell the truth could be equally disastrous. But he had no option. 'I remember very little sir, but naturally I'm able to learn. I have all the skills, but my duties for the Reich have prevented me from practising my profession. However, it won't take me long.'

'Good. Ever been to South America?' he asked.

Reinholdt was genuinely shocked. He turned and looked at the smiling face of his host, the second most important man in the land. Reinholdt said nothing. 'We'll talk later,' said Göring.

He turned his attention to Reinholdt's wife. 'So, is there anything that a wonderful singer can't eat? Something which might interfere with your voice or your performance tomorrow night?'

'Absolutely nothing, Herr *Reichsmarschal*,' said Eva, her voice confident and clear as a bell; everybody around the table lowered their voices to listen to what Göring and Eva were saying.

'That's what I like. A beautiful woman with a big appetite, for all sorts of things. Hey?' he said and burst out laughing.

Eva laughed. Reinholdt laughed. Everybody around the table laughed. Eva wondered what she should say next and where the mines were hidden.

When dinner was nearly over, Hermann Göring rose from the table before his guests had finished their coffee and *petit fours*. He pushed his huge chair back perilously close to the edge of the podium on which he was seated and tapped Reinholdt on the shoulder.

He turned purposefully to Eva and said, 'Perhaps, my dear, you could act as hostess for my guests while your husband and I discuss a few matters of no great consequence.'

She nodded gracefully in acquiescence.

'Come,' said Göring to Reinholdt in a slightly more officious tone.

Reinholdt stood and followed him. Although he held a senior rank in the SS, compared to the *Reichsmarschal* he was as nothing. He was mystified. He had not expected the invitation. He didn't know what was behind it, but to be accorded a private audience at the insistence of the *Reichsmarschal* was little short of extraordinary. Göring's personal attendants began to follow in his wake but their boss turned and looked at them. His shake of the head was almost imperceptible, but his staff understood instantly that this was a very private meeting.

The two men walked behind a tapestry and through an oak-panelled door which took them into an antechamber. Göring walked ahead, confident of who he was and where he was going. Reinholdt merely followed in the slipstream of the one-time fighter pilot. Through another door and they arrived in a room which was obviously part of Göring's private apartments, far removed from the baronial pomp of the dining hall and the reception areas. Göring motioned his young guest to a settee. He sat opposite. Between them was a huge fireplace, the fire spitting and hissing from the newly placed logs. Above the fireplace, a massive Rembrandt. Reinholdt's mouth drooped in shock.

Despite needing to give his every attention to the man opposite him, Reinholdt's eyes involuntarily scanned the room. The furniture was modern and comfortable. Yet the paintings on the wall were nothing short of phenomenal. Titians, Vermeers and Rubens and Hals in one corner. In another, a collection of modern masters, including Monet, Degas, Matisse, and Seurat. An art gallery curator would be in seventh heaven.

Göring seemed not to notice his children on the wall. Instead he fixed Reinholdt with a riveting stare. The affable host suddenly disappeared in the privacy of his apartment to be replaced by a military commander, a man who used words like bullets.

'How do you think the war's going?' he asked, point blank.

Reinholdt swallowed. What could he say? The truth or what the *Reichsmarschal* wanted him to say?

'Despite some set backs, Herr *Reichsmarschal* our troops are …'

'Cut the bullshit, Stricher. This isn't an official conversation. You're not working for Goebbels or Himmler now. You're talking to the *Reichsmarschal* of Germany. Now, how is the war going in your opinion?'

'Badly.'

'Why?'

Reinholdt swallowed. After Hitler, nobody knew better how the war was going than the man asking the questions. This wasn't for information; Göring was obviously testing how much Reinholdt knew. Truth was the only way he would get out of here intact.

'The Russian adventure has been a disaster. It's only a matter of time before the German people begin to realise the scale of the disaster. The British bombers over Hamburg and Cologne can't be put down to Allied luck or the fortunes of war for much longer. The bombing of Berlin has already informed the German people that Germany isn't a fortress any longer. Soon the talk in the streets will be that the war's changed direction …'

'And your view of the short-term future?'

'I made my view plain to *Reichsführer* Himmler that it was only a matter of time before America and Britain attack in overwhelming forces to regain an Allied foothold in France. They will also attack us through the south in Italy. And we will soon be defenceless in the Balkans. Worse, Herr *Reichmarschal*. At the same time as this is happening, we'll also be caught in a pincer movement from the east. The Russians are right now pushing us over their border.'

Göring nodded. 'I read your report. That's why you're here.'

Not for the first time in the evening, Reinholdt was stunned. 'But that can't be! By order of *Reichsführer*-SS

Himmler, there was one copy only of my report, Herr *Reichsmarschal*. I don't understand, sir. I saw it destroyed in front of my eyes. *Reichsführer* Himmler tore it up himself, telling me I was a traitor for speaking in this way and that I had better concentrate on my work as an officer of the SS, and let the Wehrmacht fight the war. He believed that I should focus on supplying the concentration camps with more inmates – Jews and communists and others – than advise on matters to do with the war. But all I was doing was trying to warn the *Reichsführer* of the potential danger of fifth column elements in Germany as the German people became increasingly aware of our defeats.'

Göring nodded. Then he smiled. Reinholdt's body sagged in relief. 'I have your report, Stricher, regardless of what you think was done with it. Your secretary, who typed the report, made a spare copy which she gave to one of my men. Don't be annoyed with her. I have to keep my eye on what that little farmer you work for is up to.

'He's such a moron he had no idea of just how prescient your report actually was. It's exactly the sort of thing I've been saying to the Führer, but despite his military genius, the Führer's reaction was precisely the same as that of your boss. But I won't bore you with Reich politics. I've called you here for a number of reasons. Firstly, I intend to transfer you from Himmler's staff to my personal staff. Secondly, I want you to make a trip for me. I want you to go to South America. I want you to examine the work that German firms like Krupp and IG Farben have been doing over there. See the state of the civil engineering projects, the factories they've been building, the infrastructure.'

Reinholdt nodded. He knew when to keep quiet.

'That's all. You'll receive a more detailed briefing just before you go. In the meantime, not a word of this conversation is to leak back to Himmler. You'll continue working for him until I arrange for your transfer to my secretariat.'

Göring remained silent, staring into the blazing logs, thinking.

'Am I permitted to ask the *Reichsmarschal* a question?' Reinholdt asked timorously.

'Depends on the question.'

'Why is the *Reichsmarschal* so interested in South America? What am I expected to do there?'

'You will do, Stricher, precisely what I've told you to do. You will examine the infrastructure that companies of the Reich are currently building in Argentina. And there's a couple of people that I want you to meet. He's an army general. He has an interesting mistress. The reports on them indicate that they could be favourable to us. His name is Perón. Her name is Eva Duarte. Perón is close to Mussolini. Of all of the jumped up little potentates in that comic opera country, he's the one that Mussolini is putting his money on. Mussolini has an instinct for these things. He might act like a buffoon but he's shrewd. I want you to contact Perón and if he won't deal, then try to influence him through Eva. She's an actress. They call her Evita, little Eva. Now she's somebody to look out for; a real whore, from everything I've heard.'

A thought suddenly struck him. Realising the connection, Göring looked up and smiled. 'Same as your wife's name! Why not take your Evita to South America. She'll love it there. You know, your old boss, Ernst Röhm, may the devil rot his boy-fucking socks, spent much time in South America. Interesting continent. Very interesting country. Mind you, so's Australia … and New Zealand … and Canada … and South Africa. You see, Stricher, I'm thinking internationally. I've also sent men like you to these other countries. Still, that's not your concern. What I want you to do is to concentrate your mind on the amazing possibilities for the SS of South America.'

It was the dinner party that enabled her to make up her mind. For weeks and weeks, she'd been planning an exit strategy, a way of resolving the titanic conflicts in her mind. But she always vacillated. The decision was life and death but now it had been forced upon her. Tonight she would tell him. She had almost told him the previous week but that look on his face, that smile of love and devotion, had prevented her from saying anything. Tonight she would steel herself and go through with it.

She was quiet all the way home in the car. Reinholdt was grateful for her circumspection. The last thing he needed was his wife chattering inanely about the excitement of South America, though he had no idea what was actually going through her mind. He was so excited, that he told Eva about the conversation with Göring as they waited outside the villa for their driver to bring their car around. Now he regretted telling her. Instead of her excitement, she became silent, introspective. He didn't understand why. These days, she was increasingly becoming distant from him. He put it down to the war going badly, or to the fact that the pace of his work had increased exponentially as Hitler demanded increasing numbers of Jews be rounded up from their ghettos and sent to the concentration camps. The fact that resources like transport and fuel were being taken from the army didn't dissuade the Führer from his manic drive to eradicate the Jews from the face of the earth. Perhaps her silence was because he was spending less and less time at home, and more in Greater Germany dealing with the camps' commandants. And when he tried to discuss his work with her, she shut him up peremptorily, telling him that she simply wasn't interested in what he was doing to the Jews. She preferred him to remain silent, to go on living the high life. Ah well, so be it. After all, she was a famous opera singer.

And at the moment, the silence was useful, because it allowed Reinholdt to think about the new dangers facing his life. Why him, Reinholdt wondered? Why had Hermann Göring selected him for this mission? Compared to Göring and Goebbels and the others in the command hierarchy, Reinholdt was a lowly functionary. Sure, his orders were obeyed by tens of thousands of men but in the scheme of things, in the volcanic atmosphere of Berchtesgaden, his name was never mentioned. He was one of a thousand ciphers in the machinery of the Nazi Party. All he did was ride a desk. Only occasionally did he get out of the building and go out to the concentration camps, and see where his orders were carried out. Hideous, Godforsaken places. He shuddered and put all thought of them out of his mind.

So, why him? Was he being set up as a tool for Himmler's destruction? Was the *Reichsmarschal* planning some devious assault on Heinrich's citadel? Was there going to be another Night of the Long Knives, as happened a decade before, when Ernst Röhm and his playthings were dragged out of their beds and summarily executed?

As the car drew to a halt in front of the portico of their home, Reinholdt realised that he was sweating beneath his uniform. His armpits were prickling from fear. But Germany was a nation living in fear. How different things were now from those early days of euphoria. As countries toppled beneath the might of the Werhmacht and the Luftwaffe and as the Panzer tanks crushed enemies to become united with the bloody earth, the German people had read the news with a growing sense of superiority, like spectators at a boxing match watching Max Schmelling pummel some weaker opponent into the canvas.

In the beginning, the victories seemed endless. Germany was expanding and like an octopus, it was spreading the tentacles of Germanness all over Europe. From a small nation, it grew by ingestion, getting fatter and stronger and more corpulent with each country it gobbled.

But then there was Stalingrad!

Despite advice from his cowering generals, the mad Austrian had this mania to conquer Russia. Why? Everybody, every invading army in history had been defeated by the murderous snows and ice of Moscow, by the malignant Russian winter. Did he think that the German army could defeat the forces of Nature herself? Did he, the madman stalking the corridors of power, think that the German army could deny Nature and become invincible like in some Wagnerian opera?

Yes, he did. How wrong he was. The German people were protected, of course. They hadn't seen the photos of thousands of men, stiff and bloodless, their bodies lying twisted like the roots of trees becoming one with the frozen earth, caught for all time in the icy grasp of the Russian soil.

It was Stalingrad that had changed everything.

It was from that moment that everything started to go wrong. Now the Americans were preparing to invade. Britain was dropping bombs again on German cities. Resistance was growing in France. Britain was back on her feet and bulldog Churchill was snarling and yapping and would soon re-take France and Africa and come upwards from the south, through Greece and the Balkans, to attack the underbelly of Germany. Italy was on the verge of overthrowing that fat buffoon Mussolini. It was all imploding. Everything was going wrong. And when the armies were forced to flee back to Germany for protection, would the Allies stop at the old borders? Of course they wouldn't. They would enter German soil and with their iron weapons would strangle the towns and cities until the lifeblood was drained from the Fatherland.

And worse … when the Allied armies trampled over the territory left undefended by retreating German armies, what would they find? The concentration camps! The record of the Reich's attempt to eliminate the scum from the cauldron of the earth. They'd find the millions of bodies which the gas ovens hadn't had time to burn; they'd find the medical rooms where German doctors and scientists had experimented on live subjects to try to solve the defects of Nature and so enrich the lives of German men and women; they'd find mountains of bones and shoes and spectacles and clothing which even the efficiency of German manufacturers hadn't had time to utilise; they'd find the record of Germany's attempt at the genocide of the Jews. In the conference rooms of the Third Reich, it had all seemed so easy. Figures, charts, plans, timetables … but the reality of all the theory was Auschwitz and Treblinka and Majdanek and Bergen-Belsen … and these were Reinholdt's problems. He was one of the implementors. He was the man the Allies would come looking for if ever they got to Berlin.

The car slowed to a halt outside their house. Eva had been unusually quiet. She stepped out as the chauffeur opened her door and walked towards the house. Effortlessly the front door opened. It was always a miracle to Reinholdt how the servants knew to open the door as they approached. Did they stand there all day looking out the front window for when the master and mistress returned?

Eva took off her wrap and gloves, handed them to her maid and ran straight upstairs. It surprised Reinholdt. Normally she was garrulous and excited after an evening such as this. She would spend her time reliving the conversation. Sometimes she was so excited she would sing a few bars from an aria. But for some reason she disappeared upstairs. He took off his cap, gloves and handed his baton to his butler. He ran upstairs after her. When he opened their bedroom door, he found her sitting at the dressing table, brushing her hair. Her reflection in the mirror was that of a woman just coming into the very essence of her beauty. He had always loved looking at her. He loved her more now than ever. With her on his arm, he was the envy of every German.

Ten years earlier when he first met her, he had been struck by her girlishness, by her lovely innocence, her coyness and unwillingness to open up to him; he'd had to prise her open. But now, in the maturing of woman-ness, she was more than lovely. She was the most classically beautiful woman he had ever seen. Her body was solid like any good opera singer. Plenty of meat on her bones. But her face hadn't put on weight. It was still firm and beguiling. Her long raven-black hair cascaded down her shoulders. He walked over and kissed her on the top of her head.

'Something isn't right,' he said. 'You're unusually quiet. Was it dining with Göring?'

She remained silent. Normally she reached up and held his hand when he stood behind her. She continued instead to brush her hair.

'Are you not well? The food?'

She didn't look at him through the mirror. She just looked at herself, as though she was examining her soul.

'Eva, what on earth is the matter?'

Again, she remained silent.

'Was it something I said? Something Göring said? Are you angry about something?'

She breathed deeply. It was a sigh. 'Are you really going to South America?'

'Of course,' he said. '*Reichsmarschals* don't make requests. I've been given orders. I obey. I have no choice.'

She nodded.

'It's for the best. Look,' he said. He pulled another stool across and sat beside her, looking now at her profile. He lowered his voice. 'You know as well as I do that the war is going badly for Germany. Forget what you read in the papers. Forget the garbage that Goebbels gives out and that stuff on the radio ...'

He lowered his voice even more so that no servants who might be close by could hear. He was almost whispering. 'The war is as good as lost, Eva. Everybody in the senior hierarchy knows it except Hitler. This could be our big break. We have some money in the Bank of Zurich. I've put away my salary, plus a lot of unspent money from concentration camp accounts. And other money which I'm allowed to spend, but I don't. Just don't ask how I've got it. It doesn't matter. It's in gold. It's enough for us for the rest of our lives; in fact, we couldn't live long enough to spend it all. There's so much special-purpose money floating around, nobody will miss it.

'Now that it's obvious the war's going to be lost, South America is a fantastic escape route. The timing couldn't have been better. Not only that, but Göring knows it as well. He obviously wants me to set up some sort of bolt hole for him and the senior hierarchy. He hasn't told me what ... I'll get that briefing just before I leave, but he's no fool. Indeed, he's the smartest of all the senior men. He wants me to be his reconnaissance scout. Great! What he doesn't realise is that once I've got you out of here, I'm not coming back. It will be a new life for us, Eva.

We'll live for the rest of our lives like landed aristocracy. And nobody will come after us. Certainly not the current leadership … they'll all be jailed by the Allies; and if we change our names and get new identities, nobody will know. We'll start again, but this time with more money than imaginable. It will be wonderful.'

He looked at her closely. He had been pondering a way to tell her the truth about the war. About their money in Switzerland. Well, he couldn't tell her the truth about their finances. It was one thing to tell her they were rich, another to tell her about the fortune over which he had control. But the time was apposite to get her out of the country, while there was still a country to get out of.

He didn't know how she would react, how frightened she would become when she knew the truth. She was rigid. Perhaps he shouldn't have told her. She turned to him and looked at him intensely.

'I'm not coming with you, Reinholdt.'

'What?'

'I'm not coming to South America. I'm staying here.'

'I told you, my love. The war is as good as lost. Don't you understand what's going on in the battle front? We …'

'I don't care about the battle front.' She raised her voice. He put his hand on his lips, motioning outside the door. She continued in a whisper. 'I don't care about the war or Germany. I'm not leaving.'

He was stunned. 'But any day, the bombers will reappear and …'

'Reinholdt, I have to find my mother and father, my brother and sister. They've been taken to a concentration camp. For the last few years, I've been secretly trying to find out where they went. Where they were taken. I can't leave Germany without knowing what's happened to them. I have to …' Her voice trailed off, '… do something for them.'

'What?' He looked at her as though she was speaking a foreign language. 'What did you say?' Reinholdt looked at her closely, then, as the words began to sink in, repeated, 'What?' He sounded inane, but he was trying to comprehend the meaning behind her words.

'Reinholdt, my family are in concentration camps. They're Jews. I'm a Jew.'

He whispered again, 'What?' He could think of nothing other than 'what?'.

'I'm Jewish. I was born a Jew. My name before we married wasn't Eva Schmidt. It was Eva Arpel. I'm Jewish, Reinholdt.'

He burst out laughing. Her face remained rigid.

'Reinholdt,' she repeated slowly, deliberately. 'I am a Jew!'

Furiously, he shook his head. 'Don't ever make jokes like this again, you stupid woman! Don't you know how dangerous it is to make jokes about a thing like that? If the servants get to hear about it. God Almighty! Everybody's being reported to the SS. Especially those inside the SS who are weak.'

'Reinholdt,' she said, her voice rising. 'I am Jewish!'

Like a whip, his hand shot up to close her mouth. 'Shut up, you fool. It's not funny. Statements like that will get you arrested, no matter who you are. I can't hope to save you.'

But there was a look in her eyes which suddenly made him realise that this was no joke. A frown creased his forehead. 'What?' he said quizzically. The enormity of the statement refused to sink into his mind. He took his hand from her mouth.

'My name was Eva Arpel before I married you. My parents were Serel and Franz Arpel. We came from Munich. I came here in 1930 because of what the SA was doing on the streets. I thought Berlin was safe.

I abandoned my family then. I've been trying to find them for years. I won't abandon them again. I have to know where they are.'

He stood from the stool and walked over to their bed. He sat heavily down on it and buried his face in his hands.

She looked at him in consternation. It was the biggest risk she had ever taken in her life. She had no intention of taking this risk but tonight's turn of events – the prospect of going to South America and not coming back – had precipitated what she had always feared. He stood from the bed. He was breathing deeply, his face red in anger or fear or fury. She didn't know which. He walked over to her and stood menacingly above her. She feared if she cowered he would hit her. Instead she looked in the mirror and continued combing her hair. His fists were bunched as though to strike. He walked rapidly over to the bedroom door, threw it open and looked in the hallway. Then he banged it shut. He strode back over to the bed and sat down. Then he stood up and came and sat beside her. The tension in his body was overwhelming him. It was as though his fury was about to burst out of the bounds of his skin and explode over the bedroom.

And now the coup de grace!

'And the other thing is, Reinholdt, I'm pregnant. I'm two months pregnant. I was thinking of having an abortion because I knew that Germany was no place to bring a child into the world. But I think it's your decision as much as mine.'

'You're a Jew? I've been sleeping with a Jew. A Jew is carrying my child? I could be shot for this. Do you know the danger you've put me in, you fucking slut? They'll drag me off to a prison camp and torture me until I die. You think people will believe that I didn't know? How can you live with a woman for ten years and not know everything about her? Eva, how could you have done this to me? Why did …'

He buried his head in his hands. Suddenly she felt immensely sorry for him. Was it his fault that she had closed her eyes to the obscenities he was doing to her people? It was her fault. Annelise, all those years ago, had told her she was mad. For ten years, Annelise had been wrong, but now she was right. Eva put her hand on his head and stroked him gently, rubbing the depression in the back of his neck the way he liked it. She could feel him breathing in and out, in and out. Not normal breathing, the breathing of anger and fear and disgust and rage within himself. She leaned over and kissed him on the top of his head as he had kissed her before she had dropped the bombshell.

'Reinholdt, I have deceived you. All these years for my own protection, I pretended to be what I'm not. It was my way of staying alive. But you loved me for myself before you knew the truth. When we were having dinner tonight, when we were riding in the car, you loved me. I haven't changed. I'm the same Eva Stricher that I have been as your good wife. See it from my point of view, my love. I love you and you love me. All the Nazi ideas about Jews, about how we're subhumans, how we're a plague. They're all wrong, Reinholdt. They're wrong. They're wrong because you don't know us. All the talk about conspiracies to take over the world and how we stabbed Germany in the back during the Great War. How we caused the Great Depression. It's all rubbish. It's all nonsense. It's what you want to believe because you're scared to believe the truth. But the truth is, my love, that you've been married to and been besotted with a Jewish woman. You haven't hated her. You have loved her. And now that woman is carrying your child. Believe me when I say to you that I'm deeply sorry for the trouble I've caused you but I did it to save myself.'

He sat up straight on the stool and looked at her. His face was red, his eyes bloodshot. They were brimming with tears. 'If I inform the authorities about you,' he said coldly, 'then you will die and I will die. If I don't inform the authorities, then I'm guilty of a crime against the State. This child you're carrying. This child is the product of the devil. I want nothing to do with it. I want nothing to do with you. Because of the blackmail, I can't inform upon you, the world can't know, but I know. I know!

She'd never seen him like this. So disgusted. Was this the way he looked at his Jewish victims before they went into the gas ovens? He spat at her, the globule hitting her bodice. In utter contempt, he hissed, 'You will be silent. I must think. One word and I'll shoot you.'

He stood and walked away from her, to the opposite end of the room. He looked out of the window. Then he walked to the fireplace and stood there, warming himself in its flickering flames. He looked deeply into the fire, as though trying to determine some hermeneutic solution. Eva looked at him in fear, as she would look at a wild animal stalking her.

Eventually, after what must have been five minutes, but which seemed like an eternity, he said, 'You'll never touch me again. You'll never sleep again in my bed. We'll continue to live our lives as we have always done. We'll put on a charade in public but inside, I'm dead towards you. In my heart, you're a non-person. You say the things that I've believed since my childhood are lies. No Eva. They're not lies. They're the absolute truth. You are the perfect example of that truth. You've schemed and deceived and conspired to bring me down. Your actions in all the time I've known you are proof of how despicable you and your race are. For the sake of my security we'll continue as we have been but contradict me in any area, at any time, before anybody, and you will die before nightfall in an accident. You'll be trampled under my car's wheels, or you'll fall down the stairs or something. Do you understand me?'

She shook her head. 'And now you listen to me, Reinholdt. I can't stop you killing me. But understand this, if I open my mouth, you're dead. If our marriage is over, so be it. I will not abort this child now. It's my security. No matter what you say, you're incapable of turning your back on it.

'But you will make investigations to find my family in their concentration camp or wherever they've been taken. You will locate them. You'll extricate them from where they are and you will somehow get them out of Germany. I'll go with them and you will never see me again. Not only that but you can tell people that I've died in the tragic accident you're planning, if you want, and then you can go back to being one of the master race. No one will ever know.'

He gulped. 'Why shouldn't I just kill you now? A lovers' quarrel. Nobody can arrest me. I'm too senior. I'll tell people that you and I had a fight after we went to the party. You grabbed a gun to try to kill me. I struggled and killed you in defence.'

She smiled. 'You could and that would end a lot of my pain and suffering. But you won't. You see, the people you kill, the orders you give, the commands you issue. They're all at a distance. You don't kill people yourself. You haven't got it in you. There's a gentleness, a love about you which makes you incapable of hurting me. No, Reinholdt. You won't kill me. Not because of the danger it could bring to you but because deep down, you love me and you couldn't hurt me. And the only reason I've disclosed tonight what I've done to you is because you want me to go to South America. For years I've been trying to find my family. I've used Annelise as my go-between.'

'Annelise?'

'Yes, she's Jewish too. You don't know this, but she's working for the SS; she's been turned by your people. She's now turning over U-boats for deportation. That was how she could come out of hiding; how else could she enter our house?'

Reinholdt's eyes opened wide in astonishment. This was all too much. 'How many of you are there that I don't know about?'

She smiled. 'Just the two of us. She saved my life when you first met me. I was starving on the streets of Berlin and she took me in. She became my friend. She helped me then like I've helped her. I have protected her, given her money, taken her away from what she was.'

'My God,' he said. 'How much more is there that I don't know?'

'Nothing,' said Eva. 'Now you know everything; my great hidden secret. So, will you help me find my parents? Do so and you'll be rid of me and my Jewishness forever. Don't do so, and I'll be true to my word. Even though it means my death, I'll tell the authorities that I'm Jewish.'

He smiled. 'I never thought you would be capable of blackmail, Eva.'

'You don't know how hard it is to be a Jew in Berlin,' she said.

CHAPTER TWENTY

SYDNEY, AUSTRALIA, PRESENT DAY

Frank Darman stood at the window of the Regency Hotel in Sydney and looked out at the white sails of the Opera House. It was without question the most exquisite sight he had ever seen. The stunning purity of the white billowing clouds which formed the roof of Joern Utzon's Opera House contrasted breathtakingly with the azure blue harbour in a symphony of man and nature. It was nothing short of awesome.

In his trip around the southern hemisphere, he had seen some magnificent sights – the majesty of Rio de Janeiro's Christ figure, the wondrous Argentinian Pampas and the thundering Iguassú Falls, the awesome Table Mountain of Cape Town and the falls at Lake Victoria. Of all the sites, though, none had excited him as much as his time in Argentina. Those Argentinians were something else. Populate the world with people who thought like that, and the world would be a better place. That was why Friedrich Nietzsche and his sister Elizabeth, and Richard Wagner and so many Germans had looked towards the wild innocence of South America as the future living places of the Aryan peoples, a world of open plains and pristine jungles, a world free of Jews and Negros and other vermin.

His visit to South America had made him realise how narrow and parochial New Yorkers were in their view of the world. So many wonders to be seen and yet all New

Yorkers concerned themselves with was taxis and the traffic in Fifth Avenue.

And once again, the southern hemisphere had exceeded his expectations as he looked at Sydney's harbour. Gentle, magnificent, sweeping, compact, majestic, human, eternal, busy. It was all of these things and more. Even the Bridge, the Coathanger as it was facetiously called by residents of Sydney, somehow had a place in the scheme of things. The only thing that was out of place was a hideous apartment building that an idiotic government had allowed to be built blocking the view of the Botanical Gardens behind the Opera House. Again the facetiousness, the irrepressible anti-authoritarianism of the people of Sydney, had dubbed the building The Toaster. But if you turned fractionally to the left you could actually avoid seeing it.

He was surprised when the phone suddenly rang.

'Damn it! Don't these Australian hotels know a God-damn thing? I said no calls. What the hell is wrong with them?'

He snatched the phone from the cradle. 'Yeah?'

'Mr Darman, my name is Luke Cassidy. I'm downstairs in the lobby. I'm a reporter. May I come up and see you?'

'Damn it, how did you get this room number?'

'May I see you Mr Darman? If not, I'll simply wait down here until you emerge.'

'How did you get this room number?' Darman repeated.

'Perhaps if I was just to come up and knock on your door Mr Darman?'

'Yeah, come on up,' said Darman, after a moment's thought. 'There's things that should be known. That problem at the airport yesterday, all that screaming and shouting; I didn't get my view across. Come on up and we'll talk.'

A few moments later the bell rang and Darman moved towards the door.

He opened the door and admitted a young man, fresh-faced and innocent. He was carrying a rolled-up newspaper, notebook and a pen. He was followed by a young woman, tall, particularly attractive with a large heavy square bag attached to her shoulder.

'Luke? Frank Darman.'

'Mr Darman,' he said shaking hands, 'this is Kylie Wells, my photographer. Thank you for seeing us. There's quite a crowd of reporters downstairs. Are we the only ones to get through?'

'Yeah, I'm impressed. How did you find my room number?'

'Kylie's going out with one of the members of staff. Naturally I won't tell you which one.'

'Naturally,' said Darman leading him over. He poured them drinks and they sat.

'You're quite a controversial character, aren't you?'

Darman nodded. 'I think that's what they would call a statement of the bleeding obvious in your country.'

'Why do you do it, Mr Darman? You started off as a historian and now you're banned from entering Germany, South Africa, Israel. Other places as well for all I know. You've been arrested three times. You make inflammatory speeches. What's the source of your mission? Why do you do it?'

Kylie had taken out the camera body, inserted a film and screwed in a lens and was already snapping photos as Darman began to speak.

'Luke, when you've got a massive wrong and injustice being perpetrated against one of the most civilised people of Europe, for a period of over fifty years, it behoves some of us to do something. Now you've got to understand that the Holocaust is one of the great lies perpetrated this century. One of the greatest in all of history. As a historian I'm always seeking facts, not suppositions, I'm always looking for the truth. Why is it that a figure of six million Jewish deaths has been placed as an albatross around the neck of Germany as the greatest crime in history, when the figure is nowhere near that and it was just an invention of the Russian army which has been built upon by the successive generations of Jewish leaders? Let me take you back, Luke, to …'

Cassidy interrupted. 'May I interrupt? I've read your speeches. I've read your documentation very carefully. I know your arguments. I'm not here to debate them. What I would like to know however is your view about the antagonistic response you've received from the public here in Australia. We're one of the most tolerant nations on earth. Did you come here deliberately to stir up racial hatred?'

Darman smiled. It was the famous Darman smile. 'No. I came here because certain individuals asked me if I would come and explain my philosophies to them tomorrow night.'

'You're talking about extreme right wing elements who use racist politics to appeal to fanatics and uneducated and unemployed people. Very similar to the way the SA and the SS attracted a mass following in Nazi Germany in the thirties.'

Darman sought to keep calm. 'Luke, it's not my policy to interfere in the internal politics of any country. I'm a guest here.'

Kylie Wells continued to snap one photo after another. The flash began to irritate Darman.

'Mr Darman, you seem to be surrounded wherever you go by lawyers. I read the case a couple of years ago when you were defended by a young woman lawyer in America.' He referred to his notebook. 'Sarah Kaplan. Why did you choose a Jewish lawyer when you're obviously an anti-Semite?'

Darman knew he would be baited but not this openly, nor aggressively. Not even American journalists were this overt. 'I find that a very offensive remark, young man. You're here to report my thoughts, not to give me your opinions.'

'But you are an anti-Semite. You do hate Jews.'

'No, I have a very good relationship with many Jewish people who also believe that the Holocaust was a myth.'

'Can you give me some of their names? I'd like to contact them.'

'And I think you'd better leave. You've outstayed your welcome.'

'Just before I go, Mr Darman … tell me something. These people who believe the Holocaust is a myth. Is Sarah Kaplan one of them? Is that why she defended you?'

'Maybe you'd better ask her.'

Darman stood up. The interview was over.

CHAPTER TWENTY-ONE

FRANKFURT, PRESENT DAY

The room was stark, bare, smelling of antiseptic. The bed made with perfectly folded hospital corners, with pillows plumped as though they had never felt the weight of a human being, let alone a frail old woman. The chair which sat perennially with its back to the room facing out of the window towards the park opposite, had now been replaced and was underneath the melamine dresser. The hairbrushes, scent sprays, even the handtowels which Sarah had bought less than a week ago were no longer there; not that Sarah noticed them when Annelise was in the room. But somehow, now that she was absent, Sarah noticed that they'd been removed, as though the people who had cleared away Annelise also wanted to disassociate the room from any human presence.

It was as though Annelise had been expunged from memory, as though she were no longer in the loop which connected one life to another.

Sarah looked with a feeling of confusion which quickly transformed into desperation; and with desperation, an awful reality settled upon her. Annelise had died in the night. What a pathetic way for such a dear old lady to go. Alone and in a hostel. She heard a nurse walk by the room and asked, 'Frau Liebemannn? Is she …'

'Last night,' said the nurse. 'She had an attack. She's in the geriatric hospital.'

'She's alive!' Sarah felt an overwhelming joy. 'How is she?' she asked.

'She's very frail. We haven't heard back from them yet as far as I know, but we're not making plans for her return. They can tell you more downstairs at the desk.'

'At least, she's alive,' thought Sarah, and then bitterly regretted her thoughts because they were the thoughts of a selfish woman who wanted to extract the last piece of information from Annelise before it was too late. She ran downstairs and was told a more complete story. Annelise had been checked by the night nurse, as part of the routine of the floor. She was worried by Annelise's colour, even though the old lady was fast asleep. She was deathly white and her skin was cold. The doctor was called. He diagnosed a heart attack. They pumped her full of medicines to stabilise her condition and she was taken by ambulance to the nearby geriatric hospital four streets away.

The hospital for elderly people had ramps instead of stairs and wide and deep lifts but otherwise it could have been any hospital, anywhere, except that the patients wandering around were uniformly elderly. No young pregnant mothers bursting with youth and vitality; no cheeky adolescents with limbs broken from over-indulgence in sport. Everybody here was old.

She was instructed to go to the fourth floor where the cardiac care patients were taken, and the lady on the desk there told her where she would find Annelise. She wasn't asked whether she was a relative. This was a hospital for the old and in many cases, the unloved. Visitors were not so much a nuisance as an exception.

Sarah saw Annelise from the distance, and knew it was her, even though she was swathed in bedclothes and her scrawny arms were invaded by tubes and needles. Beside her bed were plastic sacs on stands with clear solutions dripping down one drop at a time. Her mouth was agape, globules of saliva drying on her cheek. She had no teeth. They had been removed by the nursing staff. Her hair wasn't combed. In the week since Sarah had first met her, the old lady's hair seemed to have become less and less a priority as though she knew death was approaching and appearance was an inconvenience, an unnecessary disturbance to the short time left to her.

Sarah stood by her bedside and touched the old lady's arm. The skin was somehow drier and cool as though she was hovering between the warmth of life and the cold of death. A nurse came over and smiled.

'Are you a relative?'

'I'm the granddaughter of one of her oldest friends.'

'Ah,' said the nurse.

'How bad is she?' asked Sarah.

'It's very hard to say,' said the nurse. 'She seems to have given up. It happens to old people after many years of frailty or ill health. One day they just say to themselves that it's not worth carrying on and then their body simply gives in.' She hesitated before she said, 'Look, don't hold out any hope. Sometimes they make an unbelievable recovery but in most cases they linger for a few hours or days, maybe even weeks and then they just stop living. Annelise is in that state.'

'But I must talk to her,' said Sarah. 'We have unfinished … and I mean, there's so much …'

'Did you last see her after a quarrel?' asked the nurse gently.

'No. It's nothing like that. But she was telling me about the old days. And there's so much I still don't understand.'

'Yes, that's what many people say when it's too late. Working here has taught me so much, my dear. Unless you're very lucky, then you should look upon what she's already told you as a blessing.'

'Will she come back to consciousness?'

The nurse shrugged. 'You could wait here for an hour, or a day, a week or a month and she might never open her eyes. Or you could walk out now and she could be sitting by her bedside the next time you come in. It's just not possible to say because so much depends on what's in her mind. All we do is make her comfortable.'

'But can't you give her something?'

'We're giving her everything she needs but not more. What do you want us to do? Give her an operation, replace her heart. That might work for a couple of weeks but then something else in her body would fail. She's frail and old. She deserves to pass away in dignity.'

Sarah sat beside her for two hours, holding her hand, willing her to open her eyes, praying she would turn her head and say, 'Sarah, let me tell you what life was like at the end of the war. Let me tell you about your grandmother and what she did to save the lives of those all around her.'

But Annelise didn't say those words, or any other words. All she did was lie there, struggling to breathe, her chest rattle becoming even more noticeable. The spittle and saliva defeated Sarah's attempts to wipe it away with the perfumed towels which had been brought over with Annelise. And as it was turning towards lunchtime, Sarah kissed Annelise on the forehead and on the cheek and whispered in her ear, 'Bless you, my dear Annelise. Bless you for being a friend to my grandmother and to me.'

And she walked painfully away and asked the sister whether she could write a note to Annelise in case the old lady woke up and was conscious enough to hear it. She scribbled a dozen or so lines in her best German, sealed the letter and put it beside Annelise's bedside. There had been no movement of her face or body. If anything, she looked paler, closer to death.

'What arrangements have been made for the burial in the event of her death?' asked Sarah.

The sister shrugged her shoulders. 'I don't know. In these cases, it's difficult. If there are no relatives, she will be buried in the appropriate way. The State takes care of this sort of thing.'

Sarah took out her purse and gave the sister a card. 'When she dies, would you please ask for a proper funeral. Tell the funeral director to email me at this address and I'll transfer funds across.'

'Of course,' said the sister, 'Were you a very good friend?'

'Only lately,' said Sarah sadly.

And she flew back to America.

BERLIN, FEBRUARY 17, 1943

Reinholdt Stricher was in a frighteningly ebullient mood. Even the servants were cautious of approaching him. They, and his guests, viewed him as a man suddenly become a lunatic. The entire household was terrified of speaking with him, trying to discern what was wrong with the normally placid man. Conversation revolved around what subjects to avoid discussing in order to prevent an explosion of the kind the household had witnessed for some utterly trivial misdemeanour like not pouring enough wine, or for failing to lay out his uniform properly.

Tonight, he was jovial beyond normality. Drunkenness would explain the raucous laughter, the head tossed back like a cavalier laughing at jokes which were mundane at their most generous. Yet, he wasn't drunk. His instructions to the servants were baronial.

'Klaus, another glass of claret for my revered friend at the top of the table.'

'Manfred, more soup for the Herr Oberst.'

'Friedrich, fetch more bread for the table. We can't have our guests starving.'

At the opposite end of the table, Eva Stricher was sitting looking at her husband in consternation. Since her confession on the previous Sunday, he had slept separately from her. He had refused to talk to her except in front of servants and then he was courteous to the point of discourtesy, a comic opera speech replacing conversation. He suddenly left the house in the early morning without any acknowledgment, only to return long after she had gone to bed without entering her room.

Had she the courage, she would have confronted him but she was too scared of what he might do if the subject of her confession was raised again. And now, in front of a battery of the SS hierarchy, one or two holding a higher rank than Reinholdt's, he was a model of concern, the archetypal host. Were it not that she knew him so well, she would have sworn that he was about to explode in maniacal anger. But the restraint of his hatred of her was conditioned by the ebullience he showed before the party.

There was a momentary lull in the laughter. Guests wiped their mouths with napkins, sipped wine and ate the remaining food on their plates. The silence was punctuated by a cough and a shuffle of a chair but it continued beyond its natural course. It continued until the intrusion of a noise from outside. Guests stopped moving and listened. Some frowned. Some turned their heads towards the window in order to hear better. The noise sounded like an animal wailing, or like a pack of wolves baying in the forest. The noise was plaintive, awful, ghost-like, carried on the wind, and suddenly audible because there was so little noise in the room.

A man stood and bowed to Reinholdt. He walked to

the window, pulled aside the curtains and opened it slightly.

In hushed tones, people asked, 'What's that noise?'

'What is it?'

'Is it a siren, an air raid, maybe?'

Even Reinholdt, tinder-dry and abnormally excitable, stopped his breathing in order to listen better. The man at the window opened it wider and the wailing of five thousand women infiltrated the room. A cold gust blew in from the chill outside air. The man quickly pulled the window shut.

'What in God's name do you think that noise could be, Reinholdt?' he asked.

Reinholdt, realising what it was, dabbed his mouth with a napkin. 'As you know, we're rounding up the Jews, shipping them out of Berlin, to make the city *Judenfrei*. What we didn't realise was that there are four thousand seven hundred German women married to Jews; it appears that the noise we can hear is their wailing for their husbands. We had to separate these men from the 40 000 Jews we're deporting to the East for processing because when we lumped them all together, there was nearly a riot at the Grunewald Station. I've never seen German women behave like it. They were like animals, grasping at their husband's arms, shouting and screaming at the SS guards. You'd think that the Reich was doing them a favour by disposing of a Jew husband, but when we began to separate these men from their women, they cried and screamed, and nearly caused a stampede. So we decided to separate these particular men and we took them to a building in Rosenstrasse, just around the corner from SS headquarters. Now the bloody women ... German Aryan women can you believe ... have surrounded the building and they're just shouting and screaming and demanding the release of their husbands. What am I to do?' he asked angrily. 'I can't shoot five thousand German women, even if they are tainted!'

'What do you think will happen?' asked the man as he sat back at the table.

'I put in a recommendation to Göring to give the Jewish husbands special treatment. Make them into some sort of proper Germans. There's no other alternative. The worthy citizens of Berlin will happily close their eyes to the replacement of Jews with foreign workers from the occupied territories. Slaves. But here we're dealing with 5000 German women's menfolk, and that makes it into a delicate matter.' He looked at the party. 'Of course, these German women haven't deceived the authorities … they didn't try to hide their husbands' identities. For that, they should be recognised as true German women, even though they are married to Jews. They, at least, aren't deceivers, liars, committers of fraud and deceit.'

The men around the table frowned. The women looked at their plates not knowing what to do. Eva sat and stared at her husband, her mouth open, wordlessly.

Cautiously she asked, 'And are there any cases of Jewish women married to German men? What would you do in those cases, my dear?'

People frowned. There was a strained undercurrent at the table. Reinholdt was suddenly terrified that one of his fellow officers might put two and two together.

'We've no cases on record, Eva my love. But if there were, I'm not sure that we'd treat the two matters in the same way. After all, and I mean no disrespect to any of the ladies here tonight, a Jewish man can be used for his labour, and so has some value; a Jewish woman is merely a vessel for the continuance of their race, and hence should be confined to the hellish fires of righteousness.'

One of the men cleared his throat, conscious of the seniority of those who would be listening, and said,

'Forgive me, my dear Reinholdt, but I recall certain protocols from a certain conference held in January last year beside Lake Wannsee … I won't go into too much more detail because of security implications … but I'm sure you're aware of what it says in relation to persons of mixed bloods being married to German citizens. As I recall the words, it was something like, 'If no children have resulted from the marriage, the person of mixed blood of the first degree will be evacuated or sent to an old-age ghetto.' Surely the instructions from *Obergruppenführer* Heydrich, as well as from *Obersturmbannführer* Eichmann are quite clear in this regard.'

Irritated at the statement of the obvious, Reinholdt replied, 'Since the martyrdom of Reinhard Heydrich, we've been carrying out the protocols of the conference to the letter. But nobody at that conference thought for one minute that the German women would react like this. Who would have thought they'd risk their own lives to protect their Jew husbands? It's taken us all by surprise. It's been a nightmare. Rounding up Jews is difficult enough but having your own people fighting against you when it's for their own benefit, is just unbelievable.'

Eva pushed her chair back and stood, her face white with horror. 'I wonder if you will excuse me. I must go to the bathroom.'

She had already walked out of the room before the men at the table had a chance to stand properly out of courtesy.

By the time she returned, the conversation had moved on to the bombing raids over German cities, and what the Luftwaffe might do about them.

The night dragged on. Eva smiled and laughed … and kissed the cheeks of … and danced with … and poured coffee for … and snapped her fingers when it came time to bring coats.

And so the last guest left. Reinholdt began to walk towards the door which led to the hall, which led to his room.

'Reinholdt,' she shouted. The three glasses of claret had given her courage. 'Reinholdt, may we speak?'

Reinholdt looked at the servants and then at her. She had chosen her time well. He couldn't be embarrassed in front of them.

He smiled. 'Of course, my dear. In my bedroom.'

He turned on his heels and walked out of the room. Her maid walked over. Although told nothing, she knew everything. She knew he hadn't slept with her for the whole week. The only thing she didn't know was the reason. And because she knew the Madam so well, she had worked out, and told all the other staff that the master had been caught in some dalliance and was being punished by her mistress.

'You go upstairs Madam. I'll make sure everything is tidy down here.'

Eva squeezed her hand. 'Thank you,' she said.

As she ascended the stairs, she saw her husband rounding the top banister rail and walk down the corridor. She followed him up, her legs feeling heavy. Her heart was thumping. She felt like an aristocrat during the Revolution, walking up to the guillotine. She was dressed in her finest evening gown, the silk and chiffon rustled as she ascended the stairs. Few women in Germany, few women in the rest of the world enjoyed her luxuries, her lifestyle. She could have kept her mouth shut. She could have continued to enjoy all of this but at what cost? She had already prostituted herself, her upbringing, everything in which she believed. But even a prostitute has to be able to stop what she's doing every once in a while. Even a prostitute has to have some self-respect, to be able to look at herself in the mirror and say,

'I am a woman. I'm not merely a convenience for the frustrations and lusts of men.'

But she was worse than a prostitute. She had sold out more than herself, for her own safety and security. She had sold out her entire family. And, just as badly as her best friend, Annelise, she had sold out her people. Her religion. Her ancestors. She was worse than a traitor. She was as responsible for the mass murders that she knew were taking place as were the men in the SS who gave the orders. She had failed to raise her voice, to speak out when she knew all about the transportation of Jews to the concentration camps of mass murder. The only person she had been able to fool was herself and now she would be fooled no longer.

She reached the top step. Eva knocked gingerly on the door of Reinholdt's room. There was a growl, an animal noise. She opened the door and walked in to the second master bedroom. Reinholdt was sitting at his desk writing a note. He looked up disinterestedly, but then looked straight down at his writing. He continued.

'Reinholdt,' Eva said tentatively. 'I … since…'

He turned and looked up at her. There was a coldness in his eyes. It terrified her, made her fearful to continue. He picked up a glass of water and drank it. She felt like a school child in front of a principal.

He wiped his lips on a handkerchief. He just stared at her, making her too frightened to continue. His eyes bored into her very being. And then he began to speak. He sounded like a judge reading a sentence.

'Eva Arpel. Religion … Jew. Born of Serel and Franz Arpel. Servants to the Büchbinder family, formerly jewellers and shopkeepers of Munich. You have' … He corrected himself, ' … you had an older brother by a different father. His name was Isaac. You also have an older sister by the same father. Her name is Rose. Of course they had Jew names … Yiddish names … but I won't sully my lips by saying them.

'You, Eva Arpel, are the only progeny of Franz Arpel and his second wife, Serel. Franz is also her second husband, her first having been killed in an attack by the Black Hundreds in a small town in Slovakia. There are records of another child between Serel and her first husband, but it is presumed that this child died in infancy. Your stepbrother was taken to Dachau Concentration Camp in August 1937. He lived until 1941 when he died of typhus. Your stepsister Rose was taken to Auschwitz in 1942 along with your mother Serel. Your father Franz was transported to a labour camp in the centre of Germany, not far from where you were born. A camp called Flossenburg, near to Weiden. Not many German prisoners have been taken there, but for some reason, he ended up there. Bureaucratic bungle, or something. Anyway, he was set to work in the armaments factory, and now he's involved in mineral oil extraction making gasoline for our tanks. I believe that he's still alive. Unfortunately, your mother died four months ago in Batch 623. She was poisoned by Zyklon-B gas and her body was burnt in the crematorium. Your older step-sister, being more attractive than most of the women taken to the concentration camp, is still alive in Auschwitz where she provides sexual pleasures and other comforts to German camp guards and the occasional soldiers who pass by. However, according to the camp commandant, her youth and looks and body are failing to interest our gallant young men any further, and so she will shortly be returned to her fellow Jew prisoners in the camp, and will probably be one of the next victims in the camp's gas ovens. As to your father, he is rapidly becoming old and weak and will not see out the next few months. They have a special way with sick prisoners at Flossenburg, according to what their commandant, Karl Kunster told me. Once a man isn't capable of working a sixteen-hour day, he's taken to see the camp doctor, and given an injection of phenol. Well, saves on food, doesn't it?

'So, Eva, that's my part of the bargain. You wanted to know about your family. Now you know. And with that knowledge comes your part of the bargain. You will come with me to South America …'

She heard nothing more. Her legs collapsed under her and she fell into a dead faint on the luxurious carpet of her home.

The next thing Eva remembered was her maid using cold water to wash her face. She was sitting up in bed, her head pounding. She felt as if she had been hit on the back of the head by a mallet. She winced at the hammering as consciousness flooded back into her mind.

'Madam hit her head on a table in the master's room You have a nasty bump. You've been unconscious for the whole of the night. The doctor has been and he says that the baby's heartbeat is fine and you shouldn't feel any further effects provided you rest in bed and get a good night's sleep. By tomorrow you can get up again. Can I get you a drink, Madam?'

Eva shook her head. 'Where's my husband?' she asked weakly, her voice hoarse.

'He's in his study. He asked me to inform him the moment you were awake.'

The maid left the room. A moment later, Reinholdt appeared. Eva felt hatred towards him, but the man who entered the bedroom was a different man to the one who had mechanically barked information about the destruction of her family as though he were announcing the arrival of a train at the Banhoffstrasse. His forehead was creased in a frown of concern.

'Are you alright?' he asked. He wore the voice he had worn a week earlier when he had loved her. Her heart beat in confusion. She nodded and winced with the pain.

'Keep your head still. The doctor says you took a terrible crack on the edge of the table. Lucky I'm in the SS. He looked at me as if I'd tried to kill you. He was thinking of reporting it to the police. I just dismissed him. The baby is alright. No bleeding. Nothing.'

He walked over and sat by her bedside. He grasped her hand. 'Eva, I'm …' He squeezed her hand. 'I don't know what to say. I'm just so confused. A week ago I loved you. I loved you with all my heart. I thought you loved me.'

She remained silent.

'What I did before was cruel. Unbearably cruel. I told you the news last night as though I was using some sort of a weapon against you. All I wanted to do was to hurt you; to see you suffer like you've made me suffer. But when you fainted, I didn't see a Jew faint, or a woman who's deceived me. I saw my Eva, white and cold, on the floor. My Eva, with a face which was masked in shock. I realised then that … Oh God. I don't know. I still love you, God help me. Do you still love me? I know you're a Jew, but you're not like … I mean I'm supposed to …'

She remained silent, trying to think through the situation, despite her pounding head.

'If you don't still love me, I'll understand why. I was horribly cruel. But for a week, I've been so fearful and confused and …'

She grasped his hand. 'I do love you. Of course I do,' she said weakly.

'But how can we … ? How … ? You're a Jew.'

'I'm Eva Stricher.'

'But everything that we're fighting against is evil and Jewish and part of a … We're fighting an international conspiracy and now I find you're one of the conspirators.'

She ignored his comments. It was the same nonsense that she read in the party newspapers, nonsense which she chose not to read.

'My parents?' she asked softly.

'I'm so sorry, but what I told you was the truth. The way I told you was evil and heartless and designed to punish you. I was so hurt I forgot that you were living in hope. There is no hope. Your mother is dead. Your father is on the brink of death. Your sister,' he played with her name before saying it, 'Rosl is a camp prostitute.'

Eva closed her eyes at the horror of what he was saying. But she'd known the truth all along. It was what was on the lips of everybody who dared to whisper in secret about the concentration camps … all she'd done was to deny it to herself for all these years. Now there was no hiding from the truth or herself, despite the gentleness with which he was re-telling her the awful reality.

'Is there any hope? Rosl?' she asked.

He shook his head and gently told her, 'I'm sorry. She sees many different men every day. I know. I've been to these camps. It's horrible. Not even Jews should be allowed, should be permitted … I can say no more than how sorry I am. If only I had known, I could have done something. And your father isn't going to survive. Give up hope, Eva. Don't think about them.'

It was a stab in her heart. For she knew she could, she should, have tried to save her parents, her sister and her brother, and now it was too late. Everybody was dead or dying because of her selfishness, because of the way she had insulated herself from reality.

She looked at him as she had looked at him throughout their marriage. He was no longer SS-*Standartenführer* Reinholdt Stricher. He was Reinnie, her husband, the man who loved her. The father of her unborn child. She stroked his hand.

'My father? My sister? Is there nothing you can do ... in your position ...'

He breathed deeply and looked towards the floor. 'Your father can't work any more. He may already have been killed. Your sister. Yes, I can save her. But if I do, it will mean your death and most probably my death as well.'

'But you're ...' She said imploringly. 'You have the power.'

'And you have no idea of the enemies that are everywhere. The worse the war goes, the more fanatical everybody becomes. The more Jews you have to round up and kill. The more quickly you have to jump to attention if an order is given. The more merciless you have to be with subordinates. In the old days, it was a laugh. Sure, we were fighting a war, but we were winning. Everything was possible. Nobody really cared so long as the Generals in the front line knew what they were doing. But now everybody is looking to save himself. The Generals are blaming everyone else. Hitler's become more fanatical. He's in a constant rage, screaming, shouting. There's even whispers of deposing him ... taking him by force and putting the barrel of a gun in his mouth. But the last time it was said openly the man was arrested and shot. And the round-up of the Jews in the East is quickening in pace. It's unbelievable. Just when we should be husbanding all our resources to regain the war initiative, to repel the enemy from closing in, we're squandering precious petrol and transportation and manpower on putting more and more Jews into these camps.

'So how is it going to seem if I give an order to rescue a Jewish woman from Auschwitz or an old Jew from a labour camp? What are people going to think of me and you, Eva? The danger to you will be overwhelming.'

'But surely ...'

'Think about it, Eva. If there's an investigation they will

come to me. My record is spotless. My father was one of the first members of the SA in Bavaria. I've been SA and SS all my life. But you? It will take them an hour, no longer, to check your papers. What are they going to find? I never investigated you. I fell in love with you. You enjoy the benefits of my respectability in the Reich, but once people look at who you are, not what you are, you won't last a second. They'll drag you off and you'll just replace your sister as a camp whore. And me? I'll be shot. They wouldn't even think twice.'

'But you have Göring's protection. You're on his staff.'

Reinholdt laughed. 'You think Göring will risk himself to protect a Jew's husband? Yes, Eva. I can make a grandiose effort to save your family, but the effort will fail, it will only result in our certain death.'

She lay back on the pillow. Her body looked as if it had been deflated. For the first time since their marriage, she looked different to him. No longer radiant, no longer supreme. She looked as if she was getting old.

Reinholdt suddenly felt terribly tired. It had been the worst week of his life. But he and Eva had come through some sort of tunnel, and he was sure they would soon emerge into the light.

'Eva, listen carefully to me. I have to go to South America. Göring's already making arrangements. I was planning for us to stay there, to lose ourselves in the jungle until this damn war's over. Come with me. Please. We'll make a new life together. In a place where they won't care if you're a Jew.'

She looked at him. Despite the workload, the tensions of the war, he was still handsome, dashing. She smiled.

'No. Not yet. I'll come with you eventually, but you go and make a home for us. I can't risk anything happening to the baby. I must stay until it's born. Then I'll come out to join you.'

'It's not that simple. If you don't come with me now, when I fail to return, you'll be arrested. Göring will see to that. Perhaps I'll go there and make arrangements; and then I'll return here. I can arrange our deaths in a road accident or something. Burn the bodies with identification. Then we can go underground and escape. We'll think of something.'

She nodded, and fell back into a fitful sleep.

CHAPTER TWENTY-TWO

NEW YORK, PRESENT DAY

'An opera singer? My mother was an opera singer!' Bertha looked at Sarah incredulously. Sarah said nothing but nodded. 'This is a joke, right?'

Sarah shook her head.

'Sol?' said Bertha, turning around to her husband, sitting beside her. 'My mother was an opera singer. Okay, she had a fabulous voice. I remember it like it was yesterday. In the apartment, it used to fill all the rooms. She would sing Italian arias and stuff. When I was a teenager, somebody even said she should do it for a living and she burst out laughing. It was that funny. She was shy, she wouldn't get up on a stage. My mother, an opera singer!'

'I don't know whether she was or wasn't. That's the problem, Mom.'

'Sarah,' said her father. 'This Annelise. Tell me about her.'

And she did. Every detail, even the inconsistencies, even the lies, even the evasions. The one thing she missed out, to David's anger, was that her grandmother Eva had lived with and been protected by a non-Jewish German. David didn't think it was Sarah's role to protect her mother's feelings; he'd argued strongly that her mother and father had a right to know. Sarah's will prevailed.

'So, she was dying when you left her?'

'Yeah. I still don't know whether she's passed away. I hope to God she hasn't. She's a wonderful old woman.

She has a wicked sense of humour. But as I was speaking to her, day after day, she seemed to just get … I don't know. It's so hard to explain. It was as if she wanted to get something off her chest and when she had done it, when she'd told me, it was as if she'd given in. I left her one day. She was frail and coughing and when I came back the next, she was already in hospital. It was more than just a heart attack. Even one of the nurses said she'd given up. I can't explain it, Mom, Dad.'

'Maybe you exhausted her with all your questions,' said her mother. 'Oh God,' she said reaching across the space between them. 'I'm sorry darling. I didn't mean to say that. It sounded so cruel. What I meant was…'

'I know what you meant, Mom, but I was really careful. And it wasn't even me who did the talking. After she began to trust me on the second day, she just opened up. Even if I tried to stop her, she would have insisted on telling me more and more. And then when she got to the part about how she'd collaborated with the Nazis, the change was just unbelievable. Like she had been suppressing something all her life and now that she'd got rid of it, it was okay to let go.'

'I still can't believe that a Jewish woman would have worked with the SS,' said her father.

'SS? Who knows what happened back in those days. But what evidence does she have that my mother was an opera singer?'

'She told me.'

'But you said she'd been lying. You said you caught her out several times.'

'Yeah, I know,' said Sarah. 'That's why I'm just not sure how much can be believed.'

'An opera singer,' said Bertha shaking her head and looking down at the carpet. 'You know, it's possible. It's just possible. Her voice was something else. She never sang in public but she knew all the words to some of those Italian operas and God, could she sing.'

ADMIRALS PALAST, FREIDRICHSTRASSE, BERLIN, NOVEMBER 1943

Despite the fact that she'd worn them dozens of times before, the horns on her head still felt ridiculous. Indeed, the entire costume was absurd. Perhaps more than any other musical drama, the absurdity of the plot, the costumes and the characterisation of Wagner's *Die Walküre* brought home to her the total nonsense of her life and her work. Grown men and women, dressing-up and singing at the tops of their voices about fallen heroes and giants and ugly little dwarfs. Yet night after night, in dozens of opera halls around the world, singers and conductors and musicians performed works which the audience knew were palpable fantasies, yet for which they returned night after night to lose themselves in the fiction. What a life!

She was backstage in her dressing-room, allowing herself a time for the re-examination of Eva Stricher, a time to think about herself, and to herself: 'How can I, a grown woman, dress up with a bronze breastplate, a bronze horned helmet, a shield, a spear, and prance around the stage in a long white flowing dress screaming *Hoyo hoto*?' Yet, she was Brunnhilde and because she disobeyed the God Wotan, she would be condemned at the end of the opera to lose her Godhood and become a mortal woman, to sleep on a mountain peak surrounded by magic fire through which only a hero could pass.

As was her custom, Eva had researched the role before rehearsals began. *Die Walküre* was one of Wagner's best-loved operas. Audiences adored the maidens of Old

Norse mythology, whose work it was to fly over a battlefield and to choose which warriors were to die heroically in battle, and which were to lead their lives in ignominy. If only audiences realised, however, that far from being bejewelled and magnificent women, the original Valkyries were hideous creatures. According to legends, the Valkyries used to sit on a battlefield weaving a tapestry made of human intestines, with men's severed heads weighing down the ends of the cords and an arrow for a shuttle. Unlike the way they'd been portrayed by that arch-Romantic, Wagner, the Valkyrie rode wolves instead of horses, and delighted in pouring blood down from skies onto a battle. Reading the legends had made her shudder.

Yet it was Hitler's favourite opera and the Führer would be here tonight. It was also her first appearance in opera since the birth of little Inge. For two months Eva had been a mother, breastfeeding, nurturing, walking the child in the park, doing all the things that normal mothers do in their normal lives for their normal children. But these were anything but normal times. Since her last opera before being confined at home five months earlier, she had neither seen nor heard from her husband Reinholdt. Since June when he flew to Portugal and then sailed on a ship to Argentina, she had not heard a word from him.

She was desperately worried. Without him there was no news of what was going on at the front. Some of his subordinates occasionally visited her. She had even received a gift of flowers and chocolates from the hierarchy of the Nazi Party when Inge was born. Göring himself had sent flowers and a note of congratulations to the hospital, which had sent the nurses into a flurry.

Even the Führer had asked that his compliments be passed on to Frau Stricher when he heard of the birth of another German maiden. Everybody knew about Inge except for her father. When would he be back? What would his emotions towards her be like when he returned? When would the bombing of Germany stop? When would the Führer turn back the hornets who buzzed out of the sky and dropped bombs on innocent human beings in Cologne and Hamburg and Berlin?

How many innocent people had already died in the murderous air raids? Although the news was suppressed by Goebbels, everybody talked about it. Not openly – the Gestapo were increasingly vigilant in listening out for anti-German, anti-patriotic sentiments – but in hairdressing salons and beer halls and private houses it was the talk on everybody's lips. How could you ignore the bombing, or pretend it didn't exist when the *Staats Oper* on the Linden had been destroyed, when the *Deutsche Oper* on Bismarckstrasse was now a gaping wound, and Herbert von Karajan had been forced to find a new home?

She sat at her make-up table while her maid and dresser fussed around her, making final adjustments to her head dress, their nonsensical chatter disturbing her peace of mind.

'How wonderful to see you back, Madam.'

'The glory of the opera.'

'The Führer made a special request for you.'

'Even von Karajan preferred you to Schwarzkopf.'

She ignored the chatter. She was excited, thrilled, to have been asked to sing in Die Walküre. It was a role which Schwarzkopf should by rights be singing, one in which Eva had only ever understudied. But Schwarzkopf was out of the city, on retreat, resting. Practising *lieder* under the Hungarian bitch soprano Maria Ivogün.

The cowardly bitch had fled when the bombs started to fall. Now it was Eva's turn, not the understudy, but the equal. Was she capable? He hadn't used her voice in months. The rehearsals had been very pleasing but how would her voice be when the Opera House was full, when there was no turning back, when she couldn't look imploringly at von Karajan and ask him to rephrase his approach and make a certain intonation easier for her. And the Führer was in the audience. She had sung for him before but only ever with Reinholdt somewhere in the front row for her to look at. Then, she hadn't been singing for Hitler, only for Reinholdt. But Reinholdt was somewhere in Argentina or on the sea returning to her. Or was he? Despite his profession of love and forgiveness, would the time and distance between them rekindle his hatred of her as a Jew?

But for now, she had to concentrate on the work at hand ... she had an audience to sing for. Would her breasts start to leak milk? She was wearing wads of cotton, giving her mountains in front of her. Her dress ballooned in front just as much as a typical Wagnerian heroine. But she had never been typical. Although she was far from slender and had a voluptuous body, she was still slim enough for Reinholdt to put his arms around her waist and to kiss her tenderly.

Just as he would kiss their little Inge when he returned home! When he saw her for the first time. What an adorable, beautiful, wonderful child. If only Eva's mother and father ...

Eva bit her lip. 'Leave me now,' she said curtly to her maid and dresser.

'But Madam, I still have to adjust the straps.'

'They're fine. They're fine, really. I need to be alone. I have to think through the role.'

'Ten minutes to curtain,' came a call from outside. 'Ten minutes to curtain.' The mantra was repeated, coming ever closer and closer to her door until there was a sharp knock. The door opened and a stageboy popped his head around. 'Good evening, Madam. Maestro von Karajan asked me to pass on his respects and inform you that it is ten minutes to curtain time. He asked me to remind you that you wished to watch the opera progress from the wings.'

'Thank you,' she said.

The little courtesies of opera behind the scenes! Berlin was falling around their ears. Men and women were dying. Arms, legs, bodies were mangled under twisted rubble. There was no beer in the beer halls, there was no dancing allowed by order of the Führer. Berlin was dark and drear. There were shortages of food everywhere.

Yet … yet Maestro von Karajan presented his compliments and wondered whether Frau Eva Stricher might like to watch the opera from the wings as it progressed, and before her grand entry.

She dismissed the automobile. The air raid was over. She didn't want to be driving past the ruins of bombed-out buildings, shops and houses which she might have visited just a day or two earlier. But nostalgia wasn't the only reason. It was safer for her to walk in the middle of the road so she could quickly dodge any building which might be falling or still on fire. There was a feeling of being trapped in a car. Thank God the opera managed to come to an end before the air raid started. As the sacrificial fire burned around her and the audience stood to its feet and cheered and the last curtain call died away … as the Führer was rushed into an air-raid shelter … Eva Stricher thanked God that her performance had been marvellous. There was a power that hadn't been there before Inge was born. Something in her body had changed. Funny that she hadn't noticed it during the rehearsals, only when she was performing for an audience. A resonance, a deepening, an intensity that had never been there before. Even a confidence. She was a different singer. She was the equal of Schwarzkopf.

Nothing could hold her back now. Nothing except the British and their damned air raids. At first, the booming in the shelter deep below the theatre had been distant. Then came the sound of bells as emergency firefighters raced to the crisis, then the droning, the heavy dull mechanical droning of the bombers. Like a low continuous thunder roll over distant hills, never ending, unfolding its menace over Berlin's lakes and parks and buildings as though the gods were blowing in from the west and the winter wind was gathering momentum to shriek through the long straight streets of the city. A howling in fury against the crimes which Hitler had committed against Britain and France and Belgium and Poland and Czechoslovakia and all the other countries where his Blitzkrieg had caused hell on earth.

Down in the air-raid shelter below Friedrichstrasse she was no longer Eva Stricher, diva, star of the opera. Here she was just another Berlin citizen trying to save herself from the horror which dropped from the skies. People sat huddled together, husbands and wives comforting children and each other. Eva had no one to comfort. Instead she drew her legs beneath her chin and hugged herself in fear that a direct hit would annihilate her. Who then would look after her baby daughter? At least baby Inge was safe. She and the maid. Instructions were clear. Take the baby into the basement at the bottom of the house. It was reinforced. It was safe. Where was Reinholdt? Why wasn't he here when she needed him so badly?

And then the perpetual droning of the bombers, the noise which would never stop, suddenly came to an end. The thunderstorm had passed over. Beethoven's Seventh

Symphony of destruction. One minute, death was everywhere as squadrons of bombers moaned and creaked over the city, dropping their foul cargoes, and the next minute the last bomber had disappeared, turning north and then west, lighter by tons, to fly back to some airbase in England where the pilot would regale his friends and family with the excitement of his work, telling them how he had lit up the night sky over Berlin, how his bombs had helped bring the war to an end.

Did he ever think of the people he was killing? Did he ever wonder who was buried under the tons of rubble which his bombs created? Did he ever think for even a moment about the bodies torn in two by the blast, arms and legs and heads and guts flying outwards in the explosion or incinerated as a five hundred pound bomb evaporated what had once been a human being?

Sadly she walked through the streets. Men and women stood watching in horror as the buildings that were part of their lives, burned angrily and illuminated the sky in a spectral dawn hours before the sun rose. She walked left, then right, then left and as she turned into each street, more rubble, more fires, more horror. Ambulances and stretchers, and the smell of burning flesh or the stench of incinerated rubber tyres. Even the roads were on fire as the tar burned.

She turned finally into her own street. It never occurred to her that her street could have been bombed. It never entered her mind as she sat huddled in the bomb shelter beneath the opera; when the thoughts began to surface, she'd dismissed them just as she dismissed horrible thoughts when she was a child.

But now her mind entered the present. Drawn back from the fantasy that played around her thoughts. She was suddenly confronted with the reality of her own life. She frowned as she walked down the road that had been her home for the last two years. Even the most grandiose of mansions were not protected against a bombing raid. It was the great equaliser, the socialist leveller … like death; the rich in their mansions had as much chance of incineration as the poor cowering in their hovels. She looked at the houses in her street. Some were sporting gaping wounds while others next door stood proud and arrogant, unscathed, not even a broken window. A body lay on the pavement covered in a grey blanket. She might know this woman or man. They might have had tea. It was a neighbour.

She felt fear begin to quicken her pace. It was a long road, something awful was playing around in her mind. If these houses were bombed and that house over there was bombed, what about her own house? With the sudden realisation of impending doom she began to run. Number 23, Number 24, Number 25. Trees were splintered near her house. They had fallen into the street. Cars were stopped nearby. A van had been knocked on its side, its tyres were still burning. The police were trying to free the driver. She ran past and manoeuvred her way around the tree and then she saw the space beyond the pavement where her house should have been. She stopped and looked. Where was her house? It wasn't there. How could a house disappear? It was there five hours ago when she left. Where was it now?

There was smoke coming from the rubble where her house used to be. She walked as though she was in a dream. She stood in front of the house. It had collapsed in on itself. There were flames coming from the middle. The flames illuminated the tangle of curtains and floor-boards and window casements. Some walls were still standing. She looked up through the front walls which weren't there, and saw her upper dining room, which was. She recognised the wallpaper. She had chosen it herself. Deeper into the house, further back over the rubble, the kitchen was still there. No walls but she could see the stove and the ice chests; but the refrigerator which cooled the food wasn't there. She shook her head trying to clarify what was flooding into her mind. And then a thought passed through her numbed brain. Something her mother Serel had told her about a pogrom on her own home in Ruthenia ... how she'd somehow hidden the children on a river bank and in the morning, she'd emerged to walk through her house, to walk through where the walls had once kept out the cold and the rain. What did her mother say, 'It was the oddest and the saddest moment of my life ... except for the death of my little Eva in a field somewhere, my first Eva ...'

And then Eva's body became ice. Her eyes widened and a sound, a wail, like the deathcall of the Valkyrie from the battlefield ... 'Inge ... !!!'

CHAPTER TWENTY-THREE

ARGENTINA, NOVEMBER, 1943

The noise from the cataract was overpowering. The two men held their heads close together. Even that close, there was a need to speak in a normal voice in order to be heard. The water, millions of litres every hour, thundered over the precipitous drop of the Devil's Throat sending up plumes of spray which disappeared in the hot November weather to become clouds, multi-hued by the shafts of rainbows which hung like angels over the void.

It had taken Reinholdt Stricher a few minutes to accommodate the volume of sound all around him. It was like standing next to an aeroplane which was constantly revving at a high pitch. Even standing at the rail and looking down for just a few moments covered his homburg, his shirt and tie and jacket with a fine gossamer spray. He turned towards his companion and saw that his eyebrows, cap and military insignia were also covered with the white mist.

'You get used to it,' said Colonel Juan Domingo Perón. 'But it has its uses. I often come up here when I want to be totally alone. In Buenos Aires these days you never know which wall is listening.'

Reinholdt smiled. It had taken them a whole day to drive up to the border in their jeep. It was a backbreaking exercise, over precipitous mountain roads and through dense foliated jungles. The glamour, the excitement of being in a place so unlike Germany soon left him as the vehicle climbed and wound its way up massive hillsides, and down into plunging valleys, all the while sliding over the ill-formed and rutted tracks. They had rested at a cantina in a small village on the way and eaten the biggest steak that Reinholdt had ever seen. Even in the days of Nazi splendour, when everything was bountiful, he had never seen a slab of beef as big. Yet Perón urged him to finish every mouthful telling him that it was wonderful for the teeth, the bones and the eyesight. He had eaten the steak with corn, potatoes, beans and a flagon of the roughest red wine he had ever tasted. And the cost? Roughly what he would pay for a loaf of bread in Berlin. 'Well,' he thought as they returned to their jeep and Juan Perón's driving took on an all new and alarming dimension, 'they might live in poverty but they'll never starve.'

They ascended to the junction of the common border which Argentina shared with Brazil and had to hack their way through jungle tracks before coming upon falls which Perón told him were called Iguassú after the Guarani Indian word meaning 'great water'. They had stood before the most spectacular of all the 300 waterfalls in the nearly three kilometre length of the extraordinary phenomenon, and Reinholdt felt utterly humbled. They stayed and stared at the awesome Devil's Throat for the better part of an hour. The more it roared, the longer they were there, the more shamed Reinholdt felt about his arrogance as a Nazi, as a member of what Hitler continued to call the Master Race. Here, there was no master race … here there was the diminution of man before the might of Nature. It was truly the most amazing spectacle he had ever witnessed, the sort of thing that Europeans would beg to visit if only they knew of its existence.

And still Perón had not unveiled his reason for asking Reinholdt to join him on this devilish excursion. It wasn't just for Perón to show his guest the falls. There was far, far more to it than that. They would spend the night in a small and rundown hotel that they passed twenty kilometres further back and then tomorrow drive back to Buenos Aires. He would have to tell Reinholdt what he wanted soon or he would lose the opportunity. He was a strange man. Big, ebullient, full of life and excitement, yet there was something of the peasant about him. Something which Reinholdt found uncomfortable. He knew that Perón had been a leading member of a coup d'état against the government. For some time now he had been courting the labour movement in order to support him for some form of move that he was about to take, especially as the policies of the president, General Ramirez were hideously unpopular. But what could Perón possibly want with Reinholdt? Especially now, at the end of his visit when he had spent a couple of days in consultation with officers more senior than Perón and had reached some successful conclusions.

'So, what do you think of our Devil's Throat?' asked Perón.

'Spectacular! I've never seen anything like it. I've been to Switzerland of course. The waterfalls there are nothing by comparison. Not even the infamous Riechenbach Falls where Sherlock Holmes plunged to his death fighting Dr Moriarty. But this …' said Reinholdt, raising his voice above the noise. 'This is breathtaking.'

'Like so much else in my country. You haven't even seen a fraction of it, Herr Stricher. You haven't been to the south where the land is a sea of frozen ice, nor to the centre where the plains are so dry, arid and flat you would swear you were on another planet. We have every world, every people, every moment of history recorded on the face of this painful land.' Reinholdt turned to him. 'And I wonder how the future is going to be?' he said.

Ah, Reinholdt thought to himself. *Now, it comes.*

'The future,' Reinholdt told the Argentine Colonel, 'is what we make it. This is what has been taught to us by Adolf Hitler. We are in complete control of our destiny.'

'Really. Then why did your Führer spend so much of his time and expense sending his soldiers into the deserts of the Middle East to find the spear of Longinus?'

Reinholdt turned to him silently in surprise. There was a smile on Perón's thin lips. 'Oh yes,' he said almost gloating. 'There's very little I don't know about *Reichschancellor* Adolf Hitler, nor about Göring, nor Himmler, nor Goebbels, nor the rest of them. Great men. Very great men. But at times a little bit too romantic. It's the Teutonic blood in you, you see. We're the romantic race, we South Americans. We're the people with music in our hearts. We're the people who built the great pyramids of the Aztecs. We are the people who had the most sophisticated myths and legends before the coming of the white man. Germans have always struck me as being very, how shall I say this, down to earth.'

Reinholdt couldn't tell whether he was being insulted or not. He would give the man a little bit more rope.

'Of course I'm well aware of the Teutonic knights and Lohengrin, and Wagner and all his myths. We even had Friedrich's sister, Elizabeth Nietzsche building her colony not all that far from here and then there was a group of Australians who came to establish a settlement. They wanted to build paradise on earth. Well, they found it but they failed to tame the paradise, because they tried to remain Western. South America beat them, as it eventually beats everyone. Perhaps not this century, my dear Herr Stricher, but certainly next, Europe and Asia and North America will all be finished; the future belongs to the Southern Hemisphere; to South Africa, to South America, to Australasia. Maybe I'm wrong

Reinholdt, but I don't think so. And if I am wrong, it's because, invisible at the moment, there might yet be a deep romantic spirit within the European heart which will enable it to survive this war, and what will be its horrible aftermath.'

Again Reinholdt kept quiet.

'No doubt you're wondering why I've asked you to come on this long journey. Well, the view is enough. It's spectacular. Everybody should have the opportunity of seeing the Iguassú Falls at least once in their lives, of standing at the lips of the Devil's Mouth and looking down the Devil's Throat. It teaches you so much about your own importance, doesn't it? About the insignificance of man compared to the awesomeness of nature.'

Perón put his arm around the taller man's shoulders and led him away from the edge. 'But there's another reason I've brought you here, as I suspect you know.'

As they walked some distance from the precipice, the noise quickly diminished to a dull roar, as if a squadron of bombers were flying overhead. Now there was no need for him to shout. 'There are things which I can discuss with you here that I simply can't discuss in Buenos Aires. You really never know who is listening or who is behind a curtain or who is hidden in the trunk of a car as you're driving alone. And my life isn't exactly safe and secure at the moment after the coup in June. I know to an outsider it looks as if I'm very popular with the labour movement but I'm planning certain things which, of course, I can't discuss with you; things which will put me at odds with my military colleagues. Things which this country needs. Without going into any details Reinholdt, let me just say that they are not dissimilar to the organisation that you yourself enjoyed in the SA.'

In shock, Reinholdt turned and said, 'A civilian army?'

'Certain things are necessary, my dear Reinholdt, when the world is at war. We're being mercilessly pressured to end our state of neutrality and to declare war against Germany. The Americans, especially that bastard Secretary of State, Cordell Hull, have got everybody coming out against us.'

'But surely it's only a matter of time,' said Reinholdt. 'You're the only country in the whole of the Americas which has yet to declare a position against the Axis powers. You can't hold out against America or Brazilian pressure.'

'We're a sovereign nation. We do as we wish.'

'True,' said Reinholdt. 'And while you do, it's of great benefit to us. Without your platinum, industrial diamonds and medicines Germany would be in a perilous state.'

'We're being well paid for them,' said Perón as they walked further down the path, having to break into single file and weave in and out of the undergrowth.

'Do you know where the money comes from to buy these products?' said Reinholdt.

'No. No, I don't. I have often wondered. I assumed it was Switzerland.'

'It is but we get the Jews to pay for it. For the last three or four years, we've had a nice little racket going. Unfortunately, due to directives from the Führer, we've recently been prevented from doing it. We selected certain very rich Jews who wanted to get out of Germany but of course couldn't. They had money sitting in banks all over the world, so we had no access to it. What we did was nominate a very large sum of money which they could transfer to one of our two German banks in Buenos Aires as ransom for permission to emigrate from the Fatherland. You got dollars and pounds and Swiss francs. They got Argentinian pesos which we then used to pay for certain goods.'

Perón burst out laughing. Reinholdt continued. 'We had to do it. You see, we'd already taken everything they had in Germany and Austria and the East, but before the war began, the clever Jews had transferred most of their money to banks safely overseas; mainly Switzerland. We had no way of getting it back, which is why we devised the scheme. Smart, eh?'

'Smart,' said Perón. 'Like the German companies that set up here so long before the war. That was a masterstroke. How are they doing?' asked Perón.

Bending to fight vines and huge fleshy green leaves from plants he couldn't identify, it was difficult to talk. Reinholdt straightened and said, 'Bayer is doing very well. Indeed all the subsidiaries of IG Farben and Staudt & Co are doing well. Pharmaceutical and agricultural products always seem to do good business, no matter where they are in the world.'

'And what about Siemens Schuckert? How is the electrical business?'

'As far as I know,' said Reinholdt, 'doing nicely.'

'Ah huh. And how are they helping your war effort? You know I'm very close to Benito Mussolini.'

Reinholdt laughed. 'I wouldn't make too many claims on your friendship. You're aware that we had to rescue him from the clutches of a furious mob. If it hadn't been for us, he would have been strung up.'

'I'm very well aware of what you did,' said Perón bridling. 'Benito is a very good friend of mine and I won't abandon him just because he's run into some temporary ill fortune. I've sent him letters of encouragement telling him he can come here any time he wants as my guest.'

Reinholdt was beginning to become irritated by all this to-ing and fro-ing. Perón had raised the topic but not told him what it was about.

'Why precisely have you invited me here, Colonel?'

'To discuss the future.'

'I don't know what the future is going to be.'

'Perhaps not, my dear Reinholdt, but unless you plan for it, the future will never be the way you want it to be.'

'Go on.'

He was a fit and active man and was already walking at a pace that Reinholdt found difficult to keep up. Their jeep was now in sight, parked in a clearing. He stopped before he neared the jeep, turned and looked at Reinholdt.

'Let me be plain, bearing in mind that this conversation has never taken place.'

'Of course,' said Reinholdt.

'The war is going badly for you. Only a fool would deny that. The Allies are marshalling their forces. There will shortly be a massive attack, a re-taking of Europe. It'll probably be through France or via the Balkans or maybe from the East, who knows what's in the minds of men like Patton or Eisenhower or Montgomery. Germany will be caught in a vice and squeezed until it's dry and lifeless. You have only one friend in the world now that Benito is no longer in power. That friend is me.'

'You?'

'Yes, me.'

This irritated the German. The man was being presumptuous. A third-rate colonel from a fourth-rate army didn't lecture an officer in the SS. 'Firstly,' Reinholdt said, a note of contempt entering his voice, 'the Swiss, although neutral, are our closest Allies. Their banking system is supporting our war effort. Their transportation system enables us to skirt Allied sabotage. Secondly the war is far from lost. Our having suffered some set backs doesn't for one moment mean that we are not strong and powerful and …'

'If you continue acting the fool, Stricher, then there's no point in our continuing this conversation. You're here in order to create an escape route for SS officers. I know it. You know it. President Ramirez knows it and most especially Göring knows it. If you don't know it, then I have misjudged you but I assume that you do know it and that's the reason you're here.

'That's why they sent a man of your rank. Not so high ranking as to alert Hitler. Not so low ranking as to have no power of negotiation. Now, I don't know what you have said to Ramirez. I don't know what deals you have come to. Let me assure you that he's a fool. He was the Minister for War before the coup in July. War!' Perón burst out laughing. 'The closest he ever came to a battle were arguments with his staff officers. He's right now talking to you with one face and looking north to America with another. No matter what he says to you, Stricher, he's about to declare war on Germany. He'll buckle to American pressure.'

'He might decide to do that,' said Reinholdt, 'but the action is not without its consequences. The investment we have here is massive. We could easily bring the country to its knees economically.'

'And America would lift us up. America would throw its collective arms around us and give us preferential treatment. They would put millions in foreign investment into our coffers. Ramirez knows you're on your knees. He's just playing one side against the other trying to get the best deal.'

Reinholdt remained silent. He had suspected as much but kept his own counsel. It was part of the report that he would make to Göring.

'Why are you telling me this?' he asked quietly. 'This is against your national interest.'

'On the contrary,' said Perón. 'Our national interest is

to maintain a relationship with Europe, to offer Nazis safe haven when Europe implodes, to see a channel of SS men coming here to the safety of our shores.' Reinholdt frowned. 'My fiancée Evita is planning a trip to Italy as soon as the hostilities are over. I can't go because I'll be very busy but she will establish the relationships with the Vatican and with the Swiss banks so that your lovely people come here with all their lovely money. All the billions of dollars and tons of gold you have extracted from the Jews.'

'You're mad,' said Reinholdt looking at him closely.

'No,' said Perón, not in the least bit insulted. 'I'm merely creating the future. You will lose this war. This year, next year, at the latest, the year after. There will be a vacuum in Europe. The people will rise up here against the government because it took sides with the Allies, especially the United States. There's a huge German community here, and many German sympathisers. They'll rise up and I'll lead that revolt. I will become President. My fiancée is already beloved by the Argentine people as I am beloved by the labour movement and with the money we receive from your very good selves, Argentina will be assured a rosy future.'

'How do you know I won't repeat this conversation to President Ramirez? How do you know he won't arrest you for treason?'

'Because,' said Perón, 'in your heart, you know I'm right. Arrest me and the SS is more than just finished as a force … it's dead! It'll be hunted down around the world wherever you escape. There'll be no safe havens. There will be nowhere for people like you to run.'

CHAPTER TWENTY-FOUR

GERMANY, JULY, 1945

The line disappeared into infinity. It snaked up the hill and then down over the other side, to reappear out of the distant earth revealing far-off subterranean figures who climbed out of the very ground itself. An Escher landscape; a medieval frieze of a pilgrimage from Hell into Uncertainty. And then the people disappeared into the mists and dusts of a sunset.

Eva and Reinholdt knew with absolute certainty that the line in front of them, and behind them, continued on into an endless landscape of people trying to escape. There was nothing but the thin vapour of hope before them, and murk of despair behind.

The rain at least had stopped, though the sky was heavy with sad and pendulous clouds. For years, the skies had been full of angry insects which buzzed and droned and set the evenings on fire, night after night and then – as Germany became incapable of sending up even the semblance of self-defence – day after day, the insects dropped millions of tons of explosives onto a body already dead. All Germans could do was to hide and pray. But their prayers came to nothing. God wasn't listening.

Now the madman was dead in his bunker, laying in a char-black oily embrace for the rest of eternity with his simple, simpering Eva Braun. And, like vultures squabbling over the suppurating flesh of a dead beast, the Russians and the Americans and the British had raced towards Berlin in order to lay claim to its rubble; they were like crusader knights hacking their way towards an empty dustbowl of a Holy Grail.

Berlin's citizens … no! … the entire German nation, as well as cadaverous refugees from the concentration camps … had packed up what possessions they could carry and flooded into the streets, trudging their way up from the bowels of hell to arrive at nowhere.

The Russians had been in Berlin for weeks now. Rape was so common that women considered themselves lucky to have been taken by only ten men in a day. Some women had ninety or more Russian peasant soldiers force themselves into them during an average day. Like packs of dogs, the Russian soldiers, given tacit approval by their commanders, would rove the streets until they spied a woman; then they would force her to expose only those parts of her body which interested them … and right there in the midst of the rubble, with no concession to decency or modesty, they'd force open her legs, and push themselves inside her with the anger and aggression of invaders.

Even the artifice that German women had taken to in desperation, that of dressing up as though they were men or wearing shopping bags under coats to make them appear fat and unattractive, no longer fooled the Russian peasant soldiers. A flick of a knife and the coat buttons flew off; the shopping bags or pillows dropped to the floor. A call went out, 'Mikhail, Boris, Feyodor. Here. Quick. Another one,' and the woman would be pushed to the filthy ground, legs forced apart, and the sudden, familiar feeling of hot rods of hatred thrust into her a hundred times by a dozen different men would again reduce her to the level of an animal. And then the Russian soldiers would get up and shake themselves and walk away laughing; sometimes they left their genitals hanging out of their clothes to dry in the air so they'd be ready for the next woman who they happened upon. Berlin was a city out of control. There was nothing, no one, who felt inclined to put an end to the barbarity.

Suicides were more common than hot meals. Zukov and his generals were allowing the men of the Red Army to have their way with the civilian population. It was revenge for the millions of Russians butchered by the Germans. It was revenge for the deaths of three million Poles, for the concentration camps, for the siege of Stalingrad. It was the revenge of the subhumans against the master race and their Reich which would last a thousand years.

But Berlin was far behind Eva and Reinholdt. They were only two of millions of shuffling refugees, human detritus clogging every road and artery in the exhausted body of Europe. They were walking in a stupor, pushing a pram filled with their precious possessions in front of them. Not money, of course. Not clothes. Not jewellery. Those were not precious possessions these days ... they were luxuries, and refugees weren't allowed any luxuries. They were like mana from Heaven.

No, before them, in the battered pram which poor little Inge, their long dead child, had once used, were the essentials of life. Stale bread, limp vegetables, a spare pair of shoes, blankets for the cold nights, a razor for Reinholdt (not soap, of course), menstrual towels for Eva, and more food. Food which they conserved, which they only ate once a day in case there was no more food when they arrived at wherever they were going ... if they ever got there. It kept them alive – just!

All their money was in Switzerland. The only thing which Eva insisted upon taking was the amulet which she had secreted beneath her breasts in the hope that, in a cursory search by a soldier, it might be missed.

Eva felt the amulet on occasion, hanging heavily in her brassiere. She knew there was a good chance she would lose it to some peasant soldier who would strip search her and pull it out of her underclothes, shouting to his comrades as though finding buried treasure. It was a nightmare she lived through whenever they closed their eyes and went to sleep in some ditch, or in a field, or, if they were lucky, in a deserted farmhouse.

Reinholdt had initially taken his service Luger but then on second thoughts decided that refugees didn't carry Wehrmacht guns. And there were enough eagle-eyed soldiers watching the lines of refugees, trying to spot escaping Nazis, for him not to take a risk. Not that the allied soldiers were the only problem facing Reinholdt. The refugees, especially, hated the Nazis and the SS and the Wehrmacht, and gladly reported someone acting suspiciously in their ranks to the Allies.

Marching. All the while, marching. A thing he had managed to avoid in the SA and the SS. His marching days had been confined to a few ceremonial parades but now he was marching and shuffling and dragging his feet along the interminable path towards uncertainty; a path which could lead to his undoing, his exposure as an SS man, pretending to be a Jew. Dozens, perhaps even hundreds of SS men had done the same thing. Concentration camp guards had killed Jews as the Russians and the Americans were liberating the camps. The guards had swapped their uniforms for the lice-ridden, tattered remnants of clothes that the dead inmates had worn and in the confusion were able to slip quietly and unobtrusively into the crowds of people who clogged every road and artery. Many of the guards, of course, had been torn to pieces in just the same way as the hated *Sonderkommandos* were torn limb from limb by vengeful prisoners. How could Reinholdt blame them? He had been responsible for organising the transport for millions of prisoners to the death camps during the years of Nazi madness. How could he blame them, Jews, Slavs, Allies … what right did he have to ask for mercy?

Yet, he could only blame himself for returning. He had done the deals in Argentina a year before the collapse of the Reich. There was ample time for him to return to Eva, collect her and escape before the end … if only Eva hadn't become paralysed by Inge's death … if only she hadn't sat night after night, day after day, staring out of the windows, making little birdlike noises and whimpering. And by the time she showed some signs of recovery from Inge's death, it was too late … the borders had become too dangerous, flight impossible, the end of Germany had begun.

On the ship returning from Argentina, Reinholdt made all the arrangements in his mind. Back then, it had all looked so easy. Germany would lose the war and in the confusion thousands of SS men would slip out of the country along well established rat lines and into the welcoming arms of Juan and Evita Perón. Other colleagues in the SS had established safe havens in Canada, Australia and he had even heard on the grapevine a few months ago that there were sympathisers in America who had facilitated escape routes into mid-west American cities. Even Perón had advised him to stay. Or at least to return immediately before the final collapse.

But he had been drawn back into the miasma of Germany by two powerful and conflicting forces. One was his responsibility to the Reich, the other his yearning to be with his family; not just his mother and father but with Eva and to see and touch and hold his baby Inge. What a disaster!

As he shuffled towards the void of night at the end of the long and pitiless road, he shook his head in wonder at the way his life had gone. The last time he had seen his father and mother was in their home in Munich. His father looked old, grey and ashen. He kept shaking his head like a man suffering from Parkinson's disease. He kept muttering the words, 'Why?' 'How?' It was all too much for him. There was no way he could ever understand how the war had been lost, how things had been so good one day and so unutterably bad the next. One day he was the master of the Universe. The next day his tiny world had collapsed and the barbarians were pressing to crucify him.

And Lotte? His mother was in a state of denial. She kept calling him by a name she hadn't used since he was a boy – Reinnie. She kept promising to make him his favourite food; spicy pork sausages with potatoes and fried onions, followed by an apple strudel and thick whipped cream. She didn't seem to understand that the only pork sausages were full of sawdust and the last time they had seen cream was at the height of Germany's wartime blitzkrieg.

But that was nothing compared to the horror of his return to Eva, to the vicious bombings of the British, the merciless thunder and lightning which rained from the sky and exploded somewhere, always close by, and blew off the arms and legs and tore bodies to pieces, and the wailing of sirens and ambulances and fire trucks as they tried to bring the conflagration to an end. A conflagration which would be extinguished in the grey dawn of the morning, only to start again that night and the night after that and which would never ever end.

He had found her at the Opera. Obscenely it was still performing. She looked like a ghost. She had lost so much weight. She was still singing but her voice was hollow, drained of emotion. He had driven in a Reich car from the Templehoff airport to their home and found a charred hole where his life had once been. He sat for ten minutes looking, just looking. His driver had been too frightened to say anything but had merely gripped the steering wheel staring ahead until Reinholdt instructed him to go to the Opera.

Reinholdt was terrified that she was a casualty. His feelings were so confused. His wife was a Jew, his sworn enemy; but he was petrified that she was hurt or killed. Even the months of separation had not dulled the love he felt for her, the overpowering sense of one-ness. He had rationalised everything in his mind. So what if she was a Jew? She was the mother of his child. She was his partner in bed, in life. So what? Nothing mattered except his love for her. His anger; his fury. They were all things of the past. He ached to see his Eva, to hold her, to see his baby Inge.

He had been alone ever since he left Berlin. Evita Perón had offered him a procession of women, beautiful women with dark Spanish eyes, olive skin, long glistening black hair and perfumed breasts. He had rejected most of them. He had only failed as a husband three or four times while he was in Argentina. He felt almost proud of himself for maintaining his love and affection and his faithfulness.

And when he stood on the threshold of her dressing-room and saw the gaunt, grey pallor of her skin, he knew that his life was over. They had looked at each other for an interminable moment. And then her bottom lip began to quiver and her face flushed with tears and she ran over and hugged him. In between her sobs, she had told him that Inge had died in the bombings and they cried together. They sat on the couch in her dressing-room holding each other and sobbing.

He had tried to get out of Germany a few months after his return; to take Eva with him; but events happened too fast. It was all beyond him. Transport became impossible to acquire. Petrol was so severely rationed that forms had to be filled in triplicate just to commandeer a chauffeur. Everything now militated towards the war effort. He had even been told by Göring that he could expect to be called up into active front-line service. It was then that he decided to escape. But escape was impossible. The Gestapo was everywhere, especially keeping an eye on traitors to the Reich. Since the attempt on Hitler's life, senior men like him were being trailed, spied upon, arrested. More than his own safety, he had to protect Eva's identity. For his sake and more especially for hers, she had to be Brunnhilde, Isolde, Fricka. She must be the archetype of the German heroine, stalwart in her grief, resolute in times of despair, purposeful in times of national catastrophe.

And it worked. Of all the senior men who worked with him, he was under the least suspicion because of Eva's position. Even when the Opera closed permanently, even when the last violin was packed away and the piano was locked, even then his wife, his Eva, was still the German heroine, unassailable, beyond doubt, beyond reproach.

Hitler had been seen on the streets occasionally, patting young Hitler Youth on their cheeks, assuring old men in uniform that their fight was for the good of the Fatherland, but even as he hobbled around looking old and infirm, the Führer's staff were destroying records so that the victorious Americans or British or French or Russians would never know the truth of what people like he and others in the SS had done. The instructions had gone out. Destroy the camps, kill and bury the inmates, cover the graves with earth, leave no trace. But it was all too late.

Now he was a refugee. Now Reinholdt stumbled over potholes in his path, shuffled with the agony of walking in shoes which were full of holes and bent under the weight of a suitcase strapped to his back. The only thing that kept him upright was the pram, the only remaining memory that they had of their daughter, a little girl he had never seen.

As they walked Eva quietly made him repeat the Hebrew prayers for blessings over wine and bread which he'd been learning for the past two weeks. The morning *sacharis* prayer and the evening *ma'ariv* prayers, the prayers for Sabbath and the prayers for the end of the Sabbath, were now well-known to him. He even had the accent correctly. As she taught her husband from the reservoir of the childhood memories of her religion, so he learned things about Judaism which he'd never known. He got to understand the family relationships, and the one-to-one understanding which many Jews had with their God.

He was a good student, a keen student. He listened attentively when she explained to him the Jewish ritual for greeting children, the prohibition on kosher and unkosher food, mixing milk and meat, the order of service in a synagogue, relationships between parents and children. He even appeared to be genuinely interested, although what he was learning was intended to save his life.

As they left Berlin, Reinholdt Stricher metamorphosed into Rudolf Büchbinder. In the nights of living in shelters underneath their new house, the bombs raining down like black confetti at a Satanic wedding, they constructed the story. He was the son of Herr and Frau Büchbinder. She was the daughter of the cook, Serel Arpel and the chauffeur, Franz Arpel. They had fallen in love. They had married secretly, against her parent's wishes. He had followed her to Berlin where she worked as a maid in the Hotel Adlon on Unter den Linden. During the war, when the evil SS were sweeping the streets clean of Jews to make the city *Judenfrei*, Rudolf was picked up and taken to Theresienstadt Concentration Camp just north of Prague where he had managed to keep himself alive. There he had mixed with people from the Bialystock Ghetto and had done his best to save the children when their parents had been murdered. In May 1945, when Theresienstadt was liberated by Soviet troops he had escaped and hidden just above the bogey wheels of a train going south-west to Berlin. The continual day and night roar of the train wheels riding over the tracks had affected his hearing, which is why he continually asked people to speak slowly and clearly.

The former Eva Arpel had managed to escape deportation by assuming a Christian identity and buying false papers. Now she was free. Now she was united with her husband who, by a miracle, had found her walking in the bombed-out centre of the city selling cigarettes. She had been serially raped by dozens of Russian troops. She was a nervous shell of her former self. Every time she was questioned, she would burst into uncontrollable tears. Nothing wearied interrogators than the perpetual tears from a hysterical woman, especially as there were tens of thousands of people to interrogate. And where were they going? Their story to whoever asked was that they were trying to get to the coast ... to find a port ... to get on board a ship. They were travelling to America or Israel to make a new life.

They had practised the story many times until it was perfect. The lack of food available to them in the last months of the war made them sufficiently thin and emaciated to look like genuine victims of the starvation of concentration camps. People felt sorry for them, especially the Germans in the seemingly endless line. Whatever food the Germans had was shared with these Jews as a way of buying favour in case the occupying forces stopped the line and questioned them.

Everybody was leaving Berlin. Everybody who could get out and passed the security checks of the British and American forces.

Annelise was somewhere back there, somewhere in the bombed-out remnants of the city. Before they packed up and left, Eva had gone back into the city despite Reinholdt's pleas to beg her friend to join them, but Annelise shook her head.

'If I show my face in a crowd of refugees, I'll be killed. They know me for what I am, a traitor. Somebody who told the SS where the U-boats were hiding. I sold out my people. I have to take my punishment.'

In bitter tears, Eva said, 'How will I know where to find you when this is all over?'

'We'll find each other,' Annelise had assured her. 'Somehow we'll find each other.'

'How will you look after yourself?'

Annelise had shrugged. 'I'm in God's hands.'

'When we get to where we're going, I'll send you money. Reinholdt has plenty of money in Swiss accounts.'

'No,' Annelise had said. 'It's too risky. You'll be caught. Just leave it. I'll be alright. I've already got another identity I can change into. I'll dye my hair and pretend. Don't forget, I'm an actress. The way I performed in the nightclub, men actually thought I enjoyed what I was doing.'

They had hugged and kissed and sworn eternal love and as she left, Eva knew she would never see her friend again. She muttered a silent prayer in Hebrew and went back into the chaotic streets to join her husband on the long march to somewhere.

The whole of Europe was in chaos. Millions of people were ambling along roads in the hope of going somewhere. People didn't seem to have destinations in mind. All they wanted to do was escape. Eva and Reinholdt were the same as everybody else, but unlike most, they did have a destination in mind, if only their disguises could carry them there.

That night they stopped walking when the road became too dark to see potholes. They pushed their pram to the side of the road, a ditch overgrown with grass and moss. Eva began to cry in exhaustion. Reinholdt put his arm around her. They hugged each other in desperation. He took his knife and cut a slice of stale black bread for Eva and a slice for himself. They chewed as slowly and carefully as they could, the heavy malt flavour seeming to explode in their mouths. It was the first they had eaten since morning. It tasted horrible but it would keep them going until the following morning when the road would once more continue to stretch into the future. People began to light camp fires. They were dotted beyond and in front of them, one after the other. Along the way, he had detoured into a field and collected straw and twigs and some branches. He gathered them together, and took out a box of matches. Cupping the match in his hand, he felt the warmth of the straw as it caught fire. Then the twigs. Soon, their fire was as welcoming as everybody elses.

When he was a senior man in the SS, he had flown into country airstrips lit by kerosene lamps, long necklaces of lights stretching into the distance, converging at a point far away. Reinholdt looked up and down the road. He was no longer a God descending from the clouds to determine the fate of thousands of people. He was one of the huddled masses of humanity on the ground, terrified of life.

Brave souls who thought they could still see the road walked passed them, shuffling now instead of walking with the strength that sleep and a bit of food gives. Eva fell asleep in his arms.

An hour later, he was almost nodding off, when there was a call from far up the road.

'Büchbinder!' was the call.

'Yes,' shouted Reinholdt.

'Rudolf Büchbinder,' the voice shouted again.

'Yes,' Reinholdt replied.

'Come here, my friend. There's a Rabbi here. Just got out of Sachsenhausen. Come talk to him. Keep him company.'

A chill travelled through Reinholdt's body. His mind reeled in panic. It was what he and Eva had feared most. They had met very few Jews and most of those they had met were secular German Jews. Hardly Jews at all, Jews who had hidden from the Nazis throughout the war in basements or attics or Jews who had been in concentration camps and somehow survived. The skeletons who had left the concentration camps were somewhere in the East.

But a Rabbi! How could he possibly … there was no escape. Eva was fast asleep, the exhaustion claiming her body. There was still a lump of black bread nestling just inside her mouth. He lay her head carefully on the blanket and walked across the road, up to where the voice had come from.

'Where are you?' he shouted.

'Here,' the voice said, telling him that he was three camp fires further down the road. It was a community of refugees. Nobody spoke during the day because they were too exhausted, too frightened, but at night, there was community. There were a few Jews somewhere along the line. But they didn't feel like mixing. They still felt the horror of the brand which the Nazis had stamped them with, still the feeling that they somehow should hide.

As he walked closer, he saw the fat old man who had called him. They had spoken on the journey from Berlin days earlier. The fat old man was a retired butcher. He kept his family supplied in meat throughout the war. Then, he had been a good German, a provider. Now he was nothing more than an equal, just the same as all the other refugees, only fatter. His family lay asleep around him, sons and daughters. He was a widower so there was no wife, but he had taken up a wizened old man, emaciated with a dirty grey beard and a cap pulled over his hooded eyes. His clothes were torn and louse infested. He must have stolen a greatcoat from a solider, though there were no insignia. The old man's hollow eyes looked up gauntly at him. They nodded in recognition. Reinholdt sat beside the old man.

'Shalom, Rabbi,' he said. The old man nodded, too weak to speak. 'Where are you going, Rabbi?'

The old man raised an eyebrow and shrugged.

'Can I get you anything, Rabbi?'

A trace of a smile appeared on his lips. He shook his head. 'God will soon call me. Somehow, for some reason, God spared me the camps for this.'

'Me too, Rabbi,' said Reinholdt. 'I was in Theresienstadt.'

'Ah, I know of that place,' said the Rabbi, his voice weak and barely audible. 'Many martyrs died there I'm told.'

'My wife's family were taken to Auschwitz. All dead. She managed to escape detection in Berlin. She's over there,' said Reinholdt pointing with his head further down the line. 'Are you able to come and meet her?'

The old man smiled and shook his head.

'Will you say a prayer for my family, Rabbi?'

Hardly able to reply, the Rabbi drew breath, and whispered, 'Of course. In heaven I'll say a prayer to the Almighty for all Jews who have suffered this … this.' He couldn't find a word to express the horror of the last decade. There were no words in the glossary of humankind to describe what the Jews had been through at the hands of the SS.

Like music on the breeze, he whispered, '*Baruch ata adonai elohanu melech ha'olam …*'

The rest of the prayer was lost in the firmament. It was all that Reinholdt recognised. He had only learned a few Hebrew prayers, just enough to get by in case he was questioned by the occupying authorities somewhere along the road. Just enough to convince them that he was a Jew.

The old man finished the prayer. 'Thank you, Rabbi.'

The old Rabbi's head was heavy and he nodded forward towards sleep. Reinholdt gently put his hand behind his neck and like a baby, lay him gently down on the ground. The old Rabbi was asleep. Reinholdt knew about death. The old man would be dead by morning. He wouldn't survive the cold of the night or the rigours of the journey, or the exposure of the roads. People died every day, journeying somewhere. At least in Berlin they were protected from the elements by cellars and bombsites. Reinholdt pulled the old man's greatcoat tighter around his body to ensure the maximum warmth. Then he bent down and looked closely at the old man. Was this the enemy? Was this truly what had threatened Germany and the whole world? Was this old man part of a universal conspiracy to enslave Christianity and control all the money and businesses and sources of production?

This old man, barely able to breathe? Yes, thought Reinholdt. Yes, he was. To the very core of his being he knew that this old man and the millions like him were responsible for Germany's ills, for the ills of the world. Even in defeat he couldn't bring himself to think otherwise. Perhaps even more so in defeat, he saw the sweep of history more clearly. The thousands of years in which Jews had mutated from a tribe in the backwaters of the dying empire of Rome, to become a universal bacterium, a disease within the body of all humanity. Wherever they went, old men like this caused economic and social illness to propagate. He looked closely at the old man, breathing his shallow breaths. His last moments. Yes, he thought. Yes, this is the enemy. The enemy is a child and an old man. The enemy is tall and short. The enemy is man and woman, and all in the guise of their religion. Jews. All Jews.

He shook his head. He couldn't explain his feelings for Eva. He knew they were genuine because he ached for her when he was in Argentina, even though he knew she was a foot soldier in the army of the enemy. Perhaps she was different. Perhaps he loved her because she was such a convincing actress. But scratch below the surface and a Jew was still a Jew. He couldn't explain his love for Eva. Maybe it wasn't love for Eva the Jew, but for Eva the Aryan he had met in the nightclub and with whom he had fallen in love.

Maybe he would spend the rest of his life – whatever was left to him – trying to explain his love for Eva. But one thing he knew viscerally and that was that this old man, gentle and pious as he was, was merely one form of the many-headed monster which was the universal Jew. And once again, the hidden cartels and powermongers had caused the downfall and destruction of everything he believed in, everything he loved.

People in the fat butcher's entourage were looking at him as he cradled the old Rabbi. He bent down, and kissed the dying man on the forehead. He lay his head gently down on the ground, bunched up a scarf lying nearby as a pillow and stood silently over the old man's sleeping form.

'I've said some prayers,' he said to the fat butcher, who nodded in unctuous appreciation. Reinholdt felt a wave of anger which he forced himself to subjugate. This butcher … so fat, so self-satisfied … how had he suffered for the war effort?

Reinholdt walked away, took a handkerchief from his coat and wiped his lips of the stain of having kissed a Jew.

He hardly slept during the night. Recurring images invaded his peace. It was a cold night, wind blew through the grass of the nearby meadow sounding like the voices of the condemned, the screams of men and women and children who he had consigned to the fires of hell. Not the cleansing fires of the *auto-da-fe*, the self-righteous, self-appointed cleanser of heresy. His fires were those designed to obliterate, to expunge the memory of the race, to cleanse the world of an infestation caused by a bacterium.

So he had been told.

So his father believed.

So the Führer had said.

So he believed.

So the propaganda was written.

He had read the propaganda, listened to the lectures, watched the films put out by Goebbels. He had participated in rallies designed to alert the German people to the dangers that faced them. Not that he had ever willingly participated directly in the death and destruction of the Jewish race; except for the early days when he was little more than a boy, he'd never dirtied his hands. He had never joined his colleagues in voluntarily participating in wilful destruction. All he had ever done was to follow orders. He had been an engineer, a mechanic, a builder. He had oiled the engine which had driven Jews to their destruction. Hundreds of thousands of Jews. Millions. Maybe even tens of millions. Nobody really knew how many Jews had been killed. At the conference in 1942 at Lake Wannsee a figure of eleven or twelve million was touted. Could it possibly have been that many? At the time, it was feasible. The calculations had been done. Burn rates, gas rates, numbers of bullets, cattle trucks for transportation, train transport, petrol required, men and matériel. How quickly will a body decompose? How much of a body can burn? What about residue from bones? Someone promoted mass burials. But the problem there was that the bodies below would fill with the gas of decomposition, and that would push up the bodies above and cause a fountain of blood to erupt out of the earth.

Himmler had once seen this phenomenon happen, and was so horrified about its psychologically upsetting effect on the Death Squads, that he'd ordered a different method of disposal. An industry for mass death. Slaughter houses, charnel centers, human offal.

Jews from all over Europe, herded into cattle trains and shipped to abattoirs called concentration camps. A vast pool of slave labour to feed the German war machine for the benefit of Volkswagen and Krupp and Farben and the dozens of others who had financed the war. Those who couldn't work wouldn't be allowed the precious resources needed to keep themselves alive. The Final Solution. Extermination.

And the noises continued to haunt him at night, the deeds for which he had been responsible. Voices of those who had entered the shower rooms and screamed as the Zyklon-B entered their lungs and forced them in a dance of madness to climb above dead and dying bodies to try to escape the unimaginable horror of their death. And he had been there to hear the air escaping from the bodies of the dead as they were pulled from the gas chambers and shovelled like carcasses into the crematoria, where their bodies were turned to steam, where what remained of them was dust which escaped through the tall chimneys into the cold and unfeeling night air, to be spread over the houses and towns and fields of Germany and Poland. Unknown. Unnamed. Unmourned.

The voices kept him awake that night. Not even the joy of the lightening eastern sky, nor the stirrings of humanity as another day dawned, made him feel any easier now the voices were in his head. He had no escape.

Eva woke beside him. She breathed deeply before she opened her eyes. She reached out for him, sensing that he was awake. She felt his body. It was rigid. She opened her eyes sensing immediately that there was a problem.

'What's the matter?' she asked, her voice harsh from the cold night air.

'Last night I visited a Rabbi over the road. He's probably dead by now. He said a prayer for me.'

His body began to sob. She held him and pulled him towards her. He was freezing. She stroked his stubbled cheek.

'Shhh,' she whispered into his ear. 'Shhhh. It will be alright There's plenty of time for this when it's safe. When we're safe.'

He shook his head. 'You don't understand. I didn't know what I was doing. I was following orders. I knew why I was doing it, but I didn't know … the horror … I was immune to it. I had no understanding. You were the first Jew I had ever truly met. You made me realise how wrong everything was. And now the old Rabbi. And there will be more, won't there? I hear the voices, Eva, at night. In the fields, the dust from the chimneys. It lays on the grass and it calls to me. What have I done, Eva? You … the Rabbi … I'm so confused …'

She looked at him in concern. 'Listen to me,' she said softly. 'Listen carefully. Try to understand what I'm saying. From the moment I came to Berlin, I changed my identity to save my life. I lived a lie. Now you have to live a lie to save your life and to save mine. If anybody finds out who you are, who you really are, you'll be arrested and tried as a war criminal. And I won't escape. I'll be arrested as well. They'll never believe my story. Nobody will.'

'I can't live like this.'

'You must, Reinholdt,' she said, her voice still low, so as not to be overheard. But firm. Directing, imposing her will. 'You *must* live like this. You *will* live like this. Once we get over the border to Austria and then to Italy, we'll be alright. We'll do what you say. We'll hide in a mountain village for a couple of years. We'll be farmers or I'll be a maid or something. Then when it's behind us, we can emerge with new identities. I can't survive without you. I have no access to the money in Switzerland. It's our only hope.'

He remained silent and, despite the rays of the sun lighting up the drear landscape of central Germany, he lay his head against her warm breasts and pretended to fall into a deep sleep. It was important that he convince her of his change of heart. If he was to have any hope of survival in the new world, then he must convince her of his new identity as surely as she had convinced him that she was an Aryan German. It was a lie but he could live with that. He would have to be careful from now on. He must never reveal his true feelings to anybody but himself. To lie was to survive. Eva could trust him but could he trust her? He couldn't take the risk, not fully, not for years, not until the past had been buried.

ITALY, JULY, 1946

Every five minutes the truck was forced to stop and pull off the road to make room for another urgent convoy which was racing towards the Italian capital. The driver continued to groan as his journey was yet again delayed.

He even called back to Reinholdt and Eva, 'Fucking Americans! Italy's been conquered so often in its history, you'd think I would be used to it. Every conqueror seems to think they own the roads. When we got rid of Mussolini, the Germans were bad enough. Fucking Barbarians. Now the fucking Americans. You see how they push me out of the way? Some prick of a lieutenant decides he wants to eat risotto near the Vatican so he pushes all the traffic out of the way with his lights flashing and his horn blaring and rides through like he owns the fucking roads. How would he feel if I came to his country, if I did that in New York? Eh? Eh?'

When the convoy of two jeeps and three army trucks had passed by and disappeared down the dusty road into the distance, the truck which was carrying them towards Rome trundled back up the embankment and, when the driver changed down a gear, managed to find the security of the bitumen. Eva could hardly believe that they were nearing the end of their journey. They had been travelling for nearly a year, sometimes sleeping rough, sometimes finding shelter in barns, begging for food at the beginning, earning food more recently. Working for farmers or shopkeepers or for the American Army doing domestic chores or any other service which would result in hot food and shelter for the night.

Europe was awash with refugees. Europe had run out of sympathy for refugees. People just wanted to get on with their lives. The war crimes trials in Nuremberg weren't even making news any more. The thousand year Reich had collapsed and now Europe just wanted to get on with the job of living. Tens of millions of people who had been dispossessed by the lunacy of Adolf Hitler and Josef Stalin were struggling to find their way home or to a new life. Further millions were desperately trying to get away from what had been their homes and to find a new and welcoming country like America, Australia, Canada, anywhere outside of the garbage pail which was Europe; rubble-strewn, disease-ridden, impoverished, defeated. Nobody even asked them for identification any more. Their clothes, their matted hair, the dust and flies which surrounded them wherever they went spoke more eloquently than any identification papers of their status.

An hour later, the truck came to a halt at one of the major intersections in the north of Rome. The truck driver turned around. 'I'll drop you off here. Good luck.'

Reinholdt jumped off the tailboard first and lifted Eva down after she had passed their two suitcases to him. They had found the suitcases on the roadside beside the body of a man and woman who had died of exposure. They had left little Inge's pram, the last relic of their once happy life, and loaded up the suitcases with possessions. Now they walked towards the centre of Rome, busy with traffic, dusty with petrol fumes, and with a heady aromatic smell of coffee and fresh bread seemingly everywhere. It reminded them of how hungry they were. They had eaten last night as they bade farewell to the farmer and his wife just outside Pisa on a small farm on the River Arno. They thanked them profusely for their help, the farmer's wife kissing Eva and blessing her like a good Catholic. They had worked hard for their food from the early morning to late night. There was no charity but the meals were nutritious and hot and absolutely delicious and when they slept at night, they slept with full bellies and aching muscles.

But each new journey brought new dangers. Dangers of exposure for Reinholdt or the more immediate and present danger of starvation and injury. Yet there was no other way. They had to get to Rome. And they couldn't go by train because stations were full of police, and police wanted papers, and they had no papers to give them. That would mean internment until their story was checked which could take a week. Simpler to walk to Italy.

When Reinholdt told Eva about the reasons for going to Rome, she had at first rejected it out of hand. She wouldn't countenance any further risks to their security but, as Reinholdt continued to explain the necessity of what he was doing, she grudgingly gave in and began to look forward to a new and trouble-free life.

It took them an hour to walk to within sight of the confines of the Vatican, where they found a priest who directed them to the Institute of San Girolamo in the via Tomacelli. He left Eva in a cafe close to the Institute and, heart pounding inside his chest, Reinholdt rang the bell. He heard its tones deep inside the building. Cars passed by in clouds of acrid petrol and dust as he waited on the steps of the Institute for somebody to respond. He heard footsteps coming down a long corridor and a bolt being drawn on the top and bottom of the door before it opened to reveal a black robed middle-aged priest with a long grey beard obscuring his dog-collar, standing there looking quizzical.

'Yes?'

'I would like to speak to Father Draganovic.'

'I'm afraid Father Draganovic isn't here. He's away. I have no idea when he will return.'

'Would you tell Father Draganovic that a friend of a friend of a friend of the Order has sent me.' It was a code that the SS men had been instructed to use in order to identify themselves to friends. It was passed around surreptitiously in the last few months of the war.

'And the name of your friend?' asked the priest.

Reinholdt looked up and down the road to make sure there was nobody within listening distance. 'My friend is the enemy of the friends of the anti-Christ and all the hosts of the damned.'

Now the priest listened carefully. 'And where is the anti-Christ?'

'Living in Moscow.'

The priest opened the door. Reinholdt entered quickly. The priest closed the door and locked it at the top and bottom latch.

'Who are you?' he asked.

'I'm a friend. I have to speak to Father Draganovic.'

'He won't see you unless I give him your name.'

'Tell him I am a friend of Croatia.'

'Your name or you will not see him.'

Could he trust this priest? Everybody was a spy for everybody else. 'Tell him I'm Reinholdt Stricher. *SS Obergruppenführer* Reinholdt Stricher.'

'Very well,' said the priest. He led Reinholdt into an antechamber and closed the door. The room was luxurious. It was exquisitely wallpapered in gold flock with deep-pile carpets and leather armchairs. In glass-fronted oak cabinets were hundreds of volumes of books stretching around the room. In the centre, a long mahogany table on which newspapers and magazines were laid in neat rows, as though this wasn't a monastery at all, but some wealthy person's guesthouse in the Tyrol. He walked around the table and looked out of the window. He caught a glimpse of the rooftops of the city beyond the walls of the Institute. He sat down, picked up an Italian newspaper and tried to interpret some of the words. He was never good at languages. They had crossed over the border into Italy over four months ago, but he found the intonation, the romance of the language hard to grasp. Eva, on the other hand, seemed to have a marvellous facility for learning new languages … they'd taken an inordinately long time to travel through southern Germany, Austria, and into Italy, working for weeks, sometimes months in the same district until things settled down. And in that time, she'd somehow managed to teach herself some Italian, some Spanish and not a little English from the invading conquerors.

Before long, the door was thrown open and in walked a tall handsome priest. He was beardless and his hair was receding but there was a youth, a vigour about him. He was a typical Slav. Except for the Ustashi, it had been Hitler's intention to subjugate the subhuman Slavs to become servants of the German master race. His puppet in Zagreb, Ante Pavelic, had happily slaughtered half a million Serbs, Jews and Gypsies with a brutality second only to the commandants of Auschwitz and Bergen-Belsen. Pavelic was one of the most sought-after war criminals … it was rumoured that he might be in this very Institute.

'Welcome,' said the priest, his voice deep and resonant.

Reinholdt stood and walked around the table to grasp the man's warm hand. His was a firm handshake.

'You are *Obergruppenführer* Reinholdt Stricher? Am I expected to know you?'

Reinholdt shook his head.

'Then how do you come here?'

'I was on the staff of *Reichsmarschal* Göring for the last two years of the war.'

'I don't know your name.'

'I was tied to my desk. I was in charge of ensuring the technical support to enable the directives for the final solution of the Wannsee Conference to take place. But, more importantly, I have been entrusted with substantial funds to establish a sanctuary for SS personnel who are currently in hiding. I'm sure you know what I'm talking about.'

Draganovic nodded. There was no warmth in this man. He remained cautious. 'And what do you want with me?'

'I need the protection of San Girolamo. I need to arrange passage to Buenos Aires.'

'And why, Herr Stricher, do you think that I either will, or should, do that for you?'

'Because Father, that is what you are committed to doing. You have already agreed with Ante Pavelic to assist all Croatian SS and other Yugoslav Nazis to escape from the Americans and British and Russians. I hope that we can come to an arrangement for you to support German and Austrian Nazis as well.'

'I help Croatians. I help members of the Ustashi. These are my blood. These are the defence against the evils of communism.'

'That's all you help?' asked Reinholdt.

'That's all.'

'Yet before the collapse of Germany I was informed by my friend Franz Stangl, the former commandant of Treblinka Concentration Camp, that you have offered him and others help if he survived the war.'

Draganovic nodded. 'I may have made it known through the network. But how do I know you are who you say you are? Do you have any identification?

'Would I be stupid enough to carry identification of who I was across occupied Europe?'

'Then you have no proof,' said Draganovic.

'The proof is up here,' Reinholdt said, tapping his head. 'The proof is a number in a Swiss bank account. Plus I have access to gold deposited in a German Argentine bank, placed there on a visit I made before the end of the war. Some of the proceeds of these funds will be made available to you if you will assist me and my wife. We wish to stay in your protection and with assistance from the Vatican until we are able to leave on a boat to Buenos Aires. We would also be immensely grateful for your assistance in getting us identification papers and new identities.'

'What sort of money would you be prepared to pay from your Swiss bank account?'

Reinholdt mentioned a figure. The priest's severe countenance melted momentarily before he regained control.

'That's very generous.'

'It is to help me and my wife as well as other former SS brethren who will be coming through here. We need all the help we can get. These funds were given to me and others like me by the brotherhood in order to ensure their safe passage after the war. You may deal with the members of the Croatian Ustashi as best you will but when it comes to the German SS, where I know you have no feelings of loyalty, then we will pay our way.'

Draganovic nodded. 'And need I ask where you got the money to be able to pay your way?'

'That's not your concern, Father.'

'Perhaps not, *Obergruppenführer*, but it doesn't take a genius to guess. Still, the dead don't need wedding rings and gold teeth, do they?'

For the next two hours, they talked detail. As Reinholdt left the Institute, there was no feeling of pride in his mind for helping his former colleagues. It was a blood oath he'd taken. He was staying faithful to his promise. And the one person who he perhaps could have helped, but who refused his assistance was Hermann Göring, who'd stayed in Germany in a doomed attempt to take over from Hitler at the end of the war. Despite Reinholdt's pleas, Göring actually believed that the Allies would deal with him and allow him to run the country after Hitler's death. Now he was a prisoner and was hauled before the Nuremberg judges accused of crimes against humanity. For Göring there would be no escape. But Reinholdt knew that he would evade whatever punishment the Allies meted out. Reinholdt knew about Göring's cyanide tooth, and prayed that the Americans didn't.

No, the SS and the Gestapo and the German soldiers weren't the real concern of either Reinholdt or this Croatian priest. As far as Reinholdt was concerned, his only desire was of a personal nature. Indeed, his real ... his only ... concern was to save Eva and himself. Yet he knew with absolute certainty that if he didn't help the other Nazis by using the money and gold in the Swiss bank, his life would be valueless. If others in the former SS found he'd absconded with their escape funds, they'd hunt him down until the end of time. Unless he spent the money helping colleagues to escape, he was a dead man.

Eva Arpel, known for a short period in Berlin as Eva Schmidt, then Eva Stricher during her marriage to Reinholdt and since the collapse of the Nazi regime, known as Eva Büchbinder, wife of Rudolf Büchbinder, victims of Nazi aggression, concentration camp inmate, refugee who had escaped over the mountains of Austria and the Italian Alps into Rome to live in a new land, was bursting to go to the toilet.

She had already drunk six cups of coffee while waiting for her husband to reappear from the monastery of San Girolamo. They had worked out an escape route for her if things went wrong. If he didn't appear by ten o'clock that night, then she would leave the cafe, find a cheap hotel, assume that her husband had been arrested and she would go to one of the Jewish agencies dealing with refugees to be transported to Palestine.

She looked at the clock on the cathedral opposite. The hands in the illuminated dial moving painfully slowly now read 8.45. She had been expecting him for the last two and a half hours. She was desperately worried. There was no turning back. There was no fail-safe. If he didn't appear soon she knew with absolute certainty she would never see her husband again, nor the money that he had hidden in a Swiss bank account, money which they would use to set up new identities in South America.

When they had made the arrangements, it had all seemed so straight forward. Reinholdt had been confident everything would go well. So was Eva when she ordered her first cappuccino in Rome. But by the time she had drained the dregs of her fourth cup, she was already frightened. The noise of jeeps on the street, the petrol-laden air, the clatter of horses and carts dragging boxes and food stuffs and luggage up the steep hill had given her a headache.

She had watched the passing parade on this busy street for so long now that nothing attracted her attention. And she continued to sit at the back of the cafe, watched by suspicious waiters with black waistcoats, cuff-less and collar-less shirts, their legs cloaked by long black aprons. She felt utterly conspicuous. Her morale had deflated. She was verging on panic. It was … what … she looked up at the clock through the cafe's open front window. The clock was about to strike nine. God Almighty, four and a half hours. How much longer? If at all.

And then her heart leapt when she saw him. He stood outside the cafe, peering into the dark trying to discern her face. The mean electric light bulb hardly illuminated the cafe's interior. But he saw her. His face beamed and she knew everything was alright. He sashayed around the tables and sat down heavily.

'I'm so tired, 'he said. 'That man could talk the hind leg off a donkey.'

The waiter came over. Eva hadn't said a word, she just held on to Reinholdt's arm.

'Coffee,' he barked, 'and a cognac please.'

'Certainly,' said the waiter and walked away.

'Cognac?'

'We have plenty of money,' he whispered. 'I have one

hundred American dollars in my pocket. The priest gave it to me for starters. I have an address for us to go to stay the night. Three rooms in a small hotel. The owner asks no questions. Clean sheets, Eva! Our sheets. Beds. Running water. Listen to me. Hear what I'm saying. They're paying for everything. They've given us money, accommodation, as much food as we can eat. I told you I would make it alright.'

He was whispering urgently. 'I said I would make it good. We're going to be okay from now on, Eva.' She grasped his arm tighter. 'No more sleeping in barns and in ditches, and beside roads. No more begging for work from filthy farmers. We're safe now. We'll never have to work again.'

Suddenly he sighed. His head sagged as though his shoulders could no longer support him. Eva put her arm around his back and pulled him close to her.

'Why did the priest give us so much money? All we need is something to help tide us over until we can get to a representative office of our Swiss bank. That's what you've been saying. Why so much, when we've got our Swiss bank? What did the priest say?' she whispered. She couldn't begin to comprehend the fortune they suddenly possessed

'We have to stay in Rome for maybe three months, maybe six, until he can arrange safe passage on a boat out of Italy. Then we sail straight to Buenos Aires. It's the route that he uses for Croatians. He expects many from now on; now that people are losing interest in chasing war criminals, people like me are beginning to come out into the open again; people like us are emerging all over Europe, escaping from the Allies, men and women wanting to escape, terrified of retribution.'

'Why is he doing it? I don't understand. The people he's saving' … She found the next words hard to say.

'They're mass murderers. You know what they're saying in the Nuremberg trials. That Englishman, the lawyer Shawcross, he says that the Germans were the greatest criminals in the history of humanity. Why is this priest helping? I thought we'd just pay him a bit to help us, and …'

'Don't look a gift horse in the mouth,' her husband whispered.

'But he's a priest. He is supposed to be against evil. Until now, I've never considered … I mean, why should … ?'

'One day you'll understand all about evil. Do you think the Vatican didn't know all about what went on? One word from Pope Pius XII and the German Catholics could have stopped Hitler. But the Pope kept silent, even though he knew. He just kept quiet.'

'But why now?' she asked. 'Look, don't think I'm not incredibly grateful. Of course I want to sleep in clean sheets and have a full belly without having to work for it. I'm not a fool. But why is he helping when the war has been lost? Why is it to his advantage? What's the reason? Is it a trap?'

'The Vatican has a simple philosophy,' he whispered in her ear. 'Hitler might have been evil but the devil is in the form of communism. Hitler was fighting communism and so the Vatican supported Hitler. Communism won this war. Look at Zhukov and the way he rushed to capture Berlin. The Russians now have half of Europe. How long before they expand their empire and take France and Italy and the Low Countries and Greece with them? Soon the only non-communist country in Europe is going to be Vatican City. That's what the Pope is terrified of. That's why he's helping the Nazis.'

She still didn't understand but she let it go. 'You know, we don't have to associate with this. You're good at being a Jew, just like I was good at pretending I used to be a Christian. We could go to Palestine. Millions of refugees are going there and finding a home. It's a new country. A young country. It would be hard work but we'll be free. We won't have to associate with this priest, or people who were in the SS. We won't need to take the risk.'

'Do you know how hard the work will be? You think I don't know about Palestine. It's a malarial swamp. The Jews who are rushing there from Europe used to be bankers and lawyers and doctors. What do they know about draining swamps and planting crops in dry dusty earth on mountainsides, or in bogs with mosquitos biting them? They'll all starve to death if they don't die from malaria. Do you think I want that after what we've been through in the last year? No, my love. It's the wealth and isolation of South America for us. Argentina. We'll set up a home in Buenos Aires.

'Remember the trip I took for Göring back in '43? It was to set up relationships with a man and woman to whom we gave a lot of money. We took a gamble that they could pull it off, and it's succeeded, Eva. The SS have virtually bought the government of Argentina. That's how far we've been thinking ahead. We supported these people in their climb to the top. His name is Juan Perón, his wife is called Eva, just like you. She's the darling of the people, because she looks after them by taking from the rich and the powerful. The aristocracy hate her, but that's okay.

'General Perón has just been released from prison. The other generals in Argentina were furious with the way in which this Evita was influencing Perón's ministry, so they locked him up on some island. But the people organised a huge demonstration, and the government was forced to bring him back. They made him President, but don't believe for one minute that he's the power. No! I've met her. She's the real brains behind him. She's greedy for money. When I was there in '43, all I had to do was to mention Reichsgold and you could actually see her salivating, drooling at the lips, thinking she was going to get her hands on all that money.'

Eva was looking at him in shock. After all this time, he was finally unveiling more secrets. Why hadn't he told her all these things in the year they'd been travelling like peasants? Why hadn't he given her something to hold on to, some hope for the future.

Unaware of what she was thinking, he continued, 'There's something that you don't know Eva. Something I haven't told you until now. That I couldn't tell you until I'd seen this priest in the Vatican and knew that everything would be alright. Eva, we don't just have a little money in a Swiss bank, money which I've saved from my salary, and from other places. The SS set up many accounts with Swiss banks that were held in trust by certain members of the Reich. Certain highly trusted very senior SS officers were given access to them in order to purchase safe passage and immunity in new countries. There's a whole network. We have people who are even now in Canada, Australia, South America, Syria, Iraq, Lebanon helping comrades to leave Europe. We have numerous accounts in many Swiss banks. Each one has been given a guardian who has the number and the password. I'm a guardian of one of them. Some of the money I'll use for us. But I'm duty bound, an oath of blood, to use the money to help my former colleagues to escape from Europe and come to South America. That's why we're in Rome. That's why we had to come here. I can tell you now because the arrangements are in the process of being made. I couldn't tell you before, because in the event of our capture, it was vital that you should tell the Allies nothing.'

She looked at him in surprise. 'But I thought all that money was ours. I didn't know it was ... I don't understand. How much money is there in this account?'

'A fortune,' he said.

'But how can there be? Where did the money come from?'

'It was German government money. Money given to us from various sources. Most of it from the large corporations like Krupp and IG Farben and Messerschmidt. We've been saving it carefully. It's been in the Swiss banks for years. Now we need it to save our colleagues.'

'But you said it was our money. You said that you had been saving your wages and that you sold our war bonds. And so we had money to help us. And now you're talking about a fortune.'

'The fortune isn't just ours. It has to be used for our comrades.'

'Your comrades, Reinholdt. Not mine,' she hissed. 'You're no longer a Nazi. You're a Jew. You can't use this money. You must give it back. You must give it to the victims. You must give it to Jewish families. Do you understand?'

He looked at her sadly. 'Yes, I understand.'

'And will you?'

How could he tell her that if he did, it was a death warrant? How could he tell her that for over a year, he had hidden the truth from her because he didn't trust her. Only now was he beginning to have confidence in her. She had hidden him from people who were suspicious of his Germanness. She had lied on his behalf. Only now did he feel sufficient confidence to tell her these things.

The waiter brought the coffee and cognac. Reinholdt didn't answer Eva's question immediately, nor did he answer her by the time they finished their drinks and took a taxi to their hotel. He didn't answer the question in the next eighteen months as they played the role of tourists in Rome and visited parts of Italy as sightseers. And by the time the tickets arrived for the ship which would take them to Buenos Aires he still hadn't answered her question. And Eva had stopped asking.

After a few weeks in their hotel in Rome, Father Draganovic, whom Reinholdt discovered was close to the powerbrokers in the Vatican, organised for them to be moved into a small but comfortable villa just outside a village in the hills of Tuscany. It was ideal for their needs. Secluded, private and, by the time Eva had finished putting up curtains and paintings, very comfortable.

The next eighteen months were blissful ones in which they consciously refused to read newspaper accounts of the aftermath of the war in Germany. Reinholdt occasionally disappeared from Eva's presence to make telephone calls from the village, but she was sensitive enough not to ask to whom they were being made.

Reinholdt fished. Eva baked. And she fell pregnant. At the end of 1947, she gave birth to baby Bertha. She had wanted to call her baby Sarah after her mother, but the war was so far in the past, so far behind them, so much a hideous memory, that she reluctantly acquiesced to Reinholdt's request to name the baby after his long-dead infant sister.

At the beginning of September, 1948, when baby Bertha was already rolling over, crawling, sitting up, jabbering non-stop, and eating more than just the pureed food her mother prepared for her every day, a note arrived for Reinholdt. The courier was a local priest, a man who visited them occasionally. He handed the letter over at the front door, nodded and retreated despite Eva's invitation to join them in a cup of coffee. Reinholdt opened the letter when he returned from the town where he had been drinking with the mayor. He read it carefully, smiled, read it again and then struck a match and burned it, depositing the charred curling ashes in the fireplace.

'Well?' said Eva. 'Don't keep me in suspense. What is it?'

'Our freedom,' he said. She frowned. 'I am to go to the Institute to see Father Draganovic. Our tickets have arrived for South America. We must leave here within four days to catch the boat.'

'South America! But all that was so long ago. Why can't we stay here in Italy?' she said. 'Why do we have to go so far? South America is the other end of the world. Nobody knows who we were any more. Nobody cares.'

'It's not that simple, my love,' he said.

'But the trials are over. The leaders have been hanged and imprisoned. People are forgetting what happened. They're getting on with their lives. Another year or two and nobody will remember a thing. We could stay here. My Italian's become fluent. So has yours.'

He led her over to the couch in front of the stone fireplace. It was where they sat on cold winter nights, reading and talking about the past. It was where he tried to forget his crimes, where Eva tried to forget her deception and the treason she had committed against her people.

They sat and he turned to her. 'Eva, the trials have only been held against a handful of leaders of the Reich. There are hundreds of Nazis accused of committing crimes against humanity and who are now in hiding, just like me. Your people, the Jewish people, have a righteous anger against me and those like me. There's a man called Simon Wiesenthal, a Jew. He works in Austria for the War Crimes Section of the US Army. He's in the Office of Strategic Services and Counter Intelligence. He's gathering dossiers on war criminals for future trials. These trials could go on for the next ten years. There might not be enough lawyers and judges in the world to try the number of people who could justifiably be accused of war crimes. I'm one of them, Eva.'

'But you never killed anybody,' she interrupted.

'Not directly.' He smiled and patted her hand. 'That's not the issue. I was part of the machinery. I realise now how wrong I was. If there was a way I could turn the clock back I would do it.'

She remained silent. And then she smiled briefly. 'But there's talk in the village of an end to all of this. With the hatred growing between Truman and Stalin, there's talk of a war between the Americans and Russia. Nobody will worry about the Nazis any more.'

'This man Wiesenthal. He's making statements about setting up his own office to document war crimes. He wants to set it up somewhere in Austria. He's not a fool. He was a victim of Mauthausen Concentration Camp. I've read the documentation on him. His wife was very much like you. She was blonde and very attractive and for years she passed as an Aryan. That's why he would understand about you, but he will never give in until he has brought me and people like me to justice. A man like him and all the volunteers working for him – they'll track us down into our graves. He calls what we did the greatest crime in history and there's no way he'll let the criminals go free.'

'Maybe if I go and reason with him. I'm a Jew. He's a Jew.'

'No, my love. In a few days' time we'll be on a boat, the SS *Sestriere*, travelling to Buenos Aires. We'll have new passports, new names, new identities. A completely fresh start. He'll never find us there. We'll have Perón's protection.'

'But I like it here, Reinnie. This is my home. Bertha's happy. Why should she leave? And if we're that far away, it means I can't …' The words trailed off.

'Can't what?' he asked.

'Nothing,' she said softly, shaking her head.

He held her chin in his hands and gently twisted her head to face him. 'What is it?'

'I don't want to be so far from my mother and father, from Rosl and Yitzchok and my nieces and nephews who died in the camps. I don't know where they're buried. I don't know where to go to say prayers for them. But at least in Italy, I'm in Europe. I'm standing, connected to the same ground. At least when I hear somebody say the mourner's *kaddish* for them, I feel I'm close to them. In South America,' she shook her head. 'I've let them down so badly. Through me, everybody's dead.' Her lip began to quiver.

'No Eva,' her husband said quietly. 'Through me, everybody's dead.' And for once, he meant it.

He hadn't been to the Institute of San Girolamo for a year. The traffic was even more hysterical than when he last visited. The daytime air was filled with the dusty fumes of Vespas and Lambrettas, of cars and the ubiquitous jeeps and army vehicles which forced their way arrogantly through crowds of pedestrians. When he rang the doorbell, he was admitted immediately. No longer was he questioned about why he wanted to see Father Draganovic. Although he didn't know the young priest who opened the door to him, his appointment with the head of the Institute was known to the priests.

He was waiting in the anteroom for just a matter of minutes before Draganovic walked in smiling, and shook his hand warmly. 'My dear Reinholdt,' he said. 'You're looking good. Italy agrees with you.'

'And you Father, are looking … how shall I say … richer.'

'Your generous payment came through over a year ago, and it's been very useful in helping us with our work. I assume there's more, that you haven't left yourself short of funds to help your colleagues.'

'A bit,' said Reinholdt.

'If I'm any judge, then I know how much that bit is. Anyway,' he opened a dossier and took out two passports, two tickets, identification papers and a file containing the curriculum vitae, life history and detailed record of the existence of Señor José Phillipe Fierro and his wife Esmeralda. Reinholdt began to glance through the documents but Father Draganovic forced him to stop. 'You'll have much time on the boat to study these things. I have an appointment very shortly to see one of my most trusted friends, Monsignor Giovanni Mantini, His Holiness's Undersecretary of State of Ordinary Affairs. I mention his name so that you will recognise it later. A young man destined for greatness; perhaps in time the Papacy. But before I go to see him, there are things which I have to tell you. I will not write these things down but you must remember them.

His tone suddenly changed from the affable to the sententious, 'When you arrive in Buenos Aires, you register as José Phillipe Fierro and will make your own arrangements to stay at the Hotel Del Rio Plata. It's not an excessive hotel as I understand it, but comfortable and clean. No arrangements have been made in advance but I'm informed that there will be room for you. It hasn't been booked in advance, because we don't want your arrival to be known by certain Jews from Vienna who are tracking movements into and out of Trieste and Naples, especially ships that are going to Australia, South America and South Africa. It's a great danger. This man Simon

Wiesenthal is becoming quite a nuisance, and may have to be dealt with, though from what my agents tell me the Americans are becoming as fed up with his fanaticism as we are, so he's likely to burn himself out in the next year or so. Our problem at the moment, Reinholdt, is that there is a very large population of Jews in Buenos Aires and I have no doubt that they're assisting the efforts of Wiesenthal's agents in Argentina.'

'What about other South American countries? Bolivia, or Chile?'

The priest shook his head. 'Perón is our closest ally. Now he's President, he has set up a team which organises for the welcome of German, Austrian and Croatian Nazis. Thanks to him we have safe passage. It's this team that will be in contact with you shortly after your arrival at the hotel. The team consists of Pierre Daye, the Belgian, Jacques de Mahieu a French Waffen SS officer, Branko Benzon, a Croatian friend of Hitler and Göring and others. There's also a young man called Rudi Freude, the son of Ludwig Freude, whom you will meet. It's he who will finance you into a new business or farm or whatever other identity you require. It is to him that you will transfer the remainder of your Swiss funds.'

'Who else will be there from the old days?' asked Reinholdt.

Father Draganovic smiled. 'The less you know, the safer you will be and the safer they will be.'

'Eichmann?'

'You might meet Adolf somewhere in the capital. I don't know. Why are you asking?'

'For no reason other than interest. I want to know with whom I can have a schnapps.'

'Ah,' said Draganovic. 'Still dreaming of the Brotherhood. My advice is to forget the past and concentrate on the future. Let the past go. In the war, the things done by the Nazis to halt the spread of communism were done for the very best of intentions, but the Allies don't recognise Hitler's true purpose in stopping Stalin's march. They don't think of it as God's work, of eliminating the anti–Christ. That task is now left to me and those like me.

'But I haven't got time for a philosophical discussion with you. We have to deal in pragmatics. The people who you must meet in order to guarantee your security are the President of Argentina, General Perón and his wife Evita.'

'I know them both,' said Reinholdt.

Draganovic looked at him in shock.

'Göring sent me over to South America in 1943 to prepare the way for his own, Borman's and Goebbel's disappearance should the war be lost. They knew that Hitler and Himmler would have to be sacrificed. They thought that they could escape the wrath of the Allies. I went over to Buenos Aires and met with General Perón and his fiancée Eva Duarte. I found them charming and hospitable but I have never in all my life encountered anybody as money hungry as that woman. I gave them a fortune in gold in a German Argentine bank as custodians to ensure their sympathy. When I told her how much, I thought she'd wet her knickers. It's that money which has bought the loyalty that President Perón and his little Evita now show, Father Draganovic. Money, pure and simple. Not sympathy with any cause, nor any philosophical grandeur. Just plain hard cold money. I'm glad that Evita left enough money in the account to pay for my tickets. From the way she looked when I gave the deposit details and code words to General Perón, I had a nasty feeling she might try to take the lot and build herself a kingdom somewhere in Patagonia.'

Reinholdt put the papers back into a folder, nodded and walked towards the door. Before he left, he turned back for a final look at Father Draganovic. 'I don't believe we'll ever meet again, Father. I thank you for your assistance and I ask you not to waste time in praying for me.'

He had been travelling in the train for an hour before he dared to open the dossier which the priest had given him. He ensured that there was nobody in the compartment paying any attention to him, and took out the tickets. One was made out to José Phillipe Fierro and the other for his wife Esmeralda Fierro. Reinholdt smiled. He needed them and the passports to get out of Italy. But he had been planning very different identities for when he and Eva arrived in Argentina.

CHAPTER TWENTY-FIVE

NEW YORK, PRESENT DAY

The envelope postmarked Argentina even felt ominous to the touch. It was padded and when she turned it over and saw the spidery writing of the addressee, *Dr L Forenjo*, she hesitated to open it.

Beside his name was the stamp of The Institute security officer, saying that the envelope had been X-rayed and been passed by the sniffer dogs. But it lay on her desk for more than a minute before she felt comfortable opening it.

Sarah's past was already clear in her mind. She now knew the truth. Her grandmother was a rich and varied woman, a bit of a good-time girl in her youth who, in order to protect herself from the horrors of Nazism, had hitched a ride with a Christian gentleman to save herself from exposure. She had sung for a living in a cheap nightclub and in far more sophisticated environments. God knows what she suffered when she was arrested and interned in Auschwitz but at the end of the war she had met up again with her longstanding childhood sweetheart from Munich, Saul. They married and the product of the marriage was Bertha. Because of his ill-treatment, Saul had died in 1950 in Eva's arms. But that last part was what was in the dark corners of her mind, the part of her grandmother's story which she couldn't let go; the part on which Annelise had failed to shed light. And it was the part gnawing away at her.

Sarah was now content in her mind about her grandmother's history, if not that of her grandfather. It was even something she could talk about at dinner parties. Her grandmother had been a nightclub singer just like in the film *Cabaret*. It was compartmentalised, enabling her to get on with life.

So she didn't need this letter from Dr Forenjo. She didn't want it. But it was here. Lying like Pandora's box, tempting her to open it. And if she did open the letter, would she release further doubt and evil?

She tore open the seal and looked inside the envelope. There were certificates, photocopies of letters and several photographs. Not brown sepia photos dating back half a century but modern crisp colour photos, taken, she assumed, within the past dozen or so years. First, she read the letter.

My dear Sarah,

I feel a sense of guilt that I have caused you concern. To clarify matters, I'm sending you some documents to see if they stir your mother's memory. If not, please send them back and I shall continue my search for the real relatives of my friend, Ricardo Padrone.

My sincere regards,
Luis Forenjo
(Retired Doctor of Medicine)

She lifted up the envelope and patted the bottom so that the documents all fell out. The face which stared up at her from the photograph was that of an elderly man. There was a yellow 'post it' note stuck to the back. It read, *Ricardo Padrone, taken in Buenos Aires 1993 before he became ill*. Sarah picked up the photograph and looked at the man who was claimed to be her grandfather. He had a sort of innocence about him, alert eyes, an intelligent face. He was smiling. She could see his teeth were slightly yellowed but they were his teeth, not the awful tombstone white false teeth of the elderly poor. He had a certain arrogance in his look, a certain challenge as he stared at her from beyond the grave. There was pain in his old, lined face. Perhaps, the pain of experience or of regret.

She sighed as she looked at this elderly man. She compared his look to that of Annelise when they had first met. There was far more brightness in Annelise's face, certainly for the first day or two. But much had disappeared as Annelise unburdened herself. This face though was frozen in time, a moment in a man's long life.

She put down the photograph and picked up the other documents which were in Spanish. She could understand enough to know they were photocopies of official letters and correspondence to prove who he was. But all the while she was drawn back to this man, Ricardo Padrone. She searched for a family likeness. Did he look like Bertha? The cheekbones, the nose, the set of the eyes; the square of the jaw, the breadth of the forehead, the aquiline nose. Was any of this man a part of her genetic make-up, handed down from father to daughter to granddaughter? If she superimposed his face upon hers, would anybody say, 'Yep, no question about it, Sarah. You're this man's granddaughter'?

God Almighty, she thought. There is a resemblance. And then she put the photo down again. There couldn't be a resemblance. Not even Annelise had told her about a South American connection. But how? How could it be possible … who was this man? Could he be Saul, her grandfather, hiding in shame and fear from the condemnation of the Jewish world for being a turncoat, a concentration camp *Sonderkommando*? Could her grandfather and grandmother both have been traitors to the Jewish people?

She picked up the phone and urgently started to stab some numbers.

Her secretary didn't know what to do. Perhaps she was ill. Why would Sarah just be sitting there, staring at a photograph?

The intercom on the secretary's telephone burst into life. She jumped. It was uncharacteristic of her but brought about by Sarah's reaction to the envelope which was postmarked Argentina.

'Mandy,' said Sarah. 'Can you track down Josh Krantz for me please? Straight away.'

'Sure, Sarah.'

Within minutes, she patched him through.

'How you doing?' he asked.

'Good,' Sarah responded. 'Josh, I'm sorry to bother you. Where are you at the moment?'

'In LA. I'm doing some post production. What's up?'

'I need to come over to the West Coast. I need to spend a couple of days doing something private.'

'Sure,' said Josh. He knew not to ask too many questions. If she told him it was private without telling him what it was, then no amount of questions he asked would make her reveal the nature of her business.

'I'm wondering if there's something I can do while I'm over there; a speech or organise a dinner or a fundraiser. I know it's short notice but you guys in the movie industry seem to be able to do things at the drop of a hat.'

'Yeah,' he said, 'no problem. I'll get the network operating. Where you staying?'

'Can I crash at your place?'

'My pleasure,' he said, smiling. 'My pleasure.'

Three days later, the Los Angeles Rabbi looked at her quizzically, oddly uncomfortable in her presence. Normally a man who directs both the agenda and the attitude of a meeting, this time he felt distinctly subordinate. Indeed, he had felt discomfort throughout the entire interview and the feelings were growing with every detail she revealed. The letter from Argentina, the photograph of her grandmother with some sort of amulet or necklace, the picture of this old man who claimed to be her grandfather, but for some reason couldn't be, the documentation from the Department of Alien Affairs as well as the Department of Customs and Immigration, documents from the Department of Immigration and Alien Affairs in New York City and a swag of other photocopies of ancient lists and papers and documents which hadn't seen the light of day for fifty years, all from government departments which had disappeared decades ago.

With each document that the young woman revealed, the Rabbi's sense of concern grew. She unveiled each one as though he were a judge in a court, handing them over to him across the desk as if they were Exhibit A, B, and C. What was she trying to prove? he wondered. She had come to him for help in solving an imponderable problem. She needed his assistance. Yet her training as a lawyer made this seem a confrontational situation, with her treating him as though he were some sort of judicial officer. As the eighth document floated across his desk, he put up his hand to stop her monologue.

'Miss Kaplan,' he said. 'Sarah. Enough with the proof. You haven't even told me why it is that you are here!'

She realised she had been voluble and sat back in the chair. She smiled and nodded.

'I'm sorry, Rabbi. It's the perennial lawyer in me. Before I came to LA, I approached this matter as dispassionately as I could, almost as if I was presenting a case on behalf of a client. It's the only way I could remove myself and my emotions because ...' She fell silent.

'Let me see if I understand it,' said Rabbi Friedman. 'You've come to the Simon Wiesenthal Centre in order to access our records, to prove that this man, Ricardo Padrone is not your grandfather.'

She interrupted him and leaned forward. 'Not to prove. I don't want to approach it like that. All I want to do is find out whether this man Ricardo Padrone is any relation of mine. I need to find out how he got photos of my family; why he claims that my grandmother was his wife when there's no family history involving him.'

'But what has this got to do with the Simon Wiesenthal Centre? We're Nazi-hunters. Are you saying this man was a Nazi?'

'I have no idea who this man is. What I'm frightened of is that he was my grandfather and that he was a *Sonderkommando* in the camps.'

'Oof,' said the Rabbi, pursing his lips. 'That's a hell of an accusation. Have you any idea what the *Sonderkommandos* were forced to do?'

'I know, Rabbi. I'm well aware of how bad it would be if he turns out to be my grandfather, and he was one of them.'

He looked at her, and frowned. 'I gather that you suffer the popular misconception of the Jewish *Sonderkommando*. That they were traitors, they were evil men and women who willingly worked for the camp commandants in order to save their own miserable lives ... that they drank beer with the guards after a day of marshalling Jewish prisoners and throwing their weight around.'

Sarah nodded. That, as far as she knew, was what the Jewish *Sonderkommando* used to be – a turncoat, a prisoner who got lenient treatment if he or she did the dirty work on behalf of the guards; some, it was said, even took part in the mass murders.

The Rabbi shook his head. 'Some, certainly, were like that. Quite a few, as far as we know. But the majority, by far the vast majority, were unwilling slaves. For them was reserved the worst possible work in the camp. First, they had to be fit and strong. Then they were put to work. They were the poor devils who had to force Jews into work units, who had to have them on the parade ground, lined up in neat rows, answering their numbers and names at roll call. Anyone out of line, and they'd suffer a beating. And the ovens in Auschwitz's death camp, Birkenau, were going twenty-four hours a day. That was what the *Sonderkommando* were used for, Sarah. In May 1944, 360 000 Jews were gassed and burnt; in June, 512 000; in July 442 000 of your brothers and sisters … that is over one million, three hundred thousand human beings burnt in their ovens in less than a quarter of a year. Of course, sometimes there were just too many to fit into the gas chambers, and not even the ovens could keep up, so the Nazis dug huge pits and they threw the dead bodies into them and burnt them there, in the open. But they were clever and resourceful, because they'd allowed for drainage lines to collect the human fat which sank to the bottom. The *Sonderkommandos* had to collect it in buckets, and pour it onto the top to make the fire burn hotter …'

Sarah's face turned red. 'Stop it. Please. Why are you saying these things?'

He realised that he'd become caught up in the rhetoric of Hell. 'I'm sorry. You're right. I'm doing to you what I do to an audience … or in a court of law when I have to prove the Holocaust happened.'

She looked at his impassive face. Did he know that she was the lawyer who had defended the hideous Holocaust denier, Frank Darman?

Praying that what he said was a coincidence, Sarah continued, 'So what are you saying?'

'What I'm saying is that if your grandfather was a *Sonderkommando*, then he wouldn't have lasted long. They worked till they dropped. There was a rule of thumb that the concentration camp doctors used … if they could pass their clenched fist between a man or woman's thighs, then they were too sick, too emaciated to continue working, and they were sent to the gas chambers. Well, although they received better rations than most of the inmates, the *Sonderkommando* squad members also grew thin and weary … and they didn't have the comfort of others in the barracks who became their friends. The Jews in the barracks hated them.'

Sarah shook her head. 'But I don't understand. I thought they were like the guards themselves.'

'Some were. No question. But on October 7, 1944, just as the SS knew that the Russian army was approaching Auschwitz, word got out that there was going to be a revolt of the *Sonderkommando*. Three hundred of the squad were rounded up by the SS on the pretext of doing some outside work; but the *Sonderkommando* knew they were going to be shot, and so they revolted; they pelted the SS with rocks and packed one of the crematoria with explosives they'd stolen and blew it up. Within hours, a hundred trucks, full of SS men arrived; the *Sonderkommando* fought them with a couple of stolen machine guns and grenades. The SS sent in fifty attack dogs. Suddenly, other *Sonderkommando* units arose. But they couldn't hope to fight that sort of might. They were locked in a wooden barn which was set alight. They perished.' He shook his head. 'You think a Jew wanted to be a *Sonderkommando*? Never. Sure, those who were brutes were literally torn limb from limb. It was the Jews … Jewish prisoners that did it. Not the Allies. These traitors were so hated by the inmates of the concentration camps that when they relieved the camps, the Americans and the Russians and the British just let the Jews have their revenge. Eyes were torn out. Jaws were pulled out of faces. Limbs torn off bodies. I mean, Sarah, the hatred that was felt towards these men and women was just unbelievable. The Jewish prisoners hated the guards, but the *Sonderkommando* who'd willingly co-operated' … Again he pursed his lips and shook his head. 'Ooof! God help your grandfather if he was one of them. There's a special place in Hell for men like Hitler and Stalin. I reckon the traitorous Sonderkommando aren't very far away.'

'But did any of them live? That's the point. Could my grandfather have been one? We've been told that he died in my grandmother's arms in Berlin in 1950, that he was a victim of the camps, but somehow he managed to survive Sachsenhausen. But I have to know the truth. You see, if he didn't die in 1950, could he have changed his name to Ricardo Padrone and lived in South America?' she shook her head. 'And if so, then why, unless he had some huge crime that he wanted to hide for the rest of his life? And why would my grandmother have left him?'

The Rabbi picked up the photograph and looked closely 'How can I explain human nature to you? How could you possibly understand the horrors that went on in those days, Sarah?' He sighed. 'Why are you opening up old wounds? It's our job to catch war criminals, not yours. You're a lawyer. You're a granddaughter. You work for Josh Krantz. You've got a big position in New York. You have everything going. Why are you stirring up this pot of trouble for yourself when we're the pot-stirrers?'

She looked at him. 'I would have thought you would be the last person to ask that, Rabbi. I have to know the truth about what happened to my grandfather.'

'For others, I can understand that, but for you? Have you thought who could be hurt by the things you could find out? The only people we try to hurt, Sarah, are people who perpetrated monstrous crimes against our people. Are you going to hurt your mother, your father and yourself?'

She remained silent.

'This man,' he said pointing to the photograph. 'When this shot was taken, he was in his eighties, late seventies maybe. He looks fit and healthy, sun-tanned, at ease with life. It's a good photo. The people who were war criminals don't look like this. They were pinched and drawn from half a lifetime of hiding. They didn't go out in the sun like this man obviously did. This is a man at peace with himself.'

'Even so,' said Sarah. 'Is it possible to go through your records and find out whether he was a *Sonderkommando*?'

'We have very few photographs of *Sonderkommando*. We have a lot of Nazis taken from newspapers at the time and from captured German records but Jewish traitors were not exactly the top of anybody's list of favourites. Nobody went around taking happy snaps. Still, I'll see what we can do.'

'How are you going to do it?' Sarah asked. 'Do you have people here who can discover identities?'

'Sure,' he said dismissively. 'We've got a computer morphing programme which can take a photograph like this, scan it into a computer and then morph it back to the way he would have looked when he was in his early forties. That's when he would have come out of the concentration camps. The programme we've developed is used by the LAPD and other enforcement agencies. It's unbelievably accurate. Come back tomorrow, Sarah. Please God you'll see what this man looked like when he was in his early forties.

'We'll check on all the facts you've given us as far as we can, but let me put your mind immediately to rest. I will almost guarantee that when we examine it, we'll find that your grandfather was killed by the Nazis, or like your family history says, he died in his wife's arms. Very few came out of Sachsenhausen. Those that did, like your grandfather, *alav ha shalom*, were skeletons. If he survived even another five years, it was a miracle. Thank God, he met up with your grandmother, and thank God he had a few years of peace before his death, God rest his soul.

'As a result of those years, your mother was born, your grandfather of blessed memory passed on and so your grandmother Eva came to America.'

Sarah breathed a deep sigh of relief. 'That's what my husband, David, says.'

'Good. Then we agree.'

'Not quite, Rabbi.'

The Rabbi smiled. 'You want proof?'

'I want something more definite than supposition and prayers to the Almighty.'

'Okay, there's a cost to our services because the equipment we use is expensive and we charge to morph photos and delve into old records. We need to pay researchers.'

'Don't worry about the money,' Sarah assured him.

'I didn't think money would be a problem for you, Sarah, though I must say that after your defence of Frank Darman, that Nazi, I didn't think we would ever be graced with a visit from you.'

She was stung but it was the sort of statement against which she had been forced to defend herself for the last two years.

'Rabbi, that issue with Darman was fought to defend the First Amendment. You must realise that I have only contempt for him and his views.'

She handed over the rest of the dossier to him, assuring him that she had copies of all the documents in her office in New York. She stood and held out her hand to shake his, but he delayed a moment before standing and grasping it.

She walked out of the door and closed it gently behind her. Rabbi Friedman stared at the back of the door for a long while before he sat again behind his large desk. There was something which was making him uneasy. Nothing definite. Nothing specific, just an unease which he felt in his soul. He'd tried to reassure Sarah, but even while he was telling her things she wanted to hear, his heart and mind weren't easy.

He looked closely at the photo, trying to see in his mind's eye what this man might have looked like when he was in his forties. A spark of fear was growing. Whatever the computer showed, Rabbi Friedman knew a Nazi when he saw one. But it couldn't be. Yet … yet he'd seen that picture before. In all the tens of thousands of pictures that he'd looked at over a forty-year period hunting Nazis, he knew that, somewhere in the deep recesses of his mind, he'd seen this man before.

He'd felt that same sense of unease before … when he was closing in on the most important manhunt of his life. He remembered this feeling, this gut-instinct from when he was a much younger man advising the Israeli government on the whereabouts of Adolf Eichmann.

The past two days had been days of business, mixed with a whole heap of pleasure. The concentration of business activities in Los Angeles was utterly different from that in New York. In the eastern capital, there seemed to be an intensity, a remorselessness about deals having to be done, appointments having to be made, documents having to be read. But in Los Angeles, the appointments were looser, the breaks for lunch obscenely long, and afternoon business truncated because of a parade of parties, openings, galas, social nights, swirls and whirls.

Josh had already left for his studio by the time Sarah awoke. She was breakfasting on the balcony of his palatial home overlooking the sea when a Filipino maid brought out a mobile phone. 'A call for you, Madam.'

Sarah answered the phone.

'Sarah? Rabbi Friedman. Can you meet me in my office some time today? How about we do lunch? 12.30?'

She hardly said a word. Rabbis doing lunch? Only in America … no, only in LA.

Her heart was fluttering as she was shown into his office four hours later. The conference table was set for three people. Jugs of orange juice and water and three paper plates as well as a tray of sandwiches. He walked from around the desk and shook her hand warmly.

'I've asked Ira Lansman to join us. Ira's one of our top researchers. He was the guy who conducted the investigation into your grandfather. Before we began the morphing of the photo, I thought I'd get him to search the records. Should have that back shortly after lunch.'

She nodded but, desperate for the news asked, 'What have you found so far? Is it good or bad?' she asked. It was a totally unlawyer-like approach, overly eager, but she had to know. This wasn't law. This was her life.

'Sarah,' said the Rabbi. 'So far nothing. I've asked you in here because we thought you might be interested in seeing the morphing, you being a lawyer and all. We've got all the equipment set up. It was Ira who thought you might like to see the process. You know we can take somebody back forty years, give or take five years or so. Either way the human face doesn't change all that much between thirty-five and forty-five. Bad things start to happen to the human face after about fifty. That's when you get sags, lines and bags. So, we're pretty confident that when we've gone through the process, the guy on the photo, your grandfather or whoever it is, would look the way he looked around the start of the war.'

A young man walked into the Rabbi's office with a disconcerting degree of informality. The Rabbi introduced Sarah to Ira Lansman. He was in his mid-to-late twenties, and had a freckled face and reddish brown hair, very odd for a Jew. He was open and warm, shaking her hand and saying, 'You want to see some magic? Come to my office. I'll show you.'

Ten minutes later she was seated at his work station. The image of the photo of Ricardo Padrone had been scanned and was now disconcertingly large on his screen, staring at Sarah from a time past. With his mouse, he pressed icons and buttons and the image on the screen appeared to shudder and become wavy but then clarify. Moments after each action he explained what he was doing.

'With this programme, I can cut out most of the faults that you find on a photograph. The blemishes on the paper or on the image. Any ageing or curling. I can even deep-etch the image so that it comes away from its background. Look,' He highlighted the perimeter of Ricardo Padrone's image, pressed two more buttons and suddenly the photo appeared much more sharp as though it was almost three dimensionally jumping out of the screen. The background of distant trees and bushes and cars was gone. Now his face was stark against a white background.

'Now we'll go back in time. Ever seen morphing?'

'Only on old reruns of *The X-Files*,' she said.

He looked at her and laughed. 'That was just computer animation. This is the real thing. This is where the computer uses the image and works back through a programme to de-age the human face. We take it back stage by stage, decade by decade, sometimes year by year and flesh out parts of a face around the cheekbones which would have shrunk or puff out cheeks which would have collapsed. In some cases, we retract flesh that has been made puffy by age, like around the eyes or the bulb of the nose. We get rid of wrinkles, sag lines, skin creases, the growth of ear lobes, nose lobes, eye sacs, nose and ear hair … you wouldn't believe how the body ages, especially after the age of sixty. And of course we deal with skin colour. Just watch.'

And Sarah watched in utter amazement over the next hour as the face transformed from old to not so old, to younger, to athletic and virile. She was looking at the photograph of a man in his forties, a strong healthy, intelligent-looking man with penetrating eyes and a clean and noble face. She started to breathe a huge sigh of relief. This was not Bertha's father. There was nothing in this face which looked even remotely like her mother.

Ira split the screens and showed smaller images of the young man compared to the old man. As a testament to the genius of a computer programmer, it was awesome. But the tangible satisfaction which Sarah felt at seeing a man who patently wasn't her grandfather was so enormous that she reached over and kissed a surprised Ira on his cheek.

'Thank you,' he said. 'Normally we get denials when we do this sort of thing.'

'Not from me you don't,' she said.

'Of course,' said Ira. 'He could have had a moustache or a beard. There's no way we can predict that.'

'Don't worry, Ira,' said Sarah. 'I think he looks just gorgeous the way he is.'

But that wasn't the way she was thinking an hour later when Sarah's lunch conversation with Rabbi Friedman was interrupted. Ira appeared at the door with a folder in his hand, looking sheepish and uncomfortable.

He walked over and said, 'Rabbi, can I have a word with you alone?'

'Why?'

'I'd prefer to,' he said.

'If it concerns me,' said Sarah, 'I'd rather be here. If not, then I'll leave.'

Silently Ira opened the folder and placed it in front of the Rabbi. Rabbi Friedman looked at the document in front of him and then looked up at Ira in surprise. 'You're kidding.'

Ira shook his head.

'What's going on?' asked Sarah, her mood of ebullience changing by the moment.

Rabbi Friedman didn't answer but instead picked up the image which the computer had morphed of Ricardo Padrone. He studied it. It was an attractive photo, a handsome young man, Aryan; Germanic; certainly not Jewish and certainly not Spanish.

'This man looks very German to us,' said Rabbi Friedman. 'While we've been having lunch, Ira's been searching our records to see if there are any other photographs of him.' He bit his lip. 'There's no easy way to say this Sarah, but in a way it's good news for you. This man couldn't possibly have been your grandfather. No way in the wide world. You see, we've got an actual photograph, an older photograph, of this man; one taken when he was a number of years younger; one which came from the Nazi newspaper *Der Angriff* in 1938. This is a photograph of an SS commander. He was leading a troop and he was identified by the newspaper as one of the fine young men in Germany. His name was Reinholdt Stricher. He was one of the major war criminals who we thought had died at the end of the war.

Like Eichmann, he was responsible for transportation and the mass movement of Jews. We don't know that he ever participated directly in mass murder but he was certainly one of the leading facilitators of the Holocaust. His work in the SS was to organise for the mass collection of Jews from eastern Europe, Poland and the Baltic areas and transport them to concentration camps all over Germany and the East. So you see, this war criminal lived for years in South America, and we missed him. But your grandfather?' He shook his head vigorously. 'What chance a Nazi leader could have been your grandfather? Zero. Zip.'

Sarah smiled in relief. 'But that still doesn't explain why this man, this Ricardo Padrone, this Reinholdt Stricher, had photos of my grandmother and my mother in his possession. And why he was writing to her, asking her to come back to him.'

Rabbi Friedman shrugged. 'Who can tell after all these years; except for the most obvious reason, of course. This doctor in South America. This …' He picked up the file to remind himself, ' … this Dr Forenjo. Is he on the level? Maybe he's deluded or mischievous. Or he's got some other agenda.

'Anyway, Stricher. If it's him, then it's the same man we thought was dead. This is quite a revelation, something which we've missed. It's a very big mistake on our part. This guy was a real fiend. Another Eichmann. Now dead unfortunately, if the South American doctor is to be believed, so he can't face his accusers. But he was a real mother. A very serious son of a bitch. God only knows how he slipped through our net. We knew a little bit about him but how we let this one go, I'll never know. We thought he'd died at the end of the war. But regardless, Ira's searched our files and there's no record whatsoever of your late grandfather Saul, Solomon or any other Büchbinder having been in Sachsenhausen. That's not to say of course that he wasn't. It's just that the Nazis destroyed most of the records before the camp was liberated by the Russians. The only records we have got are ones that the Allies managed to prevent from being burned. Or records given to us by survivors. Of course he could very well have been in Sachsenhausen, but there's no way of proving it.

'The other thing is that we've found a history of your grandmother Eva. We've taken it from records of the Munich Jewish community before the war. Eva was born the child of Serel and Franz Arpel, working as a maid or a cook in the home of a Hermann Büchbinder and his family. He was a prominent Munich jeweller in the 1920s but he and his whole family were victims of the Holocaust. Maybe your grandfather was one of the children of the Büchbinder family. We don't know. Anyway, unless we're lucky, there's no real way we can get any further with tracing your grandfather. You must appreciate that millions and millions of Jews died without identity because of the destruction of records.'

'Okay, if not the victims, what about those who came out? There must have been records kept of survivors of Sachsenhausen?' asked Sarah. 'Surely the Russians or the Allies kept records of who survived.'

'Some,' said Ira. 'But it's not that easy or obvious I'm afraid. You would think it would be, but it's not. When the Russians liberated the camp those that had any energy left, literally walked out of the door, down the road and out into Germany where they became refugees. They were taken up by the war refugee associations and the Red Cross, and from then on, records were kept which we're still tracing. But only those that were so ill in Sachsenhausen that they were unable to leave the gates were recorded. These records have been kept by the

Russians, although we do have lists which they released in 1958.'

Sarah nodded.

'But it's the other man that has really taken us by surprise. This man, Reinholdt Stricher was one of the architects of the Holocaust. We knew his name but we had no idea that he was still alive after the war. Like Eichmann, he was a desk jockey. He did nothing directly to kill or murder but he was one of the men in the SS who were given the job of carrying out the orders of the Wannsee Conference and bringing into reality the final solution against the Jews. He was an engineer by training and his expertise was in transportation. He organised for cattle trains to be in the right place at the right time so that the *Eingruppenführers* and the other death squads just had to round up Jews from all over Germany and Poland and later Hungary and Carpathia and everywhere else, and ship them off to the death camps.'

'So, he knew everything about what was going on?'

'Well, if he didn't,' said Ira, 'he was blind or stupid. The fact is that back in 1950, there's a file note saying that we thought we had got a link to him in Buenos Aires, but it came to nothing. One of our investigators over there died in a head-on car accident, but when we retrieved his notes from his hotel room, there was absolutely nothing in them about Stricher. All we had was a diary note of a phone call saying that the investigator was on Stricher's trail. But nothing more. We did some investigations, but we hit brick walls. Since then, we haven't been able to trace Stricher any further. So we went back to our original assumption that he committed suicide at the end of the war, like so many others.'

Sarah nodded as she sipped some more of the orange juice. 'So if this Stricher was so pivotal to the final solution, what are the chances that he would have married my grandmother, Eva, who was a Jew?'

Ira laughed. So did Rabbi Friedman. 'Absolutely none. Zero. Not a hope in hell. He was a rabid anti-Semite. He was at the top of the SS. He left with the rank of *Obergruppenführer*. That's equivalent to our rank of an army general. Your grandmother wouldn't have survived ten seconds if he knew she was Jewish.'

Sarah smiled. 'That,' she said, 'makes me feel a hell of a lot better.'

But deep inside her, there was a nagging fear that the Christian protector that her grandmother had lived with and who guarded her, could just possibly have been this Nazi SS Fascist? No! The Rabbi had said it wasn't possible and he was right. Not possible at all.

CHAPTER TWENTY-SIX

NEW YORK, PRESENT DAY

When Sarah flew back to New York, she reported the satisfying news of her investigations to David and her mother and father over dinner the following Sunday. David already knew most of the information from long and intimate phone calls which she'd made every night she was away, but was happy for her to repeat it. It was evident that the possibility of her grandmother having anything to do with this man from South America, an SS war criminal, had been finally laid to rest. The poor doctor was wrong, and Sarah would tell him during the following week in a gentle and open way. Why he kept photos of Sarah's grandmother and mother in his chest of memorabilia was anybody's guess. But the answer had died with him.

A further search of the scant family records in the attic, photographs, questions and cross-questions back and forward at the dinner table, eliciting responses of partial information or no information at all brought the conversation to a close. It was the end of the matter.

Her mother simply didn't know anything more about her father, Sarah's late grandfather, than she'd already repeated a thousand times. All she knew was the authorised version that her grandmother had told her. A wonderful man; a kind man; a gentle man; a learned man; a simple man; a religious man. He had all the qualities of a saint and because of Grandma Eva's pain, nobody had sought to question any of the details. How do you cross-examine a frail old lady about the man who died in her arms after years of torture in a concentration camp?

The following Monday in the office saw Sarah busily trying to get on top of the work that had built up since her trip to Los Angeles. Not that it had been entirely on her own behalf. She had addressed a B'nai B'rith group as well as participating in a private fundraising function which had been organised for some time by Josh, and through the dynamism of her after-dinner speech $150 000 more had been raised than anticipated. Josh was especially pleased, not because of the additional money, but because of his colleagues' admiration for Sarah.

'Beauty, brains and style …'

'You've got to marry this girl, Josh.'

'Okay, so she's got a husband. Big deal. This is LA!'

Tuesday and Wednesday were busy days and when she came to work on Thursday, she already had a diary full of meetings, phone calls and reports which had to be written. At five to twelve, her secretary buzzed her.

'Sarah, there's an Ira Lansman calling from LA. He says it's a personal matter. Do you want to take the call?'

Sarah thought for a moment, trying to place him and then remembered who he was; the thin studious young man from the Simon Wiesenthal Centre.

'Ira! How are you?' she said brightly.

'Good, Sarah. Listen, we've had a piece of luck. Going through some of our files, I've found some more newspaper clippings on this guy, Reinholdt Stricher with his wife. I thought you might like to have a copy. We're still checking for stuff on your family but nothing much more than we told you. I wouldn't count on finding any further information about your grandfather. He literally disappeared into the same sinkhole as three or four million other people. I'm really sorry. But there's little we can do. As to your grandmother, well, we've come across the same problems that you did. There really doesn't seem to be a record of an Eva Arpel coming to the States from Europe in 1950. We've gone back to 1949, '48, '47 and forward to 1953, but there's nothing. However, we did find the same record you did of Eva Arpel arriving from Argentina; it's strange but strange things happened in those days. But maybe it's not so strange after all. See, refugees did anything to get away from hell, or to get back home. They lied, they cheated, they robbed, they made up stories. Or it might have been something comically simple, like a mistake. You have no idea how confused Europe was just after the war. Your poor grandmother might have got on a flight or a boat out of Hamburg or Rotterdam or somewhere to come to North America but ended up in South America. You remember the story of the SS *St Louis* of the *Hamburg-Amerika* line?'

'Sure,' she said. 'The voyage of the damned.'

'Yeah. Shortly before the war, eleven hundred escapees from Nazi Germany got on board the *St Louis* bound for Havana. The ship was treated like a political shuttle. They stood off the coast of Cuba for days in no-man's-land, while frantic efforts were made to find them sanctuary. But they were turned back to Germany. Eventually the line managed to offload people in Holland, Belgium, France, even Britain. But there were two hundred others who ended up back in Germany, and were almost certainly killed in the war. Well, something like that could have happened to your grandmother. An accident. Getting on the wrong boat, somebody stole her ticket. She might have gone to Buenos Aires and then turned around to go north. That would account for it.'

'Sure,' said Sarah. 'Thanks for phoning, Ira. By the way, I deposited another $1 000 in your account.'

'Thanks. We could use the money. Keeping and maintaining a record of everything that happened before and during the war is expensive work. We were lucky to find this photo of Stricher and his wife. Apparently she was a heavyweight opera singer in Berlin. She even sang Wagner for Hitler. I'll send photocopies of the cuttings across to New York by DHL. You'll get the envelope tomorrow.'

Sarah froze. Opera singer? She felt her fingers go numb, her body arching in panic. She fought to regain her composure. 'Thank you,' she said softly, her mind reeling from the connection.

They said goodbye and Sarah fought the panic in order to continue with her day. She would remain silent until the envelope arrived. She'd already put her husband and mother and father and even her staff through enough of her emotional swings and roundabouts. She would hold her fears inside her until the evidence arrived.

When she came to work the following morning after a restless night, a parcel was on her desk. It had already been through the X-ray, metal and bomb detector in the basement and carried the office seal showing it was safe for an employee to open as it had been passed by security. Sarah opened it in trepidation. Three photocopies of photographs fell out as well as a handwritten letter which she picked up and read. She was desperate to look at the photos, but controlled herself. She would deal with it at the appropriate time. The letter was written in black ink on Simon Wiesenthal Centre letterhead.

Hi Sarah. These are the pictures of the bastard who claims to be your grandfather. Hope, like me, that you can't see any family resemblance! Regards, Ira.

She picked up the newspaper photo and studied the man. He was elegant and resplendent in his Nazi uniform. His hair was slicked back and he had high cheekbones, but there was a thinness about his mouth which made him look cruel. It was the same man whose photo had been morphed by the Wiesenthal Centre.

Although it was a black-and-white photocopy of what was presumably a 1940s newspaper, she was sure that his hair was Aryan blond. He certainly looked Germanic. She knew enough of German from her recent studies to read the caption. *Gruppenführer SS R. Stricher addressing cadets at the initiation ceremony at Administration Centre no. 4 Kurfurstenstrasse 115 of Judenamt IVB4.*

She picked up the next photograph. It was a picture of Stricher taken with a gaggle of other men, also senior members of the SS. The picture was dated 1942. She vaguely recognised Himmler, but the other members of the Nazi hierarchy were unknown to her. And when she picked up the third, she saw the same young man but his Nazi uniform had been replaced by black tie and a dinner jacket. It had been taken at some social event.

Standing beside him, looking utterly confident and secure, was a stunning and radiant young woman, bursting with pride and self-possession.

It was Sarah's grandmother.

The blood drained from Sarah's face. From deep within her, a distant voice said, 'Oh God!' Sarah was staring at her own grandmother, standing as an equal beside a member of the Nazi hierarchy. This was no photograph of a victim, nor a skeletal apparition from a concentration camp, nor one of the millions of hapless and downtrodden Jews wearing a look of incomprehension at the brutality of their Nazi overlords. No! This was a woman who was a member of the master race. There was absolutely no mistake or doubt in her mind. The picture was *Bubba* Eva. Without realising it, Sarah let out another cry of horror. She read the caption. *Gruppenführer SS*

Reinholdt Stricher with his beautiful and talented wife, the soprano Eva Stricher at a reception to celebrate the 34th birthday of Maestro Herbert von Karajan at the Hotel Cosmopolitan in Wilhelmstrasse. Frau Stricher will sing a recital of Lieder by Schubert as well as favourites from Franz Lehár at the Berlin Opera next week in order to raise funds for the war effort.

Sarah dropped the photo on to her desk as though it was poison. Without touching it, she stared again at her grandmother's face.

She had seen many pictures of her grandmother when she first came to America, taken in the 1950s by friends from the Jewish neighbourhood. All pictures of her from her childhood and youth had been destroyed in the war. The first pictures she had ever seen of *Bubba* Eva were taken when she was in her forties. This woman in the old newspaper photo was many years younger but it was the same woman. It was exactly the same woman. It was her grandmother. It was Eva. Married to Reinholdt Stricher. Archenemy of the Jews and architect, along with Heydrich, Eichmann, Himmler and Hitler, of the most murderous deliberate killings in the history of humanity. The Holocaust designed to end forever the existence of the Jews.

Sarah hid her face in her hands, her head swimming, emotions of horror mixing with incomprehension as she fought to understand what she had just seen. She took deep breaths as her mind fought vertigo. The room began to swim. Slowly over the weeks she had doubted the history she knew of her grandfather. Without admitting it to herself, she had come to terms with the fact that Saul might not have been the angelic Jew who died a victim of Nazi brutality; that he might have been a *Sonderkommando*, a Jew who sold out to the Nazis in order to save himself, who cleared the remnants of gassed bodies from the shower stalls and who threw them into the ovens to be burned; that her grandfather had somehow survived the vengeance of the skeletons who walked out of the concentration camps; that he had escaped to South America and escaped his punishment. Yes! She had almost come to terms with living her life atoning for his sins.

But this!

She looked at her grandmother and her grandfather. She looked at two Nazis and she now realised the full enormity of her discovery; that both her grandparents had been Nazis; that both were part of the evil she had fought all her adult life; that they had appropriated Jewish identity to escape the verdict and punishment of civilised human beings in the aftermath of Nazism; that in her body, coursing around her veins and arteries, in every cell, indeed within the very genes of her existence, there was the essence of a Nazi. She, Sarah Kaplan was – literally – the spawn of the devil.

Sarah's staff looked through the glass partition of her office in shock as Sarah sat back in her chair, ashen-faced, tears streaking her cheeks.

The office was in turmoil. Phone calls flew from desk to desk, emails popped up onto screens, gossip replaced information. Nobody, not even her secretary and personal assistant, could offer inside information. All anybody in The Institute knew was that Sarah had taken some momentous step, and the very foundations of life as they knew it were about to be undermined. Joshua Krantz was now on the phone from the West Coast, and although people couldn't hear the details of what was being said, Sarah's tearful – and totally uncharacteristic – response told the entire office that a catastrophe was about to happen. Everyone in the office liked Sarah … she'd gone out of her way to be a gentle and sympathetic boss … to avoid the stereotype of the hard bitch boss in a man's world … but their thoughts at that moment were for their own careers.

Sarah looked up and realised that most of the men and women in the office were staring at her as she tried to explain her position to Josh. She looked down at the papers on her desk to shield her face. 'Josh, please try to understand.'

'What's to understand?' he interrupted. 'You suddenly phone me and tell me you're quitting. And you won't even give me a reason. Christ sake, Sarah, I've known you long enough to know that there's something very wrong happening in your life and I want to help.'

'But Josh…'

'Sarah, now you listen to me. You have a contract with The Institute. You know I'm not going to throw the law at you. We're close friends, and friends don't usually do that. But by Christ, Sarah, for your own sake, I'm going to hold you to the contract. Jesus, how can you even think of quitting when we're just starting out on the journey together. Now, let's stop this bullshit talk of your resigning and get down to *tachlis*. What's behind it?'

'I've told you, Josh. There's a personal matter that has arisen in my life and I can't discuss it.'

'Is it David? Is he having an affair?'

'No,' she said irritably.

'Is it you? Has somebody come into your life?'

'No,' she said louder. She realised she was shouting and looked up to see the staff still looking at her in consternation.

'Is it illness?' he demanded.

'Josh, for Christ's sake, it's a personal matter. I don't intend to go into it.'

'Sarah,' he shouted. 'There are no personal matters between us. God's sake, we nearly had an affair in Prague.

I love you and you love me. And I love David and I'm not going to have you walk out of my life and my Institute just on your say so. Damn it, I've got a stake in you, a big stake. You know my plans for the future. They involve you and David and The Institute.'

He calmed down. 'Sarah, I can hear the hurt in your voice. You can't treat me like this. Not somebody so close to you.'

She had been dreading his reaction. It was worse than she had anticipated. Instead of taking it like a business decision, he was bringing in all the emotional big guns. If it was difficult for him, how would it be for David when she went home and told him. How would it be for her parents? Could she ever tell her parents the truth? That her mother was the daughter of two Nazis who had stolen an identity from some nameless Jewish man and woman who'd probably died in a concentration camp somewhere. For that's the only way that Sarah could possibly come to terms with the awful conclusion of her life.

'Josh, let me try to explain. Something has happened which …'

He interrupted. 'Forget the explanations. I'll be there in five hours.'

'Josh, please don't come to New York.'

'Of course I'm coming to New York. I'll charter a Lear if it will get me there faster. Damn it, Sarah, you're part of my fucking life! You're half my fucking world!'

He slammed the phone down. This whole thing was turning into a disaster.

David sat in an armchair staring at the photograph, then back at Sarah. She was a little girl again, slight, ashen, unworldly. The supremely confident lawyer-woman he had known all these years, whom he loved to distraction, whom he had married, had disappeared as the superstructure on which she had built her life collapsed beneath her. The little girl was exposed. A little girl who was hurt and battered and not understanding what was happening to her. He knew if he shouted at her, which is what he felt like doing, that he would drive her further into herself. What she needed wasn't aggression, but gentleness, love, sympathy.

'And on the basis of these photographs,' he said gently, 'you quit your job?' She nodded. 'Sarah, stop being involved for a minute and think about this like a defence lawyer. You're presented with uncorroborated evidence. What you have just done is said to the prosecution, "Okay. Guilty. I quit".'

'David,' she said. 'There's the proof.'

He smiled. 'Stalin altered history. He expunged people from photographs. He changed texts in newspapers. He buried facts. Goebbels was a master at it as well. How do you know that this photo is genuine?'

'David, they didn't have computer morphing in those days. That's a genuine photograph.'

'Yeah,' he said, 'but how do you know it's your grandmother?'

'I know. It's her. I can tell. I've seen photos of her when she first came to New York. It's the same woman.'

'You ever heard of a *doppelgänger*?'

'Not in this case,' she said, 'the coincidences go beyond image. This is more than my grandmother's face. It's her singing. It's everything about her. I've thought this through from top to bottom. The only conclusion I can come to is that Reinholdt and Eva Stricher weren't Jews, but after the war, in the confusion, stole the identities from two dead Jews and passed themselves off.'

'Okay,' he said. 'It says in this photograph that she was a famous opera singer. We know your grandmother sang, but this photo caption says she was a famous opera singer.

Now from what Annelise told you, she was just a bar-room soprano. This,' he said pointing to the photo, 'is serious German opera. You couldn't compare one with the other.'

'Only my Mom said that Eva never sang professionally. We have no records. That doesn't mean she didn't.'

'Point one,' he said, trying not to sound patronising. She was still in a state of flux. 'Point two: why did she leave Reinholdt in Buenos Aires and come to America? According to your theory, they were both Nazis. They were married. They'd got some mother of an alibi. Why spoil things by coming to America where there were millions of Jews and try to live the lie here? Wouldn't it have been horribly dangerous for her to leave him?'

'I don't know.'

'Point three: why did he write that letter begging her to come back? What happened between these two people?'

'I don't know.'

'Point four.'

'Alright! Don't go on. You've made your point.' She smiled at her unintended pun. 'My point, David, is that for some reason, that's a photo of my grandmother standing shoulder to shoulder with a Nazi. And not just any Nazi. With the guy who ordered the transportation of millions of Jews. How can I represent the victims of oppression who come to The Institute, when I've got the blood of oppressors in my veins?'

'It looks like your grandmother … but this whole thing could be a massive series of coincidences, or just a series of mistakes compounded, and which generate a life of their own. Maybe the real Eva Stricher left Reinholdt because he was having an affair, and went to America. Maybe he got a detective to try to find her, and the hapless gumshoe found somebody who was the spitting image. Your grandmother. And in all innocence, he sends the photos of your grandmother back to Reinholdt. Hence the collection of photos, the letters, the confusion ... look, I'm just thinking on the run here, Sarah, but there are a dozen explanations that don't necessitate you learning how to goosestep and scream out *Heil Hitler.* Anyhow, Madam Counsellor, aren't you concerned with the burden of proof?'

'That's why I intend to find out precisely what went on back then.'

He looked at her blankly. 'What do you mean?'

'I'm going to South America. I'm going to Argentina. I'm going to find this doctor who wrote to me.'

David was shocked. He stood from his armchair and walked over to where she was sitting. He sat down on the arm of her chair and put his hand on her face, stroking her cheek.

'No, Sarah. No, you're not. That's enough now. I'm not going to allow this nonsense to go on any longer. You're taking this too far. Quitting your job is one thing, though God knows, I think it was the most stupid career move you've ever made, especially after everything Josh has done for you. But going to Argentina is something I will not permit. I've never spoken to you like this before but I really have had it with your flying in the face of danger. You left me for a year to fight Stalin's henchmen in Czechoslovakia. You got yourself thrown into prison in Turkey. Enough is enough! I'm yearning for a quiet life for a change. I don't want to have to rescue you from dangerous situations any more. You will not be going to South America.'

In all their time together, he had never spoken to her like this. Although there was a gentleness in his words, they were still patronising and authoritarian. She didn't think that words like this were in his soul. He was the master of compromise, of debate, of consensus. She realised he must be very angry. Or frightened.

'David,' she said, choosing her words cautiously. 'I won't be endangering myself. We're talking about a civilised country. I'll be going there to examine records. Nothing more.'

'And the eighty-six Jews who were killed there in 1994? And the twenty-nine people from the Israeli Embassy who were killed a couple of years earlier? Nobody's been strung up yet for murder. Coincidence, or a fascist government at work?'

'It was Iran who committed those murders. Plus a couple of Argentine policemen who've been accused. Look, I'm not saying I don't know about the swag of Nazis and Neo-Nazis there. But there are low-life scum in America as well. Nobody's going to know I'm in the country. I'll be very quiet and terribly discreet. I've got a couple of different passports in different names because of my work, all courtesy of the State Department.

'David, I won't make waves, but I don't think you understand fully the implications of what's happened to me today. My whole life's suddenly been turned upside down. My identity has always been as a Jew. I was born of Jewish parents. I'm a Jewish lawyer. I'm a young Jewish woman. I work for a Jewish organisation. And now I find that I could be the daughter of a woman who isn't Jewish at all because her mother, my grandmother, wasn't Jewish. Worse. My grandmother could have been one of the Nazi hierarchy, and my grandfather might be one of the architects of the Holocaust. I can't live with that. I've spent my entire life fighting anti-Semitism. I represented Frank Darman because there was an issue at stake more important than anti-Semitism. The issue was our fundamental freedom to say what we want and to be who we want. But I suffered badly because I was associated with his anti-Semitism and I vowed there and then that I would do everything in my power to meet it head on and to turn it around. That's why I'm going to South America. Because if my family was part of the evil then I want to know about it.'

He stood and walked over to the drink cabinet, pouring himself a club soda. He poured Sarah a glass of wine and brought it over. She was looking at him keenly to determine his response.

'And what if you find out that you're right? That your grandmother was the personification of evil, that your grandfather did do the things that you're accusing him of? What then, Sarah?'

She remained silent and sipped her wine.

Josh was in her office long before she arrived. He had been in New York since twelve o'clock the previous night and had slept badly in his 6th Avenue apartment. She wasn't surprised to see him as she walked in to the office at 8.15.

'You look like shit,' she said.

'I feel like shit, thanks to you. What did David say when you told him?'

She smiled. 'He threw his hands up and said 'Thank God you've quit. Now I'll have you all to myself.'

Josh ignored her sarcasm.

'What did you expect him to say Josh? He thinks I'm an idiot, a moron, a short-sighted fool.'

'Did you tell him why you're quitting.' She nodded. 'Yet you won't tell me.' She shook her head. 'Dear God. Aren't I family? For Christ's sake, Sarah, you're my closest friend. I thought I held that status in your eyes.'

'You do, Josh.'

'Then why won't you tell me?'

'Because it goes to the very deepest part of my being. Something about me which I found out that nobody else must know. Not until I've sorted it out.'

'Is it something to do with your visit to Los Angeles?'

'Please don't ask me.'

But he insisted. 'Sarah, I've just flown three thousand miles to beg you not to do this thing. You owe me an explanation. Not just a phone call telling me that you've resigned. You know my resources. You know my wealth better than I do. If it's a question of money, tell me what you want.'

She sat down on the sofa beside him and held his hand. 'It's a funny thing, Josh. Back in Slovakia when I was fighting to get your parent's house back, I was incredibly attracted to you. Physically as well as emotionally. You had absolutely everything. But I was terrified that I would become a part of the image if I married you. That Hollywood wasn't a reality and that my life would become increasingly a part of a dream. Your life is all image. This is a reality,' she said pointing to her desk, 'what you're doing in The Institute is very real, very important and I'm enormously proud that you have decided to do it. And I'm incredibly proud that you asked me to head it up. It's the most important thing I've ever done in my life.'

He waited for her to finish but she said nothing else. 'I don't understand the point, Sarah. What is it you're trying to say?'

She sighed. 'When I was in the Czech Republic with you, I thought you were image and I was reality. Now I realise that yours is reality and my whole life is nothing more than image. It's a facade. It's all based on quicksand.'

He put his arm around her shoulders and drew her head towards his. He whispered into her ear. 'Sarah, you're talking the biggest crock of shit I've ever heard!

Now listen to what I'm going to say because this is reality. Resign and I'll hit you with a hundred million dollar lawsuit. I'll ruin you and David and your parents and everybody else in your family that I've come to love. Your dad Sol will be in a poor house, Bertha will be selling her body on the streets, and David will have to hock his cello. Seriously, Sarah, I'll sue you for everything unless you take back your resignation. I don't know any other way of bringing you to your senses.'

'You're not going to sue me, Josh,' she said. 'You know I'll tie you up in knots in a court.'

'Sure you will, honey,' he said, 'but you tell me what other weapons I've got to stop you from destroying your life. You couldn't live without me if you tried. Let's make a deal,' he said. 'Take a month off and reconsider.'

She kissed him gently on the cheek. 'How about we go downstairs and have some breakfast,' she said. 'Let's talk this through over a cup of coffee.'

CHAPTER TWENTY-SEVEN

BUENOS AIRES, ARGENTINA, PRESENT DAY

The Hotel South America on Avenue de Mayo was ridiculously cheap compared to four-star hotels in New York. The entry hall was grandiose and spectacular, a throwback to the architectural genius of Spanish America, and was unusual in a city whose buildings owed much to French architects.

Sarah could imagine some eighteenth-century *grandee* in his black leather riding boots, fawn jodhpurs, gleaming white shirt and raffish hat, slapping his riding crop against his thighs as he commanded his mulatto servants to prepare his horse for his ride into the countryside to examine his holdings.

She looked up keenly each time the doors of the hotel opened and admitted some expensively dressed man or woman. Walking around the lobby were archetypes of international business; but these could be identified easily by their power-dressing and briefcase. She ignored them as they walked confidently through the lobby and into chauffeur-driven cars or taxis. The people she looked at more circumspectly were those who entered the hallways and lobby area looking around quizzically as though this was unfamiliar territory. Her appointment with Dr Luis Forenjo had been made two days earlier from New York. He was already half an hour late. She wondered whether he'd changed his mind, and if her entire journey to discover her origins was a waste of time and effort. Perhaps it was better that way. David had first refused to allow her to go, then ordered her not to leave New York, then begged her; yet nothing, not rows with her husband nor her employer, would dissuade her from making this journey of discovery. Why? She'd only know that after she'd spoken to the doctor, after she knew the truth about her grandparents.

David was first furious, then ultimately resigned to the fact that his headstrong wife was again on one of her journeys. He'd told her that she wouldn't discover anything, and that there were inherent dangers in what she was doing and where she was doing it. Josh had also begged her, but he knew nothing of the information she'd received from the Simon Wiesenthal Centre ... he just wanted her to continue with her work at The Institute.

But she knew deep down that if she didn't go, if she failed to resolve the sudden and inexplicable mysteries of who she was, then for the rest of her life, there'd be a cloud hanging over her, dulling the sunshine existence which she'd worked so hard to achieve.

Sarah had arrived the previous day in Buenos Aires and spent the evening and much of this morning wandering around the city centre. She had walked slowly down the Avenue 9 de Julio towards the Plaza de la Republica, glorying in the foreignness of her surroundings. And her joy was that it was everywhere ... in the air, in the smells of the street and the shops, in the colour of trees and the birds, in the way in which people walked. American imperialism, McDonald's culture, hadn't made nearly the inroads into Buenos Aires that it had in other capitals she'd visited. The world-wide trend to uniformity – McDonalds, and KFC and Pizza Hut – seemed to have met its match in the strongly nationalistic Argentines.

And the pace of life was slower than in New York. Here they seemed to have more time than in America; people ambled, they strolled, they savoured their surroundings, they stopped and made their points forcefully to their companions, prodding their fingers into chests or gripping arms to emphasise a particular urgency; then, when the point was made, they'd link arms and continue to amble down the footpath, the importance of their conversation lost in the word pictures which danced in the air around them. It was all so different from New York, where conversations were snatched, points shouted as people ducked into taxis, or ran into buildings to escape the freezing cold or stifling heat, instructions barked as appointments drew closer, and men and women growled in discontent.

It was the very atmosphere itself which was so colourful. The trees seemed to paint the sky. As Sarah walked towards the Plaza, her thoughts flew back to Central Park. So much of New York was drab. It was a cliché to call the streets canyons, but that's what they were. Dry river gulches, surrounded by tall grey lifeless buildings. Only at intervals was the endless drabness of the city broken by parks and plazas where the city fathers had grudgingly forsaken commerce for the needs of the human inhabitants. The trees bordering roadways allowed Nature to remain in the city, overwhelmed though She was by concrete, steel and glass.

Yet the trees of Buenos Aires spoke of warmth and perfume and life; bright red ceibos, deep blue-violet jacarandas, brilliant yellow tipas, delicately pink lapachos were everywhere, each vying to outshine the women who sauntered beneath them in their multicoloured outfits as they sashayed their way to work, or window-shopped; Sarah was stunned by the women ... it didn't matter what they were doing, their movements were fluid, lithe, and their walk always seemed to be seductive; the tango was present in every step.

And above the traffic noise and rush, there was music. Everywhere, music. Coming from the open windows of apartments high above the streets, from shops whose doors were open and inviting, from cafes whose tables intruded onto the footpaths, from radios carried next to their ears by impish beggars who darted between the tables, stealing food from plates to the bemusement of the early-morning breakfasters. The music vied with the perfume of the trees and flowers and the harmony of laughter to saturate the air with wonder. It made Sarah thrilled to be here.

She threw money into the multicoloured blanket on which an accordionist was sitting cross-legged on the footpath, playing a tango. Then she sat on a bench amid the cacophony of traffic and continued to watch the unconscious exoticism of Spanish women as they flounced their way to and from offices and shops.

It was an endlessly fascinating brew of a city. The buildings in the main were French style. Indeed the very centre of the city looked as if it was like one of the old quarters of Paris, except for a few notable buildings such as her hotel, the modern and artificial Hotel South America. The centre of Buenos Aires was really only Spanish because of its people, not because of its architecture.

Yet, there was an eclectic mixture of influences in the air. For the first time in days, her immediate problems didn't seem as pressing. Her spirits were brightened as she breathed in a different atmosphere from the worry and introspection that she had felt since realising that her grandmother and grandfather were Nazis. Eventually she had reconciled herself with David who had grudgingly admitted that not only was this journey important to her peace of mind, but that he would be best not insisting on accompanying her. It was, she told him, a journey of self-discovery. 'Something I have to do on my own, for myself.'

Sitting in the middle of the excitement of a strange city, her mind flew back to trace the circumstances of her arrival. The night before she left for Buenos Aires, she and David and Josh had dined in a restaurant on 48th Street. Not an elegant restaurant, but one where the chef did exciting and unusual things with ordinary food. She realised how privileged she was that she was dining with the two most important men in her life, both of whom she knew loved her. David loved her for herself and of herself. Josh, she knew, loved her because of her sense of ethics, her inherent morality and because they had journeyed together down difficult and dangerous roads and succeeded in exposing evil. But what would he think of her if he knew that coursing through her blood vessels was the very evil which they both detested to their very core?

It was something that she had sworn David to keep secret until she was ready to reveal it to the world. Even as she flew out of New York, Josh still confidently believed that her sudden decision to resign – now rescinded at his insistence – was because she was overwhelmed by the timetable she'd set herself, and the consequent amount of work she had to do. She had not even told him she was going to Buenos Aires, just that she was getting away from pressures.

As the tango the accordionist was playing reached its climax, Sarah found herself clapping and then laughed at her own ridiculousness. The elderly man sitting cross-legged on the Indian rug was only interested in her throwing more coins on to his blanket. She did, and stood, walking down the diagonal Avenue Roque Saenz

Penya towards the Metropolitan Cathedral which bordered Plaza de Mayo.

By the time she reached the Plaza, crossing six city blocks, the sun was already hot and she was tired. It was a large city centre, immaculately laid out though obviously run-down through years of neglect since the squandering of the country's fortunes by Perón and his wife, followed by the disastrous rule of the Argentine Generals. Would Maggie Thatcher have gone to war if she'd known what sort of a city Buenos Aires really was? Yes, thought Sarah … yes, she would.

What delighted Sarah most as she walked around the city was the excitability of the South Americans. They didn't talk. They sculpted images in the air with their hands. Their faces carried every emotion that their words failed to express. Men walking with other men talked as if their hands were a part of their vocabulary. Women walking with women laughed and giggled and linked arms in a colourful expression of friendship and openness. It was only when men walked with women that restraint was introduced. Not between young lovers, of course, nor between children; but Argentine men and women appeared to associate with dignity as their chaperóne.

Eventually the street opened out onto the Plaza de Mayo, a vast open square surrounded by colonial buildings and dominated by the huge cathedral. As with elsewhere in the city, trees were everywhere and fleetingly Sarah imagined the tree-lined Unter den Linden in Berlin before the war, an elegant avenue which ran like an artery through the very heart of the city. She'd often wondered what it would have looked like, before Hitler cut all the linden trees down to make the road wider so that more of his SS men could march shoulder to shoulder down the avenue. Hitler had hated Berlin and Berliners. But eventually they won out. Even Adolf had been forced to bow to their fury at the desecration of their famous avenue, and plaster the wooden telegraph poles with branches from linden trees. Had her grandfather been one of those who marched in geometric precision, rank upon rank of young Nazis, singing the *Horst Wessel*?

As she walked deeper into the Plaza, she saw a large group of women standing with placards and as she came nearer, above the noise of the traffic, she heard their chants, a low unremitting moan. These were the Madres de la Plaza de Mayo who for years now had been marching around the centre of the city demanding a full accounting of what had happened to their children. More victims of fascism. Latin-American style. These mothers knew, of course. Any mother, any father would know. In the first months, they would have lived on the oxygen of hope; but as the waiting ground down their expectancy and the months became years, they knew, in their hearts, that their precious childrens' bodies were rotting in some obscene burial pit, hidden from their eyes, their memories, destroying their peace and their hopes and right to mourn. Sarah felt ill as she looked at their hollow lifeless eyes. How could such evil have reigned in such beauteous surroundings? How could South America have been given over to the fascistic care of its armies? How could the generals have gained control of a country like Argentina? How could evil like the Nazis have flourished in such a sophisticated culture as Germany? And what was the difference between the pits which hid the bodies of millions of concentration camp victims, and the excavations which concealed the bodies of young men and women who were spirited away by the fascist generals of Argentina during the evil dirty war. Had the world learned nothing from the lessons of the Jews. A mere half a century separated the pits of the Jewish martyrs from those of the Argentine, Yugoslavia, Rwanda … genocide. Everywhere there were fascists who thought nothing of ordering mass murder for their cause … ethnic cleansing, reclaiming land, anything to ensure the success of their particular hateful mission. And the victims? Unnamed, unknown, and mourned by people who were insignificant in the eyes of the nations' rulers.

Sarah felt inclined to go up to the women and to talk to them, to tell them that she knew, that she cared … but these were mothers alone in their grief, wailing with other mothers in communal isolation from the truth, a truth held in its entirety by the government. Her heart sank as she looked at the women. There was a desperation in their faces. All they needed was to be told, 'Yes, your son is dead. He was snatched off the street and taken to prison and tortured and he died and his body was thrown into a mass grave.' That's all these women wanted. They knew their children were dead. They just wanted to be told officially so that they could mourn them, so that hope could come to an end, and be buried along with their children. So that those responsible could face the white heat of their fury.

And then she thought of the way in which she'd defended Frank Darman. A Holocaust denier, a rabid anti-Semite, a hideous excuse for a historian, laughed at by true academics. At the time, she'd had no exposure to the reality of genocide … she was an armchair theorist, a dilettante, a lover of the high-blown rhetoric of defending the Constitution and the right of anybody, even a Frank Darman, to speak his nonsense. If only she had known then what she knew now. After she'd discovered the horrors of Stalinist atrocities in Slovakia, after she'd spent the past year listening to the hideous stories of refugees whose lives had been eviscerated by madmen, after she'd done all the reading about the

Holocaust, seen the films, spoken to the elderly survivors … seen their tears, still fresh and painful and full of misery even after half a century. Yes, if only she'd known then what she was aware of today, when she defended Frank Darman, she would have spat in his face. The principle of free speech meant nothing when confronted by an enemy who could create an Auschwitz, a Bergen-Belsen, a Treblinka.

Sarah, her heart suddenly heavy, turned and walked back along the Avenue de Mayo towards her hotel, where shortly she would be meeting Dr Luis Forenjo. Her mood of elation in walking through the strange city, in experiencing new sights and sounds and the delights of being enclosed by strange languages and customs evaporated. She was back in the land of her memory. She was back in the world of fascists, of evil, of Nazis, of generals like Juan Perón and Leopoldo Galtieri and the fascist Alfredo Stroessner of Paraguay, and notorious Augusto Pinochet of Chile … men whose abuse of human rights had caused the death of countless numbers of innocents. Numbers? Yes, not people, not names, not lives … but numbers!

She knew him the moment he walked into the lobby. He was a short man with stooped shoulders wearing a heavily creased cream coloured suit and an absurd black beret. He looked like an elderly bohemian, a Parisian artist from Montmatre desperately earning a few francs painting the faces of tourists. He had the face of a disappointed man, someone who considered himself to be a failure in the eyes of his society, yet who now played the role of a bit player in the colourful pageant of his surroundings. He looked around, unsure of himself. Up towards the high ceiling, across towards the walnut reception desk, his eyes milky with age, scanning the room and squinting at the distance.

Sarah smiled and stood. She walked over to him. 'Dr Forenjo?'

He hadn't noticed her approaching from the side. He turned in surprise. 'Sarah!' he said. She held out her hand and to her surprise, he lifted it to his lips and kissed it. Despite herself, she beamed a smile at the delightful courtesy.

'I must have a drink of water. I have walked far from the bus stop. I'm not used to Buenos Aires any more. The petrol and noise … it makes me dry and giddy.'

She escorted him over, her hand supporting his elbow and sat him in an armchair which encased him in its depth and size. He was shrinking with age, yet his mouth, his forehead and his eyes were alive with intelligence and with an understanding of who he was and why he was here.

Sarah raised her hand and beckoned a waiter. 'A cup of coffee and a glass of water please. Doctor, will you have a coffee?'

'When the water has done its work and revived me, I'll have a coffee.'

The waiter bowed and headed off. Dr Forenjo was still breathing deeply from the strains of the walk. 'While you're getting your breath back, let me just tell you how grateful I am that you have agreed to meet with me,' she said. 'I'm particularly pleased that you wrote to me because you've introduced areas of my past of which I had no idea.'

He looked at her and took out a handkerchief. He dabbed his forehead, wiped his mouth and returned the handkerchief to the top pocket of his cream linen jacket.

'Your phone call was enigmatic, my dear. You said little when you asked to meet me but it's in the spareness of your words that I divine a depth. I believe that my letter has struck a chord with you despite your earlier denial.'

She nodded. 'And you have come to the conclusion that my old and dear friend Ricardo Padrone was perhaps your grandfather.' She nodded again. 'I thought so,' he said quietly.

She would wait before telling her parents the awful truth that she suspected, but she had to involve this old man in her fears, because without his co-operation, they could not be examined; she would extract whatever information he had about Ricardo Padrone; she would examine the files of the city and the country; and when she knew the absolute facts, then, and only then would she decide whether to tell her mother and father the knowledge which she alone knew, or, like her grandmother Eva, take it with her to her grave. And in the process, this lovely man had to be hurt. There simply wasn't any way around it.

The waiter returned with a cup of coffee for Sarah and a glass of water for the doctor. He sipped it, took out his handkerchief again and mopped his brow. He then drank the rest of the glass of water. Sarah called the waiter back and ordered a coffee.

'Why are you here, Sarah?' he asked.

'Because of the letter.'

'My letter didn't necessitate your coming to this country. We could have done this by correspondence.'

'There are other things, Dr Forenjo. Details which I need to sort out in my mind.'

He nodded and wiped his brow again, still sweating from the exertion of the walk. 'There are things which are strange in all of this, Sarah. I detected the strangeness over the phone when we spoke last time. You were a troubled young woman and I didn't understand why. I asked you if you were Ricardo Padrone's granddaughter. You said no, but then something else has happened, hasn't it?'

She looked at him, wanting to reach out and touch him, hold his hand, protect him from what she had discovered. Why did she need to tell him? Why damage an old man's last years with reality? But without him, without access to her grandfather's papers, she could go no further. The proof would be in the detail. Things that she would be able to see from his papers that might mean nothing to the old Argentinian.

'Dr Forenjo,' she said quietly. 'Before we discuss that, can I ask you whether you have made a thorough examination of Ricardo Padrone's papers?'

He shrugged. 'As executor I have access to them all.'

'And have you read them all closely and carefully?'

'Closely, yes. Carefully? That has a value which I cannot place on it. As far as I am aware, I've been careful. But not knowing what to look for, how do I know what I've found?'

'What did you find of my grandfather's German past?'

He frowned. 'Is this the reason you're here?'

'Could you just answer my question, doctor.'

He frowned. 'Am I being cross-examined?'

She withdrew. 'No. I'm sorry. I didn't mean to use that tone of voice. I just have some very real concerns at the moment. Please understand I'm only trying to get to the bottom of a personal matter.'

He nodded and reached out to touch her arm. She was so young and vulnerable and in some ways she reminded him of his first wife. Her beautiful olive skin, her Jewish eyes. She was a very beautiful young woman, as had been his wife.

'There were many German documents I found there. Some were very old and of no interest to me. Understand this, Sarah. I was merely acting as his agent, as a facilitator to his wishes and that was to seek out his daughter Bettina and to give her the benefits of life that he had accumulated. It wasn't my role to have his documents translated into Spanish.'

'Are these documents available to me?'

'Of course. But what do you hope to find in them? I've answered your questions. You now owe me an answer.'

She could delay and prevaricate. She could be dismissive and make some sort of excuse that all she wanted was knowledge of her grandfather. But she owed this man more. He was a man of great decency and integrity. To hide the truth from him might save him pain but it wasn't the right thing to do. Not the moral thing to do.

'Dr Forenjo, the reason that I'm here is because I have found out certain things about my grandfather and my grandmother which cause me the gravest concern. Have you heard of a man called Reinholdt Stricher?'

He shook his head.

'What I'm going to tell you will come as a very great shock. But the man that you knew for half your life as Ricardo Padrone is, I believe, Reinholdt Stricher, my grandfather.'

She sighed, not knowing how to start. She looked at his innocent face. It wasn't too late. Maybe there was another way. But there wasn't. This was the end of the road. Did he deserve to know? No! Nobody deserved this kind of truth; just as she didn't deserve to know what she'd found out.

The coffee was cold and untouched by the time she finished telling him. She spared him none of the details; how her grandmother and grandfather had been a senior part of the Nazi hierarchy before and during the war; how her grandfather had been one of the architects of the Holocaust; how they had almost certainly appropriated the identity of unnamed Jews in the last days of the war;

how they had arrived in Argentina pretending to be Jews; how she had discovered the reality of her grandparents' identity through the Wiesenthal Centre; how computer morphing had taken Dr Forenjo's picture of his elderly friend Ricardo Padrone and transmuted him into a young man who was without any question one of the evil facilitators of the Final Solution.

When she was finished, the old doctor sat back blinking, licking his lips, unable to speak. She looked at him sadly. Then she opened her dossier case taking out the photocopy of the photograph she had received from the Simon Wiesenthal Centre in Los Angeles. She handed it to him. He squinted and blinked to try to clear his eyes. She knew the minute he saw it that the photograph was of his old friend.

'Ah,' he said simply.

'Ricardo Padrone?' she asked.

He said nothing, his silence testimony to the accusation.

'The woman beside him is my grandmother. That makes me the granddaughter of Nazis.'

He looked at her. There was an immense sadness which came over his face. 'Something is wrong, young lady. I know you have all these marvellous machines which can turn back time and make the faces of old men young again. I don't understand what can be wrong. But I know that something is very wrong with what you say. I don't know what, but this,' he said, pointing to the photograph, 'this can't be. The man I knew for three decades, the man I played chess with three times a week, who rode horses with me in our younger days, the man with whom I holidayed and shared my life's experiences. That man was not a Jew hater. That man wasn't a Nazi. I'm not a fool, Sarah. I'm an educated man. And so was Ricardo. He could have hidden the fact that he was a Nazi for a day, or a week, maybe a year. But he sought me out as a Jewish doctor. He sought out my Jewish friends. He knew Hebrew, though because he was secular he didn't know much …'

She interrupted him, 'How much? Did he speak Hebrew often? How were his prayers? Did he know the *b'ruchas*?'

'He knew as much Hebrew as me. Little. We were atheists in our own small way. Doubters, unbelievers. We went to *shul* because our fathers did and our grandfathers. And because our friends from the Jewish community went. We were secular Jews, happy to go three or five times a year and to call ourselves Jews and to enjoy the privileges of living in a Jewish community. But neither Ricardo nor I could have performed like a Rabbi.'

He took a sip of the cold coffee, hardly noticing its temperature. He was beginning to construct a rebuttal in his mind, working out ways in which her irrefutable evidence could be refuted.

'He went to *shul* many times. We gave him a *tallis* and a *teffilin* to replace those that the Nazis destroyed so that he could say the morning prayers. He was a member of our congregation, like me, and like me he wasn't a regular and certainly not Orthodox, but nonetheless he was always there to make a *minyan* if he was needed. This man was no Nazi. This man couldn't have been a Nazi. This man was a Jew. And to say that he was the architect of the Holocaust is insane.'

'Then how do you explain the photograph, Doctor?'

'I don't know,' he said sadly. 'I just don't know.'

Dr Juan Santa Fe de la Rosas took his time studying the picture. He opened his desk drawer and pulled out a magnifying glass. She was attractive, dark-looking, Semitic, probably a Jew. The old man was mopping his brow with a handkerchief. Dr Rosas smiled. Was it a flush of hormones sitting next to such a pretty little thing or was it the exertion of coming in from Avellaneda to central Buenos Aires? Whatever. It was of no concern. He put the picture back into the file and re-read the report from one of his undercover agents.

'Subject arrived at Hotel South America at 10.30 appeared disoriented and confused.'

Juan Santa Fe de la Rosas wondered how such an ape of a man as the agent would know that a man was disoriented.

'Subject ascended stairs of hotel and looked around lobby for several moments. Young unknown female person …'

Female person? Why these ridiculous euphemisms. What was wrong with 'woman', or 'lady'? Female person? It was so typical of a boorish ex-policeman. Still, that was the reason the Germans had hired him. Not because of his qualifications and background in literature, that was for sure.

'… approached subject, who ordered glass of water followed by coffee. Young female person took out a dossier and showed subject several photographs, and spoke animatedly. I couldn't get close enough to hear what they were saying. At one stage female person put arms round subject's shoulders and comforted him. They spoke with heads close together for many minutes. Then they went for a walk. They sat in a nearby park on a bench, and seemed to be lost in conversation. I tried to get close enough to hear, but both seemed to be speaking close to whispers. Female tried to comfort subject, but as time went on, he became increasingly emotional. At one stage, subject rose, walked around shaking his head obviously agitated. Then he returned to his seat. Ten minutes, he rose again, and after shaking hands, departed from female person. Did not know whether to follow subject or woman …'

Ah! Good. Now she was a woman.

'… but as woman was resident in hotel, I determined to follow subject, who returned to bus station, and left twenty minutes later on a bus to return to his home. Returned to Hotel, but female person had departed scene. I then returned to headquarters to prepare this report.'

Juan Santa Fe de la Rosas sat back with his cup of coffee, and looked outside of the Ministry's windows to the park below. He was deep in thought, working out the parameters. The report from the Department of Alien Affairs as well as the dossier from the Department of Customs and Immigration lay on his desk. Tracing the 'young female person' from hotel records had been simple. She was Sarah Rose, a tourist from New York. But further checking identified her as the newly married wife of David Rose, an up-and-coming cellist. Prior to her marriage, her name had been Sarah Kaplan. By this name, she was well-known as the head of the *Moishe, Vilma and Hermann Krantz Institute for the Recovery of Property Stolen in Times of Evil*, a New York-based lobby group for getting back stolen property and supporting the rights of downtrodden people, usually refugees, against governments who had allegedly stolen their property. The Institute had recently written to the heads of many Jewish communities throughout Argentina, asking them to report on anti-Semitic activities in their local area. Both her name and that of her Institute had come to his attention because of the potential adverse implications of such an Institute for the German community in Argentina.

Now the head of The Institute was here, visiting an old Jewish doctor. Of course, it could all be a coincidence.

These Jews … they had connections round the world. The old man could be her uncle, or a family friend.

But why then had the investigator specified that the old Jew was agitated by the conversation? What did this Sarah Kaplan woman want in Argentina? Was she here to stir up trouble for the elderly German comrades?

He cogitated for a few more minutes, before picking up the phone, and dialling a familiar number, that of an elderly Argentine who had been born over eighty years earlier in Bonn. A man called Heinz Keller. It was answered after a few rings.

'Heinz, it's Juan de la Rosas. We need to have a cup of coffee, my friend.'

There was no preamble. De la Rosas only phoned where there was a problem.

'Tomorrow or the day after?' asked Heinz.

'This afternoon I think, my friend.'

CHAPTER TWENTY-EIGHT

IGUASSÚ FALLS, ARGENTINA, PRESENT DAY

The music of the falls still rang in her ears, vitalising her thoughts, and the feeling of being at the very limit of the universe stayed with her until she returned late that night to Buenos Aires.

In her hurried preparations for the trip when she was in New York, Sarah never imagined that she would have any time in Argentina to do sightseeing. She hadn't known what to expect, but she certainly hadn't anticipated that her quest to find the truth about her grandmother and grandfather would be truncated so quickly. She had anticipated that Dr Forenjo would be more forthcoming, would give her help in searching through the documents, in trying to establish how her grandparents came to Argentina, in what they had done before they came from Europe.

But once he had delivered the box containing her grandfather's letters and other personal effects, he had closed off all communication with her. He had brought down the barriers. He didn't want to know. He refused to believe that his Jewish friend of thirty years could possibly have been a Nazi. Dr Forenjo was an old man; twenty years ago he could have dealt with something as confronting as this. Now all he wanted was peace and quiet and anonymity, and so Sarah had been faced with the prospect of having no further lines of investigation open to her except the documents themselves.

And now she deeply regretted bringing the old man into her confidence. She could so easily have demanded her grandfather's papers as her mother's proxy. Why did she go the whole way and unburden herself, placing an intolerable burden on the old man's shoulders? Why tell him? Why infest him with her fears and nightmares? She had done the wrong thing, and was bitterly regretting the sadness in Dr Forenjo's eyes as he delivered the box, and said to her, 'You will not find what you're looking for in here. My life-long friend was not the stuff of nightmares.'

When he'd gone, she delayed opening the box for many minutes, as though the act of opening it would expose her to even more unknown evils. And now that Dr Forenjo wanted nothing more to do with her, where could she go to find further information? She'd read her grandfather's letters time and again. She would have them translated properly, but her knowledge of German was strong enough to ensure that she understood the gist of what he had written to her grandmother in the 1950s.

Sarah had phoned up government offices asking for records to be opened up, to allow her to see what went on twenty-five years before she was born, but Argentine bureaucracy had obfuscated, as bureaucracy everywhere else in the world does so often. Fed up with waiting for phone calls back from Ministries of Alien Affairs, Customs, Immigration and Argentine commissions dealing with these matters, fed up with sitting in a hotel room just praying for the phone to ring, she decided to take herself out and give herself a trip away.

How naive she'd been. Were this investigation for a client of The Institute, she'd have done all the groundwork in New York; she'd have set up meetings, organised conferences and interviews, gained permission to access government papers long before travelling overseas. But all her professionalism had gone out the window when she was confronted with these things for herself. And now she was suffering the frustrations which her clients suffered in dealing with officialdom; which, of course, is why they sought the wisdom and professionalism of Sarah. Ha!

And so she'd decided to spend a day or two away from the silence of the telephone. Her visit to the Iguassú Falls had been on everybody's lips. The desk clerk, the concierge, the assistant manager at the hotel, all told her that she couldn't possibly leave Buenos Aires without flying up-country to visit the world's most spectacular natural phenomenon, close to the Brazilian, Paraguayan and Argentinian borders.

The flight had been longer than she expected. She was advised to stay overnight but she didn't want to, and so she only had a relatively short time at the falls. The moment she arrived she knew she had made a huge mistake. She should have packed to stay away for at least three or four days. 'Spectacular' didn't even come close to defining the phenomenon all around her. The falls were two kilometres long and five thousand cubic metres of water every second plunged two hundred feet down a vertical escarpment where the Rio Iguassú and the Rio Parana met. But it was neither the volume of water, nor the spectacle of the plunging torrents that held her captive to the majesty … it was the noise. It was the sheer unmitigated, unadulterated, uncontrollable power of Nature. No man, no artifice, no device could possibly make an impression on the vastness, the potency of what was around her. She was in awe of forces more powerful than those dreamed of in even the most expansive fantasies of tyrants and despots.

There were guided tours but she decided not to take them. Instead, Sarah walked along the *pasarelas* from cataract to cataract. She was deafened and drenched and defeated as she stood at the lookout staring at the Devil's Throat, the *Garganta del Diablo*, where white and furious water cascaded downwards in a never-ending torrent, which commanded the entirety of the landscape. Only when the wind blew and stirred the brew of mists and clouds could she define the edge of the water. For then the perpetual billowing vapours and the rainbows which danced around the top of the falls like sprites were blown away and Sarah could see the green vegetation and the wet black rocks seeming to stand in defiance of a torrent of water so great that it defied her imagination.

She knew there were people on either side of her making touristic noises, but she couldn't hear them; nor was she concerned with them. All that kept her eyes riveted was the volume of water, the sheer majesty and power.

Among the other falls, Sarah saw many different cataracts, different versions of the same thing, but none overwhelmed her entire body, her eyes, her ears, her skin, her mind, like the Devil's Throat. And the more she stood there, the more her thoughts went to her grandparents, and all the thousands of other Nazis who had left a devastated Europe and come to this clean and verdant New World to take on new identities and live new and unsullied lives. Had Reinholdt and Eva stood here, looking at this breathtaking phenomenon of nature? Had they marvelled, as their tainted granddaughter marvelled today?

They had come here with evil coursing through their veins and been cleansed.

Had they talked about the old days, the glory days of Nazi parades and flags and banners and torches blazing and a million men and women screaming *Seig Heil*? And if they had stood here after the war was lost in Europe, what language did they speak? German? Spanish?

And what thoughts went through their minds as they stared into the void of the Devil's Throat? Did they see the burning pits of Hell, where Hitler and Göring and Goebbels and millions of Nazi murderers would suffer an eternity of torment for the crimes they'd committed? Or did they see, in the writhing water far below, the arms and legs and bodies of their millions and millions of victims, struggling to escape the ghettos and the concentration camps and the gas chambers and the crematoria? Did they care? Or were they merely tourists, holding hands and saying to each other, 'Well, we've escaped. Now, let's put the past behind us, and get on with a new life.'

She left the Devil's Throat as soon as thoughts of her grandparents invaded her mind. But the scene was still imprinted on her brain as she travelled back to Buenos Aires; and it was still there as she entered her bedroom in the Hotel South America, exhausted after a long and tiring day, desperate for a bath, her ears still full of the anger of the gods.

It was when she closed the hotel door, seeking merciful rest and serenity, that she knew something was wrong. The bed had been made. The room had been vacuumed. But her innate sense told her that somebody else had been in the room. She looked around and could see nothing out of place. She stood close to the door, holding the handle and checking to see whether it was reality or a hidden sense of danger. She smelled the air. It was the cloying perfume of hotels. She checked her possessions. They were more or less where she had left them, moved only to clean and dust. She walked into the bathroom. It was clean and tidy as it had been the day before. She looked under the bed. Nothing. She slid open the wardrobe and the light which came on as she opened the doors illuminated her clothes and her suitcases. She realised that she was mistaken and felt foolish.

But instinct again took hold on reason. Her back stiffened as though she was being violated. She wasn't being foolish. Her room had been entered. There was a masculine smell, a feel of an intruder. He'd hidden his traces, but he'd been there.

She walked over to her briefcase which she had locked the previous night. She tried the locks. They were still closed but there were tiny scratches close to the keyholes; scratches which she couldn't remember having been there previously. Again, her imagination. She felt in her pocket and took out her keys. She clicked open the briefcase. It was almost exactly as she had left it the previous day. Almost, but not quite. Nothing was seriously altered. Nothing missing. Indeed it could have been the cleaners moving it which had shaken the contents. But again her instinct told her it had been opened and examined.

She picked up her passport, the letters she had brought with her, the folder containing the details of her grandfather and grandmother. The letters her grandfather had sent; the documents she'd been given by Dr Forenjo. She examined them carefully. Everything was there. Nothing was different. She closed them and locked the briefcase.

Sarah ran a bath, stripped off her clothes and threw them into the laundry bag for the maid to take away the following morning. She lay in the bath and came to terms with the fact that she may just be being hysterical. But something deep down told her that her room had been searched. That her briefcase had been opened. Her privacy violated. Somebody had examined who she was while she was at the falls. She held her breath and sank beneath the surface of the hot water. The sound of the falls came back. It was the sound of her heartbeat.

Heinz Keller read and re-read the photocopies of the documents. 'So, the Jew, Ricardo Padrone, was really our very own Reinholdt Stricher. Amazing! What an evil bastard he was. May he rot in Hell. We thought he'd been dead all these years. All these years. And instead, he'd just run away with our money. Fucking bastard! How could a man be born a German, become a Nazi, work for the greater glory of the Third Reich, escape Nuremberg, and become a fucking Jew?'

Heinz smiled to himself. It was a whimsical smile, a smile of disgust. What a heinous crime! Reinholdt Stricher should have made himself known to the German community in Argentina the moment he landed. It would have been so easy. He would have been a hero. He could have saved himself from any investigations by the fanatics from the Simon Wiesenthal Institute. He could have enjoyed the spirit of the expatriate German community, the support, the safety and the protection which they had to offer, the money which they had to spend to ensure a peaceful retirement.

Instead, he had apparently arrived pretending to be a Jew and lived for half a century by denying his roots, denying himself. What an amazing accomplishment. What phenomenal subterfuge. How can a man, how can anybody, play the part so well for so long? Not that Ricardo Padrone was known to anybody in the German community. He didn't even figure. He was a poor Jew that had obviously arrived after the war in Argentina, become associated with the Jewish community and lived the rest of his life like that. It was all there in the documents the girl had brought with her … letters, notes, photos from old Nazi newspapers, communication from the Simon Wiesenthal Centre in Los Angeles … but how could he have escaped the attention of the old German community? Surely he must have been recognised by someone? And why stay in Argentina after the war, when there were so many Nazis there and so many Nazi-hunters? Why not go to America or England or somewhere?

But how the hell had the brotherhood not known of his entry into Argentina? Was it a simple breakdown in communication? He'd checked the old records when the searchers had brought back copies of the documentation taken from the girl's hotel room. It appeared that the German community had been notified of Stricher's imminent arrival back in 1947. He was supposed to have documents announcing that he was entering the country as Señor José Phillipe Fierro, accompanied by his wife Esmeralda. In reality, the German community was looking forward to Reinholdt's arrival, especially as he was to be accompanied by his wife, the famous diva Eva Stricher. The Brotherhood's records showed that on five occasions, the courier had gone to the old Hotel de Rio Plata when passenger ships had arrived from Italy asking at reception for Señor José Phillipe Fierro. Yet nobody of that name, or of his description, had booked in.

Heinz tried to think back all those years. He remembered that messages had been sent to Father Draganovic. There was talk of Stricher being arrested or something like that. He couldn't remember the details for the life of him. It was all so long ago. They had assumed that somehow, between leaving the Institute of San Girolamo and catching the boat, he had been arrested or met with some accident. Either way, there was no record of his death and he certainly didn't appear to have arrived in Argentina. After six months of waiting patiently they gave up on him.

How had he managed to avoid attention? Maybe the answer was his wife, this … Heinz looked at the paper again … Eva Stricher, formerly Eva Arpel. She had sung for Hitler, yet now it turns out that the bitch was Jewish. Maybe she had been giving him lessons in being a Jew while they were in Germany as the Reich was collapsing around them. And now her Jew granddaughter was here looking for the truth.

But it didn't make sense. Stricher was an SS man, for God's sake. You couldn't marry a Jew as an SS man. They would shoot your balls off if they found out. He would end up in Auschwitz soon as blink. Things just didn't make sense.

But the thing which made least sense was why he'd chosen Argentina. If Stricher had wanted to avoid the German community … say he'd wanted to keep the SS money given into his keeping … why did he settle in Argentina? If he'd wanted to hide, why didn't he go to New Zealand or Australia or one of the Arab countries? Was it because he had special connections in the Argentine government of the time? A deal, perhaps. A certain kind of security denied to other Germans because he'd made a deal with Perón and the SS money? Maybe he'd retired to a farm, away from the crowds of the city. Maybe to where this old Jewish doctor had come from. Who could tell after all this time?

But Heinz had a particular problem. The granddaughter. Now this granddaughter was out here looking for answers. She was Jewish. She was heading up this Institute in New York, working for Jewish survivors of the Holocaust and other refugees. A troublemaker. Heinz would need to speak to her. And it wasn't the sort of conversation she would want to hear.

If this man really was Reinholdt Stricher, whom everybody thought had died at the end of the war, then there was a fortune hiding, waiting to be reclaimed. Men like Stricher were given numbered accounts in Switzerland. If he was custodian of that money then it was money that belonged to the Third Reich, to the SS, to the comrades. Of course the Swiss banks would never deal with a man like Heinz Keller, but they *would* deal with the granddaughter. Killing her and taking the number of the bank account would be useless. No. Somehow Heinz would have to persuade the young woman of her origins and the debt that she owed because of the lies her grandfather had told. Now, how the hell was he going to do that? He smiled to himself as he thought of a couple of ways.

Sarah turned off the cold tap and listened again in the quiet of the bathroom. She swore and dried her hands quickly. Why did the phone never ring when she was in the bedroom, but always when she took time to go to the bathroom? She ran in, sat down on the bed and picked up the phone. It had been ringing more frequently in the last two days than when she'd first began to make inquiries, but matters were still impossibly slow dealing with Argentine bureaucracy.

'Hello,' she said.

'Miss Kaplan?' the voice was Spanish with its clear musical lilt. 'Good morning. I hope I'm not disturbing you. My name is Dr Juan Santa Fe de la Rosas. I'm with the Argentine Ministry for Alien Affairs. Miss Kaplan, your letter to the Minister and subsequent phone calls have been passed to me to answer. I wonder if I might have the privilege of meeting with you.'

Involuntarily she found herself smiling. Anybody from the State Department in Washington would get straight down to the point. *Let's do lunch,* or *I'll buy you a cup of coffee.* No nineteenth-century mannerisms for the north of America.

'To what end, Dr de la Rosas?' she asked. 'I've met with quite a few people from different ministries, only to be told that there's nothing they can do for me. Will our meeting produce similar results?'

'How can we possibly tell, Miss Kaplan, unless we meet? Anyway, there's another gentleman that I would like you to meet. Bearing in mind your letter and your thoughts that your grandfather might have been one of the expatriate German community, I've invited a person who has advised me on such matters in the past to join us, an elderly German gentleman. With your permission, of course. It's quite possible that he will be able to shed some light on matters concerned with your late grandfather's arrival and origins. He's a gentleman called Heinz Keller, Herr Dr Keller, a former engineer in Germany. He's been here since the war.'

She felt her back stiffen. 'A Nazi?' she asked.

'We've learned from long experience that it doesn't assist us to ask too many detailed questions about the past lives of our citizens, Miss Kaplan. What a man has been or done before he found peace and tranquillity on our shores is between himself and his conscience. But if you require answers that might apply to your quest for information about your grandfather, Dr Keller is perhaps the man best placed to help you.'

Under any other circumstances, she would have refused; to meet with a Nazi, even one who had atoned for his sins, was unthinkable. It condoned the infamy of their actions, as though rehabilitating them in the eyes of society. But these were anything but usual circumstances. They went to the very nature of who Sarah was. If anybody, even Adolf Hitler, could shed light on her true identity, then she'd shake hands with the Devil himself. They fixed a time and place for later that day. It was over lunch in a restaurant in the centre of Buenos Aires' business district. Sarah told the ministry official what she would be wearing so he could recognise her.

She arrived fifteen minutes early having spent the morning killing time. She knew that the man she was about to be introduced to was undoubtedly an ex-Nazi. She had never met a Nazi face to face, not one whom she knew for sure was a Nazi during the war. Elderly people with thick European accents walking along the streets of New York could be Nazis as far as she knew. There were many old Germans of dubious record living all over the world. Whenever she met one who wasn't Jewish, she always wondered what he or she had done during the war. Now, her recent personal experience made her doubt even the veracity of some of the Jewish victims.

Yet this man she was meeting with the Argentine bureaucrat … he was almost certainly a real Nazi. There was no doubt in her mind as she approached the time when she would have to shake his hand. This man had probably been standing there on the steps of Nuremberg Stadium screaming '*Heil Hitler*' as the arc lights built cathedral spires in the air above the stadium and a hundred thousand voices were raised in adulation of the very devil god himself.

She watched the door, her heart sinking in fear every time it opened and admitted businessmen. Even her throat was constricting. At precisely 1.15, the very time of their appointment, two men walked into the restaurant. One was in his mid-forties, elegantly dressed, Latin-looking, of middle height, a bookish man with round spectacles and carefully parted hair. The man beside him was vigorous and spritely but age had withered him. Like old Dr Forenjo, this man looked shrunken within his suit as though his clothes were swamping his body. But unlike Forenjo, this man was obviously wealthy. The clothes he wore, a cream linen jacket and slacks, were expensive and immaculately tailored. And instead of the beret favoured by the doctor, this man wore a white Panama hat. A man twenty years younger would have looked dapper and raffish, but despite the money he'd spent on himself, he looked like an ageing roué, an old Lothario, somebody who had charmed weak-kneed women in the 1940s and 50s and who today lived only in his memories. He was clean-shaven and, as they walked towards her, she found her eyes transfixed upon the Nazi's, as though he were a snake and she the rabbit.

Why was she frightened of him? She held the power, the youth, the vigour. One slight push and he would fall. One word to the authorities in New York and he would spend the remaining years left to him pilloried by the Jewish press. But his eyes! They were the eyes of a grandfather, clear, luminous, intelligent, loving eyes. Or was it a practised look, the artifice of the actor? The subterfuge of the deviant.

'My dear Miss Kaplan,' said the younger man. 'I'm Juan de la Rosas. It's my pleasure to introduce to you Herr Dr Heinz Keller.'

Keller held out his hand. Sarah hesitated momentarily. To touch him would be to commune with evil. Yet, a lifetime of manner made her extend her arm towards his. His skin was warm and dry, desiccated like the skin of a leather chair.

'Thank you for joining us here, Miss Kaplan. So much more commodious than my office.'

She smiled. The waiter appeared and took orders for drinks. For the first time, she heard Keller speak. His accent was a peculiar mixture of the guttural and the romantic. He had spent more than half his life in South America and had picked up the cadences of Spanish. When he had finished ordering, he returned his gaze to Sarah. She felt uncomfortable.

'Your letter has caused some concern in my department, Miss Kaplan. Your grandfather was not known to us as

Reinholdt Stricher. However, on your advice, we have traced him as Ricardo Padrone, and as far as we are aware, he was a member of the Jewish community. I have traced records of his arrival. He came here on the SS *Santa Emelia*. He arrived with your grandmother. Their names weren't Stricher on the immigration lists as I told you, but were Mr and Mrs Padrone. They gave their religion as being Jews. They gave their intention as that of immigration. His occupation was listed as businessman, hers as being a secretary. Their first accommodation was a hostel owned by the Jewish welfare and relief organisations where they stayed for three months. They then moved into an apartment in a working-class suburb of Buenos Aires and from there we had no further need to view them, until they applied for citizenship a year later which they were granted. This is as much as I've been able to find.'

Sarah smiled. 'That's more or less what I've found out as well. But what I really need to know is what this gentleman can perhaps help me with.' She turned and looked. 'Dr Keller, what do you know about my grandfather, Ricardo Padrone?'

Deliberately, she didn't use his German name. She'd let him do that.

He mused for a minute, a lawyer's technique, and then said softly, 'Little more than you've been told, I'm afraid. Perhaps the Jewish community in Argentina could be of more assistance than Dr de la Rosas or myself.'

'I've been to the Jewish community. I've examined their records. He had membership of a synagogue in an outer suburb of Buenos Aires; a very poor working-class suburb. My grandmother suddenly disappears from all the records in 1950. He then moved his membership to a smaller synagogue, ostensibly because he met and subsequently married a Jewish lady called Rosaria two years later. He also moves to a wealthier suburb and lives a normal Jewish life. But he wasn't a Jew, was he, Dr Keller? He was a Nazi.'

'He was a German,' said Dr Keller softly.

'He was a Nazi!'

'For some, Miss Kaplan, the term is indistinguishable. For others, we insist that we were merely foot soldiers in an aggressive war being conducted by Adolf Hitler and that we were merely obeying orders.'

She nodded. 'The Eichmann doctrine. It's also what they said at the Nuremberg trials. Just following orders.'

'Unfortunately, it's the truth,' he said. 'It might be hard for you to appreciate but I would ask you to look at the record of American soldiers in Vietnam under the leadership of Lieutenant William Caley. Those men were merely following orders too.'

'That man was arrested by the US military, tried and convicted by American justice.'

'German justice came to an end in 1945, Miss Kaplan.'

'German justice came to an end in 1933, Dr Keller.' He deferred. 'But we're missing the point,' she said. 'Did you know my grandfather?'

'No. I never once met him.'

'Why did he pretend to be a Jew, do you think?'

'Obviously to escape attention.'

'Why do you think that he continued to live in Argentina despite the danger of discovery or identification by other Nazis?'

'Again, I have no idea. It's something which has puzzled me'

'And you never met him here? Not once? You or any other members of the Nazi community?'

Dr Keller bridled. 'Miss Kaplan, we call ourselves the German expatriate community, for that is what we are. Many of our members had nothing to do with the Nazi Party but came here at the end of the war to get away from Europe. You can brandish these terms as insults, or you can ask our assistance in trying to help you find the reality of your family history. Many men and women such as yourself have come to Argentina with the intention of exposing deep and awful plots or of identifying war criminals. Mossad was particularly successful in uncovering the whereabouts of Adolf Eichmann and spiriting him out of the country for trial in Jerusalem. But there have been no other significant arrests. The war criminals, the truly evil men of the Third Reich have been found and convicted or are dead, and their bodies are rotting in some far away grave.'

She shook her head. 'You know that's not true, Dr Keller. As I'm sure you've been told by Dr de la Rosas, I head up a New York-based Institute. We monitor Jewish affairs around the world. One only has to read newspapers in Canada and Australia, South Africa and France to know that war criminals are still being found and are doing their best to evade the weight of justice.'

'Old men who should be left to die in peace, if only to spare their innocent families … and indeed their victim's families … any further suffering.'

She sipped her mineral water. 'Old men who are mass murderers and responsible for the most heinous crimes in history don't deserve a peaceful end. Neither do their wives and daughters and sons. Not until the thousandth generation. Rather, they deserve to die knowing that, regardless of the amount of time that has elapsed, these crimes will never be forgotten or forgiven. And worse, without putting them on trial and exposing them and their foul deeds, we've managed to spawn an entire subclass of neo-Nazis who parade around America and Canada and Germany and Austria beating up and murdering immigrants and homosexuals and Jews, emulating what their grandfathers did seventy years ago.'

The two men were swept by the self-righteousness of her anger. But unbowed, Dr Keller asked quietly, 'Is this the same Sarah Kaplan who vigorously defended Frank Darman's right to question the validity of the Holocaust?'

Sarah was stunned. How had he known? She had no idea that it had made the news in Argentina. But the crevice had been opened. Her Achilles heel exposed. 'In America, we have a peculiar tradition Dr Keller. It's called the Constitution and guarantees the right of free speech. I wasn't defending Darman or his obscenity. I was defending his right to make a public laughing-stock of himself when he claimed that the Holocaust never happened. If only to allow thousands of survivors to scream in righteous indignation that there *were* six million victims, that they were eyewitnesses to the crimes, that they had been there when the bodies were forced into the crematoria, that they knew what they knew and nothing he said could deny their truth.'

It was all getting too heated. Dr de la Rosas said, 'Excuse me, but this is getting us nowhere. I've brought Dr Keller here so that he could assist you in finding further details of your grandfather. This anger and vituperation will merely end in one of you storming out and then nothing will have been achieved. Can I suggest that you put your personal problems to one side and deal with the matters at hand?'

Sarah looked at him and nodded. Dr Keller shrugged. 'We do seem to have got off on the wrong foot, Miss Kaplan,' said Keller. 'I came here offering help in your quest. You need to find out more about your grandfather. While I never met him, I can most certainly assist you in the records of the German community here. Records which might enable you to put two and two together. The question however is to what purpose?'

Sarah looked at him obliquely. 'I have to know.'

'You have to know what? Whether your grandfather was a Nazi? If he truly was Reinholdt Stricher, then he was. Or to know whether he changed his religion in order to escape detection? Again, it's almost certain that he did. Whether he regretted his involvement with the German war machine? Something no amount of record-searching will be able to tell you. Your grandmother is dead. Your grandfather is dead. Why continue the search?'

'For some small clue. For some little forgotten thing.'

She felt her hand involuntarily clutching at the amulet that she wore every day of her adult life.

'Just something,' she said. 'Some way I can go back to New York and tell myself that this didn't really happen. That this was just a nightmare. That both my grandparents weren't Nazis pretending to be Jews.'

She clutched the amulet more firmly. Since the time when she was just a little girl asking questions about the amulet, she willingly believed her mother's story that it had originally belonged to her great-grandmother Serel. But now, that truth, and everything else in her life was undermined. The link was broken. Her grandmother and grandfather weren't Jewish, but were Nazis. They had probably stolen the clothes and the amulet and the identification of nameless and pathetic Jews who had fallen by the wayside, or who were victims of a concentration camp horror. The amulet was part of the facade, the story that those people had built. The old Jewish farmer in a *stetl* in Ruthenia; the discovery of the amulet; killing in a pogrom; Serel escaping the legions of the damned in eastern Europe and trudging, children in her arms, to Germany in the early 1900s. Maybe it was all true … but it happened to another family, and her Nazi grandparents had mercilessly stolen the lives and histories of some unknown victims, and made them their own. And in doing so, had made Sarah an unwilling accomplice to a calumny.

Sarah had believed it all, but now she knew that it wasn't true. It was all made up. A lie, a constructed family history, built in the air, a convincing story to prove that two Nazis, two Germans, two people who clicked their heels and screamed '*Heil Hitler*' were not who they had been born, but instead were impoverished Jews. She let go of the amulet. It no longer brought her comfort. It was debased. Sarah had no idea of its origins, where it had come from, who had originally owned it, how it had been discovered. Everything in her life was shaky and ill-founded. Nothing was as it seemed. Where was her reality?

'Miss Kaplan,' said Dr de la Rosas. 'Would you like to order some lunch?'

She looked at him and then saw that the waiter had been standing opposite her, pad and pen in hand, waiting for her to give him some attention.

He sat in the darkened room of his apartment, the shutters closed to tame the heat of the day. He was getting old and stupid. He was angry at his incompetence. Twenty years ago, this would never have happened. He would have worked out a subtle subterfuge, some clever ploy, something devastating to wrest the money from her sticky Jewish fingers. But age had tired him and made his thought processes border on the naive.

What had he really expected? A compliant young woman nodding happily, listening to his explanation of how the Germans had been misunderstood all these years, happily handing over the details of her grandfather's bank account, saying to him, 'Of course you can have access to the millions which are still there?'

Fool, that he was! A stupid arrogant old fool. His late wife was right. He should have retired decades ago, left the running of the SS accounts and the welfare of the comrades to others who were younger and as committed. He had enough money. He had property. He could have sold a couple of apartments and spent the money travelling the world, bought a new identity, pretended to be a Spaniard, died in the arms of a beautiful young woman in a bordello in Madrid. But no. His overwhelming naive feeling of responsibility to the German expatriate community had stayed with him all these years. Why in God's name did he think that his subtle engineer's mind could have persuaded a woman like Sarah Kaplan to agree to hand over the grandfather's bank account.

Damn him to hell! If only Stricher had had the balls to announce his arrival in Buenos Aires. He wanted to keep the SS money to himself. That was obvious. But was it? Why take the risk and come if he didn't want to associate with the Nazis? He'd asked himself the question a dozen times, but still couldn't come up with an answer. Why didn't he go somewhere else? South Africa, Canada, plenty of places. Why come to Argentina? Why take the risk of a country like this, why steal SS money and all the dangers that entailed, if he didn't want to be discovered? None of it made sense. Well, it was all too late. No answers. The bastard was dead, God rot his bones. But the money was probably still alive. Somewhere. Not even Stricher could have spent tens of millions and not been noticed. And if it was in Switzerland, he had to get it out before the Swiss compromised further, and gave all the SS money back to the Jews.

Now he was in a difficult position, and would have to do something he didn't want to do. Any action would endanger the organisations that he had built up. The last thing he needed was some precipitate action, drawing the attention of the Jews to the German community. God. It had been difficult enough when the fucking Iranians had killed all those Jews in 1994. World Jewish attention had suddenly fixed on the Buenos Aires Germans like they were under a magnifying glass. Questions, demands, investigators from all over the world. That was the last thing they wanted to live through again.

This wasn't like the old days, when the Nazi-hunters had been after everybody. Then, back in 1950, he had had to take urgent action when those bloody boys from the Simon Wiesenthal Centre in Vienna had come sniffing around. How could he have known they were after Reinholdt Stricher? He thought they were after the others. There was nothing in their documentation to say they were after Stricher. He still had the pages he'd removed from the diary they'd left in their room. He even remembered what they'd said. *On trail of Holocaust architect. Big News.* What kind of detective work was that? Who were they talking about? Eichmann? Borman? Hitler himself? They were buffoons, those boys. How was Heinz expected to know they were stalking Reinholdt Stricher, a man he and everybody else in the German community thought was long dead. Once he had had them killed in the road accident and performed a thorough search through documents, there was nothing which indicated who they were really after.

And he'd put paid to all the others, of course. The Mossad spies they had uncovered. They had been dealt with. The disappearance of Jewish Nazi fighters over the years. All had been accomplished with risk. He thought that after half a century, the risks were over, but they weren't. He'd sacrificed Eichmann. Nothing he could do. Mossad was too thick on the ground. So, give the Jews a victory. Eichmann; sacrificial goat. Anyway, he was no great loss … buying his wife flowers on their anniversary. What a stupid thing to do. It'd cost him his life. And having caught such a massive fish, the boys and girls from Mossad had retreated back to Israel, gloating and proud of their achievements … leaving the rest of the Argentine and Paraguay and Chilean German communities to get on with the rest of their lives.

But now, thanks to this girl and the bloody gutless fool Reinholdt Stricher, he would have to take another risk. Kill the girl. Get hold of this bloody Jew Luis Forenjo and shake him until the number of Stricher's Swiss bank account dropped out of his pockets. Then he'd employ an actress to play the role of Sarah Kaplan, arrange all the right identity papers and documents from the Department of Justice to prove that she was Stricher's legal heir, and then take her over to Switzerland to get hold of the money.

Yes, he'd have to kill the girl. If he didn't, if he let her live, then the moment she learned of Forenjo's death, she'd panic and bring in all the heavyweights. Mossad, World Council of Jewery, anti-Nazi leagues. Everybody! She'd have to die. What else could he do? The money, which he was sure was in Stricher's Swiss bank account, belonged to him. To him and the comrades. How could he possibly leave an amount of money like that to the possession of a girl like Sarah Kaplan? That wasn't Jewish money. That was Reich money. And he wanted it. And damn it, he would have it!

When the document box finally arrived, it was a disappointment. She didn't know what to expect. All Sarah knew was that Dr Forenjo had phoned her the previous night and told her that, as her mother was the beneficiary of the will and Sarah was a lawyer with her mother's Power of Attorney, he had applied to the Department of Justice of Argentina for relief from the position of executor of Ricardo Padrone's will and had nominated Sarah as a suitable and duly qualified person to be executrix. He had no doubt in his mind that the Minister, when he finally came to sit in judgement on the matter, would accede to his wishes as a living relative had been found and so, in anticipation, he was wiping his hands of the whole sorry affair and sending Sarah all the documentation that he had of her late grandfather's estate. She'd had his first box of correspondence. Now, she possessed the second with all the official documents.

It was a sad discussion, one with a defeated, disillusioned old man. For thirty years, he and Ricardo Padrone had grown close together in an increasingly alien world. The old norms by which they had lived in the 1950s and '60s were rapidly overtaken by the evils of the '80s and '90s. Life wasn't what they wanted it to be and Ricardo Padrone had died with a Jewish prayer on his lips in his own bed, tended by his old friend, mentor and doctor.

No, Luis Forenjo had told her, he was unwilling to meet her again and talk to her about her late grandfather. She had come to South America with the intention firmly in her mind that her grandfather was a Nazi. While Dr Forenjo could not explain the photographs or documentation she had shown him, and nor could he explain the letters he had found in the document box which he had sent to Sarah, none of this mattered. All that concerned him were the memories which he shared of life with his old friend, Ricardo Padrone.

Sadly, Sarah opened the box. It was an old document box, metal, about the same size as a computer CPU. The papers inside smelled musty. Some were obviously many years old, others much more recent. Some were in German, others in Spanish. She spread them out on her bed. She would need the help of a translator again to work with her. She might as well catch the next plane back to New York for all the good she was doing here.

She sighed as she looked at the collection on her bed. Is this what her life would be when she was old? Was a whole life reducible to a series of piles of paper, collections of letters and official documents? Was that all a living, breathing person was worth at the end of eighty years? She picked up one pile, bound together by an old brown string, letters that looked official. They were addressed to Ricardo Padrone from various organisations whose letterhead carried crowns and heraldic symbols and embossing. They were all in Spanish. She let them fall back on the bed.

She picked up another pile. These were handwritten letters. She flicked through them and tried to define the names. Some were from women, some from men. Some in German, some Spanish. Again, she would need to study them closely. Their message was in the subtext, not in the words themselves. An indication here, a hint there, a veiled reference somewhere else. No doubt when she traced the documents year by year, person by person she would build up a story enabling her to look deeper into the heart and mind of her dead grandfather.

She looked at the collection of documents laid out on her bed more carefully. Odd. There was nothing here of her grandmother, no record of Eva. No photographs; no mementos; nothing. It was as if she hadn't come over to South America with him, as if he had never existed in her life. Somewhere within the body of the correspondence was his letter to her and her response, but Sarah had already seen this. Was that it? Did that account for the sum total of her late grandmother's life with this man, this Nazi? But there again, her grandmother was a

Nazi. Oh God, thought Sarah. Now they're both dead, how will I ever get to the truth?

She picked up another document pile. These were bank statements. She did a quick conversion of the currency into US dollars that went into and out of his bank account. They were completely unexceptional amounts. $500; $930; $122. She laughed. Not exactly Ted Turner or Bill Gates. She looked at a second and third page of the most recent statements. The income seemed to be fairly regular. Probably a pension. She traced the source of the income to the left-hand column and translated it as best she could from the Spanish. Department of Old Age or Pensions or something.

She looked several lines below the entry. Another amount had been paid in. This was roughly double the pension. About one thousand American dollars. She followed the line back with her finger in order to see where that payment had come from. As with the others, it was in Spanish, but she thought it said something like, *overseas deposit*. She lifted the page to look at older pages of statements, going deeper into her grandfather's history. Again the pension of $450 and a few days earlier another amount of $900 and something US dollars paid into his account. Once again, it was an overseas deposit. She breathed a sigh. Such small amounts. Such an unimportant life. Yet, was he a mass murderer? Had he chosen his identity by abducting the life of an elderly Jew like Dracula stealing the life blood from the living?

She flicked through further pages. More money from the government, more money from the overseas deposits. What were these overseas deposits? She took the three-inch thick collection of bank statements over to the desk in her room and started to flick through them. She turned to the oldest of the pages, which dated back to

1959. Nothing there. Far more entries in the income side of the statement, but then there would be because he was a younger man who made a living from working at some job or other.

And of course, there were more outgoings than recently, lots of cheques written for fairly small amounts. She flicked through to the next page and then the next.

And then it appeared. '*Overseas deposit.*'

Four hundred and twenty American dollars. Sarah frowned. She turned each page carefully now and started to make a note of the dates on which the overseas funds had arrived in the bank account. She covered the years 1959 to 1979, amazed that her grandfather had been so meticulous in his record-keeping. Not a statement was missing. Month followed month, year followed year in perfect succession.

For each year, there were twelve deposits of roughly the same amount of money. It had started off at $US420 in the late 1950s and by the late 1970s had grown to $US750 a month. Not a lot of money but unbelievably regular. Thirty days separating each deposit.

Sarah went to the bathroom and washed her face in cold water, cupping mouthfuls and drinking them. She went back and did another sixteen years until the death of her grandfather in 1995.

By the time of his death, $1000 a month had been coming in from this overseas source. Added to his pension from the Argentine government, it was not a bad income. Nothing unusual. So why was she curious?

All the expenditure in the account, of course, ended when he died, but Dr Forenjo had thoughtfully included an accounting for the money which continued to flow in from the overseas source from 1995 to the present. Nearly $50 000. Not a large amount by anybody's standing but significant. And the money seemed to be still coming in. According to the handwritten records of Dr Forenjo a deposit from an overseas source had arrived only a few days earlier.

She walked over to the phone, looked up her address book and phoned him. He was courteous but obviously cold.

'Of course I will respect your wishes, Dr Forenjo, though it upsets me that you and I can no longer speak about my grandfather and grandmother. However, I'm phoning you as the new executrix about these amounts which are coming in from overseas. What's the source of this $1000 a month?'

'I don't know, Sarah. Since I became executor they've been coming in. They just seem to arrive. I suppose it's a pension from the German government. Many of the elderly Jews in Argentina enjoy such pensions as war reparations.'

'Isn't $1000 a month rather a lot?'

He remained silent, eventually saying 'Yes, I must admit, but I hadn't thought to check.'

'So, you have no idea where the amount is coming from?'

He told her he didn't. Her next phone call was to her grandfather's bank. Eventually she found somebody who spoke English and who worked in an executive position. She explained who she was and what she wanted. She told him that she was the executrix of her grandfather's will. The executive apologised and said that he could give no information about this matter over the phone and made an appointment for the following day.

As the crowds were emerging onto the pavements as lunchtime approached, Sarah Kaplan emerged from the Banco de Rio Plata next day in a state of complete confusion. Why on earth would the Bank of the Swiss Cantons in Zurich be sending her grandfather $1000 a month, every month?

She sat down in the cafe opposite the bank, her body numb with fear. Much of her work with Josh Krantz and the Institute in the past year had been dealing with the Swiss banks, trying to get money stolen by the Germans out of the gnomes of Zurich. They had now conceded that they inadvertently had been in receipt of stolen money and gold bullion and jewellery and other precious things during the Nazi era.

Inadvertently! It was all bullshit, of course. The wartime Swiss government had actively involved itself in complicity with the Nazis, despite the high moral ground claimed by the Swiss due to their supposed neutrality. When they were caught with their pants down, the gnomes had made derisory offers of tens of millions of dollars in compensation, rather than the billions which they'd received and kept these fifty years. Compensation! When the money was Jewish money stolen from Holocaust victims! Never once did it occur to Sarah that she could be one of the beneficiaries or that she would have to go to Switzerland, fighting and screaming on her own behalf instead of on behalf of elderly and exhausted victims of Nazi aggression.

She stood, and left the cafe to walk back to her hotel and pack. She knew that she should meet the old German again, and try to source her grandfather's activities in Argentina. But she couldn't. What would he tell her anyway? No, she would go to Switzerland, and find out more about the source of the money he was receiving. That alone might enable her to define her grandfather more clearly.

As she walked away, two young men stood and followed her at a discreet distance. One dialled a series of numbers into his mobile phone.

CHAPTER TWENTY-NINE

ARGENTINA, PRESENT DAY

Dr Luis Forenjo picked up the bishop and placed it cautiously down upon the square it had occupied during the past few years. It was a peaceful move, full of reflection, of memory. So different to the last time he'd moved it. Then, four years ago, it had been moved strategically, aggressively. Now, there was no strategy, no aggression. Just memories.

The last time he'd played a move had been before his old friend had died. Peacefully, if not particularly comfortably, in his bed. Coughing a bit, but eased by the draining of the fluid from his lungs. Yet no medicine could save him. His heart wasn't strong enough.

He smiled when he thought about that last game before Ricardo Padrone had been taken to hospital two days later with complications from pneumonia. A week in hospital, and he'd been released back to his home, to die in peace and dignity, his wife Rosaria by his side, comforted in the rites of Judaism. *Baruch ata adonai, elohenu melech haolam* …

Dr Forenjo shouldn't have won their last game and could only ascribe his luck to the fact that Ricardo was about to die. Why did he win? Ricardo's mind was still active. He was comfortable on the antibiotics and the painkillers. Did he allow his doctor friend to win, knowing that within the day, he'd be sitting in heaven, watching his old friend withering away, lonely and pining for someone to talk to, someone with whom to play chess?

Every day for the last four years, he had picked up different chess pieces, analysing the last game, wondering whether Ricardo had somehow played the game of his life, seeming to make the play difficult and torturous, yet manipulating an outcome which allowed his opponent to win … without his opponent knowing it.

How would a different approach have altered the final result? Perhaps it would. Or perhaps after so many years of playing, Luis Forenjo had finally learned a trick or two … just in time for his friend and opponent to relinquish the game of life.

He did a quick calculation. Say two games a week for fifty weeks a year, was one hundred games a year, over what? The twenty-five years of their close friendship. Two and a half thousand games! He only won one in a hundred of them, and these because Ricardo allowed him to. But the last game! Had he won that on his merits? How would he ever know?

It was Ricardo's mind which beat him every time. Not that Ricardo was a particularly brilliant or knowledgeable man but he had a Judaic mind, a universal approach to life, a mind which came from centuries of scholarship, with grappling with the eternal complexities of the Talmud and the Mishna and the Gemorra.

That's why his being a Nazi was just so incongruous. No! He couldn't explain the photos nor the documents that Sarah brought to South America with her, thrusting them at him as though they were weapons, but Luis Forenjo knew Jews and there was no doubt in his mind that Ricardo was Jewish. Nobody could pretend like that. Not in such a sustained way, not over all these years. Nobody.

He sighed. Life was lonely now. His daughters lived miles away. His son was overseas working as a doctor at

Guys Hospital in London. Now his wife was dead, now his best friend was no longer here, Luis Forenjo spent the days waiting for the nights and the nights waiting for sunrise. Sure, he was busy on some days, working for the Jewish community. But there were younger more active people now to take the strain and his role was that of adviser. Young people didn't need so much advice. Now there were computers and databases, the knowledge he had gained over decades was ... what was the term? downloadable. That's right. All the history, all the relationships, everything was 'downloadable'.

He picked up another chess piece and smiled. And then he heard the noise. When he lived in Avellaneda, there was always noise. Shouts in the street, motorcycles and cars going past, drunks shouting, fights going on. It was the poor part of Buenos Aires, where the workers and the migrants lived. It was the part which had risen up in support of Perón. It was where Ricardo had first moved when he arrived in Argentina. Not many Jews, but enough for a community. Ricardo had moved out of the area five years after he arrived to live in seclusion on a farm. But twice a week, without fail, he'd travel into Avellaneda for a meal with Luis and a game of chess.

That was in the old days. On his retirement, Luis Forenjo moved out of Buenos Aires to live permanently on his farm, where there was rarely human noises. There were often noises around his farm, noises of horses and cattle and nocturnal animals. These days he never paid any attention to noises but the noise he heard outside his farmhouse was different. This one was a confident noise, not the noise of a skulking beast. He put down the chess piece and listened. Silence. And then the noise again.

Dr Forenjo stood and walked towards the door. He lived on a small farm; an investment in his younger days, a place of tranquillity in his retirement. He opened the door to see who was out there making the noise. He didn't expect to see four tall young men standing under the light of his porch, He smiled and then realised that he shouldn't be smiling, but that he should be worried. One of the young men stepped forward and aggressively pushed him back into the room. He tripped over the rug and fell sprawling on his back. He was winded. The four men, tall, athletic, strong looking, walked into his home and closed the door. Suddenly he was very frightened. These men had the look of evil in them. There was no kindness, no compassion in their face. They were like soldiers.

'What do you want?' he asked aggressively. 'How dare you come into my house!'

One of the young men walked forward and kicked him hard in his groin. He let out a yelp and rolled over on to his side, gasping for air. He felt them pick him up and throw him into a chair. His eyes were watering, and the pain in his groin was overwhelming him. He still couldn't breathe and felt consciousness beginning to slip away. Then they slapped his face and the pain migrated upwards from his middle to his cheeks.

One of the young men knelt down and spat in his face aggressively. 'Now you listen to me, you old bastard. You fucking Jew. We want the bank account number in Switzerland. And we want it now. There's four of us and one of you. Nobody knows we're here. We've cut the telephone wires. You've got ten seconds to tell us before we beat the shit out of you. Now, what's it to be? You going to be sensible or are you going to die painfully, like a hero?'

Forenjo blinked, trying to understand what they were saying in the swirling mists of his mind.

'What's the bank account number, you old bastard?' yelled the young man.

'Bank?' hissed Luis Forenjo. 'What bank?'

'Reinholdt Stricher's bank account number in Switzerland. We want it now.'

'I don't know anything about it. Please. I know nothing about it. What bank? What Switzerland?'

'Don't fucking lie to us,' he screamed, spittle spraying Luis' face. 'We followed the girl today. She went to the bank. You told her. Now fucking tell us, or you're dead.'

Dr Forenjo couldn't speak. He lost control of his bladder as he began to feel faint.

The young man smiled. There was no pleasure in his smile. There was instead a mixture of malice and the anticipation of a future joy. The young man took out a knife from his pocket and opened it slowly and deliberately.

'The first thing I'm going to do is to cut out your eyelids so you'll see everything that we do because you won't be able to close your eyes. That should be fun for you. Then we're going to cut off one of your fingers for each time you tell us that you don't know what bank account. And when you've got no fingers left, we're going to cut off your toes and when you've got no toes left, we're going to cut off your balls. Now, let me ask you again. Where is the number for the bank account in Switzerland owned by Reinholdt Stricher? Your friend, Ricardo Padrone! You gave it to the girl. Now give it to us.'

Dr Forenjo fainted.

Half an hour later, after frantically trying to revive the old man, one of the young Nazis reluctantly took out his mobile telephone and slowly pressed a series of numbers. Regardless of the consequences, he would have to tell Heinz what had inadvertently happened.

The four young men who buried Luis Forenjo's body were too far from the airport to hear the roar of engines as the Aerolineas Argentinas Boeing 747 took off on its flight from Buenos Aires to Frankfurt. From there, Sarah Kaplan would take a connecting flight to Zurich.

As she looked down at the city lights, Sarah tried to imagine the landscape she'd just left. Buenos Aires, of course, was ablaze with lights but she had only been flying for a matter of ten minutes before the brilliance of the city disappeared into the darkness of the night, and the city, now thirty miles away, was replaced by the occasional illumination of a village in the Argentinian countryside. Nor did she know that when she flew high over the area in which Dr Forenjo had just died, his assailants were already obeying the commands of a furious Heinz Keller and were ransacking the house for clues to the password and account number for the Swiss bank. Details which she already held in her possession.

It was all contained in a letter which a translator had helped her understand, one of the letters which was in her grandfather's strongbox. The letter had been written to her grandmother Eva in New York, but had been returned unopened. It had been written a few months after Eva and Bertha had left Argentina in 1950. In the letter, Reinholdt had begged her to return to him, promising that he would leave Argentina and the dangers of discovery and find a place where they would both be safe. He swore his undying love to her. He said that he had protected her through the war and now she had a responsibility to protect him.

Sarah was the first person to have read the letter in the fifty years since her grandfather had first written it. He'd sent it to an address in New York which Sarah didn't recognise, presumably where her grandmother had lived. He could have followed her there, but he was waiting for her to return to him and the love he bore her. Sarah had been surprised that Dr Forenjo had not opened the still-sealed letter, despite the note attached which said, *To be opened in the event of my death only by my wife Eva, or my daughter Bertha*. Sarah had assured Dr Forenjo that she wouldn't open it, but would allow her mother to have the privilege of being the first person to read Ricardo's words in all these years. Yet Sarah couldn't resist. And now she was delighted.

When first she had read those words, Sarah's heart had leapt at the implied meaning. What did he mean? He said that he had protected Eva during the war! Protected her from what? From whom? Why would a good Aryan German woman need protection, especially one who had sung for Adolf Hitler. There was something here which didn't make sense. Something which perhaps could act as Sarah's salvation. Or was she clutching at straws? Her visit to Dr Forenjo, her meetings with Argentine officialdom, and finally her lunch with that hideous Nazi, Heinz Keller. Smug, supercilious bastard. Why should he tell her anything? And could he tell her anything she didn't already know about Perón and his awful wife Evita, and about the Nazis they'd helped evade prosecution and punishment? Could he tell her about her grandfather's record as a Nazi? About her grandmother, and what precisely she'd done in the war? Did Herr Engineer Dr Keller know that her grandmother was an opera singer? Did he know anything?

Sarah had ended her stay in a state of confusion, glad to be leaving Argentina, worried about what she'd find in Switzerland. She'd left with her grandfather's safety deposit box. She hadn't thought there would be anything in there which would shed light on the situation; she hadn't counted on such a man as Dr Forenjo, who obeyed the wishes of his dead friend and hadn't opened the letter.

She thought again about the rest of the letter her grandfather had written to Eva in 1950. Why hadn't Eva read it? Why was it returned unopened? It was all so mystifying. She took it out from her briefcase and re-read it as the plane levelled off at 20 000 feet and crossed the coast towards Europe, before climbing again to 35 000 feet in the South Atlantic for the rest of the journey. The original letter, written in German, was in a plastic envelope to protect it. But it was the translation that she read so avidly … where was that really interesting bit?

You know of my love. You know of my faith in you and you know that I will share what is ours. It's 'back there'. It's worth more than you can know. Its value though is more than money. It's security. It's ours. We have worked for it. We've risked everything. Remember those years in Italy and crossing the Alps? Working in farms as labourers and suffering the abuse of the peasants. Why shouldn't we have it? Why shouldn't it be ours to share? What do we owe others? Why do you think it was, that in the past five years that I've been in South America I have never once associated with comrades from the old days? Why do you think that before we left Italy I took the risk of changing the ship's tickets and going out on a later boat just in case they were due to meet me? These things were last-minute decisions, spur of the moment. I did it because when I saw the look in your eyes and I knew that we were leaving Europe, from that moment onwards I knew that my life was changed forever, that the old days were behind me and that for the sake of my new life I must break all ties. That's why I have made no attempt to gain this money. And neither without your permission will I attempt to take any. Not until you say to me, yes my husband, yes, you may.

I understand your fears. These young, earnest men who are here now from Vienna, sent by the Nazi-hunter … the young men who were searching for people like me, and who frightened you so much that you've run away from me. Why do you worry so? They'll never discover who we are. I'll avoid them … I don't think that he even recognised me … it's just my hysteria, my fear of being found. I should never have told you they'd approached me.

And even if I am discovered, why are you in danger? You were born a Jew and are again a Jew. For you there is salvation in your people. For me, there will never be salvation because all my people are dead.

I am alone. I need for nothing. That's why I've taken nothing from Switzerland. There's nobody there I trust to keep my secret. You know as well as I do there are real dangers in taking this money. My former comrades have eyes everywhere. Many years might still have to pass before I feel free but one day it will be our security.

You told me in Italy it was never ours. I deny that. Yes, it was taken from those who suffered but they're now dead and their remains are part of the dust of Europe. So, here is my faith in you Eva, my wife, my soul. Here is my faith. You will know the name of the password if you think of an opera in which once you sang. The knight whose name must never be known is the password. And the number should be obvious to you if you think of me and then look in a mirror. I've never told you these things before because I was too frightened that those who left Europe at the same time might extract the information from you, but what else do I have to bring you back to me except my sharing this information with you? How else can I draw you back my Eva, my love, my wife? And my daughter, my Bertha. She is my daughter, Eva. Mine as much as she is yours. I miss her rosy cheeks and her golden hair and her chubby little fingers touching my face in such innocence and with such delight.

Could he be believed? Could the words of a dead man be trusted? Was Eva really a Jew? At least then, Sarah could begin to understand her life. For then, it was as Annelise had said all along. Eva had sought the protection of a Christian German when she lived in Berlin. The German had turned out to be a Nazi … an SS man. And as with so much that happens in wartime, events had overtaken conscience and as the war progressed, Reinholdt Stricher, a man who might very well have been born a decent German, became an SS man, and then as things became increasingly hysterical, he had become one of the functionaries who organised the Holocaust.

Did Eva know? Could she conceivably have known of his involvement with mass murder? That was something which Sarah would never, ever be able to find out.

She held the translation, and re-read the last few lines. A letter like this from a Nazi. It was nothing like she'd expected. He was such a romantic … or desperate. But there were more important issues than literary criticism on her mind. It had only taken Sarah a few moments to work out the name of the password. The knight whose name must never be revealed was obviously Lohengrin. He held magical powers. He guarded the Holy Grail. As a knight he was sent to fight for virtue but his powers were only retained while he remained anonymous. He was the son of Parsifal, the keeper of the Grail. So the name was either Lohengrin or Parsifal, but more likely Lohengrin.

As to the number for the Swiss bank account, that wasn't as easy. It had taken her some time, but eventually she worked it out. She believed it was probably 30914111 which corresponded to the reversal of his birth day which she knew from certificates, November 14, 1903. If that was the case, then there would be no reason for her not to be given access, especially as she had the documents from Dr Forenjo and proof of her own identity as attorney for her mother Bertha, the rightful heir. She had her grandfather's death certificate, statements from his bank account and solid proof of her identity and her relationship with Stricher. It was all she needed when she represented Jewish claimants for money stolen from Holocaust victims. But now she was going to be acting the role of claimant herself.

The cabin stewardess offered her more drinks and canapés. She put the letters away and sipped a delicious fruit cocktail, declining the canapés and looking forward to the dinner she would be served before she caught a few hours sleep prior to her arrival in Frankfurt. There was so much she didn't understand. So much she needed to know. Fortunately David had been incredibly supportive of her decision to go to Switzerland. He had even offered to meet her there but she told him she didn't think she would be very long and that she should be back in New York within a week.

The question of course was how much money would there be in the account? Hundreds of thousands; millions; billions; trillions … what number was larger than trillions? She smiled for the first time in ages. She now enjoyed the relief of knowing that only half of her body was tainted … that even though her grandfather was a Nazi, her grandmother was, in all probability, who she said she was.

So how much was in the bank? In truth, it could be any amount. The Nazi monsters who had stolen jewellery, gold bullion, gold fillings and teeth and cash from their Jewish victims had amassed a fortune now worth hundreds of billions of dollars. It was to finance the war machine and the Swiss were implicated right up to their armpits. What would she do with the money? It wasn't hers by rights. By law it was her mother's, but the law didn't count in a matter like this. Morality overrode legal ownership. If it had been given to her grandfather by the Nazis to pay for the comfort and security of ageing war criminals, then neither he nor his heirs had any right whatsoever to it. She would give it to a Jewish charity, maybe even give it to The Institute where she worked so that she could continue in her work. She would send some to Dr Forenjo for the benefit of his Jewish community. There were lots of things that she could do now she put her mind to it. She relaxed back into the seat and found herself drifting into sleep.

Dr Jorg Hasselbach was anything but the archetype of the gnomish banker. He was young, tall, extremely good-looking and had a delightful twinkle in his eye when he welcomed Sarah into his office at the Bank of the Swiss Cantons in Banhoffstrasse, Zurich.

'You say we have corresponded in the past, Miss Kaplan?'

'We have indeed, Dr Hasselbach.'

She told him about her job at The Institute. He immediately remembered.

'Ah', he said. 'You have a reputation in this bank. You are considered very forthright and determined.'

She smiled. 'I don't know whether to take that as a compliment or an insult.'

'For you, it's a compliment. From me, it was an insult.' She burst out laughing. 'We don't like these constant inquiries into the Swiss holdings of German moneys belonging to Jews, Miss Kaplan. They tend to affect our equilibrium, to upset the sensitivities of our delicate government leaders. You see, Swiss bankers are dull, slow-witted numbers men. We like our anonymity, we gnomes. We much prefer the world outside of Switzerland to get excited about things like morality and decency and responsibility. We in Switzerland, on the other hand, don't particularly worry about morality and decency and issues like these. We only get excited when we're counting our piles of deutschsmarks, kroner, American dollars, French francs and Euros. We don't like people like you, Miss Kaplan, who upset us and make us come to terms with our dishonourable past, people who attract attention to us and put us under the damning scrutiny of the whole world.'

His grin was infectious. She felt herself warming towards him. A dangerous thing to do as he could soon turn out to be an adversary. She had met many Swiss bankers in New York over the last year. Most of them were officious, patronising and more or less what this bright-eyed young man described. But he was very different.

'You seem to have a devastating sense of humour for a Swiss banker.'

'Blame my training at Goldman Sachs,' he said. 'It's not easy to be an Aryan Swiss gnome in a building full of Cohens, Spiegels, Guttmans and Shapiros.'

'How did you cope with all those Jews?' she asked.

'I married one. That was my insurance policy, my way to get ahead.'

'Then why don't you get ahead right now, Dr Hasselbach, and lead the way for the Swiss banks. Give back the money that the Germans stole from the Jews?'

He drew back in horror. 'My dear Miss Kaplan. That would be against the Swiss Bankers Code of Ethics, which states that a good Swiss banker must only be concerned with money, and to hell with morality.'

And then his mask of pretended seriousness changed. Suddenly he remembered that he was dealing with difficult, emotional problems, that the lessons of history were being relearned. He thought back on the recent articles he'd read, the new histories which were being published in America, and he felt a sense of shame that he should have joked about this, the most contentious subject in Switzerland today.

'Sarah, don't think that this matter is distant from my heart. Indeed, it's a subject about which I feel strongly. You see, the war had been over for fifteen years before I was born. My father was little more than a teenager when Europe erupted around him and his parents. I've asked him about his attitudes, and those of my grandparents. I get the sort of responses you'd expect ... that they were neutral ... that in order to protect the Red Cross and our sovereignty, we couldn't take sides. But history tells us a very different story. I've recently been reading that few countries had such a huge number of extreme right-wing groups per capita and for the size of their country than Switzerland during the Hitler madness. Even today, there are still about ten neo-Nazi groups in Switzerland. Back then when Hitler was *sieg heil*-ing all over Europe, there were about forty.'

She looked at him in shock. An admission like this from a Swiss banker ...

'Yes, about forty. These societies, full of reputable, inscrutable Swiss ladies and gentlemen, published their own books, newspapers, magazines, pamphlets, bulletins ... and all were viciously anti-Semitic. There was the SVV, the BSG, the BVH, the BTE ... I could go on and on. The leaders were lawyers, army men, bankers, politicians. All leading Swiss citizens, all fervently pro-Nazi and virulently anti-Semitic. Despite what our wonderful government says, these wartime Swiss citizens were scum. *Of course* they took in Nazi money and gold! *Of course* they knew where it came from! *Of course* they conspired to assist the Nazis in the transportation of their cattle trucks and trains containing Jews going from one part of Europe to the other! Just like we're now finding out about the saintly Evita Perón's connection to Nazi money, so the world is just waking up to the immorality of Switzerland's wartime banking system.'

She was still in shock as his words washed over her. A Swiss banker speaking like this ... it was ... well, unheard of. 'Jorg, these matters have all been raised some time ago by the Simon Wiesenthal Centre in Los Angeles, yet they still seem to be shocking to you.'

'Wiesenthal might have raised the issues, Sarah, but Swiss newspapers and television have been conspicuously indifferent to reporting them. And our politicians are still taking the high moral ground, saying that the matter has been grossly overstated. We're in damage control, and it's not a pretty picture. Our government is even pressuring Swiss Jewish citizens, even new ones like my wife, to speak out against the criticism, pressuring them to say how marvellous the Swiss were during the war, how they protected their Jewish citizens. Well, let me assure you that it's not true. Not a word of it, as far as I can gather.'

She looked at him sadly. If only young Germans had this sort of insight to the immoralities of the previous generation. Instead, they were merely aping the salutes and gestures and uniforms and mindless rhetoric of their fathers.

'Sarah, let me tell you something you might not know. In October 1942, when we and most other people knew about the purpose for which the extermination camps had been built, the future President of Switzerland, Eduard von Steiger himself, held meetings and actually conspired with a leading elitist anti-Semitic group, the Swiss Fatherland Association to stem the flow of Jewish refugees into Switzerland. From then on, Swiss customs officials received orders that no Jew might be eligible for political asylum. You hear that, Sarah? Thousands of men and women and children probably died unnecessarily because of that order. Even after the war, von Steiger met with the Association again, and instructed them that the meeting was a classified occasion, and not a word was to be breathed to the outside world.

'That's the sort of people you Jews are up against in your attempts to get back the money from the victims of the Nazis. You're up against people like us. And it makes me ashamed to be thought of as one of them.'

She looked at him sadly. Under different circumstances, she thought, she could really like this man. She wished she had come to see him personally in the past instead of sending off aggressive and demanding letters.

He smiled suddenly. 'But I'm being self-indulgent. You haven't come to talk about me and my feelings towards these representations which the Jewish community is making. From your letter, I assume you want to know about the account of an elderly depositor.'

She nodded. 'A dead depositor.'

'And what connection are you to this gentleman?'

'I'm his granddaughter,' she said.

Jorg Hasselbach's jaw dropped. He was genuinely shocked. Sarah nodded. 'Yes, I've only very recently got to know of his background and there's no doubt that I'm his granddaughter. I believe he appropriated his identity after the war and became Jewish.'

Dr Hasselbach seemed genuinely flustered. 'And how do you feel about that, Sarah?'

'I prefer not to discuss my own personal feelings but I'm sure you wouldn't be too thrilled if you'd found out what I've found out.'

All the banter was suddenly gone. He realised now he was dealing with emotions which he had never encountered before. He nodded and took out a deposit box, tightly sealed.

'Do you happen to have the password and the pass number?' he asked.

'I believe I do.' She withdrew a piece of paper from her briefcase and pushed it over to him. He looked at it.

'The password is correct. The number isn't.'

She took back the paper and crossed out the number. It was an alternative that she had considered if this one didn't work. He was born on November 14, 1903. The Americans would write the month first, then the day, then year. In Europe, it was more often written with the day first, then the month, then year. She wrote down on a piece of paper 14111903, then she reversed the numbers and handed over the number 30911141. He nodded when he saw the correct figures.

'May I see your identification please, to prove that you are this person's granddaughter?'

She took out her passport, his death certificate and the correspondence that she had received from Dr Forenjo. He read them briefly and nodded. He pressed the numerical code on to the keypad on top of the box and handed the box over to her.

'Would you like me to leave so that you can see whatever is inside on your own or would you prefer I stayed to explain things to you?'

'I'd prefer you to stay, please,' she said. 'I have a feeling most of this is going to be in German.'

Sarah opened the box. Inside were numerous deeds, documents and financial statements. Some looked very old. She felt her back stiffen, as though suddenly tainted, as though she had just opened Pandora's box and was in the presence of evil. Because some of the documents and letters, old and fragile, bore the hateful Nazi swastika as well as the insignia of the German Republic. Others were far more modern and had to do with the bank's accounting procedures, presumably before the days of computerisation in the 1980s.

'I took the liberty of going through the box before you

arrived, Sarah. There are records of Reinholdt Stricher's war details up to 1943, his commission into the SA in the 1920s and the SS in the thirties, his marriage certificate to Eva Schmidt.

'But of course, I'm sure that the real reason you're here is over the question of the money.' He looked at her to gauge her reaction. He knew that no matter what he said, it would still come as a shock. 'As you'll appreciate, over such a long period, the value of gold goes up and up, and with the accrued interest and the fact that it was ploughed back into the account until your grandfather thought that the gold price had reached its ceiling … well' … He drew a deep breath. 'There's a total of 1.1 billion US dollars in the account, both the original principle which was deposited as gold bullion, and currency, plus the interest accrued over the past half century and more. As I said, the original deposit was in gold bars and bullion and United States dollars, Swiss Francs, English pounds sterling, as well as Nazi Government Reichsmarks which no longer had any value after the war. The gold was sold on his instructions many years ago when its price went through the roof. Since 1948, we've been sending some of the interest, frankly a paltry amount, to a bank account in Buenos Aires. The original amount in 1970, before the gold was sold was $US295 000 000. Naturally the gold was accorded a nominal value only of $US35 an ounce. But when the price skyrocketed at the time of the Arab oil embargo, your grandfather instructed that most of the gold be sold. It was subsequently traded in the market at over 720 US dollars an ounce. That added hundreds of millions to his net worth. Since then the only money that has been extracted from the account has been a fraction of a percent of the interest accrued and of course bank charges which are all itemised for you, Sarah. I should point out that we advised your late grandfather many times over many years of the state of his account, and begged him in writing to reinvest the money in property or government bonds or something, but he seemed quite content with just keeping it in cash on deposit, and taking a risible sum each month.'

Sarah had hardly heard a word he'd said in the last few minutes. There was the sound of blood rushing through her ears. 'How much did you say the account is worth?' she whispered.

'About 1.1 billion American dollars.'

'One point one billion,' she repeated.

Dr Hasselbach deliberately remained silent. On the few occasions he had had the pleasure of revealing these sorts of surprises, it always took a few moments to sink in. It was taking a bit longer for Sarah than it did for the African potentates and the Asian war lords with whom he sometimes had the dubious pleasure of dealing.

'One point one billion?' she said again, her face noticeably paler. 'One thousand million dollars.' Now her face was going from pale to a ruddier flush, as reality began to suffuse her being.

'Um,' said Dr Hasselbach, 'I think you've forgotten a small matter of one hundred million dollars. The amount is one thousand one hundred million dollars.'

She nodded. 'Excuse me. I didn't mean to forget … I mean … how much?'

'One billion one hundred million dollars. It's a fortune accumulated by the massive rise in the price of the gold deposits. Your grandfather was a canny investor. We were pressing him in correspondence for years to sell his gold stocks; we even sent him a warning letter a couple of years before the big rise after the oil shock saying that gold bullion might not be as good an investment as government bonds. Were we wrong! He followed his convictions, held onto the gold until it went up, and then instructed us to sell the lot. It was that which transformed his fortune from something massive into something phenomenal. Anyway, he turned out to be right and we were wrong. The Swiss banks, as did most other banks throughout the world, as well as most governments, misjudged the way in which the gold price would skyrocket and your grandfather sold out his gold stocks at $US720 an ounce. Amazing! He was close to the top of the market. Since then we've been begging him to put the money into futures, Eurobonds, other high-interest yielders, but he wouldn't budge from cash.'

He stopped talking. She wasn't listening. Her mind was still coming to terms with a figure of one billion dollars … plus another one hundred million on top. All the way from Buenos Aires she had been fantasising about ridiculous amounts but nothing prepared her for the reality of suddenly being a billionaire.

And then she corrected herself, and fought back a laugh. It wasn't Sarah who was the billionaire. It was her mother. She imagined the look on Bertha's face when she told her that she didn't have to do the cooking or the cleaning any more. And her father needn't ever mow his damn lawn again.

'Naturally we would be proud to continue to look after the money for you. There's an amount of approximately $70 000 000 a year which is due and payable as interest by the terms of your late grandfather's instructions on how the money was to be deposited in our bank. But your grandfather took a trifling amount of that money. All he wanted was $US1000 a month and that's all we've been paying. The rest has simply been accumulated.'

'And that's all he took? Just $1000 a month, when he had the potential to take tens of millions a year.'

'That's all,' he said. 'That and a small regular payment made to an account in Frankfurt.'

'Excuse me?'

'There's a trivial amount of money which we are instructed to pay every month to an account in Frankfurt. It's a stupid amount. Only about 400 or 500 Deutchsmarks a month. The cost of the paperwork is almost as much as the amount paid out but we are instructed and we do. That's the nature of the Swiss bank.'

'Frankfurt?'

'Yes. Why? Do you know somebody in Frankfurt?'

She thought for a moment about how much she should tell him. It could do no harm. Poor Annelise.

'Yes,' she said. 'I do know somebody there. A very old friend of my grandmother. The payment must have been made on her instructions.'

'Your grandmother? No, Sarah. I checked the records before you came today. The instructions to pay this amount of money regularly came in writing from Argentina in the late 1960s. It came as a letter from your grandfather.'

Sarah nodded. 'I see,' she said quietly. So her grandfather had supported Annelise all these years, even after he'd given up hope of getting Eva back, even after he'd married Rosaria, his second wife. Why? A streak of kindness, of generosity, maybe an atonement for his sins; it was yet one more thing which she would never know for sure, one more element of her grandfather for Sarah to try to comprehend, another fact to clutch onto, some straw of humanity.

Her decision not to fly directly back to America but instead to return to Frankfurt surprised David who was keenly anticipating her return. She checked in with Josh who reassured her that she had as much time as she needed to get her act together. Her need to be in Europe was almost at an end but there was one last thing to do, one final act of homage both on behalf of her grandmother and, now she realised, her grandfather. It had been Reinholdt's decision to continue paying the money to Annelise long after it was obvious that he would never see Eva again. A spark of humanity; another mystery which Sarah could never hope to understand.

The taxi took Sarah to the Frankfurt hospital where she had left Annelise comatose and at the point of death. Every instinct of her being told her that it would be too late and when she walked into the ward and saw Annelise's bed occupied by another elderly person she knew that the old lady had already passed away. The same sister who had been there on the previous occasion recognised her and came over to stand with her at the entrance to the ward.

'I'm terribly sorry. She didn't recover.'

Sarah nodded. 'Not even for a moment? I left a pen and paper here, just in case.'

The sister shook her head. 'I'm sorry. But she did die in peace.'

Sarah smiled her thanks but before she left the ward, the sister said, 'Would you like to collect her things. They're downstairs in Administration.'

It was a pathetically small bag, the life of an old person; nothing to remember her by other than an ancient ring whose gold was already worn thin by a lifetime on Annelise's finger; then there was a small necklace with a tiny *chai*, the Jewish symbol for life.

And an envelope.

Sarah took it out of the bag and held it for a moment, wondering. It bore her name. She tore it open and devoured the words greedily. They were written in a formal hand, obviously dictated to a nurse who worked at the hostel where Annelise had been when Sarah first met her.

Dear Sarah,

It was a surprise to meet you. A lovely surprise at the end of my life. I know I'm going soon, and I want you to pray for my body and soul. Not every year ... just this year when I meet the Almighty.

My body isn't working properly any more. I've told you things which are true and not true about Eva. We lived and lied through bad times. You can't begin to know how bad. But your grandmother was a shining light. The man she married was caught up in the evil but wasn't evil himself. Of that I'm sure. People do terrible things in a war. Better you don't know. Better you go back to America and forget all about Annelise and what I've said. But remember me as a friend of your grandmother. And your grandfather.

My love to you, child.

Annelise
PS Just once in your life, make love to a Negro.

Sarah folded the letter and realised that she was laughing and crying at the same time.

It was a long flight back to America. It was the time that Sarah needed to think to herself. She was so confused. Images of Eva were weaving patterns in and out of her mind. Such conflicting stories, the biography from hell.

At the beginning of the journey from Switzerland, Sarah had a profusion of messages to comprehend. Who was Eva? Was she, according to Sarah's mother and father, a Jewish refugee who had traipsed across Europe after the death of her husband looking after the welfare of a baby girl whom she brought up in America; a good mother, a decent human of scruples and ethics and a strong moral backbone, a matriarch in the ancient Jewish traditional way, a woman who had lost her husband in the most heinous of circumstances and whose life had been ruined before it had begun?

Or should Sarah believe Annelise's version that Eva's life was turned upside down by the advent of Nazism in Germany, that she had travelled from Munich to Berlin to escape the horrors of the SA and the SS; that, in order to live her life in safety and with a modicum of comfort and security, she had attached herself to a young Christian man who looked after her until the end of the war? But how then, if she believed Annelise's story, could she explain so much which was inexplicable? Her opera singing before the glittering crowds of Nazis? Her marriage to a senior functionary of the Holocaust? Her separation from him when the Nazi-hunters from the Simon Wiesenthal Centre came looking? Was Bertha the daughter of a Christian father, or of a Nazi beast? Was Annelise totally wrong in her view of her friend Eva? Had Eva been killed somehow in the war and her identity appropriated by the Nazi wife of Reinholdt Stricher? How then could she explain Reinholdt's letter telling her that she was safe because she was Jewish?

So many questions. So much doubt. And with everybody dead, there were no answers, only speculations.

Sarah had begun the journey in doubt and ended it knowing in her heart where the truth lay. She had never met her grandfather, Reinholdt Stricher, and even though there was not one element of her being which was capable of violence or aggression, she could now somehow accept that a part of her make-up belonged to a Nazi. But she could never accept that the kindly old lady who spoke Hebrew with a German accent and who spoke Yiddish with the old Polish and Hungarian women who were her friends, and who was accepted intimately as a member of the New York Jewish society without question or reservation, was anything but a Jewish matriarch. This was her Eva; this was her grandmother; this image, Sarah could accept. This she knew to be true.

When Sarah finally landed in New York, she had retrieved her grandmother from the mire of Nazism. And in her heart of hearts, she knew what had happened. The Christian man of whom Annelise spoke was Reinholdt Stricher. Somehow she'd fooled him. In a masterpiece of acting, in the performance of her life, she had kept herself alive by pretending to be an Aryan Christian, by hiding her Jewishness. How she'd done it, how she had lived amongst the elite of the Nazi hierarchy before and during the war, Sarah would never understand. But then, as Annelise had said to her, neither Sarah nor any other member of the modern world could begin to understand what life had been like for Jews in Nazi Germany.

As the plane taxied to a halt at John F. Kennedy Airport, Sarah had finally wrested her life back again. She had neither the right, nor the desire to condemn her grandmother for what she'd done. She would spend the rest of her life ignoring the fact that Reinholdt Stricher was her grandfather. She would tell Josh and David and her mother and father and would swear them to secrecy. The banker in Switzerland knew; Dr Forenjo knew; but that was all. And she had no doubt that one day the news would come out. Somebody would find out. And then she would have to stand before the world court and atone for the sins of her grandfather; but until then, she would strive, regardless of Annelise's final plea, to cut him out of her mind and her heart.

EPILOGUE

NEW YORK, PRESENT DAY

Her nervousness increased as Sarah drove closer and closer to the house. She'd already plotted out the way in which she would approach her mother; how to break the news about Bertha's father, Reinholdt's, personal history; how to guide her in her decision-making process about the billion dollars ... she said the amount again to herself. A billion dollars. Now her family was twice as rich as Josh Krantz ... hilarious. A billion dollars.

See, she'd done it again. She'd even missed the one hundred million out of the equation. One billion, and one hundred million dollars. A week ago, if anybody had told her that she was worth a hundred million dollars, she'd have gone berserk. Now, she didn't even bother to mention the figure in the same breath as the amount of one billion sitting in the account in the Bank of the Swiss Cantons. And every day she delayed her decision, the interest on the money accumulated by over $200 000. Every day! She was earning half of her annual salary every single goddamn day. Shit!

David had insisted on coming with her, but this wasn't a family discussion. This was a time for a mother and a daughter to get together and have a heart to heart conversation. David had begged Sarah not to go through with it. Just to donate the money to The Institute and other worthwhile Jewish charities. But the fortune wasn't hers. It was, by rights, her mothers. No! Not by rights at all. By rights, it belonged to countless, nameless millions who had been murdered in the most inhuman manner by the cruellest and most vile of human beings in the greatest crime in human history. By rights, her mother should have nothing to do with the money.

But what if she insisted? What if she said, 'Sarah, that's a lot of money. Maybe we don't have to give it away. Why don't we deserve some *mazel*, after all?'

What would she say? And how would she react when Sarah told her that her mother's father was a fucking Nazi, for God's sake.

She realised that she was shouting it out loud. Thank God she was in a closed car. People would think she was mad.

Bertha Kaplan retreated to the kitchen, her place of refuge. Sarah followed her.

'Mom, you have to believe me.'

'Excuse me, but I should believe you? I should believe a young woman who tells me that her grandfather *alav ha shalom* is a Nazi? What, I should believe a know-nothing daughter who knows from *gournisht* instead of my own mother who told me that the man who died in her arms was the gift of God; suddenly I should believe that he was the gift of evil?; that had it not been for those German Nazi bastards, I wouldn't have grown up like half an orphan.'

Sol interrupted, stepping between the two women. 'Enough, Sarah, you've done enough. Look what you're doing to your mother. Isn't it bad enough you come with this *farcochteneh* story about the Nazis, you have to spin this cock and bullshit story about a billion dollars. Does David know you're here? I'll bet he doesn't. He'd never allow you to do this to your mother.'

He turned to his wife. 'I'll bet David knows nothing about this, Bertha. What do you bet.'

'David should know? Never!' shouted her mother as she started to peel the potatoes.

'David does know,' Sarah told them.

'And he approved?'

Slowly she shook her head.

'Aha! See, she's here without her husband's permission. I told you David would never allow you to go on like this.'

'Mom, Dad, this has nothing to do with David. I've been to South America. I've uncovered the truth about my grandfather; and that *Bubba* Eva married him to hide from the Germans. The old woman in the home, Annelise, told me everything, but I had to check it out for myself. I have Reinholdt's letter to prove it,' she said, trying again

'I knew you shouldn't have listened to the ravings of an old woman. What's she got, Alzheimers?' demanded her father.

'She was perfectly in command,' Sarah insisted. 'But forget Annelise. What about the letter? Why won't you read it.'

'Why?' her mother said, standing. 'Because it's not from my father. That's why. Because it's from some Nazi. Because my father died in my mother's arms in Berlin. Because he was in a concentration camp, and they didn't allow you to write letters in a concentration camp. That's why, Sarah.'

Her mother walked away from her daughter and the letter and continued with the meal, sinking into the cooking as a way of excluding her daughter's nonsense.

The anger, the protestations died down, replaced by the noises of pots and pans. Sarah breathed a sigh of frustration. She'd known it would be difficult. But she'd held out hope that she'd be listened to, if not wholeheartedly believed. And how the hell was she going to get her Mom to agree to give away one billion dollars … oh, and never forgetting the hundred million.

Sarah sat in the comfortable armchair, the usual preserve of her father. She stared into the empty fireplace and looked at the basket of logs, there for decoration not usage. She was surprised by her mother's reappearance at the door. Sarah looked up into her mother's face.

'Tell me again what Annelise said about the way it was. What did she say about my mother?'

Bertha walked over and sat in the chair opposite, the two women separated by the mock fireplace. Her face was still flushed from the heat of the kitchen.

'This money in Switzerland,' she said before Sarah had a chance to answer. 'It really belongs to me?'

Sarah nodded. Bertha sat back, her head resting on the top of the armchair looking at the ceiling. She mumbled something, barely audible. Sarah could have sworn it sounded like *Oy vey*!

'You're off your tree.'

'Perhaps.'

'And so's Bertha.'

'Definitely.'

Josh Krantz looked at the document. 'One billion and ninety million dollars.'

Sarah nodded. 'We've decided to keep ten million, just to make ends meet. Mom decided that she'd like to travel first class round the world. A couple of dozen times. Compensation for not having a father all her life.'

'A billion bucks! Sarah, this is lunacy. Why?'

'Because, as I've explained to you twice, it's not mine. It's not ours. It doesn't belong to us.'

'But why to The Institute? Why not give it away yourself?'

'Because through The Institute, I'll be kept anonymous. I want nobody to know about my grandfather and what my grandmother did. If I was to start tossing around amounts like this, it'd be the talk of the town in five minutes flat. Done through The Institute, though, we can hide it.'

Josh nodded. He turned to David. 'And this is okay with you?'

'Of course not. I want a new Stradivarius. The rich bitch won't buy me one.'

Josh laughed, glad that there was humour flying around the room instead of the tension and trauma of half an hour ago. Unwillingly, Josh had agreed to being sworn to secrecy before Sarah agreed to tell him the full story.

While he was surprised, he couldn't fully understand why Sarah had taken the whole thing so badly. After all, it was nothing to do with her what her grandfather got up to. But he'd been duly solicitous and understanding … up until the time that she'd told him about the Nazi loot, and handed him over a Deed of Assignment, making The Institute the trustee of the one billion and ninety million dollars. The Deed said that The Institute must direct the entirety of the money to reputable Jewish charities, and that the entire sum must either be disbursed or committed in annual increments within a period of five years.

As they were talking, Sarah's secretary knocked on the door. She entered, carrying a large bouquet of flowers.

'They were just delivered,' she said, handing them to Sarah.

'An admirer?' asked Josh.

'Probably,' said Sarah. 'The question is which one.'

She opened the small envelope and took out the card. She was smiling as she started to read the message, but her smile soon disappeared. Instead of joy, her face turned a sickly grey colour, her mouth clenched in distress. She screwed up the note, and threw it onto the floor, as if it was poison. Instinctively, she grasped her amulet, hanging on her chest. And not for the first time recently, it brought her no comfort.

David bent down to pick it up, looking at Sarah in shock. He read the note, and, sighing, handed it over the desk to Josh. When Josh had read it, he looked at Sarah in sadness. There was nothing he could do. Nothing he could say.

The note sat crumpled on Sarah's desk. In neat, copperplate writing, it said,

Sarah

I was so pleased to learn that you're one of us. There's a meeting of the Brotherhood in New York on the 18th.

Why not join us? After all, we who share the same blood must stick together.

Frank Darman

The Gift of Evil

Book I in Amra's Journey

ISBN 0 7322 5653 4

An ancient golden amulet with a history of violence and death.

A highly organised group of killers who will do anything to keep secret their past identities and their crimes against humanity.

A brilliant young New York lawyer with a passion for truth and justice.

A Hollywood film director determined to expose the horrors committed in Slovakia under Stalin's regime.

When Josh Krantz wants to reclaim his grandparents' house from the Slovakian government, he has another agenda – to expose the evil crimes committed by Stalin's henchmen against the Krantz family and thousands of others. He engages the services of New York lawyer Sarah Kaplan, and together they travel to Slovakia to begin their fight.

Dr Laco Plastov – an archaeologist who is amazed by the engravings on Sarah's ancient amulet – joins the two Americans on their crusade. Delving into the past, they uncover the Syndicate – an organisation set up to protect the evil killers of thousands of innocent people during Stalin's regime.

Armed with information that will expose these men and bring them to justice, Sarah, Josh and Laco become involved in a deadly and strategic contest – playing for their very lives.

This tale of evil, murder and retribution is international bestselling author, Alan Gold, at his very best.

The Marmara Contract

Book II in Amra's Journey

ISBN 0 7322 5991 6

For the past fifty years, the golden treasures of Troy have been lying in the basement of the Pushkin Museum in Moscow. Now, as the millennium approaches, Germany and Turkey are both reclaiming the treasures. But who really owns the precious antiquities? And how far is each country prepared to go to claim them as their own?

American lawayer Sarah Kaplan, an expert on the reclamation of property, is drawn into the debate when the Turkish government employs her to get the treasure back. But things go horribly wrong and Sarah ends up in a Turkish gaol, accused of theft and blasphemy. Alone in a filthy cell, Sarah's only link with the outside world is the amulet she wears around her neck, passed down to her from her great-grandmother.

Engraved with the symbols of the bull and owl of Troy, the amulet's origin is a mystery. But gradually, through the interweaving of two stories three thousand years apart, the secret of the amulet becomes known.